My Brother's Keeper

Lorrieann Russell

My Brother's Keeper

Edin Road Press

This book is a work of fiction. Although certain real locations, events and public figures are mentioned, all names, characters, places and events described herein are the product of the author's imagination or are used fictitiously. Any resemblance to actual events, places or persons (living or dead) is purely coincidental.

Published by Edin Road Press
Second edition © 2012 & 2015 by Lorrieann Russell
Second edition (Pbk) ISBN 9780615736945

First edition ©2001 by Lorrieann Russell
Published by Writer's Club Press
First edition ISBN 0-595-20642-5 (Pbk) 0-595-74461-3 (Cloth)

On the Web:
www.facebook.com/lorrieannrussell

Jacket art and Interior book design by the author

Dedication

Thank you to Jesse V. Coffey for the prodding and poking to convince me this story was worth the polish and pain to bring it back to print.

To Brenda Lagasse and the late, great Thom "Fury" Michaud for graciously allowing me to borrow their names for the vile Lord and Lady Aberdoir. Thank you. You know I love you both.

Special thanks to the Great and Powerful Conanne the Grammarian, a.k.a. Patricia Morrison, for her profound and invaluable tutelage in the proper form and production of the printed page.

Foreword

Some could say that witchcraft in Scotland is probably one of the oldest spectator sports in the UK. Being a superstitious lot, the Scots have always found a way to marry the best of the Pagan religions to their Christian beliefs, and yet they so feared the practices that those fears turned them, like so many others in the world, towards an inhumanity that is still remembered. Indeed, a search through the internet on the subject turns up many a document or list of men, women, and children that had been hanged, burned, or hanged and burned as witches.

Fans of Diana Gabaldon will remember the witch Geillie Duncan, who was the secret lover of Dougal McKenzie and was imprisoned with Claire in the Thieves' Hole in Cranesmuir— she was accused of witchcraft and murder. But a search on the internet shows that there really *was* a Gellie Duncan who was burned as a witch in 1591. Unlike her fictional counterpart, the real Gellie didn't get a secret reprieve.

The real Gellie was part of the most famous case of Scottish witches, that of the *Witches of North Berwick.* Over one hundred people were accused and tried of casting a spell over the weather, to drown King James the VI and his new bride Anne as they were returning to Scotland and England. Many were tortured into confession, some confessed on their own.

The most noted of those killed in North Berwick was Agnes Sampson, who was important enough to be questioned by King James, himself. He oversaw her imprisonment and torture— which included the infamous "bridle," an iron contraption with four prongs that dug into the cheeks and tongue to a very painful degree. She finally confessed to fifty-three acts of witchcraft before being strangled and burned.

William Fylbrigge, the fictional hero of this book, represents those who also felt the wrongness of the King's vendetta and the paranoia of the superstitious and often ignorant villagers, nobles, and clergy of his time. While many nobles chose to ignore the problem as being an exaggeration of justice being meted out with a justified heavy hand, William decries it publicly for what it is— greed and abuse against those who cannot fight for themselves.

While you read this book, you'll find yourself getting caught up in William's struggle and fighting along with him. While this is a piece of fiction, remember that it was taken from the pages of history. There is a lesson to be learned here— may we all learn it and hold it dear in our hearts.

And now, on to *My Brother's Keeper*.

Jesse V. R. Coffey, editor

For the muse, in all incarnations.

Prologue

"COME ON, SEAN! Move!" William Fylbrigge kicked his stallion, Cirrus, into a full gallop, praying he'd reach the meetinghouse in Kylkannen before the sentence was carried out. Close on William's heels, Sean Wilbrun raced behind, more interested in saving his friend from his own reckless crusade than in saving the woman who was about to be burned alive.

"Slow down, Will!"

"This path is too long." Without warning, William turned sharply into the thicket and straight through the untamed underbrush of the forest pushing Cirrus to his limits.

"What are you doing?" Sean yelled from behind, but turned to follow without hesitation. "Watch it!" he shouted, as William ducked just in time to avoid a low hanging branch. "You can't save her if you get yourself killed!"

Oblivious to Sean's frantic warnings, William flew through the forest, dodging jagged rocks and brambles, even leaping a treacherous gorge over a raging river far below. With only William's safety in mind, and giving no thought to his own, Sean stayed close at his companion's side, racing his own horse, Hawk, matching William's flight leap for leap. He knew if William believed there was even the smallest hope to save the woman from the death-fire, he would take it without a second thought or die trying. It was Sean's duty—no matter how foolhardy the plan— to follow William and keep him alive.

Another sharp turn and a jump through a veil of hanging moss and they were at last free of the forest. They galloped into Kylkannen shire just as the doors to the meetinghouse were flung open and a boisterous crowd spilled into the square.

"There!" William hollered, then gave one more kick and drove Cirrus full charge directly toward the meetinghouse with Hawk nose to nose beside him. William reined in hard and jumped from the saddle before Cirrus had even come to a stop. Sean halted and leapt from Hawk just as quickly, not taking time to tether the reins, the blind determination on his friend's face moving him to leave the horses to wander if they chose.

A milling crowd swarmed about a raised platform surrounded by bundles of peat and kindling. They chanted and cheered as two hooded men bound a terrified young woman to a stake in the center of the platform.

"Burn, witch, burn! Burn, witch, burn!"

"We're too late!" Sean called rushing to keep up with William.

An expression of wild glee crossed William's face. "No, we're not, Sean. The torchbearers are not there yet!" The glee turned fierce as he burst through the wooden doors of the meetinghouse to confront the woman's accuser.

"Lord Ambrose Woodhall! What right have you?" William called out, as he pushed his way through a throng of spectators, ignoring their startled gapes.

Sean steeled his nerve, and tried not to notice Lord Woodhall's horde of mercenary witch hunters standing armed and scattered throughout the crowd, their faces hidden under dark hoods. His took his position at William's back ready to pull his lord and friend out should any of the armed hunters move on them. But even if the hunters did attack, Sean knew that William Fylbrigge would never turn and flee.

"Fylbrigge, stand down!" Woodhall yelled, red-faced, clearly outraged at William's bold intrusion. "You have no voice here."

"I have voice enough to call you a liar!" William said, defiantly pushing his way past the hunters who were moving toward him, his sight set squarely on Woodhall alone. "Are you ready to condemn an innocent woman for the sake of your manly pride?"

"Manly— how dare you!" Woodhall glared, angrily. "The trial has ended. The sentence has been given. The witch confessed!"

"Under torture!" William countered. "She only confessed to stop the pain. Any fool could see that."

Woodhall narrowed his eyes, and placed his hand menacingly on the hilt of his sword. "Her crime has been proven."

"She refused your bed," William shouted, reaching for his own blade. "That is her only crime."

Several hunters began to inch toward him, their swords drawn.

Sean put his hand on his friend's shoulder and spoke in

his ear. "Will, we are far outnumbered here. It may be best to leave now while we still can."

"No, Sean. She's innocent!" William answered, keeping his eyes fixed squarely on Woodhall, as his rival raised his sword. William reciprocated with his own blade. The two stood, eyes locked, waiting for the other to move.

Sean held his sword at the ready behind William. "I hope you know what you're doing," he grumbled under his breath.

"I have had more than enough of you, Fylbrigge," Woodhall growled, and took several steps forward. "It is insult enough that you have wrested my trade routes from me, you will not now call me a liar in my own estate. Be gone now, or I swear by all that is holy—"

"Holy!? There is nothing holy in what you are doing!" William would not allow him to change the subject. "Three burnings of innocent women are not enough for you, that you must seek a fourth?"

"Confessions!" Woodhall hissed.

"Coerced!" William countered.

The hunters circled in closely. Sean spun on his heel, taking a defensive back-to-back position behind William.

"I'm on your back, but we won't last long in this room," Sean whispered keeping his eyes on the hunters, while mentally planning their escape route.

"Stand ready," William told Sean, quietly.

"What would you have me do, Fylbrigge?" Woodhall raised a brow and grinned. "As I said, they all confessed. The law is the law and the prescription for her transgression is clear. I do not suffer the witch to live under my authority!" He took a step closer, now standing within striking distance.

"She's not a witch and you know it. What is your price?"

"Price?"

"Yes. What is it you want that will buy her freedom."

After a moment, Woodhall growled his demand through clenched teeth, "I want my trade routes restored!"

"Give the order to release her, and you shall have what you ask."

"Will!" Sean spoke under his breath, so only William would hear, "You can't throw away the treaty like that."

Woodhall narrowed his eyes and examined William's face closely. "You would cross Lord Edward of Stonehaven so easily, Fylbrigge? Will you truly risk his displeasure only days before you wed his daughter?"

"The girl is innocent. I'll handle Edward. Give the order!"

"And if I do not agree to free the wench?"

"You lose. No trade routes through your county. Besides, what do you gain by allowing her to die? Pride? Your manhood vindicated? Hardly seems a logical bargain." William took a step closer, fully closing the distance between them, his unblinking eyes locked on his rival.

"What is there in this for you, Fylbrigge? Do you fancy her? Is she to be your last conquest before you take your wedding vows?"

William grinned and shook his head. "Hardly. I gain nothing from this. I shall expect I shall lose face with Lord Edward, and will most likely deal with repercussions from him. I may even be disowned. Perhaps he'll withdraw his daughter's hand from me, much to my despair. But I would risk it all to know the woman you have falsely accused will live. Send her from this shire if you wish, send her to Stonehaven or beyond if the sight of her troubles you so." William's voice grew softer, yet controlled. He had the knack for getting what he wanted by making the other man feel the victor. It was for that reason Edward trusted him to negotiate trade treaties in the first place. "Give the order to free her and reclaim your trade routes. In the bargain, take the satisfaction of knowing it will surely be my own undoing."

From outside, the sound of the chanting crowd grew louder. "Burn, witch, burn! Burn, witch, burn!"

For an instant, Woodhall looked away from William and glanced through the open door to the gathered crowd outside. The torchbearers stood ready waiting for his order to light the death-fire. William watched Woodhall's face closely as he mulled over the proposition. The rival earl had lost control of a good deal of his county due to William's negotiations, and even Sean could feel how it must gall the man that in order to regain control of his territories, he would have to relent, yet again. However, Sean knew that William was confident that the odds on his gamble—playing on Woodhall's famous lust for power—were in his favor, and that the pompous ass was not so foolish as to throw away the opportunity before him. But, the longer Woodhall mulled his decision, the faster Sean's confidence in his advantage began to wither. We'll never make it out of here. But just as Sean began to believe the bluff would be called, Woodhall relaxed his stance and lowered his blade.

William stood firm, his blade still raised as the hunters surrounding him made a slight forward motion. Sean mimicked their advance, raising his blade slightly. The hunters glanced to Woodhall for orders. The Earl raised his hand slowly, signaling them to stand down. They immediately fell back. William lowered his blade slightly, but Sean held his ready position, still at William's back.

"Give the order."

"I have your word?" Woodhall asked carefully, watching William's sword hand.

William reached over his shoulder without taking his eyes off Woodhall. "Sean?" Sean took a small scroll from his tunic and handed it over his shoulder to William. "You have my word. The scroll is yours." He handed it to Woodhall.

Woodhall opened the scroll. It was the treaty he had signed only the day before—the treaty turning his key trade routes away from his county in return for limited protection from Edward's armies. William had made the deal seem advantageous during his proposal, but when all was said and done, Woodhall had given away far more control than he had gained. He looked up over the scroll to William, grinned, and then tore it into small pieces.

From the corner of his eye, Sean watched the shreds float to the floor, his heart beginning to race with fear that he had allowed William to lead them both into certain disaster.

William did not waver. His voice to remain steady and confident. "Give the order."

Woodhall stood back on his heels, arrogantly laughing out loud. "Why? I have what I need."

"Sean?"

Sean reached into his tunic again and pulled out another scroll and handed it to William in the same manner as before. Woodhall stopped laughing as he watched the relay.

It was William's turn to be arrogant. "I'm not that naive.

This is the binding treaty; the one bearing Edward's seal. Give the order, and you shall have it."

Woodhall snorted, glowering at the parchment.

William allowed himself a satisfied half-grin, knowing he had reclaimed his advantage.

Woodhall turned to the hunter closest to him. "Release her," he muttered irritably with a dismissive wave of his hand, then, scowling, he held his hand open. "May I have that scroll now?"

William watched the hunter walk past him toward the door. Not wanting to turn his back on Woodhall, he asked over his shoulder, "Sean, can you see?"

"Aye." Sean answered. William tightened his grip on his sword, holding his breath, until he heard Sean say, "She's free."

"May I?" Woodhall extended his hand higher in William's direction.

"By all means. Pleasure to do business with you." With a twist of his wrist, William handed the scroll to Woodhall, then bowed and smiled politely with a defiant glint in his eye. Sean grabbed him by the shoulder and the two fled the meetinghouse.

William looked briefly in the direction of the young woman's family as he ran past them toward the edge of town, gratified to see the relieved expressions of joy on their faces as they hurried her away from the odious pile of kindling.

It occurred to Sean, they would probably never know how she had come to be released. Just as well, he thought, he doesnae need any attention about this. He looked around quickly for the horses, relieved to see them grazing not far from the edge of the woods. I'll just be happy to get away from here in one piece.

They flew to the horses, each mounting with a leap into the saddles. Though no hunters followed them, they kicked into full gallop, charging back through the woods, putting as much ground between them and the town as they could before slowing the horses to walk side by side.

When they had reached the safety of the road leading away from Kylkannen, William sat back on the saddle and relaxed. "Well, I'd say that was a success. I hope the girl has sense enough to leave there. Did you see the look on Woodhall's fat face? I cannae believe we got away with that farce." He laughed, then finally turned too look at Sean. "What?"

Sean reached to his friend and swatted his shoulder with the back of his hand. "You are a madman! You could have gotten yourself killed back there! Worse yet, you could have gotten me killed, you lunk!" He laughed heartily, but after a moment, he caught his breath and grew quiet.

"What's wrong, Sean?"

"Aren't you worried that Edward will be upset that you annulled that treaty?"

"Not at all. He never knew I bargained for routes in Kylkannen to begin with. I did that all on my own. The treaty never officially existed, so how could it be annulled?"

"What about the seal?"

"You mean this one?" William flashed the signet ring he wore and smiled, completely pleased with himself. "Is it my fault Ambrose can't tell my mark from Edward's?"

"I should have known," Sean laughed, shaking his head. "I swear I spend more time worrying after you for nothing. But must you always do things the hard way?"

William cocked his head and grinned. "Absolutely."

Chapter 1

August 31, 1607
Stonehaven, Scotland

LAUREL MAY McCARY peered quietly into the chamber where Lady Mehlyndia sat watching out her window. "M' lady? Are you ready for your meal? I could bring it up for you, if you are not up to dining in the hall."

Mehlyndia turned and gave Laurel a warm smile. "Thank you, Laurel, but I believe I will wait a bit longer. You run along and see if Elinor needs you to help with the linens."

"Aye, m' lady." Laurel curtsied lightly before bounding out of the chamber and down the corridor.

Left alone to her thoughts, Mehlyndia resumed her vigil, watching the road and imagining the caravan that would carry her betrothed back to Stonehaven. *Have these many months been as torturous for you as they have for me, my love?* It had been nearly nine months since he had gone to work in her father's service, and Mehlyndia had counted the days like beads on a string, until this day—the day he would return and she would become the wife of William Fylbrigge.

She dallied by the window, imagining the celebration, the revelry of the guests, the merry tunes that would be played by the finest musicians in her father's court. She swayed to the imagined music that her beloved William would play upon his lute, charming all those who gathered as he sang a song of his own fashioning for all to hear but meant for her alone.

As children growing up together in Drumoak Castle, Mehlyndia and William were fortunate to have been taught to play music. She toyed with the harp and few singing lessons, but was never as skillful at it as William was with his lute. She remembered clearly the first time William witnessed Geoffrey, Lord Edward's court musician, perform for the duke and how he had been enchanted by the lilting music that sang from the strings of Geoffrey's lute. Edward, the Duke of Stonehaven—Mehlyndia's father and William's foster father—had indulged the lad by allowing him more free time than was customary to pursue his musical training. William always found an eager audience in Mehlyndia and Edward for his little tunes. He had a talent for weaving everyday events into imaginative ballads. She smiled, remembering how he once so delighted the duke with a silly tune about kitchen pots and pans that he was asked to sing it whenever guests visited the castle.

But what she lacked in musical talent, Mehlyndia more than made up for with an uncanny talent for drawings, sketching and painting. She spent as many happy hours capturing the faces of the people who lived with her at Drumoak with charcoal or pigments as William spent with his music. Edward praised her works and said they revealed clever attention to expression and detail and he proudly displayed many of her paintings on the walls of the castle for all to see.

Her favorite subject, of course, was William. She had drawn him so many times that he no longer needed to be in the room for her to produce an uncanny likeness. She especially enjoyed rendering his image with pigments, to capture the deep emerald green in his eyes, and the silky blue-black texture of his hair. She'd painted a small portrait just a day ago; it rested against the mirror of her dressing table. She glanced at it, smiling. Soon, my love.

"Hello, my darling."

Mehlyndia jumped, startled from her thoughts, then ran to the outstretched arms of the woman who stood in the doorway. "Oh! Bryndah! You've come!"

"Of course, I have come. Did you think I would not attend my own sister's wedding? You must think me a complete beast!" Bryndah, feigning hurt, made a monkeyish pout that soon had them laughing in each other's arms.

"Of course I knew you'd be here. I'm just surprised to see you so early in the day. I did not expect you until well past noon. I'm so glad to see you. Are you happy for me, sister?"

Bryndah's smile faded. "Happy? Of course not."

Mehlyndia drew back, stunned. "But... why?"

"You're marrying a little brute who used to kick me in the shins. I had a devil of a time trying to teach that boy some manners, and I fear I completely failed in that respect."

Mehlyndia could only stare, until Bryndah betrayed a grin, then laughed playfully. "Yes, my darling, you know I am happy for you. You are so very fortunate, you know. Father is allowing you to marry for love and not for the sake of some foreign alliance. Although I must say that my arranged marriage has not been the terrible burden I feared it would be. Thomas and I are quite well suited to each other."

Mehlyndia had never been fond of Thomas Fylbrigge,

William's older brother, but she could not explain why. He had always been perfectly polite and cordial to a fault. She honestly could not remember a single personal slight he had ever made toward her. Yet, whenever he looked upon her, she could not help but feel she was being appraised somehow, and never came close to the standard of whatever it was he was judging her against.

"Bryndah?" Mehlyndia began, shyly, "does Thomas think as well of my marriage to William as you do?"

Bryndah hesitated for a moment before answering, "Yes, naturally he approves. His brother and my sister. How perfectly charming and well-suited we all shall be. Now, let's stop all this worrying and get you ready to present yourself." Her tone was unconvincing, but the smile in her eyes seemed genuine enough.

"Thank you, sister. You mean the world to me, and I could not bear it if you did not approve."

Bryndah gave her a reassuring squeeze on the hand and led her to the dressing table. "Where are your combs, darling?"

"On the table there." Mehlyndia reached for a pair of gold combs and handed them to her sister, before settling herself down on the cushioned bench in front of her mirror. Bryndah tucked the combs into her bodice for safekeeping while she went about smoothing Mehlyndia's auburn locks with a silver-handled boar's-hair brush. Mehlyndia smiled up to her sister's reflection, then allowed her eyes to wander toward the window, watching the road for the first sign of the caravan, hardly aware that Bryndah was speaking to her.

"Mehlyndia?" Bryndah tapped her shoulder lightly with

the handle of the brush. "Have you heard anything I've said at all?"

"Hmm? Oh, I'm sorry, sister, did you say something?"

Bryndah chuckled under her breath, "I've been asking if you know if Father will bestow a title to William? Perhaps make him baron of that little holding to the north? What is it called?"

"Sutherland."

"Yes, that's it. Do you know?"

Mehlyndia wondered why Bryndah would care. After all, being the daughter of the duke, Bryndah held some rank of her own. And when Thomas became the Earl of Aberdoir, Bryndah became the countess.

Mehlyndia spoke to her sister's reflection in the mirror, "I'm not certain, of course, but I believe his rank will be higher than baron."

Bryndah looked back at Mehlyndia's reflection, an interested lift to her brow. "Oh? And why do you believe his rank would be higher than baron?"

"Well, you see, Father has kept William close to his hip for these past nine months, allowing him privilege to all the issues of governing. He adores William, you know." She smiled wistfully, again looking toward the road, until Bryndah caught her ear with the brush. "Ouch!"

Bryndah made an apologetic little giggle. "Forgive me, darling. So what do you think William's rank will be?"

"It is my guess he will be named earl to Sutherland."

Bryndah dragged the brush roughly down the remaining length of hair. "Really? That would be quite... an honor." She spoke to Mehlyndia's reflection, tossing a long hank of hair carelessly to the side. "Especially since William is not his natural son."

"He's been with us here for more than seven years, Bryndah," Mehlyndia replied, curtly. "Father has come to regard him as far more than just a foster son. He considers him a true son... and when we are wed, he truly will be his son. Well, son-in-law, but still—"

"—Still, he is so young. He has a lot to learn about government. An earldom is not something that should be left to a boy." Bryndah grabbed another hank of Mehlyndia's hair, roughly snagging the brush in her tresses.

"Ouch! Bryndah, please, not so hard!" Mehlyndia pulled away. "Apparently, Father has no fear about William's abilities. And he's not a boy. He'll be twenty-one come May next. You don't know how much he has accomplished on this tour with Father. His letters have been filled with news." She turned to face her sister directly. "Do you think that Thomas will take issue with William's promotion?"

"I'm sure he will be thrilled," Bryndah replied, in a flat tone that Mehlyndia found disturbing. "Besides, it's not like Father would name William his heir. Naturally Thomas would be the logical choice, or perhaps our son, Richard." She yanked the brush hard through a tangle, and said through her teeth, "A blood relative."

Mehlyndia pushed Bryndah's hand away from her hair and took the hairbrush from her. "Thomas is no more a blood relative than William is. Why wouldn't Father consider him as heir? And if blood is so important, remember that William and I could— and will— provide a grandson who has the right blood."

Bryndah smiled sweetly, her eyes softening a bit. "Yes, of course you're right. I meant nothing, darling. Of course you will have children." She retrieved the brush and resumed smoothing Mehlyndia's hair in a far gentler fashion, then leaned down and cooed into her ear, "Perhaps."

Mehlyndia was about to ask what perhaps was supposed to mean when the chamber door flew open, and Laurel trotted in with a happy smile.

"Excuse me m' la—"

"How dare you interrupt, you silly girl!" Bryndah snapped at the maid, pointing with the brush to the door. "Leave us this instant."

Laurel stood stunned at the unexpected rebuke, her large brown eyes grew even larger, shining with the threat of tears. "I... I'm sorry, m' lady!" she cried, and ran from the room.

"Oh, Laurel. Please, come back." Mehlyndia looked at her sister, appalled by her sudden change in demeanor. "Why were you so cross with her?"

"Are you always so familiar with the servants?" Bryndah asked sarcastically.

"Laurel is my first waiting lady, and my friend. Please, do not yell at her again." She stood, pushed Bryndah aside, and hurried to the door hoping Laurel had not gone far.

Laurel stood with her face against a stone pillar on the far end of the corridor, sobbing quietly into a handkerchief. Mehlyndia approached her quietly. "Laurel?"

"I'm sorry, m' lady," Laurel wiped her face quickly, and began to ramble into her handkerchief without taking a breath. "I did nae know you had a guest. I should have knocked. It won't happen again. Please, m' lady, dinnae be angry with me."

Mehlyndia placed her hands gently onto Laurel's shoulders and smiled, hoping it would help the girl to calm down. "Laurel, have I ever been angry with you? You did nothing wrong. My sister is simply more... formal with her ladies." She reached into her own pocket, withdrew a dry handkerchief, and gave it to Laurel. "Now, you wanted to tell me something a moment ago. What is it?"

Laurel turned a grateful face to Mehlyndia and forced a trembling smile. "Thank you, for your understanding." She drew a long breath and wiped her eyes with Mehlyndia's handkerchief. "It's just, I'm so happy here, and I never want to make you upset with me. I do try so to be good and do what—"

"—Laurel, what did you want to tell me?"

"Hmm? Oh! Yes, ma'am. The carriages have arrived."

"What? Why didn't you tell me?" Mehlyndia burst, inadvertently shaking the girl by her shoulders, and once again, poor Laurel was reduced to tears.

"I'm sorry! Please don't be angry."

"Oh, for goodness' sake, Laurel, I'm not angry, just surprised. William is here?"

Bryndah appeared in the doorway, her hands on her hips. "Mehlyndia, for pity's sake, will you come back here and let me make you presentable? Leave the foolish girl to her chores."

"I'm sorry!" Laurel cried, then turned and ran away down the stone stairs at the end of the hall.

Mehlyndia turned an angry glare on her sister. "Why were you so mean to Laurel? She's a simple, sweet girl, and

I'll thank you to not speak to her again."

"Sister, please. Come back so I can dress you properly. You have a lot to learn about the station you are about to gain. Don't worry about that silly creature. She will have forgotten all this by the time she finds the kitchen."

Mehlyndia had never known her sister to be so short tempered. Then again, she had never really known her sister well at all. They were nearly twenty years apart in age, and Mehlyndia had grown up quite alone in her father's castle— until William had joined them, of course. Could the years Bryndah spent with Thomas have somehow changed her? She had said they were well suited, but Mehlyndia had found that hard to believe... until now. *I'm just nervous about the wedding. I'm being too sensitive. Bryndah is only trying to help me get ready, and Laurel does tend to fall apart with the smallest provocation...*

"Mehlyndia, dear, we haven't got a lot of time. Please?" Bryndah's voice returned to its usual light and pleasant tone. "I promise that I will not interfere anymore with your house servants. I should certainly not want you to interfere with mine, after all. Shall we call a truce then?" She flashed that puckish pout again.

This time Mehlyndia did not laugh. "All right. Truce. Now, please help me dress. William is in the great hall. I do not wish for him to be left waiting." Mehlyndia settled down on the stool again and allowed Bryndah to continue dressing her hair.

"Oh, I don't think he'll mind waiting a little longer. You will look beautiful. Now, let's dress this hair so your groom will not confuse you with a haystack from the stable, shall we?"

Mehlyndia could not resist a small smile at that. As Bryndah fussed with the combs, she once again allowed her thoughts to wander. In a moment, Laurel, Thomas, and even Bryndah were forgotten as her mind traveled to the great hall, where she knew, at that moment, her beloved was waiting for her. Today they would meet in the great hall. Tonight would be spent in the wedding suite.

Throughout the great hall of Drumoak, bustling servants and hovering ladies made preparations for the wedding. The children of the servants scurried about with small brooms and pans, being sure to clear away every bit of dirt or dust they found. The stewards saw to it that the chandeliers were lowered to the floor, where each votive received a new candle. Swags of evergreens, entwined with late-summer flowers, were draped on the walls and windows. Long tables hewn from heavy ancient oak were arranged in the front of the hall. A place of honor was arranged for Edward, with William to his right and Mehlyndia to his left. The table was covered in a woven cloth bearing the blue, red, white, and black tartan that was specific to Edward's house.

The kitchen was easily the most chaotic place in the castle, as dozens of lavish delicacies were being prepared for the feast. Platters of roast beef, game hens, pheasants, grouse, and venison covered the counters, along with all manner of sugared fruits, sweet meat, and pastry treats. The center of the table was reserved for the most delectable of the dishes: a full roasted boar. Some of the men in Edward's guard, the ones most friendly with William, had spent all week hunting the beasts that would be served at this celebration. Richard Fylbrigge, Thomas and Bryndah's son, had scored high praise for felling the boar—one of the rare moments of acceptance he enjoyed among the men.

Edward delighted himself in checking on all the preparations, peeking around the kitchen, poking into pots, and peering into cauldrons. He discovered one particularly irresistible broth and was soon dipping a ladle into the bubbling pot. He blended in so well with the melee that Elinor, who regarded herself as "Head Lady of the Household," mistook him for one of the working men.

"Enough of that," she scolded, thumping his shoulder with a washrag. "You'll spoil the broth."

Edward turned around, a comical expression of contrition on his face. "But Elinor, it smells like a feast prepared by God's own hand."

"Oh, my lord! I'm sorry, please forgive me, I did not recognize—So good to have you back, my lord," she said, her eyes sparkling.

He smiled in return. "Thank you, my dear, it is good to be back. I am certainly out of my realm in this kitchen. I would not presume to call rank in the midst of your capable charge."

He chuckled and presented Elinor with a regal bow. She blushed so deeply, her face matched the color of the beets one of the cooks was slicing and placing into small silver bowls.

"You have my gratitude, Elinor. You have always made my household a refuge, and for that I am eternally grateful."

"My lord, it has been my blessing to be in your service. Is the Master William back as well?"

"He was with the young men of my guard last I saw him. But I must say, you may not find him as calm as I am. He is beside himself with giddiness, the likes of which I can recall in only one other bridegroom," he laughed. "That would have been me, on the happy day I wed Anne of Sutherland. How proud she would have been to see her beautiful child wed so well. I cannot help but see Anne each and every time I look upon my little Mehlyndia. She does so favor her mother, don't you agree?"

"Aye, sir, she is the image of her sweet mother, blessed may she sleep."

They stood quietly together, comfortable in each other's company for the moment, when a crash from a preparation table broke the silence, and chaos erupted once again in Elinor's kitchen.

"Laurel," she cried, turning on her heel. "What have you done now, child? What has bedeviled you so? You've been told not to stack the bowls so high." Elinor tossed her washrag over her shoulder and hurried to where Laurel was unsuccessfully trying to catch the remaining bowls. Elinor looked back to Edward and smiled apologetically, "I'm sorry, sir, I need to attend to this."

"Carry on, Elinor." Edward left the kitchen and returned to the hall. He heard the confusion in the kitchen ebb and flow as he walked away. He smiled to himself. He truly did enjoy his home, and he made a mental note, not for the first time, to remember Elinor in his discretionary will.

The past few years had been terribly unkind to Edward. He had lost his beloved Anne to a fever when Mehlyndia was only five years old. He had married for love, in a time when such alliances were not encouraged. Anne of Sutherland did possess a generous dowry, however, which appeased Edward's father, so he eventually sanctioned the union. Upon their marriage, Edward inherited a large bit of land in Sutherland, across the North Sea. It was not rich for farming; however, it was strategically placed across the gulf from his own Stonehaven. Between the two fortresses, he had holdings of four other garrisons which ensured that no surprise attacks from the sea would bring ruin upon him.

But land and wealth were not his reasons for choosing Anne; he simply loved her. What's more, he was faithful to her. Even though it was his right and privilege as duke, Edward never took a serving girl or baron's daughter to his bed. Not that the opportunity had not arisen; he simply did not wish it. Anne was the light of his life; their two daughters, his joy; Mehlyndia, his greatest treasure.

During the past five years, the hysteria brought on by King James's zealous pursuit of those he considered sorcerers or witches had left little happiness for anyone of rank who dared tolerate so much as a talented herbalist. The king had taken his place as head of the church and populated the hierarchy with like-minded clerics. Edward, though loyal to the crown, did not believe that matters of faith should be paramount in maintaining a government. However, in the interest of keeping the king content, he did his best not to draw unwarranted attention to himself or his tenants by challenging the laws. He simply chose not to participate in the hunts. Should a trial take place in Stonehaven, he kept his distance, allowing whatever sentence decreed appropriate by the bishop to be carried out. This duty presently fell to

Gregory de Dunkirk, the bishop of Stonehaven Abbey.

Dunkirk earned his respect by fear and intimidation. Those who were wise did not presume to disagree with him on any matter of a religious bent, lest they find themselves in the lower level of the Stonehaven gaol, being persuaded to change their way of thinking. Edward and Dunkirk had an unspoken understanding between them. Edward allowed the bishop to judge souls, while the bishop left matters of government to Edward's discretion. Though Edward found the death-fires of the witch trials loathsome, he trusted that those condemned had been fairly tried and judged, and most likely deserved whatever fate they met.

But on this day, neither the king nor the bishop nor any other dreary bit of politics could steal away his good humor. He shook aside thoughts of unpleasant business and focused on his home. It was his refuge, and he needed to acknowledge those who offered him solace. Elinor, indeed, should be rewarded for her care.

Lost in his thoughts, he was startled to realize he was not alone in his walk to the great hall.

"My lord," Thomas said, bowing his head slightly.

"Hello, Thomas. I didn't realize you had arrived."

"You are looking quite well."

"Thank you. The gentle weather seems to be agreeing with me."

"Indeed." Thomas fell in step with Edward. "I trust you had a successful tour of the counties."

"Yes, yes." Edward gave him half a glance from the corner of his eye. He did not wish to get into the political debate he feared was Thomas's purpose. "I will fill you in on all the details later, after the wedding. Today is a holiday. No matters of state will be discussed."

"But, my lord, I hear you have left delicate negotiations to William—"

Edward stopped walking and turned sharply to face Thomas. "Tomorrow."

"Yes, my lord. Forgive me." Thomas made no attempt to hide the irritation on his face, as he changed the subject. "I see the preparations are about complete. A bit overly opulent perhaps. A gala the likes of this has not been seen in these walls since—"

"Your wedding." Edward lifted a brow and gave Thomas a challenging grin. He would not allow this jealous, pompous son-in-law of his to spoil his day. "As I recall, Elinor had an equally impressive feast prepared for your wedding. Your brother and Mehlyndia are deserving of no less opulence. Are they not?"

"Of course." Thomas smiled with only half his mouth.

Edward chuckled, and resumed his walk toward the great hall.

Thomas bowed curtly. "I shall beg your leave then, as I would like to find my Lady Bryndah."

"By all means." Edward made another mental note about his discretionary will—regarding Thomas.

He arrived at the entryway to the great hall just in time to see an entourage of jubilant young men carry a struggling, laughing William on their shoulders through the grand doors of the foyer.

"What is all this?" Edward asked, intrigued.

Isaac Walford, the youngest of Edward's guard, answered

the duke with a grin. "Lord Edward, we caught this sparrow trying to take flight from the parapet." He looked at William, teasingly. "Could it be we have finally found your one true fear, Will? Are you afraid of marriage?" Raucous laughter erupted from the rest of the men as William was gracelessly lowered to the floor.

"Afraid?" William replied indignantly, dusting himself off. "I think not!" He straightened his tunic and adjusted his scabbard. "Terrified? Definitely!" He made a comical effort to run back out through the doors, only to be hauled back by his friends.

Edward approached him, laughing with the rest of the men. "Ah, my boy, I see these fine gentlemen have finally managed to clip your wings and bring you home to roost. A worthy captivity, in my opinion."

"It is indeed, Father. One to which I shall gladly surrender." William crossed his hands over his chest and lowered his head in a gesture of submission. Then he sneezed and grimaced from the cloud of dust that rose from his tunic. "However, I don't believe my lady would be pleased to have me in my current state. I fear I would offend even the pig keeper."

Edward clapped him hard on the back and let out a bellow, making an exaggerated wave of his hand in front of his nose. "I believe you are right. At the very least, you should douse yourself in something more sweet smelling, like garlic, and burn your garments."

The boisterous crowd that had carried William through the doors began to disperse through the hall, much to the dismay of the servants who were setting the tables there.

William's contemporaries were all the sons or wards of the nobles and personal guards in Edward's service, and they were a riotous lot.

Only days ago, these same jovial fellows stood in a much different posture, armed and willing to kill or be killed to defend Edward against Lord Ogham, Duke of Lothian. After Edward refused the rival duke access to one of the major seaports in Sutherland, Ogham had Edward's camp surrounded and could have easily killed or taken them all prisoner. William had defused Ogham's imminent show of force with an impressive display of diplomacy and his usual boldness. On his own dubious authority, William had barged into Ogham's camp in the middle of the night, apologetically claiming that Edward had sent him to clear up a misunderstanding. In a performance worthy of the stage, William assured the rival duke that access to Sutherland would indeed be granted. Ogham had been convinced and sent orders to withdraw. Of course, William neglected to mention that Edward had no idea of what he was doing, but by the time the deception was found out, he and his companions had made it well beyond Lothian's border and safely back to Stonehaven.

William smiled as he watched three of his friends engage in a battle of another sort, arguing over which of them would win a romp with a certain dairy maid who had caught their eyes.

"Come into the hall, son." Edward nudged him out of the foyer. "If you have a bold streak in you today, you should investigate the kitchen. Just don't allow Elinor to catch you!" Edward laughed as he escorted William through the doors to the great hall. Edward raised his arms and gestured to all the magnificent preparations in the room. "All of this is for you and my sweet Mehlyndia. This is a day I have long awaited."

"As have I." William smiled, looking at the evergreen swags adorning the walls and the splendid silver and gold table settings. The chandeliers were being hauled back to the proper height, each votive sparkling with a fresh candle. Even the somber-looking faces on the portraits on the gallery wall seemed more cheerful in this setting. The great hall had never looked so grand.

"Now, if you'll excuse me, I want to see my daughter while she is still mine, before you steal her away from me." Edward gave William a warm smile and another pat on the back, then made his way to the staircase on the far end of the hall.

William was suddenly overwhelmed with a sense of joy that took him completely by surprise. It occurred to him how fortunate he was to be part of Edward's household.

A high-pitched squeal shook him from his reverie. "Will—I mean, Master William! You're here!"

William spun around, startled, then laughed loudly at the comically pompous posture Laurel affected in his presence. "Hello, Laurel. You gave me a start like no warlord ever could." He took her hand and swung her around under his arm to make her laugh. "Since when do you stand on formality with me? Please don't call me 'master.' You know I hate that."

He gave her a quick embrace; she groaned at the cloud that rose from his tunic and backed away, waving her hand in front of her nose.

"All right, then. It's good to see you, Stinky."

"I think I prefer 'master' after all," he laughed. "It's good to see you, too."

"This place has been dull as a rock with you and Sean away. I've gone quite mad with boredom." She was holding her laughter in check, but there was mischief in her eyes. "If not for m' lady I would have nothing to occupy my time." She pulled Mehlyndia's handkerchief from her pocket and held it to her nose, looking at him coyly from under her bangs.

He backed up two steps to give her better breathing room. "I'm sure there is all manner of trouble for you to find. I've not known you to ever sit still. So, is she ready?"

"Ready? For what? Is something happening today?" Laurel batted her eyes innocently.

"You are an evil wench!" William burst into renewed laughter at Laurel's playful teasing. "Seriously, should I sneak in and see her? Or is that something an imp like you would encourage me to do just to cause me grief?"

Her face softened into a serious, hurt expression. "Now, why would I wish you grief? It's your wedding day, Will."

"You know I didn't mean anything," he assured her, feeling like a bit of a lout for his teasing. He smiled apologetically, then tilted his head, suddenly curious as to why Laurel was on the stairs and not attending the bride. "Shouldn't you be helping Mehlyndia?"

Laurel stiffened her shoulders, pursing her lips. "Mehlyndia has all the help she requires. It seems I'm not needed by her today," she said, scowling toward the top of the stairs.

"What are you talking about?" he asked, concerned by her sudden change in mood. "Of course she needs you."

"The countess is with her." Laurel hissed the end of the

word countess.

"Bryndah is here?" He wrinkled his nose as he spoke the name.

"Aye, and I am sure I've never met such a one as her in my life. I've met friendlier guard dogs. You were right about that one. She scared me too." Laurel took on a conspiratorial tone, leaning toward him, and said, "I don't envy you living under her roof, Will."

William leaned close to her and mocked her tone, "Neither do I." He looked at her wide-eyed expression and smirked, eager to banish any thought of Bryndah being in the house. "Laurel, if you need someone to dress, I could use a good and proper scrubbing," he winked.

She blushed violently, but chuckled. "You're right about that, but I believe I shall send Sean up for you."

"Yes, send Sean," he sighed in mock disappointment. "He will surely keep me out of trouble. Tell him I'll be in my chamber setting fire to my garments."

"Aye, Stinky," she replied, with a wink and headed down the stairs.

After one last glance to the great hall, he chuckled and headed up to his room. A sense of belonging fell on him like a warm quilt on a cold evening. He was home.

"There, am I ready now?" Mehlyndia could scarcely believe the stunning woman in the looking glass was actually her own reflection. Bryndah had transformed her hair into a cascading braid of auburn, woven with summer flowers and greens. Her brow was crowned with an intricate net of spun gold threads that caught the light of the sunset through the open window. She ran her hands across her saffron brocade gown, beautifully embroidered with lilies of the field at the hem and glass beads throughout the bodice and train. It had taken Elinor and Laurel months of painstaking stitching to complete the work of art that now graced her petite figure.

"You are a vision, child."

Mehlyndia turned to see the smiling face of her father in the doorway. "Father, you're home!" Mehlyndia flew across the room to embrace Edward. "I'm so glad to see you."

"Slow down, now, and let me look at you." Edward stood back to admire his daughter. "I tell you, nothing God has in His heaven could look as splendid as you do right now. Bryndah, look at our little one. A woman of her own now."

"Yes, Father, she is beautiful," Bryndah said, while fussing with Mehlyndia's train. "She was an appalling mess of sticks and twigs when I arrived. I have been working miracles with combs and lacing for the better part of the day," she laughed. "I suspect she will pass." Bryndah gave one last tug to Mehlyndia's train, then stood and presented her own cheek to her father for a kiss.

"Well, you have indeed performed a miracle." Edward gave Bryndah a quick peck on the cheek. "Thomas is in the hall, my dear. I believe he was asking after you a while ago."

"Well then, I suppose I should go find him. I shall see you later. Mehlyndia, dear, you do look lovely." She gave Mehlyndia a kiss on the cheek and made one final inspection of her hair dressings. "William will hardly know you." She brushed a stray curl from Mehlyndia's cheek before she turned and walked briskly from the room.

William will hardly know me? Because I look lovely?

Mehlyndia's annoyance with her sister crept back, as she watched Bryndah walk out. *Can she never give a compliment without taking half back?*

Shaking her annoyance aside, Mehlyndia stared again into the looking glass with the light of the fading sunset. She looked up into the reflection of her father's face as he stood behind her. His gaze was filled with such affection, it brought her close to tears.

"Oh, my dear child, when I look on you, I see your mother. You are her very soul come back, I am certain," he said, softly and wiped a tear from his eye. "Are you ready?"

"Is it time?"

"I believe it is."

Before they could leave the room, a small squeak came from the doorway. Laurel timidly pushed the door open and peeked into the chamber. She looked such a sight—crouching low beside the door, her eyes wide with a look of imminent flight about her—that Mehlyndia did not know whether to laugh or cry. "Forgive me, I—"

"Laurel, what is it you need?" Mehlyndia asked gently, not wanting her to race away in panic.

"Only to know that the gown is to your liking." She spied around the door like a mouse watching out for the cat, and whispered, "And to be sure you are all right?"

"All right?" Edward looked at Laurel curiously. "Of course she is all right. Laurel, what concerns you?"

Laurel answered in her customary short, breathless rambles, "Nothing, sir. Nothing... I was just checking... I must go anyway. I need to make sure that Sean is sent to help Will—I mean Master William—dress, and Elinor will be vexed that I haven't told her where I am." Laurel curtsied and hurried away.

"Well, it seems we have a genuine mouse amongst the household staff," Edward laughed once Laurel was gone. "I do believe she has caught Elinor's ire, though. I witnessed a catastrophe of immense proportions in the kitchen."

"I think her concern has more to do with a scolding she received from Bryndah, Father. She was very cross for no good reason today. She practically slapped poor Laurel with her harsh words. I have never known Bryndah to be so ill tempered."

"Unfortunately, I have," Edward sighed. "Oh, not when she was your age, to be sure. In her maidenhood, she was as sweet and cheerful as you. I'm not sure if her marriage caused her to change or if her latent sour disposition was born in her. But I have to admit, I have known her to be quite cruel indeed. Someday I shall tell you more. But not now."

Until this day, Mehlyndia had never known her sister to be anything but loving, and was not completely ready to accept that she could be 'quite cruel indeed.' Mehlyndia stared absently out her window. The sun was completely down over the hillside, and the sky was bathed in a deep purple haze.

She turned to her father, blinking back happy tears. "The sun is down."

Her father extended his arm to her. "Are you ready to get married now?"

Banishing further thoughts about her sister's temperament, she took one last glance in the glass, then accepted his arm. The next sunset I witness, Mehlyndia mused, will be as Lady Fylbrigge. "Yes Father, I'm ready."

Sean chuckled to himself that he had been ordered by Laurel to head up to William's chambers, to provide a 'proper scrubbing' to the bridegroom. Laurel had told him to be sure William did not arrive at his wedding dressed as a common horse trader and that he smelled better than the horse. Sean was more than happy to obey Laurel's command, bowing regally from his waist before obediently trudging up the stairs, going slowly to allow William time to bathe *himself.*

Sean knocked lightly on the door. "Are you ready for me now, Will?" Without waiting for a response, he let himself in.

William stood beside the bed wearing nothing but his undergarments and a grand feathered hat. "Sean! I thought you had abandoned me. I am absolutely at my wit's end here. I swear I will never be comfortable among nobles. The shoes are too tight, the trews are dreadful. I'd much prefer to wear a proper kilt, but Father insists on the king's fashion. But... just how do all these garments go together?" He shook his head as he tried to drape a formidable tartan cape across his shoulder. It slipped to the floor in a heap. He picked it up and attempted to hang it across the other shoulder, without success. "This confounded thing won't cooperate!" he growled, and tossed it onto the bed. "At least I know how to wear the hat!" He laughed and tipped his brow, as he handed Sean a goblet of wine.

Sean raised his drink. "To shoes and trews and fancy hats!" He could not help but laugh at William's wedding jitters. "You're mad, you know, Will. And quite hopeless. Laurel warned me to keep an eye on you. She feared you would arrive at your wedding dressed in bed sheets and draperies if you were left to dress yourself."

"I will not be the sort of nobleman who must be dressed by someone else, thank you! I do not care how many dressers the other fops need."

Sean had to admit he had trouble imagining William as a nobleman. He made a mental comparison of the cocky, confident William who had recklessly gone against Ambrose Woodhall only two days ago, and the nervous bridegroom before him now. "No, you surely are like no other nobleman I know."

William stared in dismay at the array of fine clothing laid out on the bed before him. "All right. Now, honestly, I can do this." He held up a stiffly embroidered doublet, shaking his head in mock disgust that someone expected him to adorn himself in lilies of the valley. "Flowers. As if the hat isn't silly enough."

"Would you prefer ducks?" Sean teased.

With a deep sigh, William prepared to don the elaborate garment. "First things first." He turned it several times in his hands, trying to decide which side was the front. "Aha! This way."

"Yes, that's right, Will. Put it on backwards," Sean laughed. "You truly *are* hopeless." Sean put his drink down on the table and bowed dramatically. "All right, my liege, your humble servant is here to help you dress, like it or not." He took the doublet from William and put it back on the bed. "You'll need to put the trews on first," he said, then handed William the puffy leggings, also embroidered with lilies of the valley.

"I hate these," William groaned.

Sean pushed William onto the chair and handed him the trews. "You'd look fetching without them, I'm sure, but it may be drafty."

William pulled them on properly, then rebelliously flattened out the puffs. He stood in front of the mirror shaking his head. "Do the king's men actually wear these in public?" He reached for the doublet, then stopped and turned to Sean. "Now?"

Sean nodded.

William examined it again, turned it front to back several times before holding it out to Sean. "I give up. Dress me, humble servant."

"You're sounding more like a nobleman by the minute." Sean took the garment and held it up in front of William. "Now watch, so you don't have to spend the rest of your life naked."

Before William's amazed eyes, Sean pulled the front of the doublet apart. The opening had been concealed behind all the embroidery. William allowed Sean to put it on him and fasten it up.

Sean primped up the sleeves; William flattened them down. Sean scowled and primped them again, slapping William's hands when he tried to flatten them again.

The belt and scabbard came next. William ran his fingers over the fine leather tooling. "Thank goodness, there are no flowers on this." He held it up for Sean's appraisal, before he secured it around his waist and adjusted it to the proper place on his hip. Sean reverently retrieved William's sword from its old tattered and worn scabbard, draped carelessly over the back of the chair. He presented it to William in a proper knightly fashion: over his left arm, hilt first.

William bowed in mock tribute and ceremoniously slid the sword into the new scabbard. Sean draped the cape around William's shoulders with a flourish, bringing the corners together at his left shoulder. "We can't forget this," he said, as he picked up a silver badge from the dressing table.

"I should say not." William grinned and took the badge that was adorned with a silver eagle—the official designation of Edward's house. "It'll be official tonight. I'll be part of the clan." He pinned the badge to his cape, securing it at his shoulder. It had been given to him as a token of acceptance when Edward had blessed William and Mehlyndia's betrothal. William had worn it proudly during the tour, but not until tonight, when he was properly wed, would he truly be part of Edward's clan.

Sean stood back to look at the fully dressed bridegroom.

William struck a lofty pose. "Well? Am I presentable?"

"Be still, my heart," Sean prattled. "Look at you. You could turn even my head!"

William glanced at him sideways.

"I mean it. You are absolutely stunning."

William admired his reflection in the looking glass. "For once in your life, you're right. I am stunning." He let out a hearty laugh and tossed his discarded and dusty tunic at Sean, hitting him squarely in the face. "Or perhaps I'm only just stunned."

Sean picked up his goblet and handed one to William. The two shared a quick toast.

With one last glance in the mirror, William took a deep

breath. "Well, I would say I am as ready as I will ever be." He extended his hand toward the door. "After you."

Sean pushed William's hand down and extended his own. "No. After you." He shook his head. "Some nobleman."

They laughed and started toward the door. They were stopped by a firm knock.

"Are you expecting guests, Will?"

"I never expect anything. Makes everything much more interesting." He chuckled and opened the door. The smile on his face faded as quickly as it had appeared. "Thomas. What are you doing here?"

"Would you leave your only brother standing in the corridor? Or may I come in?"

"Actually, we were just on our way down. You can walk with me if you choose."

Thomas ignored the comment, walking straight past William and into the room. He strode to the table and helped himself to some wine, then turned slowly to face William. "I see you have finally learned the proper way to dress yourself," Thomas said, scrutinizing William as he would a horse he wished to purchase and giving Sean a dismissive glance. "A pity that you still need lessons on what company to keep, however. William, there is a matter we need to discuss. Could we have a private moment?"

Sean bristled and started toward the door. William held up a hand.

"I don't think there is time now, Thomas. You really don't want me to be late for my own wedding, do you?" William turned to leave.

"I wouldn't be so quick to turn your back on me, brother."

William stopped, then slowly turned to face his brother. "I beg your pardon?"

"I said, there is a matter we need to discuss... privately."

"Say what you came to say, but Sean will stay here. If you will not speak, then we shall go down to the hall." William clenched his teeth to keep the confident edge in his voice, but he could feel the angry redness forming on his face.

Thomas took a step forward, locking his eyes on William's. "Lord Ogham is not amused at the way you so eloquently convinced some of his earls to shift the trade routes from his tenants. You may have held your own against his dull-minded twits, Drunbalk and Wesley, but are you prepared to take on Ogham face-to-face?" He took another step forward, glowering. "I cannot believe Edward sent *you* to the negotiations, a beardless boy. Is he trying to condemn the lot of us?"

William scowled at his brother, resisting the urge to reach for his sword. "Edward has no such concern, Thomas. At any rate, I will not speak with you further on this subject tonight."

"Then allow me a word of brotherly advice. You have angered some considerably dangerous adversaries." Thomas sauntered toward the door, a wry grin coming to his face. "You would be wise to watch your back, dear brother. It is obvious you have no one capable of watching it for you."

Sean crossed the room in less than a heartbeat, his hands clasped tightly around Thomas's throat. "That's twice! No further threats will come from you."

Thomas twisted awkwardly, trying to free Sean's hands from his throat.

William strolled toward the two. He spoke in a soft and steady voice as Sean and Thomas grappled. "We don't have time for him, Sean. But feel free to finish this later. Right now, I'd like to go downstairs to get married." He casually returned to the door. "Now, is anyone going to join me?"

Sean released Thomas with a shove, sending him flailing over the table. The wine bottle and glasses hit the stone floor with an ear-splitting shatter. Thomas rose to his feet quickly. Red-faced and furious, he stormed toward William. "You have set your course, brother. Mark my words; this is not finished!" The echo of the threat hung in the air as Thomas stalked past William and out of the room.

"How pathetic," William said, more to himself than to Sean. "He still attempts to intimidate me."

Sean set the table straight, leaving the broken glass where it lay, and returned to William's side.

The scarlet slowly fading from his cheeks as William brushed the dust off Sean's shoulder. "Thank you, Sean. You handled that quite nicely. I would have hated to ruin this fine outfit."

"My pleasure." Catching his breath, Sean grandly primped up his own less grand sleeves. "Will," he began, still struggling with his breathing.

"What is it? We're late, you know."

"Don't worry about your back. I've got it covered."

"I'm counting on that, my friend."

By the time he and Sean reached the top of the stairway leading into the great hall, William had managed to leave behind the unpleasantness with Thomas. Sean took on a more alert stance, which enabled William to concentrate on his wedding, and not the threat his brother had just made to him.

At the top of the stairs, the fragrance of wild summer flowers mingled with the aromas of the impending feast. He watched the guests, all decked out in their finest clothes, as he listened to the sounds of rustling skirts and jumbled conversations. His sense of joy in the occasion gradually returned to him. But it was the sound of the musician, plucking gently at his lute, that brought him the comfort he needed to gather his thoughts and calm himself down.

Many a time he had daydreamed about how pleasant the simple life of a musician would be. Often during the past months, while learning what government life would be like, he had longed to retreat to his tent and let it all pass from him in the stings of his lute. But he kept to his tasks, his sense of responsibility preventing him from turning from the course set before him. As much as he would like to lead the quiet existence of the simple folk, he knew it was not his lot.

William surveyed the guests from the top of the stairs until he spotted a jovial group of young men gathered near the dessert table, still arguing over which of them would win the eye of the dairy maid. He tapped Sean, gesturing toward them.

Simon MacHenry, one of Edward's guards, pointed as William and Sean descended the stairs. "Look, lads, an impostor has joined us."

Isaac Walford and Ewan McDonough, two of Edward's sentries, approached William, circling him, looking him up and down with comical expressions of astonishment at his transformation into a proper nobleman.

Ewan picked at William's fancy sleeves. "Not even wed yet and she's got him turned into a dandy!"

"And so fair of manner and face," Isaac added, placing his hand on his cheek. "You'd best be careful, Will, or you will have Ewan swooning," he said, making exaggerated fan-waving motions with his hand.

William brushed his clothing pompously and fluffed the sleeve Ewan had poked at. "I just had this conversation upstairs, you lunks. I assure you; by tomorrow, I will be back to my old, ugly self."

Sean slapped William's back and grinned. "What do you mean, 'back to?'"

"Very funny. Now, if you will all excuse me, I need to mingle with the real guests," William laughed.

Isaac slapped his hand to his chest in mock dejection. "I'm deeply wounded! I think I may need to seek solace with a certain tavern dancer." He gave William a conspiratorial wink.

"Now, now, no need to bring up my past indiscretions." William assumed a pious expression. "I'm reformed now." He leaned in close and spoke from the side of his mouth. "Besides, it was only once and she didn't even finish her dance. Save your silver, Isaac. She's not worth it." He winked back at Isaac and broke free from his rowdy comrades.

He walked casually through the room, making polite conversation with the nobles he knew by name, introducing himself to those he did not. He was charming with the ladies and raucous with the lads, until at last he found his way to the musician in the corner. He beamed a warm smile in greeting to the elderly musician as he finished his selection. "Hello, Geoffrey."

Geoffrey looked up, smiling. "William, lad, there you are!" He set his lute down and stood to embrace William, then held him at arm's length and admired his appearance. "It is good to see you so well, and so tall now! And on such a happy occasion! I was beyond honored when Lord Edward called upon me to perform for you, Will. I hope you still have the opportunity to play. You have such talent." Geoffrey bent and retrieved his lute, then leaned in close to William. "Bishop Dunkirk himself will be here tonight," he whispered. "Please, for my sake, let me do the singing."

William stood back, his smile gone instantly. "Dunkirk? I thought the vicar from Kent was to perform my wedding."

"Apparently there was a last-minute change. I heard the duke tell Elinor." Geoffrey lifted his nose pompously. "I suppose he did not wish to slight his holier-than-thouness." He resumed his serious tone, placing his hand on William's forearm. "But please, Will, I know you. Tonight would not be a good time for you to sing one of your adventure tunes. Not with the likes of Dunkirk present."

William patted Geoffrey's hand reassuringly. "I promise. I had not planned to sing at all tonight, unless it is requested by Mehlyndia. And then I shall sing for her alone. I know this is not the place for anything of an adventurous nature."

Geoffrey exhaled, nodding his head. "Good."

William glanced about the corner, then back to Geoffrey. "Where is Nora? Is she feeling better yet?"

Geoffrey's smile faded, and his eyes grew cloudy. "Thank you for asking. I'm sorry to say she has not improved. To tell the truth, she is fading away from me more each day. She stays to her bed now."

"I'm sorry to hear that, my friend." William placed a gentle hand on Geoffrey's shoulder. "I shall make a point to come and see her as soon as I'm able." He fully intended to keep his promise. He owed so much to Geoffrey and his wife. Both had befriended him early in his days at Drumoak and had helped him realize that there were genuinely good people in this world.

Geoffrey patted William's hand. "I should be very grateful for that."

The doors to the great hall swung open, sending a stiff breeze through the room.

Bishop Dunkirk and his acolyte strode in from the foyer. Dunkirk glided across the floor, straight-backed and pompous, dressed in full formal regalia. His mitered hat towered at least two feet above his brow. The young acolyte was dressed far less impressively, in a simple white cassock and cowl. The boy walked respectfully, head down, three steps behind and to the left of the bishop.

"Looks like it's about time." William said to Geoffrey, before dutifully walking toward the bishop. William suppressed the grimace that always seemed to find his face in the presence of clergymen, hoping Dunkirk would not notice it.

"Fylbrigge," Dunkirk said, coolly, "congratulations on your wedding. I'm sure the duke is pleased with his daughter's union." He held out his hand, palm down toward William, presenting his ring for the customary kiss on the large stone.

William looked at the extended hand and bowed over it

quickly, ignoring the ring. "Your Grace, thank you for being here. I am honored that you have consented to perform the ceremony."

Bishop Dunkirk withdrew his hand slowly. "I was beginning to think other arrangements had been made, as I was only told of your nuptials two days ago. I feared I had somehow earned the displeasure of the duke." He raised a suspicious eyebrow.

"An unfortunate oversight, I assure you," William replied carefully, not wanting to insult the bishop further as he was sure he already had by ignoring the ring. "I'm sure Lord Edward meant no disrespect." He felt heat rising to his cheeks, but kept his expression as natural as possible.

"I see." Dunkirk's tone was unconvinced. "Well, I'm here now. Perhaps you should send that cowering little girl to announce to Lord Edward that we are ready to begin."

William followed the bishop's gaze. Laurel peered at him wide-eyed from behind a statue in the corner. She seemed positively terrified. "Thank you, Your Grace, I shall do just that. If you'll excuse me."

"Laurel," William addressed her as calmly as his jangled nerves would allow, "would you please tell the duke we are ready to begin?"

"What's he doing here?" she whispered, pointing to Dunkirk as though she had seen a ghost.

William spoke as quietly as possible, "I believe he's here to perform a wedding. But he won't be able to do that if Edward doesn't bring Mehlyndia down."

"What happened to the vicar?" she asked, her high-pitched whisper carried loudly throughout the hall.

William waved his hand in front of her. "Quiet, Laurel, he'll hear you. I know how you feel." He made a quick glance over his shoulder to see Dunkirk watching him with his head tipped to one side. William flashed him a quick smile and turned back to Laurel. "I didn't expect him either. Go on, now. Take the back stairs."

Laurel disappeared through the kitchen.

William returned to the bishop, affecting a proper expression of respect. "They shall be here presently. Perhaps we should take our places." William directed Dunkirk to the landing at the foot of the stair, not meeting his eyes. When they had taken their places, William signaled to Geoffrey, who made the announcement that the wedding would begin soon.

When the crowd quieted, Geoffrey began to pluck the strings on his lute. William chuckled silently to himself at Geoffrey's selection. The melody was from one of the bishop's favorite hymns; years before, William had taken delight in fashioning new words to that very same hymn. Words he was sure, that would not amuse Bishop Dunkirk.

At last, Mehlyndia appeared at the top of the staircase on her father's arm. William caught his breath. She was more beautiful than he had ever seen her. The candles in the chandeliers caught the glass beads on her dress and the gold netting in her hair. When her eyes found his, he was certain that they were the only two people in the room.

Mehlyndia descended the staircase gracefully, supported by her father's arm. Finally, Lord Edward took her hand and placed it into William's. Was that a tremble in his hand? Or was it hers? He wasn't sure. It was the first time they had seen each other in nine long months. Their eyes locked, unwilling to break apart for even an instant.

The bishop's commanding, monotonous voice broke the trance, "Let us begin." The world suddenly slowed. Everything but the lady beside him and the voice in front of him vanished. He found it difficult to pay attention to the never-ending Scripture falling from the bishop's lips as his eyes wandered to his bride, and her hand in his, to her delicate fingers—I hope Sean has the ring! William tried to glance sideways without attracting the attention of the bishop. What he saw confirmed his fears. Sean was giving hand motions to Isaac, slipping an imaginary ring on his finger. Isaac motioned to Ewan, who picked up his cue and stepped backward through the kitchen door. William's heart began to beat faster. Oh, no. I cannot believe this! He turned his attention back to the bishop, who had finished his fourth Gospel reading and was now sermonizing about a wedding in Cana. William chose his moment carefully and risked another sideways glance toward Sean.

A murmur from the back of the room gave him license to turn fully for a moment. From out of the kitchen, a small maid crept along as quietly as a mouse weaving through the rows of gentlemen, and skirted ladies. A small brown pouch suddenly flew into the air, arcing above the head of the Countess of Norwalkshire. It landed lightly in the back-extended hand of Isaac, who, in a graceful sweeping motion, sent it sliding across the floor to land between Simon's feet. Simon's left foot casually pushed it toward a crouching Ewan, who then hurled it to Sean. To William's astonishment, none of the guests seemed aware of this relay. The instant Sean had the little package in his hand, the bishop looked up.

"Do you have a ring to present?"

"A ring! Yes," William answered, fighting to suppress a nervous giggle. "Right here."

Sean offered the ring to William. He took it, thanking Sean with his eyes. He bit his lip, trying to restore his breathing to normal and combat his sudden urge to laugh out loud when Sean winked at him.

"Place the ring on the third finger of Lady Mehlyndia's left hand."

William took Mehlyndia's hand and slid the ring onto her finger.

"Would the two of you now please kneel and bow for the taking of the marriage vows."

Mehlyndia immediately obeyed. The order to kneel before this man caught William momentarily unprepared, and he felt a twist in his stomach. Mehlyndia's hand reminded him it was solely for the purpose of the wedding. Worried that the bishop had noticed his hesitation, William slowly lowered himself to his knees.

The bishop read the vows and William repeated when he was told to. He listened to Mehlyndia recite her vows as well. Finally, the pronouncement was made that they were now man and wife.

"You may both rise."

"Not yet, please remain down."

William looked up, concerned but was relieved to see that it had been Lord Edward who spoke. He looked at Mehlyndia, who revealed no sign of surprise. In fact, she was smiling at him through moist eyes. William looked back up at the duke, confused.

"Please bow your head, son. We are not quite finished."

William bowed obediently, while Lord Edward withdrew his sword from the scabbard strapped to his side. He held it with both hands above the newlyweds.

"It is my privilege and honor to make this proclamation. Let it be known, from this day forth, that this man, William Fylbrigge, whom I have freely chosen, shall henceforth be known by all as Lord William of Drumoak, Earl of Sutherland. He will be heir to my seat as Duke of Stonehaven, with all of the rank, honor, and privilege that goes therein. And this woman, my beautiful daughter, shall from this moment henceforth be known as Lady Mehlyndia, Countess of Sutherland." Lord Edward placed the blade on William's right shoulder, then on his left. He placed his hand upon Mehlyndia's shoulder. "Rise now, Lord and Lady Sutherland."

William could barely hear the applause from the people in the hall for the pounding of his heart. He forced his legs to a standing position, then turned to face Lord Edward. He had not expected to receive such a high rank. Earl? Of Sutherland, no less. *Thomas will just love that.* William glanced at Sean in disbelief. Sean's expression told William he was not surprised at all.

"Welcome to the family, son," Edward said, as he embraced the new Lord of Sutherland.

"Thank you, my lord," William answered formally, then gave his new father-in-law a squeeze.

"Thank you, Father. You have made us both so happy."

As Mehlyndia and Edward embraced, William leaned back toward Sean. "I can't believe I forgot the ring. You are a lifesaver."

"I've always got your back," Sean laughed.

William turned his attention to his bride. "I believe this is where we are allowed to share a kiss, my love." Smiling, he placed his hands on her face and drew her near. They stood lost in each other's eyes for a moment, relishing the joy of the occasion.

The moment was short lived, however, as the doors were violently flung wide and a sudden gust of wind furiously swirled through the great hall. Surprised gasps echoed through the room as the guests separated, making a path for the tall, menacing figure who strode through the crowd to stand in the middle of the hall. The uninvited intruder faced Lord Edward, William, and Mehlyndia with his hand at the ready upon the hilt of his sword.

Chapter 2

A SUDDEN SILENCE FILLED the hall, broken only by the sound of swords and dirks being drawn and readied. Mehlyndia clutched at William's right arm, as he reached for the hilt of his own sword. "My love," he whispered, "I have need of this arm. Please stand behind your father."

Mehlyndia began to protest, fearful to leave his side, but the angry set of his jaw and steely expression in his eyes told her not to argue. Reluctantly, she released his arm and backed away to stand behind Edward.

"Edward of Stonehaven, in the name of Lothlanne, I demand to address this convocation!"

"Lord Ogham, sheath your weapon!" Lord Edward called out. "This is not a state occasion nor convocation. You have no voice here."

Mehlyndia trembled at her father's fearsome and unfamiliar tone and stance. William, too, had transformed from the gentle, eloquent man she loved to someone she scarcely recognized—his neck muscles taut and his eyes afire, still squarely trained on Ogham.

"Not a state occasion?" Ogham bellowed. "You have named an heir and bestowed an earldom. An earldom that meets the borders of my own holdings in the north. And to a man who has just wrested control of major trade routes from my nobles. Did you think I would not take interest in this?"

"Ogham, this is a wedding." Edward took a step forward to stand beside William. "You were sent an invitation to convene tomorrow with the other nobles on these matters. Remove your hand from your sword and discard your demeanor immediately!"

Ogham responded by flexing his fingers tighter around the hilt of his sword. "How is it, Edward, that I alone have been left out of this informal proclamation?"

William's jaw tightened; his knuckles grew white gripping his sword.

Mehlyndia dared not move nor even draw breath. She scanned the crowd of faces; most of them familiar if only by sight. It seemed to her that everyone she had ever known was in the great hall. At the far end, near the door, Bryndah stood silent, her eyes fixed on their father. Thomas though, standing close to Bryndah's side, stood grinning, staring squarely at William.

"How is it, Lord Ogham," William demanded, "that you have knowledge of a proclamation made only moments before you entered?"

Ogham shifted his gaze sharply from Edward to William. He glowered at the new earl, but remained silent. William took several steps forward, distancing himself from Edward.

"Speak! Who among this hall has given you this knowledge?"

Mehlyndia slipped back further behind her father when Ogham took a menacing step forward, his hand twitching on his sword. Sean and Isaac inched away from where they had been stationed during the ceremony, their swords unsheathed and held at the ready.

William mimicked Ogham's hand motions on his own sword. "Did you not hear my lord ask you how you knew? Have you no voice with which to answer?"

"Stand easy, Lord Sutherland," a scornful voice echoed from the rear of the hall.

Surprised mutters from the guests wormed through the crowd, all heads turning toward the door to see who had spoken. Thomas Fylbrigge stepped forward, his formal cloak billowing dramatically behind him as he strode to the middle of the hall. "Lord Ogham is here upon my invitation." He assumed a relaxed, almost charming manner as he took a place beside William, turning to face his visitor. "My Lord Ogham, I beseech you forgive the ill temper of my young brother. His youth and lack of court manners are clearly at the crux of this... misunderstanding. The honor bestowed upon him this night seems to have come as much of a surprise to him as it does to you. As it does to many of us in this room. I assure you no slight in your absence of an invitation was intended."

Mehlyndia shuddered at the proximity of Thomas to William and the devilish curl forming on his lip as he addressed Lord Ogham. She shrunk away from the landing, moving backward toward the banquet tables. Sean and Isaac stepped sideways, allowing her to pass and stand behind them as they assumed a precautionary stance near Ogham and Thomas. Ewan and Simon mirrored their movements and flanked the uninvited duke taking positions opposite Sean and Isaac.

"The snake," Sean whispered to Isaac. "I knew I should

have strangled him when I had the chance." He held his sword at the ready.

Isaac halted him instantly, holding him back with a hand on his shoulder. "Easy, Sean. If swords are to be drawn here, ours must not be first. Can you tell how many may be with him?"

Sean surveyed the faces in the crowd, ticking off each face he could identify. "Drunbalk, Woodhall, Wesley. They're not a threat where they stand."

Isaac nodded his agreement. "By my reckoning, the advantage is ours, but I don't like our distance from Will. He's only got Richard on his back."

"Gads, he's as good as naked," Sean grumbled. "Keep sharp, Isaac."

"Step down, Thomas," Edward ordered, approaching Thomas, "I will not have this night further insulted by your simpering—"

"I assure you I had no intention of causing ill feelings to overshadow this joyous occasion," Thomas replied with a contrite bend of his neck, then turned and addressed the bishop in the same patronizing voice. "Your Grace, I regret you had to witness this unpleasantness."

The bishop curled one side of his mouth and bowed slightly. "Thank you, sir. Lord Edward, perhaps it is best to hear what Aberdoir has to say."

Thomas solicitously bowed to Edward and gestured graciously to Ogham. "I can only imagine that Lord Ogham arrived just in time to hear you bestow my dear brother with this... honor."

Ogham held his foreboding stance and surveyed the

crowed with his eyes. He set his eyes on each of Edward's guards who surrounded him, then onto Thomas. Ogham's brow lifted slightly; Thomas responded in kind. At last, Ogham released his hand from his sword.

William relaxed his grip in answer. A chorus of exhales rose from the crowd.

"Lord Ogham," William said, stepping forward, putting several paces between himself and Thomas. "I find I must... agree...with my brother's explanation on the oversight of your invitation." He bowed only slightly, never lowering his eyes. "I had no anticipation of Lord Edward's honor before this evening. There was no slight intended. This is a wedding, a sacrament made before God. No other issue will be taken up this night. Only a heathen would dare defile the sanctity of such a gathering." William did not falter as he turned and looked Dunkirk in the eye. "I'm sure you agree with me, Your Grace, do you not? Unless, of course, you are indebted to these two for their... generosity to your church."

Dunkirk's eyes flared in a flash of crimson. Mehlyndia caught her breath, stunned at William's boldness in challenging the bishop in such a way, blatantly suggesting that Dunkirk was somehow conspiring with Thomas and Ogham— but to what end? Dunkirk took a step forward, and raised his hand as if ready to strike William across the face. A collective gasp echoed and silenced when Edward grasped the bishop's hand and held it firm, preventing him from finishing his swing. Dunkirk glared at Edward for a moment before he gave Ogham a curt nod of his head. "Stand down," he said angrily, then wrested his hand from Edward and stepped back to join his acolyte.

Ogham looked from Dunkirk to Thomas, then stared into William's furious eyes for a long moment. "My apologies, Lord Sutherland. It was my... misunderstanding. I will be pleased to leave you to your sacred gathering until we meet on the morrow."

William held his stance. "Until the morrow, then."

Ogham spun on his heel and stalked arrogantly to the door.

Thomas stepped away from the landing and melted into the crowd.

As Ogham crossed the threshold, he glanced up toward an open window in the south end of the hall and gave a quick gesture with his left hand. Sean looked up to the window just in time to see a hooded figure crouched on the wide sill, only half concealed by the shadows cast by the grand draperies.

"Bloody hell! Isaac, go!"

Without question, Isaac charged toward William, just as the twang of a bowstring and the whoosh of an arrow rang from the open window. "Will, move!" he cried as he flung himself full force onto William, sending him sprawling to the marble stairs.

Richard mimicked Isaac's dive, throwing himself protectively onto Bishop Dunkirk, pushing him safely away from the landing. Before the archer could draw his bow a second time, Sean retrieved the dirk from his belt and hurled it with deadly precision. The archer tumbled to the floor with Sean's blade protruding from his throat. Sean looked to where William had fallen to see Ewan and Simon standing protectively on either side of him; Richard however, had disappeared into the crowd. Sean growled as he retrieved his dirk, and wiped the blood from it on the dead assassin's cloak. *I shall have to remind Richard about where his loyalties lie.*

The hall errrupted in a tangle of screaming women and unsheathed swords. Goblets and platters crashed to the floor as panic-stricken guests leapt over tables and chairs to escape the impending swordplay.

"William!" Mehlyndia screamed as she watched her new husband disappear within a sea of skirts and legs. She felt a tiny hand clutch her and looked down to see Laurel hiding beneath one of the banquet tables.

"M' lady, please, come under!"

Mehlyndia would not move. She had seen William fall, but could not tell if he was hurt. "He'll be trampled!"

Laurel was insistent. "Please, please. Under here!"

Mehlyndia ducked to avoid the pushing of panicked women running in all directions. She crouched down and backed under the huge oak table with Laurel. Sobbing and terrified, she tried to catch sight of William but could see nothing but skirts and legs.

Edward shouted his orders above the noise. "Ewan, Simon! Clear the hall! Sean! Quickly, we have a fallen man over here!"

Mehlyndia listened carefully, trying to make sense of the jumbled noises and voices calling out around her.

"Clear them now! Everyone out!"

"Full in the throat!"

"Both of them?"

"How bad?"

"He's taken the arrow!"

"Everyone give them room—"

Laurel and Mehlyndia looked at each other, terrified, as they recognized Sean's voice saying, "He's dead."

"Who?" Mehlyndia gasped.

"I can't see," Laurel cried. "I don't know."

The melee lasted but a few moments. Ogham had few followers among the guests, and so had used the diversion to afford himself a clean exit. Edward's men herded the few remaining guests toward the big doors and cleared the hall within moments of the riot. Richard escorted the bishop and his acolyte to the safety of the foyer. Thomas and Bryndah disappeared completely amid the turmoil.

With the crowd dispersed, it took only moments for Mehlyndia to catch sight of William lying on the floor where he had fallen, Isaac sprawled on top of him in a protective embrace. Both men lay deathly still as a shining pool of crimson spread about them on the white marble floor. "William!"

"No!" Laurel gasped, clutching vice-like to Mehlyndia's hand.

"Let me go, Laurel. It's over."

Mehlyndia struggled loose from Laurel's grip and crawled out from under the table. Before she could reach her fallen husband, Edward, Sean, and Simon surrounded him, blocking him from her sight as they gently moved Isaac off of William's chest. It was then that Richard ran back into the hall and joined the rest of the guard.

"My God," Richard gasped, looking toward the bloodstain as the color drained from his face. He looked up to Mehlyndia, then thrust himself in her path. "Nay, m' lady, please stay back!"

Mehlyndia pushed her way past Richard and ran toward the place where William had fallen, but was caught in her father's arms before she could reach him. "Let me go! William!"

"Mehlyndia, breathe easy," Edward told her, holding her tightly. "He has gained only a knock on the head. See? He's waking."

"Let me go to him then!" Mehlyndia cried, frantically trying to release herself from her father.

"In a moment. Let him clear his head."

Mehlyndia shuddered in relief when she saw William stir as Sean helped him to sit up. "Oh, Father. Why has all this happened?" she asked, sobbing onto her father's shoulder.

"It is simply an unfortunate affair of government, I'm afraid," Edward answered grimly. He held her close, rocking her in his arms. When her breathing steadied somewhat, he led her to William.

"Oh, no," she moaned as she saw William sitting on the landing, cradling Isaac's lifeless body, his fine wedding garments defiled with the blood of his fallen friend. She sank to her knees on the floor and buried her face in her hands.

Laurel left her shelter beneath the table and joined Mehlyndia, dropping to her knees as well. "Isaac! Please, Blessed Mother, this can't be real."

❊ ❊ ❊

For a long time, William would not allow the others to help him to his feet or to remove Isaac from his lap. Isaac had performed his duty, taking the arrow aimed at William full in the neck. William had witnessed death before this, of course, but never so close, and never that of a friend who had sacrificed his own life on his own behalf. He stared at the blood on his hands, shuddering at the sight and smell of it.

Sean placed a hand on William's shoulder, and crouched in front of him. "Will? Are ye well?"

William slowly closed his eyes against the sight of the blood and drew a long breath. "I killed him," he said quietly, then looked sharply into Sean's eyes. "It should have been me."

Sean leaned close, taking William's shoulders in his hands. "Will... no, lad. Ye dinnae kill him. He done his duty, ye know that."

William stared at Sean for a moment, then glanced down to the half-opened eyes of the corpse and gently closed the lids with his bloodied hand. "Farewell, my friend..."

"Let us take care of him now, Will. You need to be with your lady."

The mention of Mehlyndia brought William back to himself. He had somehow lost the fact that he had been married moments before all this happened. "Mehlyndia! Where is she? Is she hurt?"

"Right over there," Sean said, nodding toward a pale-faced Mehlyndia. "Give me your hand. You don't look like you're steady after that hard knock."

"I'm fine, Sean. I don't need help."

Sean helped William to his feet despite his protests. He faltered slightly and allowed Sean to support him. When he finally gained his feet, he saw Mehlyndia and Laurel huddled together, sobbing in each other's arms. The aroma of the flowers and food mingled with the smell of the blood on his clothes, bringing on a sudden wave of nausea. He closed his eyes for a moment to steady himself as he felt the floor sway under him. Sean gripped his arm, but William impatiently pushed his friend's hands aside as he hurried toward the women. He tapped Laurel on the shoulder and she turned, looking at him through tear-filled eyes.

"Are you hurt? Tell me. Please," she asked, horrified, at the blood on William's clothes and face.

"I'm fine, Laurel." The pain in his head belied his words. "Thank you for being here for Mehlyndia." He lifted his hand to Laurel's face to brush away the tear on her cheek, then froze at the sight of the blood covering his hand. "Laurel—" He swallowed hard, trying to ignore the taste of blood in his mouth. "Isaac... I'm sorry. I know he was your friend, too."

Laurel looked away from his face. Her eyes fixed on the bloodstains on his shoulder. She reached out to him with a shaking hand and wiped his silver eagle badge with her palm. She pulled her hand back, now wet with Isaac's blood, and looked up to him with tears brimming in her eyes. "Blessed Mother! It could have been you."

"Sean," William said, looking over his shoulder, "please, come take care of Laurel."

Sean knelt at once, and she threw her arms around his neck and cried, as held her.

Mehlyndia remained on her knees, crying into her hands.

She did not see him before he put his arms around her and spoke softly, making a great effort to control the tremble in his voice.

"My love, have you already forgotten about your husband?"

Mehlyndia looked up quickly and flung herself on him, nearly causing him to fall again. "William! I was certain you were truly lost to me!"

"I'm not lost. I'm here. Are you all right?"

"Yes, I am now." Mehlyndia embraced him until he began to sway on his feet.. "You are hurt! We need to get you upstairs."

"I'll be fine. I've been clocked before." He covered his eyes with his hands until the swaying sensation passed. "This is not how our wedding feast should have ended." When he opened his eyes, he saw that Mehlyndia's gown was now covered with blood as well, and he pulled away. "I'm sorry, my love. I've ruined your gown."

" 'Tis only cloth," she said, and pulled him back to her. "It would seem it is Ogham who should apologize. This is all his fault."

"Perhaps," he said quietly, doing his best to sound comforting. If not for the pain in his head, he would have argued with her on where the blame should be laid. She's got a lot to learn about politics. He knew where to place the blame and it was not entirely on Ogham's shoulders, believing that the more likely culprit was his own brother. Probably thought he could use my wedding as an attempt to prove his diplomacy to Edward... the bastard. He was certain Lord Edward would take issue with Thomas at their first meeting.

"I should speak with Edward about Ogham's whereabouts before we go upstairs." William started to walk toward Edward but his feet were still unsure.

Mehlyndia caught him as he lost his balance. "Father, please come."

Lord Edward gave orders to Ewan and Simon with a sweeping motion of his hand. The duke waited until the two young men left the great hall before turning his full attention to William and Mehlyndia.

"Father, he's hurt. We need to get him upstairs to bed."

"I'm fine," William protested. "My head will clear. There are more pressing matters—"

"There is nothing more to do this night." Edward spoke softly, but firmly, "Mehlyndia is right. You need to tend to that hard head of yours. You'll be no good to me if you cannot keep a clear mind." He called to Sean, "See these two to their chamber."

"Aye, my lord." Sean put his shoulder under William's arm and took the burden of his weight off Mehlyndia.

"And you, little mouse," Edward said, gently tapping Laurel's shoulder, "please run and fetch Elinor to attend to them as well."

"Aye, sir." Laurel curtsied and left, still sobbing.

William made an unsuccessful attempt to push himself away from Sean and stand on his own. "But, Father, shouldn't we go after—"

"I have sent out scouts and sentries. There is nothing more we can do tonight." Edward sighed wearily. "But I do appreciate your enthusiasm, son. Please, lad, go now. Get some rest."

"As ye wish." William relented, allowing Sean to lead him up the stairs and down the passage to the left. He had to admit he really did not feel capable of accomplishing much more than several hours of sleep. After a momentary confusion at why Sean would lead him to the left corridor, away from his room, he remembered, he and Mehlyndia would be occupying the suite that had once served as the marriage chamber for Lord Edward and Lady Anne. Draped over Sean's arm, however, was not how he had expected to enter it.

In the large chair by the fireplace in the wedding suite, William rested his head on the back of his hand, staring into the fire, feeling completely miserable. An hour ago, he had stood in the great hall happily taking his wedding vows, anticipating how he would sweep his bride off her feet and whisk her through the doors into this very room. He never dreamed that it would be himself who would be swept through the door by Sean, of all people. Sean had decided to remain in their chamber until Elinor arrived to minister to William's head. He both welcomed and resented Sean's presence in the room—grateful for his friendship and concern, but growing weary of his overprotective hovering. Always two steps near...

Flashes of Lord Ogham's threatening hand on his sword, Mehlyndia's crying, and Isaac's dive on him, all swirled together in his head. He walked backward in his mind to the early part of the day. He could still see Isaac's face as he and the others hoisted him into the air to carry him through the doors of the castle. He remembered how only minutes before the wedding, Isaac had made sport of his wedding clothes. He remembered Mehlyndia at the top of the grand staircase, looking more beautiful than any creature on earth had a right to look. He watched her now, as she sat on a small stool next to his chair, her face tear-stained and her eyes swollen and red. He could not bear to look at the bloodstain on the bodice and sleeves of her gown. It was all too much.

"William?" Mehlyndia called to him softly, then reached up and brushed his hair from his forehead.

He flinched in surprise at her touch, then realized he had been staring. "I'm sorry, Melly. It's been quite a day." He stretched and winced at the stiffness in his shoulder that had been bruised in his fall. "I think we could both do with some fresh clothing."

"So it seems," she said, looking down to her gown. "All of Elinor's and Laurel's careful stitching has been spoiled. I had hoped to see our own daughter wear this one day. Now I would sooner watch it burn."

After a soft knock, Sean opened the door to allowed Elinor to enter. "Come on in, they're expecting you."

Elinor carried a large basin and several rolls of linen cloths, and a small wooden box. "Could you give me a hand, dear? How's he doing?" she whispered to Sean.

"I'm fine, Elinor," William answered from his chair.

Sean rolled his eyes in William's direction, shaking his head. "Stubborn." He took the large basin and linens from Elinor, and carried them to a small table next to William's chair.

Elinor placed the wooden box on the table next to the basin, and opened it. "I've got something for the pain, should it be too much for you." She retrieved a small brown pouch from her box and held it up for William.

William had enough experience with Elinor's painkillers to know that a small dose would most likely be more than he needed for his headache. It would probably put him to sleep for hours, and he was not willing to concede the rest of his wedding night just yet.

"Thank you. Just leave it with the water pitcher, would you? I'll have it later."

"If you've no further need of me, I'll go now and leave you in Elinor's capable hands," Sean said, bowing politely.

"Yes, of course. Thank you, Sean." Mehlyndia stood and held her hand to Sean. He took it, bowed over it formally, then turned to leave.

"Sean?"

"Aye, Will?"

"Thank you." William extended his hand, not leaving his chair. "For keeping alert."

Sean accepted William's hand and gripped it tightly. "It was my honor. Take care of your head," he said, giving William one of his 'or else' looks, then bowed again to Mehlyndia. "Good night, m' lady."

Sean turned again to leave and met Laurel coming through the doorway. Her burden was a large pail of steaming water that seemed impossibly heavy for her small frame. Sean took it from her and carried it to the table where he had set the basin. Laurel thanked him, and the two left the room together, gently closing the door behind them.

"Would you prefer I attend to him first, or to you, m' lady?" Elinor asked quietly. She waited a moment for an answer, watching Mehlyndia quietly trying to release the laces on her gown. "Come here, dear, let me help you out of this mess."

"Thank you, Elinor." Mehlyndia submitted to Elinor's ministering, allowing her to remove the wedding dress and wash the bloodstains from her arms and neck. Elinor released Mehlyndia's hair from the netting and smoothed it into shining stands, and drew a fresh dressing gown around her.

William rested in the chair haunted by his thoughts, as he watched Elinor tend to Mehlyndia. This was a sight he was never privy to before, and on this, his wedding night, it only made him feel sad. The wife of a simple musician would not have had her wedding night so defiled. He vowed that Mehlyndia would at least know a proper consummation of their marriage, and he would ensure that all the madness of this night would fade from their memories.

When Elinor finished with Mehlyndia, she approached William, an awkward expression on her face. He knew at once what her quandary was. "I'm not going to argue with you, Elinor. Do what you need to."

Satisfied, Elinor, with Mehlyndia's assistance, managed to help William stand and free him of his ruined wedding clothes and the obscene stains that had transformed them so terribly.

"Elinor?" William leaned close to her ear.

She tilted her head to him. "What is it?"

"It's foolish really, but..." He whispered to her, not wanting Mehlyndia to hear.

Elinor made an intuitive nod. "She'll see them eventually, dear."

He sighed. "But not tonight."

Mehlyndia watched the secret exchange with a crease in her brow. "Is something wrong?"

"No, love," he answered quietly. "I'll explain later." He leaned onto the chair, facing Mehlyndia, to allow Elinor to scrub the bloodstain from his back. Elinor had seen the mean jagged marks on his back before, but Mehlyndia had not. Until that moment, he hadn't given them much thought, but he knew Mehlyndia would want to know how he had come by them, and he simply did not have the energy to explain it to her this night.

When Elinor finished his back and pulled the nightshirt over his head, he sank back down in his chair. Mehlyndia took a cloth moistened with warm water, and soothed his face and neck. "Are you feeling better?"

He looked at her face in the soft glow of the fire and relaxed as she tenderly washed his skin. "Aye. That feels lovely."

She stroked his face and, never taking her eyes from his encouraging gaze, dismissed Elinor. "I believe we should allow William to rest now, Elinor. Thank you for your care. I do not know how we could ever get along without you."

Elinor winked at Mehlyndia. "Yes, ma'am. You take care now." She picked up her linens and the basin. "Don't forget the powder for the pain. It's merely a simple nightshade potion, but take care with it. Just a half pinch is enough to dull the pain. Any more than that and you will very likely sleep until midwinter. You may want to wait a bit to drink it, if you're not ready... to go to sleep," she advised as she left them to their privacy.

* * *

As Elinor closed the door behind her, she was startled by Laurel and Sean hovering in the corridor outside the wedding suite. "What in the name of all that is holy are you two doing?"

"Keeping watch," Laurel answered. "We are not about to leave them unprotected. Are we, Sean?"

"Hush, Laurel," Sean said gently. "We are just concerned, Elinor. Is he clearheaded yet? That was a devilish blow he took. I wasn't sure he had fully come back to himself before I left him."

"It will take more than a stone floor to crack that great skull. My guess is it's his heart more than his head that's hurting him. Their wedding spoiled, and Isaac and all. Poor man, so young. Terrible thing." Her breath suddenly caught in her throat. "I'm sure it shall weigh heavy on him." Elinor glanced at the door behind her. "Isaac died in his service, after all." She blinked back her tears and turned from Sean and Laurel. "I'll see you in the morning, darlings." She walked away with a heavy sigh, shaking her head.

Sean checked the door to be sure it was closed securely, still reluctant to leave his protective post. "I suppose they're safe enough for the night. Elinor seemed content enough to leave them." He gave Laurel a tired smile and walked away from the door, only going as far as a small alcove at the opposite side of the corridor. An unlit candle stood in a recess in the wall.

"Aye, they've earned their privacy." Laurel sighed, joining Sean in the alcove. "But, she's right, Sean. It'll be a heavy burden. Isaac died protecting Will." She felt for the matchbox next to the candlestick and retrieved the lone match, struck it against the stone wall, and lit the candle. "He's not like the other nobles. I don't think he actually expects his guards to go that far."

"He doesn't. But he should." Sean glanced at the closed door. "I wonder how ready he is."

"Ready?" Laurel asked.

"To accept his place."

"What do you mean?"

"He wasn't expecting to be given such a rank tonight. I could see it in his eyes. I don't believe he's completely pleased with it all." Sean took Laurel by the hand and leaned against the alcove wall. "I know him, Laurel. I think he'd be happier someplace far away."

"From Drumoak? He loves it here. With her especially."

"No, I mean away from the nobles and government duties. Far away." He gestured to an imaginary place at the far end of the corridor. "Have you ever seen him when he's with them?"

"When am I ever with nobles?"

"Point taken." He smiled, then became serious again. "He has no love for any of them, save Edward. For Edward, he's fearless, ready to take on all challenges. No matter what the odds, he charges ahead with no thought for his own safety. It's as though his only fear in life is to disappoint his father. But on his own, when Edward is not on his shoulder... do you know how he spends his leisure time?"

"How?" Laurel asked. "Slaying imaginary dragons?" She

chuckled at her own quip. "Like when we were young, in the caves?"

"No." Sean smiled at the childish memory. "He sits with his lute, singing songs to himself when he thinks there is no one near enough to hear. Sad sonnets, ballads, and tunes of longing." He laughed lightly. "Not the sort of songs he sings in the taverns, to be sure. And not the sort you'd expect to come from a cocky, self-assured nobleman either."

"Perhaps he is slaying dragons after all," she said, suddenly becoming more serious.

Sean looked at her, puzzled by the change in her mood and the wrinkle on her brow. She looked somehow different in the candlelight. "How do you mean?"

"His music," she began. The candlelight playing in her eyes held Sean's attention. "It's how he banishes his demons. Lord knows he's got a few." She squeezed his hand and brushed the frown away, resuming her soft smile. "If sad songs help him do what he has to do, then I say he's blessed to have them."

"I suppose you're right." He always knew Laurel had more insight than people gave her credit for. She was his own age, but because of her small stature and childlike features, it was easy to mistake her for far younger. But in this light, with the seriousness of her mood, for the first time, Sean realized how mature and pretty Laurel truly was. The affection he was feeling at the moment became somehow less brotherly than it had been in the past. Odd time to discover this. I wonder if she feels it.

"Fear not, Sean," she said, nodding toward the closed door. "He won't set his responsibilities aside in favor of his lute."

"I've no fear of that." Sean laughed quietly in agreement. "He'll take the reins and charge ahead, reckless and headstrong as always, regardless of what he'd rather be doing." Sean's voice quieted and his smile left him as he thought about how William would be stoic about Isaac in public, and then purge his grief in private with his songs. "And I suppose he'll come to accept that guards die when they are called on to protect him. That's our function. He'll get used to it."

"He may come to accept it. But he'll never get used to it," Laurel corrected him.

"And that's what makes him different."

The conversation was interrupted by the sound of footsteps approaching.

"Who comes?" Sean called.

"It is I, Richard Fylbrigge."

Sean groaned under his breath. "What is it, Richard?"

Richard entered the circle of candlelight. "Is he well?"

"He's still in some pain," Sean answered curtly. "But I suspect he will recover by the morrow."

"Good." Richard returned Sean's cool tone. "I am willing to stand sentry if—"

"I don't think that is necessary." Sean moved away from the wall, pulling Laurel by the hand with him, as he gestured to the closed chamber door. "They are better left to their privacy. You are dismissed for now."

Richard held Sean's eyes for a moment. "As you wish." His eyes fell on Laurel's hand within Sean's and instead of leaving, he stood frowning at them.

"Is something wrong?" Laurel asked.

Richard cleared his throat, then averted his eyes from their hands. "No, I'm sorry. I... just wanted to be sure he was well." He spun on his heel and walked away quickly, blending into the darkness.

"He's an odd sot, that one is," Laurel remarked. "Seems so sad all the time. 'Course, given who his parents are, can't say as I blame him."

"Don't waste your sweet, worrying heart on him, Laurel." Sean gave her hand an affectionate squeeze.

"Why? What's he done?" She returned Sean's squeeze.

"Not for me to tell." He picked up the candle and led her through the corridor to the stairs. Laurel didn't push the issue as they walked hand in hand down the grand stairs.

Finally alone, William reached toward his bride, then drew back, wincing at a sudden stabbing pain in his head.

"Do you want a dose of that powder now?" Mehlyndia asked, stroking the furrow in his brow.

"Perhaps later. For now, I'd like to stay awake with you for a while."

"Does your head still hurt, my love?" She leaned close and kissed him lightly on the forehead.

"A bit." He kissed her brow in return.

She picked up the moist cloth. "Shall I wash your face some more?"

"If you wish. It does help."

"Would you be more comfortable lying down, m' lord?" she cooed in his ear.

William smiled. "M' lady, if you think it would help... my head, I mean."

"Then I shall see you safely across the room."

"I shall be grateful, my lady."

She took his hand and helped him gain his feet. Somehow, being alone with her, he didn't mind so much being helped. In fact, he was beginning to enjoy it.

"Lean upon me if you must."

William gladly took her offer, as his unsteadiness was not completely feigned. The pounding in his head increased. Lying down did seem like a good idea, but his pride and stubbornness would not allow this inconvenience to rob him of his bride on their wedding night.

They reached the bed but once he was lying down, his head began to vex him more powerfully. William desperately wanted to stay awake, but he also longed to allow the creeping darkness of sleep to wash over him and take the pain away. "Would my lady indulge her husband in a bit of wine?"

"Are my lips not wine enough?" She kissed his face and his neck, and sank down onto the bed and into his arms.

Though he was enthralled by Mehlyndia's boldness, he had no idea how to respond to his predicament. He really did want the wine to help dull the throbbing in his head. But for Mehlyndia's sake, he said no more about it.

His heart raced with the touch of her kisses, the closeness of her skin, and her hair on his arm. He loved her fully and truly, closing his eyes and kissing her in the same way she had kissed him. He caressed her neck and breasts and stroked her hair. He felt her begin to tremble and his own heart began to race. He trembled as well, but it had more to do with the ever-growing pounding in his head than his excitement with his lady. The pounding seemed loud enough for Mehlyndia to hear, but he tried to ignore it. He took a deep breath, closed his eyes, and rolled onto her and kissed her hard and full.

Mehlyndia gasped as she suddenly found herself pinned beneath her husband's full body weight. Finding it difficult to breathe, she pushed on him a bit. "My love, you are about to crush your bride." To her surprise and dismay, he was easily rolled to the side. "My love?"

William lay next to her, completely unconscious.

"Oh, my dear, sweet love." She kissed his forehead and pulled the coverlet over them. She watched him breathe for a long time, then turned her back, weeping quietly, until she finally fell asleep.

Chapter 3

"**I**T'S JUST NOT right! All this good food gone to waste," Elinor muttered, shaking her head as she   patrolled the ruined remains of the wedding feast from the previous night throughout the great hall. "Not to mention the loss of perfectly good crockery," she grumbled, whisking broken bits of plates and cups off the tables into a bucket, using a small broom. "I don't know what this world is about anymore that a man and woman cannot even be married in peace. It's an outright sin." She stepped carefully around the fallen flatware and overturned trays, kicking away the mice that brazenly grazed upon the remains of a crushed cherry tart. "Blasted mouse!" she scolded, as she swatted at it with her broom.

"Ouch!" A startled child pulled back his chubby hand. It was Duncan Wilbrun, Sean's young brother.

"Duncan!" Elinor laughed. "For a moment, I thought you were a wee mouse. I'm surprised to see you away from the stables this morning. Scavenging the treats, were you?"

The child blushed and bent his head, looking coyly through his ragged bangs. "Mum said it was all right so long as I dinnae get in your way. Am I in your way?"

"No, lamb." Elinor smiled, brushing the hair from away from the lad's face. "You are certainly not in my way, but mind the crockery. It's sharp."

Elinor scanned the hall to see Agnes, Duncan's mother, was just arriving to help. Agnes waved and gave Duncan a smile. Elinor reached for the tart and held it out to Duncan. He accepted it with a grin, and opened his mouth wide for a bite. "Ahem." Elinor tapped his cheek and winked.

"Thank you, ma'am." He blushed again, then took a hearty mouthful of tart.

She brushed the crumbs from his cheeks with her apron, giving him a grandmotherly smile. "Be a good lad and find Laurel for me. Then you can come and have another treat."

"Yes, ma'am." Duncan wiped his mouth with his sleeve, then trotted off in the direction of the kitchen.

With Duncan off on his mission, Elinor continued her tour of the battlefield that had once been the great hall, joining Agnes near the stairs.

"This place will never be clean again, I'm certain," Agnes moaned, pointing at the various piles of debris. "Lady Anne's favorite table cloths, ruined!"

"Aye, 'tis a bloody sin! The curtains are down, and just look at the crystal vases. Shattered!" Elinor took in a deep breath when they approached the marble landing. "And that," she sighed, pointing to the blotchy, crimson stain. "That will not be easily removed."

"Lye shall have to be set to it, Elinor. That's all there is to it."

"Aye," Elinor agreed. "I'll see to it, dear. You go on and tend to the cooks, would you? We should be able to salvage *something* to make a stew at least."

Agnes gave Elinor a nod and a pat on the shoulder before heading toward the kitchen.

Elinor stood, chin in hand, scowling at the unholy mess when Laurel came up behind, startling her. "Great Mother! Laurel, child, you are always so quiet. You are going to be the absolute end of me one day!"

Laurel stood with mop and bucket armed and ready for battle. "I'm sorry, Elinor," she replied speaking with her typical quick, short breaths. "Duncan said you wanted to see me. I was trying to find the lye and a sturdier scrub brush than this to tackle the stain. I've been trying not to think about last night. Poor Isaac. I do not want to think about that but I cannae help it. I'm sorry I forgot to tell—"

Elinor put her hands on Laurel's shoulders. "Slow down."

Laurel took a breath and closed her lips tight.

"Good lass, the lye is just what we need." Elinor smiled, then gave Laurel an affectionate pat on the cheek. "We are all upset about Isaac, dear. I'm sure the duke will see to it that he is honored. He saved Master William, after all."

"*Lord* William," Laurel corrected. "He is now Earl of Sutherland, remember?"

"Yes, yes. With all else that happened, I had almost forgotten about that. And it suits him, too. He'll be the one to keep the peace, you mark my words. I've known him to charm the worst of them." Elinor paused and gazed toward the top of the grand stairs. "Laurel, dear, it's close to midday. Would you go on up and ask if Lord and Lady Sutherland require their breakfast. It's a shame to disturb them, but it would seem m' lady should have called by now. Run on and check, will you?"

"M' lady, it's Laurel—"

The door flew open. "Laurel, quickly!" Mehlyndia, wild-eyed and frantic, grabbed Laurel's hand and pulled her through the door.

"What is it, mistress? What has happened?"

Mehlyndia raced across the room to the bed, pulled aside the bed curtain and pointed to where William lay sleeping. "Laurel, I can't wake him! His head hurt him so last night that I thought it best for him to sleep, but now... "

"I'll run and fetch Elinor." Laurel shot across the room to the open door. Looking back over her shoulder, she called, "Elinor'll know how to put it right! Don't worry, I'll be right—" She turned too late to avoid a collision with another woman who was just entering the room. Laurel flailed her hands protectively in front of herself, raking her fingers on the woman's silk skirt as she fell to her knees.

"Dear God," Bryndah scolded, rocking on her feet to keep from falling on top of Laurel. "Be careful, you idiot child! Your manners are positively atrocious!"

Laurel recoiled at once, back-crawling away, then hurriedly regained her feet. "Please, forgive me, m' lady! I didn't see—"

"Remove yourself from my path at once," Bryndah growled. "I wish to see my sister!"

Laurel whipped her head up, fear replaced by anger, her face turning scarlet. "Gladly! As soon as *you* get out of *my* way!"

Laurel dashed to her left, Bryndah to her own right, and back again, the two still blocking each other's path.

"Move!" Laurel impatiently pushed Bryndah aside and sped out the door.

Bryndah slammed the door and stormed across the room toward Mehlyndia. "My dear, that girl needs to be severely corrected. If you don't see to it that she's punished, I most certainly will. Her behavior is intolerable. Why do you allow her to—"

"Bryndah, do shut up!" Mehlyndia shouted. "I sent her for help. Can you not see with your eyes?" Mehlyndia drew the bed curtains back to allow Bryndah an unobstructed view of the still-sleeping William.

"I see he does not take his new rank to heart." Bryndah sauntered across the room. "You need to wake him, of course."

"I have tried. He won't wake up!" Mehlyndia snapped. "That is why I sent Laurel for help."

Bryndah bit back her urge to laugh at Mehlyndia's dramatics. It was obvious from his light snoring that William was only sleeping. But, seeing that Mehlyndia was serious in her worries, she softened her tone. "Is he breathing?"

"Of course he's breathing. I just can't wake him!" Mehlyndia wailed, sending an annoying shudder down Bryndah's spine, while she sobbed into her handkerchief. "Oh, Bryndah, it is all my fault. I should have let him rest as he needed last night. I was so selfish."

Bryndah offered a fresh handkerchief to Mehlyndia, fixing the proper expression of concern on her face while embracing her sister. She kept the tone of her voice calm and reassuring, "Oh, my dear, I'm sorry. I suspect the hard knock he took to his head has more to do with his reluctance to awaken than anything you may have done."

"What ruin this has been." Mehlyndia cried. "I fear there is a shadow cast upon my marriage. How could all this have happened?"

"There now, quiet yourself. Sister is here," Bryndah comforted, with a motherly pat on her sister's back. "Let me see what I can do. I've nursed a skull or two in my day. Do you recall the time Richard was certain he could tame the warhorse that even his father would not dare to ride? I'm sure William will remember. That beast sent your fearless nephew crashing through the barn door. The next day, he also would not be roused easily—just as William is now—but eventually Richard came around and was back on his feet and back into mischief in a day or so. He has been right as rain ever after. I'm sure William will be too. Where is your hand mirror, my dear?"

"On the dressing table, near the water pitcher." Mehlyndia sat on the edge of the bed, wiping her eyes with her handkerchief.

Bryndah released Mehlyndia and walked toward the dressing table. As she reached for the mirror she paused, intrigued by a little brown pouch that lay next to the water pitcher. *What have we here?* Looking over her shoulder to see that Mehlyndia's attention was diverted, she picked it up and opened it.

She recognized immediately the scent of one of Elinor's nightshade powder concoctions. She could remember drinking it herself as a child in small proportions, when a fever or other malady had prevented her from sleeping. She also recalled how Elinor had a talent for making it tasteless— the only way to assure a child would swallow the entire dose.

Bryndah held the little pouch in the palm of her hand. *Quite a large dose, if one were to use the whole amount at once.* She knew a half pinch would be enough to put a child to sleep for several hours. Half the pouch may service a grown man for several days. The entire amount at once—she curled her lip thinking about it—was potentially lethal, especially if she were to add the contents of what was concealed in a compartment beneath the large black stone in the ring she wore. *Nightshade alone is dangerous enough, but a little opium added to the mix will make it all the more potent.*

Bryndah took two pinches of Elinor's powder and placed it in the bottom of the goblet before filling it with water from the pitcher. She looked in the mirror again to be sure Mehlyndia was still distracted, then emptied the opium from her ring into the goblet. She glanced back into the pouch. *Waste not...* Giving no more thought to it, she emptied the entirety of the nightshade into the pitcher, then tucked the empty pouch into the folds of her gown, congratulating herself for her stealth. *I imagine he will be quite thirsty when he awakens. Will he take one sip? Several? Drain the pitcher and be done with it? Thomas, my darling, you will be quite pleased with me.* She glanced at Mehlyndia's reflection. *She may drink some as well. Ah, well, 'tis a chance I shall take.* She picked up the mirror and the goblet, and walked toward the bed.

"Here, my dear, hold this for a moment." She handed the goblet to Mehlyndia, then held the mirror close to William's nose. A small fog appeared on the glass. "There, you see? He's breathing steadily and deeply. This is good sign, darling. Not to worry." She placed the mirror on the nightstand. "Here now, I'll prop him up, and you hand me that pillow. We need to get him sitting up."

Bryndah found it easy to assume the motherly demeanor toward William she always displayed in front of Mehlyndia. *After all, I was the beast's foster mother for twelve years.*

Mehlyndia set the goblet on the side table, accidentally spilling a drop or two. Bryndah kept her eye on it for a moment to be sure it did not topple over completely.

After a little trouble, they managed to sit William up against the bed pillows.

"Now, let's see if we can rouse this sleeping lunk, shall we?" Bryndah smiled sweetly as she dipped the tip of her handkerchief into the water goblet and dabbed the cloth on William's forehead. "Lord William," she said in a lilting, singsong voice, "are you in there? The day is fleeting, and you have duties to see to."

Mehlyndia sat on the opposite side of the bed, holding her breath while she clutched William's hand.

"Come along now, wake up," Bryndah scolded merrily. "No more sleeping allowed for you today."

William stirred slightly. Mehlyndia squeezed his hand. "He's coming around!"

Bryndah dipped the cloth in the goblet again, dampening it more this time. She traced his cheeks and lips, allowing the droplets to fall into his partially open mouth. "Lord William, your wife requires your presence," she twittered.

William stirred again and turned his head in the direction of the voice that had called to him. His eyes blinked and opened slowly.

Mehlyndia squeezed his hand again, and he responded in kind. She gave Bryndah a grateful smile.

"Hmm?" William yawned, and looked at Bryndah. "Bryndah?" He sat back startled, his formerly groggy eyes now fully alert.

"Good morning, my dear, welcome back," Bryndah said, laughing. "Have you decided to rejoin the living, then?" She stepped back from the bed, secretly pleased with the startling effect she knew her face was having on him. *How sweet, he remembers me.*

"William, you're awake!" Mehlyndia kissed him, then sat back up on the bed. "Thank goodness. You worried me so."

He straightened himself, keeping a wary eye on Bryndah. "What is the worry? I was tired."

Bryndah approached him with the water goblet, but he backed himself into the pillows. "Be a good lad and drink up." She brought it to his mouth before he could push himself completely off the bed. He reached for the cup, but Bryndah made sure he had taken a sip and had swallowed before she allowed him to hold it on his own. She knew how alarmed he was by her proximity and made no attempt to conceal that she knew it—and that it pleased her—as she leaned close to him and spoke directly in his ear, "Did you miss me, darling?"

He pushed himself sideways and turned to Mehlyndia. "Why is she here?" Mehlyndia's perch on the edge of the bed unwittingly blocked his retreat from Bryndah.

"You've been asleep all day, my love. I have not been able to rouse you. Your poor bruised head, I fear." She turned to Bryndah. "Thank you, sister. I should have called on you sooner."

"Yes, you should have," Bryndah pouted in mock hurt, then winked at her. She found it amusing that Mehlyndia did not seem to notice the distress on William's face. "Darling, I shall go and have that silly creature of whom you are so fond bring some food up for the two of you. It seems she has gotten quite lost in her important mission." To William, she said, "No more tricks from you, young man," then she blew him a kiss and left the chamber.

William watched Bryndah leave, pushing aside an unbidden shudder. *Seven years, and I still cannot look at her without shaking.*

Mehlyndia stood beside the bed, hands on her hips. "Are you quite finished frightening your wife to death, Lord Sutherland?"

"That depends. Are you still alive?"

Mehlyndia glared.

William blushed and smiled at his bride. "Yes, dear." He laughed, then yawned, which made him cough. He held up a hand in reassurance at the concerned crease in her brow. "Just a bit dry, I think."

"Here," Mehlyndia said, lifting the water goblet to his lips, "take a sip. Drink slowly."

William accepted the drink without protest. "I'm gratified to learn that you are so patient with the hopelessly infirm, Lady Sutherland." He took another sip. "Though, I would not blame you for not speaking to me ever again for falling asleep so quickly last night. I am so sorry, darling."

"It is quite fortunate for you, Lord Sutherland, that you already had a bump on the head before we came to bed or you would have surely gained one from me." She spoke in a haughty voice, then winked at him, her eyes twinkling.

"May I be assured it was not a lack of desire for me that put you off?"

"You may be secure in that, my love. You are my one desire in life." He leaned forward and kissed her lightly on the cheek, then turned her face to him for a more passionate kiss, until they were interrupted by a knock. "Life resumes." He sighed, gesturing toward the door.

Mehlyndia opened the door and Elinor whooshed in, wringing her hands, a panicked expression on her face. Laurel followed, carrying a tray laden with bread, cheese, dried meats, fruit, and a large covered dish.

"It's all right, Elinor. I fear I have upset you more than is warranted." Mehlyndia took the tray from Laurel.

Elinor ran to William, her hand on her chest, smiling in relief. "Thank goodness! You had me frantic with worry. I was sure that you'd been careless with that sleeping powder. Laurel said you were in the sleep of the dead. The child exaggerates so!"

"That would be my fault, Elinor, not Laurel's," Mehlyndia explained. "I simply could not wake him and I'm afraid I was in a state of near panic when I sent her to fetch you."

"Ladies, please, I am fine. You will have the entire village planning a wake if you don't stop all this fuss." William laughed. He was feeling better; the fog in his brain was lifting and he even felt hungry.

As he swung his feet around to sit on the edge of the bed, the front of his nightshirt fell open. Laurel blushed and turned her face. Elinor casually pulled William's dressing robe off the foot post of the bed and handed it to him.

"Ah. Thank you, Elinor. But after all the indignities of last eve, what is a little immodesty among friends?"

Mehlyndia turned scarlet. "William! Please."

He covered himself, holding back a laugh.

"Can you stand up?" Elinor asked, offering an arm.

"I'm sure I can." He waved her away, as he stood on his own. Feeling secure on his feet, he walked to the table. "There you see? I'm not an invalid just yet. Now, let's see what good things we have to eat here." He eagerly lifted the silver dome from the tray. "Ah, kippers, bread and berries! This looks wonderful. Thank you, Elinor."

"Eat well, m' lord." Elinor chuckled. "You need to get your strength back. The duke has been asking after you. Will you be well enough for the convocation this evening?"

"I believe so." William picked up a roll, slathering a thick layer of butter on top. "It would not do for me to be absent tonight. They need to see that I'm still whole. I imagine no one outside this castle knows for certain if I'm still breathing. If I don't show myself in public soon, the gossip vine will have a holiday." He settled himself in the chair, more interested in surveying his breakfast than looking at the women around him.

"Today?" Mehlyndia took the roll from him and turned his face up to hers with a gentle nudge on his chin. "William, you still need to rest."

He blew out a loud breath and snatched back his roll, growing tired of all her fuss and worry. "Melly, I'm fine. I've suffered worse bumps than this, trust me. Besides, I have no choice. Father is expecting me."

Mehlyndia sighed and looked toward Laurel and Elinor. "Thank you both for your help," she said, then rolled her eyes.

"I saw that." William pointed with his fork, then smiled. "You're as bad as Sean in your worry, you know."

"Not likely," Laurel snickered, curtsied politely, and then turned to leave.

"Laurel?" Mehlyndia called.

"Aye?"

"It may be in your best interest to stay out of the Lady Bryndah's way today."

"Oh, aye, miss. Ye can be sure I shall," Laurel said, beaming. "I'm glad you're not upset that I yelled at her."

William looked up, suddenly concerned. "You yelled at her?" he asked with his mouth full of bread and butter.

Laurel giggled. "Yes, sir. Right after I ran into her."

William choked on his roll and quickly washed it down with a gulp of water. "You ran into her?"

"It's all right, William. No one was hurt," Mehlyndia assured him, a curious look in her eyes at his reaction.

William felt like a fool for his paranoid attitude toward Bryndah. *You're a grown man now, for pity's sake. She has no power over you anymore.* He forced himself to smile at Laurel, who was looking at him with the same curious expression Mehlyndia wore. "I was just making sure no one... got hurt." He shrugged and cleared his throat. "Be more careful next time."

"Thank you. I shall." Laurel shook her head and joined Elinor who was waiting for her in the doorway. The two ladies left the chamber, and Mehlyndia and William were at last alone.

William watched the door close, then turned his attention

back to his breakfast. He felt his face turning red and hoped Mehlyndia did not see it. *Laurel crossed Bryndah. Just what I need; something new to worry about.* He filled his plate with kippers and bacon, knotting his brow.

"William? Is your head still foggy?"

He met her eyes, seriously. "As the moors on an April morn," he said, then dissolved into laughter, anxious to not share his private paranoia with his bride.

Her concern transformed into silly laughter. "Good, then you're head is normal again."

He leaned over the table and kissed her with buttery lips. "Let's finish this breakfast."

"It is mid-day. That, sir, is your luncheon. The rest of the Stonehaven finished breakfast hours ago."

He saluted with his butter knife. "Yes, ma'am... luncheon. Whatever it is, it's lovely."

"Would you like some wine, my love?"

He shook his head and refilled his goblet from the water pitcher, "I should like my head to remain clear. This will be better, I think." He upended the goblet and gulped the last of the water, then refilled the cup from the pitcher once again.

Mehlyndia poured some wine for herself and they finished their meal quietly, exchanging polite conversation, enjoying each other's company. During the course of the meal, William drank the second goblet of water.

When they had finished, Mehlyndia rose and gathered up her riding cloak and gloves and headed for the door. "It's a lovely day for a ride. Would you care to join me?" She batted her eyes playfully. "Husband?"

"Absolutely, wife!" He stood and made for the door as if to

leave immediately.

Mehlyndia laughed and held up a hand to halt him. "So eager are you to please your lady that you would ride the countryside barefoot in your bedclothes?"

He looked down at himself in mock surprise, slapping his forehead. "Gads, I've forgotten my boots." He laughed, searching the pockets of he robe. "I know they're here someplace."

"You've forgotten more than your boots, my love. I think half of your sanity has been misplaced as well." She winked at him, then turned to leave. "You dress. I'll wait downstairs. Don't be long, darling."

He made a quick dash to beat her to the door and opened it for her. "I'll join you as soon as I'm presentable. Sanity more or less intact, I promise." He gave her a quick kiss that she returned with one of her own before she left.

William was pleased to have these few moments alone to gather his thoughts, and he had plenty to think about before Edward's convocation of the nobles. The more he thought about the events of the past evening, the more convinced he was that Thomas had joined ranks with Ogham and was more than likely already plotting ways to gain control of Sutherland. *He won't gain it while I'm breathing!* It had also crossed his mind that Thomas had known about the archer in the window. He considered asking Edward to postpone the nobles' meeting.

I'm turning paranoid again. Sean will have me covered. I can't let the gossips think I'm a coward. William knew how rumors could spin unwarranted fears and cause ruin in a government. The last thing he wanted was for people to think him fearful of assassins or worse—that he had been hit by the arrow and was dead.

He dressed himself while mulling over the convention. *So what are you going to say?* Pleased to be rid of the stodgy formal nobleman's attire, he chose his old linen over-shirt and leather leggings. He nibbled at the remnants of the bacon and the last of the kippers and, finding them salty, washed them down with a large swig of the water. As he searched for his boots, he began to feel drowsy again. *That's what comes of sleeping late.*

Thomas sat on the window seat, casually resting his chin on his hand, his arm on the sill, when Bryndah entered the guest suite. "Well?" he asked impatiently, "Did the arrow strike?"

"No," she answered flatly. "He just took a hard blow to the skull. He'll live. For a while." Bryndah reached into the folds of her gown and produced a small pouch and tossed it casually to Thomas. "But I believe I may have solved your problem."

He caught the pouch in one hand, intrigued. "And what would this be?"

"An inadvertent gift left for me by Elinor. A bit of nightshade powder she concocts for aches and pains." She ambled to the cabinet and pulled out two glasses and a bottle of wine. "It is also good for helping one sleep. It works slowly, though. But given enough, it could put a man down for hours. Add in a bit of help—" She grinned, casually flashing the ring she wore. "—and those hours could turn to days... or perhaps... " She poured herself some wine and handed an empty glass to Thomas, then poured some for him as well.

"Call it insurance, my dear."

"Insurance that I have not disappointed Ogham after all?" Thomas squeezed the pouch and gave his wife an appreciative grin. "Bryndah, my sweet sparrow, tell me what you have learned about my *dear* brother's condition. I would be remiss in my... *peace effort*... with Ogham if he were to think I have not held up my part of the bargain."

Bryndah assumed a look of mock grief and in a trembling breath simpered, "I'm sorry to report that our former foster son, your own sweet brother, has suffered a ghastly injury from last night's treachery. I do believe it will keep him to his bed... indefinitely. Perhaps forever. I am so terribly sorry to have to burden you with this sad news, my dearest."

Thomas shook his head and sighed. "I am beside myself with grief." He raised his glass and clinked it with hers. "Edward will no doubt be calling on William soon enough. I'm sure the melodramatics will be quite entertaining. I should like to be there to watch, but I shall be otherwise engaged," he said, looking over his glass seductively, "negotiating my... *our* reward." He pulled Bryndah to him, his hand scooping the back of her neck. He kissed her with a teasing flick of his tongue across her upper lip.

"Tread easily, precious," she purred, then kissed him in the same manner. "There is still the risk of failure." She kissed him again, raking her teeth on his lower lip. "There is no guarantee the powder will do more than make him sleep. Remember, it takes time to settle. The whelp could actually recover." She drew back slowly and sipped her wine. "And if he does, you cannot openly act against him. Father would be on to you instantly. Are you certain of your dealings with

Ogham?"

"Of course, I'm certain," Thomas assured her, tracing his finger across her cheek and down the nape of her neck. "Ogham has placed a reward on William's head and is fully aware that I intend to collect on it." He emptied his wineglass in one gulp. Bryndah refilled it for him.

"But if the powder fails—"

"I shall simply find a different approach, dear heart." He tucked the little pouch into her bodice.

"To claim Ogham's bounty?"

"To silence William," Thomas corrected her, toying with the lacing around her neckline. "But for the most altruistic of reasons, of course."

"Altruistic?" She arced her neck to the side as Thomas caressed her throat and collarbone with his wineglass. "How so?"

"By preventing Edward from being further swayed by William's passionate eloquence." He traced her neckline with short kisses, stopping to lick at her earlobe. "I intend to protect your father from ultimate ruin... for our sake. And I intend to collect Ogham's bounty and claim the holdings in Sutherland."

"I think you give the imp too much credit, my pet." Bryndah's breaths began to come in short gasps. "My father is not as easily swayed by William's 'passionate eloquence' as you may think."

"Don't be so sure," he murmured into her ear. "William spins words as cleverly as a spider spins a web." He pulled away from her slightly, bringing her hand to his lips, and kissed her fingertips. "I've seen him confound the shrewdest of men. He could enchant King James himself into believing that witchcraft should be considered a holy sacrament of the church."

Bryndah froze, her eyes gleaming wickedly. "Enchant, did you say?"

Thomas caught the gleam in her eye. "I did indeed." He took the wineglass from her hand and tossed it carelessly over his shoulder. It shattered on the stone hearth. His own glass followed. They celebrated their plot right there on the table in the guest suite.

In the wedding suite, William had finished dressing, save for his boots, and was still lost in thought about how he would present himself before Edward and the nobles that evening. No more than a quarter hour earlier, he had promised Mehlyndia he would meet her for a ride in the countryside, but in his contemplation, had completely forgotten that she was waiting. He wanted to rehearse what he was going to say to the nobles when he addressed them for the first time as the Earl of Sutherland. *Half of them—including my own brother—will be ready to finish what Ogham started last night.* Facing one or two of these men at a time would be challenging enough. But all of them? Together?

He sat on the footstool to pull on his boots and happened to glance toward his dressing table. *I could always use— no, not this time. Come on, Will, pull yourself together. Some nobleman you are!* He yanked on each boot, then walked to the dressing table, opened the top drawer, and peered down to an ornately carved wooden box. *Well, it's here if I want it. No, I don't need it.* He slammed the drawer. *I've stood up to warlords and hunters without it. I don't need it to make a simple speech.* He deliberately put his back to the dresser and walked away from it, catching sight of his overcoat hanging on a hook near the door. *Melly! I forgot all about her. I'm no better a husband than I am a nobleman. How could I have forgotten about her?* He hurried to the door and grabbed his coat, but was stopped in his tracks by a sudden wave of vertigo.

This is all I need. Another headache! He closed his eyes for a moment, waiting for the sensation to pass. He stumbled to the table, picked up his goblet, and gulped down the last mouthful of water. As he stood with the cup in his hand, he felt the room begin to rock beneath his feet. He leaned heavily on the table with his free hand. He looked at the goblet in his hand, suddenly remembering who had first given it to him. *Bryndah!* The goblet crashed to the floor a moment before William did.

"William! Open your eyes!"

"Hmm... what?" He opened his eyes and shook his head, trying to clear the fog. He glanced around his surroundings to see who had called to him, expecting to see his own bedchamber, but instead was confronted with a murky blackness. As he sat up, he could feel a presence near him. Through the murk he could barely discern the form of a woman, reaching toward him. "Mehlyndia?" Suddenly the fog cleared and it was instead Bryndah who grasped his hand, standing twice her normal size. He pulled his hand away, too late to prevent her from scratching him with her fingernails.

His grotesquely inflated foster mother leaned over him, her face hideously large and close to his own.

"You've been asleep all day! Well, you'll be allowed no more of that! You've neglected your chores again." Her voice was shrill and hollow, with a strange windy echo. "You've been disobedient again!" She raised her hand threateningly above him.

"No!" he cried, startled by the small and childish sound of his own voice. "Mother... please... no!"

"You were supposed to clear the ashes from the forge! Do you wish to spend another night in the coal shed?" Giant Bryndah loomed over him, pointing a spidery finger toward something behind him. He whirled around to see the iron door of the blacksmith's shed spring out of the blackness. "You've been told not to leave your chores. Who let you out of there before you finished cleaning it?" She was suddenly in front of him again.

"Rebecca let me out. I did finish my chores." He held his hands in front of his face. But the hands he saw were those of a small boy, not a grown man.

Bryndah's eyes turned a fiery orange that flickered like flames. "You forced her to come to you. She let you out because you made her believe your lies again. You told her you were afraid of the fire, didn't you!"

"No, I... I don't like it near the forge. All she did was open the door!" William wanted to look away from those flaming eyes, but found it impossible as they stayed in front of him no matter how he turned.

"You lie! The door was locked. How did she let you out? Was it with magic, beast?" Her hands, with nails as long and sharp as talons, came down suddenly and sank into his shoulders as she pulled him to his feet.

"I don't know how she let me out!"

"You made her use her magic didn't you! But there'll be no more tricks from you, young man." Bryndah spun him around to stand with his back to her and pointed one of her talons into the blackness. "Look there! See what you have caused!"

In a flash, a crowd of ugly, grizzled people appeared in the distance. Bryndah lifted him off the ground with her claws and they floated toward the throng. The crowd began to chant. Softly at first, then louder, until it became a deafening cacophony, echoing painfully within his ears.

"Burn, witch, burn! Burn, witch, burn!"

He covered his ears with his hands, but was unable to block the sound of the chants. "Stop it!"

The chanters encircled him, laughing and clapping.

"Burn, burn, burn the witch!"

An old woman, gnarled and bent, pointed a twisted finger at him. "He's the one!"

The crowd changed their chant.

"He's the one! He's the one!"

William sank to his knees as they closed in around him, pressing against him, cheering in hideous glee. He believed they meant to crush him, but before they overtook him completely, they separated, revealing a large pile of logs and sticks. In the center of the pile, bound to a tall wooden stake, was his nurse, Rebecca.

"Let her go!" he screamed, but his childlike voice was swallowed by the clamoring mob.

Rebecca called to him, "Run away, little one! They're coming! Run away, run away!"

He tried to stand, but his legs became heavy and awkward and would not move. His arms fell limp by his sides. "I can't run, Rebecca. I can't even move."

"They're coming, Will. Run away."

Her screams and his cries made the crowd cheer and clap all the more. "Stop it!" With all his mental effort, he willed them all to vanish. To his amazement, one by one each distorted, leering face melted into the dark. *I have control! I can change this.* He looked down at his hands to see they were fully grown again. He rose to his feet. *I can save her this time!*

William's heart raced as he rushed toward Rebecca, though it seemed his steps were not moving him forward. He pushed on, but could not close the space between them. Exhausted, he collapsed to his knees, no closer to her than when he had started running. He watched, unwillingly mesmerized, as a group of men in black hooded cloaks approached, then encircled the stake. They withdrew large swords and held them toward the sky.

Bryndah appeared in front of him again, her eyes still flaming. She pointed a long, clawed finger at the hooded men. "Burn the witch now!"

Instantly, their blades burst into flame. Each of the men touched the kindling around the stake with his sword.

"No! Rebecca!" he cried, covering his face with his hands.

"Watch, William!" Bryndah's banshee voice split his eardrums, and his head was yanked back. "See what you've done! You did it, William! You made her use her magic for you."

"No!" He covered his ears and closed his eyes against the sight. With his now-adult voice, he screamed, "You're not real!"

When he opened his eyes, the jeering crowd, hooded figures, and burning stake had vanished and he found himself in the field behind the stable in Aberdoir. The air around him was still and dry, with the acrid smell of burned wood hanging like a shroud about him.

Bryndah suddenly reappeared, standing several yards away from him. She had returned to her normal size. "Go ahead, Brother Joseph," she called to someone who was approaching William from behind. "Teach the beast a lesson!"

William spun in time to see a hulking, robed figure block the sun. Before he could retreat, he felt his feet leave the ground as a massive bear claw of a hand took hold of him by the wrists. Joseph hauled him away toward the hitching post at back of the barn. William tried to yell, but found his voice muffled and garbled, his jaw locked tight by Joseph's other hand.

"Teach him!" Bryndah cackled.

William struggled against the hands that carried him. *It's not real. It's a dream.* He tried not to look at Bryndah, but no matter where he set his gaze, she was there. Her eyes became large and red, and her teeth long and sharp. He stared transfixed as his foster mother transformed into the horrible and familiar shape of the dragon from his childhood nightmares, but had not haunted his dreams for nearly seven years.

"The child mussssssst be taught," the dragon hissed, spitting flame from between its teeth.

No! I'm not a child anymore! You have no power over me!

William looked up at Brother Joseph, struggling to free his

wrists before they could be bound together. The monstrous cleric glared down, drooling, as his face transforming into the grotesque masque of a boar. Fire spewed from its mouth as it spoke, "If you wish to behave as a heathen, then you shall be treated as such!" The flames engulfed William's face, nearly suffocating him. He gasped hard and felt the fire burn in his throat as he struggled for breath.

"Repeat after me, heathen! Thou shalt not... " William watched helplessly as the boar raised his massive, flaming hand above him and brought it down hard to the side of his face.

Chapter 4

THOMAS SLIPPED SILENTLY into Stonehaven Chapel, obediently dipping his fingers in the font of holy water and marking himself with the sign of the cross. *"In nómine Patris, et Fílii, et Spíritus Sancti. Amen."*

He knelt in the first pew before a bank of flickering votive candles. Assuming an appropriate posture of prayer, he waited. The pungent aroma of incense mingled with the candle smoke, and the dank smell of the stone walls helped him affect the convincing air of melancholy he would need for his mission.

He glanced up at the stern, intricately carved faces of the marble saints that surrounded him. For a moment, he felt the queer sense that the cold, hollow eyes had all turned to look on him. Did they know what he was about? Did they judge him? Did it matter?

He glanced upon a statue of the Holy Mother cradling Her newborn son. The artisans had cleverly—or morbidly—arranged her gaze to fall not upon the sleeping child in her arms, but upon an older version of herself across the way, posed with the adult corpse of Her son lain across Her lap. Would She judge him?

High above him, the crucifix hung from the vaulted ceiling on long iron chains, its shadow dominating every part of the sanctuary. The lifeless stone eyes of the Christ figure stared down. *He would most certainly judge me.* Thomas lowered his head into his supplicant hands, blotting out the judgmental eyes of the statues. *They're stone. Wrought by human hands. Easily broken.*

He had come to clear his mind; to contemplate the wheel of events he was about to turn; to weigh the implications, the ramifications, and count the souls that would be affected. How many? He had not worked it through that far. Did he have the wit and strength to carry it through? Did he calculate all there was for him to gain? Indeed, all that could be lost? He knew at this moment he had time to reconsider. Time to abandon all thought of what he was about to do. He could simply bow, intone a benediction, turn, and leave the chapel.

Then again, he was not one who quit easily. There was power and wealth to be had, and he wanted it. Ogham would pay him well to gain control of Sutherland. Wesley and Drunbalk would certainly find it worth his price should he help them dissolve the treaties William had negotiated. Ambrose Woodhall had become a laughingstock after William tricked him and would be more than happy to line Thomas's pockets just for the chance to see William brought low.

He grinned, pleased with the simple solution he concocted to bring all these untidy ends neatly to the middle. He marveled at how easy it would be. The seed that he and Bryndah had planted over a simple drink had germinated and grown to a full and terrible blossom. *Enchant, did you say?*

He folded his hands and found the prayer that suited him.

He did not ask God to tell him what was right or what was just, but only prayed to win. He offered no prayer for the life he was about to tear apart, but beseeched the Prince of Peace for his own protection and gain, with no sense of the perverse irony of his meditation.

With bowed head and clasped hands, Thomas ran the plan through his mind again. He knew the hour was late and at sunset he would have to be in the great hall of Drumoak for Edward's convocation. To miss that meeting would be ruin before he began. He needed to see the response of the nobles to judge who he could best use in his plans. He was fairly certain William would not miss this opportunity to wave the banner of his favorite personal cause. Thomas was counting on it, in fact, when he realized the obvious flaw in his newly hatched plan. *The nightshade powder.*

If William succumbed to the nightshade, there would be no need for Woodhall or the others to give him so much as a farthing, let alone align with him. *Surely it's too late to prevent William from drinking.* Thomas wondered if Bryndah was wrong about the dose she had given his brother. Perhaps he would not drink any of it. And if he did, someone would likely find him in time to prevent his untimely demise. He squeezed his fingers together and allowed a small prayer to that effect. *Dear God, allow my brother's life to be spared this day.* Outside his prayer, he continued his thought: *I need to use him.*

He waited in silence, listening for the sound of the bishop's footsteps as his cue to begin his performance. When at last he heard the vestry door swing open and the muffled footfalls of the cleric, Thomas began to utter his prayer in a loud, grief-stricken voice. "Please, Father in Heaven, why...?"

Bishop Dunkirk placed a hand on Thomas's shoulder. "My son, why do you seek the divine guidance of the Lord?"

Before answering, Thomas looked to the stained glass windows depicting biblical heroes and tales. His eyes lingered on an image of a man with a stone clenched in his raised hand, the other hand gently resting on the shoulder of his brother as he tended his crop. *I certainly am not my brother's keeper.* He drew in a long, deep breath and slowly turned his doleful face to Dunkirk.

"Your Grace, I request to receive the sacraments as I fear a dreadful evil has befallen me."

"Of course, my son."

Edward approached his daughter, curious to find her pacing the foyer by herself. "Mehlyndia?"

"Hello, Father." She stopped pacing and nodded in greeting. "I am waiting for William."

"I was concerned to see you by yourself, pacing the floor with such a scowl on your face." He placed a hand under her chin. "Is everything all right?"

Mehlyndia's scowl disappeared and she smiled shyly at her father. "I'm just impatient. He takes longer to dress than I do," she said, chuckling. "I've been waiting for the better part of an hour for him to join me."

"Oh?" Edward said, surprised that William would keep her waiting. "Perhaps we should see what has kept him in his chamber, shall we?" He extended his arm to Mehlyndia.

"I'm sure he'll be here any moment," she began to protest, then glanced up toward the stairs.

Edward followed her gaze. The worried look in her eyes was enough for him to insist. "Well then, for my own peace of mind, will you join me while *I* see what has kept him?"

She nodded and accepted his arm as he led her up the grand stairs. Before they could reach the wedding suite, a high-pitched screech and the sound of a tray crashing echoed through the stairwell. "Stay here," Edward ordered.

"No, I'm coming—"

"Stay!" Edward left Mehlyndia and ran to William's chamber to find Laurel kneeling on the floor, her service tray askew with broken dinnerware. Next to her, by the table, William lay unconscious, the water goblet on its side, only inches from his outstretched hand.

Edward knelt and tapped Laurel lightly on the back. She jumped back, a terrified expression on her face. "I just found him! He was down when I came in to clear away the tray. I tried to wake him, but he won't stir."

Edward retrieved the water goblet and dipped his finger in the small puddle that remained in the bottom. The scent of Elinor's strongest pain reliever was unmistakable, but it was the gritty residue on his fingers that troubled him more. A quick taste confirmed his fear. "Laurel, listen carefully. I need you to fetch Elinor at once. Tell her I need a nostrum to counteract nightshade and opium, and I need it *now*. Then find Sean and send him to me, do you understand?"

"Opium? In the nightshade?" Laurel's eyes grew wide, but without hesitation she sprang to her feet. "I'll fetch Elinor straight away, m' lord!" she told him as she ran from the room calling out, "Elinor! Sean! Elllinoooor!"

Mehlyndia stood in the doorway, her face turning pale as

Laurel rushed past her. "What has happened?" She dropped her riding cloak and flew to her father's side.

Edward waved her away. "I need room, Mehlyndia, please stay back." He placed a hand on William's neck. Satisfied with the pulse he found, he gently hoisted the young man onto his shoulder and bore him across the room to the large chair by the fire. Mehlyndia followed, wringing her hands, but allowed the space Edward required.

"Who has been in here today?" Edward barked, as he lifted William's eyelids.

"Only Elinor and Laurel." Mehlyndia answered, jumping back at Edward's sharp tone. "Bryndah was by as well. But after I left him, I can't be sure."

Edward wrinkled his brow. "Do you know how the powder got into the water?"

"Powder?" she gasped, confused. "Elinor brought it for the pain in his head last night, but William refused to use it. She left it for him if he changed his mind but I'm sure he never touched—" She searched the dresser and nightstand, "It's not here!"

"Do you suppose he would have decided to take some after you left him?"

"I don't think so." Mehlyndia's voice trembled. "He seemed to have regained his wit and strength. He was eager to dress and meet me downstairs."

Edward shook William's face lightly to judge the depth of his sleep. "Son, wake up." There was no response. "William! Open your eyes!"

Elinor burst into the chamber without the formality of a knock. She carried her small wooden box and a pestle within a bowl. A flask of water was tied to her hip. "I came as soon as Laurel told me." She raced directly to Edward. "She's gone to fetch Sean."

Edward turned to Mehlyndia, noting her panicked expression. "My dear, it may be better if you wait outside."

"I wish to stay," she snapped, not taking her eyes from William. "I won't leave him now."

"Then please stay back." Edward turned his attention to Elinor and the items she carried. "Do you have what you need?"

"Aye, but I was unsure of the size of the dose he'd taken," she answered back in a hushed, urgent tone.

"The dose he took seems to be quite large. Judge for yourself."

Elinor lifted William's eyelids and examined the pupils closely. "The blacks of his eyes have taken over green! Blessed Mother! You're right, it may be more than I thought." She listened to his breathing, then shook him hard as Edward had done. William made no response. She placed an ear to his chest and listened for a moment. "His heart! It's slowing down. I'll have to hurry."

Wasting no more time, she opened the wooden chest. It was filled with several small vials of a greenish-black liquid and pouches of powdered leaves and herbs, each carefully labeled. She reached for one pouch labeled 'turnip seed', then stopped, a momentary trace of indecision on her face. "Blessed Mother, which one?" she muttered to herself. Then, as though the answer was made clear, she reached for a pouch bearing a tag marked 'powdered foxglove leaves.' She carefully placed some of the powder in the bowl. "This is terribly dangerous, but should work on him quickly. I just need to be careful with the amounts. If it isn't done precisely right, it won't be much of an antidote." Taking one of the vials of green liquid, she allowed four drops to fall onto the foxglove, added a small amount of water, chanting quietly under her breath as he missed. After a moment, she gave the mixture a quick sniff. "It's ready."

"Sir! I'm here!" Sean announced as he bounded into the room. "Laurel told me— Will! My God, what has happened?"

"Come here, Sean! Hold him straight for me," Edward snapped.

Coming around the back of the chair, Sean grasped William under each arm, and held him upright.

Edward pushed William's head back and held open his jaw as Elinor poured the entire potion into his mouth.

"Hold his jaw tight, and pinch his nose," she instructed.

Edward complied.

William began to gag at once, and in his struggle to breathe, swallowed the liquid. Edward released his hold at once. William coughed violently for a moment, yet remained unconscious.

"Hold him firm, Sean, do not falter."

Sean nodded his understanding as Edward raised his right hand and brought it down hard to the side of William's face. Sean winced but held William firm from behind the chair. Mehlyndia cringed and turned her face, sobbing loudly. Edward raised his hand again, bringing another and then another sharp slap down on William's face. With each blow, Mehlyndia cried as if she were the one receiving the blows.

"Stop it! You'll hurt him!"

Elinor went to her and held her close. "There, child. It's the only way. Your father knows what he is doing."

Sean stiffened his jaw, his own distress evident, but he did not falter.

Another slap and William began to moan quietly, "Thou shalt not..."

"He's coming around," Sean said hopefully.

Edward shook his chin, preparing for another slap if necessary. "William, wake up!"

William began to stir. "You have... no power over me. No!" He startled and his eyes went wide as the vision of the fiery hand of the boar monster vanished, to be slowly replaced by a blur of familiar surroundings. He stared, half-blind, as from the corner of his eye he saw Edward's hand rise one more time. He managed to raise his own in time to forestall another strike to his aching cheek. "Father, do you mean to wake me or kill me?"

His question was answered by a chorus of relieved sighs. As he tried to focus on the concerned faces around him, his vision remained oddly blurred. His throat burned and his hands shook violently. "What is happening?"

"I'm sorry for that, son." Edward took William's hands and held them tightly together, helping him gain control of the shaking. "It's the foxglove."

"Foxglove? It feels like fire." William looked up at Elinor, confused, and slightly alarmed. "Why have I swallowed foxglove?"

"I'm sorry, dear, it was necessary." Elinor bent over him and examined his eyes. "It may be a while before you can see clearly, but don't ye worry, ye vision will mend." She handed him the flask of water, helping to steady his quaking hand. "Here, this will help your throat."

Edward's voice was gentle and low, but William clearly heard the anger in it. "Can you tell me how you came to ingest such a large dose of Elinor's sleeping powder?"

"Sleeping—But I? No, If I had any, it was not by my own choice, Father."

"I suspected as much." Edward toyed with William's discarded goblet. "It would seem there is someone who would prefer you to stay infirm awhile longer." He stood and paced the floor angrily for a moment, then pointed sharply at Sean. "You are not to leave his side until I tell you otherwise. Understood?"

"Understood," Sean replied briskly.

"Is that necessary? I'm all right now. I just need to clear my head of this fog." William rubbed the sore spot on his face. A small trace of blood came away from a split on his lip.

"Yes, it's necessary." Edward handed William a cloth to clean the blood from his mouth. "This is intolerable. I name an heir, and in less than a day, two attempts are made on his life—one from within my own household! I've no doubt you are capable of defending yourself when you are out adventuring, however while you are here and until I am satisfied the threat is over, Sean shall remain with you."

"As you wish," William relented. His eyes fell on the goblet in Edward's hand. "I have a fair suspicion of who is responsible for the nightshade, Father."

Edward turned the goblet between his fingers. "As do I, and I shall deal with *her* myself."

"Bryndah?" Mehlyndia gasped, giving William a look of disbelief. "But she helped me wake you. How can you think—"

"Who else, then?" Edward shouted, causing Mehlyndia to shrink down on the stool. "Do you suspect Elinor? Or Sean? Perhaps you believe that little Laurel would do such a dreadful deed."

Mehlyndia stared disbelievingly at her father. "But she cares so for him. She was his foster mother."

William looked at Edward, whose eyes told him they were in agreement. He knew it had been Bryndah, but did not want to upset Mehlyndia. He was angry with himself for being careless enough to accept a drink of water from his *dear* former foster mother. He thought about what possible motive, besides her penchant for hurting him, Bryndah could have had to poison him, and the answer came to him simply.

"It wouldn't be for her ambition alone," he began, giving Mehlyndia a wary glance. "After last night, I'm convinced there is something afoot with Thomas. What, I cannot say, but I have my suspicions." He rubbed his hands together, hoping to lessen the annoying shaking. "He seemed awfully cozy with Ogham last night." Giving up on his hands for a moment, he blinked hard, trying to clear his vision.

Edward placed the goblet back on to the table. "I agree. At any rate, for the moment, we are to regard Ogham as a sworn enemy to this house. His attempt on your life must, of course, be answered."

"I suppose so." William sighed, frustrated. "Elinor, how long must I be quaking and half-blind?"

"You should be clear-eyed and steady before the

convocation," Elinor assured him.

"The convocation! How much time is there?" William asked, alarmed that he had lost the afternoon.

"We have a few hours." Edward assured him. "I suggest you prepare."

"Father, he cannot possibly be expected to—"

Edward raised a hand to quiet his daughter. "I'm afraid it is necessary. He needs to uphold his appearance as strong and well."

"Appearance!" she huffed. "I should think he more rightly needs rest—"

"You do not understand the workings of politics, my dear. He needs to be present. That is all there is to it." Edward turned away from her and spoke quietly to William and Sean, "It will be quite interesting to see who among the gathered will be the most surprised to see you, will it not?"

"Absolutely." William answered with a smirk.

Sean nodded his agreement.

Edward reached to Mehlyndia and kissed her forehead. "He's going to need time to gather his wits, my dear. I suggest you leave him alone before we convene."

"If you think it best." Mehlyndia nodded to her father, then turned a worried eye to William. "Will you be all right alone?" she asked. "Should Elinor stay in case you need her?"

"Stop hovering, Melly, I'm fine!" he scolded, then immediately felt guilty for doing so. "I'm sorry, my love." He smiled and softened his voice. "Kiss me first, then go dress and visit with the nobles' wives." He turned his face up for a kiss.

"As you wish, my lord. If it is a kiss you request, 'tis a kiss you shall receive." Mehlyndia bent and gave him a dismissive peck on the forehead, then walked away. "Elinor? Are you ready to leave?"

"Aye." Elinor replied with a stifled giggle.

"Shall we?" Mehlyndia held her arm to Edward and the three left the suite together.

"Did I deserved that?" William asked Sean when he heard the door shut.

"Absolutely."

Throughout Stonehaven, word of Lord Ogham's visit to the wedding at Drumoak was the most popular gossip of the day. By midday, noble and peasant alike had learned of Lord Ogham's unexpected appearance, his anger with Edward, and the assassin in the window, all prompting animated speculations on the current state of William's health. Many of the guests had seen him fall, but only a handful knew for certain that it was not William who had taken the arrow. Those who were privy to William's condition were not out among the crowds to reveal what they knew.

The absence of any message from Drumoak fed both sides of fire, and sparked more than one boisterous argument. There were two camps on the issue: either William had fallen and the announcement of his demise was forthcoming, or he was cowering in his bedchamber afraid to show his face for fear that more assassins were lurking in the shadows. Those who knew of William's bold adventures were quick to challenge the latter, and many a side wager was made as to whether or not William would appear at Lord Edward's convocation.

Inside Drumoak, unaware that he was the most popular topic of discussion in the highlands, William prepared for his first official appearance as earl of Sutherland. If he had been one of those in the tavern hearing the tale of the hidden assassin and his ill-aimed arrow, rather than the quarry of the archer, he would have been quick to fashion a lively tune on his lute and set the saga to raucous words of wit. As it was, he was doing his best just to keep his head clear and the quaking of his hands in check while he, once again, mulled over the words he would speak.

He was not ignorant to the mixed feelings his promotion would evoke among the nobles. He knew there were those who would support and stand by him, but he was fully aware of those who would not. His best hope for this evening was to somehow reach and motivate those who held the same convictions about the witch hunts as he did. If his speech was effective enough to move even one of them to stand with him, he would be encouraged. Perhaps even Edward would finally take his crusade seriously.

William had argued with Edward on many an evening about the burnings, and found it irreconcilable with Edward's usual levelheaded fairness that he allowed the fires to take place in Stonehaven. Time and time again, William had told Edward of the methods the hunters and inquisitors used to gain confessions, but Edward found William's accounts too unthinkable to be believed. Out of respect for Edward, William had never argued with him in public. But tonight, he would speak as earl of Sutherland, and in that estate at least, he would have the authority to defend his subjects from false accusations. Of that, he was certain.

He finished dressing. His clothes, tailored from the full bolt and dyed with saffron to a rich yellow, were now worthy of his new rank. He wore a pleated cape that hung in billows below his kilt and displayed the tartan of Edward's clan. The silver eagle badge held the cape crossed at his shoulder. On his right hand, he wore a signet ring with the Fylbrigge crest of the flying hawk, which had once belonged to his own father, Henry Fylbrigge. The two noble raptors, eagle and hawk, would soon be joined to designate his own banner and crest of Sutherland. His polished sword, which he was proud to have received from Edward as a token of respect and honor, was secure in the new scabbard on his hip.

William stood back for one last inspection of himself in the mirror. He scrutinized his image carefully, searching for any outward trace of self-doubt about his new rank.

In the reflection of the mirror, William watched Sean sitting in the chair by the fireplace, polishing his sword with a linen cloth. He allowed a smile, watching the pride and care Sean took with what was widely considered the finest blade in Edward's realm: the former blade of Henry Fylbrigge. Sean had not let it out of his sight since winning it in a tournament, much to Thomas Fylbrigge's consternation. Sean would be certain that it was prominent tonight, and William was certain he would make sure Thomas would see it.

"So? Do I look noble enough?" William asked, not turning away from the mirror.

"You'll pass." Sean looked up from his polishing and spoke to William's reflection. "How are you feeling?"

"I can see again. That's an improvement," William

answered, still looking in the mirror. He held up his hands and frowned. They still weren't completely steady. He turned and held them out for Sean's opinion. "Does it show?"

"Try hooking your thumb on your belt. Keep the other hand under your cape and you'll be fine," Sean advised. "You know, Will, I have to admit I was wrong last night." His voice held a curious seriousness that William rarely heard.

"Wrong? How so?"

"Nobility does suit you."

"You mean the clothes?" William adjusted the scabbard and flattened out his sleeves. "I don't find them at all comfortable."

"I dinnae suppose you do," Sean chuckled. "But I meant the rank, Will. It suits you. I would not have thought that when I first laid eyes on you." He held his sword to the light for one final inspection before tossing the cloth carelessly onto the table.

"Are you going to bring up ancient history?" William turned back to his dressing table, chuckling at the memory of his arrival at Drumoak. "I finally *did* come out of the barn you know. It didn't take as long as you like to remember."

"Oh, aye. But, once Edward gave you that horse, you never wanted to leave the barn." Sean laughed and slid the sword back into his scabbard. "Star was your first true love. You could hardly stay in the saddle at first. But by autumn that year, you could best me in all the jumps and races."

"Star was quite a lady, but I was a sorry excuse for a horseman before you taught me to ride." His smile faded as other memories came back. "I was a sorry excuse for a nobleman's ward as well." He usually did not allow himself to remember how timid and unsure of himself he once was, but shades of his nightmare, and Bryndah's hateful grin invaded his thoughts. *Damned dragon.* "I was afraid of my own shadow in those days."

"There is no one who could claim that of you now." Sean grinned and joined William. "No one has the bold streak you do. You scare the life out of me." He put one hand on William's shoulder and laid the other, flat palmed, on his chest. "I don't know what you did to finally find your courage, but you certainly found more than any rational person should be allowed to have." He laughed and gave William a friendly thump on his shoulder. "Kylkannen, for instance. That feat with the fake treaty. Do you know how easily those hunters could have taken us? I don't mind saying, I was sure that was going to be our last great adventure together, my fearless friend." He laughed, but the look in his eyes told William, Sean's concern was genuine.

"I suppose that was fairly reckless," William admitted with a soft chuckle. Then he faced Sean. "But it had to be done. That lass would be dead now if not for us. I didn't see anyone else standing up for her." He fumbled with the folds of his cape, not exactly sure how they were supposed to fall.

Sean helped William straighten his cape to proper order, then turned him around by the shoulders to face him. "No one else would have taken on Woodhall with nothing more than a forged bit of parchment and a clever smile. Only you. William Fylbrigge, the champion of the idolatrous peasant." Sean bowed regally in mock tribute. "May he long defend their magic-loving hearts."

"Stand up, lunk." William thumped Sean on the shoulder

and turned back to his mirror, idly examining the adjusted
cape. "She wasn't idolatrous. Just... innocent. Besides, it
doesn't matter what faith she practices. No one deserves to
be burned alive." He opened the drawer to retrieve his comb.
His eyes fell on the wooden box.

"You don't have to convince me." Sean gave William a
pat on the back before returning to his chair by the fire. "I
believe you."

"I wish Edward did," William spoke under his breath, not
meaning for Sean to hear him. He stared at the box in the
drawer, considering the contents. *You're letting the dragon
steal your fire, Will. You don't need this.* He hesitated, then
closed the drawer.

"You wish Edward did what?" Sean asked.

William looked up, startled that Sean had heard his
comment. "I wish Edward believed me." He thought for
a moment, choosing his words carefully. "He has enough
power to stand against it, yet he doesn't lift a finger to
prevent the fires. He argues that laws are laws and rules are
rules, and souls who perish must not have known the rules."
He raked the comb through his hair quickly, then tossed it
angrily onto the dresser. "It never seems to cross his mind
that it's good people like Elinor and I—" He caught himself.
"Elinor and her herbs who are breaking the *rules*." He felt
heat rise on his face. "He doesn't believe me."

"Of course he does, Will," Sean said

"He doesn't believe me when I tell him how innocent
people are made to confess to the most ridiculous charges."
William opened the drawer again. "He thinks I exaggerate.
He's never spent as much time listening to conversations

among the servants and townspeople as I have. He's not seen
their scars, or heard the tales of what goes on in the tower.
Hell, some of the things *I've* heard even I find hard to believe.
Do you remember Caleb?"

"The crippled weaver you helped set up in town here?
Aye, poor sot. Died young, he did."

"Do you know how he became crippled?"

"Not the details. But I remember the shutters of his shop
were the first to close if there were hunters in town."

"He had good reason to fear them."

Sean looked up thoughtfully. "He was from Aberdoir at
first, wasn't he?"

"That's right. Then one day...someone..." William gave
his family ring a glance. "Someone decided they did not like
his wares, and decided not to pay him for something he'd
delivered. When he protested and made public the wages
he was denied, he learned what speaking out against..." He
turned back to the mirror and spoke quietly. "Edward always
liked to point to Caleb to show that not *all* the accused had
died on the fire. That justice prevailed. That Caleb was left
only lamed and crippled, though barely able to work his
loom, seemed to go unnoticed. And since Caleb died so
young... Edward believed his death was simply a fever, but I
know better." He ran his hand over the lid of the box. *Make a
decision, for pity's sake. Use it or not?*

"Then make Edward believe you."

"How?" William turned and looked at Sean, closing the
drawer with his backside. "Invite him to tea with the bishop
and bring it up in casual conversation?" He held up an
imaginary teacup, pinky out, his nose in the air. "So tell me,

your grace; how many of those wretched witches did you have dismembered today?"

"I'm serious." There was no trace of humor in Sean's eyes. "If you could convince me it was a good idea to take on Woodhall and his hunters single-handedly, you can convince Edward to open his eyes and see the truth about what *justice* truly means. And remember this lad; he didn't believe you about Bryndah in the beginning, either."

"You're right." William leaned against the dresser. *Damned dragon, get out of my head.* "It was an unbelievable tale to tell."

"You showed him the hard truth about his own daughter and he accepted it. You are the most persuasive fellow I've ever known, Will. Use that charm that has won him over so many times. He'll listen, you'll see. You are his voice of reason." Sean spoke with a rare air of near brotherly affection. "You'll convince him, and he'll support you."

"I appreciate your confidence." William found it difficult to meet Sean's eyes. "But as I see it, I have a long way to go before Edward will support my 'voice of reason' against the hunters." He brought his attention back to his dressing table, speaking to his own reflection in the glass. "I can assure you, though, my voice will most definitely be heard. Tonight, as a matter of fact."

"Be careful!"

"What?" William asked, surprised at Sean's reaction. "You just encouraged me to—"

"Think before you charge! Be certain you are safe—"

"I have thought about it. I need to speak up, be heard. They won't follow me if they don't hear me."

Sean threw his hands in the air. "I'm not asking you to be

quiet. I'm asking you to be careful."

"The bishop himself will be in the hall this evening," William continued, ignoring Sean's words. "I do not plan to alter my speech to please his pompous, pious ears."

"Will—"

"I've challenged harder men than him—on your behalf once or twice, I might add—and just because Edward winnae cross Dunkirk doesn't mean that I have to kiss his ring—"

Sean put his hands on William's shoulders and turned him. "William Mastin Fylbrigge!" That got William's attention. "You are no longer just one of Edward's wards, free to go off on reckless rescue missions defending damsels against vindictive, jilted lovers because I fancied a lass I had no right to..." His face flushed for a moment and he turned away, taking a long breath before he continued, calmer, "Will, all I'm saying is that going against Dunkirk is not the same sort of enemy as that sot Adrian Tearlach who has it in for me."

"Tearlach is more than a jilted lover, Sean. He's a hunter."

"So? He's had three years to make good on his threat and has yet to cast so much as a shadow on Stonehaven."

William half-smiled and nodded. Sean never spoke much of his exploits with the lassies, though his reputation of being a bit of rogue was impressive, if not embellished. The incident in Aberdoir was not something Sean brought up lightly. He'd come close to being run through by Tearlach, whose betrothed lass had found Sean to be more pleasant company. In one of William's more daring adventures, he'd charged ahead, fearless, and attacked the sot from behind, saving Sean and his lady from certain disaster. Sean failed, however, to win her hand completely. William suspected that of any of the lassies that had turned Sean's head in recent years, Annlise Chase was the only one who'd turned his heart—and still owned it. "Sean, I understand the risks. But I need to do it my way."

"Then your brother was right." Sean sighed. "You will need someone at your back."

"That's your job, remember?" William smiled. "You've got me covered, right? I'm counting on you."

Sean crossed his fist over his heart and bowed. "I promise." He motioned to the door in his customary, lighthearted manner. "Now, are you ready, Lord Sutherland? Your public awaits."

"In a moment. I'm not done preening. Give me a moment, will you?" William laughed and looked in the mirror for one last appraisal. He was still unconvinced that he displayed a convincing noble-like countenance.

He opened the drawer, glancing in the mirror to be sure Sean did not notice what he was doing. Sean stood by the door. *No more thought, time to slay the dragon and take my fire back.* He reached for the small wooden box and opened the lid. *Only for a little extra confidence, Will. You want your voice to be heard, don't you?* He took a small vial of oil bearing a label that read 'chicory' and carefully let a drop fall into his hand before replacing the vial and closing the drawer. Casually, he raked his hand through his hair, rubbing the oil into his forehead with his palm as he did so. Silently, he recited the words:

Blessed Mother,
Let none be harmed within my mission.

Move my tongue to speak for thee.
I ask that those with ears shall listen,
That they may turn and follow me.

His secret ritual complete, he turned to Sean with a casual nod. "Ready. Let's go."

Sean opened the door to find Laurel standing, hand in midair, about to knock.

"Perfect timing, Laurel," William greeted her with a chuckle.

"Lord Edward sent me." Laurel spoke quietly from the doorway. "He is ready for you in the hall. He asks that you meet him at the top of the grand stair."

"Thank you. You can run on to see if the ladies need your help."

"Aye sir." Laurel curtsied politely, her eyes downcast.

"Is there something wrong?" William asked.

"Oh, no, sir." She looked at William, as though inspecting his appearance. Her eyes rested for a moment on the silver badge on his shoulder. "I shall never get used to your new clothes, m' lord." She smiled shyly and turned to leave.

"Laurel." William reached for her arm and turned her back to face him, "It's just me. I'm still the same Will you've known for years. Why do you call me 'sir' and 'my lord'? I don't like it. I thought we were friends."

"But you are a *nobleman* now. Earl of Sutherland. I'm merely your lady's serving girl. Far below your rank. I must learn my station." She looked him in the eye with a trace of angry defiance.

William braced himself. "Here it comes—"

"At least, that's what *the countess* has been telling me all day. And I don't relish going down to the ladies salon if that dried up old harpy is going to be there, spewing rubbish about my manners, calling me names, and telling me I'm not fit— "

"Ah, there's my Laurel." William interrupted Laurel's outburst by placing his finger on her lips. "It isn't likely that you will find Bryndah in the ladies salon, anyway. I'm sure the old dragon is elsewhere, looking for fresh victims." He laughed and gave her a hug. "However, if you do cross paths with her and she raises her voice or hand to you, she will have to answer to me." He held Laurel at arm's length and looked her in the eye. "Just don't provoke her. Agreed?"

Laurel blushed and gave William a smile. "Agreed. Thank you, Will. I will certainly be pleased if she never lays eyes upon me in this life as well, which be all the provocation she seems to need to catch fire." She winked at Sean.

William and Sean laughed as Laurel turned and left them alone.

"We shall have to take her with us when we move to Sutherland Manor," William told Sean. "Mehlyndia would be lost without her."

"Yes, I'm sure *Mehlyndia* would be." Sean raised his brow and cocked his head before extending his arm to the door, with a grand bow. "After you, my liege."

William ruffled Sean's hair as he walked past. "I could begin to enjoy this." He laughed and once again raised his palm to his forehead and ran his hand through his hair, ensuring there was no lingering trace of the chicory oil. His self-confidence was already rising.

William met Edward at the top of the stair, Sean dutifully by his side. "Laurel said you were ready for us."

Edward greeted them eagerly. "Ah, good! You're looking splendid. Let me see your hands."

William held his hands up and steadied them as much as he could.

"Hardly noticeable, good." Edward turned to Sean. "Has he behaved himself?"

"For once, I can say he has, my lord," Sean replied with a grin. "I did not even need to use the manacles to keep him in his room."

Edward laughed. "Well done, Sean; now, shall we?" He led them to a balcony at the top of the stairs overlooking the great hall. "Everyone I expected has arrived, as well as a few I had not. I'm sure their curiosity has gotten the better of them. I believe the odds are ten to three that you are no longer with us," Edward laughed and raised his hand to the side of his mouth. "Thankfully, I had some inside knowledge and will be sure to collect my winnings from Hal of Norwalkshire."

"So long as you have not bet against me, Father." William quipped then turned to Sean and said, "Manacles? Remind me never to make you angry," which sent Edward into a fit of laughter.

Sean signaled the two trumpeters who stood on either side of the hall. They played the fanfare that was customary when Edward held a formal meeting of his subjects. All conversation stopped, as the gathered guests looked toward the stairs.

William stayed out of sight behind a stone pillar at the

top of the stair, watching as Edward took his place on the highest landing and stood stone faced, surveying the hall silently. From his clandestine perch, William spied on the crowd though a small gap between the pillar and the wall. The same faces, more or less, that he had been amongst the wedding guests, looked up to Edward, displaying mixed expressions of surprise, concern, and indifference. Random inquisitive murmurs rippled through the crowd.

"Is it true?"

"Lord Edward looks weary."

"He's alone."

"Oh, no. Where is Lord William?"

"Ha! Pay up."

"I knew it. He did take the arrow."

In the middle of the room, William spotted Thomas and Bryndah. He was not prepared for the look of apparent disappointment at his absence on their faces. Or for the words he heard Thomas say as Bryndah clutched at his arm. "Oh dear God, no. He's not there!" *They're putting on a good act. They'll be more surprised when I go out there.*

"Oh dear God, no. He's not there." Thomas leaned closer to Bryndah and whispered, "Must we accept the lesser victory of simply being rid of him?"

Thomas had barely uttered his question when Edward raised his hands to silence the crowd. "Greetings, nobles, ladies, and loyal subjects. It is my honor this day to present to you Lord William of Drumoak, Earl of Sutherland, and heir to my seat as Duke of Stonehaven, with all rank, honor, and privilege that goes within." He turned and stretched his arm, signaling for William to join him on the stair.

William appeared, accompanied by a mixture of trumpets and spontaneous applause that started lightly and grew to the sound of thunder as he took his place beside Edward.

Thomas's mouth hooked into a grin. "Are we viewing an apparition? Or has luck returned to our side? Are you sure you delivered the dose?"

"That is no ghost." Bryndah shared his grin. "I know he drank some of the powder. Had I known of your plan beforehand I would not have gone to the trouble." She observed William carefully. "Look at him closely, my pet. Is that a tremble about his hands?"

"I don't see..." Thomas took a closer look. "Ah, yes. A slight tremble in his right hand. If I were to guess, I'd say he's still feeling the effects of... something." He nodded to Bryndah with one brow raised.

She met his eyes, with a glint. "A counter-potion perhaps?"

"Interesting notion." He met her gaze and kissed her hand. "Turn and smile. Clap your hands. Do not attract the attention of your father."

Bryndah turned and smiled demurely, clapping her hands as she was told. "How fortunate for us that I failed. Aye, my love?"

"Fortunate for us," Thomas cooed to her. "William may not agree it is so fortunate, in the days to come."

William bowed politely to the crowd as he swept the perimeter of the room with his eyes. Sentries and archers had been placed in strategic positions. The draperies in the windows were tied back, leaving the wide sills completely visible. *That's reassuring.* He smiled broadly to Mehlyndia, who stood at the foot of the stair, beaming with pride. He scanned the faces again, deliberately seeking out Thomas and Bryndah. Again, he was unnerved by their expressions. *They seem awfully glad to see me. This doesn't make any sense.* He tore his gaze from them and placed his attention on Edward.

Edward silenced the crowd with his hand again, then gestured to the boy who stood at the bottom of the stair holding a velvet pouch resting on a silver tray. The boy approached Edward regally and held the tray to him. "Thank you, Duncan." Edward nodded and turned to William. "I had this made for you months ago. It was intended as a wedding gift, but I think this is a more appropriate occasion." He emptied the pouch and held up a polished silver crest, bearing the diving eagle and soaring hawk that represented William's two fathers, "Your new emblem—the crest of Sutherland."

William smiled as Edward removed the badge he was already wearing from his shoulder and replaced it with the new crest. Edward extended his arm and they shook hands in the formal manner, locking hands to elbows. They turned back to face the crowd, applause beginning slowly, then building as William formally accepted his new rank.

"Are you prepared to address your subjects, Lord Sutherland?" Edward asked over the sound of the applause.

"As I will ever be, Father." William casually rubbed his palms to stifle the stubborn quaking in his hands and to assure himself that no trace of the chicory oil was left on them—the last thing he wanted was for Edward to know of his need to push away his doubts.

"Good. Let me go first." Edward chuckled and motioned for William to step to the side. The crowd quieted. "I take it that you all approve of my appointment. Or that at least half of you have just increased your purse a few coins." Polite laughter from the crowd momentarily interrupted Edward's speech. "My apologies for the suspense. As you can see, Lord Sutherland is alive and well, despite the attempt made on him in this very hall last evening." He was interrupted this time by loud cheers.

William acknowledged the crowd with a bow of his head, gratified by the reception. Every face, it seemed, turned to smile on him. Even Thomas wore an enigmatic smile.

Edward raised his hands to quiet the crowd. "That attempt will not go unanswered," he continued. "It is my decision that, until further notice, all trade dealings and negotiations with Lord Ogham be suspended. Violations of this ordnance will be seen as an act of aggression against this house."

Edward's words were met with a mixture of hushed whispers, a few loud moans of protest, and a loud cheer of support from those he held most loyal. "Further, let it also be known that any future treachery against Lord Sutherland, or any other member of my household, will be understood as an attack upon myself and dealt with severely." He turned his gaze squarely on Bryndah and said, "You are to support, defend, and uphold him as you do me."

Supportive cheers and applause, mostly from the young men closest to William, rang for several moments before Edward moved aside and William took his place on the highest landing of the grand staircase.

Banish my fears... When the noise subsided, William

cleared his throat and spoke in a strong, confident voice. "Before I begin, I would like to, at this time, offer my sincere condolences to the loved ones of Sir Isaac Walford, who displayed his loyalty in the extreme last evening." William's voice softened. "For those who may still not have realized, it was Sir Isaac who took the assassin's arrow that should have been mine." He lowered his head and breathed deeply. "Please join me in a prayer for his soul. Though I am grateful for my life, I wish he were here this evening to celebrate with us. God rest his soul."

Sean and the rest of the guards crossed themselves, and chorused "God rest his soul." Others in the crowd exchanged glances, and he heard at least one mumble, "Such show for a guard? You'd think he was a prince."

William glared at his brother. Thomas grinned and lowered his head as if in prayer.

After a moment of silence, William continued. "I would like to offer my gratitude for the support you've displayed thus far to my lord, Duke Edward of Stonehaven. In these times in which we find ourselves, it is imperative to remain as united and cooperative as possible. We must demonstrate that, in this realm, we have the determination to bring prosperity, security, and protection against unwarranted persecution to our subjects." He paused briefly, surveying the crowd, taking note of who held an expression of agreement and who did not. He hooked his right thumb into his belt to conceal the slight tremble that remained.

"Yet," he continued, a harder edge coming to his voice, "there are those who would sacrifice reason and justice, indeed allow their own people to suffer unthinkable atrocities, in their ambition to gain favor from higher places. There are those—possibly even some present here—" He set his sight on Woodhall, "—who do not weigh the lives of their people against injustice if there is wealth to be gained. They would bring false claims of witchcraft down on the innocent, merely to save their reputations."

A low murmur of discord waved through the hall. He made a quick side look at Edward, noting the scowl the duke wore. *He's not happy with me.* "I tell you now that the protection of *all* our subjects, be they noble or peasant, duke or weaver, dairymaid or duchess, is key to the survival of our autonomy and prosperity. I beg you to remember that your silos are not filled on their own, and your flocks and herds do not tend themselves. Your fields do not produce without the hands and backs of good, hardworking, honest people. Whether these folk uphold the dogma of the king's church, or Rome—" He looked directly at Bishop Dunkirk, "—or a faith outside either of these disciplines, they have earned your protection." He caught Edward's eye for a moment. *I hope he understands what I'm doing.*

"To those who would choose to break ranks, seeking greater fortune in alignment with Lord Ogham despite the ruthlessness of his rule, I can only beseech your consciences to reconsider the cost you will incur upon yourselves, your estates, and your tenants. I realize that the embargo ordered by Lord Edward will certainly affect the coffers of many of you, and you may feel it is your right to maintain your relationships with Ogham's representatives. You are free to make that choice, but know this—You will not have privilege of resource or tribute at your disposal from those who now stand beside you."

William paused, allowing his words to hang in the air, surveying the expressions on the faces. As expected, he found expressions of support, confusion, and clear contempt. For the most part, the expressions met his expectations. He did not anticipate the Earls of Drunbalk or Wesley to find his speech pleasant, so when they abruptly turned and strode out of the hall, he was not shocked. The fact that Ambrose Woodhall remained was a slight surprise. He was more concerned with the reactions of the earls in Edward's government. The Earl of Norwalkshire held a look of stunned anger. The Earls of Kent and Bannenvale seemed more complacent.

It was the look on his brother's face that troubled William above all else. Thomas stared up at him with a contemptible glee that sent a shudder down his spine.

William swallowed hard and steeled his jaw. "Now, if you please, we shall conclude these formalities. For last evening, a wedding was held in this hall, but a proper wedding feast was denied to all of us. So, in that light, I should like to invite you to stay and enjoy what is offered for your pleasure by way of food and music. Thank you."

Without waiting for a response from the crowd, William turned to Sean.

"Well done, Lord Sutherland." Sean extended his hand, grasping William elbow to wrist. "Congratulations."

"I'm not certain I like that name, but thank you. I suppose it only gets harder from here."

Animated conversations erupted throughout the hall. Edward watched as certain members of the crowd left immediately, summoning their wives and entourages to follow. He was dismayed, but not surprised, that William had chosen this particular time to begin his crusade to quiet the hysteria that lived among them. But he worried that his heir did not fully comprehend the potential dangers he was bringing upon himself and his household. Edward's concerns escalated as he noted more than half of the guests had departed.

Notably among those who remained, the bishop, red-faced and glowering, stood alone by the door as he watched William descend the stair.

Edward approached the bishop with as much confidence as he could find within himself. "Your Grace." He bowed. "Thank you for attending."

"Lord Stonehaven, I trust you will not trample upon the Scripture, as has your *heir* this night." Dunkirk grumbled.

Edward discarded his polite tone. "I heard no such trampling." He took a breath and lowered his voice. "What I did hear was a call for peace. I assure you, William holds the Holy Scriptures as dear to him as I do." Edward felt the crimson come to his face. "It is not God with whom he has his disagreements."

Dunkirk glared. "He does not appear to hold the Scriptures dear enough if he would stand and defend those who defile their holy teachings. He speaks of a faith outside either of these disciplines. I can only assume he refers to the practices of the heretics he so eagerly rallies to defend." The bishop's voice lowered. "Lord Edward, I advise you to council your heir more closely. His Majesty is a good and fair monarch who has labored tirelessly to make known the Scripture to his subjects, for the sake of their very souls. It would not do for young Fylbrigge to convince the heathens that what they practice is tolerable to God and king. Or to you." Dunkirk turned on his heel and walked away, not waiting for Edward's reply.

Chapter 5

"**T**HE SILVER TONGUE has at last shown signs of tarnish! And may we be the better for it." Gerald of Drunbalk, hoisted his flagon in a mock salute, then tossed a log onto the blazing fire in the center of the camp. His companion, Evander Wesley, responded with bellows of laughter.

"Aye," Wesley said, chuckling. "And we shall see how fast it will be 'afore the peasants he loves so well turn and chase him from their fields. For that's precisely what they'll do when they find he cannot defend them from our armies with mere pretty words and tunes. Edward must be daft."

"I've not seen the like, I swear." Gerald peered into his flagon, now empty. "Perhaps the lad believes he can talk the king into allowing witches to hold cabinet seats." He doubled over in laughter.

"What's his worry about the peasants?" Wesley wrinkled his brow and took a swig from his own flagon. "The lot will work for them who they be most fearful of. I say the way to keep your workin' class workin' is to keep the fear of a heavy hand in 'em and let 'em know they can't be presumin' to dally about with their chants and idols." He punctuated his comments by pointing his finger in Gerald's face.

Gerald pushed Wesley's finger away. "They be more loyal to their bellies than all else, at any rate. I've seen enough of them dutifully present themselves on Sunday to the chapel, only to go back to their old rituals upon returning to their huts." Gerald swaggered to his horse, tethered to a nearby tree, and rooted around in his saddle pack for the flagon of ale he'd packed. "Ah. There 'tis." He took a swig and returned to his stump by the fire. "And 'tis the fear that we know about their chants and idols that keeps 'em quiet and tending our flocks and fields."

Wesley nodded and turned his gaze to the fire. "It be not the comfort of the peasants I'm worryin' about. What we must deal with is Edward's blockade. He's just blocked the last access road through Sutherland. 'Course, we've as good as blocked all the access to the south, save Aberdoir that is, but without Sutherland—"

"Aye, without Sutherland, we're landlocked," Gerald grumbled. "And the south isn't all that secure either. Edward could always make his way through Kylkannen, even with our blocks. And don't be thinking Woodhall won't allow it. Fylbrigge almost had him in Edward's camp when we met at Lothlanne last week. Woodhall could turn the tide in his favor should he align with Edward. You must have noticed he chose not to ride back with us."

"Aye, that would give him the southern road to Norwalkshire. But I don't think it's likely." Wesley tossed another large log onto the bonfire. As the sparks burst from the stack and spiraled skyward, the sound of hooves on leaves approached.

Gerald was instantly on his feet, sword drawn. "Who comes? Call out!"

"Thomas Fylbrigge of Aberdoir. I approach unarmed."

Gerald shot a curious look at Wesley, then lowered his

blade. "Come, Thomas, if you be alone."

"I am, sir, I assure you." Thomas dismounted and walked into the circle of light cast by the bonfire. He bowed in greeting and stood to face the two earls. "My lords, I've come in the hope we could speak privately. Away from our respective chiefs and clansmen."

"You take a risk in seeking us out, Thomas. Do you not fear we will cut you down where you stand? Your duke has declared us your sworn enemies." Wesley smirked. "Or have you decided to play diplomat again? "

Nonplussed, Thomas did not look away. He took a few steps closer, a sly grin growing on his face. "Gentlemen, could we sit? It would be more comfortable near the warmth of your fire."

Wesley and Gerald exchanged curious glances.

Gerald extended his hand toward a nearby log. "Be our guest, then."

Thomas bowed and sat down across from the companions. "Gentlemen, I shall not waste your time," Thomas said, making himself as comfortable as he could on the log. "It concerns me, as I'm sure it does you, that Edward sees fit to risk the tenuous relationships we share for the sake of his new heir. I find no benefit for either side to this ridiculous blockade he has levied, and as such, I would like to offer you a proposal."

"And what proposal would that be? Has Edward suddenly given *you* authority to negotiate treaties?" Gerald laughed as he guzzled noisily from his flagon. "Your holdings in Aberdoir, though impressive, are too far south and not of any strategic interest to us."

"It is not Aberdoir of which I speak," Thomas replied. "I believe I can offer you a more attractive property to the north."

"Out with it, man! I've no want to sit here playing guessing games with you this night," Gerald snorted impatiently.

Thomas picked up a small branch and flicked it idly into the fire. "Sutherland."

Gerald eyed Thomas warily, though his interest was piqued.

Wesley leaned forward, lowering his flagon.

Thomas removed a flask from his own belt and took a long, slow drink.

"And how is it you would deliver us Sutherland?" Wesley asked, breaking the silence.

"When it is granted to me and I am made the next Earl of Sutherland, of course." Thomas's tone was low and confident. "I shall then align it with Ogham."

"Are you daft, man? Edward has just installed your own brother." Gerald burst out laughing. "He's not likely to recant that appointment for the likes of you."

"True enough," Thomas replied. "But should Edward's loyalties be questioned or deemed in conflict with the king's ambitions, he could find that he is overruled on his appointment, or forced to recant it himself. And I believe I know of a way to bring certain *inconsistencies* with the crown to the forefront."

The earls sat in silence.

"You are intelligent men," Thomas continued. "I should think you are able to see for yourselves how simple it is to stay in good graces with the crown these days. You simply supply the king with his precious victims—just enough to keep him out of your tenants, do you not?"

Gerald nodded. "Aye, we were discussing that before your arrival. Enough to keep the king content, but few enough to keep our workin' class in workin' order."

"Then let me ask this of you, gentlemen." Thomas lowered his voice and leaned forward. "Do you believe the king shall allow one of his key ports of entry to be governed by one who defends, indeed perhaps even participates in, the demonic practices of which we have been so warned about?"

"Edward? You're daft, man! He may be senile but we could scarcely call him demonic and live to tell of it." Wesley spat into the fire.

Thomas remained calm, his voice low. "'Tis not Edward to whom I refer."

"I see where you are aiming now, Thomas." Gerald allowed a grin to spread across his lips. "You have more backbone than I have given you credit for. So, what is our part in this?"

"You have the ear of Lord Ogham, do you not?" Thomas asked.

"Aye, more so than his other nobles," Wesley confirmed.

"And Ogham has the ear of the king himself, it is well known." Thomas sat forward, resting a hand on his knee.

"It's true, but . . ." Gerald waved his flagon impatiently, sending splashes onto Thomas's doublet. "What has that to do with anything?"

"I should think," Thomas continued, irritably wiping the ale from his clothes with a flick of his hand, "the king would take interest in knowing one of his most loyal dukes has just been bereft of his key trade routes by way of demonic trickery."

"Demonic trickery?" Wesley's eyes caught the fire and glowed red.

Gerald allowed himself a deep, muffled chuckle. "So, what display of witchcraft are you to accuse your brother of, then? I say you have a difficult task. I've witnessed him in the church; he knows the canon as thoroughly as most of the priests do, and better than some of them." He gestured again with his flagon, sending another splash, this time onto Thomas's forehead.

Thomas glared across the fire and grabbed Gerald's wrist, pulling the flagon from his hand. "Why, it is obvious, gentlemen. My brother," he said, pausing to wipe the ale from his face, "is an enchanter."

"Enchanter?" they chorused.

"Yes." Thomas pushed the flagon back into Gerald's hand, a self-satisfied glint in his eye. "An enchanter."

"How say you?"

Thomas's voice grew softer, yet more commanding, "My lords, you have both witnessed this countless times. Have you not been swayed into accepting unreasonable concessions by his unending *eloquence?* Has he not *charmed* Ambrose Woodhall into releasing a farm wench whom he had rightly accused?"

Gerald considered Thomas's assertion, recalling how only weeks before, Ambrose Woodhall had taken a fancy to the daughter of one of his overseers. When she fought his advances, he grew enraged and had the entire household arrested. After they had been interrogated in the customary manner, the family had seen fit to repent and admit to their heathen practices, promising to forever abandon those rituals and confess their faith to the king's church. They were set upon the public pillory for a week, as an example, then released. The young girl in question, however, refused to recant her allegation that Lord Woodhall had forced himself upon her, and she was thus sentenced to the stake. It was William who rallied to her defense and somehow managed to convince Woodhall to release her, although just how he had done it was a mystery.

"And you, Evander," Thomas said, looking Wesley in the eye, "have witnessed him in the taverns, while he sings his banal tunes, how he captures rapt attention as easily as this?" Thomas reached out suddenly and deftly snagged a moth out of midair then crushed it in his palm. "And has he not persuaded Edward into declaring him to be his heir? A mere fosterling!"

Gerald began to see a demented logic in what Thomas was saying, though he wondered if it was Thomas, rather than William, who so easily cast spells with mere words.

"Let me understand you, Thomas Fylbrigge," Gerald began, squinting past the fire, setting a dubious eye on Thomas. "You're tellin' us that we be the victims of a spell? Cast by your own brother? And that is how Lord Ogham lost his access to the port at Sutherland?"

"That's how he tricked us into agreein' to those ridiculous trade concessions?" Wesley slapped his knee. "I'd be glad to find a way to turn those back permanently."

"If we were to prove your claim —" Gerald began.

"That it was black magic—" Wesley continued.

"The treaties would be made null." Thomas finished their

thought with a conspiratorial grin. "It will not take much to convince Ogham. You need only to remind him of the fact that William turned him from his own wedding just last night."

Gerald took a long swig from his flagon, and shook his head, "But accusations such as you make are easily refuted, Thomas."

"Perhaps. But the clergy is easily enough convinced on very little hard evidence." Thomas reached into the small pile of kindling that the earls had gathered and chose a piece of wood with a stout middle and two smaller twigs on either side that vaguely resembled the shape of a man with upraised arms. "Ah, my poor dear brother," he said, cooing to the stick. "See what you have done to yourself? You shall prove yourself guilty *for us*, then they shall deal with you in their own... *special* way." He tossed the stick into the fire then brushed his hands together, dismissing its existence. As it caught and burned, he looked deliberately to his companions, a snakelike grin sliding across his face as the firelight reflected in his eyes. "Won't they?"

Gerald watched the fire swallow the stick, and nodded slowly, understanding the implication. "Aye, that they will."

"If all of his enchantments are not enough to convince Ogham of my brother's demonic affiliation," Thomas continued in whisper while reaching for something in his belt. "There is one thing more to offer as proof."

"More?" Wesley grinned. "Does he eat babies as well?"

"Have you ever known a man to rise and speak only hours after ingesting a large, hard dose of nightshade... enhanced with opium?" Thomas tossed the little pouch to Wesley, then sat back, swallowing a gulp from his flask. "Or to rise at all for that matter?"

"This was full? And he woke?" Wesley asked, eyeing the pouch skeptically. "Truly? He took it all?"

"It's true."

"Then it was an impotent dose."

"I assure you it was potent." Thomas sniffed at Wesley's doubt. "You witnessed him, yourself in Drumoak this night. He practically rose from the dead! Who else but one who makes use of darker powers could accomplish such a feat? He has obviously made some sort of pact that protected him from the poison."

"Damning evidence enough, I'd say. Ye be right, Thomas. He should be dead." Gerald's eyes widened as he saw the neat web Thomas had spun. "However, it will take more than the three of us, even with Lord Ogham, to bring him t' trial."

Thomas stood slowly. "I have my own source already at work. The man would turn on his own mother for the opportunity to increase his purse. He stands at the ready for me as I speak. It will be easy if the accusation is levied by someone who also enjoys a certain prominence. Someone who is eager to rid the earth of heathens, yet one for whom the value of gold and power is not lost."

"And who would that be, Thomas?" Gerald asked, eager to learn the details.

Thomas sauntered back to his horse and mounted. "The Right Reverend Gregory de Dunkirk, Bishop of Stonehaven." He mounted his horse and left the two earls sitting speechless by the fire.

* * *

Mehlyndia, sighed as she sank down in the chair by the fire in the bedchamber she and William shared. "That was exhausting. I shall be very glad to close my eyes tonight. I thought the guests would never leave." The festive atmosphere that should have accompanied William's ascent, and their belated wedding feast, had felt more like a slow suffocation than a celebration. She had smiled, chatted with all of the guests, been dutifully polite, laughed when it was appropriate, and spoke in a demure, ladylike voice at William's side all evening. Now all she wished was to be allowed her own mood and to go to sleep.

"I feel as though I've no right to sleep for at least a week after spending half this day with my eyes closed," William yawned as he closed the chamber door. "Besides, it seems each time I close my eyes, I am awakened by drastic circumstance. I don't think I'm up for any more adventures of that sort," he chuckled.

Mehlyndia did not find his jest the least bit funny. "Yes, you have had your misfortune since we spoke our vows," she said, with no trace of humor in her voice. "I fear there is a pall on our marriage, William. As if the fates have not blessed our union."

William's smile faded. He took her hand in his, helping her to her feet. "The fates work to please themselves, and nothing we do can dissuade them from what they have decreed for us." He kissed her lightly, placing a finger under her chin. "But I cannot believe that the fates object to our marriage."

Mehlyndia looked into his eyes, tears beginning to brim

on her lids. "Don't they? Already they have conspired to take you from me twice."

"And they have failed to do so, my lady," he whispered and held her close, rocking her gently. "I'm still with you, so why the tears? I promise you that our time together has not ended before it's begun."

She pressed her face to his shoulder and embraced him. "I love you. I know you hate it when I worry."

"Worry all you wish." William squeezed her, rubbing her back affectionately. "I suppose I shall just have to learn to endure it."

"Yes, you shall." She turned her face up to his with a sad smile. "Is tomorrow soon enough for your next crisis? I'm too tired for another one tonight." She placed her head on his shoulder and sighed.

"Aye, tomorrow is more than soon enough," he whispered, stroking her hair.

A light knock on the chamber door interrupted their embrace. Mehlyndia quickly brushed her cheeks and opened the door. Laurel stood in the corridor holding a tray with fruit and cheese and a bottle of wine. "Please forgive the intrusion. Elinor asked me to bring this up. She said she noticed you had not eaten much this evening and thought you might like it now."

Mehlyndia took the tray from Laurel and carried it to the table. "Thank you, Laurel, that was very thoughtful. Please thank Elinor for me."

Laurel turned to leave, but turned back again. "Is all well, m' lady?"

"Of course," Mehlyndia reassured her. "I'm just weary of

the evening."

"I'm sure you must be." Laurel turned to leave again, then stopped in the doorway. "Will you be requiring a sentry? Sean is beginning to falter on his feet." Laurel made a quick motion with her head to the left of the door frame.

Mehlyndia followed Laurel to find Sean leaning against the wall, arms crossed over his chest, fast asleep on his feet. "Oh, the dear man. He takes his duties to William to heart. My love, I believe we should allow Sean to have a night of sleep."

"So it seems." William gave Sean a light shake on the arm to wake him.

"What? Who?" Sean started, then looked ashamed. "Will, I'm sorry, I must have . . . It won't happen again."

"Sean, you're only human, and you have not left my side since last night." William patted him on the back. "Send one of the others up to take your post. We'll be fine. Please, go rest."

Sean looked at William gratefully and exhaled loudly. "Thank you, my lord. I will be back at dawn."

William sighed. "Sean, I really do not believe it is necessary, but I do thank you. And to put you and Edward at ease, I will go into this chamber and drop the bar across the door."

"All right, you win." Sean yawned and patted William on the shoulder. "Come on, Laurel. You look like you haven't slept in days yourself."

Laurel swallowed a yawn and blushed. "I'm coming." She turned to William and waved good night.

"Good night." William closed the door and dropped the bar to secure it as he had promised.

* * *

William watched Mehlyndia, transfixed by the delicate curve of her neck and the smooth, perfect features of her face as she sat before her looking glass, releasing the lacing from her hair. The candlelight caught in her eyes, making star-shaped sparkles on the last trace of tears. He approached her quietly, not wanting to disturb this vision.

When her hair was free of the netting, she reached for the brush on the dressing table.

William reached it before her, their fingers meeting on the silver handle. "May I?"

Mehlyndia gazed up at his reflection in the mirror. "As you wish."

Their eyes locked in the glass as he took the brush in his hand. He gently stroked her hair, smoothing it from top to bottom, never taking his eyes from her reflection. He traced the curve of her neck with one hand while drawing the brush through her hair with the other. He continued to brush with ever-slowing strokes. He pushed the neckline of her gown past her shoulder to the middle of her forearm. Then he allowed the brush to fall to the floor while he traced the other side of her neck, lowering her gown as he softly stroked her shoulder. His fingertips traced the middle of her back where the lacing of her gown was tied with a finely embroidered ribbon. Tentatively, almost shyly, he looked again at her reflection in the mirror.

She sat calmly with eyes closed, her head slightly arched to the side. She caught her breath as he stroked her back.

He pulled the ends of the ribbon apart slowly, freeing her from her garment. She trembled at the sudden coolness on her skin.

"My love, we have waited far too long," William whispered as he drew her into his arms from behind.

She stood and turned to him. They embraced and kissed. She loosened the lacings from his cuffs, and helped him remove his shirt. Her arms traveled along his back as she lightly dragged her fingertips down his spine, allowing only the tip of her delicate nails to touch his skin.

He held his breath until she had freed him of his kilt, then he swept her into his arms to carry her to their wedding bed.

There would be no pain in his head to rob them of this night, no intrusions from outside, no arrows, no poisons, nor duties of state to attend to. At last, they were free to give themselves to each other fully and truly, both trembling, engulfed in the ecstasy of their first love.

When the candle had burned to a smoldering stub, they lay exhausted and content in each other's arms. Sleep came easily and they lay entwined together as peacefully as if they were the only two souls on earth.

Sleep would not come so easily for Edward. He paced the floor of his salon, reliving the past two days in his mind. He had never, in his reign, made a second guess of himself on any decision and he was troubled by the nagging uncertainty that crept into his head now.

A fortnight past, he had gained territory from Ogham. A gain that he had little hope in achieving until William, in a skillful display of diplomacy, convinced the rival duke to withdraw his armies from Sutherland's borders. He had been well pleased with William at that crucial meeting. In fact, he had been pleased with William since he had arrived at Drumoak as a boy. Once William had accepted Edward's gentle manner as genuine, the lad's eagerness to please and be accepted had touched Edward deeply. No son could have made a father more proud, and Edward truly loved William as a son. He had never doubted that William would become his heir. But on this night, for the first time, a gnawing doubt was keeping him from rest.

The chicory aroma had been faint but perceptible. Edward wanted to convince himself that William had no knowledge of the implications of the use of that particular oil—a preparation used by the superstitious, when one wanted to receive a favorable response to an unfavorable request. Edward could see the logic in the choice of chicory if it had been used by one who practiced such rituals; however, to his knowledge, William had never shown an inclination to such beliefs. The only answer he could find was that it had been a gift from Elinor, and William had allowed it simply to please her.

He stopped pacing long enough to look up at the portrait of his beloved wife, which hung above his fireplace. How he missed discussing his thoughts with her. She had always been able to see through the fog of indecision and guide him. How would she guide him through something like this?

"My sweet Anne, have I acted in haste? Should I have waited longer? He is so young. Perhaps I place too much upon his shoulders." He stoked the fire in the chamber with a large birch log, and looked up to her face again. "How I miss you." He doused the lone candle that lit his chamber and climbed into bed. There was nothing to be done this night that could not be done in the morning. "It's been a trying couple of days. I'm too weary to be reasonable. Blessed sleep, beloved, until such time we meet again."

He closed his eyes, and sleep did indeed find him quickly. But the dream that came with it was not the kind to bring him peace.

He found himself again on the stair in the great hall, addressing the nobles. William stood confident and tall by his side, ready to speak as the voices in the hall quieted.

Everything happened as it had earlier, only this time, as William spoke, Edward noticed a strange glow on his forehead.

As William's speech progressed, the glow grew brighter and his words bolder. He no longer addressed the crowd but spoke directly to Edward.

"Never again!" William's voice echoed in the hall. "It's time. You must stand against it, Father."

"Not here, William. They will see what you've done." Edward's dream voice seemed frail and unsure as he pointed to the glow on William's forehead. "They don't know you as I do." He turned to the crowd in the hall. "Don't you see? They'll hurt you!"

Among the nobles, other figures appeared—hooded, shadowy men, who crept out from the dark corners of the hall. One by one, the nobles turned their backs and walked out of the room, only to have the shadow men take their places.

William seemed unaware of the shadows as he continued his speech—the same one he had given earlier in the evening. "... a faith outside either of these disciplines, they have earned your protection." The glow from his forehead spread down to his eyes, his mouth, and to his chest.

Edward watched in horror as the shadow men came up the staircase toward William, who still did not seem to see them as they drew their swords.

The shadow in the lead pointed a wispy finger toward the glow on William's face; its ethereal comrades swarmed the foot of the stairs.

Edward felt as though he had turned to stone, unable to move from his spot or call out a warning. He could only watch as flames erupted from the swords wielded by the shadow men. Still, William continued to speak.

Edward tried to cry out, but found his voice was too small and too late. He could only watch helplessly as William finally saw the lead shadow man raise his fire sword, too late to prevent the blade from coming down upon him.

Edward awoke with a start. "My God! Does he not see the danger?"

Chapter 6

THE LIGHT OF early dawn stretched slowly across the hillside. The shadows fell away, and the details of the trees and buildings in the village became bright in the early morning sunlight.

Edward stood by his window, watching the spectacle take place. A sense of relief washed over him at the coming of the light, as if God's own hand had pushed aside the darkness that had surrounded him throughout the night. Yet, the troubling dream that had robbed him of his sleep lingered still, and this promising sunrise did not bring him the comfort of answers, only more questions.

"I suppose there is no other course than to trust my own instincts on this, my love," he said to the portrait over the mantle. "As you always so wisely advised me to do." Had anyone witnessed his peculiar habit, he knew he would be declared mad, but he didn't care. He missed his wife, and even though she could not hear him, he still took comfort in speaking to her portrait. "My instincts tell me that William will lead Sutherland with an honesty and conscience that is sadly rare among most nobles, and I have done right by his appointment." He tossed off his night shirt and began to dress, pulling on his leggings and boots. "Ogham is a vile tyrant who sows his fields with the blood of his own people. A blockade against him is a kindness in that light." He turned full to the portrait. "And perhaps William is wiser than I have credited him, and with more backbone as well. Maybe it is time for someone to stand up to the king and his bishops, priests, and judges. And he's just the one to do it." He pulled his cloak over his shoulder. "But my heart is heavy in fear for him just the same."

He returned to the window and looked down at the landscape of Stonehaven. He had a grand view of his little shire from his window. This time of morning, the only movement he saw was the occasional milkmaid, busy with the cows, or smoke rising from the baker's chimney. What Edward did not expect to see was a solitary rider coming from the woodland road. He looked closer and squinted his eyes to try to identify the figure approaching the town. In the morning sun he glimpsed a flash of blue-black tartan and the colors of his own house beneath the saddle of the horse.

"Thomas?" Edward looked closer, sure he had been mistaken, but a moment more observation confirmed his suspicion. "Where would he be coming from this time in the morning?"

He decided he would pay a visit to the stable in order to greet his son-in-law upon his arrival. The last he knew of Thomas's whereabouts, he was in the guest suite in the east wing of Drumoak. Edward would be keenly interested to know how Thomas had come to be on the woodland road at dawn riding *toward* Drumoak.

On his way to the stable, Edward stopped by the kitchen where Elinor was just beginning to light the stove fires for the day's baking.

"Good morning, my lord! You are up and about early this morning. I trust you had a good night's sleep." Elinor, ever congenial, beamed as she bustled by him, her arms laden with firewood.

"Sleep did not find me as I would have liked, I'm afraid." Edward sighed and then smiled. "But this morn has dawned glorious and I see no need to waste the daylight."

"Oh, I'm sorry, my lord. You should have awoken me for a powder. I would have gladly prepared it for you." She dropped her burden in the wood box near the oven. "Is there anything I can do for you now?"

"No, my dear, but thank you for your thoughts." Edward turned to head out the door toward the stable, then paused, a sudden inspiration coming to him. Perhaps Elinor could shine light on at least one of the nagging puzzles that had plagued him in the night. "I was wondering..." He paused, thinking carefully of how he would ask his question.

"Yes?"

"If I were to desire... a favor... from someone who I was sure would turn me away... is there something I could wear or do that would, perhaps, insure the favor be granted?" He looked at her closely to see if she would understand him, vague as he was trying to be.

"You mean a beguiling charm?" Elinor asked, curious.

Beguiling charm? That is what I asked, isn't it? "No, not exactly," he answered hastily, stumbling over the words for a moment. Then he immediately resumed his pleasant conversant tone. "Just something to help me find the proper words of persuasion required to gain the favor." Edward looked closely at Elinor, but she gave no sign that she knew why he would ask such a question.

"Are you planning to give a speech?" Elinor whispered.

"Do you need something to make you more persuasive?" She blushed and added quickly, "Not that I trifle in such—"

"Elinor, you have nothing to fear from me," Edward interrupted her. "While I find your talents with herbs astounding, I do not for a moment believe you to be trifling in black magic." He raised a brow to her. "That is what you feared, isn't it?"

"Yes..." Elinor looked over her shoulder and then leaned close toward him. "You know how times are. I'm an herbalist, but there are some who would call me a... witch." She mouthed the word.

"Not I, my dear," Edward assured her. "And no, I'm not planning to deliver a speech." He returned to his original subject. "But if I were, what *would* make me more persuasive?"

"Of course, it is only a superstition..." Elinor looked over her shoulder again, then took him by the hand and led him to the far corner of the kitchen. "But I would say that perhaps an oil made from chicory," she whispered cautiously. "I have never found need to prepare such a charm. But if I were asked, that is what I would use."

Edward was dismayed that his limited knowledge of herbs had been so close to the mark. "Chicory? That's an interesting notion." He stroked his chin in thought, then looked at her suddenly. "You've *never* prepared such a charm?"

"No, sir. Never even thought to," Elinor answered.

Her demeanor and tone told Edward she was telling the truth. He leaned against a work bench, a crease coming to his brow. *If Elinor did not give it to him, where did William get it?* After another moment's thought, it occurred to him that perhaps there were other reasons a young man would perfume himself with chicory oil.

"Are there any other uses for that oil?" Edward asked casually, hoping for a logical answer.

"Why do you ask, my lord?"

"Indulge me." He chuckled. "Please, go on."

She gave him a muddled smile but continued, "Well, there are those who believe the chicory could make one able to walk about unseen by others." She laughed at the notion.

Edward snickered with her. "That could be useful if it actually worked," he quipped. *Well, that certainly isn't why he used it.* He was fairly certain that William was not trying to be invisible. "Anything more?"

"I believe it has also been used as a cure for..." Elinor blushed into her hands and let a shy giggle escape her.

Edward raised a curious eyebrow to her, prodding her to continue. "Yes?"

"Well, it could be used as a cure for..." She crooked her finger, telling him to bend close enough so she could whisper. "Troubles of a... *manly* nature, sir." The scarlet in her cheeks brightened as she looked away.

"Oh, I see." Edward could not suppress a chuckle. He had not considered that perhaps William had such a strictly personal reason as *manly* difficulties for using the oil. But given the injury on his wedding night and the subsequent close call with the poison, he thought it was quite possible and logical that William may have sought out an herbalist other than Elinor for such a personal request. He dismissed his original concern that William was relying on folk magic to deliver his speeches. Surely he needed no magical charm to boost *his* persuasive public speaking talents. *That little mystery I shall put to rest.*

Edward smiled, pleased with his conclusion. It faded quickly, however, when he remembered why he had come down to the kitchen so early in the day. *Thomas.* He looked at Elinor. "There is something you could do for me this morning."

"Certainly, what would that be?" Elinor seemed relieved to leave the subject of her craft.

"Prepare a breakfast tray enough for three, and bring it up to Lady Bryndah. If she is sleeping, then wake her; and tell her that Thomas and I shall be joining her presently."

"Right away, my lord." She curtsied and set about preparing the breakfast.

Edward walked out through the kitchen door toward the stables. He was pleased to see he was just in time to greet Thomas as he dismounted at the paddock.

Edward stood casually leaning on the gate post, not calling attention to his presence.

Thomas brushed the dust from his garments and walked toward the gate without looking up. There were a scant ten paces between them before he noticed Edward and came to a sudden halt.

"Good morning, Lord Aberdoir. You are just in time to join me for breakfast. Come with me, if you please." Edward turned on his heel, not waiting for an answer, and proceeded to march back toward the castle.

Edward did not look over his shoulder to see if Thomas was following him. He knew his son-in-law would not disappoint him. He led the way through the great hall to the grand staircase up to the east wing suite where he imagined

Bryndah would, by now, be cursing at Elinor for waking her at such an early hour. As Edward had anticipated, he was greeted at the door by a scathingly shrill caterwaul.

"Have you no sense, you blathering old woman? Leave me at once!" Bryndah's face turned scarlet at the appearance of Edward in her doorway.

"Ah, good. You are awake." Edward entered the room jubilantly, pleased with the surprised look on his daughter's face. "Thank you, my dear, dear Elinor, for preparing such a marvelous looking feast. It is just as I requested and far surpasses my expectations. As always, I am in your debt." He bowed grandly to Elinor.

Elinor curtsied, her cheeks dimpled with suppressed laughter as she hurried out of the suite.

"And now, shall we?" Edward motioned for the two to join him at the table that was set by the window.

The couple exchanged confused glances as Edward merrily sat himself in front of the breakfast feast.

"Come, come, sit with me. Pity to waste such a fine meal." Edward motioned with his knife and fork for Thomas and Bryndah to sit down. He lifted the silver cover on the platter and inhaled the aroma of the sausage and porridge. "Ah. Glorious. And look, Elinor has even provided a pot of her good strong coffee. Wonderful beverage, have you ever tried it?"

"Father, the sun is barely full in the sky. Could this not wait?" Bryndah held her hand over her eyes, blocking the morning sun.

"No, it could not." Edward picked up a napkin, snapped it in midair, and then tucked it into his collar. "We have much to discuss, we three. But as it happens, I am hungry and would prefer to fill my belly before we begin. So I say to you a last time, sit and eat." He eyed both of them intently, leaving no question that they should obey.

Exchanging questioning glances, the two finally approached the table and sat with Edward.

"My lord, to what do we owe this visit?" Thomas asked, clearly struggling to sound casual as he poured himself some coffee.

Edward continued to eat.

"Father?" Bryndah asked irritably.

"Eat." Edward looked up between bites. "We shall talk when we have finished."

They argued no further, dutifully eating the breakfast that was before them, exchanging nervous glances. The meal was well prepared, but neither Thomas nor Bryndah seemed able to enjoy what was offered.

Edward would not be rushed, nor would he be persuaded to begin the discussion he found so important as to have called it at the break of dawn.

Bryndah finished a bit of toast, then impatiently drummed her fingernails on the table while she watched Edward savor the last morsel of his breakfast.

"That was excellent. Elinor has a gift, don't you agree?" Edward sat back, contentedly patting his stomach.

"Father, please," Bryndah said, tossing her napkin onto the table. "Will you not tell us why you have awakened both of us at this ungodly hour?"

"I have not awakened both of you, my dear. I have only awakened *you*," Edward stated casually. "Thomas has been up for hours." He cocked his head toward Thomas. "Haven't you?"

"I could not sleep," Thomas answered defensively. "I merely took a ride to... pass the time, my lord."

"I see. Do you often ride in the night on the woodland road? It is thick with thieves in its shadows. You take a harrowing risk indulging in such a habit."

"I did not go far." Thomas shifted in his chair. "As I said, I could not sleep."

Edward stood slowly and leaned over the table. "Do you think me a fool? You still wear the clothes you wore to last evening's convocation."

Thomas was silent. There was no argument to be made.

Edward turned his unsmiling eyes on Bryndah. "Did you not miss your husband's presence?"

"I turned in early, Father," she answered meekly. "I thought he would be up behind me."

"You are such a loyal wife." Edward glowered in disgust. "So much so that you would attempt to poison his brother— your foster son, your sister's husband, and my own heir—on his behalf."

Bryndah jumped back, wide-eyed and frightened. "Father, no! 'Twas not I who dispensed the nightshade."

"Enough!" Edward pounded the table to silence her. "I had not mentioned the nightshade, Bryndah." He stood, leaning over her, forcing her to sway back in her chair. "William's poisoning had not been made public. So the only way you could possibly know about it is if it was your hand that tainted the water."

"Father, please, I only sought to help ease his injury—"

"Silence! Do not attempt to justify your reprehensible act. You could have killed him! Or perhaps that was your intention all along. Do you think I am ignorant of your resentment toward William? I am not a fool, Bryndah. Do not insult me by attempting to convince me that your motives came from your deep *maternal* instincts." He pounded the table, causing the dishes to jump. "I remember too well, the cowering child you sent to me seven years past, and most clearly do I remember the bloody condition in which he arrived."

Bryndah sat silent, drawing a trembling hand to her mouth.

"And you." Edward turned to Thomas. "What is your business in all of this? Do you believe I am unaware of your contempt? I find you all too eager to gain audience with those who stand against me. Your sudden exit behind Drunbalk and Wesley was not lost on me, Thomas." Edward clenched his fists, leaning on the table top. "Hear me now and understand my words. Any further attempt upon William of Drumoak by you, and I shall personally see to it that you are drawn and quartered. Should I gain knowledge that the two of you have conspired against this house again, by God, you shall both be staked!"

"Do you not see the danger you bring upon us, Edward?" Thomas flared. "The boy is too passionate for matters he has no place in which to meddle. He would bring the wrath of the king and all his armies down upon our heads for the sake of a few simple-minded peasants. He should be more interested in securing alignments with the more prosperous of our sworn enemies by whatever means is warranted!"

Edward put his face inches from Thomas. "Is that what

you have been about, Thomas? Seeking to prevent the wrath of the king from descending? Do we not pay more than our share of tribute? He has no quarrel with the way I govern. Nor has he found cause to question whom I would place in key seats." Edward's voice grew louder with each word, as he stared Thomas squarely in the eye. "Swear to me you have not crossed my orders and conspired with Ogham's camp to move against me."

Thomas clenched his teeth and snarled back to Edward. "I swear that I have not conspired against *you*. But 'tis true enough that I did seek out the more level minds of Drunbalk and Wesley."

Edward withdrew from Thomas and cleared the table with his arm, sending Bryndah into a fit of sobs. "The two of you are to leave Drumoak within the hour. Do not allow me to lay eyes upon you after that time. Expect no tribute or support of arms from this house until such time as you bend your knee and publicly swear fealty to me as your duke and to your brother, William of Drumoak!"

"You shall never see that day!" Thomas flung his chair aside. "If you feel it so necessary to destroy your rule in this duchy by placing such confidence in that wretched recreant, than so be it. I shall be very glad to leave you to your ruin. And I shall see you both rot in hell before I utter an oath of fealty."

"Thomas, no!" Bryndah ran to her husband, reaching for his arm.

"Quiet, woman." Thomas pushed her aside, causing her to fall to the floor. She turned and buried her face in her dressing gown. "Dress yourself and gather your belongings.

Then take your last view of Drumoak and this *fool* who is your father."

Edward raised his hand, striking Thomas sharply with a backhanded blow across his face.

Thomas reached for his sword, but before he could retaliate, the doors to the chamber flew open. Sean and Simon rushed into the room and pounced on Thomas, pinning him to the floor.

"Release me at once!"

"Lord Edward, forgive our intrusion." Sean growled as he sat upon a struggling Thomas. "We heard the shouting and deemed it necessary."

Simon extended a hand to help Bryndah to her feet.

"Don't touch me," she snarled, standing on her own.

"Thank you, gentlemen," Edward addressed Sean. "Your instincts, as usual, are keen. See that these two are parted from this castle at once. They are not to be seen on this estate again." Edward turned a disdainful eye on Bryndah. "You will no longer be known as my daughter."

"Father, please," she pleaded as tears welled in her eyes.

"You shall not address me as such again. I shall take my leave of you now." Edward's cold voice silenced her cries. "You have your orders, gentlemen. I shall require your report within an hour."

William also awoke with the dawning of the new day. His sleep had been deep, peaceful, and blissfully free of dragons. He was taken with the light from the window as it fell across Mehlyndia's face and hair, struck by how beautiful she looked while she slept and how childlike her features became. How he loved her at that moment.

He sat up, stretched, and looked out the window. Then, finding his tunic and leggings, he dressed. He had a busy day planned for the two of them, but could afford a bit of quiet time to gather his thoughts before he sent for breakfast.

His belongings had been transferred from his former chambers, and he surveyed the room until he saw his greatest personal treasure, his lute, resting in the corner near his dressing table, as if waiting for his hands to bring it to life. It seemed weeks since he last had an opportunity to play. Eagerly, he picked it up and positioned himself comfortably on the window seat.

He plucked the strings as quietly as possible, not wanting to awaken Mehlyndia, but loudly enough for the music to fill the corner where he sat. He played a plaintive melody that Geoffrey had taught him years before, and allowed himself to be swept away by the music he created. He hummed quietly at first, but soon, before he realized it, he was singing from his heart as he had done many times when he had been alone.

October winds lament
Around the castle of Drumoak
Yet peace is in her lofty halls,
My loving treasure store
Though autumn leaves may droop and die,
A bud of spring are you
Sing hushabye loo, low loo, low lan
Hushabye loo, low loo

When his song ended, he allowed the strings to ring until their vibrations came to a natural end.

"What lovely songbird has blessed me with such a sweet tune this morning?"

"Melly!" William glanced up, slightly embarrassed to realize he had been singing aloud. He gave her a playful, boyish grin before leaving his cozy spot to join her. "I had not meant to wake you. A thousand pardons for disturbing your sleep." He bowed to the waste. "I am at your mercy for penance, my lady."

"Well, then, sir." She sat up and held out her hand for him to kiss. "As penance for such a crime, you are hereby required to provide like tunes each and every morning to greet my day."

"Your wish is my will." He knelt and kissed her hand in happy repentance. "Shall I play a bit more?"

"Nothing would please me more, my love. But wait a moment." She reached for her charcoal and the expensive, smooth paper she kept in the stand by the bed. "I should like to sketch your face while you play." She took only a few strokes, yet had already captured the delight in his eyes as he watched her work.

William remained on his knee at her bedside and began to pluck the strings, a bit more loudly this time. He sang her a tune of his own fashioning, never taking his eyes off her skillful hands as she continued with her sketch.

As he sang his song and watched her skillful hand, it seemed that the whole of the world only existed for the two of them. He knew that soon enough Elinor or Laurel would be at the door with a tray, and their time would not belong to themselves any longer. But for this moment, he fancied himself to be a callow bard, rather than the dutiful Earl of Sutherland.

It was not Laurel with the breakfast tray that interrupted their peace, but the clatter of running feet in the corridor and the muffled yet distinct sound of angry voices coming from the east wing. He rose to his feet at once. "Something's happening." He went to the door, raised the bar, and went into the corridor. Mehlyndia put her drawing down, hastily drew on her dressing gown and chased after him.

William had expected to find someone standing sentry outside the chamber. Sean would have sent Simon or Ewan to take his post. Concern grew to trepidation at finding the post completely abandoned.

The sounds came from the east wing. William recognized Edward's furious shouts. He and Mehlyndia shot startled looks to each other. They rushed to the east wing but halted when they could clearly understand the words being spoken.

"Thank you, gentlemen. Your instincts, as usual, are keen. See that these two are parted from this hall at once. They are not to be seen on this estate again."

William pulled Mehlyndia back and motioned her to stay close to him and to remain quiet.

Mehlyndia stood, ashen-faced. "Bryndah! He has disowned her."

William did not share Mehlyndia's shock, but was surprised, nonetheless, that Edward had chosen this time in the morning to throw his daughter and her husband out of the castle. "Let's go back," he said. "Father will come to us and we'll know soon enough what has happened."

She nodded absently but did not move from where she stood. He took her by the hand with an insistent tug and led her back to their suite. When they arrived, he closed the door and held her.

She cried onto his shoulder. "I knew he was angry with her, but this is more than I thought he would do. How could he judge her so harshly?" She broke from William and moved away. "He cannot be sure it was Bryndah. I cannot believe she was the one who put the dose—"

"Melly, I have no such doubt," he said softly, his voice flat toned.

She looked at him with a hurt, disbelieving expression.

He saw no gentle way to continue what he was going to say, so he simply continued in the same steady voice. "She has done worse things than place a bit of nightshade in my drinking water."

"What are you saying?"

William found it difficult, but faced her fully. "She has shown me no kindness at all that I can recall. My childhood in her care was not one I would wish on the lowest of God's creatures." He turned his face, not wanting to elaborate.

"How can you speak of my sister so coldly?" Mehlyndia forced him to look at her, turning him by the arm. "Why do you all turn on her? Why are you telling me such vicious lies?"

William was taken aback by the wild anger in Mehlyndia's eyes. "Have you ever known me to lie to you?" It was his turn to feel betrayed. He fought his impulse to raise his voice to her, battling to keep his growing anger in check.

"Perhaps you have lied to me and I have been unaware. How many untruths have you told?"

"I have never told you an untruth," he yelled, no longer able to control his voice. "I am guilty only of withholding certain painful details from you in an attempt to protect your feelings. A mistake, I freely admit. A mistake that I shall not repeat."

"What details have you withheld, then?" Mehlyndia yelled back. "I cannot begin to understand or believe what you claim until I am fully enlightened."

"Believe it. She's evil, Mehlyndia." William locked his teeth and pried her hand off his arm, astonished at the fire in her eyes. He had never noticed until that moment that she bore an eerie resemblance to her sister when she was angry.

"I have never known Bryndah to be anything but kind and caring to me," she argued. "I admit to have known her to show her temper toward Laurel, but you cannot make me believe her to be as evil as you claim."

William growled and in his frustration, raised his hand.

Mehlyndia gasped and stepped back, throwing up protective hand. But he had no intention of striking her. Instead, he reached over his shoulders, pulled his tunic roughly over his head, and threw it to the floor. He stood before her, bare skinned to his waist, glaring. He balled his fists then quickly turned his back, leaning heavily on the table.

"Look upon my back, Mehlyndia, so you may know your sister better." His voice was hard and strained as he fought to retain control of the last shreds of his composure. "Not by her own hand, but on her order did I come by these."

"My God! What is this?"

"You wanted proof," he answered coldly. "Look close. The

marks you see did not come about as the result of simple horseplay or childhood mishap." He stood still as a stone, tensing his arms against his anger as, for the first time, he allowed Mehlyndia to see the jagged scars that crisscrossed his flesh from his shoulders to his lower back. The marks left behind were from a heavy-handed lashing Bryndah had ordered on him by Brother Joseph, behind the stables in Aberdoir. "Shall I enlighten you further?" he asked without turning.

"This is what you sought to keep from me on our wedding night. The thing Elinor said I would see eventually. Why did you not ever...?" The anger in Mehlyndia's voice faded immediately, to be replaced by a trembling whisper.

William drew a long calming breath. "I saw no need to shatter the bond you held with your sister." He spoke quietly, still not turning to her, "Until now." He reached for his discarded garment and pulled it back over his head. After several moments, he turned again to face her.

She sat at the table, staring unseeingly ahead of her. "Forgive me, please, William. I had no right to accuse you." She swallowed hard but maintained her control. "It was of my own choosing that I turned a blind eye to my suspicions about Bryndah. Still, I never imagined she could be guilty of such as this. I cannot bear to think... " She caught her breath, choking on words. "You were only a child. I suppose Thomas also..."

"You would suppose correctly." Walking to the open window, he chose his words carefully, speaking softly, looking out on the landscape. "I will not make a further attempt to spare you from the truth, though the details are difficult for me. I will say only that there is no love to be lost between my brother and I. He has made no effort to conceal from me how he regards my existence as an abomination. You have no idea what my being named Edward's heir means to him. Thomas is seething."

"I don't understand." Mehlyndia stood beside him. "Why then, if he hates you so much, did he send you to be fostered here? It seems it was your salvation to have been given to my father."

"It was," William admitted. "And it is a bitter dose to Thomas that I've thrived here. But you see, it wasn't Thomas who sent me to Drumoak, but my own father."

"Your father?" She looked at him, puzzled. "He was long dead when you arrived here."

"In his will," he explained. "It was his wish that I be sent here when I reached the age of twelve. He and Edward were close friends, and my father wished for me to learn from him." William spoke quietly, still looking out the window.

Mehlyndia stood silent while he explained.

"Thomas inherited my father's title, the land, the house, and the stables as his eldest son. He would have inherited the whole of my father's fortune as well, as his only son, but as fate would have it, I was born to my mother in her late age. When she died at my birth, my father made a change in his will." William let his voice trail away for a moment. "His fortune was divided between the two of us."

"But Thomas is sole holder of Aberdoir now. Has he stolen your share?" She placed a hand on his arm.

"No. I was given no share of Aberdoir. However, my father had holdings in Sutherland and a substantial amount of personal wealth. Father put his holdings in Edward's trust, with the intent that part of it would come to me when I married or reached twenty-one years, whichever came first." He gave her a quick smile. "You've married a wealthy man, my love." He turned back to the window and stared silently at the hills.

"That's not important."

He continued without looking at her. "Thomas has always felt that he should have inherited everything." He turned from the window and paced toward the table. "He used to call me 'the burden.' For a long time, I thought that was actually my name."

"Why, then, did he consent to raise you?" she asked. "Wouldn't your father's wealth have gone completely to him if... " She turned away, not finishing her thought.

William looked at her, understanding her implication. "If I did not survive to at least my twelfth year, Edward was to keep what my father entrusted to him and Thomas was to be cut off completely. Once I turned twelve, I was to be delivered to Edward's care and Thomas was to receive an exceptionally large amount of the estate back. It galled him that he had to wait twelve years to get it. That is the only reason I was not dropped in the river as an infant. But he felt no obligation to treat me any better than he treated his horses. Truth be told, the horses were better cared for, by far." His voice grew softer. "Upon my majority. . . or marriage, Edward was to give to me the remainder of my father's holdings. Everything except for the seat in Sutherland, that is. That was left to Edward to do with as he wished." An ironic smile crossed William's face. "Thomas has always expected to gain that particular seat for himself."

"I suspected as much," Mehlyndia whispered.

"It would have been kinder had my father sent me here from the start, but that was not how it was to be." He could see from the look in Mehlyndia's eyes that he had no further need to elaborate on his childhood with Thomas and Bryndah.

A knock on the chamber door brought an end to William's unpleasant oration.

"Good morning, Father," William greeted, as he opened the door.

"William. Mehlyndia." Edward entered and kissed his daughter. "I should like to speak with the two of you, if you don't mind. I have had to take care of a bit of unpleasantness this morning that you need to learn of."

"Yes, we were expecting you." William closed the door and motioned for him to sit down.

Edward looked surprised. "Then you know?"

"Not the details," William answered as they sat. "We heard the commotion. Please, tell us what has happened."

Edward paused as Mehlyndia drew a long, staggering breath. He cast a concerned look at William. "Is all well with the two of you?"

"We are fine, yes." Mehlyndia quickly brushed her cheeks and changed her expression to a more cheerful one. "William has merely moved me with his song this morning."

Edward took her hand and spoke gently. "Come, now, I am not a hard-headed old fool, I can see you are troubled. What has upset you so?"

William answered for her. "We overheard your last order

to the sentries, Father. Melly is distressed that her sister has been banished."

Edward sighed deeply and settled heavily onto the chair. "So you know that much, do you? I'm sorry, my dear, to have had to take such measures. Believe me when I tell you, it was necessary."

"Only moments ago, I would not have believed you." She looked at William. "I have no such doubt now."

"Oh? And what has persuaded you?"

She cast her eyes down.

Once again, William answered for her quietly, "I've explained the scars on my back."

Edward nodded his understanding.

William was more concerned at what Thomas may have done to provoke Edward. "I'm sure there is more to hear. Thomas had a look of fire in him last night. Am I right to assume that he has caused this?"

"Yes. He left the convocation abruptly and I found him returning with this morning's light."

"Returning?" William asked. "From where?"

"He chased down Drunbalk and Wesley when he left last night. I need not explain to you the implications. I took the opportunity to confront him with my suspicions over breakfast."

"Forgive me, Father. What are the implications?" Mehlyndia asked.

William answered, yet did not look directly at Mehlyndia. "He seeks to align against us. He will ally himself to Ogham's two bulldogs first. He would not hesitate to give Aberdoir to Ogham, compromising our southern borders."

Edward nodded. "For the most part, you are correct. I confronted him on that point, and he did not deny that he feels it is in our best interest to pander to the king's favorite tyrant."

"Is that everything?"

Edward looked up, scowling. "His vendetta does not appear to be aimed solely toward me."

William made a quick, scoffing laugh. "You? His *vendetta* has been to erase my very existence from the start. I assume he offered Aberdoir to Ogham in return for another archer to finish what the first one bumbled?"

"Aberdoir holds little interest to Ogham. It is of no strategic advantage to either of us, for that matter. I fail to see what else he could offer to gain any favor from that camp." Edward reached for the water pitcher. "But Drunbalk and Wesley may have motives of their own that have nothing to do with Aberdoir. Do you see?" Edward poured some water and looked at William, raising his brow waiting for William to puzzle out the answer.

"The treaties," William answered. "Thomas was angry that it was me you sent to negotiate them."

"Yes," Edward answered. "It is no secret those two dimwits are unhappy with the way things turned out." He smiled at William for a moment. "You surprised even me with the terms you managed to get them to agree to."

William allowed a smug grin. "I simply spoke in short, simple words they could understand." He sat quietly for a moment, contemplating what Thomas was hoping to gain from them. "Do you think Thomas promised them better terms? I can't see how he could accomplish such a thing. The scrolls are signed and sealed, iron clad."

"I believe that is exactly what he wants," Edward answered flatly. "But I'm fairly certain we have little to fear that he could actually null the existing treaties."

"Is that all you think it is?" William wondered. "I can't help but wonder if he has something far more personal in mind."

"Has he made personal threats?"

"Nothing I can't handle." William remembered the visit Thomas paid him just before his wedding. But he did not want to upset Mehlyndia. "He's made idle threats for years. This was no different."

"Perhaps you should tell me anyway." Edward gave him a stern look.

"He came to see me before the wedding," William began. "He told me to... " He gave a sideways glance to Mehlyndia. "... to watch my back."

"Why didn't you tell me this before?" Edward slapped the arms of the chair. "I would have thrown him out right then."

"Father, he's been telling me that for years. Why would I think it any different now?" William argued.

"Because you have other adversaries now." Edward raised his voice. "That he won't hesitate to cozy up to."

"Drunbalk and Wesley." William sunk into his chair and rested his head on his hand.

"Exactly." Edward stood and leaned over the table. "Not to mention Ogham. We've already seen how far he's willing to go."

"Politics." William sighed in disgust. "That's all it is."

"Possibly." Edward sat down again. "But there is someone else you need to consider."

"Who? Woodhall?" William chuckled at the idea.

"If only it were." Edward stared, unsmiling. "You have raised the hackles of the bishop, William. He is a powerful man. You could find him to be a dangerous opponent."

William tightened his jaw. "The last thing I wish to do is to go up against him. Yet I won't sit by and remain silent while he orders the fires. Never again." He spoke softly, resolved determination in his voice. "Someone has to take a stand. It's time."

Edward sighed loudly. "I know you believe that. But William, know when you must back away. I fully understand your convictions and I admire them. However, you must be more careful of what you say and to whom you say it. If not for your own sake, then for Mehlyndia's. And mine." Edward looked at him strangely, almost fearfully, then said, "The danger is right in front of you, all you have to do is look up to see it."

"Aye, Father." William answered, knowing his acquiescence was unconvincing. "For your sake."

"What in Heaven's name are you doing over there?" Elinor entered the kitchen from the yard, her apron full of the day's eggs, when she saw Laurel's curious position, crouched and peeking through a crack in the kitchen door. She placed the eggs in a bowl and hurried to the door to have a look for herself. "What are you—"

"Hush, Elinor. I'm trying to hear." Laurel waved her hand wildly. "Oh!" she squealed.

"What? What is going on?" Elinor tried to push Laurel away from the crack so she could see for herself. Laurel would not be moved. "Tell me what's happening, child."

"They're throwing 'em out. They've got the trunks in the hall." Laurel tugged Elinor's apron, a look of unabashed joy on her face.

"Who, Laurel? Will you please tell me?" Elinor struggled to get a look through the crack.

"Will's horrid brother and his dragon of a wife." She was positively giddy.

"What? Let me see." Elinor finally succeeded in pushing Laurel away from the crack in the door. Sure enough, she saw Thomas and Bryndah in the hall, dressed to travel, surrounded by a dozen or so of Edward's sentries. Sean and Ewan carried a large trunk between them down the grand stairs.

"Holy Mother, you're right." Elinor clapped her hands, sharing Laurel's glee.

"What are you two conspirators up to over there?" A voice came from the other end of the kitchen.

The two women jumped and spun around with guilty expressions. Agnes came into the kitchen, little Duncan in tow, her arms full with turnips and carrots. She dropped them into the bin by the oven.

"Shh!" Laurel summoned with a frantic wave. "Come see, come see!"

Agnes hurried to them. "What is all the—Oh my! They're leaving?"

"Look closer, Agnes. They're not just leaving, they're being tossed." Laurel giggled as the three of them leaned against the kitchen door, sharing the view through the crack. "I won't be taking a tongue-lashing from that shrew this day."

"I wanna see too!"

Elinor turned in time to see little Duncan charging across the kitchen floor. She reached out to stop him. Just as he was about to gain the door, she caught him, but his momentum took her balance. He and Elinor fell onto Agnes, who fell on top of Laurel, who went crashing into the swinging door. The four of them were unceremoniously dumped through the doorway onto the floor of the great hall in a heap.

All eyes turned to view the pile of serving women who had just fallen through the kitchen door. Elinor held her breath, trying desperately not to laugh.

Duncan was the first to get back on his feet. He stood with his hands on hips and a disappointed pout on his face. "Aw, is that all it is? It's just that ugly lady with Sean and his mates." He waved his little fingers at Sean. Sean waved back in the same manner, then Duncan merrily trotted back through the kitchen.

Sean gave the women an incredulous look, then shook his head, holding back a laugh of his own. Laurel was the first to lose control and burst into audacious laughter. Elinor and Agnes soon followed, sending echoes of unbridled mirth though the hall.

Bryndah turned with a venomous look on her face. "Quiet, you gang of blithering harpies!" She stormed toward them, but Sean blocked her. She pushed him aside. "Get your arse out of my way, you idiot!"

"My lady," Sean spoke in exaggerated politeness. "My arse has orders to see to it that yours is parted from Drumoak."

"You will not speak to my wife in that fashion!" Thomas's face turned red as he charged toward Sean.

Ewan jumped to block him. "Stand back, sir. You have no voice here. Our orders come from Lord Edward."

"You tell him, Ewan," Laurel called out, cheering them on. "Watch out for her fangs, Sean."

Bryndah set fiery eyes on Laurel and hissed through her teeth, making a quick dash around Sean. "You insolent little bitch!" Bryndah screeched as she lunged toward Laurel, bony fingers outstretched, ready to scratch her eyes out.

Simon took his turn to join the fray, gallantly leaping in front of Laurel. In an almost graceful dive, he caught Bryndah by her waist and scooped her onto his shoulder, her backside facing front.

Laurel doubled over, howling in laughter. "Simon! My hero!" She waved her apron in his direction, tears of laughter on her cheeks.

"How dare you!" Bryndah kicked and screamed on Simon's shoulder. "Get your filthy hands off—"

Simon smacked her on the bottom. "Now, now, my lady, mind your manners."

Thomas growled and flew toward Simon, his hand reaching for his sword.

"My turn!" Sean called out and flung himself onto Thomas before he could draw. He caught him in the middle as well, hoisting him onto his shoulder in the same manner as Simon carried Bryndah. "I've wanted to do this for a long, long time."

Elinor and Laurel clung to each other, wiping tears of unrestrained laughter from their faces. They watched Sean and Simon pompously carry the Earl and Countess of Aberdoir out to their waiting carriage. The other sentries closed ranks behind them. Ewan turned and gave a quick salute and polite bow to the ladies, flashed a full-faced grin, then twirled around to join his comrades.

Elinor shook all over from laughter. Her face was beginning to hurt from it all. Just as she was finally gaining control of her wits, the sound of more bellowing laughter came from the highest landing of the grand stairs. She looked up to see that Edward and William had arrived in time to witness the removal of Lord and Lady Aberdoir.

The ladies silenced at once and looked up at the two lords of Drumoak on the stairs. But it was not long before Edward's laughter caught them, and soon all were seized again.

William waved in greeting as he and Edward approached the women. He had managed not to fall into the frenzied laughter that had taken the others. He approached straight-faced, a look of sullen concern in his eye.

Elinor stiffened up and straightened her apron, nudging Laurel with her elbow to do the same. "He doesn't look happy," she whispered.

"Good morning, ladies." William stopped in front of Laurel, no trace of humor on his face. "Laurel, what is it?" he asked as though he had come across a tragedy.

Laurel took a breath and held it, puffing out her cheeks to contain her laughter.

"Why are you so glum?" William asked.

Laurel burst into uncontrolled laughter. "We'll miss them so."

"You must be devastated." William finally gave in, his face breaking into smiles. "I know how fond of them you are." He offered Laurel his cape. "For you to wipe your tears of grief."

Laurel waved it away, catching her breath.

"Ladies, please." William gained control of his laughter quickly, assuming a less jovial manner. "Though I fully share your sentiments, for Mehlyndia's sake, could you refrain from showing her your joy? Remember it is her sister who has been removed. You have all seen for years what Mehlyndia has only just learned of, and she is understandably upset by all of this."

"Aye, I understand." Elinor smiled at William, wiping the last tears from her cheeks. She looked at him more closely, noting that the laughter was gone completely from his face. She took a breath and forced herself into a more serious attitude, as Edward ushered them all into the kitchen.

William settled onto one of the chairs around the kitchen worktable while Edward prepared to explain to the three ladies what they had just witnessed. Though William was glad to have Thomas and Bryndah removed from the castle, something about the laughter that accompanied their departure gnawed deep in his gut.

"I had intended to make a formal announcement to the staff, but I see you are all aware." Edward took a long breath to change the mood to something a bit more serious. "Here, let's sit. Elinor, could you prepare us each a nice hot caudle?"

"Aye, right away." After a moment, Elinor produced five steaming mugs and set them down around the table.

William accepted the caudle without comment. *Laurel mocked her.* He stared into his cup while Edward addressed the others, not paying attention to them at all, absently sipping the hot brew. *The dragon won't let the laughter pass unanswered, that's for sure. Seems I'm to be haunted by Aberdoir all day.* He heard Edward's deep voice addressing the ladies, but pushed it aside, allowing himself to drift, staring unseeing into his cup. *Laurel mocked her.* He remembered only one other time he had seen anyone so brazenly stand up against Bryndah. The result of that confrontation had led to complete ruin.

"Stay behind me, little one."

"I saw you run in here." Bryndah shoved open the pantry door and charged in, furious. "Rebecca! Where is he?"

William gasped. Bryndah heard him.

"Hiding him? I suppose you are the one who let him out?" she roared at Rebecca. "Come with me, you little demon." She reached around but Rebecca blocked her, staying protectively in front of William.

"Yes, I let him out! He's just a wee bairn and the fire from the forge turns that shed into an oven."

"How dare you contradict me?" Bryndah yelled back. "I shall run this household as I see fit. I've told you before not to overrule me when I discipline the boy."

"Discipline? Is that what you call baking a child alive? Stay behind me, little one!"

"How did you find him?" Bryndah made a quick dash around Rebecca.

"I found him when I heard him banging the door and crying out." Rebecca spun, keeping William protectively behind her. "He was terrified. I let him out."

"The door was locked. I have the only key. How did you unlock it?" Bryndah challenged.

"I used the hammer and the iron poker from the blacksmith's fireplace. I had to let him out."

"Why? Just to disobey—"

"Because he could have died in there, you heartless witch!" Rebecca lost control of her temper just then and slapped Bryndah sharply across the face.

William clung to Rebecca's skirt. At the sound of the slap, even as a child of six, he knew Rebecca had just brought something terrible upon herself.

"You will pay for that."

Bryndah reached again for William, but Rebecca grabbed her arms and pushed her back toward the wall. "Run away, little one. Run away!"

William sat, solemn-faced, with the memory of Rebecca's cries echoing in his mind. He was only half aware of the conversation taking place around him, when he realized Edward was voicing his concerns of repercussions from Bryndah.

"She is like a caged animal, and will likely lash out at everyone she feels has crossed her." Edward looked to each of the women in turn. "I'm afraid that would be the three of you. Particularly you, little mouse, after the hysterics in the doorway just now."

William looked sharply at Laurel. "You didn't slap her, did you?" he blurted.

"No," she answered quickly. "Why would you think that I would slap her?"

"I didn't." William was stunned at his own sudden outburst. "I'm sorry. Silly question." He blushed and forced a smile, frustrated with himself for not keeping his paranoia in check. "I didn't mean to interrupt."

Edward placed his hand over William's for a moment and looked him in the eye. "It's all right. I understand your concern." He spoke softly for William alone to hear. "That was a long time ago, son, best left forgotten." He glanced at the ladies, indicating to Elinor that William's mug was empty, and he should have a refill.

William accepted a fresh caudle, pushing the memory away. "Father, perhaps this is a good time for me to make a request of you."

"What is it?" Edward asked.

He looked up, half cheerfully and said, "It seems I have a new manor to staff. I ask your permission to extend an offer to these ladies." *Get them as far away from the dragon as I can. Then she can't strike back.*

The three held different expressions. Laurel was clearly delighted with the prospect. Elinor and Agnes merely smiled politely.

"You honor us, dear." Elinor spoke gently, catching Edward's eye. "I should not like to speak for the others, but for myself, I am old and have served this house for most of my life. I am willing to take the risks that may come, but if you please, I should like to remain in Lord Edward's service. Still, I shall miss your presence, and my lady's as well."

"I understand." William half smiled at her. "You are welcome at any time to change your mind. And I shall deeply miss your presence as well." He was disappointed, but not fully surprised by her response. "Agnes?"

"I believe I shall also remain at Drumoak," Agnes answered

shyly.

William had expected as much. *Well, I tried. Edward won't let Bryndah back here anyway.* He turned to Laurel, the light in her eyes gave him his answer before she spoke.

"Just try to keep me away from Sutherland." Laurel grinned. "I accept." She looked to Edward quickly. "If my lord allows it, that is."

Edward chuckled and winked at her. "You are free to do so, little mouse. Go with my blessings."

William reached across the table and squeezed Laurel's hand. "Good. Mehlyndia will be pleased to have you."

Agnes spoke timidly. "Lord William, may I be so bold as to request a favor of you?" She looked down at her hands.

"Certainly. What would you ask of me?"

"I ask that you consider taking Duncan with you to Sutherland." Agnes looked at William quickly, then turned her eyes down.

"Duncan?" William asked softly. "Are you sure?"

"Aye," Agnes answered. "To be trained... as Sean was."

William looked at Edward, tilting his head in question.

Edward shrugged. "It is your decision, lad."

"Allow me this," William began. "I shall put the house in order, and when Duncan is the right age, I'll send for him. He has shown a lot of pluck, and I should think one day he will make a fine bold sentry, just as his brother, Sean. I should be glad to see to that if you like. You and he will always be welcome to visit. Sean will certainly miss the both of you once we go."

Agnes smiled, at last looking up to him. "Aye, that shall make me proud indeed. Thank you."

"Then it shall be so." William was happy to have pleased her, and touched that she would entrust Duncan to him. *My first foster son.* The thought amused him. He finished his caudle and turned to Edward. "I should also like to offer service to a few of the men."

"I expected so. I can't imagine you'd leave Sean behind." Edward chuckled. "You are free to choose your guard from among mine. I'm pleased you are thinking seriously about security." Edward stood to leave. "Ladies, I apologize for taking you away from your duties." He tapped William on the shoulder and motioned for him to follow. "We shall take our leave of you now. There is much for us to do. Please keep what you have witnessed in the hall to yourselves. I know how the gossip tree grows in this castle, but for your own sakes, please do me this favor."

"Yes, m' lord. I shall take a broom to the back side of anyone who babbles out of turn." Elinor looked squarely at Laurel, a warning in her eye.

Laurel wrinkled her nose and rolled her eyes before beaming one last smile at William. "No babbling today. I promise."

Chapter 7

"THEN WE ARE agreed?" Gerald Drunbalk extended his arm to Evander Wesley.

"Aye. We make our proposal today." Wesley grabbed Gerald's arm at the elbow to seal their arrangement.

Gerald grinned. "I should think Thomas will be pleased. Although I doubt he is eager to ruin his brother for our benefit alone."

Wesley laughed. "That much is plain to me as well. But our interest in Sutherland and those blasted treaties is genuine enough. And if we please Thomas's personal vendetta in the mix, all the better. I care not what happens to that blasted whelp of a brother of his. Let him burn. One less nuisance to deal with." He reined his horse sharply to the left to cross a stream.

Gerald followed. "I have to admit, he has given us the perfect device to spark Ogham's interest in the deed." Gerald brought his mount to a halt by the water.

"Do you think there be truth in Thomas Fylbrigge's accusation? Have we all been enthralled?" Wesley made a mocking wave of his hands and laughed, then dismounted.

"Absolutely." Gerald replied, suddenly serious. "You cannot deny that young Fylbrigge has an uncanny way with his words. Now, could it be by dark magic that he's swayed us all to his will? There, I have my doubt. I don't fully believe it exists, despite what the king believes. I think it be all a lot of nonsense." He tossed the reins over a nearby branch. "But, I know that the king and Ogham certainly subscribe to that belief, so if it benefits my purse, then I say... I believe."

"I am not so sure that it is nonsense," Wesley said. "There is something uncanny about Fylbrigge. Especially in light of the poison he presumably survived. Thomas is either mistaken in his claim of what was in that pouch, or his brother is extraordinarily lucky." He splashed his face and filled his water skin. "Or perhaps he truly has been charmed. But as you say, what we believe is of no consequence. It is what the king and Ogham will believe that is important." He grinned. "And Thomas has given us a golden seed to plant in their superstitiously fertile little gardens."

"Aye. But what then, to do about Thomas?" Gerald scowled as he washed the dust from his face. "We cannot possibly suggest he be placed at Sutherland. Ogham would never allow it. It is far too important a seat and Ogham has even less love and trust for Thomas Fylbrigge than we do."

"That's true. There has to be some other compensation we could offer Thomas that would suit his lust for authority and wealth while keeping him out of *our* hair."

"There may just be."

"What do you have in mind?"

"He is so eager to govern near the sea, perhaps he would enjoy governing *across* it." A sly grin crossed Gerald's lips. He took one more splash on his face, then returned to his mount.

"You are brilliant." Wesley laughed wickedly. "We offer him a governor's post in the New World. Let him convert the savages. Who knows, he may even survive." He remounted.

"At any rate, the offer will be enticing. One I'm sure he would not quickly refuse, should it be presented properly. Perhaps we should ask his enthralling little brother present the offer for us!"

They both laughed at that.

"Perhaps we should! I should think Ogham will agree as well." Gerald kicked his horse into a quick trot.

It was only a half-day's ride to Lothlanne, Ogham's castle in the Lothian lowlands. Bolstered by the new twist they had in their plan to undo William and rid themselves of those ponderous trade treaties—and possibly Thomas in the bargain—they set out.

By midday, the two were on the final mile to Lothlanne, her parapets growing steadily taller as they approached. A dreadfully formidable sight, she occupied the southern slopes of the mountains that separated Ogham's county from Wesley's. The river Tyne meandered through the valley below these slopes. This was the key access to the ports across Scotland, the shortest and most efficient route to the port at Sutherland. It also served as the most important trade route through the highlands to the southern border. During normal times, the river was crowded with barges and small ships bringing and taking coal and grains to and from the continent. However, on this day, the effects of Edward's embargo were already evident. A few small crafts were moving along the river, but no barges entered from the port at Sutherland.

From his private chamber in Lothlanne, Lord Ogham stood brooding over the sight of the near-idle river. He paced the stone floor and gloomy shadows of his chamber, waiting for word from his earls of what had transpired at Drumoak after he made his abrupt departure. He cursed himself for not waiting long enough to know if his archer had hit his mark. He assumed that William had been spared the assassin's arrow, as it had taken his two earls this extra day to return. That could only mean that Edward had held his convocation after all, and William of Drumoak was now fully installed as Earl of Sutherland.

"Damn them both."

His wait ended with a knock on his chamber door and the chamberlain announcing that Gerald Drunbalk and Evander Wesley had arrived and were eager to have his audience. Ogham stood next to a throne-like chair that occupied a raised landing before a large pair of arched windows. He pulled open the huge velvet draperies, allowing the sun to invade the room, then turned his back to the window, casting a long, crisp shadow across the floor.

"Gentlemen, come." Ogham beckoned with an impatient wave of his hand. He deliberately stood at the edge of the landing, knowing the back-lighting from the window would make his countenance seem larger than normal, dark and intimidating. "Waste not my time. Tell me, what news from Stonehaven?"

Gerald bowed, wringing his hat in his hand as he stood in Ogham's shadow. "My lord, Edward has set an embargo against you."

"Is that what has taken my barges from the river?"

"Aye, my lord. It is in retaliation for the attempt on the life of his heir."

"Attempt? So the whelp still lives," Ogham grumbled, stepping aside and causing a blinding stream of sunlight to fall into Gerald's face. "I suspected as much."

"Yes, my lord." Gerald replied, squinting against the sunlight. "Fylbrigge has been seated in Sutherland and has made clear he intends to honor the blockade." He took a quick step to the side, back into Ogham's shadow.

Ogham scowled and moved, purposely blinding Gerald again. He had already assumed all that had been told to him, even though he had clung to the hope that William had been dispatched and Edward could easily be swayed to release his pathetic embargo.

Wesley and Drunbalk exchanged a silent communication. Ogham noticed their secret messaging. "What more have you to tell me?" he asked impatiently.

"My lord," Wesley began, carefully avoiding Ogham's shadow. He cleared his throat. "We believe we have the means to put an end to Edward's blockade, the treaties. . . and perhaps his reign as well."

Ogham raised an interested brow. "Speak."

"Thank you, my lord." Wesley bowed quickly, then looked up, blinking against the sunlight. "We were approached on our journey from Stonehaven by Thomas Fylbrigge of Aberdoir."

"Were you?" Ogham's lip began to curl. "And what was the excuse he gave you for disappointing me? He assured me the archer would be sufficient."

"Thomas sent the archer?" Gerald asked, shielding his eyes with his hand. "I thought you had ordered—"

"I merely mentioned to him, over an ale, that his brother

was beginning to be a considerable thorn in my side." Ogham smirked and made a dismissive gesture with his hand. "It was Thomas's idea to put the archer in the window. I admit, the plan made sense to me, and I told him so. I offered him a price to carry it out." He laughed mirthlessly under his breath. "I'm glad I did not pay him in advance."

"It seems Thomas has not abandoned his hope to claim your payment, my lord," Wesley chimed in, nodding enthusiastically to Gerald. "He has given us information about his brother that you will find interesting." He crossed himself quickly, looking nervously over his shoulder. "God help us if he's right."

"Aye." Gerald crossed himself as well. "God help us indeed, that we've allowed young Fylbrigge near us at all."

"What are you talking about?" Ogham crossed himself automatically, suddenly feeling paranoid at their fearful faces. "What have you learned?"

Gerald took a step closer to the landing, avoiding the sunlight. He locked eyes with Ogham. "My lord, Thomas professes that the new Earl of Sutherland has gained his rank in Edward's line by calling upon... demonic forces."

"Demonic forces?" Ogham repeated, absently crossing himself again. "In what way?"

Gerald continued his narration in a harsh whisper. "He is an enchanter, my lord, who has bewitched us all. We were not of our own will when we agreed to the trade treaties."

"He sways minds." Wesley added, stepping close to Gerald. "And with his tricks he even convinced Ambrose Woodhall to free a condemned witch right from the stake!"

"That's right." Gerald nodded. "He makes no secret of his

support of the heretics. He's defended them at every turn."
He looked Ogham straight in the eye, stepping brazenly onto
the landing. "He's one of them."

"Have you proof?"

"He revealed himself at the convocation." Gerald's voice
grew softer but darker. "He told us to turn a blind eye to
heretics in our estates, and that we should tolerate their
heathen practices." He beckoned Ogham to lean close. "And
if we did not, then we would surely bring disaster upon our
tenants and ourselves."

"He made that threat?" Ogham asked, inches from
Gerald's face.

"He did," Gerald answered in an ominous whisper.

Ogham straightened himself slowly, then sat stroking his
beard, considering what Gerald had just said. *An interesting
threat indeed.* "That alone is not proof of sorcery, Gerald,
although it is a very good argument for treason to the crown."

"My lord, there is more." Gerald kept his menacing tone.
Not taking his eyes away from Ogham, he retrieved a small
brown pouch from his belt pocket. "Do you know what this
is?" He tossed it to Ogham.

Ogham caught the pouch one-handed and opened it.
Turning it inside out, he sniffed. "'Tis a sleeping powder of
sorts. A strong one, by the smell of it. What proof is this?"

"It's a blend of nightshade and opium, my lord." Gerald
approached the , then knelt on one knee to Ogham's left.
"Thomas told us that only hours before the convocation took
place, Fylbrigge ingested the entire contents of that pouch. It
had been *full*, my lord. Yet there he stood, fully awake, none
the worse for wear at Edward's side." He gave a quick look to

Wesley. "Isn't that right?"

"Aye, my lord, tall and proud he stood there." Wesley approached the chair as Gerald had, and knelt on Ogham's right. "He didn't even look tired."

Together, the two earls flanked Ogham, eye level, almost head-to-head with the duke.

Ogham turned the pouch thoughtfully between his fingers, skeptical of what these two had told him, but willing to believe. He closed his eyes to narrow slits, looking from one to the other, then asked, "Was Fylbrigge given an antidote?"

Wesley and Drunbalk looked quickly at each other. Wesley answered, "An antidote for such a poison would be equally lethal without some sort of miraculous—nay, *demonic*—protection. Should it be proven that he did survive a counter-potion—"

Ogham raised his hand to quiet Wesley. No one could withstand two poisonings in one day and walk to tell of it, at least not without the intervention of some supernatural protection. It occurred to him that the maker of these potions was more likely the spell caster. Still, with or without William's knowledge, the end was the same. Ogham sat back in his chair, resting his chin on his entwined fingers. "He's obviously made a pact with the devil." He slapped his knees and raised his hands, palms up. "There's no other explanation."

Wesley crossed himself dramatically against the mention of a pact. "It's obvious. You could see it in his eyes," he said.

"And hear it in his voice," Gerald added.

"How did Thomas propose this to work in our favor?" Ogham grinned, intrigued with this new information. He turned his head from one earl to the other as they spoke in rapid succession.

"The trade treaties were obviously signed under the influence of black magic," Wesley said.

"The judges will surely rule them null under those circumstances," Gerald continued, barely a breath after Wesley.

"Sutherland will be wrested from Edward's holdings—"

"Leaving full control of that tenant to—"

"You," they finished together.

This was what he had been waiting to hear. A clear way to proceed. Ogham knew they had more than enough damning evidence against William of Drumoak. But to be sure, he would need to engage the services of the clergy to waylay any doubt to the accusations. "You say Fylbrigge blatantly professed his support of heretics at his convocation?" Ogham raised his brow, drumming his fingertips together.

"Aye, my lord, in front of many witnesses," Gerald assured him. "Including the bishop Gregory de Dunkirk." He inclined his head and grinned from under his brow.

"Perfect." Ogham clapped his hands and rubbed them together briskly, then jumped to his feet. "The fool has provided us with the kindling for his own pyre. Gentlemen," he continued, tallying off his orders quickly, "we need to send messengers at once, to Gregory de Dunkirk and to Aberdoir... and, of course, to His Majesty, informing them that we are currently investigating a matter of heresy within the house of Stonehaven. I will request an entourage of the king's hunters to be sent there." He spun on his heel to face the two. "Anything else?"

"Aye." Gerald answered. "One last bit of business, my lord. Thomas would expect to be seated in Sutherland. Surely you can see that would not be wise. However, his cooperation in this is key. He is a greedy man, my lord, and I am not certain his obvious hatred of his brother is enough to guarantee his commitment."

"A valid point." Ogham scoffed at the idea of putting Thomas in Sutherland. "Do you have a suggestion?"

"Yes." Wesley grinned. "We feel he would relish the opportunity to govern an entire colony rather than a small tenant by the sea, here in Scotland. We recommend that Thomas be offered the rule over one of the burgeoning colonies in the New World. Well out of harm's—and our—way."

"An excellent suggestion." Ogham slapped Wesley on the back. "I am impressed with you both. The king is keen to expand those colonies, for whatever reason. I hear there is nothing there but trees and heathens." He extended his hand to the men in turn, thus ending the meeting.

"I want those messages sent at once. If it plays as we expect, a trip to Stonehaven is forthcoming for us all."

Despite Edward's orders of silence, lively discussions of the removal of Thomas and Bryndah from Drumoak abounded among the servants in the castle. The groundskeeper and his wife had seen the sentries carry the struggling couple to their carriage. They told an animated accounting to the stablemen, and they in turn found an interested ear or two among the rest of Stonehaven village. By sunset, the entire town knew that Lord and Lady Aberdoir had been physically removed from Lord Edward's castle, back-end to.

The little village thrived on such gossip, just as it had when wagers were made regarding William's reported assassination. Ale poured freely at the inn and maids chatted endlessly across fences and clotheslines. It would be a profitable evening in the tavern, to be sure.

The innkeeper's wife washed and stacked extra mugs and dishes, and the town's most notorious tavern dancer primped and prettied herself in preparation for the busy evening.

"Why are you bothering to rouge your knees, Cassandra? He's married now. Not likely to be stopping by the tavern to see the likes of you again."

"Ye never know, Enid. He seemed right pleased the last time I caught his eye," Cassandra answered with a wink, placing a hand on her jiggling hip. "Paid me right nicely, he did."

"Aye, and he'd had at least five pints in 'im at the time!" Enid laughed. "His mates 'ad to carry 'im out, as I recall."

The rumors and gossip finally carried full circle back to Drumoak. Edward was dismayed but not surprised when differing versions of the event reached his ears. He corrected those he felt had earned a better explanation and ignored the rest. He sank down in his favorite chair at day's end with a steaming cup of mulled wine, exhausted and eager to put a rest to it all.

"I suppose I might as well have ordered the river to change direction. It would have been easier than trying to stem the tide of this gossip." He spoke to the portrait of his beloved Anne, never aging, gazing at him in frozen elegance. "I imagine it would be quicker as well."

A knock interrupted his musing. "Enter," he called from the chair, not wishing to rise.

"Father." William entered casually. "As you asked, I have given some thought as to whom among the guards I shall extend an offer. Is this a good time to talk?"

"I suppose now is as good a time as any." Edward sighed and rested his head on his hand.

"Is something wrong?" William asked.

"I'm just feeling my age." Edward yawned and sipped his wine. "This has been a long day at the end of a longer night. I suspect I shall turn in early." He gestured toward his mug. "There's more on the table if you'd like to join me." William declined with a slight wave. "Have you decided, then, whom you wish to retain within your guard?"

"For the most part," William answered eagerly. "I know I shall ask Sean, of course, and Simon. Ewan, probably, as well if you would allow." He sat next to Edward in the chair that had once belonged to Anne.

"I assumed as much." Edward sat up straight on the edge of the chair, and pointed a fatherly finger. "But don't forget to think about some of the older, more experienced men as well. Though I would not allow you to take Galen Berra."

William nodded his agreement. "Aye, Galan has been with you for as long as I can recall."

"Aye. And he is responsible for the training of the new men. He's a good man."

"I remember," William agreed. "He trained Sean well and proper."

"Aye." Edward sipped the last of his wine and looked into the empty cup. "May I make another suggestion to your roster of guards?"

"Of course," William answered. "I value your advice."

Ever eager to please. Edward looked up from his cup. *He won't be expecting this.* "Have you considered extending an offer to your nephew, Richard?" Edward smiled to himself as he watched William attempt to camouflage his dismay. "Does that come as a surprise?"

"I admit I had *not* considered extending an offer to Richard." William tightened his lips. "I don't want to outright disagree with you, but—"

"I understand your reluctance. You are free to choose your own guard, of course." Edward looked at him, head tilted on his hand.

"Reluctance? Trepidation is more like it." William sat back in his chair. "I'm not sure I'm ready..." He left the thought unfinished as his right hand began to absently rub at a fading scar that encircled his left wrist—a habit Edward had noticed him do many times, particularly when Richard was present. "But if you feel I should consider him, I should like to hear your argument on his behalf."

"I have taken the liberty of summoning him. I should like you to stay and speak with him." Edward saw protest come to William's eyes and raised his hand to forestall his argument. "William, he is not his father nor have I seen evidence that he remotely favors him. I have been aware that the other sentries have set him apart, but he has never shown me a single disloyalty. I am willing to separate him from his parentage. Can't you?"

"You ask a lot of me." William spoke quietly, his eyes no longer meeting Edward's. "Yet, I suppose, Thomas and

I descend from the same stock, and I should not like to be compared to *him*. I will stay and hear what Richard has to say." He released his wrist, apparently unaware of what he had been doing.

"Good man." Edward stood and patted William on the shoulder. "No one could compare you to Thomas, son. You have a sense of fairness that he will never possess. Your own father, God bless him, would be well pleased with the way you've turned out." He smiled affectionately at William, then went to the table and refilled his mug from the pitcher. "Many times, when I look at you, I see my old friend looking back at me. You have Henry's heart." He chuckled quietly. "And his notorious, wild spirit."

"I wish I could have known him," William said with a thoughtful look. "Thomas and I are so different. I sometimes find it hard to believe we are truly brothers. We are as opposite as... Mehlyndia and Bryndah. That never occurred to me before." He laughed. "So, tell me about my father's wild spirit."

Edward returned to his chair, amused at William's eagerness. "Your father, Henry, had a brash, courageous streak, the likes of which I've never seen in any man I have ever known." He looked at William sideways. "With one possible exception."

William grinned.

"And popular with the ladies." Edward laughed and blew into the hot mulled wine. "Unlike you, who have rival noblemen on your back, your father was more likely to be hunted down and challenged by jealous husbands and protective fathers. He had a particular fondness for dancers."

"Dancers?" William looked at Edward, a curious blush rising to his face. "Here in Stonehaven?"

Edward eyed him slyly. He had heard rumors that William had taken a trip or two to the taverns before he settled down to married life. "Stonehaven, Aberdoir, Kent, Bannenvale, London— even as far as Cornwall!" Edward ticked off the towns on his fingers. "Any village with a tavern. But he didn't limit himself to dancers. Dairymaids, cooks, and countesses were all fair game. In fact, there were rumors he had progeny scattered about the highlands, but he steadfastly denied such claims. Not that he'd be the only nobleman with bastards throughout the land."

"He sounds a perfect cad." William laid a hand to his face, feigning shock. "Nothing like me at all. I've never been to Cornwall. And I am fairly certain I have no progeny scattered about."

Edward laughed out loud. "He even wooed a woman here at one time."

"Here?" William made a mischievous smirk. "Is she still here?" he asked.

"As a matter of fact, she is. But she'll deny it if you ask her." Edward chuckled.

"Who?" William raised a curious brow.

Edward did not answer the question. He looked into his cup for a moment, becoming more serious, remembering his old friend. "He was a good man, your father. He had a kind and compassionate nature that was both his strength and his weakness. There were those who took advantage of that compassion." Edward sighed and looked at William. "Have you ever wondered why he gave you to Thomas?"

William's smile melted into a frown as he looked into the fire. "It has crossed my mind one or two *thousand* times."

"It was because he was reluctant to accept my misgivings about his son." Edward set the mug on the arm of his chair and reached for the fireplace poker, easing the flame back to life as he spoke. "He refused to see Thomas as I did. We nearly came to blows on the subject shortly before he died. I actually had to call rank on him."

"You did?" William sat up straight, clearly taken aback. "Why?"

"Thomas had convinced Henry to leave you in his care." He gave one final stab to the fire and rested the poker back against the hearth.

"What?" William gave Edward a look of utter disbelief. "Thomas actually told my father he *wanted* me?"

"We all knew Henry was dying, and Thomas took advantage of his weakened frame of mind," Edward continued, ignoring William's confusion for the moment. He returned to his seat and settled in comfortably, stretching his feet toward the fire. "Originally, Henry left his estate to you and Thomas equally, one inheriting the whole of it should the other pass."

"I'm glad he changed his will. I wouldn't have lasted a week." William shook his head. "Was that what you fought about?"

"That was it." Edward nodded. "Henry was content to leave you in your brother's care after Thomas convinced him how much he and Bryndah worried what would become of you, once orphaned. He put on quite a performance. Worthy of one of Mr. Shakespeare's plays." Edward shook his head at the memory. "You are not the only Fylbrigge with a persuasive tongue, William."

"Apparently." He looked away and leaned his elbows on his knees, resting his chin on his hands.

"Henry asked for my advice and I gave it to him. I'd seen Thomas's true colors many times, and I was frank in my concern for you. I asked that you be sent here on his passing to be raised in this household. We had quite a row about it, but in the end, we compromised. He put the inheritance provisions in his will, and... you know the rest. I only wish he had believed me from the beginning." He picked up his mug and sipped.

"It's frustrating when you know the truth about something, and the one person you want to believe you... doesn't." William gave Edward a quick, challenging look, then turned away.

"Yes, it is." Edward fully understood William's innuendo, but chose to ignore yet another argument about the evils of Dunkirk. "So now you know everything about your father. Most of it, anyway."

"Most?" William asked, looking up, curious. "Is there more I should know?"

Edward looked at William, a crease in his brow, considering how the young man would receive the next bit of information. He took a deep breath and continued slowly. "I suppose there is no reason you should not know. I trust you to be discreet."

"Discreet? About what?"

"The serving woman I mentioned." Edward paused, took another long sip, and looked to the fire for a moment.

"Yes?"

"She was left with child," Edward finally answered, looking at his son-in-law over his cup. "She kept the identity of her bairn's sire a closely guarded secret, but it was apparent it was not the man to whom she was betrothed at the time. They did eventually wed, and he raised the lad as his own."

William stood slowly, keeping his eyes on Edward. "A bairn? So there *is* another Fylbrigge?"

"Neither she nor Henry ever publicly admitted the child was his." Edward remained in his chair, cradling the cup in both hands. He lowered his voice slightly. "However, he saw fit to ask me privately, as his friend, to see to it that the lad would have the opportunity to advance beyond his station. That he may even be trained alongside the wards and noblemens' sons, as was his blood-right. Henry would be well pleased with him. He's a fine man now. There is none other among my guard who is as loyal to me..." Edward looked William in the eye, "...or to you."

William met Edward's gaze with wide-eyed recognition as the full truth of what had just been revealed to him settled.

"Sean?" he asked in an astonished whisper.

"Sean."

"Is my—"

Edward nodded. "Half-brother."

The color left William's face as he turned away and walked several paces, then leaned on the table.

"William? Are you well?" Edward put his cup down.

"Sean? All this time... " William turned slowly to Edward, his expression a mix of astonished disbelief and amusement. "He's my brother? My *real* brother?" An almost giddy grin came to his face. "I am proud to claim him as my own blood.

Does he know?"

"No," Edward answered softly. "It's best that he does not. As far as Sean knows, he is the son of Arthur Wilbrun, the groomsman. He was very close to Arthur and regards him as his father. I suppose, in time, it wouldn't hurt to tell him. He may find it as amusing as you do. Or he may not. It may cause him a great deal of pain, and he could be quite angry with Agnes for keeping it from him. That would be grievous for her indeed. I should not like to see either of them hurt."

"I can not imagine Sean would ever lash out at Agnes."

"No, you're probably right."

"How ironic." William began to laugh. "All these years... Do you want to know another deep, dark secret?"

"What?" Edward smiled back, relieved that William seemed so pleased with this news.

"Many times, when I see Sean with Duncan, teaching him the proper way to ride a horse and how to hold that little wooden sword I made for him. He's always so patient and protective of the lad. I watch, and feel envious." William laughed. "Of Duncan!"

"Envious?" Edward smiled, noting that the joy in William's voice did not quite make it to his eyes.

"Yes. I watch and think; that is what it should be like between brothers. The older one guiding and teaching the younger. Not plotting out ways to be rid of him." His laughter faded into a sad half-smile. "But now, as I think of it, when I arrived here, it was Sean who taught me the proper way to ride a horse and how to hold a sword. No wonder you encouraged our friendship from the beginning. I've always meant to thank you for that. I suppose I've always thought of him as my brother."

"You two would have been fast friends with or without my encouragement." Edward placed a fatherly hand on his shoulder. "But I'll be glad to take the credit for knowing that Sean would be the one to bring you around when you thought this place was hell incarnate. Which brings me back to my original point: I'm a good judge of character. I know an honorable and loyal spirit when I see one."

"You're telling me I should trust your judgment about offering Richard a place in my guard." William sighed.

"I would like you to consider it."

William glanced at Edward, then looked away. "I'll hear what he has to say. That's all I'll promise."

William sat in Anne's chair brooding, waiting for Richard. It seemed impossible that Edward actually expected him to want Richard among his guard. Richard? Even as a member of Edward's guard, the man had not displayed any uncommon valor or special talent as far as William could see. Perhaps that was the real reason Edward wanted William to take him. Edward didn't want him! But no, that couldn't be why Edward was keen to see Richard as part of William's guard. Edward would not have hesitated to put Richard out if he had any inkling that he was unfit. Still, Edward should understand that, after all, Richard had betrayed William. More than once! How could he possibly learn to trust Richard as a guard if he could not even trust him as a friend? *I'll hear him out. I promised that much, but Richard will have to say a lot to change my mind.*

The chamber door swung open quietly. "Grandfather?

You have sent for me?" Richard entered timidly. When he caught William's eye, he turned to leave. "My apologies for intruding."

"No need to apologize, Richard. I was expecting you." Edward stood and motioned for Richard and William to join him at the table. "Please come in and sit."

"Thank you, my lord." Richard bowed formally to William. "Lord William, I am pleased to see you are up and well."

"Thank you, Richard." William nodded, then took a seat at the table.

"May I inquire why I have been summoned?" Richard asked, his eyes cast down as he took his seat. "I can only assume I am to be discharged from your service."

"Why say you?" Edward asked him kindly.

"The other sentries, my lord. They are not keen to have me among them. Especially after the removal of my parents this morning." Richard spoke softly, then looked up suddenly. "But I assure you, you have nothing to fear of my presence. I have sworn my fealty to you and your house, and that has not changed in light of—"

"Relax, Richard." Edward held up a hand. "You are not here to be discharged from my service."

"Then may I inquire... why you've sent for me?" Richard looked from Edward to William, confused.

"Lord Edward has asked that I consider retaining you in my personal guard." William spoke coolly but respectfully.

Richard's eyes opened wide.

"Does that surprise you?"

"Frankly, yes." Richard replied. "It is quite unexpected. But I would be honored and pleased to be considered for a post within your guard."

"You are sure to understand my hesitance." William assumed a formal earl-like tone. He placed his hands on the table in front of him, but soon, his right hand had migrated to his left wrist. "I found my trust misplaced in you before." He cuffed his wrist with his hand.

"Yes, I understand your... reluctance," Richard said as his eyes fell on William's hands. "But I should like to explain my desire to serve in your guard. I should also like to explain my actions on the last day we spent together in Aberdoir. It's clear to me that you still hold me to blame for the events of that day."

"Do I?" William replied coolly, still turning his left wrist in his right hand. "What makes you say that?"

"Because you don't even notice when you do that." Richard cupped his hands over William's right hand and wrist.

William pulled his hand away.

"Every time we meet." Richard mimicked William's wrist motions. "As though you still feel the binding."

"Perhaps I do," William said, scowling. "Maybe not in my wrists, but here." He placed his fist on his heart. "I feel it every time I look at you and remember how you turned on me."

"I did not turn on you," Richard yelled, then immediately lowered his voice. "You've never heard my story."

"Ah, a story is it?" William laughed sarcastically. "Well, then, why don't we bend our elbows and relive old times over a stout drink?" He haphazardly poured himself a mug of the mulled wine, then poured one for Richard and slid it toward him. Richard did not reach for it. "It isn't poison, Richard," William grumbled.

"I had not assumed it was." Richard reached for the mug, tensing his jaw.

Edward sat back, watching. "This is going to be more difficult than I thought." He sighed.

"I'm sorry, there was no cause for that," William said, then finally looked up into Richard's face. "Please, tell your story. God knows I've earned it. And in light of your desire to join my guard, so have you."

"Thank you, Lord William." Richard bowed his head.

"Not *Lord*." William raised his hand. "For this, we dispense with formality. This is personal. Until that day, I was 'Will,' you were 'Rich,' and we were *friends*. The only one I knew in all those miserable years in your house. So, drink up, and we shall see if we can get back to that place."

"Very well... Will." Richard spoke the name awkwardly. "Time to put the demon to rest." He took a long drink, then set the mug down with a loud thud. "The last day you spent in Aberdoir, we had slipped away from our studies to sneak into the stable to see that warhorse my father had just purchased. The one he named Lucifer."

"I remember—a fitting name for the beast." William sat back, rolling his mug between his palms.

"You wanted to get close to that horse. You talked me into—"

"It was your idea to leave the vestry," William corrected.

"Yes, but you wanted to see the horse." Richard waved his hand impatiently. "That's not important; that's not what this is about."

"Not important?" William scoffed. "Perhaps you remember other details differently as well."

"Are you to challenge me on my every word?" Richard grumbled, then pushed himself away from the table, stood, and turned his back.

"Only when necessary," William answered coolly. "Please, continue."

Richard paced the floor. "We left the vestry through the window and had made it to the back of the barn when we heard Brother Joseph coming. We managed to hide while he searched the barn, then I lled you in through an opening in the barn wall close to Lucifer's stall."

William listened to Richard recount the events of that day. Without looking at him, not even really listening, as he lost himself in his own recollection of that day and Brother Joseph's Scripture *lesson*.

"Come on, we need to get back to the vestry if we are going to save any of our skin." William pulled Richard's hand to hurry him along from the barn wall and back to the abbey. They managed to make it as far as the vestry building when they heard the unmistakable voices of Brother Joseph and Bryndah. There were two choices—run back to the stable or try to climb through the vestry window. Neither option seemed possible in time.

"Oh, no, he's got *her* with him," William groaned, clutching his stomach.

"Dinnae worry, Will, I'll run out and lead them away." Richard pushed William into the shadows of the bushes under the window. "She won't be so hard on me if I get caught, but you know as well as I do that she'll make it worse on you. So you hurry through the vestry window and I'll run to the barn. They'll follow me there and I can hide in the hay. They'll find you in the vestry like you should be, learning your Scriptures! Don't worry, I'll lead them away. Trust me!"

Trust me... I remember it very clearly, Richard. William pushed his attention back to the present.

"I ran into the open to distract them from where you were hiding," Richard was explaining. "I wanted to run all the way to the barn. But my mother and Joseph were right there. So I thought it best to stop."

That's not how I remember it. You ran right to her! William did not interrupt Richard's account, but his own memories were still clear to him, and they conflicted sharply with what Richard was saying. *You ran right to her. I saw it.*

"Richard!" Bryndah stood in the yard in front of the vestry, arms wide, bent to one knee. "You gave your mother quite a scare. Brother Joseph said you were missing." Richard ran to his mother's arms. "Where have you been hiding, my little man?"

William watched, stunned, as Richard extended a hand in the direction of the vestry. Brother Joseph followed the direction of Richard's hand directly to the place where William was crouched, under the window.

William froze, watching Richard direct Brother Joseph right to him. *He called me out. I saw him call me out.*

"I went to my mother with the intention of telling her I

hadn't seen you all day." Richard's voice intruded again on William's recollection. "I tried to signal to you to run. I waved you away, hoping you would understand what I was trying to do." He turned and looked William in the eye. "I was trying to tell you to run."

Run? William stared incredulously. *You ran into her arms and pointed me out. I saw that quite clearly.* He allowed Richard to continue without interruption, still reliving his own version.

Brother Joseph closed the distance between himself and William in less than a heartbeat and pulled William to his feet by his ear. "Do you know what happens to boys who do not learn their Scriptures?" He seized William by gripping both wrists within his massive right hand. "In case you are not aware, I shall begin your lesson immediately." Joseph picked him up off the ground. William struggled, but could not free himself. He caught sight of Richard standing with his mother, hugging her waist.

"Teach the beast a lesson, Joseph. He's tricked Richard into leaving his studies," Bryndah called out from where she stood.

"No! Rich, tell the truth," William screamed back as he was carried along by Joseph.

"She twisted her nails into my shoulder and told me not to move or say a word," Richard was continuing. "She told me to watch what would happen to me next. I couldn't move, the way she held onto me. I was terrified, I admit, but I couldn't help you. I saw the whip Joseph carried and I knew what was about to happen, but could do nothing to stop it."

She held him? That's not what I saw. William knotted his brow and sat back.

"I kept telling her it wasn't your fault, that I was the one who led you away. But she wouldn't let me speak. She would only tell me to watch what happened to evil little heretics who disobeyed the rules, asking if I wanted to grow up that way. Every time I tried to argue, she sank her fingernails deeper into me until I was bleeding... and too frightened to fight anymore."

You didn't seem frightened. William lost himself in his memory again.

"Go on, Joseph," Bryndah yelled as Joseph lashed William's wrists together with a leather thong and secured him to the hitching post behind the barn. "Teach the little heathen his lesson."

"Prepare yourself, boy. Your ecclesiastical education shall begin at once." Brother Joseph's voice roared through the stable yard. "We shall review the Lord's commandments today. One! Thou shalt have no other gods before me!" With a loud crack, the whip came down across William's back.

"Richard, tell them," William cried out, but Richard didn't answer. He only stood with his mother, watching.

"Repeat the verse," Joseph yelled from behind as he brought the whip down again. "Two! Thou shalt not make unto thee any graven image. Repeat the verse!"

William repeated the verse through tears and clenched teeth as Joseph delivered each commandment with a heavy-handed lash, each strike tearing away at his flesh. All the while he watched Richard, standing complacently next to Bryndah as she watched Joseph with a hideously pleased sneer. William could only recall the beating up to commandment nine. That's when a merciful blackness overcame him.

"She held me in place, making me watch. I was to be next if I dared call out or argue with her." Richard paused, taking a swallow of the mulled ale. "When I was finally able to struggle away from her, I ran into the barn." He stopped and looked down to his hands. "When you passed out on the post, I thought they'd killed you and I was determined to make them pay for that."

"I don't know what happened next," William said quietly. "Tell me."

"I ran into the barn. I was in a panic and not thinking clearly, and I had the wild idea I could ride Lucifer and trample down the both of them, to avenge you. I jumped on the beast's back and he bucked and reared. Then he broke down the stall and charged through the door." Richard looked at William, a half-grin on his face. "Damned horse nearly killed me but I managed to hang on long enough to ride him into the stable yard before the groomsman and his assistant reined him. I was thrown off, of course. I struck my head on the barn door. My mother, ever the performer, ran to me, crying, 'Oh, my poor boy! He's hurt.' With all the stable hands present, she took pains to take care to help me up. None of them were aware that you were tethered to the post learning your *commandments.* She shooed them away, saying she would take me right to my bed. But first, she took me around back of the barn to be sure I got a good look."

"Must have been quite a sight," William muttered under his breath, absently staring ahead.

Richard returned to the table and sat down slowly. "I'd never seen so much blood, and you weren't moving. I was certain Joseph had killed you, and I yelled at them. Joseph laughed at me while he coiled up his whip and hung the bloody thing on his belt next to his crucifix. My mother brought me up to my bed and tended my head as though it were just another childhood bump. Then she locked me in my bed chamber. I could see you from my window, Will, but I couldn't get out." He finished the mulled wine in his mug and sat back.

"I was on that post for almost two days." William looked Richard in the eye. "Two days of wondering if I would be there forever. Two days waiting for you, or anyone for that matter, to remember that I was even there." He turned away again, shaking his head. "It was the only time in my life I was ever glad to see my brother coming toward me. I was even grateful to see the knife in his hand, hoping it was for my throat—to put an end to everything. You tend to lose your mind after a while, when you're left that way. But he merely cut me free, put me in the carriage just as I was, and sent me off to Drumoak." William made an ironic laugh. "Who knew that would turn out to be the best day of my life? To finally be free of that place." He looked at Richard again. "Were you locked up those two full days?"

"Aye," Richard answered quietly. "You were well on your way here before I was allowed to leave my room. My father joyfully announced to me that we were at last free of 'the burden.' I swore at that moment I would one day leave

Aberdoir and my parents. It took me years to convince Edward I was sincere in my desire to renounce my inheritance to work in his service."

William held Richard's gaze, still struggling to reconcile his own memories with the account Richard had just given. "You make a persuasive argument... but—"

"Do you wish to see proof?" Richard interrupted him with a cold stare. "You are not the only one who carries marks from that day." He tossed his cape aside and tore his tunic from his shoulder. He bore scars resembling the claw marks of a large animal in his flesh.

William stared at Richard's shoulder. The dragon had left her talon marks. *It's true then. I've been wrong all this time.* He toyed with his empty mug for a moment, then reached for the pitcher and refilled it. He took a long breath, drank the contents down in one gulp, then set the mug down hard on the table. *Damned dragon.* He could feel Richard staring but would not meet his eyes. He recounted again the events as he remembered them and compared them to how Richard had just described them. *How could I be so blind? It was Bryndah... again. Always Bryndah. I should have known.*

"Seven years, and not one day have I forgotten," William spoke in an almost inaudible whisper, still not making eye contact with either Richard or Edward. "It's true, I believed it was you who called me out. I vowed that I would never punish anyone for an imaginary crime." He looked up to Richard, his voice betraying the grief he fought to hide. "And yet I've done exactly that, haven't I?"

"Surely you had cause to—" Richard began.

William held up his hand. "Have I not had ample

opportunity to approach you and speak of this in the years you have been in service here? But have I? No. I found it easier to live with the belief that you had turned on me. And by my own example, I see now you have been cast separate from your colleagues." William rose from his chair and turned away, looking out the window. "It is a wonder to me that you do not despise the sight of me, since I have held you in such contempt all this time."

"I have not blamed you for believing I betrayed you." Richard stood behind him. "By my cowardice that day, I did betray you. But I have had my say. Now it is for you to believe or not. I only ask of you, please, allow me to serve you now, as I should have on that day."

William looked over his shoulder. "You were under no obligation to me then. There is no debt owed to me now. We were boys, Rich."

"It would appear we have made good progress here," Edward said, joining William near the window. "Are you now willing to consider Richard in your guard?"

William gave Edward a quick, noncommittal glance, nodded, and took a long breath. Then, turning to Richard, William assumed the formal manner and tone that was due his rank. "Sir Richard, thank you for your candor. I shall indeed take this into consideration when I make my formal offers to the guard."

Richard retrieved his cloak and straightened himself. "Thank you, my lord," he said, matching William's formal tone, then walked to the door. He paused, his hand on the doorknob, turned back to William, and smiled. "Thank you, Will."

William nodded to him, and returned the smile—which faded as soon as Richard turned away. As the door closed, the emotional tide William had fought all day threatened to drown him, as again he was bombarded with unwelcome memories of Aberdoir, Bryndah and her flickering eyes and dragon claws, and Brother Joseph and his whip.

He searched within himself, struggling to evoke the cocksure renegade he had been only days ago, instead finding only the small, timid child he had been seven years before. *This is madness! You've stood up to warlords, assassins, and hunters and have not lost your wit. Why, then, do you allow these long-dead memories to steal your nerve?* William paced the floor, arms wrapped around himself.

Edward approached him from behind, placing a hand on his back. William jumped slightly, forgetting Edward was even in the room.

"It's time to bury the past, son. It can do you no good to hold onto it."

"I've put the dragon behind me once before." William swallowed hard, fighting to maintain his composure before Edward. "Dinnae worry, father. I shan't let her devour me now."

Edward gave him a pat on the shoulder and walked toward the door. "I've given you a great deal to think about tonight. I think I'll take a walk along the parapets and enjoy the night air for a little while." He left the suite, quietly closing the door behind him.

William dropped onto the floor, sitting huddled before the hearth, while the warrior and the child battled the dragon in his mind once again.

Chapter 8

24 September 1607

THE WEEKS FOLLOWING the wedding were a blur of planning and plotting. Decisions on when and how to move into Sutherland manor were delegated to Mehlyndia, with Elinor's guidance. Decisions about security and guards fell to William, with Edward's sage advice paramount to each detail. William had taken pains to be sure his personal guard was rounded out with not only his contemporaries, but several of the older men, as Edward had suggested. Sutherland would be well guarded, and if all the household preparations went as smoothly, Lord and Lady Sutherland would take residency in their new home by the first day of October.

As peacefully as these preparations had been made, no one lost sight of the fact that there was still the imminent threat of war between Edward's tenants and Ogham's. Edward's blockade had yet to be crossed; in fact, it had yet to be challenged at all. Edward assumed Ogham was biding his time, trying to lull them into a false sense of security. Extra scouts and men had been put on alert near Ogham's lines. But the daily reports were always the same—nothing new.

More surprising than Ogham's apparent acquiescence— and in William's mind, more suspicious— was the absence of any retaliation from Aberdoir. Thomas had not made a sound, apparently retreating to his home, chastened and contrite. The longer Thomas was silent, the more paranoid William became. The suspicion that his brother and Bryndah were waiting for him to relax invaded nearly his every waking thought—and had allowed the dragon to creep into more than one dream. Even with Edward's protection and the assurance that Sean was diligently on his back, William was eager to move with his bride to Sutherland, far away from Aberdoir. Only then, he believed, would he have a decent night's sleep.

Once moved and settled, William imagined, he and Mehlyndia would at last be able to enjoy married life. Perhaps they could even take a trip by sea, far away, leaving all the woe and worry of nobility behind for a time. Truth was, he would be pleased to leave nobility behind permanently and escape to a distant land to live out his life quietly among the simple folk. But he knew that to be a fairy dream. He was an earl whether he liked it or not, and he was determined to be the best earl ever to have graced the shores of Sutherland or die trying. And the best earl would have the best guard, so on this sunny early autumn morning, three weeks into his new life, he finally called the guards together to choose those who would accompany him to Sutherland.

Formal offers of service were made in a solemn ceremony in the great hall. Those willing to leave Edward's service, if chosen, stood in formation, each dressed in the formal kilted uniform reserved for ceremonial occasions. William walked the line of assembled sentries, extending a formal wrist-to-elbow handshake to each man and naming them one by one, receiving an oath of fealty from each.

The formality seemed awkward with his close friends, but

he bit his inner lip and maintained his earl-like countenance just the same. "Sir Ewan McDonough, step forward. Do you accept your post and all responsibilities that lie therein?"

Ewan placed his right fist over his chest and spoke confidently. "I do, my lord, and swear my fealty, as is my honor, to uphold and defend your tenants. Under pain of death do I break this oath."

In the same way, Edward had presented William with his new crest at the nobles' convention, William removed Edward's designation from Ewan's uniform and replaced it with a bronze badge depicting the raptors of Sutherland. Ewan bowed briskly, took one step backward, and rejoined the line. William stepped to the next man in line.

"Sir Simon MacHenry, step forward." William repeated the ceremony with Simon, and then with several of Edward's older men: Hugo McLevey, Angus Connelly, and Malcolm Donagan, whom William was pleased to have accepted his offer. Galan Berra, who respectfully declined as William had anticipated, stood aside, pleased to see his young protégés accept their appointments to their new house and lord. As each man accepted his rank and stepped back in line, he was applauded by his comrades.

When it was Sean's turn, William finally allowed himself to smile, finding it impossible to remain formal. "Sir Sean Douglas Wilbrun, step forward."

Sean stepped forward, solemnly, the absolute model of formality, which made it all the harder for William not to laugh.

"Do you accept your post and all responsibilities that lie therein?"

"I do, my lord, and swear my fealty, as is my honor, to uphold and defend your tenants." Sean paused and looked William in the eye before finishing the oath. "Under pain of death do I break this oath."

William no longer felt the urge to laugh as he bestowed the rank on Sean. "It is my privilege, and my honor, to name you as Captain of the Guard to the House of Sutherland. Do you accept this appointment?" William extended his arm for the formal handshake.

Sean accepted William's arm. "I do. Thank you, my lord, it is my honor." Sean finally smiled and bowed his head, while William placed the silver captain's badge of Sutherland on his shoulder. As he stepped back in line, loud cheers erupted from the rest of the guard.

A small commotion from the far end of the hall joined the guards' chorus. William smiled to see the ladies, Elinor, Laurel and Agnes who were watching from the grand stairs. Little Duncan stood with his chest out, smiling and waving proudly to his big brother.

"Go on, accept the accolades," William said, grinning.

Sean took a step forward, bowed regally to the ladies, then beckoned to Duncan.

The little lad trotted happily over, then stopped short, bowed first to William, then to Sean.

"That is a fine blade you have there. May I see it?" Sean asked.

Duncan beamed, and presented his pride and joy, a little wooden sword he carried everywhere. "Can I come with you to Sutherland, Seany?"

Sean glanced to William. "It is Lord Sutherland who you

need to ask that of, Duncan."

Duncan tilted his head. "Can't I just ask Will'm?"

The men laughed, Duncan blushed, and William cleared his throat. "It would be my honor for you to join the guard of Sutherland. But you have to take an oath."

Agnes gasped, drawing her hand to her mouth.

Duncan's eyes went wide. "I know the words! I know the words! Under pain of death—"

William felt a sudden sick pull in the pit of his stomach. He placed his hand quickly on Duncan's shoulder before the tot could finish his oath. "Well done, laddie," he said quietly, taking the wooden sword from the boy, and tapping each shoulder. "I promise when you are a little older, you will come to Sutherland and join my guard." William placed his fist to his chest.

Duncan frowned. "How much older? Seven?"

William looked up toward Agnes. She quickly wiped a tear from her cheek and forced a smile. He turned back to Duncan. "Hmm, Sean was twelve when he began his training, and fourteen when he received his badge. How would that suit you? Can you wait until you're twelve years old?"

"But that's..." He looked down to his fingers, counting. "A long time."

"Not so long, lad. Besides, I am counting on you to be sure to protect the ladies." He gave a nod toward Agnes. "Your mum is going to need you more than ever when Sean is away with me."

Duncan knotted his brow, looking toward his mum. "You're right. I promise, Will'm. I'll protect them." He squeezed the hilt of his little sword, then mimicked the gesture the guards had made placing his fist to his chest.

Sean gave the lad a pat on the back, sending him back to stand with his mother.

The men cheered again as Sean took his place back. William stepped further down the line, passing by several men before he came to a stop in front of Richard. The cheering instantly silenced when William said, "Richard Fylbrigge, step forward."

Richard hesitantly stepped forward, giving a sideways glance to his comrades as he did so. William ignored the surprised gawks from the other men, avoiding eye contact with any of them—particularly Sean. "Sir Richard Henry Fylbrigge, do you accept your post and all responsibilities that lie therein?"

Fist to chest, Richard replied appropriately, "I do, my lord, and swear my fealty, as is my honor, to uphold and defend your tenants."

William waited for Richard to finish his oath, giving him a prod with a raised brow. "Go on."

Unlike Sean, Richard's eyes would not meet William's. Instead, he fixed his gaze on the floor and finished quietly, "Under pain of death do I break this oath."

William half-smiled as he concluded the ceremony by placing the badge on Richard's shoulder. He was keenly aware of the ponderous silence that fell on the great hall, and as Richard stepped back in line, no applause came from the other men, only discontented mutters.

William took several steps back to address his new guard. "Those of you to whom I have not extended offers, please do not think it is because I find you unworthy. You are all the finest in Scotland, and I am honored that you have all sought posts in my guard. I know you will continue to serve Lord Edward as loyally and unwavering as you have in the past." William bowed in tribute to the men. "To those who will take service in Sutherland, I say thank you. I am honored to have you. You have all taken your oaths to me, but remember, while we are still here in Stonehaven, you are still in service to Lord Edward and must still answer to his orders. So please," he said, grinning, "do not forget to report to duty when your shift comes back around today. You are dismissed."

The men dispersed in several directions. Sean said something quietly to Simon, then turned on his heel and strode toward the rear of the hall, his boot heels landing heavily with each stride, raising an angry echo. Richard watched Sean go, then looked to Ewan and Simon in turn, hesitantly extending a hand as if in congratulations. Neither Ewan nor Simon acknowledged Richard's gesture, and he lowered his hand, curling his fingers into fist—a mannerism inherited from his father. His face flushed slightly as he walked by, nodding curtly to William as he hurried out of the hall through the kitchen. *I'll have to put a stop to that. I can't have dissention in the ranks already, for pity's sake.* When Richard was gone, William was practically accosted by several of his new guard.

"Why Richard?"

"Are you sure you know what you're doing?"

"Have you given thought—?"

William fielded as many questions as he would stand on the subject, but in the end he made it known that he had freely chosen Richard and trusted him as he trusted all of them. "Any among you who distrusted my instincts are free to resign your appointment. Do any of you wish to step down?" he asked in all honesty, fearful that half of them would desert him. "Ewan?"

"No, sir."

"Simon?"

"I made my pledge, Will. I'll not be turnin' on you."

Relieved, William thanked them all and dismissed them again.

When all had finally left the hall, William saw Sean standing against the pillar in the foyer, arms crossed over his chest. The formal uniform and gleaming sword at his side made him seem older somehow, and downright formidable—especially when he wore the disapproving scowl that always preceded one of their rare arguments. William took a breath and approached him. "All right. Tell me why you think I've lost my mind this time."

"Not here," Sean answered coolly. "Someplace more private."

"Lead the way," William replied, irritated. He had fully expected Sean to be less than pleased with his decision to appoint Richard to his guard. He would take this opportunity to set the record straight, just has he had promised he would. "Where are we going?" he asked as Sean walked briskly out of the main door.

"We haven't given the horses a run for weeks," Sean said and kept walking, not looking at William. "I thought this would be a good time. If it suits you, my lord."

Lord? He's angrier than I thought. "Suits me fine," William answered, matching Sean's cool tone.

They walked the remainder of the way to the stable without speaking. Sean kept his jaw locked and refused to meet William's eye. They saddled Cirrus and Hawk, and galloped away from the Drumoak stables toward the woodland road, Sean several lengths ahead. Before they reached the forest, Sean brought Hawk to a stop. William rode up alongside and turned Cirrus so he and Sean could speak face-to-face.

"All right. It's private," William began. "Speak. What is it you wanted to say?"

Sean looked William in the eye, removed the badge from his shoulder, and held it out to him. "I'm afraid I cannot be your captain."

"What?" William asked, stunned, refusing to take the badge from Sean's hand. "What are you talking—"

"You said if any of us distrusted your instincts, we should be ready to resign our post," Sean interrupted. "I'm sorry, Will. But I distrust your instinct about Richard. Take it." He grabbed William's hand and forced the badge into it.

William looked at the badge, then at Sean, then back to the badge, disbelieving. "I knew you would have some reservations, but I didn't expect you to refuse your post. I hope you're not serious."

"I am." Sean shook the reins and eased Hawk to a slow walk. William did the same. "This is where you convince me that I'm wrong."

"You want me to beg?" William looked at him incredulously. "It's not likely to happen."

"No. I want you to tell me why you suddenly trust

Richard."

"Why don't you tell me why you don't trust him...or me?" William countered.

"Oh, I don't know," Sean rolled his eyes, sarcastically. "Maybe it's because he's part of the darker side of the Fylbrigge clan. Let's face it, Will. Other than you, I can't say I know a single man with Fylbrigge blood in his veins that I do trust."

William burst into a sudden fit of laughter.

"What in the name of Kenneth's ghost is suddenly so bloody amusing?"

William got hold of his laughter and took a breath. "Nothing, just my 'dark Fylbrigge' sense of humor. Someday I'll explain it to you fully." He desperately wanted to tell Sean that he had Fylbrigge blood in his own veins but he held his tongue, halted his laughter, and returned to the matter at hand. "We were talking about Richard."

"Are you going to take this seriously?" Sean growled.

"Absolutely." William made a cross over his heart and bowed his head. "What do you want me to say?"

"Tell me about Richard, dolt." Sean reached out and thumped William's shoulder. "If I'm to be your captain, then I need to know everything about the men under my charge. Tell me something to convince me he's earned a place in your guard. I've seen the marks on your back—"

"It wasn't his fault," William answered with a shrug. "He explained it."

"Explained it?" Sean gave him a skeptical smirk. "He explained why he was a coward? Why he's still a coward? I'm not talking just about Aberdoir, Will."

William looked at Sean, confused. "You think Richard is

a coward? That day in Aberdoir, we were just lads. He didn't call me out, Sean. I was wrong—"

"Will, he let it happen." Sean pulled his horse to a stop again. "Lads or not, he ran away from you, right to his mother. Whether he called you out or not doesn't matter. My point is, Richard ran."

William brought Cirrus to a halt. "He was trying to distract them. To give me a chance to get inside. He told me... He explained it, Sean. We were only children!"

"You're not a child now!" Sean took a breath and lowered his voice. "I told you, this is not just about Aberdoir. Think, Will. Where has Richard been this past year?"

"At Drumoak, where else?"

"Exactly. And where have *you* been?"

"On tour with Edward, but what does that prove?"

"Were you alone on tour?" Sean asked, leaning on the horn of his saddle.

"Sean, please come to the point." William dismounted. "Let's walk."

"You were not alone on the tour." Sean dismounted as well. "I was with you. So were Simon, Ewan, Isaac, and half of Edward's personal guard." Sean took Hawk's reins and walked alongside William, toward the woods. "Richard declined the offer to go with us."

"I can't blame him," William said as he led his horse to the edge of the forest. "The way you and the others have cast him separate—"

Sean raised a brow.

"All right, I admit, I did too. But under those circumstances, who can blame him for staying behind? Does that one day in

Aberdoir really make a difference to all of you?"

"The others don't know about that day." Sean threw the reins over a branch. "I never told them about it. Did you?" He sat himself down on a fallen log. William tethered Cirrus and joined him.

"No. I thought you had," William answered, taken aback. "So then, why don't they trust him?"

Sean shook his head impatiently and answered, "Because he's a coward. None of us were surprised when he declined duty during the tour. He dinnae stay behind because we hurt his feelings, Will. He dinnae want to swear the death oath."

William was now thoroughly confused. "I don't remember taking any oaths before that tour."

"That's because you're not a guard, lunk!" Sean thumped his shoulder again. "You're the nobleman we've sworn to uphold and protect. We all pledged to defend you or die trying."

"That oath was to Edward." William thumped Sean back. "Not to me."

"True enough," Sean admitted. "But Richard declined to take it nonetheless. That is why he stayed at Drumoak."

"He took the oath for me today," William pointed out.

"I was there." Sean gave him a sideways glance. "You practically had to pull it out of him."

William had no argument about that. He admitted to himself that the way Richard spoke the oath did not fill him with a great sense of confidence.

"And don't forget what happened after the arrow sailed at your wedding."

"I dinnae remember all the details. I was unconscious for

most of it."

"Allow me to remind you." Sean looked William in the eye. "Richard was standing right behind you. He saw the archer as clearly as the rest of us did. He was standing far closer to you than Isaac, Will. It should have been Richard who pushed you aside. And had he done that, Isaac would not have had to make that dive." Sean placed a hand on William's shoulder. "Do you know who he chose to protect instead?"

William shook his head, not taking his eyes from Sean. "Mehlyndia, Edward?" he asked hopefully, somehow knowing this was the wrong answer.

"That would have been forgivable. No, Will, it was Dunkirk." Sean sat back. "Then he took pains to see to it his parents were seen safely from the hall."

"Dunkirk? I didn't know about that." William looked away from Sean, feeling the old familiar knot grow in his stomach.

"I dinnae think you did." Sean sighed.

William stood and walked away from the log, speaking more to himself than to Sean, reaching for Cirrus's reins. "So my instincts were right the first time—Richard can't be trusted completely. I should have spoken to you before I chose the guard."

Sean smirked and stood to join William, his anger softening at last. "Aye, you should have. But you would have chosen him anyway. You usually listen to your heart before your head. I'm your head talking, and I'm telling you it was a mistake, but 'tis your heart you'll follow." He gave William a friendly pat on the shoulder and retrieved Hawk's reins. "So what is it that your heart is truly telling you?"

"It tells me I cannot possibly allow you to decline the post as my captain."

"Allow?" Sean raised a brow. "Are you calling your rank on me?"

"No." William chuckled under his breath. "But Sean, I hope you reconsider." He mounted his horse. "I'm asking as... your friend. Please."

Sean looked up, then away. William saw his jaw muscle flex and relax. He was thinking it over.

Encouraged, William said, "I'll make a compromise."

"What compromise?" Sean mounted and drew Hawk in line with Cirrus.

"Be my captain, even if Richard is part of the guard, and I will be sure not to rely on him for anything that may require even a modicum of courage. I'll assign him to... guard the dishes, or something of the like."

Sean laughed lightly. "And if I say no?"

William shrugged. "Well then, I'll have no choice but to make Richard my captain."

"That's a dirty trick, Fylbrigge." Sean shook his head, though a sly grin found his face. "With him on your back, you won't last a fortnight! All right, you've convinced me."

William grinned and held out the badge for Sean to take.

Sean took his badge back, and shook William's hand firmly and heartily. "I accept the post, my liege, for no other reason than to protect you from yourself." Sean bowed his head in tribute, placed the badge back onto his shoulder, then turned Hawk back toward Stonehaven. He cocked his head to the side and grabbed his reins tightly. "Race?"

"Absolutely." William grinned and kicked Cirrus into full gallop on the road back to Drumoak.

* * *

William felt especially lighthearted by that afternoon, after having cleared the air with Sean and settled the issues of his guards. To his delight, he found himself for the first time in three weeks with a little free time. Edward had been content to finally release him from the endless strategic planning sessions on where to move armies if Ogham woke up. He was quite looking forward to a bit of relaxation with his bride. As he made his way to their suite, he hummed a little tune that happened to his mind, paying little attention to the path in front of him as he walked. As he rounded the corner, he found himself in a sudden collision with large basket of colorful silks and several bolts of linen.

"Clumsy dolt! Watch your step," Laurel shrieked as the cloth went sailing into the air, both she and William landing in a colorful heap on the floor. "Merciful mother, look what you've done! Why don't you watch—"

William slowly pulled a bright blue length of cloth off his head, assuming a proper expression of repentance.

"Oh!" Laurel burst into giggles. "I didn't know it was you. And me yellin' at you as if you were a farm lad! My goodness, let me help you up." Laurel grabbed for his hand but got herself entangled grandly in the mess of cloth. She lost her footing in the folds of silk and fell fully into his lap.

"I surrender!" William could not contain himself and broke into laughter. "Take my gold but leave me my boots."

Laurel sat scarlet-faced on his lap, staring at him wide-eyed and speechless.

"What? You want my boots too?" He reached across and

around her for his boot. Laurel lost her balance and put her arms around his shoulders to keep from falling. The two sat in this unexpectedly close position, staring at each other.

"You had better keep your boots." Laurel gave him a mischievous wink. "You'll need them to run should Mehlyndia catch us like—"

"What is all the fun I am missing?" Mehlyndia's voice came from the far end of the corridor. Laurel and William both stopped laughing immediately, turning guilty expressions to each other. William sat up quickly. Laurel slid gracelessly to the floor, landing with a thud in the pile of cloth just as Mehlyndia appeared from around the corner.

"William?" Mehlyndia stopped short, giving him a suspicious look. "Pray tell what this latest crisis to befall you could be?"

William jumped to his feet, hoping he wasn't blushing. "I have been ambushed by this rogue in the hallway, my love." He reached down and offered his hand to Laurel. "Here I have spent weeks planning the movement of armies only to learn that Laurel, armed with a basket of silk, is a far more formidable enemy than Ogham himself."

"So it would seem." Mehlyndia half laughed as she helped Laurel scoop the cloths back into the basket. "Laurel, take it in two batches so you can better see where you are walking."

"Thank you, m' lady." Laurel nodded contritely, blushing violently. "But it wasn't me that wasn't lookin' at my path!" She flashed William a conspiratorial grin that Mehlyndia didn't see. "Aye, m' lord?"

"She's right. My fault completely." William bowed in mock contrition. "My mind only on you, my love. I have come to invite you to spend the rest of this fair day out in the fresh air." He kissed Mehlyndia on the cheek.

"Yes, that would be lovely." She squeezed his hand, smiling. "And about time you took notice of me, I'd say. Laurel, leave that for now. Could you run down and prepare us a basket?"

"Lovely idea." William smiled to Mehlyndia, relieved to see her suspicious scowl had disappeared. "Laurel, please send Sean up. He'll be delighted to pull picnic duty this afternoon."

William chuckled. Mehlyndia laughed with him and put her arms around him, giving Laurel a sideways glance, then kissing him full and hard. William motioned with a backhanded wave for Laurel to go. *What was all that about?*

Laurel walked to the kitchen slowly, hoping the heat she felt in her cheeks would subside before she encountered anyone. She placed her hand over her heart, willing its beating to slow down, certain it could be heard echoing throughout Drumoak. Her brief encounter with William had taken her off guard, and the memory of him kissing Mehlyndia's cheek suddenly and inexplicably, caused her mood to change from giddy laughing girl to distraught young woman. She walked slowly to the kitchen, trying to push the sensation of sitting on William's lap out of her mind.

"Miss? Is something wrong?"

Startled out of her thoughts, Laurel's blush returned to her cheeks as she looked to see who had spoken to her.

"Sir Richard!" She placed her hand on her chest, forcing a smile. "You gave me a start."

"My apologies; it was not my intention." Richard smiled

politely and made a small bow to her. "You seemed distressed and I wondered if all was well."

Laurel was fully taken aback by Richard's concern. He had not said but a dozen words to her in a year and yet in the last few days, he had found several occasions to approach her. If she didn't know better, she would think he was following her. "I'm just in a bit of a hurry," she said. "The lord and lady have requested I fetch a basket luncheon. They are waiting for me."

"Do they plan to leave the castle, then?" Richard asked. "Perhaps they require an escort."

Laurel looked at Richard with a curious tilt to her head. She was not sure what she should be telling him, remembering how Sean had told her not to 'waste her worrying heart' on Richard. But then, she knew Richard had been handpicked by William to be part of his guard. She decided to proceed carefully. "Well, I think they are just looking for a bit of privacy. You know how busy he's been these past few days, what with getting set for the move and all."

"I see." Richard bowed politely. "I'm sorry to have delayed you, miss."

No one had ever addressed her as 'miss.' She was simply 'Laurel' or, as Edward liked to call her, 'little mouse.' Not even William had ever called her 'miss.' "Not at all." She curtsied, then hurried past him toward the kitchen, only to stop short and look back to where he was still standing. Laurel was determined to discover for herself whether Richard be friend or foe. Her instinct told her that Sean was far from the mark on his assessment.

"Richard?" she called in a timid voice.

"Yes?" he answered, a pleased smile on his face.

"I should require some help," she said with a slight lilt. "With the basket, I mean. It might get rather heavy. Would you be so kind as to carry it for me?"

"I am fully at your service, miss," he answered, his eyes twinkling.

Very pleased with herself indeed, Laurel led the way to the kitchen to prepare the luncheon for William and Mehlyndia. She would be sure to include several heavy plates and goblets to justify her plea for assistance.

Laurel found the kitchen to be the same flurry of activity it had been for days. Mehlyndia had been given freedom to choose her staff as William had his guard, and many of the maids were engrossed in their plans for moving to Sutherland. Some of them, Laurel included, had never been past the borders of Stonehaven and the prospect of sailing on a ship across the North Sea to Sutherland Castle was exciting. Duncan had cried disappointed tears on Laurel's lap that he could not go right away, but Laurel reminded him that William had promised him personally that he would be sent for in his twelfth summer—just as he himself had been summoned to Drumoak.

Duncan sat, sullen and pouting, on the workbench when Richard and Laurel entered the kitchen. "Laurel, do you have time to mend this?"

He held out his little wooden sword. Though it was a gift from Sean, it was William who had carved an elaborate flying dragon on the blade. It had rarely left Duncan's hand since Sean presented it to him long ago on a tournament day: the same day in which Edward had awarded Sean with the sword of Henry Fylbrigge for winning first place. Duncan was frowning at the hopelessly unraveled twining that wrapped around the handle as a makeshift hilt.

"Sean is too busy," he whined, "and Mum says I'm not to bother Will'm anymore."

"Oh, I'm sorry, little one, but I've got m' lady waiting for me," Laurel spoke gently to the child. "Could I tend to it a bit later?"

Duncan dropped his chin into his chubby hands, his elbows poised on his knees.

"Now, don't be putting on faces." Laurel pushed Duncan's cheeks into a smile. "I'll see to it as quick as I can finish this basket." She knelt down to give the tyke a hug.

Richard tapped Laurel on the back. "Perhaps I can help the lad."

"Would you?" Laurel gave him a grateful smile. *Judge a man by how he treats a child. That's what Elinor always says.*

"It will be my pleasure." Richard beamed at her, then crouched on his knees at Duncan's eye level and smiled kindly to him. "That is a fine side arm you bear, lad."

Duncan's eyes opened wide. "Thank you, sir. Seany gave it to me, and Lord Will'm his own self made it, just for me," he said, proudly putting his thumb to his chest. "See, he even carved a dragon on the blade."

"Did he?" Richard gave Duncan an impressed look. "And fine work it is indeed."

"But the handle is coming undone." Duncan turned the toy in his little hand.

"I've mended a blade or two in my day. Perchance I can repair this one as well. May I try?"

Duncan reluctantly handed his sword to Richard.

Richard deftly spun the twine back into place, tying it off with a flourish. He presented it back to Duncan in a knightly hilt-first position over his left arm.

Duncan clapped his hands and happily retrieved his sword, now mended and ready for battle once again. "Thank you, sir!"

"My pleasure." Richard chuckled and mussed the lad's hair. "Run along now and see if there be any dragons to slay in the stable yard."

Duncan hopped off the bench and trotted to the door, stopping to show Richard a proper bow of respect before raising his blade high and charging through the threshold.

Laurel watched this exchange quietly while she prepared the basket for William and Mehlyndia. The gentle way Richard had with the boy impressed her. Whatever misdeed Richard held in his past had naught to do with her, she reasoned. And did she not value Will's opinion?

"That was nice of you to tend to Duncan." She blushed slightly as she spoke. "He is a good little one, really."

"He is indeed." Richard flashed a dazzling smile to Laurel. "He shall make a fine, bold sentry one day. Provided he has abandoned his wooden sword by then."

Laurel found that his smile was quite dashing, and one that she had never seen before today. She was also surprised to realized that he bore an uncanny resemblance to William when he smiled. *It must be the color of his eyes. They're as green as the hills. Why have I never taken notice of him until now?*

"Laurel, do you have that basket ready?" Mehlyndia asked as she entered the kitchen.

"Oh, m' lady!" Laurel jumped, tearing her gaze away from Richard as she felt the scarlet color return to her cheeks. "I'm sorry to have taken so long. It's almost ready." She grabbed a loaf of bread from the counter behind her and tossed it into the basket. "I wanted to make sure you had all you needed for a fine luncheon in the countryside."

"I'm afraid 'twas I who distracted her, m' lady," Richard said. "Laurel and I have been... visiting." He gave Laurel a charming wink. Laurel stared back at him, enthralled by his resemblance to William. She smiled, which seemed only to encourage Richard to wink again.

"I see," Mehlyndia answered with a conspiratorial smile to Laurel.

"Uh, yes," Laurel stammered, still gazing at Richard. "Sir Richard and I... were visiting." She looked at Mehlyndia in time to see William enter the kitchen behind her. For no good reason, Laurel felt as though she had been caught in the orchard with the shepherd boy. "I'm sorry," she blurted, then stumbled through her words, "I... haven't finished the basket." She quickly went back to packing the lunch. *Fool! Will doesn't care who you speak to.*

Mehlyndia grinned, tight-lipped. "There is no worry, my dear. We have not waited long. We were simply ready sooner than you." She turned and gave William a kiss as he joined her, which was interrupted by the sudden crash of several pewter plates hitting the floor.

"Now look what I've done." Laurel quickly crawled under the table to retrieve the dishes. *Get hold of yourself! Married people kiss, for pity's sake.*

"Is everything all right?"

Laurel looked up to see William peeking at her under the table. She gave him an innocent smile. "Fine. Just fine. No problem." William shook his head and stood up. Laurel retrieved the plates and stood, bumping her head. "Blasted thing!" She scolded the table and looked up to see William, Mehlyndia, and Richard all staring at her with the same bemused expression. "Forgive me." She rubbed her head and blushed, not knowing if she wanted to laugh or cry.

"You really should be more careful," Mehlyndia chided her with a smile.

"Thank you for your concern, m' lady." Laurel coyly slipped the plates into the basket and closed the lid. "I'm sure you'll enjoy this on such a lovely day. Will you be going to the sea wall? That's a nice place to picnic."

"That is a splendid idea." William grinned. "Is that basket ready now?"

"Oh, yes. Here." Laurel closed the lid. William reached for the basket, brushing his hand against Laurel's, sending a wave of heat through her chest. She pulled her hand away quickly, hoping her face was not turning as red as she feared.

"Did you remember to ask Sean to join me?" William asked casually.

"Oh, no! I forgot to tell him!" Laurel was suddenly a puddle of tears, surprising all who stood with her, but none more than herself. It was not her failure to find Sean that had triggered her tears, she knew well enough, but she was glad to use it as an excuse for her unexpected outburst.

"It's all right. What is the trouble?" William asked with true concern in his voice, which only upset her more.

She was feeling completely foolish, fighting back her tears

trying to answer William. "I'm sorry I forgot." She brushed her face. "I'll go find him for you." She tried to dash around William toward the kitchen door.

William caught her and turned her around. "It's of no matter. Perhaps Richard would be our escort instead." He turned to Richard for a reply, still holding Laurel at arm's length.

"My honor, my lord," Richard answered with a smile.

"There, you see?" William looked back to Laurel, smiling. "Problem solved."

"Thank you... m' lord." Laurel answered quietly, forcing her breathing and her tears under control. *Let go of me now, Will, or I'm going to completely fall to pieces.*

"Are you sure there's nothing wrong?" William looked her in the eye, still holding her arms.

"William, she's fine." Mehlyndia placed her hand on William's, pulling it away from Laurel. Mehlyndia's voice was pleasant, but there was a coldness in her eyes Laurel had never seen before. "If you need some time to rest, Laurel, you may do so."

Laurel nodded and blew her nose into her apron. "Thank you, m' lady. I think I shall retire to my quarters for a little while." She took a deep breath, curtsied, and left the kitchen through the servants' door. She stopped on the other side and peeked back through the doorway, careful to stay out of view as she watched William escort Mehlyndia out of the kitchen. Richard carried the basket behind them. *You've lost your wits, Laurel May,* she scolded herself. *Will didn't understand, he never has, but Mehlyndia saw. She's going to hate me.* The memories came to her as silently and as surely as dawn spreads over the horizon. *Put him out of your head. You knew it would be like this.* She ran to her quarters and buried her face on her bed, crying as she remembered the last time she had been alone with William, in his chamber, the night before he left on his tour...

"Why does your new badge have an owl on it?" She asked William as he reverently held out the silver badge on a velvet cloth.

"It's not an owl. It's an eagle, silly girl." William turned the badge in the candlelight.

"Better for you if it were an owl, the way you enjoy sneaking around at night to raid the pantry," she teased.

"Very funny," he said without humor.

Laurel could see she had hurt his feelings. She wasn't feeling as silly as she had pretended to be anyway. "I'm sorry, I didn't mean anything." Laurel smiled and turned her attention to the badge he held. "I think it's wonderful. You're official now. Part of the clan."

"Edward wanted me to wear it while we tour the counties." He polished the little badge with the velvet cloth. "But I'm not officially part of the clan until the wedding."

"Ah, yes, the wedding." She sighed, looking past him. "I forgot to congratulate you on your betrothal, Will. I'm sorry." She gave him a falsely cheerful smile and turned away quickly to hide the tears she felt coming. "Congratulations."

"Thank you," he said, placing a finger under her chin to turn her face back to his own. "Are you angry, Laurel?"

"No." She blinked quickly and attempted another smile. "Let me see that again." She turned her face down to the badge. "It's really quite an honor, isn't it?"

"Yes." William held it to the candlelight again. "Do you think I shall live up to this eagle?"

"Aye, 'tis a noble bird," she answered, taking the badge from him, being sure to look at it and not his face. "An independent spirit. The lord of sky. No one could ever tame it." She traced her fingers on the eagle before she set it down on the dresser. "Yes, I think you will live up to it. That's you. 'Eagle Fylbrigge.' That should be your name." She finally looked at him only to find him staring at her.

He met her eyes for a moment, then awkwardly looked away. "It's Edward's crest, not mine." He turned the signet ring he wore on his right hand. "My own father chose a hawk. Not quite as noble as the eagle."

"I think the hawk is quite noble." She took his hand to get a closer look at his ring. "The hawk stands for courage and strength. Perhaps you should wear them both. It would be a fitting tribute to both of your fathers."

"That is an excellent suggestion." He smiled regally and bowed in mock tribute. "My lady, you are quite wise."

"No, I'm quite silly. I'm only a housemaid." She spoke quietly, losing her humor again. "And you are betrothed to the master's daughter and should not take anything I say seriously." She turned away, feeling the blush come back to her face.

"I've never thought of you as only a housemaid," he said. "Have I said such?"

"No."

"Have I done something to offend you? Please, tell me if I have."

"No, Will," she said, looking down to her hands. She knew she was going to cry and loathed herself for it. "I've realized we have both grown up. You are about to step up and take your place, and I will remain in mine. I always knew the day would come." She spoke quietly, not looking at him, for fear of losing the last shred of her composure. She felt a traitorous tear find its way to her cheek. She brushed it away before William could see it. "Do you know how much I will miss you? You're the only person in Stonehaven who knows all about me and who doesn't think me a feeble-minded child."

"And you are the only person in Stonehaven who knows that I *am* a feeble-minded child," William said with a joyless chuckle. "We only pretend to be who they think we are."

"You don't know how hard it is for me to pretend all the time," she said, completely serious. "I'm always pretending. Laurel, the little mouse, simpleminded little child, can't even spell her own name." She laughed under her breath. "Can you imagine their shock if they knew I'm quite literate. Not to mention the other things I'm capable of doing."

"If they knew that, it would be more than shocking." William frowned and took her hand. "It would be dangerous. For you and me both. You for knowing, and me for teaching you. I know it's hard to pretend. But Laurel, serving girls are not supposed to read, let alone spout Latin. Although I am beyond proud of you." He squeezed her hand before releasing it. "As far as the other things... I don't think I really need to warn you to keep that to yourself."

"Don't worry." She crossed her heart with her finger. "They shall never know what you have taught me, nor what I've learned from Elinor. I'll continue on in my safe but dreary world as sweet little dull-witted Laurel, the house-mouse of Drumoak."

"You are sweet and little," he said. "But I shall fight to the death anyone who calls you dull-witted." He bowed at the waist in proper knightly fashion, as he had when they played their games as children. "I am at your service as champion, m' lady."

"Rise." She used her make-believe, lofty damsel voice from their childhood games and held out her hand to him. "Save your mortal combat for someone worthy of your noble tribute."

"You are more than worthy of noble tribute, my lady." William took her hand and kissed the back of it. He discarded his pretend air and grew serious again. "Have I not already fought the dragon on your behalf?"

"Aye, sir, that you have." She smiled and took back her hand. "A battle worthy of Saint George himself. You fought her down and emerged victorious."

"And am I wrong to believe you would do the same for me?"

"I would walk through fire for you, Will." She looked in his eyes, no humor in her voice. "Would you go that far for me? I know I have no right to ask anything of you..." Unbidden and unwelcome, the tears came freely. Laurel turned away ashamed and sank down on the chair before the dressing table, burying her face in her hands.

"You know I would." William placed his hand on her back and spoke softly into her ear. "Laurel, please, tell me what's really wrong here."

"I told you." She sat up and brushed at her cheeks, forcing

herself to smile. "I'm going to miss you." Her eyes fell on the badge on his dressing stand. Without giving it a second thought, she picked it up and enclosed it in the palm of her hand.

"I'm going to miss you too," he said as he wiped her cheek.

"Thank you." She wiped her other cheek, being careful to catch her tear in the palm of her hand. "I'm glad you finally admitted it." She placed her wet palm on top of his badge and held her hands tight around it. "So... you leave tomorrow. What will you do on this tour with Edward?"

"Find all manner of trouble to get myself into, I suspect," he said, a playful grin finding him. "I have to keep Sean entertained, after all. And I'm going to show the nobles who I am and what I'm about. It's time to make myself heard." His grin faded as he turned serious again. "See if I can't make it a safer world out there for folks... like us."

"That sounds dangerous, Will. Please be careful."

"Absolutely." He bowed his head, placing his fist to chest.

"I'm serious." Laurel's fragile cheer began to crumble again. "You could get hurt... or worse."

"I'll be careful. I promise." He placed his hand under her chin and wiped away the last tear stain. "You won't be rid of me that easily."

Laurel smiled and nodded, still clasping the tear-anointed badge between her palms. With no other thought than for his welfare, she mentally began to chant:

In the name of the Lady and the Lord
I ask your favor fall on he
Who bears this silver blessed by thee

As mine own tears doth bless this charm.
Let nothing earthborn cause him harm.

She pulled him forward and kissed him lightly on the forehead, bestowing her secret charm of protection on him as she placed the badge into his hand and closed his fingers around it.

"What was that for?"

"Because 1 love you." She turned and ran from his chambers, hoping he would not try to follow. He would be leaving the next day for his tour with Edward. It would be months before his return, and he would be married the day he arrived. She hoped he would never discover the charm she had placed on him, or how badly her heart was breaking.

With William and Mehlyndia off on their outing and Laurel resting in her room, Elinor took the opportunity to enjoy the relative quiet of her kitchen, having finally shooed the rest of the servants away to tend to duties in other parts of the castle. She was tending to a pot of stew she was preparing for Edward's dinner, looking forward to sitting down with her feet up for a while, when there came a light rap on the kitchen door.

"Are you about, Elinor?" It was Geoffrey, Edward's court musician.

"Geoffrey, come in, " she called over her shoulder as she continued to stir the pot. "1 cannot leave this at the moment."

Geoffrey entered and approached the stove to examine the contents of the pot. He inhaled the aroma grandly, giving her a look of admiration. "You have harnessed heaven in a kettle. I am sure I could be sustained on this wonderful aroma alone."

Elinor chuckled and smiled appreciatively at Geoffrey's twinkling eyes. "Oh, come on then, there is more than enough for my lord's dinner." She took a small bowl from the shelf above the stove and ladled a bit of the stew into it then handed it to Geoffrey. "There's a bit of bread on the table. You may have the duty to test the duke's meal, to be sure it is fit."

Geoffrey gladly accepted his assignment and settled himself at the bench. He sopped up the gravy with a hunk of bread and tasted. "Wonderful! I should like to burden myself with such a task every day." He gave her a crooked smile and continued to eat.

"I'm sure that would be a hard sacrifice for you to make," she said, laughing. "There, that should be good to simmer now. I believe I have a moment to rest my feet." She moved the pot to the far end of the iron stove top, away from the heat, then wiped her hands on her apron and thumped herself down with a great sigh of relief. "I've been on my feet since dawn. First chance I've had to sit all day."

"Then you have earned a bit of rest, my good lady," he spoke between bites.

"What brings you by today, Geoffrey? Seems I have not had your company in months."

The smile in Geoffrey's eyes dimmed. He pushed his now-empty bowl away and sighed. "I've been tending to Nora."

"Oh, I see." Elinor gave him a sympathetic pat. "She is still to her bed then?"

"I'm afraid so." Geoffrey removed a cloth from his pocket

and blew his nose. "Her time is close."

"You have my great sympathy. Nora has struggled so long with her ailment. It was my hope that she had at last rallied."

"It is not to be." He looked at her sadly. "She suffers so, Elinor, and her mind has fallen to delirium. I have prayed for God to end her suffering and take her to Him, but still she lingers."

"Of course you have." Elinor reached for her own handkerchief.

"It is why I've come. I would ask of you, please... to prepare a potion for her." Geoffrey's eyes brimmed with tears as he spoke, "One that would ease her gently into a blissful, eternal sleep."

Elinor knew that was what he was leading to. Her sorrow for Nora, who at one time had served in Drumoak with her, rose deep within her. Nora was quite old—near seventy, Elinor reckoned—and over the past year, her health had faded quickly. Elinor was not surprised at Geoffrey's request. Had he come to her only weeks earlier, she would have gathered her powders and herbs without hesitation and prepared the mixture at once. However, in light of Edward's admonition that she refrain from mixing her preparations for the time being, she was not quite sure how to respond.

"You ask that I relieve her of this life?" she whispered.

Geoffrey lowered his eyes, his face turning red. "I only seek to end her pain."

Elinor could not help but be moved by Geoffrey's motivation and pushed caution aside. "Of course. I shall prepare something for you. You go on back to her now, and I shall be by your cottage when I have finished."

Geoffrey looked at her gratefully and squeezed her hands between his own. "Bless you, dear lady." He rose from his place. "And thank you for the supper." He turned and walked sadly from the kitchen.

Elinor sobbed quietly, then wiped her eyes and went about the business of preparing the dose she would deliver to Nora. She would have about two hours before Edward would request his dinner, and the stew would tend to itself, simmering on the back of the stove.

She retrieved her wooden case from the cupboard and examined the contents. Several small brown pouches containing various leaves, herbs, or both were arranged neatly in rows, each bearing a carefully scribed label revealing the contents. She thought it ironic that she should choose the same ingredients to mix this dose as she had used in the powder Bryndah had slipped into William's water. A shudder crept down her spine at the thought.

Pushing aside her reservations and thinking only of her purpose, she mixed the dose and emptied the pestle bowl into a leather pouch. She tucked the little bundle into her belt, then closed up her wooden case. She was careful to clear away all signs of what she had been about, worried that if anyone knew, Edward would be displeased. She replaced the box in the cupboard, took her cloak from the hook, and quietly slipped away through the kitchen door, not stopping to tell anyone where she was going.

William moved the cart briskly along the road to the sea wall, Richard keeping pace on horseback, dutifully several yards ahead and to the left. His conversation with Sean earlier in the day wormed its way into his thoughts. *And now I'm out in the open with a coward for my guard. Sean will just love that.* He found it amusing that 'picnic patrol' was just the sort of assignment Sean would have handpicked for Richard. Truth was, he was glad Sean was not with them. He would have hovered protectively close, stealing away his privacy with Mehlyndia. William knew he could send Richard off to patrol the sand dunes and he would go without question. This led him to another realization—Richard would not second-guess William's instincts, as Sean did. He put his thoughts aside to give his full attention to Mehlyndia for the afternoon.

Today he was content to simply enjoy the warmth of the sand and the sun, before his new duties took over his life and stole his time away. Today, he would relish this quiet time and place with his lady.

"I shall be close by, m' lord." Richard bowed politely as William brought the cart around to a small, protected cove off the path.

"Thank you, Richard. Stay close enough to hear should I call." William smiled at Mehlyndia while still addressing Richard. "But I would like some privacy."

"Aye. I will be on the wall where I can see you and the road." Richard bowed his head formally and smiled. "You're well concealed in this cove. Enjoy your picnic." He led his horse away.

"I don't know why we need a guard at all," Mehlyndia muttered under her breath. "Shall we never be alone?"

"You'll have to argue with your father and Sean about that." William laughed. "I've given up that fight myself. This looks like a good spot."

Mehlyndia smiled and breathed in the sea air. "It seems years since we've been here."

"It has been a long time." William gave her his hand and helped her from the cart. "I don't even remember the last time we were free enough to come walking here." He retrieved his lute and Mehlyndia's sketching supplies from the cart and led her to his favorite spot on the beach, a large, round boulder at the edge of the surf. William cradled his lute, watching the waves crash against the sea wall. Mehlyndia readied her charcoal, watching William.

The ocean waves pounded against the stones and cliffs under the shadow of Drumoak high above them. The sea wall protruded from the side of the cliff. If the tide was low, there was access to a cave in the cliff face which led to a maze of passages that William had once found irresistible. The caves also served another purpose. If one knew the way, one could find a secret passage into the family crypt under Drumoak. Or a way out.

As a child, William had invented a game of hidden treasure and dragon hunts that he took delight in playing with Sean and Laurel. He had become quite good at finding his way through the passages, hiding in nooks and sliding down the slick stones. With or without torchlight, he had come to know the caves as well as he knew the corridors of Drumoak. He smiled, recalling the time Laurel had let her torch go out and had sat crying in the dark waiting to be rescued. William had found her easily enough, but she was angry with him for a week for leaving her in the dark so long.

William had always enjoyed his treks into the caves most when Laurel was with him. Somehow, he had never felt silly or self-conscious around her, even when pretending to be a pirate or a knight of King Arthur's court. It had never occurred to him to take Mehlyndia into the caves. She seemed far too refined and fragile to go poking around the damp passages. So with Mehlyndia, his time on the beach was spent in the sunlight. And that is where he fell in love with her.

"Do you remember when we would spend hours making secret plans to come here to run away?" William asked Mehlyndia, lingering in his memories.

"You were going to build us a ship and we were going to sail to the New World all alone," Mehlyndia said, laughing. "Of course we were going to take your horse, Star, with us, as I recall."

"I remember. I loved that horse." He chuckled and looked out toward the horizon. "Do you ever wonder what it would be like there?"

"Where?" she asked.

"In the New World. Can you imagine it? Just the two of us, no king, no dukes." He looked at her strangely for a moment. "Would you wish to be married to me if I were not an earl?"

"As I recall, you were simply my father's fosterling when I fell in love with you," she reminded him. "But you are an earl now. It makes no difference."

"So you would love me if I were but a lowly stable hand?" he asked her, playfully. "Ah, but then, you would not be a countess."

"No, I would be the wife of a stable hand. A very handsome stable hand at that." She smiled and kissed him.

"You would make a beautiful peasant, yourself." He kissed her back. "I'm hungry. Let's see what Laurel packed for us."

He set down his lute and went back to the cart. When he lifted the basket, he was startled by the heft of the thing. "Did she provide us an entire stag?" He dropped it onto the beach, sending a cloud of sand up, then opened the lid and stood back, completely bewildered by the sight before him.

"What is it?" Mehlyndia asked, laughing. "You look as though you've never seen a basket lunch."

He scratched the back of his head, completely baffled. "What has gotten into Laurel? She was acting so strange back there, and now she's packed us... the most peculiar lunch I've ever seen." He reached into the basket and held up a flatiron. "Do you like your bread well flattened, my love?"

"Oh, my, that is strange," she agreed.

William affected a pompous expression as he rooted around in the basket. "And if the flatiron is not to my lady's liking, allow me offer a fine array of pewter morsels to tempt your pallet." Mehlyndia giggled into her hand as William produced four large pewter candlesticks, two silver goblets, a tea kettle, and an iron trivet. "Ah ha!" He smiled, his finger in the air. "Laurel found a bit of room to include a loaf of bread, some cheese, and a nearly full bottle of wine."

"Of course," Mehlyndia said, as if there was nothing strange at all about the contents of the basket. "What did you expect?"

William stared at the basket incredulously, one hand on his head. "I am confounded beyond reason. Has she been ill?"

"Darling, are you so dull you cannot see?" Mehlyndia withdrew the candlesticks and set them in the sand.

"Dull?"

"You didn't notice how she blushed when we entered the

kitchen?" Mehlyndia asked as though she were addressing a child.

"Well, yes, but she blushes all the time."

"You took no notice of whom she was speaking with when we arrived?" Mehlyndia's eyes sparkled mischievously.

"She was talking to Richard, but... " Suddenly, the light came to him. A conspiratorial smile crossed his face. "She was talking to Richard!"

"Exactly." She congratulated him with a kiss. "My guess is, she made that basket heavy just so he would have to carry it for her." Mehlyndia quickly picked up her charcoal. "Keep that smile, my love." She set about drawing his image.

"So you believe she fancies Richard?" He tried to speak without moving his mouth, which only made him laugh. "I wonder if Richard knows that."

"Hold still," Mehlyndia ordered. "Yes. It's quite obvious. A woman knows these things. I would say he knows. I saw the way he looked at her as well."

"Really?" William looked at her curiously. She tapped her drawing with a mock stern look, and he resumed his still pose. *Richard has eyes for Laurel? And she's looking back? I wonder if Sean knows about that.* "Melly?"

"Hold still."

"This isn't another of your games is it?"

She set the tablet on her lap and looked up "Games?"

"You recall that joust, a few years back? How you and Laurel played that little charade so that Sean would feel jealous?"

Mehlyndia sighed. "That is ancient history. And it was a complete disaster. I had no idea Sean was smitten by that...

what was her name?"

"Annlise."

"Well it did not work out did it? She was not right for him, you know. The harlot."

"Melly! That's a terrible thing to say."

She looked up coyly and tapped her drawing. "You're right, my love, please forgive me. But what else is one to believe about a woman who is properly betrothed and runs off with another man. Scandalous!"

"Uh, I was there, she didn't run off—"

"Hold still!"

He did as he was told, glad to leave the conversation of Sean and Annlise. He knew better than Melly knew about the circumstances in which the two had come together, and he'd sworn to Sean he would keep it to himself.

"Almost finished." Mehlyndia smiled as she continued to sketch rapidly. Finishing with a flourish, she turned the paper for him to see her work.

William looked at the drawing with admiration. "That is amazing. How do you do that? I can barely scratch my name with a quill."

"'Tis true enough. Your penmanship is atrocious. However, your hands have gifts I could never hope to have." She picked up his lute and ran her fingers reverently across the fine ivy filigree carving on its face. "'Tis not every musician who carves his own instrument. I've always thought this to be as beautiful to look at as it is to listen to." She held it out to him as though it were a fine treasure. "Play for me, my love."

William took the instrument from her, smiling. "Aye, my lady." Forgetting his hunger, he dutifully began to stroke the strings, bringing forth a melody he had not played for her before. Mehlyndia turned to a fresh paper and began drawing while he sang a song about faraway lands and dreams that pass. One tune led into the next, each equally sweet. As he played, he allowed himself to be lost in his thoughts. All that existed for him was his music, the waves, and the hypnotic swooping of the sea birds. Even thoughts of Mehlyndia drifted far from where his mind had taken him.

"Where are you, William?" Mehlyndia asked gently.

Without taking his eyes from the sea, he answered her quietly, "Far away. Past the horizon."

"What is past the horizon that holds you so?"

He kept his gaze on the sea. "It's what is not there that holds me. Past the horizon," he began, as he stretched out his hand as though to reach the place he saw, "there are no nobles or armies. No assassins lying in wait. No dragons... sometimes, I wish with all my heart that I really could build us that ship and we could sail away to that place, just you and I, and leave this all behind. We could face each day with no greater worry than what the weather would be." His eyes remained on the horizon as though he could actually see the world he imagined beyond.

"William, what is troubling you?"

"Nothing."

"Nothing? Then surely it must be the saddest nothing ever known. See? Look what your nothing has done to your face." She handed him her drawing. "Melancholy does not become you, my love. I much prefer it when you smile."

William looked at her drawing and had to admit that the face of the man in her sketch did seem anything but happy.

"It shows that much?" He forced a smile. "I'll try harder to smile for the sake of your drawings." He handed it back to her and kissed her gently.

"You haven't answered my question." She took her drawing and looked up at him through her bangs. "Are you still worried that Ogham is setting snares and archers out for you?"

He laughed and placed his hand on his chest. "Guilty as charged. But, to be fully honest, Ogham is not first in my thoughts. Threats and schemes go with the rank . It is the rare nobleman who has no enemies." He turned back to the sea. "I'm more worried about living up to Edward's expectations. He's placed such confidence in me. I can't fathom what he sees in me." He rested his lute against the stone, stood, and wandered away from her, idly picking up a fistful of pebbles from a tide pool.

Mehlyndia stood and followed him slowly. "William, you have a lot on your shoulders. It's only natural for you to have momentary fits of doubt." She placed a hand on his arm to gain his full attention. "Please, you seem so sad suddenly. Is that all that worries you? That you'll disappoint Father?"

"No, that's not all. It's Thomas who really worries me." He hurled a stone angrily into the water at the mention of his brother's name. "Edward was quick to put him out without so much as one scout on his back."

"Does he pose such a threat? If that be the case, let Father know. I'm sure he'll take some action against—"

He gently placed his fingers on her lips to quiet her. "It's not for myself that I'm worried." He turned away again. "I'm fully able to defend myself."

"I'm sorry, William. I know I can be dense, but I don't understand." Her face was beginning to reflect his own dreary mood.

"I'm sorry, my love, I don't think you are dense. Let me explain." He took her hand and began to walk the shoreline. "My brother has managed to gain certain allies that I'm sure he has already contacted about his displeasure with Edward's decision to seat me in Sutherland." William spoke quickly, rambling, "I'm quite sure he will retaliate, eventually, for Edward cutting him off as he did and I know he would love to have my title, and probably everything else I have. And then there is Bryndah. She worries me almost more than Thomas."

"What threat is Bryndah?" Mehlyndia looked at him, confused. "She's banished. She can't get near you with her poisons anymore."

"I'm not worried for myself." He threw another stone, growing more agitated as he spoke. "She could call out Elinor for her talents with potions. And she seems to have it in for Laurel as well."

"Elinor and... Laurel?" Mehlyndia sighed Laurel's name. "Perhaps I am not dense, but you are making no sense to me." Mehlyndia put her hand on his arm and turned him to her again. "Why would Bryndah put any effort to harming them? They're only servants."

"Because they're my friends!" William glared at her, seeing again her eerie resemblance to Bryndah. "I'm sure she would never consider her housemaid a 'friend' but she knows that I do."

"No, I'm sure she doesn't but—"

"Laurel crossed her, Melly." He raised his voice more than he had intended. "Don't you see the danger in that?"

Mehlyndia took a step back, looking stung at his tone. "I can see where it would make her angry for a moment, but—"

"Rebecca crossed her—she ended up dead."

Mehlyndia stared at him, stunned. William worried for a moment he was going to have another fight with her about the evils of Bryndah. "How?" she asked in a whisper.

Relieved that she wasn't arguing, he answered carefully, "Bryndah called her out as a witch."

"Was Rebecca... a witch?" Mehlyndia stared, wide-eyed.

"No, of course not. She merely stood up to Bryndah." William answered with a disgusted sigh. "For me."

"Then what evidence did Bryndah have?"

"She used the damned hysteria to her own ends." William flung the remainder of his stones into the sea and scooped up another fistful. "It's her favorite game and she plays it quite well. She learned all the rules from the rubbish the king himself has written."

"What rubbish has the king written?" Mehlyndia asked. "And what has this to do with Elinor or Laurel?"

"He wrote a guide for finding witches. The man is completely demented." William felt the redness rise in his face as he threw another stone in the water, as if he could cast away his anger with each toss.

"A guide to find witches?" She almost laughed at the notion. "That sounds ridiculous. Elinor and Laurel are not witches. I should think they have nothing to fear."

"Ridiculous or not, it's claimed a lot of lives." William looked at her seriously. "The clergy believes in it, and Bryndah knows how to use it."

"So... what does it say? How does one spot a witch?" she asked, a look of morbid curiosity on her face, then took hold of his hands, preventing him from flinging another stone. "William, stop that."

He looked down to his handful of stones and held one up to show her. "See this?" She nodded. "If I were to throw this into the water, what would happen?"

"It would sink."

"Nay, it will bounce."

"But a stone cannot—"

"Watch." He raised a brow and smiled, then threw the stone side-handed across the shallow tide pool. The stone skipped four times before landing in the sand on the opposite side of the pool. "See?"

"You cheated!"

"Are you certain?" He opened his eyes wide and leaned close, as though to tell a secret. "The bishop would say, 'a rock cannot bounce' and yet I made it do so. Therefore, I must be a witch."

She half laughed at him, took a stone from his hand and skipped it the same way he had. "It would appear that I am a witch as well." She laughed, brushing her hands together.

William wasn't laughing. "Don't make jests that way. It's truly that simple."

Her smile faded. "What?"

"What I just showed you could be called irrefutable proof that we have hexed the stones."

"But anyone can do that. Does the king's witch-finding guide say that skipping stones is an act of heresy?"

William sighed. "The king finds evil in the most natural things and he encourages—even rewards—anyone who calls them out. Has your cow started giving sour milk?" He held up a stone to represent the cow. "Must be that the milkmaid cursed it." He threw the stone into the water. "Has your horse gone lame? The stable boy must have hexed it." He threw another stone. "Has Rebecca—" He stopped to rephrase his last example: "Has the nursemaid let a child out of a locked coal shed without a key?" He held up the last stone in the palm of his hand. "She surely must be a witch."

Mehlyndia looked at the stone in his palm, understanding coming to her eyes. "Rebecca was your nurse, wasn't she?"

William nodded and remained silent for several moments. Somewhere over the waves a seabird screeched, and he continued, quietly. "Her only crime was that she defied Bryndah—for my sake. Rebecca slapped her. Bryndah swore she would pay for it. All that needed to be said was that Rebecca had opened a locked door without a key; it must have been magic. The judges believed Bryndah, and Rebecca... died in the fire." He closed his hand over the stone. "Laurel and Elinor both laughed at her when Father put them out. Bryndah knows Elinor's skills with her herbs." He took her hand and led her back along the shoreline toward their picnic spot. "She also knows Elinor still holds fast to the old religion. The one outside the king's—"

"My God!" Her hand flew to her mouth. "She'll call Elinor a witch. We have to get Elinor away from here, William."

"She won't leave. I asked her. I only hope she heeds Edward's advice and stays away from her potions for the time being. After all, if she needs to mix anything, I could always—" He stopped suddenly and turned his face.

"What?" She looked at him sharply. "You were going to tell me something, please don't stop like that. Tell me. What could you do?"

William didn't answer but started walking again.

She pulled him to a stop. "Please, must I be kept forever in the dark?"

He looked at her, registering the alarm in her eyes, and softly finished his thought, "I could mix the potion."

"You?" She took another step back, astounded. "But what do you know of powders and potions?"

He looked her in eye and hesitated only a moment. "A great deal, actually." He saw the color begin to drain from her face but if he did not tell her everything here and now, he knew he may not find the courage to do it later.

"How?" she asked silently.

"Elinor trained me." He spoke quickly, watching her eyes carefully. "I know her powders and herbs... and faith... as well as she does. It is a well-guarded secret, Melly, for obvious reasons. Not even Edward knows. But should you find you have need of a good sleeping powder..." He took a breath and held her hands in his. "I'm your man."

"Does Bryndah know?" Mehlyndia asked, tears coming to her eyes. "She could call you out—"

"No, Bryndah doesn't know," he answered quickly, wiping her tear before it fell all the way down her cheek.

She looked at him as though she didn't know him, a tremble in her voice. "You practice the faith of the peasant folk?"

He fought a sudden panic that was worming its way

through his chest. *Don't turn on me, Melly...* "Not entirely—"

"But you know the Christian canon better than anyone I know."

"That has nothing to do—"

"Everyone knows how well-versed in the Holy Scriptures you are."

"I know but—"

"Surely you don't blame God for Rebecca. William, you mustn't lose your faith—"

"You don't understand anything about it, do you?" he shouted.

Mehlyndia snapped her mouth shut abruptly, looking at him wide-eyed as he had his say.

"I have no quarrel with God! I have a quarrel with the king and his bishops and their barbaric persecutions in His name. My faith in God is perfectly intact. And my faith tells me that God is not demanding anyone be burned alive simply for knowing how to use the natural gifts He's given us."

"Do you realize what you have just told me?"

He looked her full in the eyes. "Aye, and I pray you understand. Mehlyndia, in these days, it is suicidal to even admit to understanding the ways of the old faiths—let alone to follow them. Please, for me, you must never mention it."

"Are you afraid I would run to the bishop?" she asked, a hurt look on her face.

"I'm afraid you would run... *from* me."

"I would never." She jumped up and threw her arms around him. "I am only surprised at what you've told me. I can see the danger quite clearly. And now at last I have an understanding of your passion against the fires. It's more personal than I imagined."

"I suppose it seems selfish now." He stood back a bit to look at her.

"Of course not." She dried her cheeks. "I only wish you had told me before. Your secret is safe with me, my love." She kissed him lightly. "May I ask you something?"

"I will answer what I can."

"You're not telling me everything. I can see it in your eyes." She looked at him closely. "Is there more to your 'faith' to tell?"

He took a deep breath. "There is. But you will have to trust me that I cannot tell you the rest. Not just yet."

"William, you can trust me to keep silent."

"It could be dangerous for you to know." He looked at her again, beginning to feel defeated. "Oh bloody hell, who am I fooling? It would be dangerous for *me* if you or anyone one else knew. Please, Melly, do not prod me more on it."

"Do not close me away. If there be more to tell, please do, while we are alone. I have told you I will not betray this confidence."

William was fully unprepared for her persistence. "Am I to have no peace?"

"Not until you tell me everything."

"All right then." He gave her an exasperated sigh. "Not only have I learned well what Elinor has taught me, but it turns out I'm good at it. Truth be told, Mehlyndia, I'm very good at it and I have employed it to my advantage. Or rather, Edward's advantage. He would shrug it off as superstition at any rate." He began to walk away from her.

"What would he shrug? Finish!" She grabbed him by the

arm, turning him to her sharply. "Stop walking away from me! What have you done?"

William pulled his arm away and yelled, "I used a spell from Elinor's book."

"Spell?" Mehlyndia whispered. "We've gone from a matter of faith to casting spells? What sort of spell?"

"Nothing drastic." His middle began to quake. "Only a simple incantation to help me find my words and have them heard, and, if... I've done it properly... people respond favorably to me." He held her eyes with his own. "I prepared the oil and uttered the chant... and my words were made clear. And... people do... what I want them to."

She walked away, one hand to her mouth, the other to her stomach. A growing fear was born in him that perhaps she would not be as willing to accept him as he had hoped. She stood with her back to him for a moment, then spun to look at him.

"You did this before your trade negotiations, didn't you?"

"Yes," he admitted, watching her reaction warily. "How else could I get anyone to agree to those treaties. My diplomatic abilities only go so far. Without the spell, my words are... ineffective, at best." He looked away from her, aghast with himself for just admitting to her what he had never even admitted to himself. "So now you know the truth. You married a heretic who must rely on a spell to do his duty."

An unexpected soft smile crossed her lips. "How is what you do before a negotiation different from the knight who spends the night prior to battle praying before a statue in the cathedral?"

He looked at her, surprised.

"And does he not anoint himself with holy water?"

He nodded.

"And this makes him a better, more courageous, knight?" She placed her hand on his face. "You think you have no skill in negotiation because you must first utter the words of a spell? Is that not the same as reciting a prayer or taking the water? Or do you evoke some evil being to do your bidding?"

"No! Of course not! That's not how it works." He was suddenly defensive again. "That's their misconception! There is no evil—"

"I know that." She placed her hand on his mouth, and spoke gently to him. "William, I have also been raised by Elinor, if you recall. Though she has not taught me her craft, she has shared her beliefs with me." She took his hand and they began to walk again. "Your spell is nothing more than a prayer, my love."

"A prayer?" She had completely astounded him. What's more, she had made a point he had not ever considered for himself. "Yes, that is just what it is. How extraordinary you are."

"Darling, the threat of danger is not lost on me. I know perfectly well that the bishop would not share my perception."

"To be sure. It would be disastrous to be found out." William allowed himself to finally relax. Mehlyndia had put his fears that she would turn on him to rest for the moment. "Richard." He was suddenly alarmed that he had forgotten Richard was with them as escort.

"Do you suppose he heard any of this?" Mehlyndia asked, wide-eyed. It was apparent to William that she had forgotten

Richard as well.

"I don't know." William had allowed his voice to get rather loud and it was not out of the question that Richard had probably heard a good deal of the conversation. He wanted to believe that even if Richard had heard, he could trust him fully not to repeat the news; however a nagging doubt would not allow him to fully believe that Richard would not betray him.

"Call him, William. I have to know."

"Rich!" He deliberately did not shout as loudly as he knew his voice had already been.

Mehlyndia clutched William's arm tightly when Richard turned and came toward them. "He knows," she whispered.

Richard approached the two, still on his mount. The look he wore told them that Mehlyndia was correct. He had heard. William felt the ghost of a shudder cross his back again. When Richard met them, he dismounted silently.

"Yes, m' lady. I heard." He spoke gently. "Please forgive me. I had not intended to listen but was concerned that if your voices carried farther than where I stood, there would be real danger."

"I appreciate that." William looked at him carefully. "Do you tell me there is no danger, then? You understand that what you have heard would be valuable to my enemies." *Thomas would be on me before I could blink. God, what have I done?*

"Aye. I am willing to swear an oath to you should you require it." Richard bowed his head, a serious expression on his face.

Mehlyndia exhaled. She was obviously willing to trust

Richard. William was not so ready. He thought for a moment, then reached for his sword. Mehlyndia gasped but did not move.

"Your hand, Sir Richard." William assumed a formal tone.

"William!" Mehlyndia stood back, her hand to her face as William drew his blade. "What are you doing?"

William ignored Mehlyndia, never taking his eyes away from Richard.

Richard met William's unblinking gaze. "As you wish." Slowly, he removed his riding glove, then extended his hand to William, palm flat up.

William transferred his sword to his left hand and quickly dragged a long gash across Richard's outstretched palm, and quickly, in the same movement, ran the blade across his own right palm. He quickly grasped Richard's bloodied palm with his own and squeezed tightly.

"Swear on your blood, and on mine, that nothing of this conversation shall be repeated." William did not blink and held Richard's hand as tightly as possible; the trails of blood running between their fingers made drops on the sand.

Richard did not waver as he had before. "I swear to you, my lord. Should I break this oath, you may be free to spill all of my blood at your pleasure."

William held on for another moment before releasing Richard's hand. *That oath was taken easily enough. Why am I not convinced?* They stood for a moment, hands down, not taking notice of the blood each was losing.

It was Mehlyndia who made the practical move of retrieving two linen napkins from the basket. "For heaven's sake. You two would allow yourselves to bleed to death for the sake of your oaths. William, was that really necessary?"

"It doesn't hurt to take precautions." William stared at Richard, whose face had not changed since he had approached them. He took the cloth from Mehlyndia and mechanically wrapped it around his hand, still not taking his gaze away from Richard. The cut was not deep, just enough to draw blood, and the cloth soon brought the bleeding to an end. It was so with Richard as well. "Do you understand why I felt it necessary to draw blood?"

"I understand," Richard said, as he wrapped his own hand and bowed his head to Mehlyndia. "My lady, please consider this my oath to you as well. I'm sure Lord William will not require that I mingle my blood with yours."

William nodded, but his expression did not change. "I think we should be getting back."

William silently sheathed his sword and went about gathering his lute and Mehlyndia's drawings. He closed the basket with Laurel's curious luncheon left uneaten and hoisted it back onto the cart. *I'm not hungry anyway.* He helped Mehlyndia into her seat, then climbed up himself. He watched Richard trot off in front of them. *And now he knows what I've never even told Sean.* He persuaded the horse into motion and headed back along the road toward Drumoak. Somehow the oath he'd extracted from Richard did not fill him with confidence that there was nothing to worry about. The further away from the beach they traveled, the heavier the blanket of paranoia fell on him. *I hope I'm wrong.*

Laurel made her way back to the kitchen slowly. She was in full control of her unwieldy emotions at last, having taken time to wash her face and sit alone in her room for a while. *Silly fool, no more of that then. He made his choice.* She chided herself as she prepared to resume her duties.

She found the kitchen to be oddly quiet. "Where is everyone?" she called, the only response being her own echo. "Elinor? Come on now, where've you gotten to?" Elinor was never far from the kitchen and Laurel found it unnerving that she had left a stew unattended on the stove, and what's more, her cloak was not hung in its customary place on the wall behind the door. She went to the door and peered out into the yard to see if perhaps Elinor was in her herb garden. "How very odd."

"Is something wrong, Laurel?"

"Sean!" She turned with a start. "Have you seen Elinor? She's gone and left the stew on the stove, and I can't find her anywhere."

"No, I've not seen her." He went to the stew pot and curiously peeked inside. "Where has everyone else vanished to? It seems so quiet around here." He tore a piece of bread and sopped up some stew right from the pot. "Needs pepper." He reached for a jar of ground pepper and added it to the pot, then turned his attention back to Laurel.

"The lord and lady have taken a ride and luncheon in the country," Laurel announced in a comical, haughty tone. "I expect they should return before sunset."

"They've left the castle?" Sean swallowed the bread hard, an alarmed look crossing his face. "Alone?"

"No, Richard has gone with them as guard," Laurel answered carefully, startled at the look on Sean's face.

"Richard?" Sean fumed. "Why was I not called?"

"Richard was... handy."

"Handy!" Sean yelled. "When has Richard ever been handy?"

"Will asked him to go with them," Laurel yelled back defensively, remembering that William had originally asked her to find Sean. "Is that so wrong, Sean? I've gotten to know Richard somewhat. He seems trustworthy enough—"

"Have you?" Sean's face turned red. "I suppose Richard has somehow charmed *you* into a false sense of security as well?"

"Charmed me as well?" Laurel jumped back, stunned at Sean's anger and his words. "Has Will been deceived?" Laurel skittered around the table to where Sean stood near the stove. "Or are you angry with me for daring to speak to Richard without your almighty permission?"

"No... Laurel." Sean met her stare, then turned away with a frustrated sigh. "You are not the target of my anger." He sat on the edge of the table with a thoughtful scowl on his face. "So... you've gotten to know Richard?"

"Not well," Laurel answered, not missing the possessive tone in Sean's voice.

"Is he wearing your token on his armor again?" Sean teased.

A sudden heat flashed across Laurel's cheeks. "That joust was three years ago, Sean Wilbrun, and I've explained t' you time and time again that it was Mehlyndia's idea for me to give him that... I hardly knew him then and I hardly know him now!"

"Hush, hush," Sean said, placing a hand on her shoulder. "That was a low strike and I should not have said it."

Laurel allowed a smile. "You're forgiven. And the truth is, Richard and I have only spoken once or twice. But he does seem to be perfectly nice."

"Nice?" Sean scoffed. "You've decided that with only one or two conversations?"

Laurel found herself suddenly amused with the look on Sean's face. *He's jealous!* "Aye," she answered, a slight coy smile on her lips. "I find him rather... dashing. Have you ever noticed how much he looks like Will?"

"Dashing?" Sean made a sarcastic smirk. "No, I never noticed... What are you laughing at?"

"You." Laurel could not hold back a delighted giggle. "You're blushing."

"I am not!" Sean protested, trying to see his reflection in a hanging pot. "I just don't understand what you find so dashing about Richard Fylbrigge, silly child!"

Laurel stopped laughing immediately and turned a cold stare onto Sean. "For one thing, he doesn't seem to regard me as a child." She felt the flood threatening again, this time out of anger. "Will you never realize I am a grown woman?"

"I was only jesting, Laurel, I didn't mean to offend you," Sean answered, reaching for her hand. "I'm being a bit of a lout, aren't I?"

"Yes." Laurel took a breath and pushed back her tide. "You can't blame me for being charmed when a handsome, polite sentry finds my company pleasant. I'm past twenty, for heaven's sake, and other than Will, he's the first lad who seems to recognize that."

"I find your company pleasant." Sean pulled her slightly closer. "And I'm a damned fool that I haven't realized before...

you are quite grown up." He lightly stroked her cheek with his hand. "And you are... pretty."

Laurel looked at Sean as though for the first time. "You think I'm pretty?" she asked, shyly.

"Laurel, I... " Sean suddenly pulled her forward and kissed her.

Laurel pulled back stunned, but not offended, staring foolishly wide-eyed at him. "Sean!" Until that moment, she had never believed Sean felt anything more than a brotherly affection for her. But the look in his eye and the way her heart was racing had changed that feeling right then. *Has he at last forgotten the wench from Aberdoir? Perhaps he has... after all it's been near three years since he's even set eyes on her.*

"Forgive me, Laurel." Sean stood back, a blush coming to his face. "I don't know what came over me. That was... I had no right... I mean, you understand that I'm not free to..."

Three years! Enough is enough, Sean Wilbrun, it's time to forget her! Laurel stepped forward and pulled him to her, kissing him hard on the mouth. He responded quite enthusiastically. She kissed him with a passion she had never felt before. She pulled back, slowly, looking into Sean's eyes. "You're forgiven."

"Thank you, m' lady." He smiled, brushing her face with his hand. "What were we talking about?" He kissed her again, lightly this time. "I can't seem to remember."

"Richard." Laurel answered quietly and kissed him again.

Sean straightened up, his scowl returning. "Oh, yes." He leaned back against the table, leaving Laurel alone by the counter. He seemed to have completely dismissed their burgeoning romance. "Richard," he grumbled. "Tell me where they've gone off to, and I'll go provide *proper* protection."

Laurel sighed. *Twit, why'd you go and ruin it?* With a disappointed frown, she was resigned to let the moment pass, and accept the fact that Sean still carried a torch for the lass from Aberdoir. *Let him have his fancy.* "Protection from what?" she asked. "Sean, Will *asked* Richard to go with them. Surely he has no fear of—"

"Exactly!" He threw his hands in the air, and yelled again. "He has no damned fear of anything! And he places his trust far too easily where he should not. His damned forgiveness will be his ruin!"

"Don't swear on him, Sean!" Laurel, answered him quietly, still stinging from his sudden lack of interest in her. "What possible danger could they find while out for a simple picnic?"

"Plenty! Will has enemies, Laurel. Ogham put a high price on his head. Four would-be assassins have already been arrested in the past two weeks alone. The danger is real."

"What? Four?" Laurel asked, stunned. "Does Will know anything about that?"

"Of course he knows." Sean's bad temper was returning. "But do you think something as trivial as a death reward on his head would keep *Fearless Fylbrigge* from merrily traipsing about the countryside with no protection other than his cowardly nephew?" Sean threw his hand up in frustration. "He promised me he would not rely on Richard for anything more than—"

"Picnic patrol?" Laurel said, nervously chewing her nails. "That's what Will called it. He seemed to think it was... appropriate for Richard."

"Picnic patrol." Sean rolled his eyes. "I suppose he's right. It is an appropriate assignment. It doesn't require even a modicum of courage."

"Is Richard truly that much of a coward?" Laurel asked carefully. "Is that why you dislike him so?"

"Yes, he's a coward, and I dislike him because I don't trust him." Sean looked her in the eye. "He covered Dunkirk and Thomas, during the attack at the wedding."

"Dunkirk?" Laurel gasped. "That lout?"

"Now do you see my side?"

"Clearly." Laurel stared at Sean. "But it's only a picnic." She tried to sound reassuring.

"And I'll bet Will's not even wearing any armor."

"He's not," Laurel admitted, still chewing her nails as she walked to the door and looked out toward the road. "But he's got a flatiron handy should he need it," she told him absentmindedly. *Of course he's protected. I charmed his badge...* She looked up, suddenly startled. *He doesn't wear the eagle anymore!* "Sean?"

"Flatiron?" Sean looked at her dumbfounded. "What are you talking about?"

"Never mind that, does he still wear his badge? The one Edward gave him... with the eagle?"

"The old clan badge? No—"

"Where is it?" Laurel asked, suddenly feeling panicked.

"I don't know, what difference—"

"What are we standing around here for then?" Laurel dashed past Sean and grabbed her cloak from the hook.

"What do you think you're doing?" he asked, following her across the room.

"Going with you, while you look for Will," she answered, throwing her cloak around her shoulders and dashing out the door.

"Laurel, wait." Sean followed after, "Why are you coming with me?"

"To keep you from fainting when we find them all well and happy," she called over her shoulder.

"Mouthy wench." Sean laughed as he ran to catch up with her.

As they turned to the road that led to the sea, it was only a moment before they saw the distinct forms of Richard on horseback. Right behind him, William and Mehlyndia rode in the small cart.

"There, what did I tell you, Sean?" Laurel jabbed Sean's arm with her elbow, and pointed toward the cart. "There they are, right as rain and twice as nice." *Thank you, Blessed Mother!*

"I see them. Save your gloating for later; it will wrinkle up that pretty face." Sean winked at her, then waved casually to the trio approaching. William waved back. "Let's keep this as nonchalant as possible. Shall we?" He took hold of Laurel's hand.

"Aye, no need for them to know you're such a worrying old woman." Laurel could not suppress her laughter and happily gave Sean's hand a squeeze.

"Old?" Sean gave her a silly smirk. "I think not—hold on, is that Elinor?" He pointed up the road.

"Yes, that's her." Laurel looked where Sean pointed and took a second look, not quite believing what she was seeing. "Why is she talking to a monk?" she asked, surprised at the curious sight. "How odd."

"No crime in that, I suppose. They seem cheerful enough." Sean gave her a curious glance; she could see he was equally astounded. Neither had ever known Elinor to say so much as hello to any cleric, let alone stand conversing in the street. "You go on and meet Elinor. I'll be back in a minute." Before he let her hand go, he gave her a quick kiss.

"Aye." She smiled, completely pleased that Sean reclaimed his interest in her. "Hurry back." She winked and happily trotted off to meet Elinor and the curiously cheerful looking monk who was speaking to her.

When William saw Sean running toward them, he worried that something was wrong. He shook the reins, livening up the steps of his horse. "Something's happening. Pick up the pace, Richard."

"Aye." Richard doubled his speed.

"Sean? What's happening?" William asked when they caught up to each other. "Is everything all right?"

"Aye, all is well." Sean ran up to the cart, out of breath, giving Richard a quick nod in greeting, then faced William. "Forgive me if I startled you. Laurel and I were just out looking for... Elinor. We found her. She is yonder on the high road. I thought perhaps she could share your ride back to the castle."

"Elinor?" William sensed there was some other reason Sean was out and about Stonehaven.

"Why is Elinor on the high road?" Mehlyndia asked Sean, shielding her eyes to look up the road.

"I'm not sure, m' lady," Sean answered politely. "She left

Drumoak without word. She even left a stew unattended and we were worried that something might be amiss, so we set out to find her."

"Lead the way." William shook the reins. He was far from convinced that Elinor was the reason Sean was out on that particular stretch of road. *I suppose overprotection is better than no protection.*

Sean got a leg up and hopped up onto the carriage before it got moving too quickly and slid up next to William. "I trust you had a nice outing." Sean said, in a sarcastically challenging tone.

"Lovely, thank you for asking." William picked up Sean's tone and dismissed it with his own. *I was right. He's being over protective.*

"I gather nothing harrowing took place?" Sean said with a sideways glance to Richard. "Your escort is still with you."

"Imagine that," William grumbled and shook the reins sharply. As he turned the cart onto the high street, he saw Elinor and Laurel and the man they were speaking to. "Who is that?" he asked Sean, surprised to see Elinor conversing with a monk.

"I don't know, but I'd like to find out." Sean hopped down from the cart as William brought it to a stop.

"Elinor!"

William called from the cart and waved her to come. Elinor saw him and excused herself from the monk, running up to meet the cart.

"Elinor? Are you all right?" William's eyes darted from Elinor's haggard face to the unknown monk in front of them, his innate mistrust of clerics putting him on alert.

"I'm glad you're here," Elinor answered, catching her breath. "I was on my way to call on Geoffrey, but this young friar happened to meet me before I arrived." Elinor looked over her shoulder and flashed a smile to the monk, then turned back to William wide-eyed. "It's Nora, she's not long now."

"Nora is failing?" William hopped down from the cart. "Oh no. I had promised Geoffrey I would come by to see her. How could I have forgotten?" He leaned in close to Elinor. "Who is that?" He pointed with his chin toward the monk.

"Geoffrey would be grateful for your company, I'm sure." Elinor spoke in a deliberately loud voice, then leaned in close to answer William's question. "New at the abbey. Seems pleasant enough, but I've got... " She casually shook the little pouch she wore on her belt.

William looked at what Elinor was carrying. "Oh." He looked away from her belt, being sure to keep a casual expression on his face. He kept his voice calm as Elinor had done but spoke loud enough for the monk to hear as he turned to Mehlyndia. "Melly, I have promised to see Geoffrey and I fear I will not have another opportunity to see Nora. Would you take Laurel with you back to Drumoak?" He turned to Richard, who, with a curious frown in his brow, was watching Laurel speak to the young friar. "Richard, please go with them."

"Aye, m' lord." Richard looked at William, then quickly back to Laurel. "Laurel?"

Laurel excused herself from the friar's company and joined Richard and William, Sean two steps behind her. "Aye, m' lord?"

"I'd like you to go on back to Drumoak," William told her, quietly.

"Why?" Laurel asked.

"Elinor's making a... delivery." He motioned to her little pouch and kept his voice as low as possible. "And with clerics walking the street,... I just think it best for you to go on back. Richard will escort you."

"Oh, I see." Laurel nodded toward Elinor's belt.

Richard smiled politely and offered Laurel his assistance in climbing onto the cart. Sean came up quickly behind her and tapped her on the shoulder. "Laurel?"

"Yes?" She turned to face Sean.

He took her hand. "I'll be back soon. Shall I call on you this evening?"

"Yes." Laurel nodded happily. "I'd like that." She blushed as Sean kissed her hand and helped her onto the cart. "Thank you... Sean." She gave his hand a quick squeeze before she let it go.

Sean made a polite bow of his head, then turned and gave Richard a falsely, friendly clap on the shoulder. "Off you go. Take them straight back now, Richard. Captain's orders."

Richard stood speechless, a stunned look on his face. "Aye... sir." He remounted his horse.

William watched this little fool's drama with amused delight. He caught Mehlyndia's eye and found she, too, was concealing a grin. *So we were wrong. Laurel has eyes for Sean. Not Richard.* William found this far more palatable, somehow.

"We won't be long; please tell Edward where we have gone." William called to Richard as the three now headed away back toward Drumoak.

"When did this happen?" William asked Sean, as they watched the cart disappear down the street. "Don't tell me, you've at last given up that Annlise Chase will see you again."

"Nothing escapes you, does it, Will?" Sean grinned and said no more.

William chuckled and glanced up. The young friar was still standing patiently apart from them, smiling pleasantly. "Has this monk given you trouble?" William asked Elinor, quietly, as they approached the monk.

"No, quite the contrary." Elinor looked at William, answering in a wide-eyed wonder. "Which is why I am taken aback. He seems quite friendly. Not what I'm used to in a cleric these days. Says his name is Brother Ian; he's just come to Stonehaven Abbey."

"Well then, if he be friendly, so shall I." William walked toward the monk, smiling in welcome, Sean protectively at his side. "Greetings friend," he called out in his famous charming cheerfulness.

"And to you as well, sir," Brother Ian replied in an equally congenial tone. "My name is Brother Ian Proctor, but if you please, I prefer to be called simply Ian. I am pleased to meet you." He extended a hand to William. "I am new to Stonehaven and was walking about to make myself acquainted with the town."

"I'm pleased to meet you... Ian." William reached for the monk's hand, realizing the bloody napkin was still wrapped around his own. He quickly removed it, hoping the cut would not begin to bleed on the monk.

Sean raised a questioning eyebrow to William when he saw the bloodstained cloth.

"Forgive me." William smiled apologetically as he stuffed the napkin in his pocket. "I have just come from a picnic by the sea with my bride. I took an unfortunate spill on one of the slippery rocks and cut my palm as I fell. It is of no concern." William shot a quick look to Sean, who he knew would ask for details later.

Ian took William's hand gingerly. "Who is it I have the pleasure of addressing, sir?"

"Forgive me, again." William tipped his forehead with his hand. "I am William Fylb—William of Drumoak." He found it awkward to use his new designation. "This is my captain and good friend, Sir Sean Wilbrun." Sean bowed politely. Ian answered in kind. "I take it you have met Elinor."

"William of Drumoak?" Ian smiled broadly. "Are you the one who has just been named Earl of Sutherland? I am very pleased to know you, sir. I've heard of you." Ian squeezed William's hand and shook it eagerly, then released it quickly when William winced. "I'm terribly sorry." Ian had accidentally caused the cut to bleed slightly.

"No trouble." William shrugged it off, amicably wiping his hand on his leggings. He found himself amused with this cheerful monk. "So you've heard of me?" William wrinkled his brow in mock fear, still grinning. "I am almost afraid to ask what it is you've heard."

Ian blushed slightly but kept his good humor. "Well, to tell the truth, what I have heard from the townsfolk, and what I've heard from my superiors within the abbey would cause me to believe you are two completely separate beings. However, I am one who prefers to come to my own conclusions about people."

"I assure you, I am only one man." William chuckled. "And I hope I leave you with a favorable impression." His smile dimmed a bit but remained pleasant. "I'm sure you're aware, then, that I am not a favorite in your abbey." His smile left him completely. "You may risk raising the ire of Bishop Dunkirk just by speaking to me."

Ian's face grew serious as well. "I would image that to be true, I'm sorry to tell you. I know the times are difficult. But I must say," Ian added, his smile returning, "you are highly spoken of among the good people of this village. My instincts tell me they are closer to the mark. You have a good face."

Surprised by his candor, William found he could not help but return a genuinely appreciative smile. At another time, he would have been interested to converse further with this curious monk, but he knew Elinor's need to go to Geoffrey, so he closed the conversation. "It was nice to meet you, Ian." William offered his hand again. "If you'll excuse us, we should like to call on our friend. His wife is feeling poorly and I promised I would come by."

"Of course." Ian shook his hand, far more carefully this time. "Perhaps we shall cross paths again soon."

"I'd enjoy that." William bowed politely. "Good day to you, Brother Ian."

"God bless." Folding his hands into his sleeves, Ian turned to head back toward the abbey, waving and smiling to people as he went.

"Now that was... odd," William said, holding his hands palms up, amazed. "He was actually pleasant."

"Perhaps he is not really a monk?" Sean said, an equally amused look on his face. "He was far too happy, and you're not covered in hives." He laughed and clapped William on the shoulder.

"That must be it, Sean. He's an impostor," Elinor agreed, laughing. "Still, I'm not so daft as to tell him what I'm about," she said, shaking the little pouch on her belt.

"Absolutely." William and Sean spoke together.

As the three of them walked the high street toward Geoffrey's home, Sean leaned to William and gestured to his hand. "So, Will, do you often swear blood oaths with stones?"

"Nothing escapes you, does it, Sean?" William replied without looking at him.

"I've yet to find a stone that made such a neat cut as this," Sean said, lifting William's hand to get a better look. "Would I be right to assume Richard also stumbled upon the same offending sword-shaped rock?"

"Sean," William began, pulling his hand away, "let's just say, I felt the need to extract an oath from Richard. I should think you'd be pleased with me. I tested his courage." He flashed his palm. "At least I know he's not afraid to bleed a little bit."

"I'm astounded. Did you have to tie him down?"

"No, I held him at bay with a flatiron."

"Flatiron?" Sean asked, confounded.

"I'll explain it all later." William held out his bloody palm to shake Sean's hand. "Deal?"

"Deal." Sean shook William's hand, then grimaced, eyeing the little blood trail left on his palm. He wiped it off on William's tunic. "I shall be sure to have the rock arrested and severely whipped for attacking you."

"Would you?" William brushed off his tunic. "I'd appreciate

that. Nasty piece of granite that was."

"You two are priceless." Elinor laughed.

"No, he's priceless." William pointed a thumb to Sean. "I've got a rather good price on me, I'm told." He laughed, then, catching the look on Sean's face, he cleared his throat. "That was supposed to be funny."

"It wasn't," Sean said flatly.

The three walked silently the remainder of the way.

When they reached Geoffrey's cabin, Elinor knocked gently on the door. "Geoffrey, it's Elinor."

"Sean, would you stay out by the door," William whispered. "I'm not fully comfortable with monks who take walks in town—no matter how friendly they seem. Keep an eye out for anything... odd."

"Agreed." Sean nodded. "I'll wait right out here."

The door swung open quietly. Geoffrey's lined face greeted them. When he saw William with Elinor, his eyes momentarily lost their gloom.

"Hello, Geoffrey." William extended his hand. "Do you mind if I join Elinor?"

"I'm so glad you've come." Geoffrey took William's hand eagerly and led him to Nora's bedside. "Nora, see who's come to visit? It's Elinor and young Will. You remember?"

Nora made no response to Geoffrey as she lay in her bed moaning. Geoffrey brushed his eyes as he resumed his seat on the little stool next to her bed.

"There now." Elinor placed her hand on Geoffrey's shoulder. "I've got what you requested. Poor dear, she suffers so." Nora suddenly made thrashing movements as though she was fending off an attack from an unseen foe. "Will she be able to drink?" Elinor asked as she watched.

"It is hard for me to keep her calm when these fits come." Geoffrey placed a tentative hand on William's arm. "Perhaps you can help, lad."

"What would you like me to do?" William asked.

"She loves music, but I just cannot bring myself to play." Geoffrey pointed to the lute in the corner, "Could you... "

"My pleasure." William picked up the lute and settled himself on a chair close to Nora. "Elinor, is your dose ready?"

"Aye. Forgive me for not taking the duke's advice, but you can clearly see the need," Elinor said as she prepared the cup for Nora.

"I would expect no less of you." William reassured her, as he began idly plucking the strings of the lute. "But you needn't take the risk on your own, you know."

Elinor blushed. "Won't happen again."

William shook his head. "At least not today, right?" He turned to Geoffrey, "Geoffrey, is there a particular song I should play for her?"

"*Greensleeves*, if you please. That is her favorite, and I know you play that one so well."

"*Greensleeves*, it is." William deftly transformed his random plucking into the recognizable melody of *Greensleeves*. It was one of his favorites as well, and one of the first he had learned to play. He hummed softly as his fingers danced across the strings.

The music did have a calming effect on Nora. Her thrashing stopped completely after only a few moments. When she was finally still, Elinor was able to help her to drink the potion that would finally bring her rest.

"Blessed rest, good lady," Elinor whispered to Nora as, finally, the cup was emptied of the potion. "She will first sleep, then slip peacefully."

Geoffrey held Nora's hand and stroked her forehead. He kissed her gently as he sat next to her. "Bless you Elinor. And you, Will, for making this tranquil for her. May we all find such easy leave of this life."

William continued to play softly, banishing his own demons as surely as Nora's with the ringing of the strings. He closed his eyes and rocked slightly as his hands automatically took control. As though the music came from another musician, he listened and drifted away to that far-off shore in his dreams. He sang softly, lost in his song, forgetting there were others with him. He played for the better part of an hour until he was brought out of his reverie by Geoffrey's hand on his shoulder.

"She's found her peace," Geoffrey said.

William silenced the last ringing of the strings with the flat of his hand.

Elinor kissed Geoffrey on the cheek and hugged him close while he let his tears flow unchecked. "I shall return later to help with the preparations," she promised.

"Thank you, dear lady. I owe you both so much." Geoffrey reached for William's hand. "William, I have no words... thank you."

"I'm glad I could do this for her. And for you." William handed him the lute. "It's a fine instrument," he said absently, finding himself at a loss for what to say at such a time.

They stood quietly for a moment before a light knock on the door reminded them that Sean still stood outside. The door opened slowly. "Will, forgive me, please come out for a moment."

"A moment, Sean." William turned to Geoffrey. "I wish you peace. Let me know when funeral arrangements have been made."

"Aye, she will be put to rest tomorrow in a simple ceremony. Please, you must attend to your own duties now. I am grateful you have come. Please, now; go spend time with your bride." Geoffrey's eyes welled up. "Cherish her, William."

William just managed to keep hold of his own emotions. "I do, my friend. With all my heart."

Sean leaned through the doorway again. "*Lord* William, I'm sorry to *rush* you, but—"

"I'm coming Sean. Goodbye, Geoffrey." William turned and left the cottage. Elinor followed.

"Sean? What is—" William stopped short at what he saw as he left the cottage. A dozen or so horsemen dressed in long black-hooded cloaks and tunics bearing the crest of the king's church patrolled the streets. Though they bore the mark of the cross and shield, they were by no means clerics. These men were more akin to mercenary soldiers. "Hunters?"

"Blessed Mother." Elinor could barely speak. She reached for William's hand and held on tight. "They look as though they're searching."

William knew she was right, and he knew what it was they were searching for. These men had one function, which they performed quite well. They sought out witches, real and imagined—mostly the latter—and they fed the hysteria.

"I've never known them to search without a clear order,"

Sean spoke as quietly as Elinor had. "They are looking for someone specific."

William's stomach tightened. He involuntarily squeezed Elinor's hand. After the conversation he had just had on the beach, his paranoia was gaining on him. *Why should I assume they're looking for me?*

Chapter 9

ROTHER IAN WENT about the business of settling into his small, stark quarters in the abbey. The few possessions he owned fit neatly into the trunk at the end of his small bed. He had a supply of candles, parchment and quills, the odd prayer book or two, and his one personal belonging—a wooden flute he kept hidden away. He never played it, as it would be frowned upon by his superiors, but he often liked to just hold on to it, remembering the times when he was young and could play freely.

He was unusual for his calling. He enjoyed life outside the walls of the abbey, and enjoyed meeting the people in the towns and villages he traveled through. He relished the company of children, and he especially liked tending the herb gardens. In his prior abbey, he had free reign in the gardens and could easily lose himself, marveling at the first blossoms of spring. As schoolmaster, he was well liked by his young charges. He was patient and gentle with them, teaching not only the Scriptures, but also songs, games, and gardening methods. It was for this reason he was transferred to Stonehaven. Abbot Joseph had no patience with what he saw as frivolous distractions. He believed children should be taught with a stern and heavy hand, and Brother Ian had steadfastly refused to accept Joseph's approach to teaching.

It saddened Ian to know that his young students would now be facing the harsh methods his fellow brothers employed, but the choice was not his—he'd been ordered away. In Stonehaven, he would not be teaching the children. He had been assigned to the scribe's desk where he would be expected to spend most of his waking hours in a small, windowless vestibule transcribing Scripture onto scroll after scroll.

He finished putting his meager belongings into the trunk and sat heavily on the bed. He had questioned his calling many times, but never really seriously considered leaving the clergy—until now. He looked up to the crucifix above his bed, clasped his hands, and as he had done every night, prayed for guidance. He had no doubt in his faith or his devotion, yet he wondered if he could better serve his brothers and sisters if he were free of the confining walls of the abbey.

In his wanderings of the town that afternoon, he had spent time listening to local gossip from the people he encountered. Most of the talk seemed to center around this new young earl, William of Drumoak. The townsfolk seemed to have a genuine affection for the man; many eager to retell about his fabled adventures with his companion, Sean Wilbrun, and of his heroic rescue of a young woman just as she was about to be burned alive. Depending upon who was doing the telling, these stories involved him confronting one or dozens of hunters at a time, barely making it away, or leaving them all in his dust. The one element all these retellings had in common was that the story teller was eager to claim William of Drumoak as a close, personal friend.

However, this same young man seemed to be a singular obsession with Bishop Dunkirk, who held nothing but contempt for the young earl. He referred to William as the heretic heir of Drumoak and anyone who disagreed with that assessment was sure to find himself on Dunkirk's bad side.

Brother Ian's impression upon finally meeting William face-to-face was that he seemed amiable enough, if not a bit self-reserved. But then he had encountered many people who seemed reserved in the presence of clerics—the lady Elinor seemed positively petrified, though she tried to hide it. William certainly didn't appear to Ian to be the mythical epic hero the townspeople described, but he certainly wasn't the fire-breathing heathen Dunkirk believed him to be either. Ian found him to be a pleasant, polite young man, one he would gladly like to know better if given the opportunity.

He sat brooding for a bit, then pushed his dark mood aside to prepare for evening prayers. The prospect of a walk around the abbey cheered him, as he found he really did loathe the small quarters he now called his home. Though he was a bit early for chapel, he decided to walk down that way anyway.

The halls of the abbey were long and dark, and generally very quiet, the only sounds being the muffled swishing of his robe and soft sound of his footsteps. As he passed the vestry, however, the halls were anything but quiet, as he was met by the sound of several loud voices coming from Dunkirk's meeting room. Brother Ian recognized Bishop Dunkirk's voice.

"We require only one other corroborator. I'm sure we will have no trouble persuading the old woman."

Brother Ian pressed himself against the wall, carefully staying out of sight. He dared not risk a look into the room to see who was speaking, but he could see shadows on the wall that indicated there were at least six or more men, all wearing some sort of long, hooded cloak.

"Why have you not yet secured her?" The bishop sounded irritated.

"We had no opportunity to approach her without raising his suspicion," one of the hooded men answered. "Your own orders were that he not be made aware until we are prepared to move."

"But I saw her myself, walking alone in town," Dunkirk growled at the other man. "What caused you to delay?"

"She was met by one of your own clerics, Your Grace, who then stayed with her when he and his companion arrived. We did not wish an encounter in broad daylight," the man spoke, defensively.

"One of my clerics? Impossible. They are not about the streets during the day, they have their assigned—" Dunkirk stopped mid-sentence.

Brother Ian realized that he was very likely the cleric in question. He pressed himself further into the shadows and listened more closely.

"Wait." Dunkirk sighed. "Of course. He hasn't begun his vocations as yet. I can see he shall be as much trouble to me as he was to the abbot in Aberdoir."

Brother Ian caught his breath. He *was* the cleric the hunter spoke of and he had a very good idea who the woman he had delayed had been.

"It may be, gentlemen, that we may just have to go to Drumoak and get her. Secrecy be damned," Dunkirk grumbled.

"We have men watching her movements should she

venture away from Drumoak, we shall be ready," the hunter reported. "If she does not, then we shall go when the moon sets and take her."

"Excellent. Once the woman has been secured, return to await my orders. If all goes as planned, we shall have him by the morrow." Dunkirk sounded pleased with himself.

"Your Grace..." The hunter's voice was tentative. "If I may be so bold..."

"What is it?" Dunkirk sighed.

"Why bother with the old woman? Why not go directly to Drumoak and arrest him tonight?"

"You obviously haven't understood me. We need her to corroborate the charge, first." Dunkirk hissed the ending of the word 'first.' "You also obviously have no idea about this man. He's wiry as a cat. If you go there now, he and his captain will best the lot of you and disappear into the mist without a trace. That is another reason we need her... insurance. If he lives up to half the tall tales told about him, he won't take flight while she is in our custody."

"Understood, Your Grace." The hunter relented.

"Good." Dunkirk lowered his voice. "I shall send a page to Aberdoir. We shall require Lord Thomas's testimony as the one who has brought the accusation. His wife, too, has even more compelling information that we shall hold in reserve should we need it."

"Two charges?" The hunter laughed, mirthlessly, under his breath. "You're taking no chances, I see. I assume Lady Bryndah's accusation will be held as a trump, should Thomas's claims be dismissed?"

"Of course," Dunkirk replied. "I will recommend that

Abbot Joseph accompany Lord and Lady Aberdoir to Stonehaven as well. As I recall, he knows some personal history that may be quite useful." Dunkirk clapped his hands sharply, summoning his page. "Gentlemen, take your leave now. Go."

It took Ian no more than a half-breath to make his decision. He would not be in chapel for prayers that evening. He quickly and silently let himself out of the abbey through a side exit, carefully avoiding the hunters.

"God, guide my steps and give me strength this night." The sun had just settled past the hills, giving him shadows to hide within. *The moon will set early tonight, not much time!* When clear of the churchyard, Brother Ian ran as fast as he was able, toward the front gates of Drumoak.

"Please!" The monk rattled the gate, breathlessly. "You must allow me to enter. It is urgent!"

"On whose business are you?" a guard inquired in formal tone.

"No one's! Just my own. Please! I must speak with the young earl."

The guard hesitated for a moment, then opened the gate.

"Bless you! Thank you." Ian entered, bowing his head gratefully.

"Wait here. Don't move. Ewan! Come!"

Brother Ian leaned against the gate as he tried to regain his breath, then stood alert when he saw Ewan, eager to beseech this new guard to let him to enter the castle.

"Aye? What is it, Simon?" Ewan called, as he casually walked to join his comrade.

"This monk says he must speak to Lord Sutherland. He says it's urgent."

"What business does *he* have with Lord Sutherland" Ewan eyed Ian skeptically.

"Please, good sir, it's a matter of life and death." Ian dashed toward Ewan. "The moon has almost set!"

"Not so fast." Simon blocked Ian, then turned to Ewan. "Better tell the captain."

"Aye," Ewan answered then turned to walk away.

"Please, hurry!" Ian shouted, distressed at Ewan's apparent disinterest. "I must warn them. Don't you understand? They are coming tonight! There isn't much time, the moon—" Ian suddenly lost his breath and grasped his chest in pain. Simon helped him stay on his feet. Ewan turned back, but Ian waved him on. "Hurry!"

"Go! I'll stay with him," Simon shouted to Ewan, not turning away from Ian.

"They're coming tonight!" Ian called frantically at Ewan as he ran, more urgently, toward the castle. "You must hurry!"

"Who is coming?" Simon softened the tone of his voice.

"The hunters! Tonight." Ian grasped Simon's arms, then breathlessly collapsed to his hands and knees. "Please I must warn—"

"Hunters?" He hauled Ian up by his arm.

"What is this about?" Sean's voice echoed from the entrance.

Ian turned sharply to look in the direction of Sean's voice. "Please! Sir Sean, I must warn him. They're coming tonight."

"I remember you." Sean helped the man up by his robe. "Who is coming?"

Ian stood panting, unable to catch enough breath to answer.

"Who is coming?" Sean demanded a second time.

Simon answered for Ian, "He said hunters were coming."

"Hunters?" Sean took hold of Ian's robe again, shaking him as he asked, "Here? What purpose?"

Simon got between them. "Give him a minute, Sean."

Sean relented and allowed Ian to compose himself enough to continue.

"I heard them," Ian spoke between staggering breaths. "The bishop and several hunters... they're coming for her tonight, the lady Elinor... but it's him... they want to lure him..."

"Who?" Sean demanded.

"Lord Sutherland!" Ian yelled.

Sean let the cleric go, then turned sharply to Simon. "Go tell Will. Now! I'll take our friend here to Edward's suite. We can speak there; do not alarm the women. Clear?"

"Aye" Simon ran up the stairs two at a time.

"Go!" Sean snapped his orders. "Ewan, alert the sentries. I want every one of at their posts. Do not allow anyone to enter or exit the gates. Especially Elinor! Go!" Ewan was gone in a flash.

Sean quickly trundled Ian up the grand stairs to Edward's chambers, then banged loudly on the door. "Lord Edward, we have urgent business!"

The door swung open immediately. "Sean? What is it?" Edward ushered the two in without hesitation.

"We've got an emergency, sir," Sean answered briskly.

Before Sean could continue, Simon and William burst into

the room. William stopped short, a confounded expression on his face.

"Ian?" He looked to Sean. "What's this about?"

"Thank God!" Ian leaped toward William too quickly to be stopped, grabbing his arms urgently. "Lord Sutherland, you must go! You must flee this place. Tonight. Before they come for you."

"What? Brother Ian, release me!" William pried himself free. "What are you talking about?"

Sean and Simon pulled Ian away from William and forced him to sit. Edward poured some wine into his goblet and brought it to him.

William shot startled, confused glances between Sean and Ian. "Will someone answer me, please?"

"Calm down." Edward forced the goblet at Ian. "Drink."

Ian took the goblet and immediately drank the entire contents, then turned an agitated eye toward the window. "The moon. It's almost time. You have only another hour, no more, until the moon sets." He handed the goblet back to Edward.

"Now, start at the beginning." Edward poured more wine for Ian, then handed an empty goblet to William, who stood ashen-faced, waiting for an answer.

"Before who comes?" William asked, impatiently. "What is he talking about?"

Sean picked up the wine bottle and filled William's glass. "Drink." He put a hand on William's shoulder and pushed him down into a chair across from Ian. "You'll need it." He turned back to Ian. "Now, slowly. Tell them what you told me downstairs."

Ian took a long, hard breath to steady himself. "I heard the bishop speaking to the hunters. They come for the lady Elinor tonight."

"Hunters. Damn! I knew it." William stood quickly, Ian's panic reflected in his eyes. "What has Elinor been accused of?" William leaned over the table.

Sean pulled him back to his seat. "They do not intend to accuse her of anything as far as I understood, my lord."

William raised his voice. "So why are they looking for her?"

"To witness against you." Ian forced his words to come slow and clear. "And to be sure you—"

"Witness?" William yelled, attempting to stand.

"Calm down, Will, let him finish." Sean leaned on William, keeping him from flying off the chair. "To be sure of what, Ian?"

"To be sure he does not leave Stonehaven before they come for him." Ian slammed his hands on the table, sending echoes through the room. He stood, looked William in the eye and continued in a calmer, yet still urgent, tone. "Apparently, your noble reputation has not gone unnoticed by the bishop after all. He intends to use her to bait you, so they can levy their charge."

William squeezed his fists on the table in front of him. "What is the charge?" he asked, quietly but angrily.

Ian leaned over the table. "You must know the sort of charge brought by hunters." He reached out and placed his hands on William's balled fists. "You must flee. These men will not be stopped. I've seen it too often! Please! I've come from the abbey in Aberdoir, I know who the accuser—"

"Aberdoir?" Edward and William shouted together.

"Aye." Ian spun in his chair to answer Edward.

"Thomas," William hissed in disgust. "I might have known." He sat, teeth locked tight, shaking his head. The panicked look in his eye quickly turned to utter anger. He poured himself more wine and drank it slowly. "I feared he had been all too quiet since you banished him."

"Take heart, William, we are forewarned," Edward assured him. "That will be our advantage."

"My lord," Sean interrupted. "We need to take Elinor into protection. They won't gain their pawn and false evidence if they can't find her."

"Yes," Edward agreed. "She should be in her quarters this time of night. Go, Sean, bring her here. Hurry, time is valuable."

Sean motioned to Simon to follow. They left the suite quickly.

William turned to Edward after Sean left the chamber. "We'll have to send her away from here, you know. God only knows where, but she won't be safe here."

"Neither will you." Edward looked down, frowning into his goblet. "I think it wise that you prepare to travel, William."

"I suppose so." William grumbled and pushed himself away from the table. *Then Elinor and I can hide out in the land of God only knows where forever. Won't that be a grand life.*

Edward spoke softly to Ian. "If all you've told us is true, you have done us a great service. I understand the risk you took in coming. Is there anything more you can tell us?"

He wrinkled his brow and rested his head in his hand as if

to think. "Yes." He looked up at William, a sympathetic look in his eye. "They said there was another charge they would hold in reserve should they require it, but I do not know the details on—"

"Another charge?" William interrupted angrily. "Is not one false accusation enough?"

"It is a trump." Ian spoke with a tone of distress. "I've seen this done before, usually when they feel there is not sufficient hard evidence to prove the first charge. It would seem they are determined—"

"Trump?" William repeated, astounded. "What could they possibly..." He threw his hands up in frustration. "Why can't Thomas just leave me alone!" He turned sharply to Ian. "Why should I trust you? Tell me that. Maybe you're here as part of their plan?"

"No! Please, you must believe I have no love of what they do. You must leave here. If they gain ground, it will be impossible to turn them back. Please—"

"What ground is there to gain?" William shouted. "I've done nothing wrong!"

"Enough!" Edward silenced the argument. "Brother Ian, I believe you. Leave us to take the necessary precautions. You must return to your abbey quickly now, before you are missed, and you must go now before we lose any more time. Go!"

"I'm sorry, Ian." William sighed and sunk into the chair. "I'm grateful you have come to warn me. I had no right..."

"Please, sir. Leave here while you can," Ian begged one more time before turning and leaving the suite.

William waved him away, resting his forehead on his

hand. When Ian was gone, William asked Edward, "What do you think? Should I spend the rest of my life running away, hiding from my brother?"

Edward looked away, without answering. After a pause he said, softly, "Tell me, what type of evidence Thomas could possibly have against you."

"False." William sat at the table, staring off in front of himself. "Evidence of his own invention."

"William." Edward pulled William's chair away from the table and turned it to face him. Placing a hand on each arm of the chair, he leaned in as close to William as he could without touching him. "Tell me about the chicory oil."

William looked at Edward in utter disbelief. "How did—"

"I know the scent of chicory when I smell it! The night of the convocation, you had it about you. I foolishly allowed myself to believe that you needed help in the marriage bed and had sought out a charm from Elinor." He placed a hand on William's shoulder and looked at him, unblinking. "I somehow don't believe that to be the case anymore. Chicory is also used in beguiling charms, William. Folk magic. Who prepared it for you?"

"No one prepared—what are you asking? Don't tell me you believe—"

"Answer me!" Edward straightened himself by pushing against the arms of the chair. "I cannot refute a charge if I know it to be true."

"True?" William gasped, thunderstruck. "You believe me guilty of sorcery?"

"No, of course not." Edward snapped back angrily, then closed his eyes and took a deep breath before continuing in a controlled but angry voice. "I don't equate the use of folk superstition with sorcery. But *they* may. I need to know how to answer the charge."

"I'm innocent!" William shouted, suddenly on his feet, looking Edward in the eye. "Is that not a good enough answer for you?"

"You haven't given me an answer! Who prepared the beguiling charm?"

"Father, I—"

Sean burst into the room, breathless, before William could finish answering Edward's question. "She's not here! There was no sentry on her quarters. I will find out why. I had ordered every sentry to duty with specific instructions to watch after Elinor!"

William felt only a momentary bit of relief at having Edward's attention diverted, but it passed as soon as Sean's words hit him. "Is she with Laurel? Or Agnes?"

"No, they have not seen her," Sean answered.

"Geoffrey." William suddenly remembered. "She would have gone back to see him. She said she would call on him tonight. I know she's there helping ready Nora for burial."

"Would she go alone?" Sean asked, alarm in his voice.

"She saw the hunters today," William answered. "I'm sure she had the sense to ask someone to go with her. Are all the sentries accounted for?"

"No, I could not find Richard."

"Perhaps he is with her," William said hopefully. "Then she's not alone. That's good."

Sean gave him a skeptical look.

"I take it you're not convinced that she is safe with

Richard?"

"No, Will. I'm not." Sean glanced in Edward's direction, then back to William. "I hate to disagree with you." He took a step closer to William. "I've trusted your judgment in the past, but right now, the way I see it, all that stands between you and disaster is the son of the man who is trying to destroy you. That, somehow, does not fill me with a warm, content feeling. If Richard fails to protect Elinor, the way he's failed you in the past—"

William raised his hand to quiet Sean's argument, the truth to Sean's words ringing loud and clear in his ears. "I see your point." He turned to Edward. "She's at Geoffrey's. I'm sure we'll find Elinor there, Father."

Edward nodded his agreement. "Sean, go, find her. Bring her back here, immediately."

"I'll go with you." William jumped to his feet to follow Sean.

"No! Have you lost your mind?" Sean spun around on William. "They're going to be looking for you. That's not Ambrose Woodhall out there. Those are the king's hunters!"

"I've faced hunters before." William yelled and moved past Sean to the door.

"Not when they've been looking for *you*." Sean ran past, then jumped in front of William. "This is not the time for reckless heroics!"

William raised his hands to push Sean aside. "It's Elinor!"

Sean grabbed William by the arms, pushing his back against the wall, holding him firm. "Not this time!"

William stared at Sean, stunned at the fierce look in his eye. "Sean—" He pushed against him but Sean held firm. "Let me go, will you!"

"Not this time." Sean tightened his grip. "Don't play champion tonight, Will. It's too dangerous."

"Sean—"

"Stand down, William! Sean is right." Edward placed his hand on William's shoulder and lowered his voice. "Not this time."

William looked from Sean to Edward and relented in frustration. "Fine. You win." He stopped fighting against Sean's grip, but Sean still would not let go. "You can release me now. I said you win!"

"Promise me you will not follow me."

He held William's arms tighter, staring him straight in the eye with his famous 'or else' look. William was sure the look was not an idle threat this time. "Promise, or I swear I will shackle you to the wall, myself."

"I promise. Now, please, let me go."

Sean released him and stood back, taking a long breath. "I'm sorry, Will. You made me your captain, after all. Your protection comes first."

William accepted Sean's hand. "I suppose I have to get used to that." He half smiled. "Watch your back, Sean. The hunters will be out at moon set."

"And I'll keep them off your back, Will." Sean placed his fist over his heart and nodded to William. "I promise. As your captain... and as your friend."

"I'm counting on it." William mimicked the motion with his own hand over his heart. *As my captain, my brother.* "Sean..."

Sean turned to look at William, one hand on the door.

"Yes?"

William fumbled for his words before he said, "Be careful." It was far less than he wanted to say. *Brother...*

Sean made a quick nod. "Absolutely." He opened the door and left William and Edward alone in the suite.

With Sean gone, Edward turned his attention again to William. "Now, it is of no matter to me if you choose to believe in an old folk superstition, but it is exactly the sort of thing that could sway the minds of these fanatics. Please, assure me on this. Should the worst come, there is nothing *compromising* to be discovered that I cannot defend."

William stared at Edward, feeling the fire raise in his face again. He suddenly felt as though he had been reduced to the young boy who had first arrived in Drumoak, instead of the fully grown man who had just been made Earl of Sutherland.

"Compromising?" William asked angrily. "Do you tell me you would not defend me if there were something *compromising* to discover of me? I have seen you turn a blind eye on many occasions! You've let innocents be mangled and die without knowing the truths, just to keep arm's length from Dunkirk!"

"They earned their fate! I'm sure the judges do not send innocents to the stake," Edward argued, as he had many times on this subject.

William slammed his fist on the table. "Children? Mothers with babes in arms? How can you be so blind? Do you honestly believe what you have just said?" He turned away from his foster father in anger and disbelief. "How many have you already allowed to die on the stake on far less evidence than could ever be found on me? Would you abandon me to meet their fate."

"Just answer the question!" Edward's patience ran out. He grabbed William's arm and turned him forcibly to look him in the eye. "What are you hiding!"

"Nothing!" William yelled, suddenly not recognizing the man he had called 'Father' so freely all these years. A sudden, sickening revelation came to him. *He will abandon me. Even for me, he won't stand up against Dunkirk.* He turned his back, took a deep breath, then told Edward the only lie he had ever spoken to him since his first day at Drumoak. "There is nothing to be found out about me, Father. It is madness. Thomas is grasping at straws for his revenge. I should think you would see that to be obvious."

"So you don't rely on chicory charms on a regular basis?" Edward asked, in a more reasonable tone of voice.

William turned and answered, "Of course not."

Edward looked on him for a moment before he nodded his acceptance. "I'm sorry, son. I know I'm an old fool."

"Forgive my anger." William looked away, still feeling angry and betrayed.

"Understandable." Edward sat in his chair and stroked his beard thoughtfully for a moment. "We cannot keep this from Mehlyndia, though I do not relish the task of informing her. There could be grave times ahead for the two of you."

"I can take care of myself. I'm more concerned for Elinor, Father. They only want to use her against me." William looked out Edward's window, straining for any sign of Sean and Elinor.

"Perhaps we worry for nothing." Edward spoke quietly. "After all, what is there Elinor could possibly tell them about you?"

He still doesn't believe me! William shook his head irritably. "They will do what they do and they will make her say anything they choose. She will tell them I breathe fire and fly through the night sky if that is what they wish to hear."

"Elinor's not about to lie," Edward scoffed. "I'm confident our worries will be proven wrong. Sean will bring her back, and we'll find a way to get her safely away from here. You'll see, this madness will end soon enough."

William sighed, set his teeth, and turned away from Edward, lacking the will and energy to argue any further. He watched out the window, squinting into the darkness for any trace of movement. The only light he could see came from the cottages of the town. "The moon has set, I suppose we shall see how much truth there was in the monk's warning," William said quietly as he watched the last bit of moonlight vanish from the hills.

Mehlyndia appeared at Edward's chamber door. "What warning? I heard raised voices. What is happening?" She came to stand by William.

He tried to soften the worried expression he knew he wore before she became too frightened. The look on her own face, however, told him he had been unsuccessful.

"William? What's happening?"

"Sit here, there is something we need to tell you." Edward took Mehlyndia by the hand and led her to the table.

She looked from her father to her husband. "Are we experiencing another unfortunate affair of politics?"

"You might say so," William answered, still looking out the window. "Damn, I cannot see a thing outside. It's too bloody dark."

"What is outside?" Mehlyndia looked toward the window.

Edward sighed, loudly. "We have received a warning... a plot has been set in motion, apparently aimed at William."

"Ogham again?" Mehlyndia gasped.

"Not this time." William kept his eyes on the village. In the shadows cast by the house lamps, he caught sight of four vague figures on horseback appearing in the waning moonlight. He strained to see, and found there were several more in other parts of the village. In every part of town, he could see shadowed, hooded figures slinking in the darkness. "There they are," he said flatly.

"Who?" Mehlyndia jumped up, startled. "What is happening?"

"Are you sure?" Edward went to the window, ignoring Mehlyndia.

"There." William pointed out one spot. "And in the shadows there, and near the tavern."

"Will someone tell me!" Mehlyndia ran to the window, pushing William aside to look for herself. "I can't see anything."

William pulled her away from the window. "They've set hunters."

"Hunters?" She gasped and grabbed William's arm.

William brushed away Mehlyndia's hand, intent on leaving the suite to join the search. "Father, I cannot wait around here until Sean returns. I'm going to find them for myself." He moved quickly toward the door.

"No!" Edward stopped him by grabbing his arm. "You gave your word. And I intend to make you keep it. You are not going out there if I have to chain you to the wall!"

"Father!" Mehlyndia cried.

"It's dark. I'll be careful." William pulled away from Edward. "I know how to remain hidden." He turned to leave before Edward could offer further protest. "I can't stay here!"

"William, no!" Mehlyndia suddenly threw herself around him from behind, nearly sending him off his feet.

Exasperated, he stopped. Mehlyndia did not release him, but held him from behind in an awkward, backward hug. "I've stopped. You can let go."

"Swear to me you won't go out there."

"I've already had this fight! Now, if you please, you are making it difficult for me to breathe." William was also having difficulty gaining control of his anger as well.

Reluctantly, she released him.

William stood with his back still to her, pushing his anger away. "I feel as though I am abandoning them to the fates."

"It would serve no one for you to make it easy for them." Edward's tone was firm, but gentle.

"Could we return to our suite for the moment, then?" Mehlyndia whispered for only William to hear.

"Yes, I think we should." He turned to Edward. "Father, we're going back to our chambers. I'll be there when Sean returns."

Richard stood outside Geoffrey's cottage waiting for Elinor to finish helping prepare Nora for burial. She had told him about the hunters that she, Sean, and William had seen earlier that day, and how she had been nervous about being out alone that night. But she had promised Geoffrey she would return. Richard, as well as everyone else who knew Elinor, knew that when she made a promise, she would move heaven and earth to keep it. So, reluctantly, he had agreed to accompany her when she came to him asking for an escort. He waited outside, listening to snippets of conversation that came from the women within the cottage.

"She's finally at rest. It's such a relief."

"Was it hard?"

"He made it quite easy, with his song."

"Song?"

"William; you remember, Hester? We saw him leaving earlier."

The women spoke in soft, sympathetic tones. Richard could see Geoffrey silhouetted in the candlelight as he sat quietly by the window allowing them to do their work. He watched, only half-interested, the shadows of the women, until he heard a strange sound come from behind him.

Richard turned his attention from the conversation inside, listening instead to the sounds of muffled footsteps from the alleys. Several times he thought he heard someone close by and turned sharply to look, only finding darkness and shadows. He looked up the high street, back toward Drumoak. *The street lanterns should have been lit by now,* he thought, *it's far darker than it should be.* He searched the sky and realized the moon had just set past the mountains. Still, he wondered why the light-bearers had not lit the torch lamps along the streets yet. The only light on the street poured through the cottage windows and from the tavern.

Sudden movement across the street took his attention. He heard the unmistakable sound of horse hooves and muffled voices. He strained his eyes in the darkness to see where the noise came from. More scuffling sounds, this time closer and louder. He reached for his sword and unsheathed it quietly. He ventured away from the cottage door, walking ten paces or so into the street, sword at the ready, peering into the darkness toward Drumoak. Out of the blackness, a lone figure emerged, walking in his direction, his sword also at the ready.

Richard proceeded carefully, keeping his eyes locked on the man approaching him. The lone swordsman did not waver and kept a determined and steady pace, walking deliberately toward Richard. "Call out!"

"Richard!" It was Sean who answered. "Quiet!"

Richard relaxed and sheathed his sword. He stood and waited for Sean to meet him. He watched as Sean became more recognizable in the half-light cast by the stars. From behind and to his side, Richard was distracted by scuffling sounds in the shadows. He turned to see if he could identify what was making the sounds, but with the moon gone, it was far too dark in the shadows for him to see. Richard silently cursed the light-bearers for forgetting their duties that night.

Suddenly, the scuffling sounds were drowned by the sound of galloping hooves and blades against scabbards coming from the high street. He turned back toward Sean in time to see a hooded hunter ride out of the darkness. "Sean! Behind you!" Richard yelled and ran toward Sean.

Sean turned in time to see the horseman raise his sword, bringing it down swiftly toward him. Sean raised his blade in time to deflect the blow. The horseman rode past him. Richard ran to Sean's side.

"Go back, Richard!" Sean yelled as another horseman rode out of the darkness. "Get Elinor. Keep her there!"

"But—" Richard protested as he drew his sword.

"Go protect Elinor!" Sean turned and pushed him back. "Do it!" He spun back around in time to deflect another strike. The horseman fled past him toward Richard, then abruptly reared and turned back to Sean's direction.

Richard was halfway to the cottage when he heard blades clashing. He turned to see Sean fending off another strike, a third horseman closing in on his back. Sean managed again to block the strike, but was knocked off his feet as the third horseman bore down on him. Richard drew his sword and charged back toward him. Sean managed to regain his feet but was unsteady as he raised his sword in defense. *He can't fight them alone; like it or not, I'm going to help him!*

"Behind you!" Richard yelled as he saw what Sean had not, the third horseman coming from behind with his sword raised. As Sean turned his head to call to Richard, the horseman brought his blade down sure and swift, knocking Sean's sword from his hand. Before Sean could react, the horseman turned sharp and brought the hilt of his sword down onto his forehead, sending him crumbling to the ground.

To Richard's horror, he was too far away to defend Sean as the horseman reared and swung his blade down a third time on Sean, leaving a vicious gash from his shoulder across his chest.

Richard charged toward Sean, sword at the ready, intending to mix with the horseman. But before he could cover the ground between them, the hooded rider kicked in and sped past him, ignoring him completely. Richard wondered why they would not engage him as well, and why their sole target seemed to be Sean. He raced to Sean's side and knelt beside him.

Sean looked up, dazed and bleeding. "Go back, Richard... get Elinor." He fell back, limp and silent before he could finish.

Richard looked behind him, just in time to see Elinor leaving the cottage. One of the horsemen came on her from behind, scooping her onto his mount. She screamed once before the hunter silenced her with his hand across her mouth. He turned his horse abruptly, made a sharp whistling sound, and charged away toward the prison. Six other horsemen emerged from the shadows and followed the first, away from himself and Sean, abandoning the battle.

Richard turned back to Sean, who lay bleeding in the street, as silence fell around them. "Sean?" He picked him up as gently as possible. "Wake up, Sean." Sean made no response. "Please, my God. Sean!" He lifted Sean and held him firm and headed back to Drumoak as quickly as his burden would allow.

Sean stirred slightly and moaned. "Get Elinor."

"I have to get you back to Drumoak!" Richard quickened his pace back to the castle.

"No... can't let them take her," Sean pleaded weakly.

"I have to get you back," Richard answered briskly, moving even quicker.

"No... warn Will." Sean grabbed listlessly at Richard's arm.

Richard kept to his mission without looking at Sean. "You need help, Sean. I have to get you back. You're more important." He ran past the gate, gratefully gaining the doors of Drumoak.

Laurel stood near the stove, teakettle in hand, as Richard burst through the kitchen door. "Laurel! Quickly, go find Agnes!"

"Sean!" She dropped the kettle onto the stove top and ran to Sean. "What's happened?"

Richard pushed her away. "Get Agnes!"

Agnes appeared at the sound of the shouting. "What's happened? Sean!" She ran to Richard and helped him lay Sean onto the worktable. "My God!"

Laurel leaned over Sean, taking his hand in hers. He lay still and ashen-faced; his eyes were open but glazed, and staring. "Sean, can you hear me?"

Sean turned his head in her direction.

"You're late... you promised to call on me." She smiled miserably through her tears. "I've been waiting all evening." She held his hand tight.

"Forgive me," Sean said, barely audible as Laurel's tears fell onto his face.

"Agnes... he needs help," Laurel cried.

Agnes had already put the large kettle on the stove, and was tearing strips from a bolt of linen.

"Help me with these," Agnes ordered, as she mechanically set about preparing the dressings for Sean's wounds.

Richard impatiently pushed Laurel aside, resuming command of the situation. "Sean, you're back at Drumoak, you're going to be fine. Agnes is here—"

"Elinor..." Sean turned his glassy eyes toward Richard. "Where is she?"

"They've taken her—"

"No... gave... an order... what have you done..."

"I had no choice! They'd have killed you out there."

Sean stared, unseeing, and groaned, "You've killed him, Richard." He closed his eyes and lay still on the table.

William and Mehlyndia hurried to their suite. Before the door was completely shut behind them, she let her questions flow. "Does Father know? You didn't tell him, did you? What is happening?"

"Calm down. No, I did not tell him. What's more, you must not tell him." He took her by the hand and led her to his dressing table. "I have to show you something." He opened the top drawer and removed a small wooden box and a leather-bound book. He held them reverently for a moment before placing them on the table.

"What is this?"

That faraway look, the one she had witnessed on the beach, returned momentarily. "This is my kit. It is very important to me." He opened the lid. Several small pouches with labels, glass vials with cork stoppers, and bundles of dried leaves were arranged neatly in small compartments.

Mehlyndia looked through the kit, not touching anything. She knew Elinor did not like for anyone to handle her pouches and powders and assumed William felt the same. She traced her hand over the cover of the book. It was tooled with an image of a flying hawk. The same image that was on the ring he wore on his right hand—his father's crest. Etched under the hawk were the initials 'W.F.'—William Fylbrigge— the name she knew he preferred over William of Drumoak.

She began to open the cover to leaf through the pages.

William put his hand over hers. "It is not for you to read."

"What is it?" she asked.

"It's my journal. Everything I've learned is in this book, and things I've found on my own. My chants—*prayers*," he corrected himself, "powders, potions, charms, songs." He made an ironic laugh. "Even a few Scripture verses that I find comfort in on occasion. I've made an entry in this book almost every day since Elinor gave it to me the day I decided to come out of the barn." He put the book on top of the box and pulled a leather satchel from the drawer. "I've taken great care in how I've written it." He looked at her shyly. "I've... charmed it."

"Charmed?" Mehlyndia whispered, drawing her hand away from the book as though it was afire and could burn her fingers. "What sort of charm?"

"To keep it private," William explained, rambling in an agitated way that Mehlyndia had never known him to do. "To anyone else who reads it— and no one should— this book would seem like a simple collection of verse and songs... at least I hope so. I'm not especially good at charms,... they always seem to fall short for me... and I've never had cause to test this one." He placed the book and the kit inside the leather satchel, then wrapped a long leather strap neatly around. "If my charm fails, I suppose this book could tell quite a tale. I want you to keep this in a safe place."

"William, you're frightening me." Her eyes were beginning to brim with tears. "What other charms have you—"

"None... a few... But I don't make it a habit," he answered sharply as he checked the leather wrapping one more time.

"Must I convince you as well?" He held out his bundled book to her. "I'm not a sorcerer! My God and yours are one and the same. I thought you understood that. Please don't be frightened of me."

"I'm not frightened of you." She lied, hoping her eyes would not betray her, but feeling foolish at the same time. This was her husband after all, whom she loved more than she could say. She'd known him for years. *But I never knew about Aberdoir, nor Bryndah, and now this! Perhaps I don't know him at all.* She took the bundle tentatively from him and held it with only her fingertips, away from herself. "I'm frightened *for* you."

"With the hunters swarming about, frankly, so am I." He placed his hand on her face and kissed her softly. She recoiled from his touch without meaning to. He looked at her closely with a sad recognition in his eyes. "You are frightened of me."

"No, I'm not." She clutched the book closely, pulled him to her, and kissed him. "I love you."

He nodded. She could see he was unconvinced.

"What is happening? Why are the hunters in Stonehaven?"

"The monk who came to warn us told us they were looking for Elinor," he said, looking out the window into the dark streets. "Sean has gone to Geoffrey's to bring her home."

"Elinor?" Mehlyndia sighed, relieved. "Thank goodness, I thought you would say they were looking for—"

"They want her to give evidence... against me."

She grabbed his hands, her relief turning back into panic as a cold wave sent shudders down her back. "How do they know?"

"They don't know anything." He threw his hands in the

air, releasing himself from her hand. "Thomas is grasping at straws and has unwittingly stumbled onto the very thing that could damage me the most... and Elinor knows the truth."

"But she would never betray you. How could you think that?" Mehlyndia protested, her voice trembling in fear.

"Have you been so sheltered in your little world that you do not understand what could happen to her should they find her?" he burst out angrily, slamming the window's shutter. "You are as naive as Edward! They'll hurt her to get all they need, and when they do, she will be of no further use to them." He put his hands on her shoulders and leaned close to her. "And then they will come for me." He spoke slowly and in a low voice. "Do you understand now?"

Mehlyndia could hardly catch her breath. She trembled fiercely at the wild look in her husband's eye. She had never seen such a look on him before. There was no trace of the self-assured warrior who had stood up to Ogham at their wedding. Instead, he held the look of a caged animal, frightened by the snare, yet ferociously determined to fight his way free.

William pulled her into a tight embrace. "I would give all that is in me to change this, but it is what it is. Thomas has set out to destroy me and he will use whatever, or whomever, he deems necessary. You understand why you must hide this book away? If it were to be found..."

"I *don't* understand." She wiped her eyes. "Why keep it? Why not burn it if it is such a danger?" She grabbed the book and headed to the fireplace.

"No!" William reached to stop her. "You may not understand why, but it's... all that I can call mine. I've put my life into this book. It will be all there is left of me…" He placed his hand on the cover of the book, tracing the hawk. "… if Thomas wins." He took her hand and folded her arm around his book. She hugged it close to her and stared into his eyes.

"Surely Father will not allow them to take you," she whispered, trying to sound braver than she felt.

"He will not stand against them, Melly." He released her, walked away, and leaned on the mantle. "He has so much as told me that. Especially if he learns that I lied to him. I've assured him there is nothing to discover of me." He gestured toward his book. "He can't know. He'll abandon me completely if he learns I've practiced this craft. He says he doesn't equate this sort of folklore with black magic, which it isn't, but still, he won't defend me against the bishop."

"I still cannot believe Father would allow them to take you!" she cried, shaking as she gripped the book. "He loves you. Sometimes I believe he loves you more than he loves me."

"He loves me, yes. I believe that be true enough. But he loves his autonomy as well. He would sooner open the blockade and allow Ogham free reign within the very gates of Stonehaven, than to intercede in a witch trial."

"Witch? No! William, you must—*we* must leave here. Now. Before they come."

"I can't leave until I know Elinor is safe. And where am I to take myself?" He raked his hand through his hair and sighed. "Thomas will follow me endlessly. Am I to hide forever?" He idly stirred the embers in the fireplace with the poker, then turned to her suddenly with a new hopefulness in his eyes.

"But you don't have to hide. You can go wherever you choose. Board the next ship bound to Sutherland. Or better yet, the New World. Perhaps there is peace there. You need not stay where there is such—"

"Not without you." She shook her head. "Not for any reason."

"But—"

"No," she said. "We go together or we stay."

A knock on the door interrupted them. Mehlyndia quickly lifted the lid to her trunk and put William's book deep inside. William opened the door. Laurel stood pale as a ghost in the doorway.

"What is it?" William asked.

"It's Sean," she whispered. "He's badly hurt. Richard just brought him back. He's downstairs."

"My God!" William ran past Laurel and out the door.

"Laurel, what of Elinor?" Mehlyndia grabbed the girl by both arms. Laurel burst into uncontrollable sobs. Mehlyndia released her at once. "Forgive me, I did not intend to hurt you."

"It's not that, m' lady." Laurel took a trembling breath. "It's Elinor. They took her."

Chapter 10

WILLIAM FLEW THROUGH the doors to the kitchen. "Where is he?"

Richard stood over the worktable where Sean lay, a mean gash across his forehead and left eye, and a large gaping wound from his collar to his chest. He bled unabated through the tablecloth that Richard was holding on him. A crimson stain spread on the table, pooling on the floor. Nearby, Agnes tore strips of linen and put them into a kettle of boiling water.

"Sean!" William placed a hand on his neck. He was still alive but barely breathing. "How did this happen?"

"We were attacked on the street," Richard answered.

"Hunters?"

"Aye." Richard turned to William. "Sean approached me as I waited for Elinor to come from Geoffrey's cottage. One of those hooded devils came out of the shadows behind him. I was too far away to stop him."

"Elinor. Where is *she*?"

Richard swallowed hard before speaking. "The hunters took her."

"No!" Rage and panic grew in William so fast he had no time to think of his actions. He threw himself onto Richard knocking him to the floor, his hand going for his nephew's throat. "You let them take her? How could you do that? Do you realize what you've done?"

Richard fought to remove William's hands from his throat. He managed to get a hand up and grabbed William's throat with one hand, gaining enough leverage with the other to roll him to his back, pinning him by the neck with one hand. William struggled to keep his grip, but Richard pried William's fingers from his own neck and got a knee onto each of William's arms, effectively ending the fight. William stared back, furious.

"Get off! How could you let them take her?"

"The last thing I want to do is fight you, but you are going to listen to me!" He put his free hand over William's mouth and sat on his chest, keeping his knees on his arms. "When I saw Sean on the street, I started to go to him but he ordered me to stay at the cottage with Elinor. But there were so many—four horsemen attacked Sean before he had a chance to fight! They struck like a swarm of locust. Four blows came nearly at once, and two more after he was down. I left my post then, but they scattered before I got to them, and they just... left him in the mud, bleeding. He would have died out there had I not left my post, don't you see? When I ran toward him, Elinor came out of the cottage. Before I could stop her, another hunter on horseback was on her, and he just hauled her up onto his horse and was gone *that* fast. So were his companions." He released William's mouth and neck. "I had no warning. I had no idea they were after her. All I saw was Sean go down, so I acted as I have been trained— to defend *my captain!*" He stood up and away from William, extending a hand to help him get off the floor.

William was not prepared to accept such a simple defeat.

He looked from Sean to Richard to Agnes. Frustration and anger mixed with a growing panic. "We cannot just stand here. We have to get Elinor. Do you understand?" He turned to Sean, grasping his shoulders. "Sean! Please, wake up! I know you hear me."

Richard shook his head and placed a hand on William's shoulder. "Will—"

William whirled and lunged again at Richard's throat but stopped himself short, instead knotting his hands in the cloak that Richard wore. "You should have fought!"

"Stop! This will not help him!" Agnes shouted from where Sean lay as she applied hot bandages to his face. "There is no time for blame and anger. I need help! Please."

William calmed himself enough to focus on his injured brother. "Richard, I..." He left his thought unfinished and went to Sean.

"Hold him steady, now." Agnes gave her directions sternly, holding back tears while tending to her wounded son. "We need to remove his tunic to dress the wound. I don't know which of these..." She fumbled through Elinor's kit, picking up and dropping various pouches with shaking hands.

"Yarrow root and barley," William told her automatically.

She looked at him, confused. "I do not know which is which."

"Here, let me." He took the kit from her, reached for the yarrow root and grated a bit of it into the bowl. Next, he added a palm-full of ground barley leaves, giving no thought to the amazed look on Agnes's face. He dribbled hot water into the mixture and stirred it into a paste. "Here, put this on the bandage to draw out—" He looked up suddenly to

Agnes's astonished face. "Agnes?"

"How did you know how to do that?"

Not looking her in the eye, he said, "I remembered—" He gave a quick glance to Richard, then looked away. "Elinor used yarrow and barley on me... when I was hurt."

Agnes seemed satisfied with his answer and turned her attention back to her son, resuming her charge of the situation. William knew she was far more capable with the bandaging than he could hope to be and gladly yielded to her authority. Richard helped them as well and, between the three of them, they managed to stop the bleeding and to clean and dress Sean's wounds.

"He sleeps now but he's bled so much, I fear the wounds are grave," Agnes said, choking on her words. "It's in God's hands now; we've done what we can." The confident, efficient physician she had been moments before melted into a distraught mother as she held Sean's hand to her face and wept openly.

"My God." William stood opposite Agnes, looking down at his companion. Sean's pallid face and shallow breathing told William, Agnes was right; the wounds were far deeper than the lashes on his back had been and ,in his heart, he knew his humble medicinal herbs would be of little help. He gently held Sean's other hand in his own. "Fight, Sean," he whispered, noticing for the first time the bloodstains on his own sleeves and hands. *More blood!*

"He hates it when I fuss," Agnes said quietly, wiping Sean's face with a cloth. "I always tried to stay stern when mending the cuts and scrapes he had as a child." She lifted his right hand, tracing the ghost of scar from an old wound.

"He tried to hide them from me. Even when he broke his wrist, I scolded him while I bound it. I did not want him to know how frightened…"

William glanced at the scar on Sean's wrist remembering how he'd broken it while racing out of Aberdoir with Annlise on his saddle. He did not think it wise to remind Agnes of that at the moment, as she shared Mehlyndia's dislike of Annlise. Instead, he turned to Richard, who stood aside, a pained expression on his face. "Are you unhurt?"

"Aye," Richard answered without looking up. "Why was it so urgent he be looking for Elinor?"

William did not answer Richard; he simply buried his face in his hands and sat silent, elbows on his knees, not having the strength in him to explain the details yet again. Elinor had been taken. There was nothing he could do to change that now, and what's more, he knew at that moment that any hope he had for leaving Drumoak with Mehlyndia that night had just vanished. *The monk was right. They've gained their ground. It's started.*

The kitchen door slowly swung open and Laurel quietly looked in. Mehlyndia and Edward followed her into the kitchen. Simon and Ewan stood silently behind the duke. William did not move from his spot.

Edward stepped to Sean's side. "Severe?" he asked Agnes. She nodded without speaking, still holding Sean's hand. Edward gave her a sympathetic squeeze on her shoulder. "I'm so sorry, my dear. Ewan, would you and Simon please see to it that he is brought to more comfortable quarters."

"Aye," Ewan replied quietly.

"Agnes, I trust you'll stay with him?"

"I would not leave him, my lord" she said, not taking her eyes off Sean.

"Sean?" Laurel called to him softly. "Can he hear me?" she asked Agnes. "He'll be all rightwon't he, Agnes?" She looked around to William, then Richard. "Will?" She sat down next to him on the bench. "Tell me he'll be all right."

"I cannae," William answered her quietly.

"My salon would be more comfortable than this kitchen. Please, everyone, come upstairs." Edward herded the group from the kitchen. When William did not leave his seat, Edward turned back and tapped him on the shoulder. "Come with us, son. There's nothing for you to do here. Agnes will care for him."

William looked up to Edward, then back to Sean. *But he's my brother.* Reluctantly, he stood and joined Edward to leave.

"Will?" Laurel whispered as he stood. "May I go with you, please?"

William held his hand to her.

She took his hand. "Thank you."

Mehlyndia gave William a curious look and glanced at Laurel. "Is she always that familiar?"

"My God, Mehlyndia, don't you see what's happened?" William suddenly turned a furious eye on her, locking his teeth as he spoke. "Laurel is as close to Sean as I am. I want her with us. She's part of this."

"If you insist," Mehlyndia answered in a rather ugly tone. "Bring the child along." Laurel retrieved her hand from William and stood back.

"I do insist." William glared at his wife, completely furious that Mehlyndia had chosen this, of all moments, to display a fit of misplaced jealousy. "And she is not a *child*. She's a full year older than you." He took Laurel's hand again in one of his and Mehlyndia's in the other, leading them both to the stairs. Mehlyndia squeezed his hand.

"I'm sorry, I do not know why I said that." Mehlyndia cried as William pulled her and Laurel along. "Laurel, please, forgive me. That was unforgivable."

Laurel sobbed quietly into her apron with her free hand.

"Thank you, darling." William leaned to Mehlyndia and gave her a quick kiss on the cheek. He gave Laurel's hand a squeeze and hurried them quickly up the stairs, relieved to have, at least, that small crisis under control.

Edward lit all the lamps in his chamber as William, Mehlyndia, Laurel, and Richard filed in. "Are we all here?" He looked about. "Good."

"My lord? Forgive me." Richard spoke first. "Can you explain to me what has happened?"

"William has not told you?" Edward asked surprised.

"Not yet. I had my attention on Sean," William answered, exhausted. He did not feel it necessary to tell Edward about the altercation that had occurred between him and Richard in the kitchen.

Edward looked to Richard. "You were escorting Elinor to Geoffrey's this evening?"

"Aye, my lord."

"I was under the impression Sean gave the order to ensure she did not leave the castle."

Richard cast his eyes down. "I heard no such order. I suppose we were away before it came."

"She knew the order." William shook his head and turned

away. "I know Elinor. She was intent on keeping her promise to Geoffrey to prepare Nora for burial. All the guards in Scotland would not have held her back. She would have slipped out alone if you had not gone with her."

"Aye, she and some of the townswomen were also attending the old woman." Richard looked up at William on impulse. "They were quite moved at your part in her passing, Will."

"What?" William was only half listening, his thoughts only on Sean.

"The women," Richard continued. "Geoffrey told them how easily Nora's passage came when you played the lute and sang for her."

"Oh." William had almost forgotten the event entirely. "This has been quite the day."

"Yes, well," Edward interrupted, "we have more pressing issues to discuss now."

"Yes, we have to go get her!" William suddenly turned to Edward. "We can't just leave her in there. Why are we just sitting?"

"I have no authority in the church, William. I cannot simply go get her." Edward's voice was harsh.

"She was not taken to the church." William held a challenge in his voice. He crossed the room quickly to the window, gesturing angrily toward the prison. "She was taken to the gaol. You *do* have authority, Father! For once, use it before they hurt her!"

"She was taken on authority of the king's deputies. I do not have the right to challenge that—"

"You do! Father, this is Elinor! For God's sake—"

"I cannot invade the gaol in the dark of night!" Edward pounded the table loudly. Laurel and Mehlyndia jumped back at the sound.

"Then Sean and I will go get her!" William yelled wildly and headed quickly to the door. Raising his hand to reach the knob, he came to a dead stop and stood frozen, staring at the blood on his hands. *Sean and I? My God...*

Edward approached him quietly from behind. "William, rash acts of heroism will not stand to help Elinor now." He put his hand on William's shoulder and spoke close to his ear. "It would be suicide for you to go out there, surely you must see that."

"I cannot simply abandon her, Father. Don't you understand?" William turned and faced his father-in-law. "There still may be time to stop them." He tried to push past Edward to the door but the duke held his ground.

"What are you intending? To invade the gaol by yourself?"

"I will walk in unarmed and surrender if I have to. It's Elinor."

"William, no!" Mehlyndia ran to the door. "You are speaking like a mad fool! Or do you wish to be known forever as 'William, the Martyred Saint of Housemaids'!"

"What?" William looked at her, stunned at the venom in her words. "Is that all she is to you? A housemaid?"

"You're not thinking clearly!" Mehlyndia yelled. "You simply can not risk your life for every—"

"Every what?" William railed furiously at his wife. "Every *servant?* Is she too far beneath my *station?* What about Sean? Am I to forget him as well because he's not of my rank? My God! You sound like Bryndah!"

"That's not what I meant!" Mehlyndia cried at his accusation. "I meant... you're an earl, it's too danger—"

"If being an earl means I am to no longer allowed to fight for the people I choose to love in this world, then I will gladly relinquish the title!" William tore the silver crest of Sutherland from his shoulder and threw it to the table. "Take your bloody crest and your title, and relieve me of the burden!"

Mehlyndia picked up the crest and held it in her palm. "That is not what I meant," she whispered again. "William, please... you know my fear."

William stared back; the fear and hurt in her eyes deflated his anger. "I can't just sit here, Melly. Earl or not, I can not abandon Elinor."

"Wait." Edward took the crest from Mehlyndia. "William may have given us the solution." He tossed the crest coin-like, pacing the room. "Yes, that just might solve all of this." Edward spoke softly, as though he were thinking aloud.

They all looked at him, bewildered.

Edward turned to the puzzled faces around him to explain. "My assumption is that Thomas has been motivated by his greed. He wants William's title, and wealth. Suppose William no longer had either. Thomas would have nothing to gain by attacking a commoner; now, would he?"

Mehlyndia's eyes grew wide. "You can't be serious, Father."

"No, Melly, he's right." William felt strangely hopeful for the first time since he had seen the hunters on the street. "Thomas has always wanted everything that I've inherited. He would have drowned me as an infant if not for my father's will."

Edward allowed a slight grin to cross his lips. "Perceptive as always." He looked at Richard, who sat silently next to Laurel. They both held the same incredulous look on their faces. "Richard, would you like to be the Earl of Sutherland?" Edward asked, in a near-comical voice.

"What?" William and Mehlyndia asked together.

"Would I like to be...?" Richard stared at Edward a completely, befuddled look on his face.

"Go ahead, bend your knee before me," Edward told him.

Richard obeyed with a look of great trepidation.

Edward tapped both of Richard's shoulders with his right hand. "I hereby name you Earl of Sutherland. There. Get up, Lord Richard." Edward took the crest and pinned it to Richard's cloak at the shoulder. "Good."

"It looks better on him anyway," William muttered.

"Grandfather?" Richard began, "Please... explain to me what you are about. This is all a farce. Correct?"

William glanced at Edward, not quite sure if he had just been stripped of his title in earnest or as a ruse to confound Thomas. He half wished it to be true.

"Farce? I am quite serious," Edward told him casually.

"What?" William and Mehlyndia said together, again.

"However, it is short lived," Edward continued. "When the dust settles, the title shall return to William."

Mehlyndia and William both exhaled. As much as he longed for a simple life, he admitted to himself there may be more he could accomplish as an earl than he could as a peasant.

Edward stood and walked across the room to his wine cabinet and saw it was woefully empty. "Laurel, we are in need of more wine and perhaps some bread and cheese. Would you please fetch it for us." He smiled at her warmly and added, "Bring enough for yourself as well, little mouse."

She gave a glance to William. He nodded that she should do as Edward asked. "Aye." She reluctantly left the suite.

"Now, then." Edward turned back to the others, he clapped his hands and rubbed them together briskly. "We need to make it known to Thomas that I have just disowned you, my boy. Then we shall see if he is as ready to continue his little vendetta if there is nothing more than perhaps your lute and stockings to take from you."

"Of what has my father accused William?" Richard asked, more confused. "What has he to do with the hunters who took Elinor?"

"God, we still haven't told him." William groaned and sat in his chair, resting his head on his hand. "I'm sorry, Rich. Father, you tell him."

"Your father has made grave accusations, I'm afraid." Edward sat across from Richard to explain. "We assume he's called out charges of sorcery of some sort against William."

"Sorcery? Against Will?" Richard was stunned. "But I thought their target was Elinor?"

"She is nothing more than a pawn to be sacrificed, Richard," William answered wearily. "They want her to corroborate some sort of trumped-up evidence against me. My guess is they could have chosen any number of people for this purpose, but I see Bryndah's shadow on their choice of Elinor. It could have as easily been Laurel." He didn't say it out loud, but if he were to have guessed Bryndah's actions ahead of time, he would have thought Laurel the far more likely target.

Richard toyed with the crest on his shoulder. "Forgive me, but if they have already set the hunters, is it not too late for this charade to be successful?"

Edward sighed. "I admit it may be, but my gamble is that when Thomas learns there is no gain in what he is doing, he will recant the charge. After all, there is no evidence that William has practiced whatever it is Thomas has dreamed he has practiced. There can't be." He glanced at William. "Right?" William nodded absently.

"Father, this is all well and good to protect me, but it does not help Elinor."

"You're right, son." Edward sighed. "We shall send word to the bishop now then. I shall demand Elinor be returned to Drumoak." He looked at William. "It *is* time I interceded."

William relaxed for the first time that evening. "Thank you. I'm grateful beyond words, Father. I only hope it's not too late."

Laurel arrived with the wine and cheese. Her eyes were red lined and swollen, more so than when she had left only minutes before. The tray she carried trembled as she walked toward the table.

Richard instantly on his feet, took the tray from her and put it down. "Laurel? What is it?"

She ignored Richard and ran to William. "Sean is failing." She spoke in a whisper. "Agnes fears he won't see dawn."

William was out of the chamber before anyone could stop him.

Laurel sat at the table next to Richard, sobbing into her

handkerchief, her head reeling with thoughts of Elinor, alone and terrified in the gaol, and of Sean and the wound that would steal him from her just as she was learning what he truly meant to her. *Blessed Mother, why have you taken him from me now? Why?*

Richard placed his arm around her. "Laurel, I'm so sorry. I tried to—"

Laurel pushed herself away, refusing to accept his offer of comfort. *It's his fault! Everything is his fault. He didn't save Sean; he let them take Elinor! And now... Sweet Brighid! Will!* She looked at Richard in horror as the entire gravity of the situation came to her. *I trusted him, and he has let this happen! Sean was right all the time.* "You let them take her!" Laurel growled under her breath.

"Was I to allow Sean to die?" Richard answered defensively. "I thought my duty was to my captain, not the house—"

"Your duty is to William!" Laurel said, pointing toward the open doorway William had just vanished through. "And you have failed him miserably." She felt the crimson come to her face but would not allow the tears to show.

"How was I to know?" Richard threw his hands in the air. "Tell me! How was I to know that the taking of an old house woman could lead William to ruin? Perhaps it is Elinor you should throw your blame on. After all, she knew the hunters were about, yet she bade me take her to Geoffrey's."

"Silence, the two of you." Edward slammed his hand on the table. "No one has been brought to ruin just yet."

Laurel turned to him with a start. "Forgive me, m' lord." She looked down at her hands.

"Grandfather," Richard stammered apologetically. "We

should draft your message. We shall need to have a page deliver it as soon as possible."

"Yes." Edward opened the drawer to his writing table and removed two clean scrolls, a fresh quill, and ink. He thought for a moment, then began to write. "I shall keep this short and to the point, simply demanding the safe return of Elinor and no further harassment of my household." He finished his letter with a flourish, rolled it, then tipped the candle to it and placed a seal with the crest on his ring into the wax.

He readied the second piece of parchment and sat brooding over the blankness of the page. "God bless William for being willing to suffer this humiliation." He set his pen in motion. "Richard, according to this proclamation, you are now the Earl of Sutherland." He rolled up the second scroll tightly and slipped it down inside the other, without putting his seal to it. "But only until the charges are dropped and your father calls off his vendetta."

"Grandfather?" Richard asked. "What if this ruse does not compel my father to relent?"

Edward sat back with a frown, then answered, "Then, Richard, you are to assume the duties that go with the rank."

"Father!" Mehlyndia gasped from her chair by the fire. "You said it was a farce."

"Calm down, my dear." Edward sighed, wearily. "It shall not come to that. I'm confident Thomas will call off his dogs. There is little to fear." He looked at Richard, shook his head, and lowered his voice. "But if he doesn't..."

"God willing, I remove this from my shoulder by the morrow." Richard looked Edward in the eye. "And place it back onto William, where it belongs."

"God willing," Edward agreed and picked up his scrolls. "Now then, we only need to send these to the abbey."

Laurel was on her feet instantly. "May I take them, m' lord? Please? I need to go to the abbey for Agnes also." She blew her nose and forced her composure to return. "She requests a cleric for Sean. I told her I would ask your leave."

"Yes, of course." Edward let out another heavy sigh. "Will you be careful, little mouse?"

"Aye." Laurel wiped her face and straightened herself stiffly.

"Father? Should you not send a sentry? This is dangerous for her." Mehlyndia gave Laurel a worried glance. "Suppose they take her as well?"

"I shall be careful," Laurel answered Mehlyndia and smiled sadly. "Thank you for your worry, m' lady."

"Laurel will raise less suspicion if she is alone," Edward explained to Mehlyndia. He turned and spoke gently to Laurel. "Do you understand the urgency and the danger? Mehlyndia has raised a valid point. If they are merely baiting William with Elinor, the risk may be the same for you."

"Aye, sir. I know the risk." Laurel stiffened her jaw. "But Agnes requires the cleric for the sake of Sean's soul and I will not refuse her. There are two other souls at risk tonight as well, each of them dearer to me than I can speak in words. It is little to ask of me to do this for them."

Edward nodded. "I am impressed with her spirit and courage. Very well. Listen carefully. I want you to request to see only Brother Ian on Sean's behalf. I'm sure he will answer this need. Then you are to be sure to deliver both these scrolls to the bishop himself. You will probably raise his ire by waking him, but it must be done, Laurel. Elinor's and William's lives may well depend on it."

She swallowed hard then clenched her jaw. She would do almost anything for Elinor and Sean. As for William; she would walk through fire. "I'm ready."

"Godspeed to you. Go."

With a deep breath, Laurel took the scrolls from Edward and left the suite quickly. *Blessed Mother, guide my steps.*

Chapter 11

L AUREL WALKED AS quickly and calmly as she could force her legs to carry her, across the streets of Stonehaven to the abbey, clutching her precious burden of Edward's scrolls tucked under her cloak. She did not have far to go as the shadow of Drumoak fell on the churchyard. *Don't be afraid. You're not truly a mouse. Prove it.* She told herself over and over what she had to do. Sean's need for a cleric was her first mission, and it had to be Ian—Edward had been clear about that. She must deliver the letters Edward had written. For reasons she could not explain to herself, she was far from confident that the request to free Elinor would be honored without a concession of some sort. She also had her doubts as to whether Edward's grand charade of stripping William of his rank would actually call off the hunters. *Better to send armed men to fight those monsters and demand an end to this foolishness.* But then again, she felt that if there was the slightest hope the ploy would fool them into ending the hunt, then for William's sake, she was willing to go to the abbey alone in the dark and demand to wake up the bishop.

As she arrived at the door to the vestry, she saw a light shine through the window from inside. *I won't have to wake him after all.* She was not sure if she was pleased by this or not. She took the giant wooden knocker in both hands and banged on the door as loudly as possible. *Please let it be another person who answers... please, not the bishop, please not the bishop...*

"Who comes?"

It was the bishop who came to the door. Laurel fought her impulse to run into the darkness, forcing herself to remember why she had come and that she must be strong.

"I am Laurel May McCary, Your Grace. I've come from Drumoak. We have need of a cleric to perform a Holy Sacrament, sir. I ask that Brother Ian return with me to Drumoak." She amazed herself at how she had managed to keep the tremble from her voice.

The door opened fully. "Come in, my child. Tell me of your need."

The false concern in his voice was evident to the Laurel, but she bowed her head respectfully and entered when told. "Thank you, sir."

"Tell me why you request Brother Ian?" Dunkirk asked in an ersatz solicitous tone. "And who is it that is in need? Lord Edward is well, I hope?"

"Aye, sir, Lord Edward is well," she answered, keeping her voice steady. 'Tis for one of the sentries that I seek Brother Ian. Sir Sean Wilbrun has taken a grave wound and is not expected to last the night." Laurel's painfully real tears welled in her eyes. Frightened as she was, her heart was still breaking. "I request Brother Ian only because they met briefly this afternoon and Sean seemed to enjoy his company." She cast her eyes downward. "He had no other acquaintances among your abbey, but he mentioned to me how Brother Ian had inspired him to reread part of the Scripture." Laurel was embellishing. A risk she thought she should take, hoping a mention of reading Scripture would impress the bishop into granting her request.

"Did he?" Dunkirk raised a doubting eyebrow. "Do you know the passage he was interested to learn?"

"Matthew, sir. Chapter seven," she stuttered out nervously. It was the first thing that came to her mind.

"One of my favorites." Dunkirk gave her a skeptical grin. "Verse three in particular, *'judge not, that ye be not judged'.* Interesting choice."

"Verse one," Laurel corrected, without thinking. "You recited verse one... " She looked up, catching his irritated glare. She swallowed hard. *Holy Mother! What possessed you to correct him like that?*

"So I did." The bishop stood, scowling. "You know your Scripture well for a girl. Who has read it to you?"

"I read it myself," she answered shyly.

"Did you?" His lip curled at one corner. "Prove it to me, and I shall send Brother Ian with you."

"Sir?"

"Prove you know your Scripture." He rocked back on his heels, folding his hands into his sleeves.

"Please sir, there is not much time... Sir Sean... " Laurel's tears brimmed as she spoke. *The pious ass is enjoying this.*

"It won't take long. Finish this verse for me, and I'll send for Brother Ian." He lifted a brow. "Ready?"

Laurel swallowed hard and nodded, completely terrified she had failed her mission. "Yes."

Dunkirk grinned. *"Sanctus, Sanctus, Sanctus, Dóminus Deus Sábaoth. Pleni sunt cæli et tera glória tua. Hosánna in excélsis."* He tilted his head, a wicked gleam in his eye. "Can you finish that for me?"

With a trembling breath, she blinked back her tears and stared in Dunkirk's eyes.

He laughed under his breath. "I didn't think—"

"*Benedíctus qui venit... in nómine... Dómini.*" Laurel held back her frightened tears long enough to finish. "*Hosánna in excélsis.*" She felt the scarlet rise to her cheeks, not sure if it was caused by anger, fear, or contempt, or a combination of all of them, but she would not be put off any longer. "Please, Your Grace, he's dying."

Dunkirk stared down at her, clearly thunderstruck that she was able to answer his challenge. "How is it the sacred Latin spills so easily from the lips of a subservient wench?"

"I finished your verse, please—"

"Answer me!" He shouted at her, causing her to jump back two steps. "And do not attempt to lie. Someone has obviously taught it to you outside these vestry walls. We do not throw the Lord's pearls before swine in his abbey."

Swine? He calls me swine? "Lord William of Drumoak saw to my ecclesiastical training." She answered more angrily than she intended. "He knows the Holy Scripture better than anyone."

"William of Drumoak?" he asked flatly. "The heretic heir to the Duke of Stonehaven? Astounding." He rocked back on his heels again.

She wanted to retort that no heretic would be so knowledgeable in Scripture, but she held her tongue. *I should never have brought him up. God, now what have I done?* Laurel steeled her nerve and made one more plea. She swallowed her pride and clasped her hands together, falling on her knees before Dunkirk. "Forgive my ill manners, Your Grace.

But please, there is not much time. For the sake of Sean's soul, sir, please allow Brother Ian to come back with me to perform the Rites."

He gave her a completely contemptible smile. "I see no reason to deny such a pious request. Especially to one so... *well schooled.*" He clapped his hands loudly, startling her severely. In an instant, a young acolyte appeared at his side, coming from within the bishop's private quarters. "Fetch Brother Ian. Tell him he requires the elements for the Sacrament Extreme Unction." He made a quick, sending motion and the boy hurried away. Dunkirk turned a malignant smile to Laurel. "Now, then. Is that all you require of me this night?"

"No, sir. there is one more thing." She tightened her jaw to keep her trembling under control. "I have a message to deliver from Lord Edward." She held out the scrolls Edward had given her.

"I'm not surprised. What have we here?" He unrolled the first scroll and read it. "I see." He made no expression to give her an indication of his intention. He stood silent for several long moments, contemplating the contents of the scroll.

Laurel was not sure which of the two scrolls he was reading and dared not ask.

Before he read the second scroll, Brother Ian appeared in the hall behind him. "I've come, Your Grace. What do you require of me?"

"There is a man at Drumoak." Dunkirk spoke in a cool, disinterested voice. "You are requested to perform the Last Sacrament. It should only take a moment or two. He'll most likely be dead by dawn."

Just another dead sentry! Laurel fumed that Dunkirk

should take Sean's life so lightly. She turned her face quickly so the bishop would not see the scowl of contempt she knew she wore.

"Oh no! That is terrible news." Ian crossed himself quickly. "Poor man. I shall go at once." Laurel noted that the charity lacking in the bishop's tone was made up for tenfold in Brother Ian's. She was taken aback by his empathy.

"One moment." The bishop stopped him. "Allow me a moment to read this request." He read the second scroll. Laurel was still unsure which he was reading. A slick grin spread over his face as he read.

Laurel's stomach began to turn. She was not quite sure what the response Edward had hoped for was, but she had a feeling it was not the one the bishop would render. *Neither of those scrolls should have made him grin that way.*

The bishop finished reading the scroll and rolled it back. "So, he senses what we are about." He tucked the scroll into his sleeve. "Not that it matters. You may go now."

Not that it matters? Laurel stared at him; she wanted to tell Edward what his response would be, especially to the request to release Elinor. "Sir?"

"You have done your duty, now leave while I am still in a charitable mood." Dunkirk glared at her from the doorway.

Brother Ian put an arm around Laurel and hurried her away while the echoes of Dunkirk's laughter rang through the doorway.

In the privacy of his vestry, Bishop Dunkirk read again Edward's scrolls, laughing to himself. *How pathetic.* Then one after the other, he put the scrolls into the crackling fireplace and watched as the parchment burned to ashes.

From the corner of his chamber, a figure emerged. He had been privy to most of the bishop's conversation at the door. "What was written?"

Dunkirk made a dismissive wave of his hand toward the fire. "Nothing to concern us. The usual plea for clemency for the cook."

"And the other?"

"It would seem they suspect the true target of our hunt. Edward has suddenly seen fit to disown his heir." The bishop beckoned the man to sit.

"Has he? Does that change our plan?"

"Not at all." Dunkirk laughed. "It's obviously a charade. Edward did not put his seal to the order. But we should move quickly. The heretic is apt to run to avoid capture."

"Don't worry. He won't flee."

"Are you sure of that?" Dunkirk raised his brow to his companion.

"Absolutely. We hold his *nursemaid*. The perfect bait."

"I wondered why you insisted on her. Would not someone of his own peerage have made more sense?"

"He has an odd sense of loyalty to his subordinates. He sets them above himself. Particularly his captain."

Dunkirk grinned wickedly. "You have neatly arranged for that obstacle to be alleviated. As you suggested, it was Wilbrun who was the first to be felled by the hunter. I have just sent a cleric to perform his Last Sacrament."

"Excellent. And you have secured the old woman. So, we have all we require to proceed."

"Yes, and more. We've learned something very interesting

this evening. Another log on the fire, so to speak." Dunkirk reached for the wine.

"Have you? Tell me."

"This town is full of gossips." The bishop poured two glasses of wine and offered the second to his companion. "An elderly woman passed on today. She had long suffered fits of delirium I'm told."

"What of her?"

"I have a witness willing to testify how she passed. She doesn't even require *interrogation*, only silver. Easy enough." He sipped his wine.

"How did this woman die?"

The bishop leaned close to the man, as the cat who had cornered the mouse. "He sang to her."

"Interesting."

"I am feeling benevolent. I believe I will honor Edward's request and release the woman." The bishop looked over the rim of his glass, a wicked grin sliding across his lips.

"At what price?"

"More of an exchange, than a price. Him for her. You see?"

"When can we move?"

"With the sunrise."

The man reached across the table and offered a heavy pouch to the bishop. "The second half upon his delivery."

The bishop reached across and took the pouch, placing it in the pocket of his robe. "Thank you, my lord. Your contribution to the church will bring you many blessings."

William sat silently on the stool at Sean's bedside as Brother Ian approached quietly holding a small box in his hands.

William watched the cleric go about setting up the small altar on the bedside table: a small crucifix, two white candles, a small vial of oil, and one of holy water. He felt disconnected to the whole event, as though it were a dream, and any moment he would wake up as a child again, cowering in the barn while Sean patiently coaxed him out into the sunlight.

Ian lit the candles, reciting a prayer quietly over each one. He picked up the water and oil in turn, intoning his Latin benedictions rapidly under his breath.

William watched with a sense of irony. The elements of this ceremony were no different than those he or Elinor would use. *Candle, water, oil. Prayers to the God who made us all, and to the Lady, the Mother of God. It's the same. Why must I hide?* This ceremony was for Agnes's comfort, and William did not wish to offend her by reciting aloud a prayer of his own. But for his own comfort, he recited silently: *Blessed Mother, take thee up this soul and guide him safely...*

Ian continued the rites by laying his hands on Sean, still reciting his prayers in murmurs. *"Per istam sanctan unctionem et suam piissimam misericordiam..."* He poured the water and oil in small doses into a silver dish, swirled it, prayed over it, and then dipped his finger into the mixture to make the mark of the cross on Sean's forehead. *"...Deus omnes praeséntis et futúrae vitae paenas, Paradísi portas apériat, et ad gáudia sempitérna perdúcat."*

Watching Ian bestow the sign to Sean brought a sudden wave over William with such unexpected force, he thought he would drown in his chair. *But that makes it final.* A deep tremble began to worm its way through him as the reality of what was happening fell over him. Impulsively, he retraced the cross Ian had marked on Sean's forehead with his own hand. *Why didn't you let me go with you? There would be no need of this.*

Ian finished his rites and reverently placed the elements back into his kit. He placed his hand gently on William's shoulder. "Do you wish to receive Holy Communion on his behalf? It would be a comfort to your grief."

William could not find his voice to answer this simple, well-intended offer. He didn't want comfort, he wanted answers. He wanted Sean to wake up and wonder what all the fuss was about, just as he himself had done when Edward woke him from Bryndah's poison. He wanted Elinor to come in with a tray of soup and bread and not be suffering God only knew what at the hands of the hunters. He wanted to know why he could only sit helplessly watching life slip away from his closest friend— his brother. *I never got a chance to tell him.* He looked at Ian with his unspoken demands in his eyes. Expecting a detached, disinterested gaze in return, he was thoroughly unprepared to see that Ian's eyes held a look he could only interpret as complete understanding and genuine empathy. He felt the wave come on him again and did not fight it this time.

"Release it, my son. There are none here who will judge you." Brother Ian set the silver dish on the stand to free his hand and knelt next to the stool William occupied. To his own surprise, William welcomed Ian's comfort and surrendered himself to the monk's compassionate embrace. He purged his grief onto the cleric's robe, unabated, for several minutes.

When he had found release, he sat back, feeling both relieved and appalled that he should so freely open himself to this man of the church. He wondered if Ian would so freely offer his consolation and help if he knew of his devotion to the Old Ways; he put the thought aside. Ian had shown him nothing but compassion, and William chose to believe goodness came in all faiths. And in the end, it didn't matter what Ian would think. Sean was dying, and whether he be received by Ian's God or William's Goddess, he would still be dead.

Agnes approached Ian quietly and requested the Sacrament on behalf of her son. Ian blessed her, offered her Holy Communion then, stood quietly embracing her as he had William. "Thank you, Brother Ian." She wiped her eyes and knelt next to Sean.

William knelt next to her. "Agnes?" he asked quietly. "Can you tell me?..." He discovered it difficult to form his question. "Am I to say farewell to my brother?"

Agnes looked at William, her eyes already swollen, now brimming anew, she looked away from him. "It doesn't matter now. He's dying."

"It matters to me." He turned her gently to him. "Please, I swear on my life and all that I am, I'll tell no one if you wish."

Agnes gazed on him through her tears for a long moment. She took his hand and placed it on Sean's shoulder. "Then say farewell to your brother. I regret I never told him. Tell whom you choose. He would have been honored to know." She covered her face in her hands and turned away, leaving William alone at Sean's bedside.

"I'm the one who is honored."

There was only a small window in this room, but it was enough to show that the sun was only moments from appearing in the sky. Sean's breath grew lighter as the three stood over him. Agnes kissed him lightly on the cheek. "God bless you, my son."

William watched as Sean's breathing slowed and finally ended as the first light of the new day came through the window.

Ian made one last sign of the cross over Sean, then reached for Agnes's hand. "He has finished. God be with you."

She nodded and remained in her chair, staring into the lifeless face of her son.

William turned away quickly, not wanting to look at Sean. *This is impossible!* He motioned for Ian to follow him from the room. He was relieved that no one was hovering outside in the corridor, assuming they must be in Edward's suite awaiting word. He was grateful for a moment of privacy. "I want to thank you for your care... in there." He found his words coming heavy. "Sean was... as a brother to me. He is sorely missed already."

"'Twas my honor." Ian spoke gently. "I can see you were very close."

"Do you know how he came by his fate?" William asked, his voice soft but suddenly angry. "He was cut down to protect Elinor, and *me*." He glared at Ian and spoke through his teeth. "And they took her anyway."

"No." Brother Ian's eyes opened wide. He placed his hand on William's arm. "They took her? Then you must leave. They'll come for—"

"Let them!" William brushed Ian's hand away. "She was taken on *my* account. Isaac died on *my* account. Rebecca died on *my* account. Sean— " He lifted his hands, palms up, in a gesture of mock surrender, staring contemptuously at the stains of Sean's blood on his sleeves. "See the bloodstains? It's not just Sean's. It's all of them. Their blood is all over me, these people I care deeply about, and for what purpose?" He closed his hands into fists and lowered his arms, demanding an answer with his eyes from a man he knew could not offer him one. "I've killed my own brother, Ian."

Ian spoke softly, laying a hand on William's shoulder. "None of it is by your own making. Do not carry guilt where you have not earned it."

"Have I not earned it? Sean was out on my order." William looked at the monk's gentle eyes and could not find strength to argue further. *Not by my making? I wish I could believe that.* Exhausted, physically and emotionally, he wanted nothing other than to go up to his bed and sleep for a hundred years. He turned from Ian for a moment to compose himself, not willing to display his emotions further to this man. He took a long breath and abruptly straightened himself up. "Thank you for your kindness, Ian. Do you require me to escort you back to the abbey?"

"I'll go alone. It would not be safe for you."

William offered no protest. "As you wish."

Ian turned to go. After several paces, he turned back. "God be with you, young man."

William nodded. "Thank you." He watched Ian walk away through the corridor. William turned away, heading toward Edward's suite. *God be with me? What God? The one who has just stolen my brother?*

He reached the grand staircase just as the morning sun streamed through the stained glass windows in the east wall at the top of the stairs. The cheerful colors that splashed through the glass as he reached the highest landing seemed obscenely out of place as they danced across his blood-stained sleeves. The light caught in his eye, accentuating the fatigue he was fighting. He paused on the landing, closing his eyes against the assault from the window. "I don't know what more you can ask of me!" His voice echoed in the space around him. He turned his back to the light and dropped himself on the step, huddling his face in his arms on his knees. "God, why are you determined to take them all from me?"

A soft voice came from behind him. "Will?"

"He's dead. Laurel, he's gone." William kept his face hidden on his arms. Laurel sat next to him on the stair and put her arm on his back. "I should have been with him. I should have been on his back... how many times has he been there for me? I should have been... Laurel, I sent him out, alone... " He sobbed onto his knees, unashamed, grateful to have Laurel with him.

"It wasn't your fault."

"It's all mine. I brought it down on him." He finally looked at her, not caring if Laurel saw the streaks on his face. "Sean was struck down by the enemies that *I* earned. Not his own. Sean has not gone recklessly through the country challenging the hunters, the judges, and the bishops at every turn... It's not Sean who Dunkirk regards as 'that heretic at Drumoak.' Had I listened to him and kept quiet... the hunters would not be descending on Stonehaven. I killed him as surely as if I had swung the blade..."

"Will, stop." Laurel took his hands. "You did not kill Sean."

"He died in my service." He balled his fist and pulled away from her. "Just like Isaac. I suppose I can expect Simon and Ewan to follow? Isn't that what guards are for? They've sworn their death oaths to the almighty Earl of Sutherland. Am I to watch them all die? Is that what this title has brought me?" He put his hand on his shoulder, expecting to find his crest, and remembered Edward's charade. "Let Richard keep the bloody crest. It's been nothing but grief to me. I never wanted it, Laurel."

"Sean knew you didn't want it." A tear trailed down from the corner of her eye.

"I'm sure he did." William reached up and brushed the tear from her cheek, ignoring the one on his own. "He knew me well."

"Aye, he did. I suspect he knew you better than you know yourself." Laurel smiled softly and dried his cheek. "You had no secrets with Sean."

"Except one."

"Aye?"

"Did you know he was my brother?" he asked, in a whisper, allowing his grief free reign on his face.

"Brother?"

"I never had a chance to tell him." He impatiently brushed his face with his sleeves. "But he was by far the finest of all my father's sons. I've lost my brother, Laurel."

Laurel put her hand on his shoulder and allowed him to lean on her. They sat huddled together silently on the stairs for several moments before William finally took a long breath and stood up. He held his hand to help Laurel to her feet. "Time to be courageous again. They're all waiting upstairs.

Can't go in blubbering like an infant; now, can I?"

"No one expects you to be courageous all the time." Laurel smiled sadly. "You're only human, and you look absolutely exhausted."

"I am," William admitted, then shrugged. "I'll rest after I tell the others about Sean."

"I'll tell them if you like." Laurel motioned toward his chambers. "Go get some sleep."

"Thank you." He gave her a hug. "But I think I should tell them. Come on. Let's get it over with." He led the way.

The corridor to Edward's salon seemed longer than usual, and oppressively silent. For a moment, he did consider returning to his own bed and allowing himself to drift away from everything. *Plenty of time to sleep later.*

William opened Edward's door without knocking and entered the room; Laurel followed and gently closed the door. Mehlyndia sat quietly watching the sunrise. Edward, Ewan, Simon, and Richard sat silently around the table; it was apparent that none of them had slept. All turned and looked toward William. "He's gone," he told them, simply.

Mehlyndia came to him and they embraced. The rest sat quietly, heads bowed.

"When?" Edward was the first to break the silence.

"At the dawn."

Edward stood and nodded. "I'm sorry, William." His grief was evident in his eyes, but he did not allow it to control him as he addressed the rest of them. "I believe we are all feeling the same loss. But we cannot allow our sorrow to blind us to what may lie ahead." He cleared his throat. "Laurel did a fine service for us in the night, but I fear it may have been in vain as there has been no response from the abbey. Perhaps armed guards would have made more of an impression." He looked at the sentries. "Had there not been the need for the cleric, I would have sent you both last night."

It suddenly occurred to William that he had no idea how Brother Ian had come to be by Sean's deathbed. The news that it had been Laurel who had gone to the abbey hit him full in the chest. "You sent Laurel? She carried the request for Elinor's release? My God! You put her at risk in such a way?" He shouted far louder than he intended. "Is Elinor not bait enough, you send Laurel out as well?"

"You are not yourself this morning, William. Stand down. It was her desire to do so. It was against my better judgment for the reason you call out."

"Nothing happened, William." Mehlyndia sighed. "Laurel returned safe and sound, as you can see."

William controlled his impulse to snap back at Mehlyndia again for the tone of jealousy in her voice. "Forgive my anger. As you said, Father, I'm not myself." William took Mehlyndia's hand, giving it a quick squeeze. "I need some sleep, as you all do, I suspect." He rubbed his eyes. "I'm going to bed."

"One moment." Edward stood at his window, looking into the streets. "God in Heaven!" He waved William to come to the window. "They are returning Elinor! Our ruse was a success!"

William ran to the window to see for himself. What he saw did not fill him with the same joy Edward was feeling, but instead sent a dreadful chill through his bones. "Look again, Father."

"What is it?" Edward's smile faded as he followed William's gaze. "I see," he grumbled. "Perhaps I've spoken too soon?"

William nodded, still looking out the window. "That's too many men for just a simple escort."

"My thought as well."

William gave one more look at the approaching squad of hunters and sighed. "Damn."

"What is it?" Laurel asked timidly from behind William. He moved aside to let her see. "Oh no." She clutched at his arm. "They're just bringing her back... right?"

William turned her away from the window and spoke quietly. "You don't really believe that, do you?"

Laurel held back frightened tears and shook her head. Mehlyndia slowly approached the window and stood beside Laurel, looking out for herself. "So many?" she whispered.

"You two, stay together." William looked Mehlyndia and Laurel each in turn. "Mehlyndia, whatever misplaced suspicions you're harboring against Laurel, put them aside. I need to know the both of you will... "

Mehlyndia grabbed his arm. "What's happening."

William answered quietly. "It's starting."

"What is starting—" Mehlyndia began.

Laurel took hold of her hand, and interrupted. "We're together." Laurel looked at William, then turned to Mehlyndia. "Right? There's nothing for him to worry about."

Mehlyndia stared in surprise at Laurel, then began to cry. "Right. I'm sorry I was short with you before." She looked back at William. "Are those the hunters you told me of?"

"Yes." William led the two women away from the window. "Let's hope I'm wrong—"

"Ewan, Simon, take your positions by the gate," Edward said, turning from the window. "They see fit to bring Elinor back but they send more than a dozen armed men with her."

"Should we place more sentries?" Ewan asked.

"Yes—" William began to answer.

"No," Edward countered. "It would not be wise; they are on king's business."

"You're going to let them in?" William shouted. "You can't be serious!"

"Of course!" Edward shouted back. "However distasteful that may seem to you, we must allow them in, or they will surely send many more to follow." He turned to the two sentries. "Now go! Wait by the gate."

"Stop!" The two sentries stopped short, looking between Edward and William. "Father, there are more than a dozen of them. If you won't fight them, I will." In his rage and growing panic, William reached for the hilt of his sword and drew his blade, making a dash toward the door. "Ewan, rally my guard!"

In a flash, Edward drew his blade and held it at the ready in front of his heir. William came to a halt before his father and raised his blade defensively.

"Do you really mean to challenge me, son?" Edward stared, unblinking.

"I don't want to fight you," William answered, his heart racing. "But you leave me little choice." His hand trembled as he raised his sword. "Ewan, Simon, why are you still standing there? I gave you an order. Rally my guard."

Ewan and Simon stood, silently exchanging glances.

"I gave an order!" William yelled, barely able to keep the

tremble in his hands from finding his voice. *Have they turned on me as well?*

"My lord," Ewan spoke tentatively, "We have not yet reached Sutherland."

"What? Simon?"

"I'm sorry, my lord," Simon stammered, sheathing his sword. "Until we reach Sutherland, by your own instruction, we take orders from Lord Edward."

William could not believe what he was hearing. Ewan and Simon must have understood the danger, he thought, and yet they would stand down to the hunters. "My friends... don't you see... " William lowered his sword and spun on his heel to face Richard. "Richard? Don't you understand what is happening?" He turned back to Edward. "Father?"

Edward lowered his sword and slid it into the scabbard. "Ewan, Simon, take your places at the gate." He gave his orders once again. "Do not challenge them."

Ewan and Simon bowed to Edward and turned to leave the suite. Ewan looked back to William before he left. "I'm sorry, Will." He left, closing the door quietly behind him.

William stood, staring at the closed door. "Do you know what you've done?" he asked Edward, barely able to speak.

"I will not bring a battle onto my own hearth side" Edward answered in a gratingly calm voice. "Or would you have me risk the blood of all those who stand around you?"

William looked around helplessly at the frightened faces of Mehlyndia and Laurel. The sight of Mehlyndia's tear-streaked face and the shaking in her hands tore through his heart like a knife. "No, of course not, Father." Feeling, trapped, betrayed, and completely defeated, he slid his sword into the scabbard. *No more blood.*

"They'll be here shortly," Edward said. "From what I saw from the window, Elinor seems unharmed, William. Our fears seemed to be greater than the true danger." He gave William a pat on the back.

"You still don't believe me, do you?" William shook his head and walked away.

"I believe my eyes."

His eyes, he believes and not me. Blessed Mother, what will make him understand? Will nothing change until he sees for himself? Is that your plan, God? Must I be the one to show him? William dropped himself heavily into Edward's chair. He waved Richard to come to him. "Rich?"

Richard went to William and crouched next to the chair. "What is it?"

"Edward won't fight them." William spoke so only Richard would hear. "I can't fight alone... I want you to promise me something."

"What would you have me do?"

William placed a hand on Richard's shoulder and came as close as possible to him to keep his voice from carrying. "It won't be safe here for Mehlyndia. I want you to take her away from here, far away, to the New World if you must, but as far away as you can."

Richard protested, "It will not come to that."

"Promise me, damn it! I need to know you will take care of her! If I'm to face sorcery charges, they'll come after her next, believing her to be a... consort of the devil."

Richard gave William a disbelieving scoff. "Consort? But you're not the devil—"

"I know that!" He glanced over his shoulder to see Mehlyndia and Laurel looking curiously in his direction. He lowered his voice, then said to Richard, "But you know damned well they'll find a way to prove that I am. And if it comes to that, Mehlyndia is in tremendous danger for the simple crime of being my wife." He took hold of Richard's shoulder and knotted his fingers in his cape. "Swear to me you'll take her away."

"I swear." Richard took William's right hand in his own, a tribute gesture to the blood oath he had made the previous day. "I will take her away."

"Thank you." William relaxed a bit. He gave Richard a grateful, sad smile. "Look on the bright side. You are now an earl." He left his chair to rejoin Mehlyndia.

"What was that about?" Mehlyndia asked him.

"I hope you don't have to find out," was all William would say about it. He turned her to him and looked her in the eyes. Impulsively, he drew her in and kissed her hard, then spoke in a low whisper, "I love you more than I can tell you. You know that, don't you?"

"I know, my love." Mehlyndia put her head on his shoulder. "We shall be free of this madness soon. Father will put a stop to it."

They were interrupted when the knock came. William took a deep breath and turned to the door. Ewan entered solemn-faced.

"They're here, sir. In the foyer. They've brought—"

"Is Elinor unharmed?" Edward asked, before Ewan could finish.

"Aye, she seems well, sir," Ewan answered. "But, they've

also brought—"

"There, you see?" Edward turned to William. "Let's go downstairs and put an end to this foolishness. Come." He motioned for everyone to follow him from the room. Edward left first, followed by Richard and Laurel. William took Mehlyndia's hand and held it tight as they followed the others.

"Ewan?" William asked as Ewan stepped in pace with him. "What else did they bring?"

"Surrender orders." Ewan cast his eyes downward. "My lord, we should have followed your orders. I'm sorry."

"Water under the bridge, Ewan," William muttered, sarcastically. "Save your grief for later."

Ewan livened his step and caught up with Edward to provide the escort. Moments later, they arrived in the great hall, to be met by an entourage of men dressed in the black-hooded uniforms of the hunters. Elinor stood in the center of the men, pale and wide-eyed, but otherwise unharmed.

The hunter in the lead stepped forward and bowed politely in Edward's presence. William's heart sank as he recognized the ferret-like grin and strangely golden eyes of Adrian Tearlach.

"Lord Edward, we meet again."

"Do I know you? Who is it that am I addressing?" Edward remained several paces away.

"I am hurt you do not remember me. We met several years ago when you allowed one of your dogs to abduct my betrothed." He grinned slightly. "I am Adrian Tearlach."

Edward glowered. "I remember you. I remember you cheated in the joust . You tried to kill Wilbrun that day."

"If I had tried that day, he would have been dead—" he chuckled. "—long before now."

Richard drew his sword and rushed toward Adrian. "You son of a—"

Edward forestalled him with his arm. "Hold your peace, Richard!"

Adrian grinned. "Thank you, my lord. I see you are still a reasonable man."

"Not for much longer. State your business."

"Of course, I am here as an official deputy of His Majesty." Adrian removed an official-looking scroll bearing the seal of the cross and shield and opened it. "By authority granted us by His Royal Highness, King James VI by way of proxy of Bishop Gregory de Dunkirk, we hereby order the immediate surrender of William Fylbrigge, forthwith to face charges of—"

"Explain this!" Edward interrupted, grabbing the scroll away.

Adrian stood his ground calmly. "Read for yourself then. I shall not stand on formality. I shall simply order my men to seize your castle and take him out by force."

Edward read the scroll, then handed it to William. He took it and scanned the document. No mention of his title, rescinded or otherwise, was indicated on the order. Edward's gamble had been wrong. Thomas would pursue his vendetta after all. Whether William was earl or commoner made no difference.

He read the words slowly, once, then again, loud enough for Mehlyndia to hear the gist of the charges. "... William Fylbrigge, known to have revealed himself... displayed his dark and satanic craft by ways of speaking... taken control of the will of God-fearing men... tools such as his voice... called to demonic consorts though means of song..." William looked up, mystified, as he dropped the scroll on the floor beside him. "I've not bewitched anyone. This is madness."

Mehlyndia gasped. "How did they find out?" she whispered close to William, but loud enough for Adrian to raise a brow.

"Find out what? There's no truth here!" William snapped at her angrily under his breath, feeling betrayed. "Unless you believe me to be in consort with demons, how can you even ask? Are you to turn on me now as well?"

"No, my love. I... " Mehlyndia threw herself around him. "I'm frightened. Of course I know it's a lie."

William was not fully convinced. He pulled her arms from him, keeping his eyes set on Adrian, who seemed amused with Mehlyndia's panic. William deliberately turned his back to the hunter and leaned close to Mehlyndia, speaking as quietly as possible. "Say no more. They will construe anything you say against me. I only hope Tearlach did not hear you just now. You may have just sealed my fate. Please, stand back with Laurel."

Mehlyndia stared at the hunter as she took several steps backwards to where Laurel stood, ashen-faced and silent. "I love you," she spoke silently. William answered in kind then slowly turned around to face Adrian.

"Are you quite finished?" Adrian yawned. "As you can see, we have other business to address." He nodded toward Elinor. "Lord Edward, you will be pleased to learn that your request for the return of this woman has been granted. She has been questioned, and her testimony noted as corroborative to the charge set forth against him."

Elinor's eyes grew wide. "I told you nothing! You lie!"

The hunter closest to her pushed her roughly to the floor. "Silence!"

"Leave her alone!" William moved toward the hunter quickly, his hand going for his sword, but Richard held him back. "I'm over here! I'm the one you're here for, let her go!" he yelled through clenched teeth as he tried to push himself past Richard.

"Stand down!" Edward turned and glared at William.

William reluctantly held his place behind Richard, his hand on his sword, still ready to fight. He looked at Elinor to see if she was hurt.

She looked back to him, her face pale and frightened, but also determined. "Stay back," she mouthed silently from behind Adrian.

Edward growled. "If you have come to return her, then do so and leave us!"

"There is one condition to her release." Adrian took a step forward and grinned.

Edward met Adrian's eyes, unwavering. "What is your price?"

"You've read the arrest charge." Adrian stared Edward down and pointed toward William. "She will be released only upon his surrender." He motioned to two of the hunters behind Elinor. One pulled her arms roughly behind her while the other secured them with a leather strap. They pushed her down to kneel on the floor. Another stood threateningly behind her, his sword in hand. Adrian leered at Edward. "It's your choice, of course. One or the other shall remain with you. I care not which you choose." He signaled to the swordsman behind Elinor, who raised his sword above her.

"The charges are false! They have been contrived out of treachery."

"Then he shall have nothing to fear in surrendering. He will merely be questioned and when we are satisfied of his innocence, why, of course, he shall be returned to you."

"Give me that guarantee," Edward challenged.

"Father—" William turned sharply to Edward. *He believes them! He's going to stand aside.* "Don't make bargains with that bastard!"

Edward raised his hand to silence William's protests without taking his eyes away from Adrian. "Give me your assurance that he will only be questioned, then returned."

William felt his heart sink. He knew what it meant to be *merely questioned* by hunters. After everything he had argued to him over the years, Edward still did not believe what he had told him of the prisons and trials. *He's going to allow it.*

"You have my solemn word." Adrian placed his hand on his heart. "However, know that we are ordered to take him, willingly or otherwise, by whatever means I deem necessary." He turned to William. "What say you, rabbit? Will you make it difficult by trying to flee into the mists as you have done before?"

William stood silent. *Father, don't believe them! They'll say anything.*

Adrian shrugged his shoulders at William's silence. "We have no further use for this woman and have been given leave to dispose of her at our pleasure." He signaled to the swordsman, who raised the sword higher, ready to bring it down on Elinor. Adrian looked directly at William. "Her life is in your hands."

William's mind raced through thousands of words, trying to find the ones that would make all this end. *No more blood! Not again, not for me. Never again.* He looked at Elinor's terrified expression and suddenly it wasn't Elinor he saw, but Rebecca who was held by the hunters, screaming to him to run away. He heard her cries as the fire consumed her as he stood and watched. *I can stop this here.* His heart beat hard in his chest as the only solution to the situation crept on him like a shadow, the decision made in a blink of an eye. Edward would not resist them and William would allow no more bloodshed on his account. He placed his hand on the hilt of his sword and drew the blade from the scabbard slowly. "Richard, stand aside." Richard raised a startled brow to him but obeyed and took two paces to the side.

The swordsman raised his sword slightly higher above Elinor, not taking his eyes from William. "Do you challenge?"

William stood fast, sword in hand, jaw tense, not turning his eyes from the swordsman. He raised his sword out before him and held it straight. The swordsman's lip curled in a satisfied grin as he met William's glare and prepared to bring the blade down upon Elinor. "Her blood for yours, then?" He began his stroke.

"Stop!" William yelled, still holding his sword at the ready. The swordsman's blade stopped inches above Elinor's head.

"Lower your blade, Fylbrigge," the swordsman growled. "I shall not stop a second time." He raised his sword again.

William stood, feeling the tremble return to his hand. He held his breath for what felt like hours, hoping Edward would at last take a stand, but as he had known and feared all along, Edward remained silent. *What other choice do I have?* William took two steps forward, then slowly turned the blade toward the floor. Without breaking his stare, he bent one knee and lay the sword on the floor beside him. He bowed his head, slowly folded his hands behind himself, and remained on one knee. "Release her."

"William, no!" Mehlyndia moaned from behind him.

Laurel cried. "Will, what are you doing?" Her words were lost in Mehlyndia's sobs.

Simon and Ewan drew their blades, ready to mix with the hunters. Richard drew also and jumped in front of William. "I shall not allow you to surrender so easily."

The hunters would not be intimidated or deterred by this pitiful show of defiance. Adrian turned to the swordsman, giving him his order with a dismissive wave of his hand. "At your will."

William looked up quickly to see the swordsman raise his blade once again above Elinor. He pushed Richard aside with such force, it sent him flailing onto the floor. "Stop!" William ran towards the swordsman with a blinding fury and lunged at Elinor, pushing her out of the way just as the sword came down, grazing his shoulder. The strike was not serious, but enough for him to lose his footing. The swordsman recovered his stance before William could regain his feet and in a flash, brought the hilt of the sword down between William's shoulders, knocking his breath away. He fell, dazed to the floor.

"William!" Mehlyndia screamed. She ran toward him. Richard was on his feet instantly and caught her before she could run into the throng of hunters. Ewan and Simon made aggressive moves toward Adrian and the swordsman, but were blocked by several other hunters.

William groped for his breath and attempted to stand, when the swordsman knocked him flat with another blow to his back, putting a foot on his neck and raising the blade above him. "Drop your swords or I end this quickly where I stand!"

"Father, stop them!" Mehlyndia pleaded through panicked tears. "Why don't you stop them?"

Edward stood silent. Richard, Ewan, and Simon were forced to relent as none were close enough to prevent the swordsman from carrying out his threat. They lowered their blades slowly, and William knew the fight had ended. Edward had given him over without challenge.

The two hunters who had bound Elinor moved onto William. One held his shoulders while the other bound his wrists behind him and roughly pulled him to his knees. He struggled to regain the breath that had been knocked out of him when he was struck. The cut on his shoulder stung and bled through his tunic, his own blood now mingling with Sean's on his sleeves. Still dazed, he fought to keep his head clear as he searched for the faces of his family. He found Edward's and waited for him to stand up for him, but he remained silent. In his addled state, he even searched for Sean. *Where are you? You promised to stay on my back!* He saw Laurel, small and terrified, clinging to Mehlyndia, who stood stone-faced while she watched what was happening. "Mel—"

Before William could speak her name, a cold metal strap with a large, flat iron bit was forced across his mouth and chin from behind. He gagged furiously as the mouthpiece was driven past his teeth and secured behind his head with a jarring clank of an iron lock. William cried out in complete fury at what was being done to him, but could only make a muffled growl.

"He has surrendered!" Edward bellowed. "It is not necessary to further humiliate—"

"We have our orders that he is to be bridled. He shall be given no further opportunity to utter his demonic chants." Adrian motioned to the men.

Two hunters brought William to his feet, then half-dragged, half-pushed him out of the foyer. The others closed ranks and followed.

"You gave me your assurance!" Edward called out as William was taken away. "You said he'd only be questioned!"

Adrian laughed wickedly. "And so he shall be put to the question!"

William tried desperately to twist around to look back on his family, but was held fast by the hunters who led him. More angry than frightened, he refused to make it easy for them to move him. He kicked and twisted and struggled every way he could. His jaw ached as he bit down hard on the hateful thing in his mouth, but he used the pain to focus his energy on fighting the men.

"Enough of this." The largest of the hunters came behind William and grabbed his bound wrists, lifting them up suddenly, almost higher than his head, and held them firm. William stopped, instantly dropping to his knee, fearing his arms would come apart from his shoulders.

"It takes very little effort to disjoint a man," the hunter

spoke in a low and threatening voice in William's ear, while raising his arms still higher in this unnatural position.

William released a muffled furious scream through the bridle.

"Now, walk!" The hunter kept William's hands high behind him, pushing him to move.

The walk from Drumoak through Stonehaven to the gaol took little more than a few minutes, but seemed a lifetime. Several times, William glanced to the buildings as he was pushed along, seeing people peering from their windows. Some held expressions of shock as they recognized who the hooded men were pushing along. Others watched in an almost gleeful fascination. Hope turned to despair as he watched the faces of people he thought may rally for him vanish behind shuttered windows and slamming doors. People he had known and had called friends hid from him in fear of catching unwanted attention from the hunters.

With each step closer to the prison gate, and with every face that hid from him along the way, the hopelessness of his situation chewed away at his resolve to fight. As he was shoved through the prison doors and the dank, putrid smell of the place assaulted his senses, he had no delusions that the worst was yet to come, and that for the first time in seven years, he would have to face the challenge alone. Sean was not there to cover his back.

Part II

Chapter 12

28 September 1607

IN THE NAME *of the Lady and the Lord, please bless this one...* Laurel mechanically set about her morning duties in the kitchen. *Blessed Mother, 'tis the third dawn and still no word has come* As she had done almost constantly since William was taken away, she recited her prayers silently, finding little or no comfort in the ritual but clinging to it all the same. The third morning had dawned gray and damp, bringing the promise of rain. She stoked the fire in the oven to take the chill out of the kitchen and rubbed her hands on her arms. *It's so cold here; it's cold there too, I suppose. I hope he's warm enough. What about meals? Is he all right? It's been three days; why has no word come? Blessed Mother, please.*

A little hand tugged on her apron. "Laurel?"

Laurel jumped and looked down. "Oh, Duncan, you startled me." She crouched down to his level. "What is it, little one?"

"Are you still sad?" he asked, his eyes wide.

She answered gently, "Yes, little one. I'm still so very sad. Just like you."

"I'm not sad. I'm being brave." He stuck out his chin. "I'm the man in the family now, Mum says."

"I see." Laurel gave him a tender smile. "You be brave, but it's all right if you feel sad, too. I know you must miss your big brother. I know I miss him terribly."

"Mmhmm." Duncan nodded, then tugged on her apron again. "Laurel?"

"Yes, little one?"

"Doesn't Will'm miss Sean?" His lower lip began to quiver.

"Oh, Duncan. Of course he does." Laurel crooked her finger under his chin. "I'm sure that Will misses Sean most of all."

"Then why did he go away?" Duncan's brave front turned into a heartbroken pout. "He didn't even come to help us put the stones on Seany's cairn after the fun'ral." He dug into his pocket and pulled out a small stone, polished smooth by the sea. "I saved this one for Will'm to put on the very top. When will he be back?"

"He's—" Laurel didn't quite know how much to tell Duncan, but she knew she had to tell him something. "He's away for a— a while. But, you know what? I am absolutely sure that whatever he's doing right now, he'd much rather be here to help you place that stone on top of Sean's cairn."

"Promise?" Duncan sniffed.

"Cross my heart." She pulled Duncan closely and hugged him tightly. *Nicely done, Laurel, you didn't even have to lie. I just hope he doesn't ask.*

"When's he comin' back?"

Laurel sighed. "I don't know, little one."

"I bet it won't be long." Duncan wrinkled his brow in thought. "After all, he forgot to take his sword with him. So he'll have to come back to get it, and then we can put this stone where it belongs."

"Now, how do you know he forgot his sword?" Laurel

smiled, hiding the lump in her throat.

"Lord Ed'rd put it on the wall." Duncan tugged her through the kitchen door to look out into the great hall. "See? It's right over there, right next to Seany's." He looked up at her. "I guess Lord Ed'rd is sad about Sean too, since he put his sword up there like that."

The hearth wall of the great hall— known as the 'gallery'— had long been informally referred to as 'The Wall of Dead Nobles,' simply because all of the portraits displayed there were of the long-dead nobles of Stonehaven. One did not necessarily have to be dead for his portrait to adorn the wall, of course, but the jest among the servants when an earl or baron passed was to say, "So sad, Lord So-and-So has made it to the wall." Laurel remembered how angry the Viscount of Kent had been, on one visit he made to Drumoak, at finding his own face included in the gallery. He had made quite a fool of himself, in Laurel's opinion, insisting the painting be removed until he was properly deceased. As it happened, the man passed away less than a fortnight later from some malady of the stomach that Laurel had always associated with his bad temperament. The viscount's portrait had remained on the wall, and since then a new superstition evolved about the gallery—it was bad luck to hang a living face among the dead nobles of Drumoak.

As lads, Sean and William had made quite a merry game of mocking the stern, serious faces of the nobles in the paintings. None of the painted faces seemed to be quite happy with their lot in life. William would puff his jowls and grimace— 'practicing' he would say— for his 'dead noble' painting. The only portrait he had never mocked was the one of his father, Henry Fylbrigge, who adorned the wall in a place of honor beside a bronze sculpture of the Fylbrigge coat of arms. The elder Fylbrigge's face was as stern and sour as the rest, but somehow there was a trace of mischief in his deep green eyes—the green eyes that all the Fylbrigge men seemed to share.

When Laurel entered the hall with Duncan, she glanced up at the spot where Henry had hung for as long as she could remember and stopped short, catching her breath. Henry had been moved to the opposite side of the coat of arms and, in his place, hung a portrait of William, dressed in common garb, lute in hand, a look of contentment on his face. She had never seen this painting before, but recognized the work as Mehlyndia's. Even more disheartening than its presence; the paint was not yet dry. *But Will is not dead! Why must Edward choose now to hang the portrait?*

William's sword hung just below his portrait with Sean's. The blades had been polished and mounted, crossed over a silver shield William had yet to carry that was emblazoned with the raptors of Sutherland.

"See, Laurel." Duncan pointed to the swords, proudly. "That's *my* brother's sword. Right there on the wall with Will'm's."

Laurel took some comfort in knowing that the lad had no idea of the implication of the portrait hanging with the swords.

"That's a good place to put them. When Will'm comes home, he'll be able to find his sword real fast."

"Yes, Duncan," Laurel whispered, unable to take her eyes from the wall. "Sean would be proud to see."

She knew it was meant as a tribute, but the sight of those swords stole away the last of her composure, remembering the last conversation she'd had with William: *"He was the finest of my father's sons..."* Edward has placed Sean among the nobles, and Laurel was overcome with the image of Sean's deep green eyes looking into her own only days ago. *I should have seen it all along.* She turned quickly from the wall and went back into the kitchen, hiding her face in her hands.

Elinor had come in from the yard as Laurel came sobbing into the kitchen, Duncan shyly following her. "What is it? Laurel? Do you have news?" Elinor asked, coming eagerly across the room.

"No, Elinor." Laurel blew her nose into her handkerchief. "Still nothing."

"Then what has upset you so, child?"

"She's just still sad, Elinor." Duncan put his brave face on. "Sean's sword got hung up with the old men in the hall."

Elinor looked at Duncan curiously. "The gallery? Oh, I'm sure you must be mistaken, Duncan. One sword looks much like the next."

"It's Sean's," he retorted stubbornly. "The one he won in the joust when I was real little."

"Ah, Henry's sword. Well, yes, I suppose it's back in its place—"

"It's not Henry's, it's Seany's!" Duncan insisted. "An Lord Ed'rd put it there because he's sad and misses Seany too!"

"Well, we shall see later." Elinor gave him a pat. "I've got to take this tray to your mum, sweeting. She's not up and about yet, is she?"

"I'll take it to her, Elinor." Little Duncan took the tray

with fruit and bread from the table. "She's still sad too. I think everyone will be sad forever. So I'm going to be brave."

"You've been a good, brave lad for us all, Duncan," Elinor spoke quietly to the boy.

"I'm the man of the family now." He took a breath and carefully carried the tray from the kitchen.

"Poor lad." Elinor sighed. "He's truly heartbroken. He loved Sean very much, you know. And to believe that Sean's been honored on the wall—"

"He's right," Laurel said, pushing back the tide of tears she knew was coming. "Go see for yourself. Be prepared for the sight. 'Twas not Sean's sword alone that upset me."

Elinor gave her a curious look, then pushed the kitchen door open and peered into the hall. "Holy Mother!" she gasped as she came back into the kitchen, covering her mouth with a hand. "Has word come from—"

"I don't think so." Laurel turned away and busied herself with preparing a breakfast tray for Mehlyndia. "It's her work, you know— the painting." She took a breath and tried to sound conversational. "It's really quite charming. And so life-like." She slammed the tea kettle onto the stove top. "Edward knows how we regard that wall! He should not have hung it!"

"I'm sure his intentions were honorable. It's meant as a tribute, Laurel," Elinor argued, but it was obvious that she had not even convinced herself. "Laurel? Sean's sword... Duncan was right. It wasn't Henry Fylbrigge's sword any longer, everyone knows it to be Sean's. Why is he honored among the dead— the nobles?"

Laurel caught Elinor's slip of the tongue. *The dead nobles. You consider Will to be lost as well?* "You shall have to ask

Agnes about that, Elinor."

"Agnes?" Elinor looked at her, confused. "How would Agnes know?" Her eyes opened wide; she had puzzled out the answer. "I do remember there was a rumor that Sean was fathered by someone other than Arthur Wilbrun, but I never believed it." She put her hand on her chest. "Do you think it was Henry Fylbrigge?"

"That should have been obvious to us all. After all, neither Arthur or Agnes, or even Duncan for that matter, have green eyes."

Elinor nodded and smiled sadly. "Aye, ye right. And Sean had that same bold streak in him that Will had— *has*."

That's twice. Blessed Mother, have you bade them all to forget him? "The tray is ready for Mehlyndia." Laurel turned away, eager to leave the subject.

"Will you bring it to her?" Elinor poured hot water into the teapot to add to the tray. "She won't allow me near her. I fear she blames me for everything. "

"She knows deep down it wasn't your fault. It's all this waiting. It's difficult for all of us."

"Three days." Elinor sighed. "Not a word." She looked out through the doorway toward the prison. "I can't bear to think of what may be happening over there."

Laurel followed her gaze. "Nor I." She picked up Mehlyndia's tray. "You would think at least Edward would insist on making sure he's all right." Laurel turned her eyes away from the doorway, not wishing to look at the shadow of the prison any longer. "Elinor? They won't... I mean, not until they prove anything? Will they?"

Elinor looked at her with weary eyes. "I don't know." She

turned back to the door. "They do as they will, I suppose."

Laurel shuddered as she thought about what may be happening to William during his 'questioning' at the prison. "It's not fair! He's a good man." Her face turned red, another flood of tears threatening. "Elinor, I swear I am going to get some answers before this day ends. If I have to resort to breaking into the gaol myself!"

"Don't talk such nonsense, Laurel! It would do him no good for you—"

"*Somebody* has to do something!" Laurel snapped, holding the handles of the tray tightly, her hands shaking in anger. The teacups and dishes rattled loudly as she rambled, "It's been three days! Edward sits in his salon talking to himself, ordering that pictures and swords be arranged on the wall. The sentries wait around for his orders, but they never come. I wish to heaven that Sean was here. He would have taken on those demons by himself. Sean would not be sitting by idly waiting while Will is—" She lost her composure and dropped the tray to the floor with a loud crash. "Damn, let me clean this. I'm sorry, Elinor." She dropped to her knees next to the mess.

"Let me do that." Elinor bent to clean up.

"And Mehlyndia!" Laurel continued her rant, shaking and sobbing on her knees. "Painting pretty pictures, then taking to her bed, ready to accept this as all over and done— even donning a widow's black shawl! He's *still alive,* damn it! Why do they not do something?" She cried into her apron.

Elinor put her arms around Laurel's shoulders. "Child, calm down. There is nothing to be done until they call for witnesses."

"Elinor, has it occurred to you that they won't call any witnesses if he confesses?" Laurel wiped her eyes and looked up.

"Why would he confess to false charges?" she asked, surprised.

"You know as well as I." Laurel snuffled. She took a fresh handkerchief from Elinor and loudly blew her nose. "He's talented. More so than I ever hoped to be."

"Laurel!" Elinor hushed her voice. "You are not suggesting that he's actually guilty? I have taught you better. He would not misuse his gifts—"

"No! That's not what I meant. I know he's not bewitched anyone! That's *their* lie! I'm worried that... he'll tell them about what he's been taught and they'll use it against him. He hasn't done anything wrong." Laurel spoke in an urgent whisper. "Even if he did dabble in the more mystical part of the herbs on occasion, you know it would be for only good purposes. That much you have taught us very well."

"Laurel? *Has* he dabbled?"

"No," Laurel answered quickly. "I don't think so. No, I'm sure he hasn't." She turned her face away from Elinor. "He didn't know—"

"Laurel?" Elinor made her turn back. "What didn't he know?"

Laurel's brown eyes grew wide as she looked at Elinor. "Please don't be angry with me." She bit her lip for a moment before continuing. "Before he left with Edward on the tour, I—"

Elinor stared at Laurel fearfully. "What did you do?"

"I charmed him," Laurel answered quietly.

"What?" Elinor whispered. "Why? What sort of charm?"

"To keep him safe," Laurel answered between sobs. "I didn't want him to get hurt. I was worried for him. It wasn't anything terribly drastic, just a simple protection blessing. He doesn't even know about it. I wasn't even sure it had worked. But then, after the arrow and the poison and everything, it seemed it *had* worked." She rocked on her knees next to Elinor.

Elinor held Laurel close and rocked with her. "How did you place the charm?"

"I blessed his badge. The eagle Edward gave him. The one he was wearing on his wedding night when the arrow— " Laurel buried her face on Elinor's shoulder. "And he had it on his shoulder when he drank the poison, and when you gave him the foxglove. Elinor, even I know perfectly well that was a foolhardy gamble! Foxglove?"

"Yes, I admit, I wondered why the Blessed Lady bade me use it." Elinor pushed Laurel back at arm's length. "It should have killed him! But he recovered. Laurel, child, did you ever tell him?"

"No. He never knew." Laurel sobbed. "I know that it is wrong to charm someone unawares. I know you've taught me, well intended or not, I should have told him."

"Tell me the spell you used."

"I don't recall, it came to me at the moment. I asked that he be protected as long as he wore the badge. I blessed it with tears."

"Your tears?" Elinor asked, alarmed.

"Of course—"

"Blessed Mother." Elinor shook her head. "Child, pray

I worry too much, but I've told you every charm extended comes at a price. The Lady and the Lord do not bestow their blessings for free, my dear. You say you placed the charm for protection and you seemed to have been quite successful, but he's not wearing it anymore. And it was your tears— oh my. Pray the cost is not too dear, for it will surely be due from both of you."

"His world has already begun to crumble, as has mine." Laurel wiped her eyes and rocked back on her knees. "Almost at the instant Edward replaced the eagle with his new crest, the hunters arrived. I only wanted to keep him safe." She buried her face in her apron and cried for several moments.

"Dear, there is nothing wrong in your intentions. It was a lovely thought. But don't ever do it again!"

Laurel gave Elinor a quick hug. "I promise, I won't. But I'm glad Will never found out. At least he won't be able to tell them about it."

"Even if he did know, why *would* he tell them?"

"Elinor, think!" Laurel burst into new tears. "He's told us what they do to make people confess. He's been there for *three* days." With great effort, she banished the unbidden images that suddenly filled her head and set about clearing away the last of the spilled tray. She prepared a second one to take to Mehlyndia and left the kitchen, still sobbing.

Her eyes fell on the new portrait on the 'Wall of Dead Nobles.' *I'll make it right for you— for both of you. I swear on my life, I will make it right. Blessed Mother, forgive me. Whatever tribute you demand, please place the burden on me alone. I meant him no harm*

Elinor sat on the bench, brooding over Laurel's revelation. *She charmed him! How many times did I warn them not to trifle with charms and spells. Why did I ever consent to teaching those two? I suppose it could be worse; a protection charm isn't such a dangerous thing.*

She sat quietly, mulling it all in her mind. It was a logical assumption to her, that of her two young protégés, Laurel was the more likely to venture into the 'more mystical' uses of the herbs. William had taken interest in everything she had to teach, asking questions, memorizing the names of the herbs and the ways they were used. She had to admit, he probably knew them as well as she did by now, but he never seemed to regard any of the magical uses as more than superstition. Therefore, the notion that William would have used the herbs or oils for anything remotely related to the charges he now faced seemed impossible to her. But then, she had never thought Laurel would have secretly cast a charm upon him either.

Still, she reasoned, William surely needed no magical aids to be beguiling when he spoke. That came quite naturally to him. *You're worrying for nothing! I'm sure there's nothing he's hiding, so there's nothing they can make him confess to.*

As sudden as a summer thunderstorm, she recalled the conversation she had with Edward the day he had thrown Thomas out.

"You mean a beguiling charm?"

"No, not exactly, just something to help one find the proper words of persuasion required to gain a favor."

"Well, let me think on what you mean. Of course, it is only a

superstition, m' lord, but I would say that perhaps an oil made from chicory. But in my day, I have not found need to prepare such a charm. But I have heard of it."

"Oh, Blessed Mother!" She rushed to her cupboard and withdrew her kit and threw it open quickly, displacing the contents. "Where is it?" She riffled through her ingredients. "Basil, caraway, cloves, dill— it's not here." She slammed the box and returned it to her shelf, pulling her book down. Just as William's book, hers was bound in ornately tooled leather, though hers was considerably thicker.

She flipped through the pages quickly then stopped, thunderstruck, when she came across the torn stub of parchment in the middle of her book. "Oh, sweet Brighid! William, what have you done?"

Laurel came back to the kitchen. "I left the tray. She probably won't take it."

Elinor waved quickly for her. "Laurel! Come here."

"What is it?"

"Do you know where William keeps his book? His kit?"

"It's probably in his chamber someplace. Why?"

Elinor opened her book to the torn page. "This is why. A page is missing."

"What page is missing?" Laurel asked, alarmed.

"I hope I'm wrong. Dear Mother, what have I led you two into?" Elinor flipped through the pages of her book again. "Perhaps there's a chance he never used it. No, of course he used it! Edward must have suspected as much. That's why he asked about it. The duke, of all people, knowing before I did," she muttered to herself, as though she had forgotten Laurel's presence. "What ruin could this bring?"

Laurel slammed the book closed. "What is missing?"

Elinor took a long breath. "A beguiling charm."

"Will? Why would Will need— oh, no." A horrible realization came to Laurel. "The negotiations. Elinor, if he used it for that and they make him confess— " She clutched Elinor's hand, terrified tears blurring her vision. "Elinor, are you positive? Could it be something else? Something less damning?"

"I admit, I'm not positive." Elinor returned the book to her cupboard. "The Lady grant that I'm wrong, but I'm almost certain that's what was in this section of my book. Perhaps *beguiling* is the wrong word. It's more of the sort of charm used to bolster his own sense of self-assurance, or confidence, when facing a difficult challenge. Or..." She caught Laurel's eye. "...a difficult adversary."

"Such as the Duke of Lothian?" Laurel whispered.

"Aye," Elinor answered, matching Laurel's whisper. "God knows William is persuasive enough *without* a charm, but with it, I dare say he's beguiling indeed."

"Those treaties!" Laurel gasped. "Will told me himself he thought Edward was asking too many concessions from Ogham and that only a fool would agree to them, but he was determined to see them through. Sean was right." She sobbed again into her hands. "He said Will's biggest fear in life is to disappoint Edward. That he'd do *anything* for that man! And look at where it's brought him." The crimson returned to her face as her anger took over. "Edward rewards him by leaving him to rot."

"Hush!" Elinor took hold of Laurel's arms and gave her a rough shake. "You know Edward is distraught over this. He's doing what is within his means to help—"

"What is he doing?" Laurel broke away. "Hanging portraits? Is that how he helps? Edward has his precious treaties; he doesn't care what happens to Will now. He's a beast—"

Elinor slapped Laurel sharply across the face. "How can you think that? He loves William."

Laurel gaped in stunned surprise.

"Oh my dear, forgive me." Elinor placed a now gentle hand to Laurel's reddened cheek.

Laurel put her hand over Elinor's. "It's all too much!" She stared into Elinor's eyes, anger draining away, embracing the older woman and crying again on her shoulder. "Is there a way to put it right? Can we reverse the charm? Anything?"

"Reverse? No, my dear. What's done is done." Elinor rocked Laurel in a motherly embrace, the anger now abated. "I fear William, alone, will come to learn the consequences of what he's done. If, indeed, he has used the charm, the best we can do for him is to keep it between us. It would do him no service for anyone else to know what he's done." Elinor stepped back and placed a hand under Laurel's chin. "That's why we need to retrieve that missing page. We need to find it before anyone else does."

"Find what?" Richard entered the kitchen, startling the two women. He looked at them curiously. "What are you looking for? Perhaps I can help."

"No, I don't think so," Laurel answered, quite sharply. "You've been enough *help* already." She ran past Richard and out of the kitchen. Her only thought was to find William's book to see if Elinor's missing page was in it. She had no idea where to look. *I wish I could just ask him!*

Richard followed Laurel from the kitchen. "Laurel, wait! Please, I'd like to help you."

She stopped on the foot of the stairs and turned on her heel to face him. "If you truly want to help me, then find a way to get me into the bloody prison so I may speak with William!"

"What?"

"I need to speak to him! Is that so hard to understand?"

"I understand that you are upset. We all are—"

"Are *we*? What have *you* done to achieve his freedom today, Richard? Oversee the hanging of his memorial?" She glared at him, pointed toward the wall. "A grand help that is, indeed."

Richard followed her gesture to the wall, then turned his gaze back to her red-faced. He lowered his voice. "You know we cannot do anything until we are called to testify. There are other strategies which Edward and I—"

"So you've just neatly moved into his shoes, then?" Laurel huffed, scowling at the silver crest adorning Richard's shoulder. "Taken over his duties? How very convenient for you that Edward placed that crest on your shoulder. It gives you a lovely excuse to simply sit and wait for someone else to rally. Well, *I* am not content to wait any longer, Richard." She poked Richard's chest with her finger. "If you won't take me to the gaol, I shall go alone."

"You don't understand. I am working on moving—"

"Moving?" She cut him off. "Into Sutherland? He's not

dead. Richard, he's still the rightful earl of Sutherland—"

"Moving Mehlyndia away from here as he swore me to do!" he shouted, silencing her immediately. "I made an oath to him that I would see her away from here. I've been making arrangements to have a ship moored offshore, not far from the seawall." He lowered his voice. "He made me swear to this should he be taken, Laurel, and I intend to keep my vow."

"Taken or dead?" Laurel challenged. "He's still *alive*, Richard. Why do you all so easily dismiss him as lost?" She lowered her voice, pleading. "You should be moving to gain his release from the gaol, not planning to carry on without him."

"I have not given up the hope of his release, Laurel," Richard argued, but his tone was unconvincing.

"Haven't you?" She casually reached to his shoulder, lightly stroking the crest he wore. "*Lord* Richard?"

Richard gently took her hand and looked hard into her eyes. Laurel met his gaze, suddenly uncomfortable with the way he looked on her, as though he were seeing through her. For an instant, she saw the resemblance to William in Richard's green eyes and found she could not look away.

He finally spoke, breaking the uncomfortable link. "I should have realized "

"Realized what?" Laurel pulled her hand away.

"Even Mehlyndia has not worn such distress in her eyes since he was taken." Richard stepped back, a pained expression of his own on his face. "You're in love with him."

Laurel stepped back, unable to stop the scarlet from coming to her face. "Is that so wrong?" she asked quietly, new tears forming on her eyelids.

"Does he return your love?"

"He married *her*, didn't he?" She looked away from him, hiding her traitorous eyes from his sight.

"Aye, he did." Richard gently placed a hand on her face and turned her back to look at him. "But 'tis not Mehlyndia who is asking for help to storm the prison."

"Richard, he doesn't know." Laurel took a breath and brushed the tears away. "I never told him."

"How could he not know? A love so bold does not remain hidden."

She blushed violently and stepped away from him. "Please, let me pass. I need to find something." Her tone left no room for misunderstanding. She would not speak further on this subject with Richard.

He nodded resolutely. "Perhaps I can help you find this thing you're looking for."

"No," she answered shortly and hastily pushed her way past him.

Richard reached out suddenly and grabbed her arm. "Laurel—" Again he took her captive with his eyes.

"What?" She found it impossible to turn away from him. She could see he was wrestling with what it was he would say. "Let me go, please."

"I know he practices Elinor's craft," he blurted, in a harsh whisper.

Laurel gasped and stared, stunned, pulling her arm from him. She stepped backwards and stumbled on the stair. Richard caught her before she fell and held her tightly, leaning over her.

"And I know that you do as well."

"No. You're wrong." Laurel struggled to gain her feet, but he held her firm on the stair. "Let me go!"

"Fear me not!" Richard relaxed his grip slightly. "He confided in me. I know it is a secret well guarded between the two of you." He released her arms and extended a gentlemanly hand to help her up. "Be assured, miss, that I shall not betray that confidence. Your secret shall die with me."

"How could you know?" Laurel tentatively accepted Richard's assistance in standing. Then, finally on her feet, she pulled her hand away quickly, as though the touch of him reviled her.

"It's a long story; please, believe me." He looked to his now empty hand, his face turning red. He turned his palm up, revealing the last healing trace of a slice wound. "I swore a blood oath to him, vowing to keep his secret. Believe me, it is the last bit of information I would want to become common knowledge at the moment." He set his persuasive eyes on hers again. "Please tell me. What are you looking for?"

Laurel stared at his hand, then to his eyes, momentarily caught up in the resemblance, once again feeling captive by his gaze. *Look away. He's not Will, Laurel. Sean didn't trust him. It's his fault Elinor was taken. He could have prevented all of this.* "No, I can't."

"Laurel, please. You can trust me."

"No!" She quickly wheeled around him and ran back down the stairs to the kitchen. *Trust him? No, too many have trusted him already.*

Blessed Mother, please tell me where to turn. She grabbed her cloak from the hook and dashed out through the kitchen yard and away into the street. She ran as fast as she could, half blinded by tears, guided by an inner voice she dared not challenge, that told her to run to the one place she would have least expected to find help—the abbey.

Laurel ran without stopping through the streets of Stonehaven to the abbey, with only one thought in her mind— find Brother Ian. *Yes, Mother. It has to be Ian.* She tired quickly as she ran. Ignoring the pain in her side and chest, she pushed herself onward, driven by the frustration and anger that everyone in Drumoak had seemed to abandon William, and the fear that Elinor's missing page would somehow be found among his belongings. *I have to get in there! I have to see him. He has to tell me where he keeps his book. Edward says he'll take action when he's called to, but if he finds that page he'll stand down.*

She wasn't sure how she was going to avoid the bishop to find Brother Ian. She wasn't even sure she knew why she felt compelled to seek out the young monk, other than he had seemed so genuinely concerned for William's welfare on that terrible night. Her instincts told her that if there was only one soul in Stonehaven who would help her, it would certainly be Ian.

She reached the chapel and collapsed on the steps. She clutched her chest, regaining her breath before running the remaining distance to the abbey. As she sat gasping for air, she looked beyond the abbey to the prison. She had never really taken a good look at the formidable stone structure that was built atop a craggy cliff overlooking the sea. The back wall meshed with the jagged cliffs, towering over the pounding waves and jagged rocks below. The only entry she could see was right through the front gate, which was guarded. The only windows were small and barred and would be impossible to climb through.

Climb through? Stupid thought, Laurel, you don't even know where he is in there. She looked up to the tower turret on the back wall of the prison. She had heard they did not use the tower for every prisoner, only those deemed to be *special* cases. She wondered what 'special' meant, and if it was better to be in the tower or down below, or if it made any difference to the prisoner. She had regained enough of her breath to stand just as the door to the chapel swung out, nearly sweeping her off the step.

"Oh, I'm so sorry, 1 didn't know anyone was there." A pleasant, apologetic voice came from behind the door.

In her great relief, Laurel impulsively jumped up and threw her arms around the young monk who emerged from the chapel. "Brother Ian! 1 am so glad to see you!"

"Miss McCary?" Ian staggered back, startled.

"Yes, please, I was going to the abbey to try to find you." She released him and stood back, blushing. "Will you speak with me please?"

"Of course, of course. But we have to move someplace less open. I have slipped away from my chores and do not wish to be confronted." He took her hand and led her back inside the chapel. "No one else is about; I've checked. We can speak here." He took her to a small alcove near the back of the sanctuary.

"Brother Ian, 1 don't know where to start. I need your help." She fought the urge to cry again; she needed to stay in control.

"Is this about the young earl? I saw them take him out. I have been heartsick about it."

"Yes, Brother—"

"If you please, I intend to leave this calling. Please, I'm just Ian. I have grown weary of the ungodly practices I have encountered among certain clerics."

"I fully understand that." She took his hand, pleadingly. "I hope that doesn't mean you won't help me."

Ian smiled and folded both his hands over her own. "What do you need from me?"

"They've abandoned him." Her voice felt small in her throat. "They only sit and wait to be called to testify. I fear they have all counted him lost." The redness returned to her face as her anger returned. "Please, Ian. I need your help. I wish to see him. In the prison."

"See him?" Ian hushed her, looked over his shoulder carefully, pulling her further into the alcove. "Prisoners are not allowed visitors, Laurel. I don't know how you could get in to see him."

"I have to see him." She grabbed his arm and stared up at his face. "There is something he must tell me, and I have to know that he is well. Please, is there nothing you can do?"

"They've made no contact with the gaolers?" He looked appalled at the notion. "Surely Lord Edward has inquired—"

Laurel shook her head.

"He has not requested a cleric be sent?"

"Nothing," Laurel answered.

"This troubles me greatly." Ian rested his chin in his hand. "After all, it's little trouble to request a cleric attend—" Ian looked down at Laurel suddenly, a light of inspiration in his eyes. He took her face in his hand, strangely pushing her hair away from her neck, and up from her forehead. "Yes, you may pass at that!"

"Pass? What do you mean?"

"Laurel, would you be willing to cut your lovely long locks?" he asked her, a glimmer of excitement in his voice.

"Cut my hair?"

"It may be just the key you need to enter the gaol." Ian looked positively giddy.

"If it will get me into the prison, I shall shave it," she answered, catching his enthusiasm, though she had no idea what he was about.

"That won't be necessary. However, we may need to wrap you up a bit, here." He blushed, indicating her chest. "And we may need to work on your walk somewhat."

"What are you talking about?"

"Have you ever considered becoming an acolyte, my dear?"

"Acolyte?" She looked at him, totally bewildered.

"The young boys who tend the altars and act as page servants, among other duties, within the abbey," he explained excitedly.

"But I'm a young *woman*, Ian."

"Yes, yes, but you are a *small* young woman." Ian stood and circled around, surveying her up and down. "With the proper haircut and clothing, you would look very much like a young boy."

She did not know if that was a compliment or not. She had never considered that she looked like a young boy. "I don't understand."

"Clerics— like me— have free access to the gaol, you see. Often we are called upon to hear confessions, administer rites, and such. It is not uncommon for us to be accompanied by an acolyte on these visits." He sat back, pleased with himself.

"Where are the scissors?" She smiled, feeling hopeful for the first time in days.

"Come this way, quietly." He led her through the back of the chapel to a door that joined the abbey at the back wall. "Be very quiet and stay close to me, now." He took her hand as they made their way through the narrow corridor, up a narrow stone stairway, and down yet another long passage. "Stay back a moment." He peered around the corner. Satisfied that the way was clear, he took her hand again and quickly led her to his room, quietly closing the door behind them.

"This is perilous business we are about. But I am as entitled to the service of an acolyte as any of the other brothers in this abbey. Dunkirk is not familiar with all the boys, so I think we may just slip by." He dashed to the foot of his bed and rummaged through his trunk, as though searching for treasure. "Ah, this is just what I need." He held up a pair of gardening shears. "They are the closest thing I have to barber scissors. I used to use these to tend the herb gardens in Aberdoir. Don't worry, I can use them."

"You know about herbs?" she asked.

"Oh, yes." He beamed at her. "The brothers keep a large herb garden. We use them to make medicine." He leaned around, almost comically, and peered over her head. "Did you know herbs could be used like that?"

"Aye, I knew." Ian's unbridled enthusiasm was contagious, and despite the grimness of her mission, Laurel could not help but to be amused by the delight in Ian's eyes at her interest in his herbs.

Ian held up Laurel's waist-long locks. "I hate to cut this hair. It's really quite beautiful." He placed the hair down on her shoulder. "Are you certain?"

"Do what you must," Laurel answered quietly. "It's only hair. It will grow back."

"As you wish." Ian sighed as he began to clip.

Laurel had never cut her hair, which she regarded as her only attractive feature. William had complimented her, even said she was pretty, one summer day when she had it hanging long instead of twisted up in a braid and secured at her neck as she usually wore it. She had made a point to wear it down more often after that. *He won't think me pretty anymore,* she thought, watching lock after lock fall to the floor.

Ian interrupted her reverie as he prattled on happily about his herbs. "You know about herbs then? That's marvelous. If I were planning to stay, I'd be after Dunkirk for leave to start a garden here in Stonehaven." He lowered his voice, so as not to attract attention, "But alas, lately even the monks have been harassed by the hunters."

"The monks? Really?" Laurel turned to him, surprised. "I should think they would, at least, be free to use God's natural gifts."

"I'm afraid not. We are as fearful as the country folk in that respect." He continued clipping quietly. After several minutes of silence, Ian placed a gentle hand on her shoulder. "Laurel, may I ask, do you know what exactly the young man has been accused of?"

"Yes," she whispered and cast her eyes downward. "They accuse him of enchanting— bewitching with his words." She turned to look at him. "They've even called out his songs, Ian! They claim he uses his own voice as a tool of the devil." She fought to keep at bay the tears that threatened to steal her courage.

"That would explain the bridle."

"Bridle?"

"The metal gag I saw him wearing when they took him away," Ian explained in a gentle voice. "They will make him wear it to prevent him from *enchanting* anyone in the prison." He returned to her hair. "Just a bit more now."

"Ian?" A sudden shudder went down Laurel's back. "It's been three days. Surely, he's not wearing it still." She shuddered, appalled at the thought of the bridle.

"I don't know," he said, but the look in his eyes gave her his real answer.

She turned away from him silently, allowing him to finish his work on her hair. She tried to push the thought of the bridle out her mind as she watched her hair fall to her lap and to the floor. "You shall have to clean this away when you're done."

"I'll take care of it. Not to worry." He made one final clip, then turned her to face him. "There. You are still quite pretty, but you will also pass for a boy." He smiled kindly.

There was no mirror in his quarters, but she did not really care to look at herself anyway. She was surprised that she felt a blush come to her cheeks when he called her 'pretty.' *Sean called me 'pretty' the first time he kissed me. The last time.*

"Now, you will need a robe." Ian spun around on his heel, searching his austere quarters for what he needed. "Acolytes usually wear a simple white cowl and cassock." He quickly removed the sheet from his bed and cut a small whole in the middle with the shears. "You will need to remove your cloak and the frock you wear." His face turned pink. "Put this over your head first." He plopped the sheet over her so that her head poked through the hole in the middle.

As Ian turned around, Laurel wiggled out of her own garments under the protection of the sheet. *I never expected to spend the afternoon undressing in the abbey,* she mused. "I'm ready. You may turn around."

"Now, we need a sash— ah! This will do." Ian pulled the cord from the curtain that covered his window.

Laurel watched, amazed at how he seemed to pull things from midair. *Is he a monk or a traveling magician?*

"Now, we tie this about your waist, gather up here, tuck in there, and, oh yes, your cowl." Ian magically whirled the pillow cover from the bed and cut the closed end off, and plopped that over her head as he had the sheet. "Now, we fluff a bit here, and yes!"

"Do I pass?" Laurel suppressed the urge to laugh at what she imagined she must look like dressed all in the bed linens.

"You would fool your own mother." Ian smiled as he assessed his own handiwork. "Now, we need to give you a name— a boy's name. And you must try not to speak. Your voice is quite feminine, even for a girl."

"Sean."

"I beg your pardon?"

"I should like you to call me Sean. In his honor," Laurel

spoke quietly.

"Very well. Sean, you shall be." He placed his hand on her face softly. "A fitting tribute."

She took a breath and steeled her nerve. "What next?"

"We go to the prison." Ian's smile faded. "Laurel, uh, *Sean*, you are apt to see things inside that you have never known to exist among human beings. Things that should not be allowed to exist. Please, think hard about. You still have time to turn back.."

Laurel blinked back her tears and called up her mettle. "I want to go."

"You understand what you risk?" Ian placed a hand on her shoulder. "You are breaking the law in masquerading as a boy. Should you be caught the penalty is very harsh. Do you still wish to take the risk?"

"Yes." She swallowed hard. "I've come this far, Ian."

"One more thing." He bit his lip. "When we enter the cell, we may find him—" He took her hands in his and drew close to her, faltering for his words as he spoke, "It is not likely to be pleasant. Are you prepared to confront the condition in which we may find him?"

Laurel stared at him closely. *Condition? No, I'm not prepared. But I'm going.* "I must see him," she whispered, determined to prove she would not turn back. She had tried desperately for the last three days to imagine that William sat quietly on a nice little cot, just waiting for his trial, perhaps pacing the floor and looking out the window. She knew that image was only a fantasy, yet she clung to it tightly.

"God guide our steps and grant us strength," Ian murmured. "Come." He held his hand to her. She took it slowly and gave him a resolute nod as they silently left his quarters. Hurrying through the same narrow hallways and stone staircase, they made their way back to the chapel.

"Put your cowl up," Ian whispered. "Should we encounter anyone, do not make eye contact. Allow me to do all the speaking."

Before they left the abbey, they passed by the pantry door. "Wait here, in the shadow." Ian moved her as close to the wall as possible, then slipped into the pantry.

Laurel's heart pounded wildly in her chest as she stood alone in the abbey. *Please hurry.*

Almost instantly, Ian returned to her. He carried a small sack and a water skin which he tied to the rope on his waist, along with the wooden box she had seen him bring to Drumoak. "Ready?"

She took a deep breath. "Ready."

"Here we go." Ian led her through the chapel and boldly out the front door into the churchyard. "Keep your eyes down and walk slightly behind me." He spoke quietly as he walked cheerfully across the yard.

Laurel had to double her steps to keep up with Ian's long stride, but she managed to stay on his heels.

"Almost there," Ian called back cheerfully.

Laurel looked up to see that they were only a few paces away from the prison gates. She had never been in such close proximity to this fortress. Everything about it felt oppressive. Even its shadow seemed capable of devouring her.

Ian merrily came to a halt to address the guard by the gate. "Greetings to you, sir," he said, bowing politely.

The grizzled prison guard greeted Ian with a stern,

growling voice. "What's ye business?"

"Mercy visit. I come to offer the Sacrament and perhaps receive a confession." Ian held up his tools and spoke in a polite, confident manner.

The guard stood at least a foot taller than Ian, had the girth of an ox, and the disposition of a starved lion. His callused and scarred left hand gripped a mean-looking hammer, fashioned on one side with barbed spikes. His right hand— missing the small finger— casually tossed a set of keys. His face was lined and leathered, one eye hideously scarred closed, the other glaring down contemptuously. Jutting his chin toward the quivering acolyte behind Ian, he grumbled, "Takin' 'im in with ye?"

Laurel shrunk down inside her cowl as far as she could, stiffening her muscles to gain control of her trembling.

"Yes." Ian nodded politely. "This is my assistant, Sean. May we enter?"

"Who'd ye come to see?" the guard grunted. "The heretic, or one o' the assassins who was out to get 'im? There be four o' 'em, ye know." He made a cynical laugh.

The assassins are still here? Laurel's stomach tightened as she recalled what Sean had told her of the four men who were eager to collect Ogham's bounty.

Ian maintained his polite composure, though Laurel could see his jaw muscles tensing. "If the one you refer to as 'the heretic' be William of Drumoak, than if you please, he is the one whom I've come to attend."

"If I please?" The guard mocked Ian's polite tone. "Ye ain't likely to get a confession from 'im." He loomed over Ian and spread a rancid, toothless grin across his face. "We been tryin' for days to get one.'"

Laurel made a mousy gasp beneath her cowl. Her knees began to wobble at the sound of the guard's voice. *Trying for days? For a confession? Dear God!* She took several shallow breaths and squeezed her fists under her makeshift sleeves to steady her nerves.

Undeterred by the gruffness of the guard, Ian maintained his self-confident air. "I'm sure my approach will be somewhat different than yours, sir. Perhaps I shall find that he is prepared to make his peace with God. If that is the case, then I am obligated to assist him."

Laurel was astonished at Ian's performance. She began to wonder in earnest if Ian was truly a monk or a street performer.

The guard made a disinterested grunt and casually opened the gate. "Just so 'app'ns you're in luck. He ain't too busy at the moment. Harold will take ye on up." He motioned to another man, equally grizzled but not quite as intelligent looking, who stood just inside the gate. "Harold! Mercy mission to his nibs at the top."

Harold looked up and yawned, displaying a mouthful of rotted teeth. "Right. Come on, then, this way." He motioned to Ian and Laurel to follow him, then turned and ambled through the prison door without looking back at them.

Laurel's heart raced inside her chest as she knew she had reached the point of no turning back. The instant she crossed the threshold into the prison, the door slammed behind her, causing her to jump and gasp loudly. The moldering walls and floor were slick and damp. The smell of the place threatened to choke her. She pressed her cowl across her mouth, blocking some of the smell, as she scurried to keep up with Ian and Harold.

"Ye new here? I don't think I know you." Harold glanced over his shoulder and spoke in a surprisingly conversational tone as they walked through the long, damp corridors.

"Yes. I've only arrived in Stonehaven earlier this week." Ian used a lofty, pious tone. "I like to make it a practice to bring God's mercy to those most in need of comfort."

Once again, Laurel marveled at Ian's performance. *He should be on the stage!*

"Well, there be plen'y o' comfort needed here, I can tell ye." Harold laughed coarsely, his laughter echoing ominously off the walls.

Laurel was disgusted by the relaxed attitude of this loathsome man— as though he were a mere tinker by trade— and how conversant he was with Ian. She imagined him kissing his wife and saying each morning before leaving, *I'll be home early tonight, m' love, only one man to torment today.*

The smell of the place was making her sick. Every odor known to human existence seemed to reside in very stones of the walls. She kept her eyes straight ahead, only risking an occasional sideways glance, turning away terrified at what she would see: cramped and filthy cells with barred doors, shackles hanging from the walls, red-hot iron pikes sticking up out of pits of burning coals, and diabolical looking machines that turned her blood cold to imagine what they could be. Laurel wretched but held her stomach, trying not to hear the moans coming from within the cells. *Blessed Mother, is this place truly Hell?* "Oh!" she screamed as her ankle was suddenly groped by a twisted and filthy claw of a hand. She clapped her hand to her mouth to prevent herself from crying out as she frantically tried to pull herself away from the beast that held her. *Is it human?*

Harold casually turned back and withdrew a short-handled hammer from his belt and slammed it against the door. "Back!" he bellowed, his voice reverberated against the walls. The hand recoiled instantly. Harold shrugged, looking at Laurel. "Don't mind 'im, he ain't learned the rules yet." He snickered and proceeded on through the dark corridor.

Twice, Laurel came close to stepping on a rat that skittered along the wall. Harold merely waved the torch across the floor. "Jus' kick 'em aside if they cross ye."

Laurel wondered how far they would have to walk before they came to where William was being held when Harold finally stopped in front of a huge iron door. He took a large ring of keys from the wall and sifted through them until he found the one he required to unlock and open the door.

"Hope you have legs for climbin'," he grumbled irritably as he led them up the twisted stone stairs.

Laurel realized they were climbing the stairs to the tower she had wondered about. She took no comfort in the notion that William must be regarded as a 'special' prisoner. The air was no better in the tower than it was below. Indeed, she found it even more oppressive as they climbed the seemingly endless stairs. Just as she thought she could not climb another step, Harold finally stopped before an iron door on a small landing. Laurel looked up hopefully to Ian. He glanced behind to her and nodded for her to remain still.

Laurel watched impatiently as Harold fumbled with one of his key rings and methodically sifted through them, taking several long minutes to decide which key would unlock this particular cell. Before he opened the door, however, he took a mean-looking club from his belt.

Laurel shrunk away, wondering what Harold needed that club for. She gasped when he raised it, thinking he was about to bring it down on Ian, but instead he only pounded on the door, sending bone-rattling echoes through the tower.

"Ye best not be asleep in there! You know the rules!" The pleasant conversational manner was suddenly replaced with pure brimstone. "Eyes wide!"

Laurel held her jaw tight to stop the sudden chattering of her teeth. She reached for Ian's hand under his sleeve, astonished that he stood as calmly as he had been the first day they met on the high road.

Harold pushed open the door, went into the cell, and began to yell, "Wake up! I told you, no sleepin'. Look up!" He motioned for them to enter.

Laurel suddenly found she had trouble moving her feet. *Why is he yelling?* She held her breath and followed Ian into the cell, keeping her face down as Ian had instructed her, fighting the growing impulse to run from the tower. She wanted desperately to keep her eyes shut, but at the same time she wanted to look up to see William.

"Would you oblige me, sir, to slacken the chains to allow his arms down please?" Ian asked politely. "And for my needs, I shall require his hands and feet to be unshackled."

"Just hands," Harold grumbled. "This ain't no merry picnic in the pines!"

"As you wish," Ian demurred.

Laurel winced at the sound of metal gears turning and

chains rattling and a muffled groan when the rattling finally ended. She could not bring herself to open her eyes. *Chains? Shackles?* She swallowed hard, fighting the rising bile in her stomach.

"The bridle as well, if you please," Ian requested. "We are in state of grace; no evil shall befall us should he try to utter a curse."

"Yeah, I suppose ye be safe enough." Harold resumed his conversational tone while addressing Ian, but the brimstone returned when he addressed his prisoner. "Head forward!" he commanded.

Laurel heard the scraping of a key and the loud click of a lock, followed by a soft cough. "I'm in no gracious state so dinnae say a word until I've gone out tha' door or it goes back on ya with a rusted lock and I lose the key!" Harold growled before finally stalking out of the cell, slamming the iron door behind him.

Ian exhaled loudly and took Laurel's hand. "Blessed God! We made it." His hand was trembling as badly as her own. He put his arm around her and spoke quietly into her ear. "Open your eyes, Laurel but, please, try not to upset him. Stay calm."

"I'll do my best." Laurel opened her eyes slowly, holding her breath.

The room was so dark she could hardly see, the only light coming from a small window near the top of the wall where only a glimpse of the growing storm clouds shown through. She shivered in the dank air and pulled her makeshift robe tightly around herself as she waited for her eyes to adjust to the dimness of the cell. She strained, searching the cell, until she was finally able to see him. *Will!* She rubbed her eyes to be sure the figure slouched against the wall— knees up, ankles manacled, his arms hanging oddly limp at his sides— was truly William and not a discarded pile of rags. She shivered uncontrollably when she realized he was naked, save for a filthy wrapping about his loins. She pressed her hand against her mouth and turned away quickly. Her knees finally betrayed her and she sank to the floor, biting her fist to prevent William from hearing her cry.

"My God. Ian, why doesn't he say something?"

"I'm not certain he knows that we are here."

"How can he not know? Isn't he awake?"

"I'm not certain about that either." Ian looked over his shoulder to William. "His eyes are open; come on, it will be fine." He held her arm, helping her to her feet.

As her eyes became more accustomed to the dimness of the cell, Laurel saw the empty shackles dangling from long iron chains that snaked across a ceiling beam and ended on a geared spool on the opposite wall. *Blessed Mother! What have you allowed to happen to him?*

Ian knelt quietly next to William, retrieved broad candle from his box, set it on the stone floor and lit it. The light was small, but enough. "Young man? William? It's Brother Ian. Can you hear me?"

William turned his head in the direction of the voice, his eyes glassy and unfocused. "Brother?" His voice was dry and little more than a whisper. He began to cough. Ian took the flask from his belt and held it up for him. William looked at the flask, then looked at Ian and shook his head.

"It's only water." Ian held the flask up again. "Take some."

"I can't lift it," William muttered.

"Forgive me." Ian put it to William' lips for him. "Slowly."

William managed to take several small swallows from the flask before he coughed and began to slip to his side. Ian caught him and helped him to sit up. "Thank you," he whispered, then looked up to Ian. He blinked a couple of times before his eyes widened as if he only then realized the man with the water was truly there. "Brother Ian?"

"Aye!" Ian replied, encouraged. "It is me."

"Is it time?"

"Time?" Ian asked.

"You brought that. Your elements for last rites."

"No, it's not time for that yet," Ian answered quietly. "Unless you'd like to receive—"

"No." William shook his head. "Not yet. Why are you here?"

"We're here to help."

"We?" William blinked and looked around.

Laurel knelt down, next to Ian. He looked at her but did not seem to know who she was.

"Will, it's me," she whispered, straining to keep her voice steady. "Don't you know me?" She moved closer to him.

Ian gently placed his hands on her shoulder and pulled her back a bit. "Give him room, Laurel. He's disoriented, give him time." He gave William another drink of water. "Slowly, there."

William squinted his eyes, looking closely at Laurel. A slow, stunned expression of recognition came on him as he finally realized whom the small face belonged to. "Laurel?"

"Yes." Laurel reached out to embrace William.

"Careful—"

Ian jumped to hold her back, too late to stop her from throwing her arms around William's neck. She withdrew quickly at his sudden cry of pain.

"Laurel, come away." Ian nudged her back.

"Will, I'm sorry, I didn't know." Again her stomach threatened to purge itself as she realized that the dark marks covering William's chest and arms were not merely shadows or tricks her eyes were playing on her. "Burns?" She looked at Ian helplessly, wanting yet not wanting to know what had caused the marks.

"Probably." Ian answered in a soft voice and squeezed her shoulder. "I warned you to be prepared."

"I thought I was." She approached William more carefully. "Will?"

"How did you get in here?" William's voice was hoarse but was becoming a bit louder, and it held a trace of wonder.

"I've come as an acolyte." Laurel tore her eyes from the wounds on his flesh, and forced a steady tone to her voice. "Ian has turned me into a boy." She pushed her cowl back to show him her hair. "I've given up my hair. It was the sacrifice to fool the guard." She forced a smile. "I suppose I truly do resemble a mouse now."

"Never a mouse," he said, still staring at her, astonished. "Still pretty."

Laurel swallowed back her tears, determined to remain strong for William. *No, never a mouse. You are the only one who never called me a mouse.*

"I've brought you some food. I expect you're hungry?" Ian pulled some bread and some soft cheese from his sack, and an apple, which he sliced with a small knife he had also taken from the kitchen. "It is meager and is what I could find in a hurry. I'm sorry it isn't more."

"Hasn't he eaten?" Laurel looked at Ian, horrified at the thought. "All this time?"

"Not likely." Ian cut the apple and cheese into small slices, but when he saw that William was having trouble swallowing, he cut them even smaller. "Better?" Ian asked hopefully, but saw that no matter how small he made the food, William just couldn't seem to swallow it.

"What's the trouble?" Laurel asked Ian when William would not accept the food.

Ian sighed and sat back. "I'm terribly sorry, sir, I should have known." He shook his head and spoke quietly to Laurel. "He's worn that unholy thing the whole time, I fear. The rust causes sores. Apparently, it's too painful for him to eat." He turned back to William and raised the water skin for him. "Drink, then. We have plenty of water."

William gratefully drank all that was offered. Laurel bit her lip again to keep from crying out. *Dear Mother, is this the price you demand from the gift I gave in love? Or is it the price he must pay for the charm he cast? Is either charm such an offense to you that you demand such a cost as this?*

"Laurel has taken a large risk to come here," Ian explained while William drank. "Had I known you had not been attended to, I would have come sooner. I'm so terribly sorry." He bowed his head as if taking the full blame of William's situation on his own shoulders. "Laurel, tell him what you came for, we don't have much time."

Laurel suddenly realized she would have to ask William

about Elinor's book in front of Ian. There would be no privacy, and he would know what she had wanted to keep secret. "Tell me I can trust you, Ian. Before God Almighty, tell me!"

"I take the same risk you do. You have my word," Ian assured her.

Reluctantly, she accepted his assurance. She found it ironic that she was more willing to believe Ian— whom she had only known for a few days— at his word than she was to believe Richard. "Thank you." She looked at William, fighting to remain in control of her nerves.

"What is it?" William asked between swallows.

"Will," she started slowly, "Elinor found a page missing from her book."

William put his head back against the wall and groaned, "Oh no." He stared at her, then dropped his head and began to shake. "I meant no harm. Why must I be damned?"

"No, Will, please look up." Laurel coaxed him gently with her hand beneath his chin. "There is no harm done. But if you've hidden it somewhere—somewhere that it may be discovered—I need to know so I can find it and make it safe if they search. Do you understand? Can you tell me where to find it?"

William looked up and tilted his head, a completely new expression on his face. He looked at her as though he just noticed her in the room for the first time. "Laurel? Is that you?"

Laurel glanced up at Ian, startled and confused. "What's happening? Will? Yes, it's Laurel."

"I worried about that as well," Ian told her quietly. "A

man's mind plays tricks in this place. Especially when he hasn't slept."

"What? Ian, what more do I need to know? Does he even know I'm here?" She suppressed the urge to grab the monk and shake him for answers. William's situation wasn't his doing, she knew, but the monk seemed to be far too aware of what was happening with William's mind. "How do you know what's happening?"

"I'm more aware than you know." Ian did not meet her eyes but pushed up his sleeves to his elbows and hesitantly showed her his own wrists, both encircled with jagged scars. "I was fortunate. I lived to tell with only these as reminders." He pulled his sleeves back down. "Give him a moment, his thoughts will settle and his clarity will return. But be prepared. He's apt to slip away into his mind again. Be patient and careful of what you say."

"Ian, I'm sorry."

She had no answer for him. But the mystery of Ian's uncanny understanding became painfully clear to her as she realized his empathy came from personal experience. But her first concern was for William. Ian was strong and whole yet he had also experienced time in a dungeon, and in this, a new hope dawned upon her. *Sometimes people do survive! Blessed Mother, please let Will be among them.*

"Will?" She placed her hand on his face, her new found hope bolstering her courage. "Where is your book?"

William responded to her new tone and turned to look into her eyes. "Mehlyndia has it, Laurel," he answered matter-of-factly.

"She knows about it?"

Laurel spoke louder than she had intended, startling William. His eyes glazed over, as though he were suddenly afraid of her and he began to shake again. *He's changed again. Be patient.* She lowered her voice.

"I'm sorry, I didn't mean to yell. Mehlyndia has it?"

William nodded.

"I'll ask her for it, then. Don't worry, it'll be safe." She reached for the water. "Here. Have some more."

William drank and took a breath. Slowly, his shaking began to subside. "She won't give it to you. I made her promise but, if you show her..." He looked down to his right hand; it moved slightly, as though he were attempting to lift it, but the effort seemed too great for him, and it lay limply at his side.

Laurel lifted his hand gently. "Your signet ring?"

William nodded.

Carefully avoiding the wounds on his wrists, she gingerly attempted to remove the ring from the small finger where he wore it. But his fingers were a bloody mass of purple and, to her horror, she realized that each knuckle seemed twisted or disjointed. He groaned as she tried, without success, to slide the ring off his finger. She set his hand carefully on his lap.

"Will, I can't get it off without hurting you. The finger is... I think it's broken. Is there anything else I can show—"

"Take it anyway!" The frightened look in his eye vanished, replaced by a staunch defiance— the same look he wore while staring down Ogham at his wedding.

Laurel stared back, startled again by this sudden change. "How?"

"Just pull it off!"

"No! I don't want to hurt you," she argued.

"Take it!" William yelled as much as his weakened voice would allow. "I won't feel it."

Laurel didn't know what to do. She knew she couldn't possibly get that ring off his finger without causing more damage to his already mangled hand. "Ian? What can we do?"

"Let me." Ian took William's hand in his. "Close your eyes and bite. I'll be as quick as possible."

"Do it." William shut his eyes tight and clenched his teeth.

"What are you going—" Laurel gasped.

"Forgive me." Ian held his own breath as he forced the finger straight and pulled the ring from it.

Laurel covered her ears and cried out even louder than William did at the sound of the snapping of his small finger. Ian embraced her from behind and spoke close to her ear, "It's all right, he was prepared, and it's over. I've got the ring."

"How could you do that?" she cried, not looking at Ian.

"Laurel," William called her, motioning with his eyes toward his hand. "It didn't hurt." The streaks on his face and his staggered breathing told a different story. "Give it to Mehlyndia."

Laurel didn't argue, though she wanted to scream again. "That was the first lie you've ever told me, William Fylbrigge." She took the ring and slipped it onto her thumb, trying to regain her brave facade. Ian patted her back and stepped back from her.

"Last lie as well," William answered, between breaths. "Tell Melly I want her to give you the book."

"I'll tell her." She toyed with the ring for a moment, swallowing hard to steady herself. "I'll make this right for you, Will. I promise. I swear to the Blessed Mother, even if I have to walk through the fire, I'll make it right."

"Please, don't say that!" William's eyes went wild and he pushed himself forward, almost falling to her lap. "Never Laurel, no fire." Ian caught him and helped him to sit up. "Let me go, don't let her say that." He began to shake and thrash, yelling as loudly as his throat would allow. "Get out of here now, please far away, run away. . . no fire!"

"Will, stop. I'm sorry," Laurel cried, terrified at William's panicked thrashing.

Ian struggled to help William calm down, but he would not be stilled. One arm raised, then fell to the stone floor, causing the wounds to bleed. He cried out, but still continued his struggling.

"Ian, he's going to hurt himself. Will, stop!"

"Go, Laurel. Run away. Run away, little one " William cried. "Before the dragon comes back."

Laurel helped Ian hold William still. *What dragon is he fighting now?* "Ian, I know what to do."

She pushed him aside and carefully wrapped her arms around William and held his head to her shoulder. He resisted, but she held him anyway and began to sing into his ear the first tune she could think of.

"Alas, my love you do me wrong..."

He stopped thrashing almost at once.

"...to cast me off cast me off discourteously " She gave Ian a hopeful glance; he seemed to understand and began to sing with her. "For I have loved you well and long, delighting in your company." She rocked William gently while she sang, until he finally calmed down enough for her to help him sit alone. Ian continued to hum behind her. Laurel made a note to herself never to mention fire around him again. *Fool, you should have known better.*

William's breathing steadied and he sat back, joining Ian softly in the song, singing in a weak but clear tenor, the last verse. "... for I am still thy lover true, come once again and love me." When he had finished, he dropped his head and quieted completely.

Ian took Laurel by the hand and led her away toward the door. "How did you know to sing to him?" he asked, an astonished look on his face.

"He mentioned the dragon." Laurel wrapped her arms around herself. "He's fought her his whole life. I just helped him find the weapon he needed to fight it."

"Weapon?"

"His music, Ian. It is how he always finds his peace." She answered and went back to William. "Will?" He looked up; the storm had passed leaving no trace of panic in his eyes. "Don't worry. I'll take care of you." She felt the tears come back to her face. "I love you."

William closed his eyes and sat back.

Ian went to the door and listened closely. "The guard is returning."

"Will, we have to leave. I don't know if I can get back in again later, but I shall try." She wiped her eyes. "I'll give Mehlyndia your ring and I will do whatever I can to get Edward moving for you, I promise. Edward will hear more than he ever wanted to hear from me."

"Let him have the rest of the water before they make it up the stairs." Ian told her as he listened to the footsteps approaching. "It's all he'll get until we come back tomorrow."

As Laurel helped William with the water, he looked at her. "Laurel"

"Yes?" She allowed him to swallow the last of the water.

"I love you, too." William looked her in the eye. "I always have."

These were words she had longed to hear for years, but instead of the elation she had always imagined they would bring, she felt her soul being torn apart. Then again, she had always known he had loved her. Laurel leaned close enough to whisper to him without Ian hearing. "Blessed be, beloved, until such time we meet again" She kissed his forehead, as she had when she placed the charm. "May our Blessed Mother and Father guard you."

"Thank you, Laurel." He almost smiled. "You as well."

"He's coming. Quickly!" Ian retrieved the candle, and motioned to Laurel to stand and put up her cowl. She jumped and made it to Ian's side just in time for Harold to get to the door.

"Time's up!" Harold pounded on the door then pushed it open. "Holiday's over. Sit up." He strode in, giving no notice to the monk and the acolyte, and went directly to William.

Laurel turned away, unable to watch as Harold reached for William's left arm with one hand and the shackle above him with the other. She grabbed hold of Ian's hand and held tightly at the sound of William's cries and Harold's grumbling warnings for him to remain quiet.

"Head forward! Open your mouth."

Ian pushed Laurel through the door quickly. The two hurried to the bottom of the stairs where they found the iron door was locked. They had to wait for Harold to finish what he was doing with William.

"It's inhuman! They're monsters! And the bishop who calls himself a holy man allows this?" she hissed through her clenched teeth as she struggled not to lose her stomach on the stairs. "They're killing him!"

"Quiet! He's coming!" Ian hushed her quickly. "You'll give us away!"

"I can hardly breathe, Ian."

She bit her lip hard. Tears covered her face as she stood trembling in the stairwell. Ian pulled her cowl up over her head to hide her face.

"Steady. You've done well, thus far. We'll be out soon." Ian steadied her trembling with his arm about her shoulders.

Harold came down behind them quickly and performed his key search ritual before opening the door. "Bit young for this sort o' work, is he? Ye gets used to it."

He chuckled and clapped Laurel on the back before he led them through the door. Laurel wanted to tear him apart with her bare hands.

When they finally arrived back to the light of day outside the prison, the fresh air that met her face was the sweetest she had ever experienced in her life, but the thought of William still in the tower would not allow her to enjoy it. *Blessed Mother, if it be the last thing I do on this earth, I will get him out of there!* She pulled the cowl further over her face to block the sudden brightness of the daylight.

"God bless you, sir." Ian spoke in his pious tone, addressing the guard at the gate. "Good day. I shall return to attend him again tomorrow, I expect."

"May not 'ave to." The guard nodded toward the abbey. "Looks like they're getting ready."

"Oh?" Ian casually looked over his shoulder. "Oh yes, so I see."

"Been watchin' the carriages come by all day," the guard commented, then yawned.

Laurel stole a peek to where Ian was watching. Outside the abbey, she saw several carriages and a group of people conversing around the bishop. A horrendously corpulent cleric, dressed in the regalia of a high ranking priest, or perhaps an abbot, was offering a hand to a regal-looking woman who was climbing down from an ornate carriage. Laurel's heart went to her throat when she recognized Bryndah. Thomas emerged from the coach behind her. He bowed pompously, took Dunkirk's hand and kissed the bishop's ring. Other men in noble attire were gathered on horseback, casually conversing with each other.

"Won't be surprised if they start buildin' it tonight so long as the weather's good that is." The guard leaned back against the gate, watching the group around the abbey. "Saves 'em time in the end, ye know."

"I beg your pardon?" Ian turned back to the guard.

"You know, buildin' the platform, gatherin' the logs and peat 'n such. Best t' get it done early, then it's ready right away."

"I should think a verdict would be necessary first, sir," Ian replied curtly. "We shall take our leave of you now." He turned to his acolyte. "Come, Sean. We've chores to attend to." He walked away from the gate quickly, Laurel keeping pace behind him. When they were out of hearing range of the guards, Ian leaned to her, saying, "Do not go to the chapel; go around the back, then directly to Drumoak."

"Ian? What was he talking about?" she asked, hurrying along behind. "Is it the trial? Is that—?"

"I'll explain when we get there. Please hurry." Ian practically lifted her off her feet, pulling her along.

They walked as quickly but inconspicuously as possible. They were almost clear of the churchyard when Laurel heard snatches of conversation from Thomas and his gathered throng.

"You must remember him, Joseph?"

"Certainly, I remember him. Untamed little whelp."

"All this was to be expected after all, he has that way about him."

"We shall all be the better for this in the end."

Laurel and Ian cleared the chapel wall and were finally out of view of the gathered group. "Run!" Ian grabbed Laurel's shoulder and pulled her along.

She did not have to be told twice. They ran full out, across the back of the churchyard, then behind the tavern and past the high street, directly to the gates of Drumoak. Laurel imagined they made a curious sight to the townspeople as they galloped across the streets of Stonehaven, but she cared little for anything other than getting back to Drumoak. Laurel managed to overtake Ian and ran directly through the open gate several yards ahead of him, her makeshift robes flapping in the wind behind her. Eyes fixed on the grand doors to the castle, she took no notice of the sentries by the gate and charged past only to be caught around the middle and lifted off her feet.

"Hold on there, laddie. Where is it you believe you are going?" Ewan lowered her to the ground. "You cannot go charging castle walls—" He pushed the cowl away, then stood back, a dumbfounded look upon his face. "Laurel McCary? Is that you? What in heaven's name?" He looked up to see Ian running up behind her, equally fast. "What is all this?"

Laurel replied between gasps, "Ewan, please, we need to go inside. I'll take responsibility for him."

"Go on then." Ewan waved them by, staring open mouthed at Ian. "I should be very glad to hear this tale in full."

"I'm sure you shall." Laurel called over her shoulder to Ewan as she led Ian to the kitchen, where she finally collapsed to her knees, exhausted, terrified, and completely overwhelmed at what she had just accomplished.

Chapter 13

L AUREL HUDDLED ON the floor shaking, her arms wrapped around herself as she at last released all the terror she had held in check during her mission. Ian enfolded her in his arms and rocked with her on the floor.

"Ian, it can't be real," she cried into his robes. "Blessed Mother, it can't be real."

Elinor ran into the kitchen. "What's all this? I heard crying—Brother Ian?"

"Please, something to calm her, dear lady," Ian said, stroking Laurel's shorn hair as he pressed her against his shoulder. "She's terribly upset. She's been incredibly brave."

Elinor poured some ale from a pitcher on the table, then knelt down next to the two. "Laurel, dear, here. Drink this." She looked at the bed-sheet-turned-cassock and gave Ian a bewildered look. "What is this?"

"A disguise, my lady. Please, give her a moment." Ian held Laurel close as he helped her get up from the floor. "I would not have expected such nerves from one so meek. She is astounding."

"What has she been about?" Elinor pushed the cowl away from her face. "Child! What have you done to y' locks? What have y' done?"

"What no one else in this castle was willing to do." Laurel took a long, trembling breath and sipped the ale. "I went to see Will."

"In the gaol?" Elinor gasped. "Merciful Lady! How did you get in?"

"Ian helped me," Laurel said, giving a grateful nod to Ian. "There is no way I can ever thank you enough."

Ian patted her hand and smiled gently. "No thanks are necessary. The urgency to attend him was apparent to me when you came and told me no one had yet been to the prison to see him. The urgency is more so now that we have seen him."

Laurel saw he was struggling to keep his own calm and confident facade. But now that they were safely back at Drumoak, she could see he was shaking from head to toe almost as badly as she was.

"Dear lady, might I have some of that ale?"

"Of course." Elinor poured some ale for Ian and handed it to him. He took it with a trembling hand and sipped it slowly. "Is he well?" she asked, after a moment.

"No, he's far from well," Laurel answered through tears, slamming her cup onto the table. "They're monsters, Elinor. They've broken him—body, mind, and spirit. I hardly recognized him and he... almost dinnae know me."

"No!" Elinor said, sitting hard on the bench next to Laurel.

"We have to get him out of there, Ian," Laurel said, twisting her hands into the folds of his robe. "We can't leave him there."

Ian put his hands on either side of her face, his blue eyes sparkling with the threat of tears. "There is little we can do about getting him out. His only hope is a positive outcome to his trial."

"What trial? It shan't be a trial, it—" Laurel cried, pulling away from Ian. "—it will be a farce. He's told me himself what a mockery those trials are. No one is ever *released*."

"I was," Ian whispered, slowly lowering his hands. He held out his wrists for her to see.

Laurel timidly touched the marks on Ian's wrists. In the light of the kitchen, she could see them more clearly than she could by the small candle light in the dank prison cell. Each of Ian's wrists were etched with the furrows left behind from something that must have been terrifyingly painful, though they seemed slightly different than the scars she assumed William would wear—should he survive. Where William's wrists were marred on all sides by the biting shackles he wore, Ian's seemed to have been cut on the inner side only and, from the look of them, the cuts had been very deep indeed. She shuddered at the reality of the marks and, after a moment, asked quietly, "Were you charged with sorcery as well?"

"No, not exactly," Ian said somewhat reluctantly, then pulled his sleeves back down over his wrists. "I was charged with abetting a woman who was." He frowned, and looked away before he continued. "Her husband had been ambushed by robbers, badly beaten and left for dead. I provided her with yarrow root and barley, and instructions of how she should use them to heal his wounds. He was not expected to live but when he did, rather than being praised for her skill, she was accused of sorcery. And because I came to her defense, I was arrested and put to the question—as they like to call it. I was certain I had seen the last of my days, but luckily the magistrate who presided in our case had little patience for superstitious twaddle, as he called it, and we were both found innocent and set free."

He gave her an encouraging smile, though, for the first time, Laurel wondered if Ian was telling her the whole truth or merely trying to ease her mind.

"So you see? There is always hope."

"Yes, there is hope, I suppose." Laurel tried to smile so as not to let Ian know that she was doubting his story. *True or not, he's a dear man to care so much. His secrets shall be his own.* "I'm glad you won. Yarrow and barley..." she said quietly, "Will is certainly in need of those now."

Ian's eyes lit up a bit and his smile became more genuine. "Yes. Laurel, you do know about the healing herbs, don't you? We'll be certain to take some to him tomorrow." He hesitated a moment, then said, "I know it's painful for you... but I believe your presence alone is a far more effective balm for him than any herbs we could bring. Will you go back to the prison with me?"

Laurel swallowed hard and nodded resolutely. "Yes, Ian. I'll go back. But will they allow us to treat his wounds?"

"Yes." Ian nodded. "I've given some thought to this. Laurel, did you see the entourage outside the abbey as we left the prison?"

"Aye, I did. The devils," she growled through her teeth. "It looks like Thomas and the dragon have gathered their dogs. I was going to ask; the guard said it may be tomorrow?" She tried to forget the comment the guard had thrown aside: *You know, the platform 'n such. Get it done early, then it's ready right away.* "Does he mean the trial will be tomorrow?"

"Yes," he answered. "It seems they've gathered enough witnesses. If his trial is to be tomorrow, they'll require him to be... made presentable. We'll have an opportunity to treat his wounds then."

"Made presentable." Laurel felt her stomach turn. "Patched up for show, you mean. To cover up what they've done to him."

Ian lowered his eyes. "Unfortunately, yes." He sighed. "But think about it this way: if we don't attend to him, Dunkirk will just send someone else who'll be far less interested in his well being than you and I."

"Not while *I'm* breathing. It will be us, Ian." Laurel set her jaw in determination. "We shall minister to him with the expectation that he will leave the trial a free man, with healing in mind. Elinor, we'll need more than yarrow and barley. He needs bandages and perhaps ground root of Solomon's seal, and boneset as well... something strong to dull the pain, but won't muddle his thinking—"

"Yes, yes, I'll put it all together." Elinor nodded eagerly, leaning to Laurel and whispering, "And dill seed. Place one in his boot."

"What for?" Laurel asked, giving Elinor a wary look.

Elinor nodded and leaned to answer Laurel, but was interrupted by Ian. "To use as a charm to help him win his case. Every little bit helps. Take the dill. It can't hurt," he said, a sly grin on his face. Elinor turned red.

Laurel stared at him, shocked, heat rising to her face. "How did?—"

"I know?" Ian smiled, kindly patting Laurel's hand. "Don't allow my cleric's robe to fool you. I'm an herbalist first; apothecary actually, fully schooled in the medicinal...and the more superstitious uses of what God has provided. Dill in the boot is a common enough belief that the king himself would put it in his boot, should he find himself a defendant."

Laurel exhaled, giving Ian a wide-eyed gaze. "You are beginning to astound me."

He smiled. "In another time and place, we may find leave to enjoy our common craft, but alas, we have an urgent chore before us." Ian's smile faded.

"Edward must be told," Elinor said. "And Mehlyndia as well. Poor thing still won't eat."

"Poor thing?" Laurel looked up suddenly, her anger returning in a flash. "I should force her to eat it! She should be glad to have it. She lay languishing in self-pity doing *nothing,* while her husband is beaten and starving." She got up from the bench and stalked across the kitchen. Her eyes fell on Elinor's book, resting on the counter. Laurel placed her hand on the book, suddenly remembering the reason she went to the prison in the first place. "Elinor, he told me Mehlyndia has it; to make her give it to me, and by the Gods, I shall scratch her eyes out if she refuses!"

"Laurel, please!" Elinor caught Laurel, turning her back around. "You're not yourself. You don't mean what you say."

Laurel glared at Elinor, angrily pushing the older woman's hands away. "I mean every word. Mehlyndia could have just as easily gone to this good man as I did. It should have been her who was trying so desperately to see Will and I tell you, I could see in his eyes he would have rather seen her than me. He's dying! And she has all but forsaken him!"

"Dying?" Elinor gaped at Laurel, then turned to Ian. "Is it that bad?"

Ian took Elinor's hand and spoke quietly, "If something

is not done, trial or no trial, he will not last much longer. If not for the little food and water we brought to him today, he would have none at all. And they do not allow him to sleep but for a few moments. I've seen this forced sleeplessness done before." He looked down. "I know it seems trivial and some claim it's a merciful form of—"

"Merciful? He's losing his mind!" Laurel said, shaking again.

"I didn't say I agree, Laurel," Ian said, placing a calming hand on her shoulder. "It's atrocious! I only meant—"

"I understand," Elinor interrupted him. "No need to say more." She stood and paced the room for a moment. "Well, I believe we each have our own task. I'll gather the medicinal herbs and roots you'll need for William. Laurel, you need to retrieve that article for safekeeping. Ian, I should think you have to let Edward know that the trial is imminent. I'm also fairly sure he is unaware of the treatment William is receiving. Perhaps you should enlighten him."

"I should be glad to." Ian clasped Elinor's hand. "Pray he will do something to make it easier for the young man."

Elinor gave Ian a grateful, sad smile. "I'll take you up then."

"Thank you, Ian." Laurel gave the cleric a brief embrace. "I can't tell you how grateful I am for your help."

Ian brushed her cheek lightly, banishing a stray tear. "It is my honor. We're not all monsters, we clerics."

"No, you're not." Laurel turned away from Ian to hide the blush she felt growing on her face. "Elinor, I'll go see Mehlyndia. Believe me, I'll get that article from her. It's time she gets herself out of that bed!"

"Laurel, you do what you must, but please, try not to lash

out at her. I suspect there is more about her than we have come to know just yet." Elinor motioned to Laurel's mock robe. "I suggest you put your own clothes on before ye go up."

Laurel glared at Elinor. "No. She will see what I had to do. I'm not ashamed. Perhaps the sight of these sheets will help her to remember that her husband is still among the living— it's too soon for her to be mourning his death!" She turned and stalked out of the kitchen.

All the way through the hall and up the stairs, Laurel marked her steps by the loud beating of her heart, trying to ignore the images that invaded her mind. Her grief turned to anger as the safe, peaceful fantasy she'd nurtured for the past three days—William sitting quietly on a nice, little cot of straw while awaiting his trial—gave way to the ugly reality of what was actually happening to him. She felt an odd certainty that Mehlyndia had somehow created a similar fantasy of William serenely awaiting a host of white horses to come take him to heaven.

As she approached Mehlyndia's door, she was surprised to find that Richard had, for the moment, left the duties of earldom to resume his former role as sentry. He stood outside Mehlyndia's suite, giving Laurel an incredulous double look as she approached him. "Miss Laurel? Is that you?"

"No," Laurel spoke in the lowest voice she could offer. "My name is Sean. I'm an acolyte to Brother Ian of Stonehaven Abbey. I have come to see Lady Sutherland."

Richard stared at her with a suspicious lift to his brow. "Is she expecting you?"

Laurel pushed her cowl back, revealing her face to him. "I sincerely doubt it, Richard."

"It is you!" Richard gaped at her. "Laurel, what in God's name are you trying to prove?"

I almost fooled him. "Not just trying to, I *have proven* it is not impossible for a mouse to become a lion," Laurel said, a defiant set to her jaw. "While you have sat with Edward, planning your life as Earl of Sutherland, *I've* taken action on behalf of the *true* earl."

He stared, stunned. "Have you lost your mind? I've never seen such fire in your eyes."

"Then you have never looked closely enough," she said, widening her eyes. "No, Richard. I have not lost my mind. But I have done what no one else in the castle has seen fit to do." She placed her hand on the door handle, eager to be past him. "I suggest you go see Edward. You will find Elinor and Brother Ian of the abbey in his chamber explaining everything to him."

He moved her hand away from the door and seized her wrist. "What are you talking about!"

She jerked her hand away from him impatiently. "Go! I shall not waste my time telling you what I have only the strength to tell her. Please, if you have any compassion left in you for your uncle, go seek Elinor and Brother Ian in Edward's suite." The last thing she wanted was to have Richard anywhere near Mehlyndia while she asked her for William's book.

"As you wish, 'Mouse Who Roars,' but the explanation had better suit me. I grow weary of your secrets!" He strode away from her toward Edward's suite.

Laurel stood and watched until he had cleared the corridor, then exhaled grandly and brought her trembling under control. *I grow weary of them as well!* Slowly, Laurel opened Mehlyndia's chamber door, without knocking.

Mehlyndia lay on her bed facing the open window. "Please, I asked to be left alone."

"Forgive me m' lady," Laurel said. "But I have urgent business with you." Laurel was astounded that she kept the tremble from her voice.

"Business?" Mehlyndia turned to look at her. "What business could you possibly—" Her mouth gaped open when she saw Laurel. "Is that you?"

"Yes, it's me." Laurel kept her voice respectful, but she would no longer pretend to be the simple-witted, dutiful, submissive little servant. Today she would take charge—for him. "Please, get out of bed. I have to speak to you."

"What have you done to yourself?" Mehlyndia asked incredulously.

"Only what was necessary," Laurel said with a casual shrug as she approached Mehlyndia, adding, "to get past the prison guards."

"The prison?" Mehlyndia sat up and finally left her bed.

"Yes, I went to see your husband," Laurel said, in an informative, cold voice as she slowly crossed the room toward Mehlyndia. "I entered with Brother Ian as his acolyte. The clerics have free access to the prisoners, you see. They allowed us in to see him with no difficulty at all."

"No one can see him," Mehlyndia scoffed. "Father said the prisoners are not allowed visitors before trials."

"They allow clerics," Laurel repeated, staring Mehlyndia

down as she got closer. "Mehlyndia," she spoke her name with a forced authority, "he wants you to give me his book." She hated being so cross with Mehlyndia, knowing her mistress's grief was truly genuine, and knowing she risked being dismissed from her service for her boldness. But for William, she would risk more than a mere dismissal of employment.

"Book?" Mehlyndia asked, feigning ignorance. "I know of no book."

"You know you do." Laurel sighed. "There is something inside it that is very damaging to him. I must take it into safekeeping."

"William told me to give it to no one! I will not dishonor his memory—"

"He is not yet a memory! And you dishonor him by your inaction!" she shouted, incensed at Mehlyndia's dismissal of her husband. "Am I the only one in this castle who is willing to stand up for him while there is still the hope he'll be set free? While he still draws breath?"

"There is no hope! You have gone mad! You have not been to the prison, and no haircut or bed-sheet will convince me !" Mehlyndia cried grabbing at Laurel's makeshift robe. "He told me not to tell anyone of his book!"

"*You have not told me of it!*" Laurel whipped her arm away. "I have known of it for many years. It is no secret to me, so you have kept your word."

"You've known? How—you?" Mehlyndia glared, the light of understanding coming to her eyes. "I should have known. He was so eager to get you away from here. You've studied the craft with him?"

"Aye." Laurel astounded herself with the command in her voice, though her knees were starting to sway. "Now if you truly care for him and wish any glimmer of hope to help him, you will give it to me."

"Why? It's safe where it is," Mehlyndia argued. "No one will find it."

"Where, in your trunk?" Laurel snapped, pointing to the trunk. The stunned look on Mehlyndia's face told her she was right. "You see? It's not so difficult to find." She took a breath to steady her anger and quell the shaking in her knees. "Mehlyndia, listen to me. If they search here, which they are apt to do, and they find this thing I need—William will have *no* hope at all."

"He told *me* to keep it." Mehlyndia put her hand to her forehead and began to sway, dropping down quickly onto the edge of the bed. "I feel dizzy."

"Perhaps you should eat something." Laurel went to the table and picked up the tray she had left hours before and brought it to Mehlyndia, dropping it next to her on the bed, rattling the dishes. "It's a sin to waste this."

"Laurel... " Mehlyndia looked at her suddenly with frightened eyes. "I'm not hungry."

"He is," Laurel yelled, then thumped the tray again.

"Who?" Mehlyndia jumped back, startled.

"William! Your husband." Laurel glared, then scooped up several of the discarded drawings that were strewn about the room and held one up as a reminder. "The one you have abandoned as dead." She tossed one drawing onto the bed. "The one you will not fight for." She flung a second one onto the floor with an angry swing of her arm. "He's *starving*. I'm sure he would be grateful to have this little bit of fruit and cream you leave rotting on the tray."

"I have not abandoned him," Mehlyndia cried, shrinking away from Laurel. "He was *taken* from me. There is *nothing* I can do."

"You can give me his book! You can cut your hair and enter the prison as I have!"

"Why do you tell me such vile lies?"

"I do not lie. He is in the bloody tower!" Laurel stormed to the window and pushed the shutters open, revealing the view of the hideous tower. "He was amazed that *I* went to the lengths I did to get there. I wonder why it was *me* who was the one to do it. I am nothing but a little mousy housemaid, after all. *You* are his *wife!*"

"Laurel! Now I know you are mad!" The fear in Mehlyndia's eyes was slowly being replaced by anger.

"Mad? No, just determined. Cut your hair and come with me into the prison tomorrow; see for yourself if that is what it takes to convince you," Laurel challenged.

"I have not your courage, Laurel." Mehlyndia sank onto the bed and suddenly burst into tears. "William would be beside himself with worry if he thought I was trying to break into the prison."

"He is beside himself with grief that no one but me has even attempted to see him." Laurel's angry resolve softened as Mehlyndia sobbed into her pillow. "Forgive me. I only wished to make you understand the need." She placed her hand on Mehlyndia's back and fought back her own tears, remembering the lost look in William's eyes. "He has no hope left in him, m' lady. He believes that he has been cast off as lost." Mehlyndia sat up and looked at Laurel, wiping her eyes. "Keep the book if you wish, only promise me that you will hide it well. But, please do *something* other than lay here in self-pity while he suffers in the tower."

"Self-pity? Laurel, I... have not felt well. I suspect that I'm..." Tears brimmed anew in her eyes as she suddenly ran from the bed to the water closet, one hand to her mouth, the other to her stomach.

"Mehlyndia?" Laurel followed, anger turning to concern.

After a few moments, Mehlyndia emerged, pale, and weary-faced. She waved Laurel away, then leaned against William's favorite chair by the fire. "So tell me, what is in the book that needs to be hidden?"

"It is safer if you do not know."

"If you wish me to believe you, then tell me everything."

Laurel was beginning to feel too exhausted to argue any longer. She simply removed William's signet from her thumb— the only finger large enough to fit his ring— and held it out to Mehlyndia. "He asked me to give this to you as proof. The bloodstain on the band is his. I won't tell you what it took to remove this from his hand. Mehlyndia. Please, give me the book."

Mehlyndia took the ring from Laurel with a trembling hand. "My God. It's true. You have seen him. He's truly starving?"

"He's suffering far more than hunger, m' lady, and cannot afford to wait any longer for someone to rally for him. The hunters may or may not come and search his belongings—I admit I'm not certain they will— but if they do and what's hidden in that book is discovered, he will surely be damned."

"I had assumed he just sat and waited for the trial. They are not supposed to hurt noblemen."

"It is not an inn. It's a prison. I don't believe his rank matters to them." Laurel sighed. "We need to find witnesses *for* him and we need to build a defense. We cannot sit and wait any longer. The accusers have assembled, the trial comes tomorrow, and we have *nothing* to fight back with. The best we can hope for is that this thing I seek will never be discovered by anyone else."

"Tomorrow?"

"That's what Ian assumes, and he has seen enough of these to know."

"I'm so sorry. I've been so foolish."

Mehlyndia suddenly swayed on her feet again, as if to faint. Laurel rushed to help her stand, the anger pouring away from her as she led Mehlyndia to sit on the bed next to the tray. Despite her queasy stomach, Mehlyndia ate the dried fruit and bread that had been brought. After a moment, she reached into the bodice of her gown and removed a small brass key with a ribbon that hung around her neck.

"In the trunk. Under the linen."

Laurel gratefully took the key and went to the trunk. After a moment, she found the leather bundle down in the piles of sheets. She opened the little satchel and extracted the book as quickly as she could. She found what she sought almost immediately; a piece of parchment with one torn edge, folded into quarters. She unfolded it and read the title: *'For Persuasion.' Elinor was right, it is a beguiling charm.* She took the paper and tucked it into her belt, then opened the kit and removed the small vial of oil that was closest to the top—the one called out in the charm, chicory oil. "Thank you."

"Take it away," Mehlyndia said, wearily watching Laurel from the bed. "Take the whole thing if it helps."

Laurel flipped through the pages of the book to see if there were any other *dangerous* entries. To her surprise, she found that only the first two or three pages had anything to do with herbs, and they were benign ingredient lists for fever remedies and the like. The rest of the pages were filled with poetry, musical notations, and personal journal entries. Near the front of the book, she came across what looked like a treasure map he had drawn as part of a game he had made up with Sean in his early days at Drumoak. She smiled slightly at the thought that there was no need to hide this book from anyone. It was completely innocent. *A simple book of verse and childish memories.*

"He asked me not to read it," Mehlyndia stated flatly. "I suppose you have that privilege as well."

Laurel blushed and reluctantly closed the book. "Forgive me. No, I should not have read it. I only worried there was more that should be hidden."

"Is there?"

"No." She cast her eyes downward and spoke in a whisper, "He's filled it only with his songs and relics of his childhood. There is nothing here that could harm him now."

"Songs?" Mehlyndia chuckled. "He'd be pleased you think they are just songs."

"Why?" Laurel looked at her, confused. "That is all I see."

Mehlyndia smiled sadly. "He told me that he charmed the pages to appear that way. He said he wasn't sure if the charm had actually worked, since he never found cause to test it."

"He *charmed* it?" Laurel shook her head, half smiling, dragging her hand across the cover. *Dear Mother, I hope he paid his tribute for this small charm at least.* She looked up to Mehlyndia. "Then perhaps it would be better to keep it in plain view. It would seem less suspicious that way, should they come to search. "

"No, it shall be hidden." Mehlyndia went to Laurel and gently took the book from her. She ran her fingers over the initials on the cover and held it for a moment before returning it to the leather satchel. "Charmed or not, he wanted it to remain private." Mehlyndia put her hand to her head and swayed again.

"You truly are ill." Laurel helped her back to the bed. She began to feel guilty for her harsh attitude. But she felt vindicated by the result—she'd found the chant. "Do you need something for your head?"

"No, I know what the trouble is. Any other time I would be pleased, but I cannot feel any joy about this. My courses have not arrived this month."

"You're... "

"Yes, I am fairly certain that I'm with child, Laurel."

Richard tromped the corridor on his way to Edward's suite. He had no idea what Laurel could have possibly been about in her costume, but the look on her face and the grim tone of her voice told him she was more of a *man* than he was. She had stung him with her words, *"How very convenient for you that Edward placed that crest on your shoulder. It gives you a lovely excuse to simply sit and wait for someone else to rally."* But, he loathed to admit, she had been right. Since William had been dragged, bound and bridled, from the foyer, Richard had struggled with his oldest enemy—the coward he knew himself to be. Had he obeyed Sean's last order and stayed with Elinor, she would not have been taken and used for bait, and Sean would not have been so distracted by yelling at him to go back that he probably could have deflected the death-blow. Sean's last words—*"You've killed him, Richard"*—made painfully clear sense to him now.

When he arrived at the duke's suite, he found that Edward's door was ajar. Laurel was right, Elinor and the young monk were there. Richard stood outside and listened as the monk described to Edward the condition in which he had found William. The graphic depiction of the wounds and how it was assumed William had come by them sent shudders down Richard's back. He fought the impulse to leave. *Just another act of cowardice. Stay, listen to what you've caused.* He drew in his gut to steady his breathing, then casually tapped the door. "Forgive the intrusion. May I join you?" he asked, keeping his voice calm.

Edward looked up, ashen-faced, then waved Richard to an empty chair at the table. He made an informal introduction, "You know Ian. He's brought distressing news."

"Yes," Richard began, "I remember him. Forgive me, my lord, but I was listening from outside. Did I hear you say that the trial will be tomorrow?"

Edward nodded. "It would seem." He turned to Ian. "You say you know this abbot you saw outside the abbey?"

"Yes. He seemed to know William as well," Ian answered. "Abbot Joseph from Aberdoir. He's an abomination in cleric robes." He scowled, shaking his head. "Such a man should not call himself a man of God. You're from Aberdoir, you must know him."

"Unfortunately, yes," Richard grumbled. "I had hoped I would never cross paths with him again in this lifetime."

"He's the same Joseph?" Edward asked.

"Oh yes." Richard thumped the table in disgust. "And I'm sure he's been paid quite well for his testimony."

"Well it would seem that we are once again forewarned by you, Ian. Let's hope we are better prepared this time." Edward looked out the window toward the prison and spoke quietly, as if to himself, "I must admit that I had expected better treatment toward him, given his rank."

Richard toyed with the crest on his shoulder. "He has no rank," he said quietly.

Edward turned and looked at him, alarmed.

"Perhaps Dunkirk took note of your charade after all. William no longer has the protection of nobility."

"But he is still known—"

"Have you never visited a prison, Lord Edward?" Ian asked pointedly, a sudden angry edge in his voice. "Forgive me, may I speak plainly?"

"Please do." Edward turned to face Ian.

"Thank you." Ian stood and joined Edward at the window. "I mean no disrespect to you, sir, but I find it troubling that you are so unaware of what happens in your own realm. I've been to many a gaol such as this," he said, pointing past the window sash toward the prison, "and I will tell you that I have seen, all too often, people perish before trial is even brought. Many do not survive the initial interrogation. The fact that William has lasted this long is nothing less than miraculous."

Edward began to turn away.

"My lord." Ian placed a hand on Edward's arm until he looked Ian in the eye. "The inquisitors do not await the outcome of a trial before they carry out their tortures. They begin right in and the stronger the will, the fiercer the pain, until they get what they want. Should the victim confess, the accusers are spared the time and trouble of the trial altogether, and the poor soul is dispatched right then. Few actually make it to trial." Ian grabbed him when Edward tried to turn away again and spoke louder, "Even those fortunate enough to be exonerated, oft' times are left crippled and maimed beyond repair, left to a life of pain. I wonder if you would have been so quick to surrender him had you known this."

Richard looked sharply at Ian. "Do not accuse Lord Edward—"

"Stand down, Richard," Edward said wearily, waving a dismissive hand to Richard. "I did not surrender him," he said, rubbing his eyes between his forefinger and thumb. "It is not my wish to make an example of William. I shall not explain my motives to you, sir, but I will say, in my own defense. . . ." He looked at Ian and raised a hand as though to explain, then lowered it with a loud sigh, defeated. "I did, indeed, believe he would be spared from the chamber. You are justified in your accusation. I am guilty."

"Forgive me, my lord," Ian said, head bowed. "I am not here to judge—"

"William, himself, accused me on more than one occasion of turning a blind eye," Edward spoke quietly, looking out the window. "I chalked it off to his youthful passion. Had I believed him, we would not be having this conversation. I've as good as done this to him myself."

"Have you gathered any witnesses in his defense, sir?" Ian asked quietly. "There is precious little time left."

Edward looked at him with a helpless expression and made a sweeping hand movement around the room. "Only those you see here."

Laurel appeared the doorway. "Don't forget me!"

"Laurel! My dear, come here." Edward approached and enclosed her in his arms. "Good grief, child, you put this old fool completely to shame. Had I half your pluck, we would not be dealing with any of this." He released her and stood back.

"I acted on heart, not mind, sir," Laurel told him.

"Then you have a heart worthy of my deep respect." Edward put his arm around her and led her to the table to join the others.

Laurel blushed and looked away from Edward and caught Richard's eye. She nodded a greeting. Richard bowed his head contritely. "Forgive my anger before, Laurel," he said. "Edward is correct. You have shamed us all." Impulsively, he took her hand in his. "Please, don't take such a risk again. I loathe to think what would become of you if you were caught."

"I'll do what I must," Laurel replied shortly, pulling her hand away. "How many witnesses do we have?"

"Not nearly as many as we need." Edward sighed. "But that does not mean we are beaten. Ian, you say you believe they will begin tomorrow?"

Ian nodded. "Yes, that was my understanding."

"Then tonight we gather our defenses," Edward said with a clap of his hands. "Door to door. William has befriended half this county; there must be at least a few hearty souls willing stand up and testify for him. Laurel, are you willing to walk?"

"Aye sir!" Laurel's said, jumping to her feet. "'Twill be my pleasure. Elinor, will you walk with me?"

"Yes, of course," Elinor nodded, enthusiastically.

"Be honest, be patient," Edward instructed them. "Many will be frightened, as is understandable, but we must win them over. Above all, be careful! We need no more adventures than we already own."

"Aye, sir. I shall rally all of Stonehaven if I must," Laurel assured him, placing her fist to her chest. She looked to Ian and Elinor. "Shall we?"

"Not so fast," Elinor said, taking hold of Laurel's sheet. "Change into your own clothes please. And you must cover what is left of your hair."

"Oh, yes..." Laurel blushed. "Come on, then; meet me in the foyer. I won't be but a minute." She turned and hurried from the room.

"That lass is astounding." Ian grinned, then he and Elinor followed Laurel from the suite. Richard remained in his chair, watching.

"What keeps you, Richard?"

"On my way." He replied red-faced, and headed for the door.

"Richard." Edward halted him, placing his hand to Richard's chest. "A moment."

"Aye?"

"I should like to send you in a different direction."

Richard looked at him curiously. "Where?"

Edward cocked one eyebrow. "I'd like for you to pay a visit to your parents. Ian tells me that they are guests of Dunkirk in the abbey."

"Why?" Richard was shocked at this suggestion. He had spent a great deal of energy distancing himself from them. Why should he want to visit them, now of all times?

"There is still the matter of the unknown charge." Edward rested his chin in his hand and began to pace as he spoke, "I'm confident—with enough witnesses—we'll defeat the absurd charges that he enchanted anyone with his voice and silly songs. But we still do not know what the second charge is, so we do not know what defense to build against it." Edward looked Richard in the eye and placed a hand on his shoulder. "I want you to find out what it is. Use whatever pretense you deem appropriate. Make your father believe you've turned traitor against me if you must, but get me that information."

Richard thought for a moment. "My lord, you will make it known to the others that I act on your order, correct?"

"Only after you have returned," Edward assured him. "I understand your hesitation. You are free to refuse."

Refuse? And be forever branded coward in your eyes as well? "It looks like I must visit my parents," he said with a resolute grin, pleased that Edward had given him this part to play— an opportunity to redeem himself—and this time, he was determined not to falter. He turned to leave again.

"One more thing."

Richard stopped. "Yes?"

"Be sure to wear that crest." Edward grinned.

Richard looked at the crest on his shoulder and nodded. "Understood." He turned to leave again.

"And Richard." Edward took hold of Richard's arm.

He stopped, looking from Edward's hand to his eyes. "Yes, my lord?"

"Faintheartedness will not serve us now," Edward said in a deadly serious tone. "Do not falter."

"I shall not, Grandfather." Richard turned to leave again and this time Edward did not stop him.

"Come on, Harold. We got work to do." Jerol, the one-eyed prison guard, thumped his dozing companion on the shoulder. "They're wantin' that confession."

"This time in the night?" Harold groaned as he reluctantly left his chair by the prison gate.

"What's the matter? Lost the stomach for yer work?" Jerol turned his lone eye on Harold's considerable girth. "Goin' soft are ye?"

"Soft?" Harold snorted indignantly. "Not likely. Was just hopin' to be done with those blasted stairs for the night. Knees givin' me trouble, Jerol. Must be age creepin' in."

"Well, we only got to go up and down once tonight then, don't we? They won't be taken 'im down for another day or so." Jerol fumbled with a mass of key rings and lock picks, looking for the one he wanted. After shuffling nearly every key on the ring, he found the one he needed and unlocked the door that led to the tower. "Bloody thing is always the last one I find."

"So what are we about then? Hope it doesn't take all

night," Harold whined.

"Waiting on his *glorious self* to come tell us first," Jerol spoke with a sarcastic smirk. "He's got something specific in mind." He searched through a tool closet at the foot of the stairs. "Now where did I leave that damned crank handle?"

Harold reached over Jerol's shoulder and took it off the shelf in front of him.

"Ah, thank you, must be goin' blind in m' good eye." Jerol tucked the crank handle under his arm. "Wish they'd just let us do our job in peace. It ain't like we don't know what we're doin'. Grab a weight for me, would ye?"

"Suppose they got their reasons." Harold sorted through the closet for the weights. "So long as I get my wage, I don't care what turns their fancy. Four or six stone, on that weight?"

"Six, they're hoping for a quick night of it," Jerol answered, still rooting through the closet for odds and ends necessary for the night's work. "Why can't they stick to normal hours? Gives me a 'eadache workin' in the dark all the time. Ah, there it is." He handed a long, flat dagger to Harold. "Good edge on this one. Tha'll do it then. We'll be ready when they come."

"I jus' wish they'd get here, then, so we can get started an' be done with it." Harold winked at Jerol. "Cassandra is dancin' at the tavern tonight."

Jerol grinned and smacked his companion on the back. "Knees, you say? Ain't your knees you're hopin' to favor tonight, is it?" He bellowed with laughter. Harold joined in heartily and the two prison guards returned to the gate to await their instructions.

It was near sunset when Richard left Drumoak for the

abbey. He held little hope that Laurel and Elinor would bring back more than a dozen souls from their door-to-door campaign to rally witnesses. He had never known the people of Stonehaven to rally for anything other than to *watch* a burning. His stomach turned at the thought. *They even seem to enjoy them.* Dunkirk had ordered at least a half-dozen burnings while Edward and William were off on their tour. Each time the villagers had swarmed to the stake, as if drawn by some irresistible force that stole away their consciences. Even in the days that lead to the fires, the people seemed to be taken into a giddy fascination with the preparations. The streets would be teeming with gossips and workmen, just as they were now, as Richard walked to the abbey. He shook his head, disgusted. *They're hungry for another. Laurel will find no sympathetic witnesses in this town.*

"Who calls?" Dunkirk said as he opened the front door of the abbey.

Richard bowed respectfully and kept his voice as confident as possible. "Sir Richard Fylbrigge, son of Thomas of Aberdoir, Your Grace. I was told my father might be your guest and I wish to meet with him if that is possible."

"Does your duke know you are here, Sir Richard?" the bishop asked with a lilting grin.

"No, Your Grace," Richard answered smugly. "I've come on my own. He would most certainly not be pleased to know I am here, sir."

Dunkirk raised his brow and extended his arm toward the inside of the abbey. "Please, be my guest. This way."

Richard was ushered through the entryway to Dunkirk's private quarters— a comfortable sitting room with an inviting fire burning on the hearth. Thomas and Bryndah sat on cushioned chairs in a cozy circle, conversing with another man who sat across from them. To his dismay, Richard recognized the stout, piggish silhouette of Abbot Joseph.

"We have a visitor, Lord Thomas," Dunkirk announced congenially as he took his chair.

"Richard? I must say, this surprises me... somewhat," Thomas said, looking up over his wineglass.

"Hello, Father. I am sure my presence is unexpected," Richard said with a polite bow of his head. "Mother, you are looking well."

"Thank you." She extended her hand for him to kiss, then grinned. "How is it Edward has let you off your leash tonight?"

"He is unaware of my absence." Richard gave her a sarcastic smirk. "He is preoccupied with... other issues."

"I'll bet he is." Thomas snickered and sipped his wine, then motioned to Abbot Joseph. "You remember the Abbot of Aberdoir— oh yes that's right, he was the schoolmaster when you were last at that abbey."

"Good to see you again," Richard said pleasantly as he bowed respectfully to the fat abbot, but the words felt like acid on his tongue.

"I'm sure." The abbot smirked, then stood and turned to Dunkirk. "Gregory, we have business to attend to. I believe they are waiting on us."

"Yes, of course," Dunkirk said. "If you'll excuse us, we need to see to matters elsewhere." He stood and offered his chair to Richard. "Please, Sir Richard, make yourself comfortable. My lord, my lady." Dunkirk bowed to each, then left the sitting room with Abbot Joseph.

Richard wanted to exhale and collapse into the chair, but he kept his demeanor appropriate for his mission.

"So, tell us," Thomas began, curling half his lip into a grin, "how would you like us to forgive and forget?"

"Father?"

"Oh, come now." Thomas poured a glass of wine and passed it to Richard. "Do you mean to tell me you have not come to beg for his freedom? To beseech us to have mercy on your *liege*."

Richard took the glass, holding it by the stem, turning it between his fingers. After a moment, he grinned, looking up over the glass. "As a matter of fact, I have not." He took a sip, then, matching the acrid tone in Thomas's voice, said, "It would better suit me should he be left to rot."

Thomas leaned forward, clearly surprised at Richard's attitude. "Oh?" He looked to Bryndah, who wore the same expression of interest. "What has changed?"

Richard casually took the crest from his shoulder and tossed it onto the table next to Thomas's bottle. "He is no longer... *my liege*."

Thomas picked up the silver crest bearing the eagle and hawk. "It was true then?" He rubbed the crest between his fingers as if it were gold. "Edward truly *has* disowned him?"

"Not completely," Richard said. "That was a ruse to persuade you to drop the charges. I'm sure you reasoned that out on your own. However, in light of... events," Richard allowed a sly grin slip across his face, "I stand next in line to inherit the title in reality."

Bryndah sat up straight. "Is that so? So why come to

us with this? You've made it abundantly clear we mean nothing to you, Richard. You forsook our home for Edward's long ago."

"Yes, well, it hasn't turned out for me as I had hoped all these years." Richard's grin turned sour. "I am no longer content to remain among the lowly guard. I had hoped to at least be named captain of William's personal guard, after all I am... *family*, but he, of course, chose Sean Wilbrun above me." He spoke the name between his clenched teeth, then turned a truly wicked grin to his father. "How unfortunate for William that his favorite bulldog has been put down."

Thomas grinned over his glass, and Richard's stomach turned at how easily his performance came to him. It made him wonder if he did in fact harbor these latent resentments.

"At any rate, Edward has seen fit to name me as William's successor, should he not win his case."

"There is little chance he will win, Richard," Bryndah said, cackling. "We have him."

"That brings me to my business." Richard leaned forward, praying his lies would be convincing enough to gain their trust. "Edward has not been idle in the days since the arrest. I wonder if you are aware of the multitude of witnesses he has amassed to refute your charges."

"He will need a multitude," Thomas scoffed.

"Nevertheless, he has sent messengers to most of the villages where William has ever been," Richard said, then looked up over his drink. "Make no mistake, Father, he has many devoted followers who are willing to rally for him." Richard wished it was true. He wished Edward had even considered sending messengers. *God, Will, forgive us.*

Bryndah sat back in her chair, ringing her finger around the top of her wineglass. "I still see no problem—we anticipated as much."

Richard raised his brow, allowing his smirk to return. "Have you? I take it that means you have more evidence to add to the case against him?"

"Absolutely. Iron clad evidence," she said, leering at him as a spider observes a fly on a web. "Have no fear, my sweeting, you shall be earl in earnest by sundown tomorrow." She took the crest from Thomas and handed it back to Richard.

"Richard, you risk a great deal in coming here," Thomas said. "Surely there must be some other reason you've come to see us than to simply show us your new bit of jewelry."

"In fact, there is," Richard said as he pinned the crest back onto his cape. "You are still the shrewdest man I know, Father." Richard saw by the look in Thomas's eye that he had flattered him. "And if... *when* I am fully installed in Sutherland, I should think we would both benefit a great deal by joining ranks *against* Edward." He chose his words carefully, calculating each inflection of his voice to sound convincing. "I have no love of this place, or him, or my *dear Uncle* William." He sniffed at the name and took a drink. "I should think the time is right to change the lines of succession completely." Richard fought the bile that was threatening to betray his cover while he held his gaze on Thomas, unblinking. "I'm sure you can imagine the reward that stands to be gained in an alliance such as you and I could create."

"Indeed, I can, and when the judge decides those ridiculous trade agreements were secured under black magic they will be dissolved. Drunbalk and Wesley will join us, and Lord Ogham himself will welcome us to his bosom with open arms." Thomas raised his glass.

"We'll be unstoppable." Richard clinked his glass with Thomas's. "With the Fylbrigge family fortune at last all in one coffer."

Bryndah clinked her glass with the others. "You are your father's son after all. I'm gratified that I did not fail in your upbringing as I had feared."

"So you are certain you will counter the defense cleanly?"

"But of course. Should the little heathen convince the judge he is not an *enchanter*," Bryndah said, grinning, "we will simply bring forth our second charge, and they will be obligated to test him. *Surviving* the test will only prove his guilt. Of course, the poor lad could be innocent."

"What sort of test?" Richard covered his distress with a convincing tone of eager glee as his innards threatened again to betray him.

"The poison, of course." Bryndah smiled sweetly, though her expression tore on Richard's nerves. "You must be aware of the poison. He survived a full hard dose of nightshade and opium."

"Yes, but he was given an antidote?" Richard said, confused. "Elinor mixed some concoction, I believe that is what the rumor is. Anyone could have survived that."

"The antidote was foxglove." Thomas smiled and reached for Bryndah's hand. "Do you know of any who could survive such an *antidote*, my love?"

"No, my pet." Bryndah's eyes flashed. "How astonishing. I've always been led to believe that foxglove is quite lethal all by itself, let alone after a large dose of nightshade. It would take the work of a witch and his own demonic pact to survive two such poisonings. Don't you think? We shall be sure to inform Bishop Dunkirk that he must add foxglove to the test." Bryndah looked at Richard with a horrific gleam in her eye that turned his blood to pure ice.

"That's brilliant." Richard grinned and tipped his glass. "After your test, guilty or innocent, the end result is the same. He'll be dead." *And you'll have murdered your own brother with the full blessings of the church.*

"Exactly." Thomas laughed, then refilled each glass. "A toast, then." He raised his drink. Richard and Bryndah raised their glasses as well. "To Lord Richard, the Earl of Sutherland, long may he—may *we* reign."

The three clinked their glasses and drank. Richard wished to heaven they would choke on their wine.

The setting sun stole away the last of the light that shown through the mean little window at the top of the tower cell. *Another day lost.* Left alone in the dark, William's mind wandered back to the day—*was it only days ago?*—he and Sean had raced from the woodland road back to Drumoak. *You were supposed to stay on my back, Sean.* He conjured an image of Sean in his mind, sitting astride Hawk, cocky head tilted to the side as he challenged him to a race. The image was so real that for a moment, William believed he could reach out and grasp his brother's hand—*I think I've always known you were my brother.* In his half-dream, he did reach, but the shackles around his wrist jarred him back to the present, stealing Sean away from him again. *My God, I wish you were here now—for both of us.*

"*Look what you've gotten yourself into. You always have to do things the hard way, don't you.*"

William looked up, startled, searching for the source of the voice he'd heard. He saw only the blackness of his cell and the faint trace of the rising moonlight coming through the hole in the wall. He dropped his head, dismissing the voice as just an illusion brought about by his solitude.

"*I swear I spend more time keeping you out of trouble.*"

He looked up again and searched. The voice was familiar and clear as a bell in his ear. But there was no one with him, and there were no sounds coming from beyond the iron door. For days he had struggled to keep control of his wits, but he feared now he may have finally slipped completely into dementia. Days of forced sleeplessness had blurred his sense of what was conscious thought and what was a dream. He was not even certain that Laurel had truly come to see him, or if he had only imagined her. And if she had truly come, why would she have been dressed as a boy? Had she been alone? He couldn't remember. Surely this voice was just another product of this same delirium. *You're not real,* he thought. *Go away.*

"*Go away?*" the voice replied. "*After all it took to get here? I'm not going anywhere.*"

William stared, disbelieving, into the darkness, now unsure if he was truly alone in the cell. *Of course I'm alone. Awake and alone, what else could I be?* Then again, he had stolen a few moments of sleep here and there when the guards had grown bored with banging on the door. It was quiet for the moment; perhaps he was sleeping now and dreaming the voice. His hands and arms were numb, held tight and high in the shackles above him, so moving them to see if he was awake was impossible. He had been left sitting on his crossed ankles, thus numbing his legs and feet as well. *I'm sleeping... dreaming.*

"You're awake, Will," the voice told him, patiently responding to William's thought.

I must be going mad.

"Only if you allow it."

William blinked hard into the darkness. He thought perhaps the moonlight was playing a trick on his eyes as well as his mind as quite faintly, in the corner of the cell, he thought he saw a trace of a shadow move in the moonbeams.

Who is there?

As he squinted into the shadow, to his amazement, it grew brighter and slowly began to take shape. He no longer worried if he was dreaming or awake. It would make no difference if he were demented, so he allowed himself to be drawn into the strange shadow form. He watched, enthralled, as the mist became substance and turned to look full upon him.

Sean? William stared at the unmistakable image before him. *How can it be you? No, you're not real. You can't be.*

"You've been calling me for days. Have you ever known me to ignore you? Look for yourself." The shadow smiled and turned full around, as though it was proving its existence. "You see? It's me."

No! You're not Sean. Sean is dead. I watched him die.

"Yes, that is true." The shade placed a shadowy hand over its wispy chest. "But a promise is a promise."

Promise?

It rose from the floor slightly and seemed to drift in the air as it came closer to William. *"Your back, Will. I'm on it."*

No, you're dead. You can't help me now. I've conjured you, you're not real. Go away. William closed his eyes against the apparition and began to tremble.

"Open your eyes. If you didn't want me here, why have you been calling to me?"

William hesitantly opened his eyes. The shade was still there and appeared to sit casually in midair with Sean's unmistakable smile on its face. *How could I have called you? I can't even speak.*

The mouth of the shade remained fixed in a soft smile, not moving with its words, as it answered, *"The same way you're speaking to me now, Will. From within."* The voice seemed to come from someplace behind William's ear rather than from the spot where the apparition was floating. *"I've been close by, but you couldn't see me. Until now."*

Why now?

"You're dying."

So then, let me die. William closed his eyes again and allowed his chin to drop to his chest. *I'm more than willing.*

"That's not my job." The voice seemed closer to his ear, almost inside it, yet the figure remained across from him. *"I'm supposed to prevent that. I'm here to help you fight. Same as always."*

I can't fight anymore. William kept his face down. He never did like to let Sean see him when he felt weak and afraid. *I've nothing left to fight with.*

"You're still alive. You must have something."

No. Sean, please. I want to quit. William felt a slight breeze, like a soft hand, brushing against his face. He opened his eyes expecting the shade to be next to him, but it was still across the cell, hovering against the wall in the moonlight.

"You can't quit." Sean's *'or else'* expression crossed the shade's face. *"It's not your time."*

Better to die in here, right now, than out there. They've abandoned me to the fire.

"You're wrong. You're not abandoned." The shade hovered closer to him, and extended its wispy hand, William felt the breeze-like touch of the hand resting on his shoulder, just as Sean had always done when he was being serious. *"You didn't dream her. Laurel was here and she's kept her promise, Will. She's out there right now gathering an army to help you."*

She needs to be careful, Sean, she's reckless. He looked up to see the shade laugh. *I know. So am I. And look where it's led me.*

"I've got her covered too," it said, then floated back toward the far wall. *"Trust me."*

From the window, the faint sound of distant voices wafted up to the cell. The shade turned as though to look through the wall, then turned a sad face to William. *"It's going to be a long night, Will."*

They're all long. William closed his eyes and dropped his head again. *Will you stay with me?* William waited for a reply, but was met with only silence. *Please?*

"Wake up! Coming in!" William was startled from his vision by the hateful banging he had heard all too many times over the past days, causing him to bite down painfully hard on the bridle. He had grown so accustomed to its presence, and the taste of rust, that he could not recall if he had felt it during his ethereal conversation. That at least would have told him if he had been truly dreaming or not. He searched the cell for any trace of what he thought he had seen but found only the blackness of the cold stone walls. Even the moon was gone behind a cloud. *Sean?*

The darkness was suddenly split by the harsh brightness of the torch that Harold held in front of him. "Watch your step, gen'lemen."

William blinked back the light trying to clear his vision as the large guard he had come to hate and dread the most entered first, followed by two clerics.

Why must they always come in the night?

"Now then, gen'lemen, how much d'ya need, and how long should I go?" Harold said in a tone that sounded as though he were making a simple barter for workhorses rather than the business he was truly about. He tossed a burlap sack clumsily onto the floor, sending an unmistakable echo of metal on stone clamoring through the tower.

William closed his eyes against the torchlight, listening as the trio worked out the details of their business.

"We only require a simple 'yes' or 'no' from him, nothing more," Dunkirk answered in a concise, businesslike tone. "I think we've waited sufficiently long enough to make your task relatively easy. He looks ready. So, I'd say no more than a couple of hours. What do you think, Joseph?"

"Certainly no *less* than an hour, Gregory," Joseph answered in a polite conversational tone, chuckling. "After all, the gaoler must be allowed to earn his wage."

"Quite right." Dunkirk grinned amicably. "Harold, I'd give you all night to earn your wage, if necessary, but we actually do need him to testify before the judge. Bring him to the brink if you must, but no further."

"If we get what we require, his testimony before the judge will be irrelevant. A confession will certainly save us all a good deal of unpleasantness." Joseph sighed. "But I suppose there is the remotest possibility that he'll be stubborn."

"Yes, that's always possible," Dunkirk agreed. "To the brink, Joseph, no further. Agreed?"

"As you wish," Joseph answered pleasantly. "Harold, I thought you were to keep him awake?"

"Eyes wide!" Harold hollered gruffly.

William reluctantly opened his eyes in time to see Harold removing a large iron handle from the burlap sack; he placed it into the chain crank on the far wall. *Sean? Now would be a good time for some help.*

Harold addressed the two clerics politely, "All right. Which of you will stay to oversee it, then?"

"I'll stay," Joseph answered congenially. "That is, if you don't mind Gregory. You do have guests to attend to, and I know this sort of business distresses you greatly."

"Indeed it does. I am grateful for your consideration." The bishop smiled and bowed his head to Joseph. "I'll see you when you've finished. I have a lovely port we can share." Dunkirk left the cell, pausing only long enough to give William a scurrilous sneer, leaving Joseph and Harold to their business.

Joseph smiled at William as he paced across the cell. "So, we meet again. I must say, I'm not surprised to find the likes of you here."

William stared at the abbot's hands. The memory of how easily he had been lifted off the ground with just one of those beefy fists sent echoes of panic through him as the right hand came toward his face.

"Take that off him for now if you would, Harold," Joseph said, indifferently pointing to the bridle.

"Forward!" Harold ordered.

William obediently dropped his head forward. He had learned early on it was not in his best interest to resist Harold's orders. The bridle was removed from his mouth but left draped around his neck like a collar, the metal bit pressing against his throat. William remained silent. He knew the rules.

"Nothing to say, boy?" Abbot Joseph asked. "Cat got your tongue?" He took a step closer and bent over his prisoner. "Oh, you'll speak. I know just what to do to insure it." He stood up to his full height and casually examined William's shackled wrists, giving each chain a sharp yank. "Do you remember the commandments, boy? Should I test you on them?" A wicked glint came to his eye.

William looked away from Joseph and stared at the dark corner of the cell. He remained silent, fighting to push down his fear to make way for the growing anger inside him. Anger would help him fight the urge to quit.

"How many commandments are there? Do you at least remember that?"

"Eleven," William said softly, a challenge in his voice. *I'm not a child anymore. He has no power over me.*

Harold let out a low, guttural laugh.

"Eleven?" the abbot repeated, sniggering as he spoke. "And what, pray tell, would number eleven be?"

"You should know. You're the cleric. Don't you know the

Holy Canon?" William spoke to the dark corner, drawing strength from his anger and from the memory of the apparition that had been there. *Where are you, brother?*

The abbot took hold of William's hair and turned his face upward. "The least you can do is look me in the eye. There are ten, heathen! You don't even know that much?" He brought his own eyes within inches of William, knotting the stout fingers in his hair, daring him to answer.

William met Joseph's eyes defiantly. "Eleven."

"You heretical wretch, prove it if you dare!" The big hand released William's hair by tossing his head roughly to the side.

William kept his eyes fixed on Joseph, unblinking. The notion that he truly did know the Canon better than this pious monster brought an ironic, rebellious grin to, face. "John 13:34. 'A new commandment I give unto you, That ye love one another; as I have loved you, that ye also love one.' Perhaps you never heard that one."

The torch fire reflected wickedly in the abbot's furious eyes as he stood to his full height, looming above William. "No more of this foolishness; it's time to get what I came for. Time to *confess*." Joseph barked his first order to Harold, "Raise him!"

Harold gripped the crank handle and yanked it hard, bringing an earsplitting rattle of metal chains and the groan of the gears echoing through the cell. Each jarring clank jerked William further away from the floor. He clenched his teeth as hard as he could, refusing to cry out despite the unbearable pain in his arms and shoulders as he dangled from his wrists. *I know the commandments and I shalt not bear false witness against myself! Blessed Father and Mother, please give me strength.* Harold pulled the crank handle until William's feet were at the abbot's eye level, then removed iron shackles from William's ankles, only to bind them together again with a long leather strap.

"How heavy is it?" Joseph asked.

"Six stone," Harold answered.

"Good. Proceed."

Harold bent and reached for a large lead ball that was fitted on one side with an iron hook. Lifting it with both hands by the hook. He raised and lowered it, judging its heft, then nodded in approval.

"I'm going to ask you a simple question, Fylbrigge," Joseph grunted as Harold lifted the weight high enough to force the hook between the tethers at William's ankles, allowing it to dangle beneath him. "You are to answer simply, 'yes' or 'no'."

William bit down hard as his wrists now bore the sudden extra weight of the lead ball that threatened to separate his ankles from his legs. Still, he refused to cry out.

"Fylbrigge, answer me this," Joseph said, pointing to the crank handle, indicating to Harold to resume on his mark, "yes or no? Have you yet renounced your pact with the devil?"

"What?" William asked incredulously through his clenched teeth. He saw the snare presented to him. Either answer would show him guilty. "I won't answer!"

Joseph gave a nod; Harold jerked the crank.

-clank-

"It is a simple enough question." Joseph yawned. "Answer yes or no."

William bit down harder as each clank caused the lead

weight to bounce beneath him. "I... won't answer."

-clank-

-clank-

"Yes or no?" Joseph asked again.

"I will... not... answer!"

"You will eventually. We have plenty of time." Joseph pointed sharply at the crank then to the ceiling. Harold pulled the handle in rapid repetition until there was virtually no chain between William's wrists and the ceiling beam.

Sean! Please don't leave me now. William ground his teeth and searched the blackness for the apparition, willing him to be there to help him find his strength, praying that he hadn't imagined the visit from his lost brother.

"It's about twenty feet to the floor, boy," Joseph hollered up from the floor. "All it takes is one word, and you will be lowered, gently, and left for the night." He paced the floor with his hands folded in his sleeves. "We'll take away the chains and the bridle. We'll even let you get some sleep. Wouldn't you like to be free of all this? Free to sleep? Doesn't that sound lovely? Give me an answer, and you can get some rest."

It was then that the voice returned to William's ear. *"Fight it, Will. You're not alone."*

I can't. It's too much.

"You can! Trust me. I'm with you."

William's eyes darted about, searching for the shade that had accompanied the voice before, but he could not find it. *Where are you?*

"You must be exhausted, lad," Joseph cooed. "No sleep for days. One word, is all it takes."

"Liar!" William screamed.

Joseph waved his arm, giving Harold his order. "Drop him."

Harold pulled the handle from the crank, sending William into a free fall until the chain went taut, his feet only inches from the floor.

William felt certain his arms had come away from his shoulders as his wrists bore the whole of his body weight and the lead ball that dangled from his ankles. It seemed every joint in his body had been pulled open. The shackles bit into his flesh, sending crimson rivulets trickling down his arms. He choked on his own blood as he bit into his tongue at the jarring conclusion of his free-fall. The pain was excruciating and though he hated to give the abbot the satisfaction, it was impossible to hold back a cry of agony as he felt the lead weight bounce around his ankles as once again, he was lifted toward the beam.

"That could not have been pleasant." Joseph snickered as Harold pulled the crank handle. "Shall we try again?"

"I... will not... say it."

"You're not alone, Will. Keep fighting," the voice told him, traveling behind William's ear.

I made no pact. I won't say it. It's a lie. Please believe me.

"I believe you," the voice assured him.

"Answer yes or no. One word. Say it!" Joseph raised his hand, signaling to Harold again.

"It's a... lie—"

"Drop him!"

"AH!" William no longer attempted to stifle his screams on each drop. And with each scream, his own blood threatened to drown him. His wrists and ankles bled freely, and he held the secret hope he would simply bleed to death right there, putting an end to his nightmare, but Joseph would not allow such an easy escape from his suffering.

"Bring him down," Joseph ordered.

Harold released the chain slowly this time, lowering William until his knees rested on the stone floor. He removed the wrist shackles but kept hold of William's arms while Joseph heated the blade of a flat dagger in the torch flame.

"I can stop your blood from flowing quite simply with this." Joseph brought the blade close to William's wrists. "Yes or no?"

"Let me bleed."

"Now, now. I don't want you to bleed to *death*, do I?"

William met Joseph's eyes as defiantly as possible, but his resolve was almost gone. "I won't answer."

"You *will* answer my question. Yes or no?" Joseph pressed the hot blade against William's wrists, sealing the wounds to stop the bleeding. "Have you renounced your pact!"

"I made no pact!" William cried out so loud, the echoes hurt his ears.

I can't keep this up, Sean.

"I'm right behind you." Was that a breeze on his back? Or was it truly Sean?

Joseph sighed and stepped back for a moment while Harold refastened the shackles over the burns.

"Shall we try again? Yes or no?" Joseph gave Harold the signal to raise William's feet to his eye level again. "I think I shall make it easier for you." Joseph cut the leather straps from William's ankles, sending the weight crashing to the floor. "There now, isn't that better?" He placed the blade back into the torch flame.

Though relieved with the release of the weight, William knew this small respite would come at a price.

"The blade will burn as easily as it will cut, and if I'm quick, you won't even bleed. But it would be *such* a pity should you not be able to walk to your trial." Joseph removed the dagger from the torch and showed the glowing, red blade to William. "One cut, just above your heel, will be all it takes to put you forever off your feet." Joseph brought the blade to the back of William's heels, and laughed under his breath. "'Twould be a shame should you actually be found innocent after such a cut. You'd be left a hobbled beggar. So, tell me. Yes or no? Have you yet renounced your pact with the devil?"

Sean? Do I fight to live crippled? Or give him an answer, and face the death fire? What kind of choice is that? William waited for an answer. Only silence came back. *God, he wasn't real.*

"Yes or no?" Joseph demanded.

"I made no pact." William held his breath and closed his eyes.

"Fool." Joseph ran the blade quickly across his heels, cutting and sealing the wounds in one agonizing stroke.

William screamed, anger fading to despair knowing the damage was done.

"Answer the question!" Joseph yelled, then put the blade back into the torch fire until once again it glowed fiery red.

"Why?" William cried, "what's... the use?" The frightened child that had lurked within him his entire life had come out to claim the last of his resolve. *Sean, where did you go?*

Joseph motioned to Harold to lower the chains so that

William's eyes would be level with his own. "Would be a shame should you not be able to see your trial." Joseph held up the glowing blade, to be sure William could see it. "Yes or no?"

God, Sean, help. William closed his eyes tight against the abbot's face and the hot dagger. He knew what was coming next and for the first time, truly considered answering yes or no. *Sean, can I quit now? Please? I don't want to live crippled and blind.* It was then that the frightened child inside him fully returned and he began to cry.

"What's this?" Joseph cooed, and laughed under his breath. "Tears?" William felt the heat draw close to his face. He heard the hiss, and felt the quick sear as Joseph caught the tears with the tip of the knife, as they fell from his face. "You're close to the end now, aren't you? Look at you, shaking all over, just like you used to do when you took lessons from me. I would have thought you'd have outgrown that by now. I've heard so many stories about mighty fearless William Fylbrigge and your courageous rescue of that poor, misunderstood wench in Kylkannen. How disappointed I am to learn that the mighty William of Drumoak is nothing more than a quivering, sniveling bairn." He sizzled off the tears as they traced down William's face, catching them closer to his eyes each time. "Yes or no, boy?"

"Don't give in yet, Will." Sean's voice returned to William's ear. *"He's bluffing. Keep your eyes shut."*

Bluffing? He means to do it.

"Trust me!" Sean insisted.

William held his eyes closed as tight as possible against the heat of the blade, and though grateful he was not yet burned, anticipating the touch of the iron was becoming just as frightening as the prospect of losing his eyes. Maybe Sean's voice was right. Maybe Joseph was bluffing.

"Yes or no?"

I trust you, Sean. Blessed Mother, do as you will. I trust you. "I won't answer." William held his breath and waited for the knife. But it was not the touch of hot iron that he felt across his eyes, but the touch of a cold wind that seemed to embrace him from behind. His kept his eyes closed and allowed his head to drop forward as his mind settled into fog. The only sensation he was aware of was the taste of blood and tears on his tongue, a bright sting on his cheek, and the windy hands that wrapped protectively over his eyes.

"Yes or no!" The abbot's insistent bellowing echoed through the cell from way below, bringing William out of the fog.

Confused, he cautiously opened his eyes and found he had been raised back to the beam and was facing the small window near the top of the cell. The first half-light of dawn was stealing over the clouds. *I must have blacked out. It wasn't Sean I felt. It was only the wind from the window. But... I can see it; I'm not blind!* He looked down to where Joseph stood in the circle of torchlight. He saw no sign of the dagger and no longer felt any pain about his heels. *Delirium. Thank God. The knife wasn't real.* But he wasn't dreaming anymore, and the pain he was feeling in his arms and back was excruciatingly real.

Joseph glared up to William. "I'm growing weary of your foolish game, boy! This has gone on too long."

Hanging at the beam, facing another agonizing fall to the

floor, delirious and mangled, William knew he had reached his limits. Even if the dagger had been a dream—*was it? Why can't I feel it?*—there was nothing in him left to fight. *I have to end it Sean. I'm finished. I'm sorry.* He waited for the voice to come to his ear, but none came. *He was a dream. Oh God, I'm alone after all.* William opened his mouth and began to form the one-word answer that for better or worse would end his ordeal when incredibly, it was Harold who interrupted him, inadvertently robbing the abbot of his victory.

"Excuse me, Abbot," Harold said politely. "But my best guess is, he's reached the brink. That last one nearly done 'im. One more drop an' he won't make it to trial. I don't care either way, mind you, but Dunkirk was clear."

Joseph's piggish cheeks flared red in fury as he grudgingly gave Harold his order. "Lower him slowly and replace the bridle and carry on as before. I shall be glad to take my leave of this as well."

Harold nodded and lowered William gently, this time leaving him low enough to sit against the wall, his hands mercifully on his lap instead of above his head.

"Your pact has protected you well this night," the abbot said and abruptly stalked out of the cell.

William closed his eyes and slouched back against the wall. *I made no damned pact.*

"None of that! You know the rules. Eyes wide!" Harold shook his face. "Forward! Open your mouth!" Harold replaced the hateful bridle and locked it with a sharp clank.

I know the rules. He wasn't really here, I conjured him up in my own mind. I survived alone. Why did you leave me alone?

Harold slammed the iron door, leaving William alone

in the cell with the first rays of dawn coming through the window.

"Sleep, Will. You're not alone."

William closed his eyes and stole an hour of precious sleep.

Chapter 14

EDWARD PASSED THE last hours of the night alone in his salon, brooding about everything that had taken place. "Anne, I've at last run out of strategies. When I am bested by a little housemaid, it is time for me to concede." He stared longingly into the face of his wife on the portrait above the mantel. "You would have done better than I, I'm sure. You would have believed him. And I would have believed you."

He walked to his window to watch for any sign of Richard or Laurel's return. "I've sent them on a fool's mission, my love. Too late and too little. Had I acted at once, the urgency would not be so great."

The moon had set hours before, but the sky had been crystal clear and full of stars the entire night. The starlight did not illuminate as well as the moon had, but it was enough for him to make out the shapes of the houses and buildings in the village below him. The first movement he saw came from the abbey— a solitary figure moving swiftly toward Drumoak.

"Richard is on his way back. Let's hope he got what we need."

Edward decided to meet Richard at the foyer instead of waiting for him in his suite. He gave one last look to his wife's image and went quickly to the door. Richard was already in the hall before Edward made it to the bottom of the stairs. He was so intent on his urgency to meet with Edward that he almost collided with him as they met on the stairs.

Edward grasped him by both of his arms. "Do you have answers?"

Richard nodded while trying to catch his breath.

"Kitchen, then; it's closer, and we shall know when the others return." Edward moved him along quickly.

Once in the kitchen, Richard dropped heavily onto a chair. "I know what they plan to do."

"What do we need?" Edward asked.

Richard looked up helplessly. "A miracle." He slumped back against the chair.

Edward stared at him, waiting for more. When Richard said no more, he grabbed him by the tunic and sat him straight up. "Tell me!"

"It is as you thought— they are hoping to overturn the treaties. That was at the crux of this, but my father is greedy and wants everything William has. I convinced him that I had betrayed you."

"How did you do that?"

"As you suggested, I showed him the crest and made out that I wished William defeated so I would inherit his title. I offered to align with Aberdoir against you." Richard cast his eyes downward. "He took the bait."

"What is the second charge?" Edward asked, impatiently.

"The poison," Richard answered. "The nightshade you revived him from."

"The poison?" Edward asked, bewildered. "But he was the *victim* of that crime. They cannae punish him for being the victim."

"They will claim he survived a double poisoning by way of a pact he's signed with the devil. That's the true crime that they accuse him of— that he's in league with the dark lord himself. They plan to prove it."

Edward's brow creased severely. "How?"

"A test." Richard stood and paced the kitchen. "They plan to force him to drink another dose of poison. If he survives, it will only prove his guilt, and off to the stake he goes. Of course, if he dies, it will mean he's innocent. Pass or fail, he ends up dead."

"This is madness!" Edward threw his hands in the air. "What do they gain in this?"

"Your treaties, embargoes, and borders will be forfeit! They'll claim that William tricked them into signing the treaties through black magic." Richard raised his voice. "My father will be paid handsomely by Drunbalk and Wesley. He'll collect the bounty from Lord Ogham." Richard stopped pacing and dropped himself onto the chair again. "And now, he believes he will rule Sutherland by my side as well." He sighed. "At least he shall be disappointed on that point." He toyed with the crest on his shoulder. "Grandfather, I swear, Sutherland will not welcome the likes of my father within her borders."

"Neither will Stonehaven when this all passed," Edward promised.

A loud commotion in the hall took their attention. "They've returned." Edward left his seat quickly. "Let's hope they can tell us something more promising."

They were both astounded to find not only Laurel and

Ian, but most of the population of Stonehaven filing noisily into the great hall. Young and old, mostly peasants, some of higher standing, clamored past the huge doors. Laurel stood on the stair landing to address them. Elinor entered last and closed the doors behind them. Laurel spotted Richard and Edward and excitedly motioned for them to join her.

"Our mouse has taken over, Richard." Edward smiled and clapped Richard on the back as he stared, overwhelmed at the little maid on the stair.

"She has indeed!" Richard agreed.

"All right, everyone, please listen." Laurel quieted the crowd by waving her hands. "We've not much time." She waited a moment for the chorus of murmurs to settle. "We've explained the situation to all of you. Is there anyone here who feels they cannot accept the responsibility we ask?"

A tentative hand went up in the middle of the crowd. A young woman they had recruited from the tavern stepped forward. "M' name's Cassandra Fraewender. I've got a question." She spoke in rough, bawdy accent. "I mean, they was offerin' to pay us to say what they want. You makin' any offers?"

Laurel's faced flared red at the woman. "Pay you?" She spat her words. "This is a man's life we are speaking about!"

"Allow me, Laurel." Edward came forward.

Laurel stepped aside, resisting the urge to pounce and scratch the vulgar woman's eyes out.

Edward addressed the woman. "Miss Fraewender, is it? Do you know the man we are talking about?"

"'Course I do!" Cassandra put her nose up indignantly.

"'At's him ain't it? 'Angin' on the wall there." She pointed with a thumb over her shoulder to William's new portrait. "'E's a sweet fellow. Musician of sorts, ain't 'e? Plays in the tavern on occasion," she answered, with no apparent respect for Edward's rank, a seedy, lewd and wanton smile on her face.

"Yes, that would be he." Edward rolled his eyes toward Ian and Laurel, then asked Cassandra, "Do you like him?"

"What's not to like! I said 'e's a sweet fellow. Always nice as nice is." Cassandra grinned wantonly, jingling her change purse. "Left me a decent tip or two on occasion."

Laurel's face turned scarlet. She had heard the rumors of William's exploits in the tavern but was glad Mehlyndia was not in the hall to hear this.

"Would you like it if he were to be killed on what you say?" Edward asked Cassandra, straight-faced. The room silenced instantly.

"Killed?" Her bawdy grin faded. "On what I say?"

"Killed." Edward took a step closer to her. "Testifying to the highest bidder may seem like a shrewd business deal to you, young woman, but this is a man's life you bargain with." Edward's voice echoed through the hall. Before another sound could be made, he looked out at the faces gathered there. "If there are any others among you who look to profit from your testimony, I invite you to turn and leave at once. I shall not play the same game the bishop plays. There will be no repercussions to any who choose to leave. I shall leave the hall for a few moments, and those who wish to leave may go. I'll address the remainder when I return. Richard, Laurel, Ian, and Elinor, come with me. Five minutes only." He spun on his heel and led them up the stairs.

When they reached Edward's suite, Ian marked the time on the mantle clock. Laurel closed the door, fuming. "I am sorry about her. I had no idea! They seemed so genuinely concerned when we called upon them. Every one of them knows Will and claim him as a friend. I cannot believe—"

"It's all right, Laurel. Calm down." Edward took her by the shoulders. "Child, I am thrilled that you have brought almost the entire village."

"Let's hope a few of them stay. Pay them! Of all the—" Laurel stopped, aghast, suddenly caught off guard by Edward's smiling face as he looked at her with absolute delight in his eyes. "What's so funny? This is no time to laugh."

"I am just, for the first time, seeing your fire," Edward said, giving her a genuinely warm hug, "and I'm terribly grateful to have you on our side."

"Thank you, m' lord." Laurel hugged him back. Edward's words of praise came as a surprise. At that moment, she decided, whatever the consequence, she would no longer pretend to be the timid, dutiful, dim-witted housemaid they all assumed she was. "Let's hope there are enough souls in the hall to rally when we return. We shall need every one of them."

"What about the other charge?" Richard asked.

"Yes, that is still the biggest concern." Edward wrinkled his brow and sighed. "That one shall be very difficult to challenge."

"You've found out what it is?" Ian asked, excited.

"I sent Richard on a special mission while you were out gathering your army." Edward flopped into his chair. "What he has learned may make the lot of those downstairs of no consequence."

"What?" Laurel turned to Edward, her heart dropping to her feet. "Why?" She began to panic when Edward would not answer. "Richard? Tell me!"

Before he could answer, the chamber door swung open as Mehlyndia slipped in quietly.

"Are you well?" Edward asked her, taking her hand.

Mehlyndia allowed herself to be led to a chair. "Yes, I'm feeling better. I need to be part of this."

"One minute left," Ian tolled.

"We do not all need to go down. I shall address the crowd." Edward grudgingly stood and headed for the door.

"I'm going with you," Laurel piped up, determined to find out why her army may no longer be necessary.

"As you wish. I dare not try to stop you from doing anything." Edward smiled appreciatively. "The rest of you, put your heads together. Richard, explain the details. Come along, Laurel, it's time."

They left the rest of the group and headed to the hall. "How bad is it?" Laurel asked Edward.

"Bad enough. But you've made me believe in miracles, my dear. There just may be one waiting for us." Edward took her hand and hurried her along the corridor.

"It's very quiet down there. I hope *some* of them stayed." Laurel was almost afraid to look into the hall. When they did get to the staircase, she could see instantly that her army had dwindled down to no more than a scout party, but she was still gratified to see the two dozen or so people who stayed behind, willing to testify on William's behalf.

"Are there enough?" she asked Edward, encouraged but

still wary.

"More than!" He smiled. "You've done it, Laurel. One charge down, I can feel it!"

They walked down the stairs to instruct the people who would rally to William's defense. Laurel was disheartened but not all together surprised that there were no nobles among them. In front of them all, a determined and defiant Geoffrey had taken the role of leader of this ragged tribe of peasants.

"I am gratified by each of you." Edward descended the stairs and stood within the crowd of peasants, extending his hand to each of them in turn. "I realize the difficulty this may bring to you. Though I offer no monetary gain, rest assured, each and every one of you will not be forgotten by me nor any member of this household. And if— *when* William is exonerated, I'm sure he will personally thank each of you in a way meaningful to him."

"'Tis little to ask of us," Geoffrey said as Edward clasped his hands. "William would not hesitate to stand up alone for any of us who are here for him."

Edward shook Geoffrey's hand. "You're absolutely right, Geoffrey. Thank you."

"Tell us what we must do, m' lord," Geoffrey said. "We're ready."

The ragged people behind Geoffrey cheered their agreement.

Laurel stood aside, trying desperately to hold her emotions in check. *Geoffrey is right. Will would stand up for any one of them. Edward should have stood up sooner. But it's not too late. Blessed Mother, please let it not be too late.* She took a long breath and swallowed hard, turning her attention to Edward as he began to instruct the group that stood before him.

"All right, then, here is what we must do..."

Later, with the peasant army instructed and dismissed until it was time for the trial, Edward sat brooding in his chair. Across the room, Richard and Ian mulled over their elaborate and complicated rescue plans to save William from the stake, should the witnesses Laurel rallied fail to persuade the judge. Mehlyndia sat curled up on the window seat, cradled in Elinor's motherly arms, with Laurel sitting nearby. Edward stared at the portrait of his wife, silently conversing with her. *They are acting under authority of the crown, and I have no power to overrule. All those souls who have faced what he now faces, I had the power to spare with but one word. I let them perish, and now, the one time I would choose to step in, I can do nothing to save him.* He looked up to his wife's loving image, lost in the hopelessness of the situation, only half listening to the conversation around him.

"You are certain? We shall be allowed to take him after the test?" Richard asked Ian, for the hundredth time.

"Yes, they will allow you to do as you wish," Ian answered wearily. He had gone through what he knew of these things countless times. "At the conclusion of the test, he'll 'die'. They will simply admit their error, rejoice that his soul was saved before God, and let you take his body where you will. The fact that he must die to prove his innocence is meaningless to them."

They remained quiet for a moment. Edward left his chair and paced the floor, deep in thought at what they had planned. "Then it must be convincing and we must be sure to remove him quickly. Inducing a deep sleep is easy enough, but he will have only so much time before we must wake him." He thought about the morning not long ago that he had woken him from Bryndah's dose. "And that shall be a difficult trick within itself. A slap in the face would certainly be out of the question given his physical state."

"I shall be prepared and waiting with the proper dose to bring him 'round," Elinor reminded Edward.

Edward nodded, his chin in his hand. "Then I shall trust you, my dear." He looked to Ian. "You'll put the potion in the sacramental wine then?"

"Yes, prior to their test." Ian nodded. "It is a gamble, but it is the best we can do." He sighed. "The one comfort we can take in this test... it is certain that he won't face death on the stake."

"Unless he's found guilty of enchanting and they do not have need of this test." Edward sighed. "If that happens, you will have the *other* potion, correct?" Edward asked quietly.

"Yes," Ian answered in kind.

"Will it work quickly?" Edward looked to Elinor.

"Aye." Elinor wiped her eyes on her apron. "It takes only a moment. He'll not even see the flame."

Edward sighed heavily. "In that case, Ian will have to wait until the last moment."

"I've done it before, sir. I'll know when," Ian assured Edward gently. "I'll take care of him. I promise you I will do everything within my power to spare him from feeling the fire."

"Thank you." Edward took a deep breath and sat himself

at the head of the table. "Now, let's assume we shall be successful instead of anticipating gloom. We have a sea journey to plan."

Laurel had been dozing by the window while the men worked out the details of their rescue. After spending the better part of the night walking the streets of Stonehaven with Ian and Elinor, she was exhausted. Though she tried to stay focused on the matter at hand, she found it impossible to keep her eyes open. Images of the horrid jail, William's mangled hands, and her journey through the streets to rally the people to fight for him invaded her thoughts and meshed with the voices in the room around her. She finally gave in and allowed herself to drift into a light, fitful sleep.

She found herself back in the street, Elinor and Ian by her side. They led a flock of hundreds of goats, some small, some large, through the town. She had no understanding why, but she knew she had to get them back to Drumoak, but they wanted to wander and hide in the shadows. She tried to herd them back together. Several disappeared into the alley.

"Ian, they're leaving us. Make them follow. Sing."

Ian began to sing, Elinor joining in. The goats followed. Elated, Laurel began to sing. "We're going to make it."

From out of the dark, the sound of galloping hooves echoed around them. "No! They'll frighten them all away!" Laurel yelled. "Elinor! Ian, keep them together."

The horses rounded the corner, each bearing a hooded rider. They rode through the herd, scattering them to the four corners of town before vanishing into the shadows once again. Laurel spun, counting the flock that remained. Less than half.

"Sing, Ian! Make them follow you. That's what he used to do."

Ian nodded and began to sing. The goats gathered again. Fewer this time, but still an ample flock. They only needed to pass by the prison, then they were clear to enter Drumoak. Laurel glanced to the highest tower. A flickering light shown through the small window in the top of the tower.

"We're almost there, Laurel. Look, there's the gate." Elinor pointed toward Drumoak. "Aye! we're going to make it."

Laurel herded the goats to the gate, when a mournful wailing wind sliced through the air. It started low and grew louder. It took on a voice. She stopped in her tracks, mesmerized by the sound. Ian and Elinor heard it as well and covered their ears against it. The goats heard it, began to panic, and again scattered into the dark until there were no more than a dozen remaining. "Are there still enough?"

Louder and louder, the wailing echoed through her ears until she felt her blood run cold. She recognized the voice and could understand the words that it carried on the wind: "I made no pact!"

Laurel sat bolt upright on the window seat. "Will!" she called out, startling everyone into silence. She stared, bleary eyed, at the faces around her, then realized she had been sleeping.

"Laurel, you were dreaming." Mehlyndia embraced her. "There, calm down."

Laurel clutched Mehlyndia, waiting for the panic to pass. "Ian... Elinor?" Laurel called, shaking in Mehlyndia's arms.

"What is it?" Elinor came to her quietly.

Ian looked up from where he sat.

"Did we hear it?" Laurel asked between staggered breaths. "Or was it a dream?" She grabbed Elinor's hand. "While we were out there. Tell me."

Elinor's eyes welled up as she squeezed Laurel's hand. "Aye," she whispered. "We heard. So did half the townspeople."

"What?" Mehlyndia asked, beginning to shake as badly as Laurel. "What did you hear?"

Ian was suddenly by their side. "My lady, it's best you don't know." He patted Mehlyndia's hand. "It would do you no good, and it shall only upset Laurel more to discuss it." His voice was gentle but his words were stern. "I don't mean to seem cold, but we need to get back to our plan. There's precious little time left."

Mehlyndia reluctantly nodded. "Yes. Make your plans." She released Laurel. "Are you all right now?"

"Yes, thank you." Laurel sat up straight and blew her nose. "I'm sorry I interrupted." She had pushed the memory out of her head, but now remembered clearly what had happened while she was out in the night. Just as they were leading the people past the prison to Drumoak, they had all heard the scream that came from the tower. She had passed out in the street and was helped back to her feet by Geoffrey. How could she have forgotten?

"I'm glad you're awake." Ian held his hand to her. "I believe they need your help. Come, join us." He led her to the table to join Edward and Richard.

"My dear, I'm sorry for your distress." Edward smiled sadly. "Ian is correct, I believe you can help us."

"Any way I can, I shall." Laurel took a breath and steadied

her nerves.

"Good." Edward patted her hand. "As you know, we have a ship moored off the coast, waiting to take Mehlyndia, and you as well, if you wish to be away from here."

Laurel suddenly realized she had no thought of the future beyond William's trial. It was as though it did not exist. "I know of the ship."

"We need to get Mehlyndia there without drawing attention from the hunters who are patrolling Stonehaven," Edward explained. "So we need to be secretive. I seem to remember you and William playing about in the catacombs when you were children."

Laurel blushed, remembering how Edward had reprimanded the two of them when he found out. "Yes. I remember."

"Do you know if there is a path through the caves from the castle that will deliver you to the seawall?" Edward asked hopefully.

"Yes. It is confounding, but there is a path," Laurel answered, weary but glad to be of help. "It starts in the crypt."

"Excellent!" Edward smiled. "Little mouse, you are a treasure!"

She smiled sadly, pleased with his praise but ever so weary of being called 'little mouse.' "Thank you, m' lord."

"When was the last time you were there?" Richard asked Laurel.

"It's been a few years, but I remember following Will from the crypt to the seawall." Laurel thought for a moment. "I hated that game, but he liked to explore down there; God only knows why. There are dangerously sharp rocks and slippery steep drops. We were mad to play there."

"Are you up to such a journey, Mehlyndia? It could be dangerous for you." Edward took his daughter's hand. "The thought of it all breaks this old man's heart." He turned to Ian. "Are you certain in your assumptions? Must she take this risk?"

Ian looked at Edward sympathetically. "My lord, she is with child. The father has been accused of entering into a demonic pact. In their view, her bairn is the devil's spawn and they will come for her. She cannot stay here."

"It seems outlandish to me. I can hardly believe they would—" Edward began then stopped short. "I'm sorry, Ian. My stubborn disbelief has already caused enough pain. I won't allow it to hurt Mehlyndia as well."

"Thank you, Father." Mehlyndia squeezed her father's hand. "It is best for everyone. I was prepared to make that journey alone, but if there is the smallest hope that William will be with me, I gladly take the risk."

Edward held Mehlyndia close to him. "I admit, it is a good plan. Should the worst befall William, you must be far away from here. And if we are successful in our deception, we will bring him through the caves to join you. After all, if the world thinks him dead, he can't possibly stay on this shore. You both must leave." Edward looked to Richard. "You understand what I'm saying? This test will force my hand. You must be prepared to accept that rank now."

"Yes." Richard swallowed hard. "I understand."

Edward nodded sadly. "You've explored those caves as well, haven't you, Richard?"

"Yes, but like Laurel, it's been a long time," Richard

admitted. "But I find no other option. It won't be safe to travel on the open road."

"I know the caves better than Richard does. Sean and Will, of course, know them even better than I do," Laurel spoke wearily, almost daydreaming.

"Unfortunately, neither Sean nor William are able to guide us, Laurel." Edward paced for a moment.

"If we had more time, I could take you there now." Laurel sighed. "I can almost see the way from the crypt to the seawall." Whether it was fatigue or doubt she could not tell, but her spirit was starting to fade.

"But there is no time. You must come with me, Laurel." Ian took her hand and spoke gently to her, "I need to see Dunkirk and persuade him to allow me to administer rites. And we must go soon, before the sun is fully up. You will need a proper acolyte robe to be convincing in full view of the bishop."

She looked at Ian with tired eyes and nodded. "I know."

"Laurel, perhaps you can remember the path enough to draw it out?" Mehlyndia asked hopefully. "I'll draw it for you!" She reached for Edward's quill and parchment. "How do I start? Close your eyes and try to describe the way through the caves."

"If I close my eyes, I shall not open them for hours." Laurel sighed.

"Think, little mouse. You know the urgency." Edward patted her shoulder for encouragement.

Laurel closed her eyes and began to remember the last time she had played the game with Sean and Will in the catacombs when they were younger— that wonderful summer day that she held close to her heart.

* * *

"Will! Sean! Come on, you two. This isn't funny! It's dark! I can't see anything!"

"Hold on, I'm coming."

"Will?"

"How did your torch go out, silly girl?" William looked around dramatically. "Did the dragon blow it out?"

"I was startled by a rat."

"A rat?" He made a skeptical grin.

"A big rat!"

"I don't see any rat trails. I think you just got scared and dropped it in the sand."

"Will, just lead me out, please. I don't like it here."

"Is the damsel afraid? Have you heard the dragon? Shall I slay her for you, m' lady?"

"There is no dragon. You're making that up."

"Ah, but there is. And she breathes fire, and she just might be right... behind this..." he teased, then suddenly jumped sideways and dropped the torch to the sand, shouting, "Rock!" The flame went out and the two were in the dark again.

"Stop it!" she screamed at him. "You're frightening me!" He made no sound. "Will?" He stayed quiet. "William Fylbrigge, where are you?" she cried, flailing her hands out in front of herself in the darkness, trying to find him. Suddenly, she felt someone grab her quickly around the middle and spin her to the sandy floor of the cave. Before she knew what was happening, he rolled himself onto her.

"I'm right here."

"You're scaring me to death, Will. Let me up." She lay on her back in the sand, stunned to have him on top of her.

"Nothing to be afraid of. It's just me." He propped himself on his arms, but remained belly to belly, holding her in place.

"Please. I don't like the dark."

"I do."

"That's because you are a raving madman." She finally began to laugh. "Why, sir, do you approve of the dark so well?" she asked him in her make-believe damsel voice.

"Better to hide from the dragon. And because no one can see us." He lowered himself close to her ear and whispered. "And no one will see me do this." He kissed her shyly but fully.

Laurel did not fight the kiss, even though it had taken her completely by surprise.

"Unhand me, sir," she protested, secretly hoping for another kiss.

"But I have saved thee from the dragon, m' lady. Am I not entitled to my reward?" He stayed close to her, his voice soft against her ear.

"There is no dragon." Her voice matched his.

"Then it is only honorable for me to give back the reward I've stolen." He kissed her again, more deliberately this time. Laurel responded in kind, elated at the unexpected turn this game had taken.

"Will? Laurel? Where are you two? Come on, we've got to leave. The tide is rising!" Sean's voice came from beyond the passage from which William had just come.

William jumped up quickly and helped Laurel to her feet. They still stood in the dark, so she could not see the look on his face to know if he was embarrassed or ashamed to be found with her. He squeezed her hand briefly, then called to Sean.

"Over here, Sean! We've lost the light."

Sean followed the sound of William's voice to where he and Laurel stood in the dark.

As the light from the torch touched his face, Laurel could find no hint in his eyes that he had felt as she did when he kissed her. She hoped the heat on her cheeks would leave when they reached the sunshine of the beach.

Sean came around the last turn. "There you are. The tide is coming. We have to hurry."

"We've got time. Don't be a worrying old hen, Sean," William mocked.

"Who worries? You've got my lunch sack," Sean teased.

"Let's go then. I hate the darkness in here." Laurel sighed no longer sharing their cheerful mood.

"What's with you? I Thought you liked the caves." Sean looked at her irritably.

"Nothing. It's getting late." She retrieved William's discarded torch and re-lit it from Sean's.

"She's right, it's getting late. Besides, we've done as much damage as we can here." William laughed and resumed his make-believe voice. "I should not like to be the pirate who tries to sneak through that fortress!"

They all had laughed together as they made their way out of the cave, being careful to avoid the rock slide trigger that Will and Sean had set as part of their game of treasure hunters.

Laurel had remembered the details of that afternoon every day of her life and had never told anyone of it. Often, she wondered if William ever thought about it, or if he even remembered it as she did. She ached at the memory of his kiss, the way he felt so close to her, and the many times she had reached back to that summer day, longing to make it real again. Especially now. As she let herself get lost momentarily in this secret memory, it occurred to her that something else had reminded her of that day earlier. "The book!"

Mehlyndia looked at her, startled. "Laurel!"

"Mehlyndia, he drew a map! There is a map of the catacombs in his book." Laurel jumped up and headed to the door.

"What book?" Edward asked.

Laurel turned and shot a look to Elinor. She, just that instant, remembered that she had the torn page still in her belt.

"Just an old journal William once kept. Nothing very important," Mehlyndia spoke quickly. "I think I know where it is."

"Elinor, come with us!" Laurel motioned for them to leave together.

Laurel ran so quickly that Elinor and Mehlyndia could barely keep up. "Laurel, wait!" Mehlyndia called to her, but she would not slow down.

By the time Elinor and Mehlyndia finally did catch up to her, Laurel was already in front of Mehlyndia's trunk, trying to open the latch. "I need the key! We have to get his book, Mehlyndia, please."

"Are you sure it's not dangerous?" Mehlyndia hesitated.

"Yes, I'm sure. I took the spell out." Laurel said quickly, without thinking what she was saying.

Ian and Richard had followed Mehlyndia and were just rounding the corner.

"Spell?" Ian asked, a concerned look on his face. "What do you mean you took the spell out? Is *that* what you asked him for?"

The three women turned to look at him all at once. Richard grabbed him by the back of the collar and pushed him into the room quickly, shutting the door behind them.

"What are you talking about?" Ian demanded. "Let me go!"

"Nothing has changed! He's innocent. Have no fear of that." Richard explained hurriedly, shaking the monk in his hands. "Please, you must believe that."

"Richard, stop, we need to explain it to him." Laurel pushed herself between the two men. She assumed the commanding air that had so surprised Edward earlier. "Ian, please, listen carefully."

He looked at her with confused concern in his eyes as Laurel slowly reached into her belt and unfolded the quartered piece of parchment.

"I only show you this because I believe you will understand." Laurel held the parchment up for Ian.

"Laurel, no!" Mehlyndia gasped.

Laurel ignored her and pushed the paper into Ian's hand. "Don't disappoint me, Ian. My heart tells me to trust you."

Ian looked into Laurel's eyes. "I will certainly try not to disappoint you." He took the page from her and read it slowly. His eyes misted as he read silently the words that were written in a precise and careful script. "Yes, Laurel. I understand it." He read the verse aloud:

~ For Persuasion and Confidence ~
Anoint with oil made from chicory,

Divine Mother, show me the way
Remove my doubts and banish fear
God and Father, creator of days
Guide my words that they be clear

Allow no harm within my mission
Move my tongue to speak for thee
I ask that those with ears shall listen
That they may turn and follow me

Written in a quicker, less elegant script, William had added:
In the name of the Lady and the Lord
May their way be mine.
~w.f.~

"This explains so much," Ian said quietly, almost to himself, then looked at the apprehensive faces around him. "Do you all understand what this is?"

"Damning evidence, should it be found by Dunkirk and his crowd." Richard spoke coldly.

Ian looked at Richard sadly and sighed. "Yes, that much is obvious because they don't understand it. Judging by the look on your face, Sir Richard, I take it you don't understand what this is either. Do you believe it to be a spell?"

"Forgive my ignorance, but yes!" Richard answered defensively. "Is it not?"

Mehlyndia and Laurel exchanged startled glances. Laurel feared her distrust of Richard was about to be proven. What's worse, she had just betrayed William's secret to a member of the clergy, but somehow Ian worried her far less than Richard. "Richard, it's not—"

Ian held up a hand to quiet her. "Allow me," he said softly to Laurel, then turned to Richard. "In another time or another place, this would not be seen as anything other than a simple, honest prayer for confidence or guidance. No different than might be uttered by the bishop himself before a sermon. William simply wished for the courage to speak his heart and to be understood. Even the reference to Divine Mother could be construed as the Holy Virgin, although..." He placed a gentle hand on Laurel's shoulder. "My instinct tells me, William practices the Old Faith, yes?" He looked into Laurel's frightened eyes. "There is nothing to fear from me, Laurel."

"But if *they* knew... they don't understand the way you do." Laurel's eyes welled up. "Ian, they can't know about it."

Ian crossed his hands over his heart. "They shan't learn about it from me. I can clearly see the implication this prayer would present, given the charges against him." He folded the paper carefully and gave it back to Laurel. "It is not a tool for evil, I know that as well as you do. Be assured, I shall not mention its existence. You have not misplaced your trust in me." He looked to Richard. "Do you understand now?"

"Aye," Richard answered quietly. "It's a prayer."

"I told William as much myself," Mehlyndia said, choking back tears. "He only wished to please my father. To be confident enough to carry the negotiations. And he believed that this simple chant is what gave him his words. He feared it would be discovered that he relied on it so, and yet it is so—"

"Benign," Ian finished for her. "It is a simple, lovely prayer. Nothing more." He placed his hands gently on Mehlyndia's shoulders.

"Thank you, Ian." Mehlyndia cried softly. "If only we could use it to persuade the judge, but as you say, he would certainly not see it with your perception."

Laurel put the parchment back into her bodice. "Now, we need to get back to business. Mehlyndia, would you please give me the key to your trunk?"

"He was so adamant it be kept private. Are you sure?" She reluctantly handed Laurel the key.

"If it helps the two of you sail away, I think he will forgive us." She opened the trunk and retrieved the leather satchel containing William's book. She released the ties and gently pulled the book from the pouch. *Please let me be right.* She opened the book and leafed through the pages until she came across the rough little drawing she had seen earlier. She turned a few pages either way to see if there were more. This was the only one she found. It was titled 'Where the Dragon Lives.'

Laurel stared at it quietly for a moment as she realized that William had mapped out and documented the place where he had stolen his make-believe reward of a kiss from her. He had made a little notation on the place that read

"Laurel is rescued from the dragon!" She felt her face turn red and tears threaten at the memory of that day and at finding out, after years of wondering, that he actually had thought enough about it to put it in his book. *I love you too. I always have.*

"This is it." Laurel simply passed the book to Mehlyndia. "We should not take the whole book. Take only that page." She turned away abruptly, hiding her face in her hands.

"Laurel, what is wrong?" Mehlyndia took the book, then looked at the page. "It seems you three had a merry game that day. He wanted to keep it."

Of course, Mehlyndia did not know about the kiss or the true feelings Laurel carried inside her for William. Laurel assumed Mehlyndia would simply understand that a happy childhood memory recalled at such a desperate time would naturally evoke tears. Mehlyndia went to her sewing box and retrieved her scissors. She carefully cut the map from the book, being sure not to damage any of the other pages. "The drawing is so crude, are you sure?—Laurel, look!" She held the severed page for Laurel alone to see.

As Mehlyndia and Laurel watched, the crude drawing, now separate from the rest of the book, became clear and detailed. The path from the crypt to the seawall clearly marked. Lengthy notations of dead ends, and hidden dangers became visible on the page. Mehlyndia looked at Laurel with an astonished glint in her eye. Laurel smiled and whispered into Mehlyndia's ear, not caring what the others would think, "It's the charm."

"Is that the map we need?" Richard asked impatiently.

"Yes," Laurel answered. "But you cannot be in this spot,"

she said, indicating the dragon's lair, "at the high tide. The sea takes over quickly."

"Then we must plan our movement to match the tide." Richard took command back from Laurel. "You two had better return to the abbey." He turned to Laurel and took her hand. "Please, be careful. Laurel, I should not want any harm to befall you."

For the first time, Laurel saw that Richard did seem to truly care for her. She stared back at him in amazement that she had not seen it sooner. "I shall. You as well." She gave Richard's hand a gentle squeeze before turning to Ian. "Are we ready, Brother Ian?"

"Come with me first, then," Elinor said, as she headed for the door. "I have the powders and roots you need in my cupboard. Laurel is very good with the herbs, Ian." Elinor looked at him shyly. "Trust her on the doses."

"I had a notion she was. I'll trust her absolutely." Ian looked at Laurel's cropped hair, and smiled. "Come along— Sean. It's time to return to the abbey." The two left the room together, Elinor close behind.

"You've been gone all night, Joseph. I expected you hours ago." Dunkirk hurriedly ushered Joseph into his quarters. "I hope you did not take it too far. If he's dead without a confession, the treaties will stand, neither one of us will be paid."

"Relax, he is still breathing." The abbot lowered himself into the cushioned chair by the fire. "For now."

"Were you successful?"

"If you are asking if he confessed, the answer is no."

"Did Harold not do his work properly?" Dunkirk asked. "Has he gone soft?"

"No, he performed as I instructed. The boy just has more tolerance than I would have ever thought possible." He shot a sly sneer to the bishop. "Which only proves our point. He's relying on his pact."

"How did you pose the question?"

"As you suggested. 'Yes or no, have you yet renounced your pact with the devil.' He refused to answer with one word."

"Refused?" Dunkirk asked, disbelieving. "How hard is it to make a man say no? Especially when he's dropped!"

"Harder than I expected! Do not accuse me of failure." The abbot glared at him. "At least we shall have part of our reward to look forward to. We are assured of that, are we not? Thomas owes us at least half. Even if the treaties are not turned back, we've held our end of the bargain. We've brought him to trial, haven't we?"

"Yes, you're right," Dunkirk admitted. "Forgive me, Joseph, it has been a long night. I suggest we both get some rest before the proceedings get underway. The judge the king has sent— Peter Garland is his name, I believe— shall not arrive until this afternoon. He is riding with Ogham and his lot."

"Have you dealt with him before?"

"Oh, yes. He's a fair man, for the most part. It is quite possible we may have to concede the first round." Dunkirk chuckled.

"I suppose there is always a risk of *fairness* in these things," Joseph agreed. "But I feel confident we have more than we need. After all, we still have our trump." He let out a loud yawn. "Gregory, I shall retire to my quarters for the time being. It was a longer night than I expected."

"Yes, of course, you must be exhausted. I will call on you in time to prepare."

The abbot yawned again and took his leave.

Chapter 15

"WE WILL ENTER the abbey through the chapel as we did before. It's still early enough in the day that there should be no one about. But stay close all the same." Ian held her hand tightly as he gave her his instructions. "And remember, should we meet anyone—"

"Yes, I know. I shall not speak. I'm ready, Ian," she reassured him.

They managed to make their way easily through the chapel and passageways to Ian's quarters. They entered silently and quickly closed the door behind them.

"No one has been about. Look." He indicated Laurel's hair cuttings still on the floor around his desk and her discarded garments from the previous day. "We are fortunate no one found these. I had forgotten about it." He kicked the mess under his bed. "We shall worry on that later. Make yourself as comfortable as you can until I get back."

"Be careful, Ian."

"I shall. It may take me some time, Laurel. Please, whatever you do, do not open the door or venture away from this room. I will need to approach the bishop to volunteer for duty."

"Duty?" She looked him confused for a moment.

"Yes, prison duty." Ian reminded her. "One thing I've come to know about this abbey is none of the other brothers seem to take the time to tend to the souls of those most in need." He looked disgusted. "That was apparent to me yesterday! I will appeal to whatever piety, if any, may be left in Dunkirk that he send me to offer the Last Sacrament to William."

"That sounds so defeating."

"I know, but that is how I must appeal to him. I'll return as quickly as possible. Please, stay put." Ian took her face in his hands and spoke quietly. "God grant me half of your courage and I will move mountains to get him away from here. For you, my dear."

Laurel stared back into Ian's eyes. "God, grant me half of your strength. Please take care. I promise I won't move from this spot."

He quickly left the room, closing the door quietly behind him. He thought it wise to approach the Dunkirk before trying to find the robe for Laurel to wear. It was about the right time of morning for the bishop to be about in the vestry, and Ian would naturally be on his way to his work desk in the transcription room, so his meeting would not seem so contrived.

He rehearsed his approach in his head, trying to find the proper tone of voice, the proper words, and inflection. His biggest fear would be that he would meet with Abbot Joseph first and lose his confidence. Something about that man drained the will right out of a person, and Ian had never been able to stand his ground against him.

As he approached the bishop's salon, he heard voices from behind the closed door.

"I suppose there is always the risk of *fairness* in these things. But I feel confident we have more than we need.

After all, we still have our trump. Gregory, I shall retire to my quarters for the time being. It was a longer night than I expected."

"Yes, of course, you must be exhausted. I will call on you in time to prepare."

Ian hid behind the corner when the abbot left the bishop's quarters. He was relieved to see him disappear down the narrow corridor to the guest suite. *Good, I don't need to deal with him!* Steeling his nerve he, knocked on Dunkirk's door.

"Come."

"Forgive the intrusion, Your Grace." Ian bowed respectfully. "I was on my way to the chapel and happened to see that you were already awake." Ian was hopeful he was still blissfully unaware of where he had been in the past day.

"Ah, Brother Ian," Dunkirk greeted him cordially. "We have not had much opportunity to speak since your arrival. In fact, I haven't seen you since you attended the unfortunate guard at Drumoak. Have you settled in?"

"Yes, thank you," Ian replied. "It seems I've come to Stonehaven in time for a bit of excitement," he ventured boldly, but keeping a casual air about him. "I don't know the details, of course, but there seems to be quite a buzz about the village. A trial of sorts to take place, is it?"

"Yes, unfortunate circumstances, I'm afraid." Dunkirk shook his head wearily. "It is always such a pity when one so young and promising turns to the dark."

If Ian did not know better, he could have easily believed the bishop was sincere in his lament. "A shame, yes. Has he repented at all?"

"Alas, he has not." The bishop sighed heavily.

"Has he been offered the Sacraments, then?" Ian kept his voice calm and confident even though he felt his heart begin to pound.

"Yes, and he has refused them." Dunkirk held his hands up, then dropped them. "Such a shame he shall meet his judgment with no thought for his immortal soul."

Ian knew this to be a blatant lie. No one had attended William so no one had offered the Rites. He was also fairly certain that whatever had kept the abbot awake all night, it was not concern for William's immortal soul.

"Your Grace, if you please, I feel compelled then, as a man of God, to try one more time to reach him; to offer him the peace to face his Creator with a repentant spirit."

The bishop looked at him strangely. Ian worried he had spoken too quickly. "Actually, Brother Ian, you may take an unpleasant burden from me. Since you already asked to help."

"Yes?"

"It is only right that he face his trial with some modicum of dignity, given his rank," Dunkirk said. "I was going to prepare him myself but find I am weary of the prison. Would you take the burden from me?"

Ian was dumbfounded and suspicious— Dunkirk seemed far too eager in his request.

"There may be a minor wound or two that may need attention as well."

"A magnanimous gesture, Your Grace," Ian replied carefully, struggling to keep the contempt from his voice. *A wound or two? The man is half dead!*

"Yes." Dunkirk looked up and met Ian's eyes. "It's the least

I can do for the poor lad." He looked away. "Send an acolyte to Drumoak to retrieve appropriate garments for him to wear and then you may go do what you must."

"As you wish." Ian bowed respectfully, holding his hands tightly together within his sleeves to hide their trembling. He turned to leave.

"Brother Ian," Dunkirk called him back.

"Yes?"

"Do not worry yourself on his account should he refuse to repent. He has made his own pact and stands to face a far harsher judgment than any mortal man could impose."

"I understand, but for the sake of God, I am obliged to offer." Ian felt the crimson rise to his face and turned quickly from the bishop. He was gratified that his goal had been reached far easier than he had imagined; however he came away with a distinct feeling that he had somehow played into whatever the bishop had planned. *I cannot worry about that now. He still is not aware of my true motives.*

Ian left the chamber quickly, not wanting to be stopped further. *Send an acolyte to Drumoak! I know just the one,* he thought. But he still needed to get a proper robe for her to wear. He made his way through the kitchen, retrieving food as he had done before, including a skin of ale and one of water, then proceeded through to the dormitory where the acolytes had their quarters. Quietly, he crept into the dark room. The boys were still sleeping but would be awakened by the bell soon. He wished he knew which boy was closest to Laurel's size and height but knew he only had time to retrieve the first robe he could lay his hands on. He approached the first cot quietly and opened the trunk at the foot of the bed. As he hoped, this boy had his robe within easy reach. He found a cassock, cowl and sash and slunk out of the room as quietly as he had entered.

He made his way back through the kitchen, taking another loaf of bread on his way, and quickly ran up the stairs to the corridor where Laurel was waiting in his quarters. He entered the room so quickly that she gasped in surprise.

"Ian!"

"God in heaven, my heart is not bold enough for this espionage." He leaned against the door, breathing heavily for a moment. "Sean, I have a mission for you." He grinned and held out the robe for her. "Change quickly!" He explained that they would be in attendance for William, and she was to go to Drumoak to retrieve his clothes.

"I will wait for you in front of the abbey and we will proceed from there."

As she had the day before, Laurel managed to squirm her way out of her own garments and into the acolyte garb Ian had provided. "I'm ready."

Ian took a quick inventory of the tools they would need. He checked the kit he required for the rites; a flask of wine, two of water, food, a bundle containing yarrow and barley roots to tend the wounds, bandages... and two vials, one promising hope, the other offering mercy. On an impulse, he retrieved his flute from the top of his trunk. The singing had managed to calm William the day before when he had gotten lost in a delusion; after the scream he had heard from the tower during the night, Ian assumed the need for music may be even greater today.

"Let's go, then. God guide us!"

* * *

She stood silent and statuesque in the shadows of the corridor as the monk and his acolyte hurried passed her. *They didn't see me. Good.* Quietly, she approached the monk's door.

Excellent, no locks.

She let herself in and surveyed the little room. *Interesting, he requires no bedclothes?*

She moved smoothly and quietly to the work desk, intending to search the drawers, but her interest was diverted by the strange jumble of cloth on the floor, half concealed under the bed. *What have we here? These are not the clothes of any monk I have seen.*

As she picked up the discarded frock, she felt a silky lock of hair brush her hand. *What is this?*

She lit the lamp on the desk to better see what may be hidden on the floor. She picked up a long lock of chestnut colored hair and stroked it. *What a shame to shear such lovely locks. Yes I'm sure, she must look very much like a boy indeed.* As she picked up the discarded belt, something—*a letter?*— fell to the floor. She picked up the parchment and unfolded it. A feeling of pure and terrible elation came to her as she read the words on the page, and pieced together all these clues in her hand.

Such a pity, dear sister, that you shall suffer the loss of your husband and pet scrub girl on the same day. She laughed to herself as she took the evidence with her back to the guest suite to see her husband.

"Dear God," Laurel whispered under her breath. As she and

Ian left the abbey, they were greeted by Adrian Tearlach and a dozen or so of his men. "What do they want?"

"Let me do the speaking," Ian told her quietly. "Good morning, gentlemen."

"Good morning." Adrian bowed politely. "I am to accompany an acolyte to Drumoak. Is this he?" he asked, pointing to Laurel.

Laurel's heart almost burst from her chest but she bit her lip and held her breath, being careful to keep her face safely hidden beneath her cowl.

"I was not aware there was to be an escort," Ian said respectfully. "He's merely going to retrieve garments for William of Drumoak."

"I am not obligated to justify my actions to you, sir." Adrian snapped, then turned sharply to Laurel. "Young man, what is your name?"

Terrified, she held her breath and in the lowest voice she could muster, she bowed her head and answered, "Sean, sir."

"Well then, Sean." Adrian gestured with an outstretched hand. "Lead the way."

Laurel hesitated for only a moment, desperately trying to catch Ian's eye but knowing she could not afford to give herself away. She bowed again without speaking, grateful for the cowls the boys were forced to wear, then turned and walked as calmly as possible toward Drumoak. She folded her hands within her sleeves and dug her nails into her arms to steady her trembling. *Dear Mother, why are they going to Drumoak?* Then she knew—to search.

She fixed her eyes straight ahead to the gate, not wanting to glance around to see how many hunters were with her.

She saw Ewan standing sentry by the gate and suddenly hoped he would not recognize her. Ewan looked up at the approaching group of hunters led by an acolyte. She saw the indecision on his face as he stared at her. *Ewan, please don't call me by name.*

Ewan called something over his shoulder that she could not hear, then Simon came to join him. The two exchanged wary glances as Laurel came to a halt in front of them.

"Allow me entrance please; I am on an errand from the abbey." Laurel caught Simon's eye; he recognized her but did not betray her cover as he surveyed the group that surrounded her.

"State your business," Ewan requested in a formal tone, giving her the same wary look Simon had.

"I am to retrieve proper vestments for William of Drumoak. He is to be prepared for trial this day." She held her teeth together. "I know not their mission," she added hurriedly, motioning to Simon with her eyes.

Before Ewan or Simon could respond, Adrian made a quick motion to his men, who quickly, drew their blades, surrounding the two sentries. "We shall search his personal effects. I do not require your permission. Enter, boy," Adrian ordered and pushed Laurel forward.

Terrified, she marched through the doors. Edward was at the foot of the stairs as they entered the great hall.

"What is the meaning of this intrusion?" he barked at the hunter. Then, giving a glance to the acolyte, his eyes widened as he recognized Laurel but did not give her away. "What is your business?"

"Reconnaissance," Adrian answered with a smirk. "You

are to remain in this hall, sir. We shall search the personal quarters of William of Drumoak."

"No!" Mehlyndia suddenly appeared on the landing. "Get out!" she screamed and ran down the stairs, caught by Edward before she could do anything foolish. "You've no right!" she cried out.

Edward held her tightly. "Quiet, Mehlyndia. This is not the time for hysterics!"

"Who else is in the castle?" Adrian asked.

"Household staff," Edward answered angrily.

Adrian signaled to two of his men. They bowed briskly and went through the doors to the kitchen and toward the servants' quarters. Moments later, they escorted a terrified Elinor and Agnes into the hall. Duncan clung to Agnes's apron shaking, but he remained quiet. *Little one! Oh, please don't recognize me.* Laurel realized that Duncan was her biggest danger at the moment, but he kept his head hidden behind his mother's skirt.

"Keep these and any other servants you may come across here in this hall." Adrian ordered four of his men to surround them. "You as well, Lord Edward. I'm sure you understand." Adrian smirked as two other hunters approached him.

Edward glowered at him but did not resist. He held Mehlyndia's hand and she followed him down the stairs. She had yet to see Laurel standing with the hunters.

Adrian suddenly reached out and snatched Mehlyndia's hand and pulled her away from her father. Laurel gasped in surprise, then instantly bit her lip.

"Let go of me!" Mehlyndia screamed. Edward turned to help her but was quickly surrounded and herded into the hall with the servants.

Adrian held her wrist tightly. "You will lead us."

"No! Let go." She tried to twist away. Adrian gave her a backhanded slap on the face, sending her to the floor.

"Mehlyndia!" Edward called out. He tried to get past the guard, but was blocked.

Adrian pulled Mehlyndia to her feet, then mockingly bowed to her. "My apologies, Lady Sutherland. Where are my manners?" He grasped her by the wrist again and yanked it toward the top of the stairs. "Will you, *please,* lead us to the private quarters of William of Drumoak."

Mehlyndia looked to her father.

Edward nodded to her. "Lead them."

Adrian gave him a wicked grin. "Wise of you, Lord Edward."

When he turned and looked at Laurel, she thought she would sink to her knees.

"Sean. Come. Retrieve the vestments you require while we search."

As Laurel hurried to the stairs, a slight breeze pushed the cowl away from her face. She casually pulled it back, fearing little Duncan would recognize her. *Please, little one, look away.*

"That's not Sean, that's—" Duncan spoke up, pointing a chubby finger toward Laurel.

Agnes clasped her hand over Duncan's mouth quickly. "No, Duncan, that's an acolyte. He simply has the same name as your brother," she explained in a deceptively calm voice.

Duncan squirmed around and managed to get away from her. "But, that's Lau—"

"Duncan!" Edward snapped. "Do not contradict!"

Wide-eyed and stunned, Duncan looked up at Edward, and shrank away behind his mother's apron.

Relieved, Laurel pulled her cowl over her face further and joined Mehlyndia and Adrian on the stair. She worried that Mehlyndia, in her fear, would give her away, but Mehlyndia glanced at her for only a moment.

"Lead the way." Adrian gave Mehlyndia a sharp yank on her wrist. Adrian made a beckoning motion to his men without turning. Four hunters followed them up the stairs.

Mehlyndia led them to her quarters. Laurel desperately wanted to speak to her but dared not. Adrian unceremoniously pushed the doors open, slamming them against the wall, and strode in with his men as though he lived there. He pushed Mehlyndia into William's chair and motioned to one of the men. "Keep her out of the way." The man drew his sword and rested it on the arm of the chair, effectively keeping her in her place.

The three remaining hunters and Adrian haphazardly searched the room from one corner to the next, overturning tables, emptying drawers, and slashing at the bedclothes. Adrian picked up one of the drawings of William and laughed. "Touching." He crumpled it and tossed it into the fire. Laurel stood like a stone in the corner.

One of the hunters picked up William's lute and roughly ran a thumb across the strings. "Leave that alone!" Mehlyndia growled at him. "You can see it's a simple lute."

The hunter sneered at her and turned it over in his hands then tossed it to Adrian.

"Ah, yes." Adrian caught it and spun it around in his hands.

"I believe this was called out as a tool of his evil craft, was it not?" He held it up, examining the fine carvings William had etched onto it. "The woodworking is simply exquisite," he said. "Who made this?"

"My husband," Mehlyndia answered through clenched teeth. "It makes music. Not evil."

"Does it?" Adrian snickered. "Well, I'm sure he won't miss it." In a quick swing, he smashed William's lute—his pride and joy— against the hearth. Laurel thought her heart would break as the fine wood carvings shattered against the stone.

Mehlyndia buried her face in her hands and sobbed. Laurel had to plant her nails into her wrist again to keep from running to her.

The search continued through the dressers and under the bed, until Adrian stood before the trunk. Finding it locked, he looked to Mehlyndia. "Open this."

Reluctantly, Mehlyndia drew the key from her bodice. She looked quickly to Laurel, then held it up for whomever Adrian would choose to take it.

"Sean. Bring it here," Adrian ordered.

Laurel took the key with a shaking hand and brought it to Adrian. He took it briskly and opened the truck, flinging the lid up. He flipped the linens out with his sword, taking a moment to mockingly admire the embroidery on a pillowcase. "What is this?" he asked with a raised brow. Laurel held her breath as Adrian withdrew the leather satchel embossed with the hawk.

"A leather satchel," Mehlyndia answered calmly.

Laurel was astonished at the way she *under* reacted.

Adrian sliced through the binding with his sword and

emptied the satchel. William's ornate book and wooden kit tumbled onto the blanket. *My God! His kit! Why is that not hidden?* Laurel struggled to pushed her panic down.

"More lovely woodworking," Adrian teased, then flung open the kit.

To Laurel's astonishment, the kit contained not William's elements for potions but merely his woodworking tools. *Well done, Mehlyndia!*

Adrian grumbled and put the tools back into the kit, clearly disappointed that he had not found the holy grail of evil doer tools. He picked up the book. "Is the leather tooling his work as well?" he asked, feigning interest. "Quite the talented fellow... *wasn't* he?"

"I don't know who did the tooling," Mehlyndia answered with a scowl.

"Well, the initials 'W.F.' on the cover tell me it belongs to your husband. Does it not?" Adrian raised his brow.

"Yes, it's his," Mehlyndia admitted in a calm voice.

Laurel would have never guessed Mehlyndia could have handled this as well as she was. As Adrian opened the book, Laurel held her breath. *He charmed it. That's why I couldn't read it. Please let the charm hold... Dear Mother...*

Adrian made a disgusted chortle and flipped the pages, pausing here and there to grin or snicker. "I feel sorry for Sutherland. Their earl was a *terrible* poet." He assumed a lofty pose and cleared his throat. "I quote... 'Of all the meadows 'neath the moon, that God hath dressed in floral / No bird hath song, nor flower bloom, as fair and sweet as Laurel' *Sickening.*" Adrian slammed the book and tossed it disinterestedly to the bed.

Laurel's knees turned liquid as she exhaled in relief, hoping Adrian did not notice. She hazarded a glance to Mehlyndia, hoping to see the same relief on her face, but Mehlyndia only scowled at her. So relieved that Adrian had dismissed William's book, Laurel had only just realized the poem he had read aloud was about... *me? Oh no. She's going to hate me. Was it a real poem? No, of course not, it was only the charm.*

"All right, Sean. Your turn," Adrian snapped at her. "Get the clothes and boots, and what have you. We're ready to take leave of this place."

"I require help, sir." Laurel looked to Mehlyndia. "My lady, if you please?"

The hunter standing over Mehlyndia removed the sword from her chair and allowed her to help find the clothing. Mehlyndia sorted through the disheveled clothing the hunters had tossed onto the floor and found a proper tunic and leggings for William, his fine tartan cape, and a stout pair of boots. She wrapped the clothing in the cape and pushed it into Laurel's arms. "Here. Dress him properly. It's the least you can do." She glared at Laurel. For an instant, Laurel feared that in her anger, Mehlyndia would give her away. But then her eyes softened. "Please take care of him, *Sean.*" In a more tender voice, she added, "Tell him I love him."

Laurel nodded, blinking back her tears. "Yes, m' lady." From the corner of her eye, Laurel caught the glint of something silver on the nightstand beside her. With a quick glance, she saw the eagle badge only inches from her hand. She casually dropped the bundle, then, while bending to retrieve it, she palmed the badge. "I shall be sure to tell him."

"Touching," Adrian interrupted. "My lady, thank you for your cooperation." He bowed and smirked at her, then abruptly left the room, signaling to his men to follow.

As one of the hunters pushed her through the door, Laurel looked over her shoulder to Mehlyndia, hoping for a glance of encouragement, or understanding but Mehlyndia only lowered herself to her bed and sobbed into her pillow. In the corridor, she saw a shadow by the stone pillar, and stole a closer look. *Richard. Hiding in the shadows. What if they had hurt Mehlyndia! Dear Mother, he truly is a coward.*

She was hurried along with the hunters down the grand stairs. Edward and the servants were still herded together in the hall directly beneath the portrait of William. Laurel's heart sank at the image of the lute in the painting, knowing how he would be devastated to know what had become of his treasured instrument, his talisman against the dragon.

"Lord Edward," Adrian called as he descended the stairs. "We shall take leave of you now. Our search was disappointing. However know that until after the outcome of the trial, your castle will be at our disposal. We shall take note of all the comings and goings in these walls."

He waved to his men. They lowered their swords and briskly fell in formation as Adrian led them from the hall, Laurel in the middle of the group. She risked showing her face as she passed through the doors.

"Good bye," she called to Duncan, with no idea why she felt inclined to do so.

When they were clear of the gates, Adrian clapped her on the back and she panicked for a moment, but he only laughed. "Good, stout lad. I'm impressed with the way you kept your head. Perhaps one day you would consider joining our band." He grabbed her face and shook it. "That is, when you're at least old enough to grow a proper beard!"

Laurel turned scarlet, not knowing how to react. *I'd quicker cut off my own tongue than join the likes of you.* She clutched the bundle of clothing tightly, suddenly fearful that the hunters intended to accompany them to the prison as well.

"What? Not interested?" Adrian laughed. "Just as well. You look too much like a girl anyway." He clapped her on the back again. "Go join Brother Ian. Tell him we shall be collecting the heretic at sunset. Dress him properly now, you promised!"

Laurel nodded but did not speak as she ran, clutching her bundle, toward the abbey. *Dear Mother, thank you. They're leaving me alone.*

When she caught sight of Ian, standing as he promised in front of the abbey, Laurel broke into a full-out charge to meet him. Terrified and angry tears stained her face as she ran.

Ian met her halfway and quickly took the bundle of clothing from her. "Come on, let's get past this foolishness. The streets have become too full and active for my tastes." He hurried her along with a shaking hand. "Are you all right?"

"Aye," she answered through halting breaths. "They searched... Ian... it was terrifying." *The lute. Oh, Will, your beautiful lute.*

Ian came to a stop. "Did they find anything?"

She took another breath. "No. Mehlyndia was brilliant

and hid his kit. His secret is still safe, Ian. But they're guarding the castle. They'll know if anyone leaves though the gate." She allowed a small grin. "But no one will be guarding the crypt or the caves. They're safe."

"Thank goodness we anticipated it." Ian took her hand and they began to walk again.

As they passed the meetinghouse between the abbey and the prison, they were nearly run over by a horse and wagon that abruptly crossed their path. "Careful there, rev'run, best to watch your steps!" the man on the wagon called to Ian.

Laurel looked up to see what the commotion was about. The streets were indeed full of people, rushing from here to there, excitedly chatting and calling to each other. She was disgusted at the festive atmosphere, as though some sort of harvest fair was in the preparations. A group of women were standing close by, gossiping to each other. Laurel recognized the woman who called herself Cassandra talking with some of the others she had known had fallen away from her army.

"Looks like it should be a grand turnout tonight!" Cassandra was speaking in her crass, loud voice. "Seems the whole town is 'ere waitin'! Pity, though. 'E's a good tipper."

"Is that all you think about, Cass?" Another woman carrying a basket of bread was with her. "Seems a shame to me all 'round. And him just married and all."

"And so young!" said another. "I 'ate to think about it." She shook her head with the others.

One looked to the sky, squinting one eye then sighed. "An' not a cloud in the sky t' put it off, neither. Pity."

"C'mon lets pick out a good spot." Cassandra laughed and the trio wandered off in the direction of the meetinghouse.

"Oh my God," Laurel moaned when she saw the construction taking place in the square.

She began to swoon and felt her knees begin to fold as she saw the ground come up to meet her. Ian caught her before she hit the dirt.

"Don't look! It's up to us to make sure it doesn't come to this. You cannot lose your heart now. Close your eyes for a moment, and catch your breath."

She did as he told her, closing her eyes tightly, hoping beyond hope that she was mistaken about what she had seen taking place in the square. *They could be building a stable... or a new barn...* She drew a long breath and opened her eyes and stared, disheartened. The wagon had come to a stop in front of a newly constructed platform that stood close to twelve feet off the ground. It was a simple flat wooden structure with a staircase to one side and one rough hewn stake in the middle. Several men were unloading bundles of logs, peat moss, and kindling around its base. She struggled to regain her wit and nerve, knowing this loathsome pile of wood was intended for William.

"They can't! Ian, they can't do it. How do we stop—"

"Laurel, please!" Ian helped her to her feet. "Don't lose your courage now! You know what the plan is. Remember, you got the witnesses we need. It won't come to that." He tried to calm her. He kept his reassurances going until they had finally reached the prison gates.

"You come to get 'im, then?" Harold asked, nodding toward the meetinghouse.

"We've only come to prepare him," Ian answered calmly.

"Looks like they're ready for 'im in the square. Should be

quite a sight." The guard took a look at the sickly looking acolyte and laughed. "He still don't have the stomach for this, does he! Be a man, boy!" He slapped Laurel on the back.

It took every bit of her self-control for Laurel not to scream at him.

"It is trying business for one so young." Ian kept his calm. "If you please?" He extended his hand to the gate.

"Yes, yes." Harold spit on the ground. "Always such a hurry," he grumbled. "Ye be needin' anythin' special, then?"

"Wash water would be appreciated. We are to clean him up," Ian said. "And a chair, if you please."

"All right, then." Harold opened the gate, then banged on the main door. "Jerol!"

"Aye?" The one-eyed guard stuck his head through a small window in the door and turned his lone eye onto Ian. "Back again, are ye'?" He swung the door open.

"They be needin' a bucket and scrub water," Harold said as he ushered Ian and Laurel into the prison.

"And a chair," Ian reminded Harold.

"By all means," Harold growled, then bowed sarcastically. "His nibs requires a chair as well, Jerol."

"He be lucky if I find the water!" Jerol grunted as he lumbered off through a dark corridor.

Laurel pressed her cowl over her mouth as she crossed the threshold into the prison. She could not imagine how it could be possible, but the place seemed even more rank that it had the day before. Then she saw a row of slop buckets lined against the wall and fought to keep from purging her stomach. *Dear Mother, let the wash water be clean.*

When at last they had reached the iron door that led to

the tower, Harold slowly retrieved the key ring from the wall and fumbled for the key he needed. *He intentionally takes a long time!* When he had retrieved the proper key, he led them up the twisted staircase that led to the dreadful tower cell.

As before, when they reached William's cell, Harold became a bellowing beast and pounded on the iron door. "It's time! Look sharp in there!" he hollered as he pushed opened the door. "What's this? Sleeping? Open your eyes! I thought you knew the rules."

"I believe your part in this is over, sir," Ian spoke softly but firmly, standing in the doorway.

"Eh?" Harold turned to Ian and snorted. "Aye, I'll leave ye then."

"The irons, if you please," Ian reminded him, pointing to William's chains. "We are required to dress him."

Harold made an irritated grunt, then took his time retrieving the key he required. "Forward!" he yelled one last time. William startled, then bent so Harold could remove the bridle. "Good clear sky tonight. Not a rain cloud to be seen." He laughed and pulled the bridle from William's mouth. "Foul luck on your part, boy."

Laurel shuddered as the guard threw the bridle over a hook on the wall. It clanked loudly against the stone. Laurel jumped again as the door bumped into her when it was pushed open wide.

"You need this?" Jerol trundled in with a large wooden chair.

"Thank you," Ian said curtly. "Do you have the wash water?"

"Keep yer knickers on, I only got two 'ands, ye know!" Jerol barked and went back out. A moment later, he carried in two buckets of water and plunked them down next to the chair.

Laurel took a quick look and sighed quietly in relief that the water in the buckets was clear and clean.

"Thank you." Ian said again.

"I'll be locking ye in 'til it's time." Harold and Jerol left together, slamming the door behind them.

Ian and Laurel stood like stones until the guards' footfalls on the stairs faded.

"He's gone." Laurel sank to her knees, unwilling to try to keep her legs from shaking.

Ian put his hand on her shoulder. "Nerves now. He needs your strength." Ian stood and taking a flint from his pocket, and lit the lone torch that rested in a sconce on the wall. It was the first time Laurel actually got a good look at the squalid cell that had been William's home for nearly a week.

Free of his shackles, William had fallen sideways and was lying on the floor, one arm covering his face. Laurel took a deep breath and knelt next to him.

"Will?"

He made no response.

"It's Laurel. Please look at me." She gently rubbed his back and her heart began to race when she saw the new wounds that he had acquired since the day before. "Ian, help me roll him over." Laurel sat herself on the floor as Ian gingerly turned him. She cradled his head on her lap and called him again. "Wake up, Will. It's Laurel." Slowly he opened his eyes.

"Laurel?" William blinked then closed his eyes again. "You're not real."

"I'm real," Laurel assured him. "I promised I'd come back,

remember?" She stroked his face. "Ian, look," she whispered, pointing out a mean-looking gash on William's cheek. "Did you bring the barley?"

"Yes." Ian unloaded his pack and searched for the crushed barley and a cloth. He wet the cloth, made a paste, and applied it carefully to William's cheek. "This may sting."

William winced and tried to turn his face away. "No more." He opened his panicked eyes and searched around him. "Take it away, please."

"It will help heal—" Ian began, as he tried to hold William's head still.

Laurel pushed Ian's hand away. "Not yet, Ian." She looked at William. "Will, it's Laurel." She waited until William found her face with his eyes and settled down. "Ian didn't mean to hurt you. You have a burn on your face; he was only treating it for you."

"Burn?" William's eyes opened wide. "Is it cut as well?"

"Yes," she answered, careful to keep her voice calm. "We have some barley mash and a cloth. Do you want me to treat it?"

William looked up to her, his eyes filled as he turned his face. "Leave it," he told her. "Look at my heels. Please, tell me if it was real."

Ian gave Laurel a startled look then, examined William's heels. "Oh, dear Lord. Both tendons have been severed," Ian explained.

"Oh, God," William cried. "It was real?"

"I'm afraid so," Ian answered quietly.

"We can treat it, can't we?" Laurel asked, shaken at the look on Ian's face. "It's only a cut. We've brought balms and—-"

"No." Ian placed a hand on her shoulder. "We can clean the flesh and treat the burn, but that's all. It's Joseph's hallmark, I'm afraid. He's been hobbled."

"What?" William still lay on her lap, not looking at her, silent tears falling from his eyes. He obviously knew what the cuts were about. "Forever?"

Ian sighed. "Possibly, but there's always a chance I'm wrong."

Laurel looked away from the wounds, heartsick and furious. "Enough!" She sat rocking him, crying for several minutes, while Ian prepared the rest of the items he brought. *Blessed Mother, surely you've taken enough from him now.*

As William lay with his head on Laurel's lap, his mind began to slip into the fog; he did little to resist. He felt himself gently lifted by someone—*Is it Laurel? Who is with her? Why can I never remember?* The hands that carried him seemed gentle enough, but he felt pain where ever he was touched and moaned in protest at first. Eventually, though, as he found he was no longer on the cold stone floor, he settled down, accepting the help. For the first time in days, he found that he was sitting in a chair—high backed with large arms, much like his favorite chair back in Drumoak. *Am I home, then?* He put his head back and closed his eyes again. He was still cold, no comforting fireplace in the room. He wasn't home. *Sean?*

An answer came immediately, like a breeze in his ear. *"I'm with you."*

The dagger was real. I thought you saved me from it. William began to shake in the chair, only half aware that there were two living people with him.

"Do your eyes still work?" the voice asked.

William opened his eyes. "Yes, they still work," he answered aloud. "Thank you."

"What works?" Laurel asked.

"I'm sorry it wasn't enough."

"You did what you could," William said, staring past Laurel to a spot on the wall, watching the shade slowly appear. "I'm just glad you're with me."

"Will?" Laurel turned his face to hers. "Who are you talking to?"

"Talk to Laurel, Will." The shade pointed his wispy hand toward Laurel. *"I'm with you. But you need to stay with the living."*

William forced his eyes to look at Laurel. "He's with me." He looked back to the shade, smiled faintly, and closed his eyes.

"Will?" Laurel stroked his face gently. "Ian? What's happening now?"

"His mind has slipped since yesterday." William heard a vaguely familiar male voice speaking. "William? I have some ale for you."

William opened his eyes and drank as he drifted in and out of his dream state. He saw Ian clearly now, though he was unsure who he was. "Thank you."

"Can you see me now?" Laurel asked.

"You're real?" William looked closely. "He was right."

"Who was right?" she asked.

William didn't answer.

"Never mind, Laurel. He's not fully with us yet." The man

knelt in front of him. "William, it's time to get ready."

"Who are you?" William tried to focus on the man.

"It's Brother Ian," Ian answered calmly. "Don't you remember me?"

"Ian... yes." William stared, but his vision began to blur. *I know him. He took care of you, Sean. He'll take care of me too. It's time to get ready... time to let go...*

"No, Will." The shade floated closer, shaking its head. *"It's not time to let go. Stay with the living."*

"Stay with the living." William nodded, then closed his eyes and slipped back into the dark.

"He's not clear-minded." Ian sighed. "It's going to be difficult to explain things to him before the trial."

"Trial?" William opened his eyes, then closed them again.

"Will, try to stay with us. I know it's hard. We have a lot to tell you." Laurel straightened him up in the chair, but it was apparent he wasn't going to stay that way without help. "Ian, what else have they done to him? Why can't I keep him with me?"

Ian tapped her shoulder and pointed out the crank handle in the chain spool that hadn't been there on their first visit, then motioned to the shackles and the beam. "Do you understand?" he asked.

Laurel stared at the crank and the chain, suddenly understanding all too clearly what had happened during the night. "Oh!" she gasped, swaying backward against Ian.

"Leave her alone!"

"It's all right, Will." Laurel got hold of her breath and struggled to keep her voice calm. "It's only Ian."

"Ian?" William looked at her, confused, as though he had no idea who Ian was. He turned to look at him, but his eyes set fixed on the Ian's robe rather than his face. "Please, Joseph... not again, go away!" he cried out childishly, seemingly terrified by the sight of Ian's robe.

Ian followed William's gaze to his sleeves. "He thinks I'm Joseph." He pushed his cowl as far off his head and neck as possible and pushed his sleeves up. "Look!" Ian called out. "It's only me. Ian."

"Ian?" William settled down immediately, his terror inexplicably changed to indifference, as though another person had taken his place in the chair. "Do you have more ale?"

"All you need. I've brought you some food as well. It's very important you eat, sir."

"Thank you." William drank, then took a long breath as clarity slowly returned to his eyes. "Is it today? The trial?"

"Yes. We came to help you prepare," Ian said, lowering the flask, handing it to Laurel. "And to help you win." He took a hunk of bread and tore it into small pieces and placed some on William's tongue. "Do you know what you are up against?"

"Yes. But they lie." William chewed slowly, then swallowed hard with a grimace, then turned an angry eye on Ian. "I made no pact."

A sudden cold shudder went down Laurel's back. *I made no pact.* She remembered the horrific scream from the tower. But the light was returning to William's eyes and she began to feel encouraged that he may be coming back.

"I know it is a lie," Laurel assured him. "You made no

pact."

Laurel's encouragement about William's state of mind began to fade as she watched the defiant glint in his eyes glaze over and take on the look of a terrified child who was facing a punishment he hadn't earned. She looked to Ian to see that he too could see that William's state of mind had begun to deteriorate again. It would be more difficult than they anticipated to explain the details of their rescue plan.

"I made no pact," William pleaded and began to cry. "Please believe me."

"I said, I believe you," Laurel spoke gently, as though it were little Duncan she was tending. "But you need to calm down so we can help you." She brushed his face and waited for him to calm down.

After a moment, he quieted, staring past her to the corner, eyes still glazed. He nodded and smiled to the corner, then muttered, "stay with the living". She waited a moment, then slowly he brought his attention back to her.

"Do you remember the charge?" Laurel asked, hoping to bring him back around.

"They say my voice is evil." William cast his eyes downward as if to find his hands. "They called me an enchanter."

"Yes, that's right." Ian tore some more bread for him. "We have good news for you. Laurel has rallied witnesses. We have more than we need to challenge the charge."

William looked up hopefully. "To win?" he whispered in amazement. "He was right."

"Yes, we may win that one," Ian confirmed.

"Who was right, Will?" Laurel asked, confused.

William smiled faintly. "He's still got my back," he

whispered and closed his eyes for a moment. "He promised."

"Has someone else come to see you?" she asked.

William's smile again dissolved completely into a frown of utter despair. "All night." He dropped his head and would not look up.

"Will? It's all right, don't answer. I'm sorry." Laurel coaxed him back. "Here, finish the bread."

"I didn't say it." William's words came between sudden sobs. "He told me to fight, he was on my back. I didn't say it. It's a lie. All night. I didn't say it." He glared at her as though he expected her to challenge him on his word, and jarringly, his expression transformed from despair to complete fury. "I won't say it!"

Laurel shuddered at the sudden wild expression in William's eyes as again a completely new persona seemed to overtake him. "What is happening? He keeps changing."

"He's been tortured, Laurel," Ian whispered.

"I know, but... his mind?" Laurel was beginning to believe she was losing her own mind.

"He hasn't had more than a few moments sleep for days," Ian patiently explained, though Laurel could see he was fighting to keep his own wits about him. "A lack of sleep can bring on this sort of dementia to the strongest of men *without* the addition of physical torture. All we can do is be patient with him."

They watched as William went through his paces again, each emotion seemingly claiming its own distinct personality. Defiance embodied the warrior, terror became the child, despondency and hopelessness fought to control the man he was, while 'William' seemed to be lost somewhere on the battlefield that was his own mind.

"I made no pact," William spoke out loud, looking past Ian to a shadowed corner in the cell. "I didn't say it."

"Yes, we believe you," Ian assured him, then turned William's face to his and made sure their eyes met before he spoke again. "Do you know why we are here?"

"To help me." William answered, suddenly lucid again. "Tell me how."

"There is a second charge to fight." Ian spoke slowly. "The poison. Do you remember the poison?"

"Nightshade." William nodded. "For my headache."

"That's right," Laurel answered.

"I remember." William looked at her calmly. "The dragon put it in the water." His gaze turned inquisitively conversational. "What of it?"

Laurel looked at Ian, feeling helpless, as she tried to keep up with William's ever changing demeanor. She forced her voice to match his now conversant tone. "They claim you survived the poison by way of a pact with the devil—"

"I made no pact!" William's warrior self, growled. "They could not make me say it! *You* cannot make me say it. He tried all night." His eyes dashed fiercely from Laurel to Ian and then to the same empty corner in the cell. "I will not say it!"

Laurel jumped back, frightened by William's reaction, finally understanding that any mention of the so-called 'pact' would send him into a frenzy.

Ian put his hands on William's face to calm him down and to regain his attention. "Son, we are friends here. I know it's a lie! But they will test you, do you understand?"

"I have *been* tested," William pleaded, anger melting into desolation. "What more can they do to me?"

Ian released him slowly, allowing him to catch his breath. "It's pointless to try to explain the details to him any further," he told Laurel quietly, then laid a hand on William's shoulder. "Have no fear, lad. We are going to make it easier for you." Ian reached for the water and spoke to Laurel, "I do not know how they expect him to stand trial in this condition! He cannot possibly defend himself! He's alert one moment and lost in fog the next."

"Let's just get him cleaned up for now, Ian. Don't ask him anymore." Laurel's face mirrored William's distress. "It's too much."

It took more than an hour to treat the wounds and clean William of the filth and blood that covered him. Once washed, Laurel applied the yarrow and barley to his wrists and wrapped them with bandages. He bit his lip against the pain but did not fight her. Though the wounds were deep, once cleaned, Laurel was encouraged that they did not seem to fester and would eventually heal. His hands took longer and were more difficult to treat. Several fingers were broken, and each one caused him to cry out as she set and bandaged them. Ian gave him more ale to drink and allowed him to catch his breath between treatments. Incredibly, William's mind seemed to clarify as they ministered to him.

"Are you ready?" Ian asked as he prepared to reset William's disjointed shoulders.

"No, but do it anyway."

William clenched his teeth and submitted to Ian's

ministering. Laurel shed as many tears for William as he did in his pain as his joints were snapped back into line and wrapped tightly with strips of linen. Laurel applied the balms to his ankles and heels, and wrapped them as well.

Once his shoulders, arms, and hands were taken care of, it was time to set hips and legs. William sat quietly while the two tended the wounds below his waist, just simply watching. Instead of taking comfort from his apparent lack of distress, Laurel grew uneasy. Surely, it had to be as painful to reset the joints in his legs as it had been for his shoulders, yet he barely even winced when Ian snapped his knees into alignment. Laurel caught Ian's eye and saw he had the same concern.

Casually, Ian told William, "Close your eyes for a moment." He took William's left foot and ran his thumb across the sole. "Which foot was that?" he asked William.

"Which foot was what?" William asked, his eyes still closed.

Ian sat back with a loud sigh. "I feared as much," he said quietly to Laurel. "There's damage to his back. Even without the cuts to his heels, he's not going to walk again."

"Oh, no." Laurel turned away. "Dear Mother, enough is enough!" she cried out loud. "Must you take everything from him?"

"Laurel." William opened his eyes. "I'm still alive," he told her calmly. "She hasn't taken everything. Please don't cry anymore."

Laurel sat on the floor next to his chair, skeptical of the clarity of his eyes. *Does he truly understand what's happening?* She wiped her eyes and got hold of her breathing. "Are you with me now?" she asked.

"Yes." William nodded, a half smile coming to him as he looked down. "And I'm naked."

William's mind stayed with him while Ian and Laurel pulled the tunic over his head and gingerly persuaded his arms into the sleeves. He made no protests as they went about dressing him. A loss of dignity was the least of his troubles. Ian lifted him as Laurel shimmied his leggings up. "A kilt would have been a better choice," she muttered, struggling with the doeskins.

"The leggings serve better to conceal the wounds," Ian told her.

"'Twould serve more justice if all of Stonehaven could see them. Then they'd know what Dunkirk has done to him." With the leggings on, she stepped back while Ian lowered William gently down into the chair. "Boots, now. We're almost done, Will."

"Feeling warmer," William said, quietly. "Thank you."

Laurel was almost grateful he couldn't feel the boots they had to force onto his swollen, bandaged feet. When they had finished dressing him, the only visible clue to his condition was the gash on his face and the wrappings on his hands and wrists.

William drank more ale and finished the food Ian had brought him, slowly. His mouth was a mass of sores from the bridle, but his hunger apparently won out over the pain. When he seemed clearheaded enough to listen to what they had planned for his rescue, Laurel held his face and explained the details of their plan.

"Before the test, you will have the right to request the last Sacrament," Laurel said, being sure he had his eyes still on her. "You must swallow your pride and request it. The wine Ian will give you will put you to sleep. Do you understand?"

"Yes. Sleep." William looked toward the small window. "Almost time." He turned to Laurel. "Will Melly be there?"

"No, Will." She sighed and looked down. "She is waiting for us below. Ready to move away from here."

"Good, then." He lowered his eyes. "She won't have to watch."

Laurel saw the truth that he was hurt that he would not see her face in the trial chambers. A sudden wave of anger warmed her face at the thought of how Mehlyndia had spent the past days wallowing in her misery, painting pictures instead of trying to see her husband. Laurel pushed her anger for Mehlyndia aside; it would serve her no purpose here. She remembered the promise she had made just before she left Drumoak.

"I have a message from her for you." She raised his chin with her hand. "Mehlyndia wanted me to tell you that she loves you." He smiled and nodded. "There is something else you should know, Will." She placed a hand on his shoulder. "It's good news, actually."

"Yes?" William smiled. "I need good news."

"She carries your bairn."

William stared back, tears brimming, though this time, not from the pain. "Thank you for telling me." He smiled. "She's safe then? Richard kept his word."

"Aye. She followed your map," Laurel told him, then smiled. "Clever drawing, Will."

William looked confused for a moment, "Map?" His eyes opened wide and he cast a wary glance to Ian. "You could read it?"

Laurel leaned close to his ear, and assured him, "Only after it was taken out of the book."

"My charm worked, then?" William smiled, then closed his eyes for a moment. "One less worry."

"Yes," Laurel said. "I have one more thing to give you, Will." Laurel took the silver badge from her belt. "Your eagle." She struggled with her conscience for a moment about telling him about the charm, and in the end, she said a prayer and decided to keep it to herself. *Dear Mother and Father, I know you demand your due. But he has already paid more than his share. Should you demand tribute, take it full from me. He needs to be allowed to be with his wife and child. Please, bless this one...* She pinned the eagle to his cape, then kissed his forehead as she had done before. "That's because I love you," she told him, before he could ask. "May the Blessed Mother grant that you pass this eagle to your son with your own hand, when he is grown."

"Thank you." William looked at her, a skeptical sadness in his eyes.

Laurel knew he hardly believed he would live to see his son born, let alone grown, but somehow, from deep within herself, the knowledge came to her. She had appeased the Mother, and a strange feeling of peace came over her as she removed her hand from William's shoulder. She closed her eyes and rocked back on her heels while a sensation of sweet release washed over her. Whether it was her own exhaustion or a divine gift from her Lady, she was not certain, but at that moment, in the midst of the nightmare, she had been given a gift and she knew without doubt—*he'll give the eagle to his boy. Thank you Mother.*

"Laurel?" Ian took her hand. "Are you all right?"

She opened her eyes to see Ian looking at her, alarmed. "Aye."

"I was beginning to worry." Ian squeezed her hand. "This has been difficult for you and we still have the trial to face. Will you hold up?"

Laurel took a breath, the peaceful wave now only a memory. "I will."

There was little daylight left coming into the small window. "The escort will be here anytime now." Ian looked to the window.

The sounds from the gathering crowd had grown steadily louder during their time in the cell. Laurel wondered if William heard the noise and if he understood what it was about.

"William," Ian asked, still looking toward the window. "Is there anything I can offer you right now?"

"Yes." William looked up at the window.

"Ask then, while we have time."

William's expression shifted from one emotion to the next, again, as he stared at the window— anger to sorrow, then sorrow to resignation, before he spoke. "I know what I am to face out there." He closed his eyes for a moment. "I heard the hammering all morning."

Laurel stroked his cheek gently. "Yes, they have prepared already." She clenched her teeth. "They don't even wait for a verdict."

"Ian, I'm not afraid of death." William whispered and dropped his head. "But—" Resignation made way for despair.

"Yes?" Ian asked gently.

"The fire," William answered, barely audible, with a terrified expression in his eyes. "I'm frightened of that."

Ian placed a gentle hand on William's shoulder. "I understand." He took the box that held the elements he used for the religious rites and opened it slowly, then took out the small vial of greenish liquid that Elinor had prepared. He held it up to show William. "I promise you. You will not face the fire."

William looked at the vial and then past Ian's shoulder. "Would that be quitting?" he asked softly to the corner, as though he were asking it for permission to accept the vial.

Ian began to answer, but Laurel put a hand on his arm. "He's not talking to you," she whispered, studying the look on William's face.

"What?" Ian whispered back, confused.

Laurel put her finger to her lips and nodded toward William. "Look," she said silently. They sat quietly, watching William as he stared into the corner. Every so often, he would nod his head, look down, then look back to the corner, as though he were engaged in conversation. After a moment, the terror that had been in his eyes lifted, and his breathing calmed. He smiled as if he were a child who had just been reassured there were no monsters lurking under his bed. "Of course I trust you," he said, looking from the corner, to the vial, then back again. He nodded his head as though his conversation had come to a close. He looked from the corner to Laurel, then to Ian, took a great breath, and said,

"I'm ready."

* * *

While Laurel and Ian were tending to William, Edward awaited the message that the trial would commence. The presence of the hunters outside the gate had put everyone on edge. The atmosphere inside Drumoak was intolerably oppressive. He found it nearly impossible to believe that in one week, everything in his duchy could have changed so drastically. There was little hope that William would be able to claim the seat in Sutherland. That was painfully obvious. But was Richard a wise or logical choice to succeed him? Edward had only chosen him in the heat of the moment and was far from convinced that Richard could ever lead Sutherland, as he had hoped William would.

He put thoughts of the future of Sutherland aside. He had more than enough to deal with in the present. There was no denying the truth that no matter what the outcome of William's trial would be, this would be the day he would lose his children. If the map Laurel had provided was as good as it seemed, Mehlyndia would be aboard the ship that would take her far away to the New World. It broke his heart to think there was the real possibility that she would sail alone. And if William, by the miracle of Elinor's potion, would be able to join her, what sort of life lay ahead for him in an untamed world? Ian had said he was badly injured and would require a good deal of care once he was free. Edward wondered if sending him off on a ship with winter coming on, in that condition, was more cruel than kind. He put that worry aside. William was strong, he reasoned, and had overcome so much in his young life all ready. He convinced himself that, in time, William's injuries would heal and he would eventually push this nightmare far behind him, just as he had left Aberdoir behind before.

His brooding thoughts was ended with a knock on the chamber door. "Come."

Ewan entered Edward's chamber. "You have a message, my lord." A young page, who had been sent from the meetinghouse, approached Edward bearing a message in his outstretched hand. Edward took the scroll from the boy and opened it.

"And so it begins," Edward said softly. "The judge has arrived." He rolled the scroll. "I assumed as much when I saw the crowds. They waste no time. Send word to Geoffrey that it is time to meet. Pray we still have as many souls as we require."

Ewan bowed and left the room, the page following close behind him.

"Anne, this is it. I stand to lose a great deal today." Edward looked to the portrait. "Save a son, lose half my holdings. Save my holdings, lose a son. Either way, I shall lose Mehlyndia. She will leave me on the outgoing tide, my love. God willing, she will have her husband with her." He washed his face in the basin on the nightstand. "And it is all my doing. I put too many demands on the boy. Had I simply allowed him a choice and allowed him the freedom to seek out his own path, perhaps none of this would have befallen him."

"Father?" Mehlyndia approached him slowly. She was dressed in common clothes meant for traveling, her hair pulled back in a single braid, tied with a coarse linen ribbon instead of the silk she usually wore.

At the sight of his beautiful daughter, now dressed as any peasant might be, Edward's grief grew tenfold. "My dear child, what have I brought on you? Can you forgive me?" He embraced her.

"Father?" she asked, glancing about the room. "I thought I heard you speaking to someone."

"Yes, that was just my foolish habit. I wondered if someday you might discover that I often speak to your mother." He looked again at the portrait of Anne. "She never responds, but I fancy that she hears me. Do you think me daft?"

Mehlyndia looked up to the portrait and to the face of her mother. "I do not think you are daft, Father. I miss her too. I scarcely remember the sound of her voice, but I remember how safe I felt in her arms." She took her father's hand. "What do you suppose her answer would have been?"

"Answer?"

"Should you have given William a choice?"

"What would *you* have said?"

"That he would have freely chosen to accept the responsibilities you put on him. As much as he would have loved to have been left to drift and dream and play his songs, he knows he could better follow his conscience in your service. He knew what he risked, Father. Yet he chose to speak his mind." She turned away. "So in truth, it *was* his choice."

"It could be your mother speaking. You are very perceptive, my dear." Edward wiped his eyes quickly before she turned around. "And now look where we are. Are you ready to travel?"

"Yes." She looked down at her clothes with a curious tilt

to her head. "I've never worn such a frock. I find it strangely comfortable. No wonder William preferred to dress as a peasant." She half smiled. "He shall not recognize me when he sees me." Mehlyndia dissolved into tears. "I want to see him again before I leave. Just for a moment, Father. Could I not sit in the back of the meetinghouse and blend in with the crowd?"

"Mehlyndia, you will not have time to go through the caves if you wait. You must be on the ship when the tide retreats," he said, holding her. "There will be nothing for you here when this is over. My holdings will surely be challenged. I stand to lose a great deal. Should we manage to rescue William through the catacombs, he surely cannot stay on this shore. You must leave now. God willing, you'll see him soon and the two of you will find a new life across the sea that is free of politics and these 'unfortunate affairs of government'."

"How will I know?" Mehlyndia stood back and wiped her face. "How will I know if we've won?"

"You'll know when they bring him onboard," Edward said, trying to reassure her.

"And if we lose, I shall know when I see the light from the bonfire," she said, then cried onto her father's shoulder. "It can be seen from the sea, Richard has told me! Father, I cannot bear to think of it."

Edward held her close and let her cry as she had when she was a child. "I have arranged with the captain of the ship to watch for my signal. I have set an archer in the parapet who will send the sign. Two flaming arrows, one after the other, shall mean we have won and that all is well. The captain will know to wait for the small boat that will bring William, Elinor, and Laurel to you, and you shall all sail away to a new life in a new land."

"And if we lose?"

"Then there shall be only one arrow and you must set sail at once." He looked into her eyes for a light of understanding. "For your own sake, my dear, should you see only one arrow, do not look further to the shore."

She nodded her understanding and hugged her father again tightly. "I shall never forget you, Father."

A light tap on the door told Edward it was time to go. "Yes?"

Elinor stood peering around the half-opened door, Mehlyndia's traveling cloak draped over her arm. "Are you ready, dear? Simon has the map and is waiting for you below. It's time to go."

"Yes, Elinor." She wiped her eyes and assumed a no-nonsense attitude that was reminiscent of Laurel's miraculous transformation. She turned to her father one last time and smiled sadly. "I love you."

"God speed to you."

Chapter 16

30 September 1607

EDWARD WALKED SILENTLY from Drumoak to the meetinghouse, escorted by Ewan, who was now the captain of his own guard. The streets of Stonehaven had become festive as though the midwinter celebration was about to take place, instead of the anticipated immolation of an innocent man. Edward had seen this phenomenon before yet had paid little attention, assuming that the people who had been brought to the stakes had always earned their fates. How many burnings had he allowed to take place without intervention? He did not want to think about it.

When he was halfway to the square, he saw that Geoffrey and the folks he'd rallied already waiting for him; just as Edward had feared, their number had dwindled to a mere dozen or so. Theirs were the only somber-looking faces to be seen amidst the carnival atmosphere that had taken over the rest of the town.

"My lord, we are prepared," Geoffrey said in greeting. "I regret we have grown fewer since this morning. People place their fears ahead of justice." He cast his eyes downward. "But you can be assured, we shall not turn away." The small group around him cheered in agreement.

Edward took Geoffrey's hand, clasping it within both of his. "You have my gratitude. It saddens me that the people of my own Stonehaven have chosen to make a festival of this madness."

"The day is forthcoming when they will seek help and find none." Geoffrey turned his face from the crowd.

Edward and Geoffrey walked the remaining distance to the meetinghouse together, their ragtag army following behind. Ewan walked protectively to Edward's right. They would enter the building in a formal procession when the judge arrived. Edward cast his eyes toward the prison, then to the milling crowd that lined both sides of the street, creating a human corridor through which William would be led to trial. "Why must they make this so difficult?" Edward asked to no one in particular, staring at the door to the prison, both anticipating and dreading the moment it would open.

The crowd stirred on the far end of the street and made way to allow an ornate and regal carriage to pass. It was followed by two more carriages that made their way, parade-like, to the meetinghouse. The first carriage stopped in front of Edward. The footman quickly dismounted and placed a velvet-lined step in front of the carriage door before he opened it for the occupants to emerge.

"So much pomposity!" Edward grunted irritably to Geoffrey.

"That is what true evil looks like, my lord," Geoffrey grumbled in response. "It does not exist on the face of the young man they accuse."

Bishop Dunkirk, dressed in full formal regalia exited the carriage first, followed closely by the abbot of Aberdoir. They stepped aside formally while Thomas came out next. Thomas held his hand to his wife and then Bryndah, too, joined the contemptible group. She carried a small leather satchel and a prayer book that Edward was certain was for show alone. He had never known Bryndah to utter a single prayer in her entire life. They proceeded into the building without so much as a glance in his direction. He had expected Richard to be with his parents as part of their deception, but Richard was missing from his father's entourage.

"Ewan, have you seen Richard? I've not seen him since before dawn."

"No, my lord. I've been watching him," Ewan answered. "Could he have gone with the Lady Mehlyndia and the others to the crypt?"

"I don't know." Edward scanned the crowd again. He hoped that Richard had not fled from the proceedings. He wanted him to stand against his father as one who would be a firsthand witness against the true character of the man who had brought the charges against William. "Let us hope he has not."

The second carriage pulled up when the first was led away. Again, a footman hurriedly placed the step out and opened the door to the coach. A tall, thin man with severe gray eyes and a long, drawn face emerged from the coach. He wore the long black robe and white collar that told Edward that he was the judge. Edward had not seen this man before so he had no idea what sort of fairness he would dispense at this travesty of a trial. To Edward's surprise, the tall judge approached him and extended a hand in greeting.

"I assume you are Lord Edward, the Duke of Stonehaven?" the judge spoke in a deep drone that rattled from his throat.

"I am." Edward accepted the handshake briefly. "And who

am I addressing, sir?"

"I am Peter Garland, magistrate for the crown." His tone was cordial and businesslike, belying nothing to Edward about his character. "Will you be presenting the defense?"

"I will," Edward answered curtly.

"Are you prepared?" Garland asked.

"As much as one can be prepared for such a farce... Your Honor." Edward had not intended to insult the judge, but he found it difficult to hold his tongue.

Garland half smiled. "Rest assured, my lord, both sides will have equal opportunity to present their cases. After all, a man's life is at stake. I do not take that responsibility lightly."

"I meant no disrespect." Edward bowed respectfully. When he stood straight, he happened to glance at the pile of kindling in the square. "I am painfully aware of what is at stake."

Garland followed Edward's gaze. His lips tightened briefly and a look crossed his face that Edward could not read completely, but if he were pressed to offer an opinion, he would say the judge looked disgusted. The look was gone by the time Garland turned back to him.

"Typical." Garland muttered ambiguously, then bowed slightly and continued into the meetinghouse.

Geoffrey leaned forward and whispered to Edward, "What do you make of him, my lord?"

"I'm not sure, Geoffrey. I am mildly encouraged that he will give both sides equal opportunity, as he said. But we shall see if his words are valid soon enough."

The third carriage replaced the second. The occupant of the coach did not wait for a footman to place a fancy step. The door flew open and Lord Ogham jauntily strode from the coach. He was followed by Evander Wesley and Gerald Drunbalk and, much to Edward's dismay, the Earls of Kylkannen and Norwalkshire as well.

"We've lost ground," Edward whispered to Geoffrey. "Hal and Ambrose have turned on me."

Ogham extended his hand. "Edward, my dear *friend*. So good to see you."

Edward stood unmoved.

"I see you still have no idea how to respect a fellow duke. Nothing to say? Or are you silent because your favorite mouthpiece is otherwise engaged?" A wild glee came to his eye. "If that be the case, I look forward to never having to endure your insufferable prattle ever again." He laughed and went into the meetinghouse, Drunbalk and Wesley close behind.

Edward caught the eye of Hal of Norwalkshire. "I see you have chosen to renounce your loyalty, Hal. You understand the ramifications."

"I have joined the side of common sense, Edward," Hal answered in a matter-of-fact tone. "Your embargoes have drained my coffers and have stymied my exports." He looked around at the crowd, then looked Edward in the eye. "You brought all this on yourself. You put your faith and the security of your holdings into the hands of a heretic. I'm here to see that justice is done." Hal did not wait for a reply as he stalked past Edward to join his new comrades.

Ambrose Woodhall emerged from the carriage after Hal, pompously preening the ruffles in the collar and sleeves of his flamboyant scarlet doublet.

"I had hoped you were of a different heart, Ambrose. After all, I made no provisions on your trades. Why do you stand so adamantly against me?"

"It's a matter of personal vindication on my part, Edward. I shall not be made to appear the fool before my own subjects again," Woodhall said, indifferently primping the ridiculously large feather in his hat. "I should have assumed his true nature sooner. I'm not at all surprised to learn that young Fylbrigge be an enchanter."

"The charges are a farce," Edward grumbled. "William is no more an enchanter than you are a peacock."

Woodhall froze, mid-primp. "Well, we shall see, won't we? My money says he is. Pity there will be no gallant hero to ride out of the mists to save *him* in his last hour." Woodhall released a contemptuous laugh, then walked away from Edward.

There were no more carriages to make an entrance. "None of my nobles have seen fit to rally, Geoffrey. We are all the defense William will receive."

"Do not discount us, m' lord," Geoffrey said, a defiant glint in his eye. "There are still more of us than there are of they."

A sudden murmur went through the crowd, beginning near the prison. The heavy iron door squealed on its hinges as it slowly swung open and two hunters—their hoods thrown back, revealing their faces—stepped out. Edward tightened his jaw in anger, impulsively squeezing his fist around the handle of his sword as he recognized the smug face of the hunter in the lead.

"Tearlach," he growled to Geoffrey. "I should cut him down where he stands."

"Cool your temper, m' lord," Geoffrey replied, placing his hand on Edward's fist. "It will serve no one for you to strike out in anger."

Edward forced his hand to relax and fall away from his sword. "Yes, Geoffrey. You are the wiser of us," he said, though he could see his own anger reflected in the old man's eyes.

Two more hunters stepped out through the prison door and fell in line behind the first pair. The four took several steps forward then turned in formation to face the door. Two others appeared from within the prison, pulling a rough-hewn, two-wheeled, wooden cart by two long poles extending from the front. A high-backed chair with thick wooden arms and legs, fitted with manacles for hands and feet and an iron collar at the neck, was situated between the wheels.

"I don't like the looks of this," Edward said, shaken by the sight of the cart.

"Can you see him?" Geoffrey squinted toward the prison. "My eyes are not sharp enough to see that far. Is he walking?"

"He has not been brought out yet. It does not appear they'll allow him to walk," he told Geoffrey, scowling at the cart.

To Edward's surprise, the next two people to emerge from the prison were a monk and a small acolyte. "Ian and Laurel, Geoffrey. They've been made part of the processional. Bless her heart, our little mouse has surely shown her mettle."

Laurel and Ian did not stop with the procession but walked deliberately, heads down and hands folded, to the meetinghouse. They did not stop to speak to Edward before entering, but Laurel risked a glance up to him and he saw that her face was red and streaked with tears. She wore such a look of distress that Edward's heart sank.

Undercurrents of excited voices snaked through the crowd when the next figures appeared at the door. The sounds grew steadily louder and more rhythmic as one group, then another, began to chant.

"Burn the witch! Burn the witch!"

"My God." Edward looked in anguish at the appearance of William and the two hunters who carried him from the prison. "What have I done?"

One man held William around the chest, while the other held his feet. They hoisted him unceremoniously onto the cart, as though he were nothing more than a sack of grain rather than a living human being. Once seated, one of the hunters fastened his wrists and ankles into the manacles on the chair. Even from the distance he stood from the prison, Edward could see William clearly, and the expression of pain that twisted his son's face sent a terrible shudder through his core.

Adrian hopped onto the cart and took a deep bow, then extended a hand, displaying William to the crowd. "Good people of Stonehaven, I give you Lord William, the *former* Earl of Sutherland, the heretic heir of Edward of Drumoak!"

The crowd responded with jeers, catcalls, and mirthless laughter. William slumped forward. Adrian pushed him back against the chair, making a show of securing the collar at his throat. Then, with the air of a street performer, he stood tall, tossed his cape over his shoulder, and held the bridle aloft to the delight of the crowd.

The people cheered, clapped, and changed their chant. *"Silence him! Silence him!"*

With a showman's flair, Adrian forced the bridle bit into William's mouth and locked the bridle with loud click. "Silenced!" he called, then jumped from the cart and bowed with a flourish to more enthusiastic applause.

Edward set his jaw in disgust at the response Adrian's performance was receiving from the crowd. "These are the people from whom we sought help?" He surveyed the faces in the crowd. Many of those who now stood taunting William, cheering his torment, had stood in the great hall of Drumoak that same morning, pledging their support. "How many of these *hypocrites* have proudly counted themselves among William's friends. Why must he be made to suffer such humiliation as this?"

"'Tis always a spectacle, m' lord." Geoffrey shook his head. "But more so for those of rank, I'm afraid." His voice choked. "And I know of no one less deserving of such abominable treatment."

A sudden wave of memories rushed onto Edward as he watched the hunters pull the cart toward the meetinghouse. William wore the same haunted and terrified look in his eyes now that Edward had seen on him when he had first arrived at Drumoak.

Edward sat with Sean on the bench outside the Drumoak stable with his back to the barn door. "I've got two apples here. Pity to waste this one. But I'm just not feeling hungry today. Sean, would you like it?"

"No thank you, sir. Just had my dinner," Sean answered

and glanced over his shoulder toward the barn, then nodded a signal— the lad was watching.

"Well, maybe one of the horses would like this one." Edward set the apple down aside him on the bench. He watched out of the corner of his eye as a small hand crept up from behind the bench and reached for the apple.

"Son, there is a warm bed and a hot meal inside waiting for you."

The boy's hand stopped short of grasping the apple, then withdrew slightly.

"We've been prepared for a long time to welcome you to your new home." Edward did not turn but spoke casually to the sky. "The horse in the far stall is named Star. She's very gentle. I thought she would suit you as a first mount. Of course, she needs a gentle rider as well."

"I've never ridden." The quiet voice came from behind. "I'm not allowed."

"She's yours, now. You're allowed." He carefully turned to face the lad he had waited twelve years to meet. "This is your home now. I'd very much like to meet you." Edward slowly extended a hand in greeting. "You can trust me, lad. I won't let anything happen to you again. I promise." He sat, hand extended, smiling gently, as his new foster son warily accepted his hand.

Edward then remembered William a year after his arrival, more confident, growing handsome, ready with a quick jest or a kind word, ever eager to please. He remembered when William became ill with a fever in his sixteenth winter, when he had been determined to stay in the cold barn with his sick mare instead of his own bed. The fever had worsened to the point that it seemed they would surely lose him. Edward never left his bedside until the fever broke. He felt the same fear now, as then, and hoped with all his heart he would soon experience the same profound relief he felt when William had recovered from his fever.

It was not the Earl of Sutherland Edward looked upon today, nor his heir, son-in-law, or foster-son, but his *son*. The son he loved as his own and had pleaded with Henry to allow him to raise, to keep him *safe*. His own words—*You can trust me, lad. I won't let anything happen to you again. I promise*—sliced through his soul as though they were the sword of judgment wielded by God Almighty, Himself. Outwardly, he stood stoic, yet inwardly, he crumbled, muted by his grief and guilt, watching the cart draw closer.

"Burn the witch, burn the witch!"

The chanting echoed horribly in William's ears as he was led past the crowd. He bit down against the bridle and closed his eyes, willing himself not to hear the jeers and catcalls made by people he once considered friends, hoping instead to hear his lost brother. *Are you still with me?*

"Burn the witch! Burn the witch!"

Sean? Where are you? No answer found him. He looked at the faces in the crowd and in his half delirium, saw them stretched and distorted, hideously disfigured and scarred, just as they had always appeared in his dragon dreams. *My God, Sean, please don't leave me alone now.*

"Burn the witch! Burn the witch!"

No! This isn't real. It's a dream. Right? It's always only been a dream before. He had thought he had prepared himself for the procession to the meetinghouse, but his last shred of hope left him when he saw the structure that was readied for him. *It's a dream. It's not real. God, it can't be real. I can change it.* He closed his eyes, willing the crowd to vanish as he had done so many times in his nightmares. He opened his eyes, hoping to see them gone; instead he was confronted by more gleeful, ugly faces who seemed to take delight in calling his attention to the piles of kindling and peat that surrounded the platform and stake.

"Burn the witch! Burn the witch!"

I shall not have to face it. Ian promised. Laurel promised, I shall not have to face it. Blessed Mother and Father, please, please be with me. I meant no harm. He closed his eyes against the sight and turned his head the other way as far as the collar would allow. When he opened his eyes again, the face he saw was Edward's. *Father! It's not too late. Please, you can stop this. Speak! Please.* He tried to speak through the bridle but found it impossible to make more than a muffled moan. He looked at Edward, pleading with his eyes for Edward to say something to him.

But Edward stood in his typical silence, offering no words of encouragement nor comfort. William would even welcome words of anger—*anything* would be better than the stoic silence Edward maintained. Could it be that he still did not believe what was happening? *He said he believed his eyes; can he not see me?* He knew his wounds were mostly concealed beneath his clothing but still, could Edward not see the gash on his face or the bridle? Was this confounded cart not enough? He closed his eyes against Edward's silence while the hunters pulled him through the meetinghouse doors. *Father, why must you still remain silent?*

Chapter 17

The Trial

... remove my doubts and banish my fear...
"You don't need that anymore, Will."
I thought you'd left me to face this alone.
"Look around. You're not alone."

AUREL CAUGHT HER breath when William was
gracelessly hauled into the meetinghouse. Ian stood
by her, but here, in full view of the world, she would
not be able to lean on him for comfort or support. She dug
her nails into her arms beneath her sleeves as she had done
when the hunters searched Drumoak. She could hardly
bring herself to look at the horrible little cart that they had
used to transport him. Her heart broke for him, imagining
how badly the manacles at his wrists must pain him. The
collar about his throat looked as though it were about to
strangle him. It was little comfort to her to think that he was
probably completely unaware of the shackles on his ankles.
She worried that he would be made to remain bridled and
forced to sit in the frightful chair throughout the entire trial.

William's eyes darted frantically around the room, then
fell and stayed locked on Laurel. She saw his breathing steady
as he set his eyes on hers. "We need to stay where he can see

us," she whispered to Ian.

The cart was brought to a halt with a thump in the front part of the meeting hall. The hunters callously dropped their poles, causing the chair to list forward, William with it. They took little notice that William was being strangled by the collar that was now supporting his weight as they walked to the back of the room. In a panic, forgetting her cover for a moment, Laurel dashed forward and picked up one of the poles to balance the cart. Ian grabbed the other.

"Your Honor?" Ian called to the Judge. "If you please..."

Garland looked up over the scroll he was reading. "You two." He pointed to two hunters who were standing close by. "Bring him down off the cart, please."

Laurel shuddered to see that it was Adrian who stepped forward with the large hunter she remembered wielding the sword above Elinor. They stood on either side of the chair and lifted it. "Pull away," Adrian snapped at Ian and Laurel. They quickly pulled the cart out from under the chair. William groaned as the hunters lowered the chair, with a thump, to the floor.

"Thank you." Garland barely looked up from his scrolls as the cart was hauled away.

"Are we ready to begin?" Garland placed the scroll down. At his right hand on the table, he lifted a large, round, polished stone that was flat on the bottom and knocked it once onto the table. "Take your seats, please."

The bishop and abbot were seated to the left of Garland, Edward to the right. The witnesses for either side filled out the benches in the hall. Ian and Laurel, being clerics and therefore expected to be impartial, were allowed to sit on a bench facing the defendant. Geoffrey and his band were directly behind Laurel and Ian.

A sudden burst of laughter at the back of the room took every one's attention. Garland shook his head impatiently and looked out into the crowd. "Quiet, please," he ordered.

Adrian and his men continued their conversation, laughing at some private jest.

Garland pounded the stone on the table. "Tearlach!"

The room silenced as Adrian turned slowly to face the judge. "Are you addressing me?" the hunter asked, raising a brow.

Garland glared. "This is not a festival!"

"Change your tone with me—"

"Your jurisdiction ends at that door! In this room, I am the authority."

Adrian smirked, bowing his head. "My apologies." He stifled another chuckle. "Go on then, start the trial."

Garland pounded the stone again. "You have been to enough of these to know the procedure. Now, come back here and remove the collar from this man. Then move his seat *respectfully* to the defendant's box." He looked back to his scroll, then added, almost as an afterthought, "Oh, and remove the bridle."

"But your honor, the charges—" Dunkirk began to protest.

"He cannot defend himself if he cannot speak, Your Grace," Garland said in a dismissive voice looking over his shoulder to Dunkirk.

"One for our side," Laurel whispered to Ian. She was hopeful that the next order would be to remove the manacles and was disappointed when the order didn't come.

Adrian approached William with a simpering smile and leaned close to his ear. Laurel was near enough to hear the taunt.

"What's the matter, rabbit? Can't run anymore? I told you I'd catch up to you one day."

Adrian grinned as he removed the collar. William slumped forward slightly and released a loud exhale through the bridle. Adrian gave a sharp hand motion to Ian. "You. Help me move this."

Ian tensed his jaw and went to help Adrian move William, chair and all, to a small boxlike booth reserved for the accused. It was closed on three sides. The front resembled the divided kitchen door in Drumoak with a solid base that locked securely with an open iron grid work on the top. Ian set his side of the chair down gently, but Adrian dropped his. William groaned with the thump of the chair. Ian looked sharply at Adrian, scowling his disapproval.

"My apologies again." Adrian laughed, then started to walk away.

Ian grabbed him by the elbow. "The bridle," he said, angrily.

Adrian rolled his eyes. "Yes, yes."

He removed a large ring of keys from his belt and began sifting through them. Several snickers came from the spectators, which only encouraged him to make more of a show of looking for the key.

"Ah. There it is." He held up the last key on the ring.

"Enough of this." Ian angrily grabbed the key from Adrian and went to William, to unlock the bridle himself. Adrian grabbed the key back and pushed Ian aside.

"Forward!" Adrian ordered as harshly as Harold had done, waiting until William bowed his head. "Good boy." Adrian laughed as he removed the bridle, hooked it to his belt, then slammed the iron door and locked it.

"As if he could run away," Laurel grumbled under her breath, scowling at the booth. As Ian took his seat, she casually nudged him slightly to the right, to be sure William could still see them from behind the grate in the door.

Garland seemed satisfied that the defendant was now properly situated and began the proceedings. "You are William Fylbrigge?" he asked in a deep, formal voice.

William looked up and answered, "I am."

"We shall address each charge." The judge unrolled the scroll and began.

"William Fylbrigge, you are accused of calling upon the forces of evil for the purpose of beguiling the gentlemen you see around you into accepting concessions and treaties that are not amenable to their tenants. Each has testified that he was coerced by evil persuasion into acceptance of the terms.

"You are accused of the casting of spells upon these men, specifically in these same said negotiations, through the use of divination of a diabolical nature to gain the knowledge of the terms of trade and changes in routes, using this knowledge in conjunction with the spells of enchantment.

"You are accused of mesmerizing, by means of your speech and songs given to you by way of consortium with the demonic, to solicit favors and bend minds to your own will, causing God-fearing Christian people to accept as tolerable acts of blasphemy, heresy and witchcraft. Specifically, the Earl of Kylkannen who, by way of your voice and demonic persuasion, was driven to overrule a lawfully ordered execution of a woman who confessed to her use of witchcraft.

"You are accused of bringing about the death of one Nora Guinness, the wife of Geoffrey Guinness, musician to the court of Stonehaven, using a lute and your voice as deliverer of her death."

"No! That isn't what happened!" Geoffrey gasped. "I shall put that to right, when my turn comes," he told Laurel quietly, leaning over her shoulder.

"Last, you are accused of being in league, by way of a pact you have entered into, willingly and deliberately, with the dark lord himself, as evidenced by an immunity to certain poisons and potions known to be lethal to humankind." Garland looked at him with one brow raised on this last point. "How plead you?"

"Not guilty." William bristled and scowled at the judge. "I made no pact!"

Rustling murmurs flowed through the room. Laurel could not discern any words but was certain she had heard laughter from the direction of Thomas. She caught William's eye and flashed her support to him with a quick smile, encouraged that the mention of the pact this time did not send him into his fog.

"Quiet in the hall!" Garland banged the stone once. When quiet resumed, he continued, "Do you have anything to say to in your defense?"

William turned away from the judge and then looked to Laurel. *Answer him, Will.* She feared he had slipped away again as she watched him silently look away from her, then from one face in the crowd to the next, as though waiting for the answer to come from one of them. William looked back to her as though he had forgotten why he was there. *Oh no, he's already drifting.*

"We are waiting," Garland reminded him. "Do you have anything to say in your own defense?"

William's eyes found Garland's as he answered simply, "No, I don't think so."

More rustling spread across the hall. "Will? What are you doing?" Laurel whispered.

Ian casually pushed her cowl up further over her head and leaned close. "You must be more careful."

"Your plea is innocent, yet you have nothing to say?" the judge asked in an unemotional voice. "How do you wish to prove yourself?"

With an unexpected clarity, William answered, "I only say the charges are false." His voice was quieter than it had been before his ordeal but carried clearly throughout the room as the crowd stilled. "I have made no pact with *your* devil. I have cast *no* spells on these men."

Laurel hoped William could hold on to this sudden lucidity. She was beginning to be able to anticipate his changes by the look in his eyes. At the moment, she could see William's 'warrior' was in charge.

"You must offer us proof," Garland said.

"I cannot."

"You cannot?" Garland looked at him closely. "Or you *will* not?"

William answered in his warrior voice, "How am I to persuade you with my voice that I am innocent, if it is my voice that has brought me here? What words could I use, then, that would not be turned against me?"

Again, the noise in the room grew to a level unacceptable to the judge. He slammed the stone to the table. "Silence!" He turned and scowled at William. "You present a valid point, but do you truly believe it wise to remain silent?"

"Wise? Perhaps not. I only know I shall place my faith in the witnesses who have come on my behalf," he spoke slowly, defiantly. "And in *my* God— the one who *I* trust."

More noise from the hall interrupted them.

The bishop pounded the desk with his fist. "You see! He mocks the name of the Lord!"

"Order. I shall be the judge of that!" Garland said, his voice rising above the noise.

"That's twice he's overruled the bishop!" Ian took Laurel's hand and squeezed. "Encouraging, to say the least."

When silence had been restored, Garland continued, "Very well, Fylbrigge, since you offer no defense statement of your own, we shall proceed. I shall hear first the accusers."

Each in turn, the rival nobles spun their tales of pain and woe, of how they had been the victims of William's black magic, coerced into agreeing to the terms of trade they had signed.

Wesley went first, nervously crossing himself as he took the stand. He told his tale with dramatic waves of his arms and fearful glances in William's direction. "I awoke the next morning and did not remember I had even attended the meeting. Yet my good friend, Gerald Drunbalk, swears I was beside him, happily signing the scroll. I swore I had been away, riding in the country. It was then I realized I had been the victim of an evil spirit." He wiped his brow with his handkerchief and crossed himself again.

Edward rolled his eyes and called out, "Don't you mean *distilled* spirit?", evoking laughter throughout the room. Garland tapped the stone to the table once to settle the noise.

Ambrose Woodhall, equally as dramatic as Wesley had been, sniveled through his entire testimony. "He convinced me I was wrong to pursue charges against the witch, even after she confessed to her crime! He used only his voice and the words became unclear, but I soon found I had indeed released her." He dabbed his eyes with the corner of his handkerchief. "It is clear to me now that he defended the witch as one of his own." He set a frightful eye on William and, as Wesley had done, he crossed himself.

"This is sickening! You'd think we were to church by all the crossing they're doing!" Geoffrey snorted. "When do we get our turn?"

Garland ignored Geoffrey as he dismissed Woodhall. "Cassandra Fraewender, come forward."

The tavern dancer sauntered to the stand, batting her eyes at Thomas and winking at Adrian on her way. She settled herself in the chair and crossed her legs, revealing a good amount of calf as she did so. "I'm just a simple workin' class lady." She began her bawdy tale in her usual crass manner. "I make m' livelihood dancin'. I know it's not as genteel as being a housemaid, but it's what I do. And what I don't do is reveal me womanly charms in public." She ignored the snickers that wafted throughout the hall and spoke over them, "Yet when he played his music, I was taken by his magic. And before I knew what I were doin', I'd flung me frock clear across the room!"

Wild laughter exploded in the courtroom. Even William spared a small grin at this unbelievable testimony.

"She flings her frock to any man who merely looks in her direction," Laurel told Ian under her breath. "Who does she believe she's convincing?"

"Quiet, you'll give yourself away," Ian warned her, then casually adjusted her cowl, fully concealing her face.

Garland dismissed the dancer and thanked her for her testimony. Cassandra's statement, as lewd and inarticulate as it was, had been heard, taken into account, and Laurel feared, would weigh against William as heavily as the rest. Laurel's heart fell when the dancer was not laughed out of the courtroom as she hoped.

The next witness was even more disheartening: Hester, a lifelong friend to Nora and Geoffrey and one of the women who had helped Elinor prepare Nora on that terrible night.

"How could she turn on us?" Geoffrey lamented as the woman told her skewed account of Nora's passing.

Hester spoke in a hushed, haunted voice, twisting her apron in her hands. "She had been ill for months. A sort of dementia bedeviled her badly, and she was prone to fits where she would spout strange words in a different language, known only to her. In the end, we feared she truly had been possessed of a demon. He came on that last day." She pointed to William, then pulled her hand back quickly as though she feared he could somehow reach out and grab it. "Poor Nora was spouting her blasphemies and thrashing about." She crossed herself and fixed her sight on William. "He called out to the demon inside her— called it by name with his song!

He sang and played the strings and called the demon back into himself and took her last breath from her on the spot!"

William only stared back at Hester in disbelief that this woman could actually speak such vicious lies about him. He wondered if she had been paid to testify as he suspected Cassandra had been, or if she'd been threatened by the hunters— which seemed more likely. He supposed it didn't matter to the judge. Hester's testimony had been an outright lie, he knew, but she had also been far more believable in her oration than the dancer or even Woodhall had been. William would not look at Hester as Garland dismissed her from the stand. He looked to Geoffrey, who sat stone-faced and sullen behind Laurel. *Geoffrey will put it right. He knows the truth, he knows it was Elinor's dose. Elinor!* William worried that Geoffrey would have to implicate Elinor in order to prove how Nora had actually passed. Elinor would be in danger again, after everything he had gone through. His eyes darted around the spectators, searching for her. *She's not here. She's with Melly. Waiting below? Laurel said they were waiting. What are they waiting for?*

The testimonies went on for what felt like years as he struggled to keep his eyes open and his mind clear. *How many more? Who are all these people? They don't even know me. Why do they lie?*

Several other townspeople offered their versions of tales they had heard of how William had miraculously appeared on horseback and bewitched the magistrates to release the witches from their fates. Others told of how he had appeared in the taverns as if out of the mists, spun his spells around his songs, and taken their wills from them for sundry reasons that never seemed to agree. But they were sure he had mesmerized them somehow before mysteriously vanishing back into the night, their pockets lightened.

During these unending orations, Laurel kept a close eye on William. She watched, feeling helpless, squeezing her fists together each time she saw the telltale glaze in his eyes as he slipped in and out of his fog.

"He drifting again," she whispered to Ian. "He's not staying with us."

"He's done remarkably well," Ian said, his eyes on William. "Still, I hope to call a rest if I get a chance. Physical tortures aside, the five days he's spent awake are what is taking his mind from him, now."

"Six days," Laurel corrected him.

"But he's only been—"

"He was awake all night with Sean the night before he was arrested." Laurel looked to Ian, her eyes wide and once again filling with tears, remembering how she had tried to persuade William to sleep before going to Edward's suite. "He was already exhausted before they took him."

"My God, you're right. I'd forgotten."

After the last of the tavern patrons had offered his testimony, and before Garland could call the last witness for the prosecution on the charges of enchantment— Thomas— Ian gave Laurel a decisive nod, stiffened his shoulders, and stood up. "Forgive me, Your Honor. May I speak, as an impartial?"

"This is out of order." Garland turned to Ian with an

irritated scowl. "Can you not wait until we have finished?"

"No sir, I'm afraid I cannot." Ian stood, addressing the judge defiantly. "You wish these proceedings to be fair, do you not?"

"Of course!" Judge Garland turned an insulted glare toward Ian.

"Then I must bring something to your attention, Your Honor." Ian extended a hand toward the box. "The defendant is unconscious."

Surprised gasps and murmurs and even chuckles filled the room.

Garland peered through the iron grate at William, who had dropped his chin to his chest and drifted. "So I see," he grumbled impatiently, then motioned to the hunter behind the booth. "If you please—"

"Before you wake him," Ian jumped in front of the hunter, hands held up. "Please, consider he has not been allowed to sleep during his entire confinement," Ian spoke quickly, pleading. "And his mind is not fully with him. I ask we allow him to rest before we proceed with the defense."

The judge looked again at William sleeping in the box. "Ah, I see." He raised one eyebrow and looked at the bishop and the abbot. "*Tormentum insomniae?*" he asked in a matter-of-fact way.

Laurel fumed beneath her cowl, fully understanding the Latin term Garland had spoken. *Ah, I see tormentum insomniae... ah, plums and apples... just another wretched soul.*

"Yes, it is customary in these cases," the bishop answered in a similarly off-handed manner. "You can see he is otherwise whole."

"Whole?" Laurel balled her fists beneath her robe to prevent herself from shaking. "He is less than half of himself!" she blurted.

Ian spun on his heel quickly. "Shh."

"I see no reason to call a stop. Take your seat, Brother." Garland waved his hand, signaling one of the hunters. "Wake him, please. We shall continue with Thomas Fylbrigge, the Earl of Aberdoir."

The hunter shook William sharply through the iron grate. He woke up instantly and looked up, wild-eyed and startled. "I know. I know the rules," he called out, surprised, evoking unsympathetic sniggering throughout the room.

Ian sat down with a disappointed sigh. "So much for a fair trial. I should have let him sleep." Ian shook his head.

"Did you expect differently?" Laurel answered, equally disappointed. She looked at Edward, wishing he would have spoken up with Ian. "How can he just sit there? He claims Will as his son. You would think—"

"Sean, hush." Ian suddenly placed his hand on her mouth and motioned with his eyes toward Garland who stood, arms folded, glowering at her.

"Are you quite finished, young man?"

Laurel shrank under her cowl. "Forgive me, Your Honor."

"Thank you." Garland gave her a stern eye, then turned his attention back to his proceedings. "I shall hear now from Lord Thomas Fylbrigge of Aberdoir."

Thomas approached the stand slowly. His posture demure and respectful, he wore the look of one deeply distressed by what he was about to do. He gave William a forlorn sounding sigh, then shook his head and sank into the witness chair.

Laurel leaned to Ian, being sure to keep her voice as quiet as possible. "Look at him! He brought all this on, yet he seeks to seem contrite!"

"Pay attention, Will. Stay with the living."

William looked up sharply. *I hear you, Sean.* Mustering what mental strength he could find, he forced his attention to the man in the witness chair. *Oh God, it's him.* He allowed his head to droop again.

"Eyes wide! Stay with the living!"

William started at the suddenness of Sean's voice ringing in his ear. *Sean? Please, don't—*

"Fylbrigge! Eyes wide!" Garland was yelling.

William opened his eyes with great effort, pushing his concentration back to the man in the witness chair.

Thomas began slowly. "You must understand, Your Honor, the pain it brings me to say what I must." He placed a sorrowful hand on his chest. "This man is after all, my own young brother, whom I, myself, raised in the absence of our father and mother." He took a long, trembling breath. "I accepted him into my household and loved him as a son. I even raised him with equal privilege as my own son Richard enjoyed."

"You have no love of him, Father! Speak the truth!"

A chorus of surprised whispers and curious comments brought yet another halt to the proceedings, as all heads turned to Richard, who was pushing his way to the front of the room.

"It's about time," Edward muttered. They were the first words William had heard him say.

"Stand down! You are not in order!" Garland boomed over the noise as Richard made his way through the crowd. "I will not have these proceedings interrupted again!"

"I am Richard Fylbrigge, son of Thomas Fylbrigge of Aberdoir," he announced. "He is the one who has brought light to these charges, is he not? I've come to bring light to his deceit!"

"You will have your opportunity!" Garland kept his control over the hall, by banging the stone on the table. "Stand down or I shall have you removed."

Richard grimaced at Thomas and strode to the table to join Edward. He sat heavily, never taking his eyes away from his father.

"Continue," Garland ordered Thomas.

Thomas glared contemptuously at his son as he continued his testimony. "As I say, it grieves me that I should have to be the one to reveal the true nature of my own brother before you." He turned from Richard and faced the judge fully. "Even as a boy, he had a way about him. We would find that the children of the servants had left their chores undone, only to learn that William had somehow persuaded them to follow him away from their duties. They would release the flocks or scatter the hens on his behest. These children knew better and yet would follow him as if they had no will of their own to refuse him." He turned and stole a look at William, giving him a half grin before turning away.

William wished at that moment that he truly did possess the dark powers they claimed he owned. He would gladly call fire and lightning down upon his brother's loathsome head.

Thomas continued, pitiful in his assumed grief. "He

coerced Richard as well, convincing him to turn away from the pious studies he once pursued. His mother and I harbored high hopes that he would choose an ecclesiastical calling. He had shown a tendency in that direction until he was led away from it— by him!" He shot a look of shear fury at William. "Richard was almost *killed* when William caused the horse he rode to rear."

Richard stood and shouted, "You lie! You know why I was on the horse! It was not his fault the beast reared!"

"Silence!" Garland demanded. "You will have opportunity!"

Richard scowled, and sat down slowly.

Thomas spun in the chair, facing the defendant's box, and looked straight into William's eyes. "What about Rebecca, brother?"

At the mention of her name, William felt the heat rise in his face, and a violent tremble snake its way through his body.

"Do you remember what you did to her with your tricks?"

"No, I was a child, for God's sake—" Echoes of Rebecca's screams invaded William's mind, and his dream world began to cloud his head again. *Run away, little one. I can't run, Rebecca. I can't even move.*

"A child, yes! But you got your way just the same."

William looked up at Thomas's sadistic sneer as he stood and approached the booth, never taking his eyes away.

"You called her out."

"No!" William met Thomas's eyes, willing the shuddering in his chest to end. "It was not me."

Garland banged the table. "Explain to the rest of us, please."

"My apologies." Thomas turned contritely back to the judge. "His nurse, Your Honor, Rebecca Chase. I'm afraid it was my own fault, really, to engage her services for the boy. She had a tendency to be severe with her disciplines when he misbehaved—"

"No! She was never—!"

"Fylbrigge! Silence!" Garland shouted.

"It was obvious to me, and to Lady Bryndah as well, that he disliked Rebecca, hated her in fact. Isn't that right, my dear?"

Bryndah nodded, mimicking Thomas's distressed contrition, dabbing at her obviously dry eyes with the corner of her handkerchief.

"He played terrible tricks on her. He'd lock himself in his room, or perhaps in the coal—"

"Father! Tell the truth!" Richard yelled.

"— shed." Thomas ignored Richard and proceeded with his testimony. "Rebecca would find him and let him out, but he had convinced us that she had used magic to open the doors for him! He used his burgeoning talents even then, convincing us that she used magic on him regularly to punish him."

"Liar!" William screamed and summoned all his will in an attempt to free his hands, but he could barely move them and the pain in his wrists and back prevented him from trying further.

"It is my regret that we believed his tales and the poor woman perished on the stake." Thomas looked at William with a snakelike grin. "It's time to repay that debt."

"I never accused her. You lie! *You* killed her!" William

cried out, desperately trying to ignore the spasms of pain it caused him, and the images of Rebecca crying out through the flames that flashed in his mind. "You and the dragon killed her!"

Garland pounded the table again. "Silence, you'll get your chance."

"You killed her!" William yelled again, his mind fogging over again. "You killed her."

"Fylbrigge!" Garland pounded the table twice more. "Settle!"

William dropped his chin to his chest and sat silently. *They killed her, Sean. The dragon and the snake. It isn't my debt. I didn't kill her.*

When William had finally settled down, Garland asked Thomas, "Do you have anything more to add?"

"Yes." Thomas replied, turned his sneering face away from William. "Over the years, in his time at Drumoak, I saw him manipulate those around him. Those he considered family. I saw how he would bend them to his will with his uncanny charms. Why else would a duke of high standing and respect name a *fosterling* as his heir? Why would his daughter consent to wed one with no other ambition but to spend his days idle with his tunes and tricks?" He turned to speak to the bishop. "On the night of his wedding, I visited William in his chamber. I went to offer my congratulations on his wedding and to offer my advice on some matters of diplomacy. I did this in the spirit of good will, to offer him the benefit of my own, considerably greater expertise in these things. I went to him peacefully, completely without thought of malice. But at first sight of me, and without the slightest provocation he set his guard, Sean Wilbrun, upon me. Wilbrun had no light in his eyes; he was not acting upon his own will, I could tell. And he held me with such force as to strangle me." Thomas turned now and glared at William. "With one word uttered from your mouth, Wilbrun released me and came back to his own mind again. Yet the threat was clear. It was then that I realized you suspected I had found you out. Found out what you are. And what you are capable of doing."

Thomas finished his testimony, with a dramatic sigh, then returned to his own chair.

"Liar," William growled under his breath, shaking with anger.

"I knew I should have strangled him when I had the chance," Sean's voice chimed.

I should have let you.

William watched Thomas lean toward Bryndah and whisper something to her. She grinned, nodded and looked directly at William. She made no effort to stifle the vile smile that spread across her face as she set her eyes on him, sending echoes of his childhood fears of her coursing through him. For a moment, William even imagined he saw a flickering flame come to her eyes, as it had in his nightmares. She placed a leather satchel on the table and stroked it as if it were a cat, never taking her eyes off him nor allowing her grin to fade.

William tried but found it nearly impossible to take his eyes off Bryndah. *The Dragon is readying her fire.*

"Look away from her, Will. She has no power over you," Sean reassured him. *"You're not alone."*

"Fylbrigge," Garland's booming voice called William back

to attention. "Do you have an answer to these testimonies?"

William pulled his eyes away from Bryndah to meet the judge's. But her eyes stayed in his mind just as they had when he was a child. He felt the terrible and familiar tremble that would begin in his middle and spread to his chest and arms; a tremble he had not felt since that last day in Aberdoir. How is it she still had the ability to terrify him, even now? Even after his horrendous night at the hands of Joseph, he could look his torturer in the face and not feel the same fear that her simple smile and the motion of her stroking hand brought to him.

"Look away from her!" Sean's voice, intense in William's ear, called to him.

William closed his eyes against Bryndah's image and fought the paralyzing terror that threatened to consume him, still searching for his voice to answer the judge.

"We are waiting," Garland droned impatiently. "What is your answer to these testimonies?"

William rallied his resolve and finally finding his voice, said only, "They lie."

"Young man, do you understand what is asked of you?"

"They're all liars," William's warrior shouted back to Garland.

"What is your proof?" Garland demanded.

William looked past the judge to Bryndah. She still held her gaze on him, stroking the satchel. He had no idea what, if anything, was inside, but her simple movement of stroking amplified the trembling. She seemed to know the effect she had on him and grinned wider with an evil glint in her eyes. Images of Aberdoir and the nights he spent terrified and alone in the stifling coal shed next to the blacksmith's forge and how he had called for Rebecca rushed back to him as he watched Bryndah's hand. He could see Rebecca standing up to Bryndah as no one else in Aberdoir did for him, and what it had cost her. He fought to keep down the frightened child inside that threatened to defeat him, as he forced himself to concentrate on the judge and the trial. *It's a trick of my own mind. The dragon won't burn me again. Open the door, Rebecca, please.* William closed his eyes against the dragon, struggling to stay out of the fog but not wanting to open his eyes.

"Fylbrigge? What is your proof?" Garland repeated the question, louder this time.

"*God* knows they lie!" William cried out. "*He* knows. *He* knows I made no pact." As he had in the tower, William lost control of his emotions rapidly as the last shreds of his angry resolve shriveled away to grief and despair. "Don't make me say it. I made no pact." He closed his eyes as the voices in the room echoed around him. "Lies."

Laurel was saying, "Ian, he's fallen away." Her voice suddenly sounded like Rebecca. *Run away.*

"Your Honor, I must request a short recess." Ian's voice meshed around Laurel's. "You can see the effect the past days have had; he cannot answer for himself! His thoughts stray. Allow me to open the door."

Open the door, open the door, Rebecca, open the door. I can't move, I can't run away.

"Fylbrigge! Eyes up!" Garland pounded the table.

William sat back instantly, responding to the command as he had been trained by guard in the prison. "I know the rules." He slowly opened his eyes as the echoes in his mind at last stopped. The child slipped back into the dark, allowing 'William' the opportunity to respond.

"What is your answer to these testimonies?" Garland repeated his question in a less threatening tone of voice.

"They lie. I've not ever bewitched anyone."

"What of the alleged pact—?"

"I made no pact." William dropped his head and quietly sobbed into his chest.

Edward had hardly taken his eyes off William for the better part of the trial, and could see that William was drifting back into his own fog. "Your Honor," he began quietly, before taking the stand. "May I please approach him? For a moment? Please?"

Garland nodded, irritably. "For a moment, only. These proceedings must continue."

"I shall be brief. Thank you."

Laurel caught Edward's eye as he left his seat. "Bring him back," she whispered. Edward tapped her shoulder lightly as he passed her.

Edward approached the hideous defendant's box, battling down the lump in his throat. He had remained silent throughout the entire course of this farcical trial, aching to reach out and embrace his son. But now, the closer he got to the box and the easier it was for him to see what remained of William, the more difficult he found it to maintain his stoic façade.

Edward crouched before the booth and reached in through the grid, laying his hand gently on William's uninjured cheek. "William? Son. Look up." Edward kept his voice as low as possible. He wished he could have had this moment privately but knew that would not be granted him. William looked up with eyes Edward barely recognized.

"I made no pact, Father. They lie."

"I know that," Edward assured him in the gentle manner that had won the child over years earlier. "But you must stay in control of yourself."

William closed his eyes. "I can't. It hurts too much. And I'm losing."

"No. You are giving up. You can't do that just yet. Open your eyes, son."

William opened his eyes and set them on Edward. "Do you believe me now?"

The simple question cut Edward to the soul. He found it difficult to meet William's eyes, but he did not turn away. "Yes, I believe you. Please, forgive me."

William looked into Edward's face as if seeing it for the first time. Slowly, the light come back into his eyes. "Forgiven. Thank you, Father."

Edward patted him gently on the face and stood to resume the proceedings. "My apologies for the delay, Your Honor." He cleared his throat and took the stand.

"Lord Edward, do you offer rebuttal to the claims made previously?"

"I most certainly do. Specifically to Thomas of Aberdoir." Edward chose not to sit, instead pacing back and forth in front of the judge's table. "He claims it was William's will that I made him my heir and named him Earl of Sutherland. I say before you, and before God, that it was of my own free will that I chose him. I chose him for his loyalty, his passion, his sense of fairness, and his cleverness. I chose him for his sense of humor. I chose him because he has talent. I chose him because he has come to be as a son to me." He leaned over the table and spoke directly into Dunkirk's face. "And I tell all present and God Almighty, at no time during his presence at Drumoak have I witnessed or had cause to suspect that William used any means other than a God-given sense of compassion to win over the hearts and minds of the people he has encountered."

Edward turned and abruptly pointed to the earls seated in the gallery. "Should it be blamed on the messenger that the idiots who received the message could not understand it?"

Drunbalk made an indignant snort and looked away as Edward continued.

"You all had ample opportunity to judge the treaties and offer challenge to them! You, Wesley! You yourself countered two of the provisions, and we agreed to *your* terms. And you, Drunbalk, do you forget so easily that we cast away an entire scroll on your behest! You all knew what you were signing. William explained it to you very clearly, in short easy words so you would not misunderstand. The only enchanting that took place during those negotiations was provided by the ladies in the tavern!"

Stifled laughter wormed through the room.

Edward spun and looked out into the spectators, pointing to Cassandra. "And you! Are you to be believed? There is not a man in this town who has not had opportunity to view your womanly charms. And was it not you who stood in my own hall this very morning asking for payment for your testimony?"

Surprised murmurs and stifled sniggers interrupted his speech.

"It was the music. I tell you he charmed me with the music!" Cassandra stood and screeched at Edward.

"It was the silver in his pocket that charmed you!" Edward bellowed back at her.

"I don't have to stay and be accused by the likes of you." Cassandra put her nose in the air and stormed toward the door, where Ewan had been standing throughout the proceedings. He took a wide side step to block her path. "Move, you oaf!"

"As you wish, my lady." Ewan bowed deeply to her, stealthily catching the string of her purse as he did so. The pouch dropped loudly to the floor, spilling her coins everywhere throughout the meetinghouse. "That's a lot of silver for such a simple working dancer. You made a shrewd choice, miss. Edward would have never met that price."

"No! Don't touch it! It's mine!" Cassandra scrambled to the floor frantically trying to retrieve the coins. Again, chaos descended on the hall as spectators watched the crazed dancer crawl on the floor between the chairs and people.

Edward looked toward William to see if he understood what was happening. He was gratified to see, for the first time in many days, the hint of a smile on his son's face as he said, silently, "Thank you, Father."

"Took care of her!" Laurel beamed at Edward, allowing the cowl to slip from her head. Ian instantly pulled the cowl back over her face.

"Please be more careful," Ian reminded her. "She was easy

to discredit. But I am more encouraged with Will. Look, he's with us. I don't know what Edward said to him, but it seemed to be what he needed."

Laurel looked at William, thrilled to see he did seem fully back from his mind battles. "Let's hope he stays with us."

"Silence. Order!" Garland picked up the stone and slammed it to the table. Quiet resumed in the room. "That is the last outburst I will tolerate. Spectators, leave. Now! I wish only those who have come to testify to remain."

Ian squeezed Laurel's hand excitedly. "That is a good sign!" he whispered. "He is serious in his fairness after all. He will not bend to the sentiment of that bloodthirsty crowd out there."

"I hope you're right!" Laurel squeezed back.

When the spectators had cleared, Garland looked stunned to see so many peasants remaining in the hall. "Are you *all* here to testify?"

"We are, Your Honor," Geoffrey spoke for all of them. "There is not a one among us who will corroborate the nonsense presented afore us!"

"Do you all have firsthand knowledge of the negotiations that have been challenged?" Garland asked.

The confident smile faded only slightly from Geoffrey's face as he responded respectfully, "Sir, we do not, but I believe Sir Edward has countered their claims."

"Yes, I believe it is my job to judge that point, sir," Garland replied smoothly. "Make your statement, please."

Geoffrey gave William an encouraging smile, which William returned as his old friend approached the stand. "I am Geoffrey Guinness, a musician and woodworker. I have lived my entire, too-long life in Stonehaven and have known this gentle young man since he arrived here, some seven years past. 'Twas I who set the lute in his hands and taught him to play it," Geoffrey spoke with the eloquence and passion of a poet. "He has a rare talent, Your Honor, and though I may have taught him the music, it was God who gave him his gift to play it. Does he beguile with his tunes? Most assuredly, he does— just as a lark in the field beguiles on an April morning, or the sound of a child's laughter beguiles his mother. To assert the notion that lovely music played by gifted hands is an act of the devil is to say that God did not teach the songbirds to sing!" Geoffrey swallowed and gained his breath to continue.

Laurel studied Garland's face closely. She could not find any trace that Geoffrey had moved him. "He must be made of iron," she whispered to Ian.

"No, Laurel, I believe Geoffrey is gaining ground for us," Ian responded quietly.

"Your Honor, I am a simple man, devout in my faith in God, and I swear before you now, I have never found cause to assume any diabolical presence within his nature. But if I must offer proof to you, I have this to tell." Geoffrey paused, took a long steadying breath, then continued in a sad trembling voice, "He was indeed present when my Nora passed from this life to glory. It is also true that he played his music for her in her last moments."

Hushed murmurs responded to Geoffrey's affirmation. Laurel and Ian exchanged startled glances.

"It has been stated that he sang a demonic song. What song did you hear him sing, sir?" Garland voice was noticeably kinder.

Geoffrey smiled sadly. "He sang her favorite song, sir. One called 'Greensleeves.' A song of gentle love, one composed by the very King of England. To be completely truthful, he only hummed the tune while he played. He sang no words at all."

"Do you believe it was his song that brought about the death of your wife?"

Laurel squeezed Ian's hand. William leaned forward, eyes fixed on Geoffrey.

"No." Geoffrey's eyes welled. "It was not his song. His song was a blessing, not a curse. It did not call out any demon, but only serve to calm the delirium she suffered. He merely played at my request that her passing be tranquil."

Laurel relaxed and saw William do the same. He sat back in his seat and closed his eyes, smiling.

"Do the witnesses behind you have knowledge of this event?" Garland asked.

The people behind Geoffrey all answered that they did.

"Do you all agree with what he has testified?"

"Yes," they answered, together.

"Does anyone have any more to add?"

Laurel bit her lip. "Please, let him be content with what has been said."

"No," was the unanimous response.

Laurel sighed in relief and looked at William. He exhaled slowly, opened his eyes, and thanked Geoffrey silently.

Geoffrey answered with a sad smile.

"In the interest of time, since there are so many," Garland said, to the band of peasants, "I will ask you all at once. Have any of you witnessed the accused casting spells?"

"No," they chorused.

"Calling up demons?"

"No."

"Mesmerizing, confounding, or otherwise calling upon dark forces to gain favors?"

"No."

"Do any of you have any knowledge of any pact he may have made?"

"No."

"Thank you, people. Mister Guinness you have anything more to add?"

"No, sir."

"Then you may all leave now." Garland tapped the table gently with the stone and dismissed the peasants. "I shall hear from Richard Fylbrigge next."

Laurel squeezed Ian's hand again. For the first time, she truly believed they had a hope to win.

Edward smiled to Geoffrey. "You could not have been better," he whispered to the old man.

"My honor, sir. I spoke only truth." Geoffrey patted Edward in response. He looked at William. "God bless you, Will," he said, then left the hall with the rest of the witnesses.

Laurel took some delight in seeing the furrowed brows that both Abbot Joseph and Bishop Dunkirk wore as they watched Geoffrey and his entourage leave the hall. All that remained was Richard's testimony against Thomas. In the surge of hope that fell upon Laurel, she had almost forgotten the last and most dangerous test they must win. The poison had not been addressed. Her eyes fell on the wooden box on Ian's lap and she reminded herself— *we're ready for them.*

Richard stood to take his place. As he walked to the stand, Laurel felt a sudden wave of dread, noting the slight unsteadiness in Richard's walk and the sweat on his brow. *He looks positively terrified!* This in itself did not trouble her so much. All of the witnesses had been nervous. But Richard had shown, on more than one painful occasion how fear had clouded his judgment, and the results had been disastrous. *Dear Mother, let him keep his wits about him this time.*

"You are Richard Fylbrigge?" Garland continued when Richard had taken the stand.

"I am."

"What testimony do you offer?"

"To refute the claims made by my father on events of my uncle's childhood." Richard clenched his fists as he spoke.

"Do you have firsthand knowledge of these events?"

"Oh, yes!" Richard glared at his father from the stand.

"Tell us first, then, about the horse," Garland told him. "What was the defendant's part in your mishap?"

Richard nodded and with a deep breath, began his testimony. "He had no part in it. I attempted to ride the unbroken beast of my own will. It was not William who caused the horse to rear; it was the inept rider upon his back." He turned a contemptuous eye on his father. "William could not have coerced the animal in any case, since he was unconscious and bound to a post at the time!" His voice echoed almost as the judge's had as he spoke.

Laurel felt more encouraged by Richard's tone. She knew the tale of that last day in Aberdoir was a painful subject for William, and she now worried more about William keeping himself together than Richard.

"My mother had ordered him beaten," Richard continued, his jaw tensing as he spoke. "The abbot who sits behind you, in fact, was the man who carried it out. I acted completely on my own in an ill-fated attempt to rescue William from the post. I jumped on the horse, the horse reared, I fell off— that is everything there is to tell of that mishap." He took a breath and continued, keeping his fists clenched as he spoke. "It is true enough that William was raised in my father's house, but not out of any *brotherly* compassion on my father's part. He stood to lose his inheritance and a substantial amount of wealth if William met an early demise. So my father raised him. Barely. William did not coerce the servant children away from their chores! More often than not, he was hiding from my parents, and they would leave their chores to help him hide or to be sure he was safe. You see it was the servants mainly, and me, who truly cared for him. Not my parents."

No wonder he has always felt so at ease in the friendship of a mere housemaid, Laurel thought. She looked to William, worried that this testimony may cause him to drift. He sat quietly, eyes cast downward, but he seemed to be in control of his mind at the moment.

Richard continued, "As far as William leading me away from an ecclesiastical calling, I tell you now, I never in my life entertained such a notion. I learned all the Scripture I could stomach from the barbarian who sits there." He pointed at Abbot Joseph. "A man who—"

"Barbarian!" Joseph snorted angrily. "How dare—"

"Barbarian!" Richard looked the abbot squarely in the eye. "A man who would demand a young boy recite Scripture while he is bound to a post and whipped until he was unconscious." Richard's voice echoed as he paused, then added in a low tone, "'Tis not William of Drumoak who is evil in this room."

The room went silent as Richard and the abbot locked eyes, Joseph red-faced and glowering, and Richard allowing a slight grin of satisfaction at Joseph's apparent loss for words.

Garland broke the silence, "Sir."

Richard slowly faced the judge.

"Do you have anything further?"

"Yes." Richard relaxed his stance and faced the judge. "You need to know the truth about Rebecca to fully realize the treacherous nature of William's accuser." William looked up at the mention of her name.

"Then continue." Garland gave him a stern look. "In a less confrontational manner, if you please. I understand she perished upon an accusation brought by the defendant. Is this true?"

"Yes, she perished on the stake." Richard drew a long, deep, breath. His voice took on a slight tremble. "But William neither accused nor played tricks on her." Richard paused and looked down.

Laurel checked on William. He stared straight ahead, expressionless save the tear that formed on one eyelid. Laurel had never heard Rebecca's story until this testimony. She only knew that Rebecca had been William's nurse at one time, but nothing more.

"What was his relationship to Rebecca?" Garland asked.

"She was the most important person in his world, Your Honor."

"Thomas of Aberdoir has testified that the accused

disliked her. Do you refute this as well, then?"

"Yes," Richard answered quietly. "Rebecca was far more than a servant, or his nurse, Your Honor. She was, to him, his mother, and he loved her as such. He even called her 'mum.' My parents knew this, as well."

Mother? Laurel looked quickly to William. As she feared, the glaze was coming to his eyes. But he remained quiet.

Richard went on, "And she loved him as well, from the moment of his birth. She was the only person willing to stand up against my mother for him." He pointed toward Bryndah, his hand shaking. "It was you who accused Rebecca of using magic, Mother, and you who told the abbot that it was William who had called it out."

Bryndah's eyes flared but she remained silent.

Richard looked at William before he continued; his eyes etched with the same pain William wore. "After Rebecca's trial, my mother took him to the stake, and forced a small torch into his hand. She held his arm, and made him put it on the pyre to start the death fire." He swallowed, turning away from William. His voice faltered as he continued. "Then she made him watch, standing so close that he came away with red marks on his face. My father stood behind him, telling him— a child of only six years— that it was his fault. They made him light the fire and then stand there to watch her die."

"My God!" Laurel covered her face with her cowl. *That is what he never spoke of! Blessed Mother, that is what the dragon has done?* Ian had taken her hand again for comfort. She looked up to see that William was looking at her through glassy, unfocused eyes, clearly adrift in his mind. "He's gone again, Ian." She cried quietly.

"I think it better for the moment." Ian hushed her gently.

Richard resumed his testimony. "My father would have you believe it grieves him to offer evidence against his brother. He lies! Two nights ago, I visited him and my mother in the guest chamber of the abbey. I will fully admit in their presence now that I was there under a false pretense. I made them believe I wished William to die so I could inherit his rank. Ask them!" He glowered at his mother and she stared back with venom in her eyes. "Yes, Mother, I lied. A talent I seem to have inherited from you!"

Voices once again rose to a roar, even though most of the people had left the hall.

"Silence!" Garland pounded the table.

Richard continued with uncharacteristic bravado, "Your Honor, I come to testify that my parents' motives in bringing William to trial are not so pious as to rid our world of an evil spirit. They wish to rid our world of an obstacle to their lust for wealth and power. Their claims are based solely on lies and greed. They know William is not an enchanter. They know this so-called pact he's allegedly made is a lie as well."

Bryndah was suddenly on her feet. "Lies? You speak of lies? I will show you proof! Father Dunkirk? Do you often employ young women as acolytes?" She made a dash around the table and charged toward Laurel without waiting for an answer.

Laurel gasped and tried to move away. Ian was on his feet, trying to get between the two, but Bryndah was agile and before anyone could stop her, she reached out and forcefully yanked the cowl from Laurel's face. Richard managed to get behind his mother and pull her away from Laurel.

"Let me go, you treacherous beast!" Bryndah screeched at Richard. "You are no son of mine!"

"Order! Silence at once! All of you! Take your seats!" Garland banged the desk hard. "Countess, explain your accusation of this young man!" Garland's booming voice echoed through the hall.

Amazingly, the judge, even though he could fully see Laurel's face, believed her still to be a young boy. She made quite sure to keep her mouth shut.

"Young man? That is a woman, Your Honor. A house servant in Edward's household!" Bryndah picked up the leather satchel and untied the lacing. "This is my proof!" She reached into the satchel and withdrew a long hank of Laurel's severed hair. "Compare it, Your Honor. You will see it has come from her head!"

No! Sean! Do something! God, please don't let the dragon hurt her.

The hunters took Laurel by the arms and roughly pushed her to the stand before the judge. Garland took the lock and held it to her head, examining the freshly shorn ends of Laurel's closely cropped hair. She stood still as a stone.

"Hair alone does not prove a gender." Garland looked closely at her, then stood away. "Adrian, examine him, if you would."

Laurel set her jaw but did not struggle as Adrian approached her with a sickening grin. "Sean? Have we been deceived?"

"No," Laurel answered in her lowest voice and stood stoic

as Adrian moved his hands across her breasts.

Sean, please, can't you stop them?

"She's well hidden, Will," Sean's voice assured him.

"Are we wrapped or are we breastless?" Adrian laughed.

"I'm a boy," Laurel insisted. "Would any mere girl have held her nerve while you searched Drumoak?"

"Good point, Sean." Adrian tilted his head. "Your Honor, in my opinion this acolyte—" He began to run his hands across her breasts again. "Is not a—"

"Leave her alone!" Richard suddenly lunged toward Adrian, pushing him away from Laurel. "Don't touch her!"

"Her?" Adrian burst into a fit of laughter. "Thank you, Sir Richard, you have just saved me from an embarrassing mistake! I was ready to believe her charade and declare her a boy!"

No, Richard! What has he done?

"He panicked," Sean's voice answered. *"Typical."*

Two hunters immediately descended on Richard and held him in the same manner Laurel was held. The judge regained his control of the room with a shout. "Quiet! Secure her. Sir Richard, I shall tolerate no more outbursts from you. You shall also be secured for the remainder of these proceedings."

Adrian bound Laurel's wrists behind her, then secured Richard, and pushed the two of them down to sit on a bench at the front of the room.

Garland turned to Bryndah. "Countess, I see you are correct in your claim. How it pertains to this case, I am not sure." He looked at Laurel. "There are civil laws, however, prohibiting young women from masquerading as males. Do you know the laws?"

"No, sir," Laurel whispered.

Civil law? Sean! Edward can save her. William looked hopefully toward Edward and his heart sank. Edward, as always, sat silently, just watching. *Will he not even rally for Laurel on such a simple charge?*

"You have doubled your crime by assuming a clerical role!" The judge crossed his arms over his chest and shook his head. "You have broken both laws of church and state, young woman!"

"No! I only sought to help!" Laurel cried.

"Help? You have apparently not thought your actions through clearly," Garland yelled, then turned to Bryndah. "Countess, pray tell, what is her connection to William Fylbrigge?"

Bryndah sauntered to the stand, smiling at William and Laurel on her way. She carried her satchel close to her. *What more could she have?* William felt the tremble begin as he watched her.

"Her connection should be obvious, Your Honor," Bryndah began. "She's in league with him. I found the evidence of this woman's deceit in the abbey." Bryndah held up her satchel. "It is apparent to me that this monk is fully aware of her deception and therefore part of Edward's attempts to hide the truth about his heir."

"No, Ian had nothing to—" Laurel started to protest.

Garland raised his hand to silence her.

"Perhaps I'm mistaken on that point," Bryndah admitted in false contrition. "It's quite possible Brother Ian has been bewitched into helping her."

Ian stared, ashen-faced, at Bryndah. "What a vile accusa—"

"Perhaps she has taken his will, Your Honor," Bryndah continued, wide-eyed and dramatic. "A trick she, I'm sure, has learned from the accused. Or perhaps she taught it *to him*. They seem to be quite close and quite familiar with each other. Unnaturally close given his station and hers." Bryndah turned slowly to Laurel and spoke in simpering tones, "You are such a loyal little servant at Drumoak, but you have never fully learned to keep in your proper place."

"You're lying," Laurel growled.

"I've witnessed her several times— unknown to her, of course— in private company with the heretic himself."

"You are evil!" William cried out. "Leave her alone!"

William looked at Bryndah closely, convinced he could see the flickering in her eyes and the talons growing from finger tips. *She's becoming the dragon.* Bryndah looked at William and grinned, sending icy waves down his back. *Fangs! Do you see them? She readying her fire, Sean, is it real?*

"Dragon!"

"Quiet!" Garland yelled at William.

"Look away from her," Sean's voice ordered loudly in William's ear.

"I wonder how far she would be willing to go in her loyalty to the handsome young heir of Drumoak." Bryndah set her fiery eyes on William. "It seems she would go as far as to masquerade as a boy, to what ends I cannot say for sure, but my guess would be to bring you something you may need. To enhance your defense perhaps, to make it possible for you to *talk* your way out of this!"

She grinned wickedly. William saw the fangs growing longer as she smiled at him.

"I have no idea what you are talking about!" Laurel snapped back to Bryndah. "I have nothing he needs."

"Don't you?" Bryndah spun to face Laurel. "It is obvious by his lack of testimony today that you failed in your mission. You did not bring him what he would most need to argue his case!" She reached for her bag. "Your Honor, I have proof that the accused has indeed used spells."

She flung open the bag, retrieved the small quarter-folded bit of parchment, and held it aloft. William recognized the page at once. He didn't move but stared at it as though it were an arrow coming straight at his heart.

"Look here, you filthy heretic, she has delivered us the proof of your evil, and hers as well!"

"No! That's a lie!" Laurel screamed. "He's not evil!"

"Evidence!" Bryndah held the parchment high as if it were the flaming sword from the dragon dreams. "Evidence he cast the spell!" Bryndah handed the parchment to the judge.

Edward stood in his seat. "What evidence?" he demanded. "More of your contrivances?"

"It is not my hand that signed this, but his. Look at the initials. W.F." Bryndah pointed to the bottom of the page.

"Where did you find this?" Garland asked.

"With her discarded garments and the hair, Your Honor."

Garland read the paper several times, then walked to William and held the page before him. "Do you recognize this?"

William looked at the page, the very familiar page he had taken from Elinor's book. The one he had hidden away. *How? Laurel, how?* The words that had always brought him comfort and confidence now seemed to burn before his eyes.

He didn't know how to answer. He looked at Laurel, who sat terrified, bound on the bench. She had risked so much for him; how could this have happened? His eyes rolled back and closed. *I'm lost.*

"*Stay with the living!*" Sean's voice demanded.

William opened his eyes again.

"Do you recognize this?" Garland asked again.

"Yes," William answered miserably.

Garland walked away and read the page again, his expression betraying nothing of his thoughts. "Do you recite this often?"

"No," William answered, struggling to stay out of the fog.

Garland turned to Laurel abruptly. "Do you know what is on the parchment? It will do you no good to lie."

"It's a *prayer*," Laurel spoke through halted tears. "He did not ask for it; he had no knowledge I carried it. I meant no harm! Please, believe me, he didn't know—"

"What *was* your intent, then?" Garland interrupted her. "This is a curious thing to leave so carelessly about when you know the nature of what is accused."

"I wanted to destroy it," Laurel answered. "I feared it would be misunderstood."

"Do you have any knowledge that the accused may have actually used this incantation?" Garland asked in his typically unemotional tone.

"It's a *prayer,* not an incantation!" Laurel corrected, through terrified tears. "And no, I never heard him say the words."

"Where did you find it, then, that you felt so compelled to carry it with you?"

Laurel stared at the judge, then to Ian, to Richard, and finally, to William. He spoke to her silently, mouthing the words "tell him." She shook her head in protest. William pleaded with his eyes and spoke aloud, "Tell him." She stared, set her jaw, and abruptly turning away from William.

"Where did you get it?" Garland asked again, impatiently.

"I..." Laurel looked at William sorrowfully, then said, "... wrote it for him." She closed her eyes and dropped her head. "He refused to accept it."

"Laurel, no! What are you saying?" William called to her, but his voice was drowned by the sounds that rose in the hall.

"*You* wrote it? Do you admit, then, that you do have skills in these dark arts?" Garland lowered his face close to hers.

"Laurel, no, don't," Ian whispered under his breath.

"I do." Laurel cried. "William is unaware. It was my doing. All of it! He never knew. It was I who placed the charm on *him*... that one on the parchment. Long ago! He had no knowledge. I only wanted to help him."

"Laurel, no, why?" William could not believe what she had just done. His entire being shook as the implications of her admission became clear. "Don't take this from me, you've done nothing!"

"Do you understand what you have confessed?" Garland asked her quietly.

"Yes," Laurel answered through her sobs. "He had no knowledge. Please, he is innocent."

"And what of this monk?" Garland gestured to Ian. "Is he aware of your craft?"

"No," Laurel whispered. "The countess was correct; I

charmed him as well."

Ian groaned and dropped his head to his chest. William knew they felt the same— Laurel had just taken the full burden of his crime onto her own shoulders.

"She admits it! Witch!" Bryndah screeched.

"No!" Richard struggled to stand. "It's not true! Laurel, tell them! Please!"

"Silence!" The hunter on his shoulder pushed Richard back into his seat.

"Witch!" Bryndah pointed at her again. "She has confessed. The two of them. You cannot believe her foul lies, they conspire together."

"No! He has no knowledge of what I've done!" Laurel screamed, frantically struggling against her bonds. "It was all my doing. He never knew. None of it."

"Laurel, why?" William cried out. "Don't take this—"

"For you. I did it for you. Forgive me!"

"Order!" Garland took control of the room. "Am I to understand, young woman, you freely take responsibility for this so-called prayer and further, you have just fully admitted to casting charms. Do you understand you have admitted to witchcraft?"

"Yes." Laurel lowered her head again and sobbed loudly.

"The punishment is mandated, Your Honor!" Dunkirk shouted, pounding his hand on the table. "There can be no leniency! She confessed!"

Garland turned to face the bishop. "I am the authority in this room!"

Dunkirk grabbed Garland's stone and hurled it toward the judge, narrowly missing the man's head. "And I am the authority in matters of blasphemy! On these two things the law agrees! The witch must burn! What does she matter to you?"

There was silence in the room. Even Garland seemed taken aback by Dunkirk's outburst. He stared at the bishop, what little color there had been in the gaunt cheeks paled to a chalky gray. An odd look crossed his face. "What does she matter?" He said quietly. "The decision to condemn someone to the stake is not one I make lightly. I should think a man of your profession would understand that."

William held his breath in hope this small show of compassion was genuine.

Dunkirk glared. "There is no decision to be made. The law is clear and she has confessed! If you do not follow the law, I will simply have Tearlach do it. She confessed before all these witnesses. Go on, ask any of them if they did *not* hear her admit she cast the spell?"

Garland looked about the stunned faces. No one would meet his eyes.

Speak, father! Tell them she's innocent.

Garland shook his head, then faced Laurel. "I have no other choice, then. You have freely confessed. A sentence must be carried out."

"No!" William screamed out. "Leave her alone!"

Garland spun on his heel, facing William. "She has just exonerated you against the charges of enchanting. Do you now claim you are, in fact, in league?"

"No! No, We... made no pact... she is not... no! Laurel, please, don't do this. Not for me. Father stop this! You can stop it! Please."

"Then you *did* have knowledge of her enchantments?" The judge glared at William.

"No! She couldn't have... Laurel, why are you taking this from me?" William leaned as far forward as he could to look through the grate on the booth. "Don't lie for me Laurel, please."

Garland turned back to Laurel and spoke sharply, "Have you only confessed in an attempt to spare him?"

"I am not lying. He is innocent!" Laurel yelled. "I told you, it was I who cast the spells. Shall I prove it?" She turned wild-eyed and began a dramatic chant. "*Amore divina, Matris, et Patris, benedico vos—*"

Astonished gasps and stares came from the people at the prosecution table. Those who knew no Latin crossed themselves and shrank away. Thomas, as well, feigned dismay but knew perfectly well what Laurel had said. Edward, as well, understood the words but stared aghast that they had come from Laurel. Dunkirk and Joseph wore matching looks of outrage.

"Silence! Speak not your obscenities. You have sufficiently proven yourself as the witch who should be held accountable." Garland closed his hand around Laurel's mouth. He leaned close, speaking quietly, though William could the hear the slight tremble in his voice, that one could almost construe as remorse. "I have no choice." She did not resist him, and he lowered his hand and stood tall, the momentary illusion of compassion, suddenly gone as he motioned to the hunters. "Take her away."

Laurel looked over her shoulder to William one last time, as she was pushed from the hall. "I love you," she spoke silently. He answered in kind. He knew that the Latin words she had chosen were not obscene as Garland had assumed. But the fact that Laurel knew them and could speak them as fluently as any cleric was more than enough insult to Dunkirk for him to not enlighten Garland. *She did it deliberately.* In her last act of desperation to save him— the act that sealed her own fate— she had merely bestowed upon him a blessing. *By the divine love of the Mother and Father, I bless you.*

As Laurel was led away, William slumped back in the booth and fully allowed the fog to overtake him.

Sean, it isn't real. I can't let this happen.

"Did you think she would do less for you?"

Why? Why would she give herself away?

"You know why. She told you herself. She'd walk through fire for you, Will."

No! I don't want her to take this from me.

"She promised you that would not face the fire."

Not like this. Please, not like this.

"It was her choice, Will."

No more blood on me. I have yours on my hands, and Isaac's, and Rebecca! I can't bear Laurel's as well. Please, not Laurel.

"We knew the risks. It was our choice. She's given you back your life."

No!

William pushed the voice away from him. As much as he wanted to win, to be allowed a second chance for life and to see his wife and the child she carried, he would have gladly welcomed his last breath at that moment if it would change what had just befallen Laurel. He wanted to stand and scream that he willingly and knowingly prepared the chicory and chanted the verse himself. He would even admit to making the damned pact the abbot had tried to torture out of him if it would bring her back. But he found no voice, no strength to take a stand and no spirit left in which to rally.

Finally after what seemed hours, order was restored. Garland paced the front of the hall as he composed himself to continue. He turned to Bryndah who still occupied the witness chair. "You have made another accusation that has yet to be addressed."

What was left of William's spirit to fight left him completely. He knew what was coming, and he knew that they had made plans to help him but he could not remember what they were. *Did they make plans for Laurel as well? Was her confession part of it all?*

"Yes." Bryndah assumed an amazed and wide-eyed air. "The poison. He survived a large dose."

"How is it he came to ingest it?" Garland asked in monotone.

"That was my accident, Your Honor," Bryndah admitted demurely. "He had suffered a severe blow to the head the night before, and the powder had been prepared to relieve his pain. I added it to the water to make it easier for him to ingest. I had *no idea* he would drink the entire pitcher in one sitting!"

"You lie, Mother!" Richard shouted, struggling against the bonds on his wrists. "You added opium to the nightshade! You tried to kill him!"

"Silence!"

"Your Honor, I know that what Richard says is true,"

Edward finally spoke up out of turn. "I will testify to this!"

He's standing against the dragon. A little late, Father.

"I see. Well, that shall be another matter we may need to consider when we are finished with the *first* defendant!" Garland frowned at Bryndah. "It seems we will have quite a few unfinished issues at the end of this trial." Garland turned to Thomas and the clergymen. "Gentlemen, I am going to make a ruling on the first charge brought forth before we proceed with the next. I understand you are prepared for the testing?"

"Yes, Your Honor." Bishop Dunkirk nodded solemnly, as though it pained him to continue.

Garland nodded his understanding, then turned to William. "William Fylbrigge, look up. I am ready to render a decision of the first charge brought against you."

William looked at the judge. *The first charge. The enchanting charges. Sean, this is it. The fire goes with this charge. Laurel and I will go together.*

"*Stay with the living, Will. Pay attention.*"

"Are you listening?" Garland asked as William drifted back.

"Yes," he answered quietly.

"In light of the confession we have all witnessed, that has been accepted by this assemblage, I rule that on the charges of spell casting, enchanting, and so forth, I find you *not* guilty."

Edward sighed loudly. "Thank the heavens!"

Thomas creased his brow and sat forward in his chair.

William closed his eyes and sank back in the chair. *No fire. Laurel took it from me.* He should have been elated, but Garland's voice boomed on and his words echoed painfully in William's ears.

"The witch has confessed that it was she and not you who cast the charm, for reasons she alone is aware, although it is apparent to me that songs and words alone can be manipulated by anyone, with or without demonic supervision. You appear to have a talent that has gotten you into trouble, young man. I am fully aware of your passionate stand, speaking out on trials such as the one in which you now find yourself, and am compelled to believe now that you have been acting under the influence of the enchantment that was placed upon you. What else could compel someone of your standing to put himself at such risk?"

What else? The burning of my mother was not compelling enough? William looked up at him, incredulous that this man would believe such nonsense.

"Therefore," Garland continued, picking up his scrolls and rolling them, "in the argument the nobles set forth, I must also rule that they were, in fact, influenced by an enchantment as they purport; however it was not of *your* fashioning. Therefore, the treaties they have protested will be made null."

Cheers erupted from Ogham and his earls. "Amen!" Ogham gloated to Edward. "Do you doubt us now, Edward?"

Edward's elation melted from his face as he glowered at Ogham, but he looked again to his son, and gave him a relieved smile. "It doesn't matter," he said. "It's only politics."

"Thank you, Father." William nodded, grateful and despondent at the same time. He had been spared the fire. But Laurel would take his place.

The bishop and abbot exchanged pleased expressions

when the ruling was made. It was not lost on William that they seemed as though they almost expected this outcome. He could not remember all of the details of the plan that had been made to save him from the test. He only remembered something about going to sleep, and sleep at the moment would be like gold to a pauper. He tried to keep his focus on the judge as he continued.

"There is, however, one more piece to your puzzle, Fylbrigge." Garland stood, chin in his hand. "And I am afraid I can see no alternative but to proceed with the test."

"Your Honor, what is the point? You have found him innocent of the charge," Edward protested.

"The point is, it is still against the laws of man and God to join in a pact with the devil," Garland said, dismissing Edward's protest. "We have not disproved this claim as yet, only that his enchantments were dispatched by a different witch." Garland turned to Adrian. "Release him and bring him forward please."

Adrian unlocked the box, then removed the manacles from William's hands and feet. "Come on out." He beckoned William with a wave of his arm, then jauntily stepped aside. "Come on, rabbit, hop on out!"

"You know he can't." Ian stood up angrily. "He needs help."

"How foolish of me." Adrian snickered, then turned with a malicious grin to William and grabbed his left wrist and pulled. William let out a bloodcurdling shriek of pain, as he tumbled out of the chair onto the floor.

"Must you be so cold-hearted? Stand away; I shall bring him to the stand." Ian furiously pushed Adrian aside, and knelt next to William.

"As you wish." Adrian shrugged and sauntered back to his seat.

William closed his eyes and lay struggling to regain his breath while Ian tried to find a good way to get him off the floor.

"Allow me, Ian." Edward knelt next to Ian, speaking gently. "I had no idea of the extent... can we get him on his feet?" he asked as the two of them helped William to a sitting position.

"I'm afraid not, my lord," Ian answered quietly. "We'll have to lift him."

"My God. I'll do it, Ian, thank you. Sit down." Edward brushed William's cheek gently. "Are you ready?"

William opened his eyes to look at his father. "As I ever will be."

He tried to smile for Edward's sake but failed miserably as Edward lifted him, childlike, and carried him to the witness chair, setting him gently into it. *Is this the life I'm fighting to keep?*

"William, I didn't know." Edward knelt close after William was settled into the chair. "This test they will do, do you understand it?" he whispered, choking on his words.

"Take your seat please, Lord Edward," Garland droned, unemotionally.

Edward nodded at Garland, then looked at William one more time. Leaning forward, he placed a kiss on William's forehead and whispered, "God grant I see you soon, son."

"Good-bye, Father; go sit down."

Edward slowly rose and returned to his seat.

Garland stepped to the front of the table and stood next to the witness chair. "Do you understand what is to follow?"

William nodded silently, then risked a glance to lan trying to pull the details of the rescue plan from the dark part of his mind. lan casually tapped the top of his wooden ritual box. *Am I to take the rites?*

"You have been accused of joining in a pact with—"

"I made no *pact!*" William growled through his teeth.

"So you have said." Garland sighed. "Yet you have an amazing amount of stamina for someone in your unenviable position."

"Stamina?"

"Yes, and the more I think about this, the more I am convinced that the test truly is necessary. I'm amazed you're still breathing."

"My crime now is that I'm alive?" William asked incredulously.

Garland ignored him and turned to the clerics seated at the table. "Gentlemen, how long has he been confined?"

"Nearly six days, Your Honor."

"Six days." He paced away. "And in that time, has he been allowed to sleep at all?"

"Oh, he may have managed an hour or two here and there," Dunkirk answered with a dismissive wave of his hand.

"I see," Garland continued. "And has he had any food or water?"

"No, Your Honor," Dunkirk replied in his businesslike tone.

"Actually," lan interrupted, "I brought him food and water today, when we prepared him for trial." He gave Dunkirk a wary glance. "And when I tended him yesterday, as well."

"Yesterday?" Dunkirk said. "Who gave you leave to see him *yesterday?*"

Ian was done being coy. "God gave me leave! Jesus Christ gave me leave! It is my *duty* as a man of the cloth. *Remember they who are in bonds, as though you are bound with them; and them who are mistreated, as being mistreated yourselves!* " He glared at Dunkirk, daring him to contradict Scripture.

Dunkirk stood and planted his hands firm on the table before him. "What?"

"Hebrews 13:2." William replied, quietly. All heads turned to him. "Or was it Hebrews 13:3?" he asked, looking at Ian.

"Three," Ian replied with a half grin, then turned his glare back to Dunkirk. "You told me yourself that Lord Sutherland had *refused* to take the Sacrament, when you had never been to see him at all— or had you only been in to witness his torture?"

"Gentlemen, enough!" Garland growled. "Both of you, stand down. This is important for me to know. Has Fylbrigge gone nearly an entire week without food or water or hasn't he? Brother Ian indicates that he alone has brought sustenance to him. Was what you brought him yesterday the first he'd received during his incarceration?" Garland asked Ian.

"To my knowledge, yes," Ian said, then added, with a defiant challenge in his voice, "but he was close to starvation, and I'm certain he could not last more than another day, Your Honor. I see nothing miraculous in the fact he is still alive—"

"That will do." Garland turned a stern eye on Ian. "I am merely trying to establish the facts, sir. I will take that into consideration." He turned back to Dunkirk. "Other than the

Tormentum insomniae and lack of sustenance, what other methods have you employed?"

Joseph answered for Dunkirk, "The normal, accepted means to elicit a confession, Your Honor. I have to say, I have never known any man to withstand as much. It's clear to me that he was relying on *something* not of the natural world."

"Indeed?" Garland asked, an intrigued look in his eye. "So you were present when he was tortured?"

"Only the last time, Your Honor," Joseph answered. "I believe Tearlach oversaw the other sessions."

Edward growled. "You assured me he would not be harmed!"

Adrian shook his head, rolling his eyes. "You really *are* naive, aren't you."

"Enough! So there was more than one session?" Garland craned around and raised a brow to William.

"Every night," William answered quietly.

"You become more extraordinary by the moment." Garland turned back to Joseph. "Explain to me what was done in your presence. I'll assume it was no more or less than Adrian could add."

William sat listening and drifting as Joseph recounted in graphic detail the *normal and accepted means* he had used to elicit a confession, reliving it with each word he heard. Joseph was thorough, recounting the repeated drops, the dagger, the chains, and the weight— and what had happened when William thought it was Sean who had saved his eyes from the hot dagger.

"That was to be a last resort?" Garland asked, a slight grimace in his face. "To blind him?"

"Yes, I never intended to put the blade to his eyes, only to cause him to believe I would. I felt the threat alone would break his will," Joseph explained calmly without so much as a glance to William. "But he swooned and I had to abandon that tactic." Joseph let out a coldhearted chuckle. "After all, it's difficult to intimidate a man if he's asleep."

Twice, William heard Edward grumble under his breath but could not understand his words. William drifted, remembering the arguments he had had with Edward where he would be the one describing the tortures, but Edward would scoff and tell him he was exaggerating. Edward was not scoffing now. *How ironic, Father, that you would not believe me when my tales were never near as horrid as what you're hearing now.*

"So," Joseph continued in the same heartlessly casual manner, as though the entire subject bored him, "I ordered another drop. I do not believe that Fylbrigge was even aware of that last one."

"Not aware?" Garland asked. He grimaced again, though the magistrate covered it quickly. "How could you tell?"

"He did not cry out, Your Honor," Joseph replied, looking at William with falsely mournful eyes, "when his back cracked."

Cracked? The word started the tremble in William's middle again. *Is that what happened?* he asked Sean as he allowed the fog to gain on him.

"Stay with the living, Will. Pay attention."

"And still he has not confessed?" Garland's voice brought William back.

"Alas, he has not," Joseph concluded with a doleful sigh

of mock pity.

Garland rested his chin in his palm and turned full to William. "Is Abbot Joseph's testimony an accurate accounting?"

William sat silent for a moment, keeping his eyes away from Joseph and those who sat near him, and looked to his father. He wondered if Edward believed Joseph's retelling to be as exaggerated as he had always maintained his own to be. But Edward's downcast eyes and creased brow told William that at long last, Edward had been convinced. "Yes, it's accurate," he answered quietly, still looking at his father.

"Tell me," Garland began, resting a hand on each arm of the witness chair, locking his pale eyes on William. "How do you account for your near *inhuman* physical fortitude?"

"Look at me. I'm as broken as any man would be. There is nothing *inhuman* about me."

"To what then do you attribute the fact you have survived thus far?" Garland held his position over William. "Frankly, I've not seen many who have gone more than two days in the tower chamber, enduring far less than what has been described to me here. Yet, you have managed to hold out for nearly six, and by the look of you, you could continue perhaps for another five." He pushed himself away from the chair and, folding his arms across his chest, he asked in his low, demoralizing tone, "If not for some unearthly pact that protects you, why are you not dead?"

Why am I not dead? The thought of another five days in the tower made William want to cry out in despair and laugh hysterically at the same time. *That's a good question. Why am I not dead, God? You tell me. Is it a reward for my good deeds or punishment for my sins?* William's mind reeled through his arguments with God and himself, searching for the answer to Garland's question. *Why have you allowed me to survive through all of this only to leave me broken and useless? Are the clerics right? Do I worship the wrong God? Is that my crime? Why am I still alive, Sean? Why won't you let me die? If it's because of the promise you made to me, then I release you from it.*

"It's not my promise that's kept you alive."

What then?

"You know the answer. Tell the judge."

"Fylbrigge?" Garland tapped William's shoulder, startling him away from Sean.

"I wish to live" was the only answer William could find.

"You wish to live?" Garland shook his head. "Should that we all possess such a *will,* we would all live to an old age indeed. Was it merely your wish to live that resisted the poison, as well?"

"No. I was given an antidote in time and was revived."

"Were you? It would be equally as large a dose, I should imagine."

"I don't know." William looked directly into the judge's eyes. "I have no knowledge of such things."

"I see," Garland scoffed. "You have no knowledge that nightshade is poison, and foxglove as well? Every school child learns this."

"Yes, but I do not know the preparation—"

"Ah, I see, you know the elements to be lethal, but not how to concoct the mixtures? Is that what you tell me?"

"Yes." William felt the tremble in the pit of his stomach again. He had a sickening fear that Bryndah would somehow produce his whole book from her satchel and reveal all his potions and chants. *No, Laurel said the charm had worked. She doesn't have the book; they're only guessing.* He was relieved when the questioning took another turn.

"Do you know how you were given the nightshade?"

"The drag—She put it in the water." William pointed his chin toward Bryndah, being sure not to look her in the eye. "The morning after my wedding."

"It was far more than you would have required for a headache, was it not?"

"Yes, I suppose so," William admitted.

"In fact, the amount you were given was potentially lethal, was it not?" Garland leaned back against the table, still keeping his icy gaze locked on William.

"There was a good deal of water," William argued, "and I had eaten enough—"

"So you have enough knowledge to understand that much as well?" Garland raised his brow. "That food and water would lessen the effect."

William looked at him carefully. *He is trying to trick me.* "It is what I was told."

"I see." Garland nodded. "So you believe the dose was diluted to a point where it was not dangerous?"

"It only caused me to sleep," William answered slowly.

"So you do not believe you were in danger from it?"

"I don't know—"

"Who administered the antidote?"

"I don't know, I—"

"Who prepared it?"

William swallowed. He would have liked to say he didn't

know, but he reasoned they already knew that Elinor had made the first dose for him. He hoped she was safely away with Mehlyndia. "Elinor."

"She is quite talented in her mixtures, I'm told."

"Any housewife can mix a remedy for a headache—"

"This was not simply a remedy for a headache," Garland interrupted with a sharp rap of his hand on the table. "It was a counter-potion for nightshade. Such a preparation, made in careful proportions, would require a great deal of skill."

"I suppose so." *Is he going to charge Elinor?*

"But she is not at issue, so we shall leave that for now." He grinned and turned away, dismissing his discussion of Elinor with a wave of his hand.

William, though relieved, was now confused, wondering what game this man was playing.

"I will freely tell you, I am not ignorant to simple chemistry. Diluted or not, nightshade can be lethal. Especially if we are given to believe Richard Fylbrigge's accusation that it had been enhanced with a bit of opium." The judge paced back and forth in front of William. "Why else would Lord Edward go to the trouble of having an antidote prepared? If you were merely sleeping, I should think it would be easy enough to wake you. I've woken you several times in this room today."

"It would have taken several hours for me to wake on my own, and I was needed to speak—"

"Ah, so the *only* reason you were given a second dose was to wake you quickly?"

William hesitated for a moment before he answered. He hadn't given much thought to the poisons, but now, a realization came on him like the rising sun— the doses *were* lethal. *Both* of them, and yet— *How did I survive those?* He looked up at Garland, fighting to stay out of the fog and find the proper answer to his question.

"Fylbrigge?" Garland sighed. "Please answer me. Was the only reason you were given the second dose to make you ready for your speech?"

"To wake me quickly, yes. There was little time."

"So Lord Edward ordered this Elinor to prepare the antidote. Now, in my limited knowledge, I am quite aware that foxglove is used quite effectively as a stimulant. It is *also* quite poisonous. Yet that is what you were given, were you not?"

"I was not told what was in the antidote," William answered slowly, knowing that to be a lie. *Why foxglove, Elinor? Of all things, why did she choose that? And why did it work?* "But, that's not what brought me to my senses."

"Oh? Tell me. How *were* you brought to your senses?"

"My father struck me. It brought me about. The second dose was small, only enough to help clear my head."

Garland rocked back on his heels. "So do you believe that the second dose was not large enough to be lethal?"

"Yes." *But it was. I was shaking for hours,* William thought, now beginning to wonder if there truly was something *inhuman* about him.

"Then you should have no fear to put it to the test." Garland turned toward the table.

"What kind of test?" William knew perfectly well but still was unsure of the plan. *Rites? I'm to take the rites? How will that help?*

"I have instructed our apothecary to simulate the

dosages for me." Garland opened a wooden box containing a goblet and two small vials. "Interestingly enough, when we administered these doses to a would-be assassin, the combination proved to be toxic. Even though it was diluted, and with the absence of opium." He lifted the goblet from the box and placed it on the table. "Tested on another, he too succumbed. In fact, there have been four men tested in all, none of whom survived. Of course, none of these men had been suspected of making pacts which protected them, and our apothecary did not mutter any magical chants about the doses." The judge picked up a full pitcher of water and filled the goblet. He placed a portion of the vial in the goblet, then dumped the rest into the pitcher, simulating Bryndah's action. "Of course, this is a drastic method to determine your innocence. You do have the option to decline, but then we would have to determine your guilt or innocence by other, less convenient means." He caught William's eyes with his own.

Ian spoke up. "Your Honor, may I make a request?"

"Speak."

"Thank you." Ian stood and bowed respectfully. "It is apparent, the proof of his innocence may well come at the cost of his life. Therefore, I must request, for the sake of his soul, Your Honor, that I be allowed to offer him the Last Sacrament before you proceed with your test."

"I thought you had done that when you went to the prison to dress him," Dunkirk said, scowling.

Ian hesitated. "I offered it, but his mind was too muddled at the time to accept. He seems more clear headed now, and so I'd like to offer again."

Garland turned to William. "Do you wish to receive the last rites?"

William looked at his father. Edward was nodding, his eyes widened. "Yes," Edward mouthed, while Garland's back was turned.

"Take the rites," Sean's voice confirmed.

"Yes," William answered quietly. "I wish the to take the rites."

"So, you understand completely what is to come?" Garland asked in the most gentle voice he had used thus far.

William looked straight ahead, past Garland to the wall, and saw again the misty shadow that had come to his cell. *I can see you now. Does this mean I'm nearly finished?* The shade inclined its head. William took a long breath then with no sense of anger nor fear, keeping his eyes fixed on the shade that was forming, he simply spoke the truth of the circumstances in which he now found himself.

"When I drink your poison, since I have not made the pact you claim I have, I shall die right here where I sit. But my innocence will be proven and my soul will be clean." He dropped his head for a moment. The room became deathly silent before he continued slowly. "However, should I survive your dose, you shall have your proof and I shall die, out there on the stake, aside Laurel. Either way, my life is forfeit."

Garland looked at him gravely and nodded. "You understand perfectly." He turned to Ian. "You may perform your rites, sir."

"Thank you, Your Honor." Ian bowed and with trembling hands, brought his ritual kit. He knelt before the witness stand and prepared the wine, bread, water, and oil that he would use.

William watched Ian remove the small silver tray he had seen when he had administered the rites to Sean. *It's the same, Sean, do you remember?* The shadow hovered at Ian's shoulder as though overseeing the task the monk performed.

"*I remember.*" The shade lifted its head and William could see quite clearly the somber green eyes. Sean's eyes. "*You said good-bye to me, Brother.*"

Good-bye, Brother. You knew?

"*I know now.*"

Ian mingled the oil and water on the tray and mumbled his prayer softly, then poured the wine prepared with Elinor's potion into the small chalice from his kit before he tore a small piece of the bread. Ian held the bread to William's mouth and intoned a benediction. William accepted it, responding correctly to the blessing.

Ian picked up the chalice and said quietly so only William would hear, "I'm sorry it has come to this."

William smiled at him.

"You're smiling. Are you not afraid, then?" he asked in his ever-gentle way.

William looked at the chalice in Ian's hands. "I'm terrified, but my brother is with me." He looked past Ian's shoulder to the shade. "I'm not alone."

Ian looked at him curiously for a moment. "We never are," he said kindly, then asked, "Do you wish to confess now, before your God?"

William's smile faded and he looked in Ian's eyes. "My God is aware of what I am about. I shall confess nothing in front of you, nor them. Not after all this." He spoke low enough for only Ian to hear and to plant the proper seed of deception in the judge's mind. "Let's just be done with this. I'd like to go to sleep now."

"Aye." Ian nodded. "Drink it all. Swallow it as quickly as possible. It will take a few moments to settle." Ian brought the cup to William's lips and he drank the wine as Ian had instructed, in one large gulp.

Elinor had not taken time to disguise the taste, and the bittersweet tinge made William shudder as he swallowed. *It's almost over.*

"God bless you, my son." Ian set the goblet aside and took the silver dish and, as he had done for Sean, he dipped his finger in the oil and water, then placed the sign of the cross on William's forehead. *"In nómine Patris, et Fílii..."* Ian's voice faltered.

William finished for him, *"et Spíritus Sancti. Amen."*

Ian smiled sadly as he placed the tray back in the kit. "Have no fear. Justice will be done."

"Not for Laurel," William responded quietly, almost silently. "Please take care of her."

"Aye. I promise." Ian crossed himself, then stood and bowed to the judge. "He's ready, Your Honor."

"Do you have anything you'd like to say, Lord William?"

"I made no pact," William asserted for the final time as the terrible and familiar tremble started in his hands. *Is it from Elinor's wine? Fear? It doesn't matter. It's time to let go.* "Bring your cup."

"May God have mercy on your soul." Garland held the goblet as Ian had done. William closed his eyes and swallowed the entire contents as he had the wine. He could taste, quite easily, the nightshade in the water and, as a testament to his own talent, he knew there was far more nightshade in that one drink than had been in Elinor's entire pouch. *Is this a test, or is Garland deliberately trying to end this quickly?*

Garland refilled the goblet and brought it to him again. He swallowed the full contents of that as well, choking down even more nightshade. *Was Ian aware there would be so much?* The antidote was already beginning to take effect as the nightshade settled on him.

Garland poured a third goblet from the pitcher but before he could drink, William felt a strange pulling sensation from deep within him. As the poison and potion took hold, he began to quake. A violent shudder thrust him back in the chair. Eyes wide but fading, he looked from one face to the next, until he came to the face of his older brother. Thomas clasped the talon-like hand of the dragon who sat on his left, the boar-beast next to her, and the bishop next to him. The four of them meshed together as his eyes began to fail, transforming into a single horrific four-headed beast, perched on the table, waiting to devour him. He blinked hard once, then twice, then watched as slowly the monster melted away before his eyes. Behind it, Sean, ethereal sword in hand, had slain the beast. William took an enormously deep breath that he would not remember releasing. *Can I let go now?*

"Let go."

William watched the faces in the room grow smaller and dimmer, as at the same time, Sean became brighter and more substantial. "That took a lot of heart, Will." Sean grinned, then made a beckoning motion with his hand. "Come on, we've got something to do."

William stood and reached out to his brother and embraced him. Then he looked down, mystified that his hands were whole and strong, and he realized he was *standing* and that nothing hurt. He felt neither hungry nor tired, just *free.* He turned back to where he thought he had just been, but found only empty space. Sean patted him on the back and the two walked together into the darkness.

Chapter 18

"I N NÓMINE PATRIS, et Fílii, et Spíritus Sancti. Amen."
Ian made the sign of the cross with his hand
while kneeling before the witness chair. "It would
appear, Your Honor, the man was innocent after all." He
stood slowly, head cast downward. "He's dead."

Garland placed his hand to William's neck for a moment,
then withdrew it, a frown crossed his eyes as he nodded and
walked away. "This matter is hereby settled," he said, quietly.
He unrolled a piece of parchment and placed his signature
to the bottom with a flourish. "Let it be known, that William
Fylbrigge is declared innocent of all charges. God rest his
soul." He banged the stone on the table once. "Lord Edward,
you are free to gather him at your will. I am..." He hesitated
for a moment, looking away from Edward before he
continued, "I am sorry for your loss." Garland gathered his
scrolls under his arm and addressed the men who sat with
Ogham. "Gentlemen, I would like you all to clear the hall.
Thank you for your time and cooperation. Your Grace, Abbot
Joseph, please, take leave as well. Leave them to their privacy.
Tearlach, release Richard Fylbrigge, if you please, then escort
Lord and Lady Aberdoir to my chambers. I shall join you all
presently."

Quietly and efficiently, the meeting hall was soon cleared.
All who remained; Edward, Ian, Richard and Ewan, stood

Lorrieann Russell

around the lifeless form in the witness chair.

"Ian?" Edward began quietly, stone-faced. "Is it true?"

"You've not much time," Ian told him, keeping his voice as low as possible. "He's not dead now, but there was far more nightshade in that goblet than we expected. I could smell it myself."

Richard placed his hand on William's neck as Garland had done. "You're wrong, Ian. There's no life here. We've failed."

"No, we haven't. Believe me. He is merely sleeping," Ian assured him. "But you must get him back to Drumoak without delay."

"Ewan, bring the cart around. Set some men out to ensure our way is kept clear." Edward gave his orders quietly, not looking away from his son. "You're certain, Ian? He's only sleeping?"

"Aye." Ian nodded.

Ewan left the hall to get the cart, leaving the doors open. The crowd outside had grown restless during the long trial but when the doors swung wide, they began to cheer and clap, and it wasn't long before the chanting began.

"Excuse me, Lord Edward." Ian extended his hand to the duke. "I have a promise to keep."

Edward accepted Ian's hand and shook it firmly, then inclined his ear to the sounds from the square. "Oh, my little mouse. I would have never thought such a brave heart could exist in one so meek. Is it too late for me to stop it?"

Ian nodded slowly. "Alas, my lord, it is. Garland was right that she sealed her own fate when she confessed before the bishop—even if it was a lie. The best we can do is offer the mercy Elinor's dose promises."

"I should have spoken sooner."

"Aye, m' lord, I agree." Ian bowed and took his leave of the meetinghouse, leaving Edward alone with William.

The festive atmosphere in the square sickened Ian. Jubilant, laughing people clapped their hands as though a merry puppet show were about to take place. He made his way to the platform, wishing he could blot out the sounds of the crowd.

"Burn, witch, burn! Burn, witch, burn!"

"Looks like it's on after all!" Cassandra Fraewender skipped past, not watching her path, almost knocking into Ian. "Come on, Enid, there's still room in front!"

"You go on, Cass," Enid called back to her, not following her bawdy friend. "My back is vexing me. I'd rather just go home, and have a nice hot caudle and put m' feet up. Tell me the details tomorrow."

"Go on with ye, then." Cassandra waved her friend on as she finally took notice of whom it was that she had just missed colliding with. She turned a lewd smile to Ian. "Evenin', Father. Lovely clear night. Should make it right pretty."

Ian looked at her with weary pity. "I'm sorry for you, child."

"Sorry? For me?" She batted her eyes playfully. "I've a purse full o' silver and m' life's m' own. So what's t' be sorry for?"

"You sold him for silver. The only thing you forgot to do was kiss him." He turned his back to her and continued to the foot of the stairs of the rugged platform and addressed the two guards who stood there. "I have come to perform rites," he lied, knowing these two dull-witted guards would not challenge him.

"Suit ye'self. We start in ten minutes. Be down before then or you'll be prayin' for rain. We can't be stoppin' it once it's lit."

"I understand." Ian climbed the stairs, keeping his eyes fixed only on the next step ahead of him, trying not to hear the obscene chanting from the crowd. *"Burn, witch, burn!"* With each step, the trembling inside him grew stronger but he would not allow it to keep him from fulfilling his promise.

He reached the top and approached her slowly. She kept her head bowed, eyes closed against the night, while she wept silently. Ian placed a gentle hand on her face.

"Ian!" Laurel gaped at him through her tears. "You mustn't stay. There are only moments left."

"I made a promise." Ian looked deeply into her eyes, relaying all the grief he felt.

"Did we win?" she asked quietly.

"Look down there." He motioned toward the door to the meetinghouse. A flatbed wagon, laden with clean straw pulled by a single horse, had been drawn up to the door. Ewan held the reins. A moment later, Richard emerged from the building, followed by Edward who cradled William's lifeless body in his arms. Edward laid his burden gently in the straw and solemnly climbed onto the cart to sit beside Ewan as he led the horse in the direction of Drumoak. Richard remained standing outside the meetinghouse.

"Oh no, Will! Is he gone?"

"Sleeping, Laurel. We did it. They believe him dead. He's been declared innocent of all charges and is now on his way to the crypt and then to the sea. I wanted you to know." He could not bear to tell her he harbored a secret fear that they had truly failed, that William would likely never leave the crypt. "But at what cost?" His eyes brimmed as he spoke to her. "If not for you— Laurel, why would you speak such a lie to save him?"

"I love him," she answered simply, as she watched the cart disappear behind Drumoak.

"He loves you too."

"You must go, they're coming."

"I have something for you." He placed the kit on the platform and removed the chalice and the last bit of wine from his flask, emptied the wine into the chalice, then removed the small vial of the greenish liquid and emptied it all into the cup "I made a promise. I intend to keep it."

"What promise?"

"He asked me to take care of you." Ian held the cup to her. "Drink this. All of it."

"From Will?" Her eyes welled with tears. "Elinor's potion."

"Yes. Drink." He held the cup to her and she drank in one long sip until the cup was empty. Ian could smell the strong scent of the nightshade and the bitter taste of the opium Elinor had added to the potion to ensure its lethality, but for Laurel, there would be no hidden antidote. He muttered the prayers silently, as she looked at him with a sad sort of grace and gratitude, before she swallowed the liquid.

"How long?" she asked as the poison sent a shudder through her body.

"Only moments," Ian answered quietly, brushing the tears from her face.

"You must leave now, then."

"No. Not until... not until you sleep."

She nodded briefly and looked past his shoulder, smiling at something she saw. Ian turned but saw only the night sky. "I'm not alone," she whispered, still looking at her private vision.

Ian looked over his shoulder again but still saw nothing. *I'm not alone.* Exactly the same words William had used. "We never are," he told her, the same way he had told William, only this time, he was beginning to believe what he said.

The chanting suddenly became louder and more excited. Ian glanced to the side and saw the torchbearers approaching.

"Come down now!" the guard called from the foot of the platform.

"Ian, you must go now." Laurel's eyes slowly closed.

"Not yet." Ian could not bring himself to leave her until he knew she was gone, even if it meant risking the fire himself. "Not until I know." He closed his eyes, embracing her one last time. A gentle wind washed about him, soft as a touch. Within the wind, close to his ear, softly, almost imperceptibly, he heard a voice.

"Ian."

Ian turned, startled, believing someone had climbed the platform and was speaking to him from behind but found he was alone with Laurel. "Who—?"

"Stay with the living," Laurel whispered, then, with a great sigh, dropped her head and Ian knew she was gone.

"Last chance!" the guard yelled. "No more warnings."

"Ian, stay with the living," the voice in the wind echoed Laurel's last words.

Shaken, Ian kissed her forehead, crossed her, then stepped

away. He picked up his belongings and descended the stairs nearly stumbling off the last two.

"'Bout time. I thought for sure you'd decided to join her." The guard grunted as he signaled the torchbearers.

Ian sought out the relative quiet of the alleyway to gather his thoughts. Had he heard the voice? Laurel had seen something in her last moments. The sight had not distressed her, in fact, it had seemed to bring her comfort. He leaned against the building, shaking. *It was a comfort. It's true. She wasn't alone. William wasn't alone.* "Is there comfort for me as well?" he asked to the space around him.

His answer came almost at once, in the form of the same detached, gentle voice carried in the breeze. *"Play, Ian."*

Standing away from the crowd in the shadows behind the meetinghouse, he reached into the folds of his robe and withdrew his flute, brought it to his lips and softly played "Greensleeves" as the smell of burning wood and peat began wafting its way through the alley. He played, finding his comfort, as he had so many times, in the sound of his music. He played, unheard amidst the clamoring crowd, unhurried, until his song was finished. Then he stood quietly in the dark the of the alley.

"God in heaven, please guide my steps, tell me what you want of me." He paused and looked about him into the dark of the alley, listening for the answer, fearing yet hoping the voice would find him again. "Please, tell me. I cannot stay here within this calling, yet you bade me stay with the living. Have you need of me here, then? Where am I to go now, Lord?" He closed his eyes, hugging himself against the wall. A breeze carried smoke from the smoldering kindling to his nose. He covered his face with his cowl, waiting for his answer. As the smoke grew thicker and the air about him thinner, he began to cough and struggle for his breaths, but still he waited. Light-headed, he sank to his knees in the alley. Just as he was close to fainting, a cool and gentle wind washed over his face, encircling him, pushing the smoke away. Embraced by the wind, Ian listened until his answer found him.

Turning his back to the square, he left the alley by the back of the meetinghouse and ran— as he had on the night he had warned them— directly to Drumoak without fully understanding how, but knowing without a doubt that he had received his answer. *I'm going with him.* He smiled through tears as he gained ground toward the castle wall, catching sight of the cart as it turned the corner. He stopped in the shadow, watching as Edward lifted his son from the hay, then turned back, taking a last look on the square. "He's alive, Laurel!"

A moment later, the sky was alight with the death fire as it engulfed the platform and the make-believe acolyte who stood upon it. He watched only for a moment, then ran to where he had seen Edward enter the bowels of Drumoak.

"You can't be serious!" Thomas waved his fists as he followed Peter Garland from the judge's chambers back through the meeting hall. "This is outrageous!"

"Stand down, Lord Thomas." Garland waved a dismissive hand to him, not slowing his stride. Adrian Tearlach kept pace with the men, his hand on the hilt of his sword, walking protectively between Thomas and Garland.

Thomas grumbled at Adrian and rushed past him to keep up with Garland. "Your Hrace, the trial has ended! We have won!"

"Have you?" Garland came to an abrupt stop and spun on his heel to face Thomas. "That is not how I see it. The accused was found to be innocent. Your charges against him have been dismissed." Garland angrily gestured with his hand toward Drumoak. "An innocent man, *your own brother,* has died! You see this as a victory? Or was his demise your sole purpose from the beginning?"

Thomas stood before the judge biting his tongue. *The treaties were overturned, Ogham is pleased with the outcome, and I shall be well paid. I am finally free of my dear brother. Father's estate shall be mine, free and clear. And Richard, treacherous as he is, is now Earl of Sutherland. Shall be an easy enough task to turn that to my own advantage as well. No, hold your tongue, Thomas, don't give yourself away, now.*

"Of course that was not my sole purpose! I grieve for the loss of my brother, as any man would." Thomas replied, feigning shock at the judge's accusation. "But to bring charges upon Bryndah now? What is the point?"

"She poisoned your brother," Garland stated simply. "The fact that he survived her attempt is immaterial. There are laws against attempted murder, Lord Thomas. The fact that he is now deceased, not of her hand, is of no consequence. She poisoned him and will stand trial for that crime." Garland turned and began to walk away at a brisk pace.

"You take the side of the heretic?" Thomas yelled as he chased after the judge, barely able to keep up.

"He proved himself innocent of that charge!" Garland

swung around and stopped again, nearly causing Thomas to bump into him. "I am starting to believe that it was the wrong Fylbrigge who stood trial here today! Do not give me provocation to charge you as well, sir!"

"Your Honor?" Adrian interrupted suddenly as two hunters approached, a struggling, screeching Bryndah held between them. "Where do you want her?"

"Escort her to the tower to await trial," Garland ordered. "I should think they can pull something together in about week."

"You will pay, Garland! I have powerful allies! I will see you hang for this!" Bryndah shrieked at him as the hunters pulled her, hands bound behind, from the meetinghouse. "There will be no peace for you when we have been vindicated!"

"Adrian," Garland grumbled, placing a weary hand to his chin.

"Yes?"

"Put that to better use, will you?" Garland pointed to Adrian's belt, where the bridle that William had worn hung alongside his scabbard.

"Aye, sir." Adrian smirked and twirled the bridle around his finger. "With pleasure."

Bryndah howled in fury as Adrian put the bridle to use. She continued her histrionics as she was led clear of the front yard of the meetinghouse into the street.

As Bryndah was being led past Richard, he caught her eye and bowed grandly to her with exaggerated rolls of his hand and a deep comical bow. "Good evening, Mother."

The hunters paused briefly to allow some of the crowd to

pass by, none taking much notice of Bryndah as they were all held in thrall at the flames that consumed the platform. The fury in her eyes turned to terrible glee as the flames engulfed the top of the platform. Richard's blood boiled in his veins and he spat at her in disgust as he saw her angry struggles turn to fits of muffled laughter as she watched Laurel's immolation.

Richard held his ground, resisting the impulse to lunge at her as the hunters led her away to the gaol on the far side of the square. Every fiber in him trembled with rage at how the events had played out. The sleep William had fallen into, to Richard's mind, was not sleep. It was far too deep and far too convincing. He had put his hand to William's neck and felt no pulse, and he blamed himself. In his mind, it was all his fault that William was even brought to trial because he had disobeyed Sean's direct order to protect Elinor. It was his fault that Laurel was brought to the stake. Had he kept his mouth shut, her deception would have been upheld. He turned his eyes to the top of the flames, grateful that he could not discern the woman who stood within it. "Forgive me, Laurel!"

"You waste your pity!"

Richard wheeled to see Thomas approaching him, haloed by the firelight. "The witch earned her fate! You should be pleased *Lord* Richard! You are now truly the Earl of Sutherland!" He began to laugh wickedly as his eyes flickered with the flames.

An all-consuming rage rushed up on Richard. The flames roared in his ears, and the sound of the cheering crowd fed his own inner fire to rail against the man who stood before him. With no more than a half-second of forethought, he reached for his sword. In a single elegant and deadly motion, he raised the blade high and brought it down swift and true upon the gloating face of his own father. Thomas had no time to even change the expression on his face before Richard's blade sent his sneer to the ground, a heartbeat before it was joined by the rest of his body.

Richard held his after-strike stance like a statue for several seconds before he realized he had just struck dead his own father. As the horror of his act came to him, he dropped the sword where he stood and backed away from the corpse. The world moved in slow, distorted motion as he saw the hunters move toward him. He spun quickly and looked once again upon the flames of the death fire. Before the hunters could reach him, and before his innate cowardice could dissuade him, he dove full and fast into the base of the blaze. "Forgive me!" he screamed as he surrendered himself willingly to the flames.

Ian ran down the dark, twisted stairs, following the sound of Edward's voice and the waning light of Ewan's torch.

"Elinor, quickly!" Edward's voice echoed against the walls. "It's been nearly a half an hour!"

Ian hurried, reaching the doorway into the crypt in time to see Edward lay William on a slab in the middle of the crypt. Elinor lifted his eyelids as Edward placed his ear to William's chest. "Dear God, Ian was wrong."

"No, my lord." Ian rushed from his from place in the entry. "He's alive, I know he is."

"No." Edward covered his eyes with his hand. "He is gone."

Ian impatiently pushed Edward away and tore William's tunic aside, placing his ear directly to his skin and listened. For a moment, he heard nothing. *Why did you lie to me? God, you tell me to go with him, yet...* He listened another moment before he heard an almost imperceptible thump, then a few seconds later, another. "It's faint." Ian grabbed Edward's hand, and grinned up at him. "But his heart beats still. Listen."

Edward placed his ear where Ian had and let out a great sigh. "He's alive!"

"Thank you, Blessed Mother!" Elinor rushed to her potions. "I feared our deception was all too complete."

"I, as well," Ian said as he cradled William gently, bringing him to a half sitting position. "But his heart is far too slow to keep him alive much longer without the stimulants in your antidote."

"My lord, shall I go alert the archers?" Ewan asked from his watchful position near the entry.

"You must wait until we have him fully back with us, Ewan," Edward answered, helping Ian to hold William steady. "Elinor, are you ready?"

"Ready." She rushed to Edward with the same cup she had used to revive William after Bryndah's attempt.

"Yet another dose." Ian shook his head at the irony of what they were doing as he tilted William's head back and held open his jaw. *Would it not occur to the bishop that his protection comes from God and not the devil?*

Elinor poured the dose into William's mouth. As he had done before, Edward held William's mouth and nose closed to force him to swallow. It took several long seconds before Edward felt the muscles in William's neck respond. "He has swallowed."

"How long do you think it will take?" Ian asked as he gently laid William flat.

"Hard to say," Elinor answered, brushing the hair from William's face. "He's fallen so deep."

"Yes." Ian sighed. "There was far more nightshade used for the test than we expected, good lady. It is miraculous that his heart still beats at all. Perhaps he truly is charmed, and that is God's jest on all of them."

Elinor looked at Ian curiously for a moment, then back to William. "Charmed?" Her hand strayed to the silver eagle that adorned his shoulder. "Perhaps he is." She smiled at Ian, tears sparkling on her lashes, then her smile faded. "Where is Laurel? Shouldn't she be with you?"

Edward took a long breath, then gently answered for Ian. "I'm afraid we have lost our little mouse, Elinor."

"Lost?" She stared in disbelief at Edward.

"I have not in my life witnessed such an act." Edward looked away. "I could never hope to match what she has done. She took it from him when he was almost lost. She claimed his imagined crime to be her own."

Elinor wept into her apron. Ian put a gentle arm about her shoulder and allowed her to lean on him. "I'm so sorry, dear lady."

"Were you with her, Ian?" Elinor asked through her sobs. "Did you give her my dose?"

"I took care of her." Ian patted her back. "She felt nothing, and she wasn't alone." *And neither are we.* Ian was certain that the cool breeze that had found him on the platform and in the alley, had somehow found its way into crypt as the dank smell of the place was momentarily pushed from his face and replaced by a gentle, sweet smelling breeze.

Edward placed one hand on Elinor's shoulder, gently lifting one of William's bandaged hands with the other. "Elinor, when he awakens he'll require a great deal of care. More, I fear, than you can provide alone."

"Aye, m' lord," Elinor agreed, wiping her face. "He's in far worse shape than I could have imagined." She took William's hand from Edward. "Oh, it's a sin. His hands. He had such beautiful hands. They won't be about his lute for a long, long time— if ever. It breaks my heart that he won't have his music to help him through." She sighed and examined the bandages. "You've done a fine job tending him, Ian."

"His hands will mend in time. After all, Laurel set them, you see. You taught her well." Ian smiled sadly. "With the care she took with him, I'm sure he won't be forever without his music." He paused and swallowed, before making his promise. "I'll see to it myself, that he plays again one day."

Edward looked up hopefully. "You'll go with them, then? I would not presume to ask it of you, but I would be beyond grateful to you, Ian."

"Aye, sir." Ian nodded. "It is why I came back here— to offer my service. I'd like to go with him, as there is truly no reason for me to stay here. I was once an apothecary and I can be again." He half-laughed, forcing himself to remain calm, realizing he'd just committed to completely altering the course of his life. "That is, if you won't mind sharing your skills with another herbalist, dear lady."

"It will be my honor. Bless you." Elinor smiled, swallowing her tears. "I knew there was a reason that I liked you from the start. And once Will is back on his feet, I'm sure the two of you will be fast friends as well."

Edward and Ian exchanged somber glances.

"What is it?" Elinor asked, then looked down toward William's boots, noting the deformed twists in the leather. "Oh, no."

"I'm afraid he will not be on his feet again, my dear." Edward said. "The night of his wedding, I heard him quip to Mehlyndia how he was not quite an invalid yet. I hope she is prepared to care for him now that he is."

"She shall," Elinor consoled. "And so shall I."

"And I," Ian promised.

"My lord?" Ewan spoke softly from the door. "Is there any change?"

"Not yet," Edward answered quietly.

"It's time to go back, Will."

"Must I go? Look at that thing they think is me. It hardly seems human."

"If you don't go, this will have all been for nothing."

"Will it? Edward believes me now. He won't let it happen again. Doesn't that matter?"

"What about your son?"

"My son?"

"You need to give him that eagle."

"Go back, Will. Stay with the living. You still have a lot of work to do."

"It's going to be painful."

"Only for a while."

"Will you stay with me? Both of you? Please."

"We'll be with you when you need us."
"Go back."

"He's moving," Ian whispered. "Look."

Edward watched as William's eyes fluttered open slightly and closed again. He put his ear to his chest again and listened carefully. "He's coming back!" He grinned through tears. "William? Wake up, son."

Again, William's eyes blinked, this time staying open, though glassy and dilated as they slowly turned to look upon his father. "Back."

"Yes! Welcome back, son."

"Now, sir?" Ewan asked hopefully from the door.

"Yes Ewan! Two arrows! Go!"

"Aye, sire!" Ewan hurried up the twisted staircase to signal the archer.

"Is there any sign?" Mehlyndia asked Simon as she leaned on the rail of the ship.

"Not yet, m' lady," Simon answered. "Are you feeling better?"

"The sea air helps. It's the waiting I find impossible to bear." She strained her eyes to see the outline of Drumoak far away from the ship. The moonless night was clear and dark and the stars shone sharp against the endless velvet of the night sky. "Are you sure we shall be able to see the sign from this distance?"

"There should be no difficulty."

Mehlyndia strained again to see. She wished that Elinor

had come with her. She wanted very much to collapse in her maternal arms and hide from the things that frightened her, as she had when she was a child. "How long will they wait before they set sail?"

"Only until the tide makes it necessary, m' lady. That was what Lord Edward instructed."

"Simon?"

"Yes, m' lady?"

"Please, no more formality. I am no longer a countess nor Lady Sutherland. I am simply Melly, the wife of the local wood carver. Perhaps we shall have an orchard or a small farm to tend." She turned to smile at him. "Do you think he'll like that?"

"Aye m' l— Melly," he corrected himself and patted her hand. "Yes, I think it will suit him." He turned back to his watch. "It should not be much longer."

"What do you know of the New World, Simon?" She tried to keep her voice calm with this idle chatter while watching the sky for her father's signal.

"Only that we are fools to set sail the first of October." He laughed lightly. "But then, I've never known Will to do anything the easy way."

Mehlyndia looked closely at the horizon until she saw a faint orange halo which revealed the silhouette of Drumoak. It came from the center of Stonehaven.

"Have you given thought to what you shall do should we set sail alone?" Simon asked tentatively, his gaze on the shoreline.

"I see it too, Simon," she answered him quietly. "They've lit the bonfire."

They watched silently while the aura grew more obvious. Even from the distance they were from the coast, they could easily see the flames rising bright and fierce into the clear night sky. They watched in silence as the blaze grew higher, every so often sending sudden, angry flares skyward.

"I shall alert the captain," Simon said softly then turned to leave.

"No!" Mehlyndia put her hand on his arm to stop him. "We have not seen my father's signal."

"But the flame," Simon said, pointing to the shore, "surely it means—"

"He told me to wait!" she cried through clenched teeth. "We shall not move until we see the arrow!"

They watched the flame for what seemed like hours as it rose and fell, flared and waned. She wondered how long it would take for the flame to be exhausted. How long did such an atrocity take? She watched without speaking or turning away until the flames subsided to nothing more than the faintest orange glow against the horizon. The darkness enfolded them while they still stood waiting for the signal that was promised from Drumoak.

"The tide is beginning to turn." Simon placed his hand on hers gently. "The captain will sail soon, with or without a sign."

Mehlyndia did not respond but held her gaze toward the parapets of Drumoak. "Look!" She raised a hand toward the shore as a single light arched across the sky. "One," she said, then gripped the railing, almost sinking to her knees. "He's gone—"

"Nay, Melly!" Simon squeezed her hand. "Look again!"

Mehlyndia looked to the shoreline, just as the second arrow streaked across the sky and fell gently into the sea.

Epilogue

Excerpts from William's Journal

3 August 1600
I came in from the barn last night. The nurse has given me this book. She says it's for me alone. The place is warm and clean. So far it seems all right, but I've made sure to find the doors.

william

2 September 1600
I must be the biggest fool to ever walk. Why I believed them all these years, I shall never know. Drumoak is wonderful, and so is Lord Edward. And I shall be happy to never lay eyes on the dragon again in my life.

I've taken Star to the meadow almost every day. She's like the wind, and it is like flying to let her run. I don't even fall off anymore since Sean taught me how to stay in the saddle.

Laurel is nice. She was a little shy around me at first and kept calling me 'Master William.' No one ever called me that in Aberdoir. I asked her just to call me 'Will' and she liked that. She and Sean have shown me the way to the caves beneath the cliffs. We plan to explore them often.

william

12 November 1600

At last, something besides this book to call my own. This silly little wooden box. Geoffrey allowed me to use his tools today for the first time, and I carved the little hawk on the lid. It's not as easy as it looks and I made quite a mess of the carving, but mine looks better than Sean's does, even though he won't admit it.

Geoffrey will teach me the lute as well! I cannot imagine ever learning something as wonderful as music back in Aberdoir. I don't think they even know what music is. I wonder if I could ever play it as well as Geoffrey.

William

14 July 1601

Laurel, Sean and I took to the caves under the seawall today. I made a fool of myself with Laurel. I kissed her. I don't think she has those feelings for me because when Sean came around, she walked away from me. I think she fancies him.

I have never had such good friends as Laurel and Sean. It is as if we three are all one person. Even in the better days at Aberdoir, Richard never knew my thoughts the way they seem to.

I asked Mehlyndia once if she'd like to go with us, but she seemed to think us too silly to even consider going into 'those horrid caves' as she called them. She doesn't care to spend her time with Laurel or Sean as much either, but she seems to like me well enough. She goes on a lot about things like 'proper stations' and 'breeding'. It makes us all sound like horses rather than people. Still, I like her well enough, I suppose. Maybe some day she will come and play with Sean and Laurel too. I think I'd like that.

William

19 May 1603

Mehlyndia went to visit Aberdoir today. She'll be back in a week. I hate it when she goes there. But I hate it more when they come here, so I stay out of sight. I know Mehlyndia wonders why I do that. I may tell her when we're older. But not now.

I have Sean and Laurel to spend my days with, but I miss her a lot when she's gone.

William

15 October 1604

At long last, Elinor showed Laurel and me how to make a simple charm today. Just a little one that is supposed to make our footsteps quiet. Mine failed miserably, and Sean heard me coming from the other end of the castle. But Laurel's worked perfectly. It made her absolutely quiet as a mouse. The trouble is she's been sneaking up on me all day, just to gloat.

Now if I could only find a charm that would make it easier for me to talk to Mehlyndia. I still get all twisted in the middle when she comes into the room.

William

25 December 1604

Geoffrey helped me put the finishing touches on my lute just in time for the Christmas ball. The carvings came out better than I thought I could do, but then, he's a good teacher. My playing is far better than it was a few months ago, and Edward asked me to play for the guests tonight. I never thought I could do it. There were so many people, but they seemed to enjoy the music. Even Sean seemed impressed. Mehlyndia liked it very much and asked me to play several times. She is so much nicer than her sister. I hardly believe they're even related.

I wish I had the confidence to tell her that to her face. I don't know why it's so hard to speak to her suddenly. I find myself tongue-tied at the most awkward times, yet I can tell Laurel anything and not be the least bit shy. I wonder why?

William

5 September 1605

Edward sent Sean on a simple errand to deliver a letter to Aberdoir that turned into quite an adventure! I went along for the company, and before I knew what was happening, we were racing out of Aberdoir with hunters on our heels. Sean and Annlise seem to be very smitten with each other. I never would have imagined them together, to be honest. I always assumed he and Laurel would pair. And Laurel would be safer for him I believe, as Annlise is not exactly free for him to woo as she is betrothed to a rather dangerous man— a hunter at that. Sean nearly got himself run-through by the sot. Love seems to have dulled his wit, as I've never known Sean to be so careless. He doesn't seem to want to talk about it with me though. I suspect that he's embarrassed that it was me who rescued him.

William

27 March 1606

I cannot believe he allowed it! Edward stood away and allowed it instead of clouting the rude sot! Blessed Mother please be with Caleb and Martha, two simple, country folk, and yet the superstitious fools of Stonehaven fear him for his physical lameness. My stomach boils for him each time I hear the catcalls. Caleb, my friend, I should have stood up for you and your gentle wife, when I had the chance, even if Edward was standing with me.   I swear, should I ever be in Father's place, I shall never allow a man be accused of being a demon simply for being crippled. Laurel thinks I should be careful how I speak up. She doesn't know of my friendship with Caleb and Martha, and I've never told her about Rebecca.

William

1 December 1606

Sean has been back to Aberdoir several times over the past couple of months on the pretense of running errands for Edward and he's come back long-faced and sullen each time. He must think I'm daft to believe he's not truly been seeking out Annlise. Tonight when he returned, he had that "don't ask or else" look about him. I didn't ask. I suggested we hoist a pint or two at the Thorn and Thistle, instead. After a few rounds he confirmed my suspicions and said simply, "Will... women! Och!" Then he drank another pint. It was the first time in a very long time that I've seen him take any interest in the dancers.

William

12 December 1606

It's decided. Edward will take me on his tours of the

counties. We leave with the new year.
William

31 December 1606

Mehlyndia accepted my proposal and Edward has agreed. I am beside myself with joy. We shall wed when the tour has ended on the last day of August.

Sean congratulated me with a pint. Laurel congratulated me as well, but I feel somehow she disapproves. I wish she would tell me what the trouble is, and why she has become suddenly distant from me. Although, strangely enough, she kissed me tonight and told me she loves me. I love her too, I suppose, but I don't think she meant it the same way I do. I'm sure she only thinks of me as a brother. If I thought she felt differently, perhaps I would have courted her instead of Mehlyndia. Fine time to realize this! She did give me a new name though, Eagle Fylbrigge. Funny, I feel more like Chicken Fylbrigge.

William

30 May 1607

Has my head ever been as sore as this? I am told I hoisted my age in pints last evening and by the throbbing in my skull, I can well believe it. Isaac has spent the morning laughing at me, asking if I enjoyed the dancer as much as the smile on my face tells him. Trouble is, I can hardly remember her. That is the last time I let Sean talk me into singing in that tavern. I seem to be somewhat of a legend this morning and would love to know what I have done to earn such status.

I fear that Melly will be done with me should these tales

reach her. Ah well, I'm not wed yet, after all.

That is all I have to say for now as I need to sleep off this confounded headache. I wish Elinor were here. I could use one of her remedies.

William

5 August 1607

My day is coming, I feel it. I know, given the chance, I can make a difference. I can turn hearts. Edward will not speak out, that much is clear. I have not seen anyone else take this banner, so if I do not carry it, than who shall? I know there are others who feel the same, they only require someone to lead them.

Blessed Mother give me strength. It shall be me!

William

16 August 1607

Blessed Lord and Lady help me, I used the chicory today, and it worked! The treaties have been signed. Edward says it is all of my own doing. That I was the one who convinced them to make the changes. He told me he is proud by my courage. That astounds me. I have no courage! But at long last I have found a way to make some.

William

17 September 1607

The world has gone mad. Edward places his faith in me, and I cannot maintain my own peace of mind. The years I spent pushing Aberdoir aside have come back to me like a recurring nightmare. Bryndah failed this time but is still a threat to me. Why I allow her vile face to haunt my sleep is a mystery to me. She has no power over me anymore.

Edward entrusts me with the ruling of a key tenant. I cannot hope to live up to his expectations. What is worse, he tells me that I should not speak my mind where my conscience leads me. He would have me stand aside, as he does, for the sake of my rank. I had hoped this rank would have given me a greater voice from which to forward my cause, but I see now that it is more of a hindrance, than help. I have less freedom now than before it was bestowed. Why all this has been placed on me is for the fates alone to know, I suppose, but I would give my last breath to take my bride and be free of this place.

William

4 October 1607
Mehlyndia has asked I keep this book for William, while he cannot. I shall do my best. ~ Ian

We have been at sea for two days now, and he has scarcely opened his eyes but for moments at a time. But his sleep is natural and untroubled, and this is a good sign. I am confident he should be fully back to us in another day or so. In the meantime, his wounds will have time to heal. His wrists and face seem to be far better all ready, and should heal completely in time though there shall certainly be scars. He moves his arms about in his sleep, but not his legs. Mehlyndia has been told of the damage to his back, but remains optimistic that William will walk again. I have not the heart to explain to her that the cuts to his heels will prevent him from ever walking normally again, if at all. In time, she'll come to learn this on her own.

Elinor takes care to see that the dressings are changed often. Oddly, she is keen that he keep the little eagle on his shoulder. She has pinned it to his bed-shirt.

Mehlyndia has kept to herself for the most part. She seems fearful to touch him. She was not prepared to receive back her husband as he is, I fear. Although, I must encourage her to sit by and speak to him, as that is the only time he seems to open his eyes.

Ian

10 October 1607

William still has not yet awoken as completely as I had hoped. He opens his eyes, but there is little light behind them. He is able to eat with help, and now and then he will say a word or two, but he does not make sense. Yesterday he said "staying", then drifted back to sleep. Perhaps this is well for him, as there is still healing to be done.

Ian

31 December 1607

The year ends with a new beginning. William spoke a complete sentence today for the first time since we set sail. He is not as clear in his mind as I had hoped, and I had to tell him my name several times. He knows his Mehlyndia well enough, though he seems to have forgotten they are wed. Twice he has asked for Sean, and we explained that Sean is no longer with us, but I'm not convinced he will remember tomorrow what we have told him today. Perhaps it would be a kindness to allow all that happened to remain lost to him.

I shall leave it in God's hands.

Ian

10 January 1608

He has relapsed back to near silence and I am discouraged. For ten days, William has spoken very little and still spends most of his time asleep or staring out the portal. When he does speak, it is not to any of us who sit here with him, but to some unseen being that seems to dwell in the corner of his cabin. I am not so quick to dismiss this as a delusion as I might have been before, especially when the few words I've heard him say are things like, "stay with the living" and "I trust you."

Mehlyndia has yet to witness any of these odd conversations, and I am reticent to report them to her. She is so easily upset, and I am fearful for her child. Until there is more positive progress to report, I shall simply tell her he is still sleeping.

I am beginning to wonder if this endless sleep will be his lot forevermore.

Ian

2 February 1608

At last, I have found a way to reach William. For my own comfort, and to pass the time, I played my flute and he responded. I'm a fool to have not thought of it sooner. I shall play more often now. It can only help the both of us.

Ian

12 February 1608

Ian writes for me, as I cannot seem to grasp the quill. I awoke a few days ago to a new world. It's a mystery how I came to be here and how I've come to the pathetic state in which I find myself. It must have been quite an adventure. I am told my name is now to be Philbrick, though I have not been told why I must change my name. Ian assures me that eventually it will be made clear.

Melly has grown large at the middle and tells me we are wed and that I am to be a father, yet that too seems impossible. I don't recall getting married and I certainly don't remember creating a bairn. But I am pleased with the news.

I only wonder what else has been lost to me. I certainly won't remember much from this book. Although the poetry is not bad, I wonder why I've written so much of it.

Ian, for William

5 April 1608

We have left the ship at last, and the captain has set sail back to Scotland for supplies. Melly hopes to hear all the news there is to know from her father when the ship returns in the fall. I suspect she is very homesick, but will not say so to me. We have settled in a fledgling settlement called Port Edin, on the northern coast of New France. There are little more than a few cottages, but the people seem pleasant enough. Ian and Simon have helped to build the cottage that Melly and I shall call home until a proper house is raised. I would have liked to help them.

I find I am quite dull-witted these days.

Whatever lies hidden in my past, it seems it shall remain

so, as no one seems eager to enlighten me, and Melly grows impatient when I ask the same questions more than once. It seems to upset her to talk about our old home. I do not wish to upset her, so I do not push, even though the few memories I have seem to grow dimmer each day.

Elinor says the child should come next month sometime. Perhaps I'll be stronger by then and less troublesome to everyone so there are not *two* helpless bairn to be looked after.

William

31 May 1608

A son was born to us at dawn. No greater gift is given a man than this. Melly is resting, content with our son on her bosom. Both she and Elinor have suggested we name the child Sean William. I am told that Sean was my brother, we were close, yet I cannot recall even his face. Still, sometimes I feel as though someone is close to me in that place between sleeping and waking— perhaps it is him. In any case, the name feels good and right to me. I think he would be pleased to know we've named the child for him.

William

18 September 1612

The house frame was raised by our neighbors and friends today. Ian helped place the last post, then I was hoisted up with the winch by Simon and Ian to put the last nail to the beam myself. Melly covered her eyes until I came down. It made for a riotous celebration. Little Seany found a way to climb the scaffold and scared me to death. Where his bold streak comes from, I shall never know.

I thank God that Melly seems well pleased with me, even as I am.

William

3 January 1613

A daughter, born this morning. Died soon after. She was called Laurel. Melly is holding up well but is heartbroken. As am I.

William

12 October 1613

The new governor, a man named Peter Garland, has arrived in Port Edin. He looked at me strangely, when I was brought to him, almost as though he knew me, though that would be unlikely. It is the one they call Tearlach that worries me more. I don't like him.

Preview:

"In the Wake of Ashes"

Chapter 1

September 1612

Port Edin Settlement, An Island off the Coast of New France

WILLIAM OPENED HIS eyes and breathed in the early autumn crispness of the fresh sea wafting through his bedroom window. Another beautiful morning.

The sun had barely peeked over the horizon, yet the sky already held the promise of a warm, clear day. He lay in bed listening to the gentle rolling of the ocean and the call of the sea¬birds. Such a lovely song.

He closed his eyes for a moment content to just listen to the sounds of life, and as was his custom, offered a silent prayer of thanks for the sun¬rise.

A gray tabby hopped up onto the bed and chirped to him in greeting.

"Shall be a diamond day by the looks of that sunrise, Dragon." He scratched between the cat's ears and allowed her to walk on his chest and rub her head against his face. She folded her paws and hunkered down on his shoulder, purring. "Yes, 1 agree. 'Tis far too early to be rising, but it would be a sin to waste such a morn as this laying about wouldn't it." In reply, the cat closed her eyes, resting her chin on her paws. He chuckled and stroked her back. "Fair enough, another moment or two, then."

Next to him Mehlyndia stirred, and rolled over, dropping her arm across his chest and upsetting the lounging cat. Dragon made an insulted snort, stood and stretch then sauntered, tail up, to the far end of the bed.

William brushed the hair away from his wife's eyes. "Good morning, Melly."

"Hmm?" Mehlyndia blinked then yawned and looked at her husband. "You're awake with the dawn again. Trouble with your sleep?" she asked, nuzzling up to him.

"Who could sleep on such a morning?" He smiled, giving her a squeeze. "Especially today. Come on. Help me up. We have a busy day ahead. The men shall be here soon. It won't do for me to be still abed when they raise the beams, will it?"

"I'm sure they're all still firmly asleep, my love." She gave him a quick squeeze and sighed before, reluctantly pushing herself up to sit. "But, I suppose you are right. The ladies will be here far ahead of the men, I'm sure. We have a grand feast to prepare. While all the men are busy raising the house, we'll be raising the bread to feed them." She drew on her dressing robe, stretched and yawned, then walked around to William's side of the bed. "I'm sure I will be on my feet most of the day," she said, as she pulled his chariot-chair close to the bed. "Ready?" She held both hands to him.

"Ready." William threw the covers aside, reached for her hands, took a long breath and pulled himself up. He held onto her, one arm around her shoulders, the other persuading his right leg, then the left, to dangle from the edge of the bed. He sat for a moment recovering his breath. "You must be tired of this," he muttered, as he did every morning.

She gave him her traditional reply and then kissed him. "Not yet." It was a ritual played out almost every morning since they arrived in Port Edin. She positioned the chair along side the edge of the bed. "The wheels are beginning to wear. They hardly roll properly anymore. You really should have Ian mend them for you."

"Ian?" William laughed. "I think not. He's talented with his flute and quick with his herbs and poultices, but he's hopeless in the wood shop. He'd make the wheels square, and then where would I be?" He reached up and locked his hand around Mehlyndia's shoulders, as she locked hers under his arms, behind his back. "Now," he said and shifted his weight forward to allow her to ease him into his chair. William always took care to keep this little bit of morning business cheerful, though he hated every minute of it.

"It's getting harder to do this," she said, taking a breath once he was settled into his chariot.

"Does it hurt?" he asked, concerned, placing a hand on her expanding middle. "I don't want you to risk—"

"No." She patted his hand on her belly. "We're fine, love. But it won't be long before I'll need Elinor to help me." She walked behind him and pushed the chair closer to the window so he could look toward the road.

"Don't wait too long to ask for help," he said, looking up at her over his shoulder. "You and the little one should not have to be lugging about the likes of me." He sighed, and then turned away from her, resting his elbow on the windowsill, his chin in his hand. "I'm not quite the husband you expected, am I."

"Am I complaining?"

"You never do." He half smiled, but his cheer had left him.

"No gloomy moods today, Mr. Philbrick." She turned him to look at her, with a gentle hand on his shoulder. "It's going to be a glorious day. There'll be friends and family about, and plenty of food. We're long overdue for a happy event, I'd say." She put her hands in the small of her back, and arched, stretching again. "We're to have a new home, at last, to make room for this growing clan we've started."

"Aye." He smiled at her finally, and then gave her tummy an affectionate pat. "This little one will have a proper roof above him well before he arrives."

"Are you so sure it's a son then?" She laughed as she went around behind the dressing screen to change her clothes. "There's the remotest possibility I could provide you a daughter, you know."

"Now that would be pleasant," William mused, looking out the window, "a Fylbrigge daughter."

"Philbrick," she corrected him as she came out from behind the screen, fully dressed. "I know you're not fond of that name, but it's the one we must use now."

"Philbrick," he repeated with a sigh. *The one thing I'm sure of about myself—my name—and you make me change it.*

Seany, their five-year-old son, interrupted their conversation. "Papa?" he called, standing in the doorway, blanket in hand, rubbing his eyes.

"Seany? Come here, lad." William held his arms out as the tyke went to him and climbed up onto his lap for a hug. "Did we wake you up too early, son?"

"No. Is it time to build the house yet?" Seany asked, his

face stretching into a yawn.

"Almost," William laughed. "As soon as Ian and the rest come. Are you ready to help with the heavy lifting? I'll need you to carry my hammer for me."

"William, you shouldn't tease the boy," Mehlyndia said, holding a hand to Seany. "He's too little, and will only be in the way."

"I am not too little," Seany protested as he took his mother's hand and hopped off William's lap. "I'm big enough to carry Papa's hammer. See?" He bent his little arm to show off his muscle. "I'm strong!"

"That you are." William mussed the child's hair. "I should think we can find a job for you today. We'll need all the hands we can find to get the frame up by sunset."

"We?" Mehlyndia raised a brow to him. "Surely you're not planning to—"

"We." William shot her a quick look. "You don't expect me to just sit and watch all day do you?"

"No, I expect you'll be in the thick of it and scaring me to pieces, as always. I suppose it's too much to ask you to be careful?"

William chuckled, "I'll be as careful as I ever am."

"That, sir," she rolled her eyes heavenward, "is exactly what I was afraid you'd say." She laughed as she kissed him on the forehead. "Come on, Seany, let's leave Papa to his thoughts now and get you some breakfast." She patted the boy on the bottom and scooted him across the room.

"Breakfast!" Seany burst into giggles and trotted away, dragging his blanket behind him.

"I'll bring yours to you, my love," Mehlyndia called over

her shoulder as she chased after her son.

"Take your time," William said, watching them go. I'm not going anywhere. He sat quietly, enjoying the breeze on his face, half dozing while he listened to the sounds from the kitchen, the scrape of the spoon on the mixing bowl, the shuffling of the dishes as Mehlyndia went about getting Seany's breakfast.

"How many cakes would you like, darling?" She asked.

"Fifty-eleven." Seany spouted with a giggle.

"Oh, you'll not eat more than fifty-ten," Mehlyndia said, laughing. "We'll save that last one for Papa."

Seany's laughter echoed throughout the little cottage and as it always happened, the simple sounds of his family and home filled him with a feeling of peace. He closed his eyes for a moment, and offered another silent prayer of thanks, knowing how fortunate he was to experience this lovely morning. He should not have been alive.

William Mastin Fylbrigge—now called Philbrick—had spent the last four or so years bound to his chariot chair, with precious little recollection of his life before he was put there. He knew he had been whole and strong before he had come to this shore, though he could scarcely remember his old home across the sea. He remembered nothing of the circumstances that had brought him here, or how he came to be in such a sorry condition.

On rare occasions, Mehlyndia would speak dreamily about a place called Stonehaven on the eastern shore of Scotland, and the castle she called 'Drumoak'. She would ask him if he remembered the time they had done this or that, or the party for so and so from wherever. Did he miss the grandness of nobility? He would nod, and smile, perhaps laugh as if the memories were clear. He hated to admit to her that he could barely recall Stonehaven, let alone the details of the events she described. She humored him by laughing along, however, he knew she was not fooled when he pretended to remember.

He did know that they'd left Scotland rather abruptly, not quite five years ago and not long after they married. Most of his waking memories of the place were shady at best, but in his dreams, he saw clearly, images of a large hall with a grand stairway, colorful glass windows and endless corridors lined with gleaming stone pillars. The dreams of this place were comfortable and familiar, and at times seemed so real he believed them to be true. In his dreams of Drumoak, he was always whole, able to walk, run, and do fine woodwork carvings with his hands. Most times, he would see himself as though watching from the side. He could watch himself performing simple tasks without difficulty, or ascending the great stairs two at a time then sliding down the wide polished granite banister. He would see his own face cheerful, young and unmarked rather than scarred and lined at the eyes, as it was now. His hair would still be black as a raven, free of the rebellious white streaks that framed his face now, belying his twenty-five years as far older.

In his dreams he traveled the corridors and rooms, knowing how they looked, felt, even how they smelled, knowing every stick of furniture, every drapery. He would walk the castle, inventorying each painting, vase and statue.

And there would always be music. Sweet, clear music that he believed was of his own making somehow, yet he could never see how he was creating it. His life in this castle had been one of privilege; he was certain of that much.

Along with images of the castle, there were also memories of faces. He would see Elinor, cheerful in her kitchen, busily preparing a meal or organizing a feast. Mehlyndia would be there, as well, dressed in elegant silks and intricately embroidered gowns quite unlike any she had ever worn in Port Edin. He remembered an elderly gentleman with a graying beard and a warm winning smile. Edward? Was this man his own father, or was he Mehlyndia's? Truthfully, he was unclear on that, but in his dreams, he called the man 'Father'. In one dream, Edward called him 'son' and had given him a horse he named Star. He must have been my father.

On occasion, he would encounter a young lad not much older than Seany, with chubby cheeks and mischief in his eyes. He carried a little wooden sword with twining for the hilt and adorned with an elaborate carving of a dragon on the blade. The boy charged about the castle, sword raised, eager to vanquish the vandals of his imaginary game.

But the two figures William saw most often, he could never find names for; a young woman, with large brown eyes and long chestnut colored hair, and a man, close to his own age, with stern but gentle eyes colored the same deep green as his own. They would stand together as though watching him, as he walked the corridors, always present, never farther than the nearest door or window, yet never close enough for him to touch. He was always greatly pleased to see them, though they seldom spoke to him. They would wave, smile, and if they did speak, their voices would come from a place just behind his ear, rather than from their mouths. He knew he had loved them. In his most recent dream-visit to Drumoak, the woman's name had been on the tip of his tongue, and he was certain he had spoken it. But, when he awoke, her name, face and her companion, faded back into the misty place in his memory that stubbornly hid away from him during his waking hours.

His dreams of Drumoak came often. At times, he would awaken from them with a warm, content feeling as the visions faded. But most often, they would leave him with a sad sense of loss, more profound than he could express. He knew he had once been happy within those castle walls, and suspected that whatever had brought him to his current physical malady had happened away from there, though he could not for the life of him imagine what it had been.

Aside from his useless legs, and the premature white streaks in his otherwise black hair, he carried a goodly number of scars. Most of the marks—the ones that encircled his wrists and ankles, and the hook shaped crease on his left cheek—were still fairly prominent, though they had softened a bit over the years. He had only limited use of his hands, as his fingers were somewhat gnarled at the joints and he could not straighten them completely. He could grip and hold his woodworking tools well enough, but he lacked the dexterity to do any of the fine carving he had seen himself doing in his dreams. Even holding his quill was a challenge, and his nightly journal entries were written in large block letters instead of the careful tiny script he once used.

He sat idly examining his fingers, tracing the scars on his left wrist with his right hand, wondering again how he had come by them. He was certain Mehlyndia knew, but she refused to speak of it. In fact, whenever he would ask her of it, she would become so upset she would almost swoon, and William hated to cause her distress, so he would not prod her for details. He was certain that Elinor knew the truth as well, but like Mehlyndia, she would grow pale, and turn away at his questions. He reasoned that eventually he would come to know the truth on his own, and there was no gain in causing Mehlyndia and Elinor distress.

His reverie was interrupted when Dragon hopped up onto his lap. "Ah, are you ready to begin your day then?" He chuckled as the cat made herself comfortable, kneading his knees with her front paws. "Is that it? You believe I'll allow you to sleep on my lap all day? I don't think so." He laughed as he picked her up and set her on the windowsill. "Go on, earn your keep, you hairy beast." With a gentle nudge, he persuaded the cat to jump out the window to the front yard. As he watched her disappear in the grass, he saw a tall man with a cheerful smile and a light-hearted lilt in his step approaching the cottage.

"Good morning, Ian." William called from his window.

Ian looked up and waved, "Hello, Will." He walked directly to the open window and rested his arms on the sill. "How does the morning find you?"

"I'm well enough, I suppose." William reached a hand in greeting to Ian. "Melly's getting breakfast, have you eaten?"

Ian shook his head and frowned, "I'm fasting today."

"Fasting? With the feast that—"

"You're too easy, Will," Ian laughed. "You believe anything I tell you."

William shook his head, suppressing a grin. "No wonder

you left the clergy. You're evil."

"Did you only now puzzle that out?" Ian grinned, giving William a pat on the shoulder, "Let me come 'round. I'll see you in a moment." He walked away from the window, still chuckling.

I don't know what I'll do if that man is not cheerful one day, William smiled as he waited for his friend to join him.

Ian Proctor had sailed with William and Mehlyndia when they had left Scotland aboard the Lady Anne. William was not certain, but since Ian was never present in his dreams of Drumoak, he assumed they had met aboard the ship. But then, he did not remember the ship journey except for the few days when they had anchored off shore. Ian had been one of the first faces he had seen when he woke up after spending months lost in some sort of delirium. His face seemed vaguely familiar, but he assumed that was because Ian had helped Elinor and Mehlyndia care for him during the crossing.

All William really knew about Ian's life before Port Edin, was what the man had told him, himself. He had once been a cleric — priest or a monk of sorts — and had chosen to leave his calling to make his way in the New World as an apothecary. William had a difficult time imagining Ian as a cleric. His sense of humor was quick with a sarcastic bite to it, and no one enjoyed bawdy tales and laughter more than Ian. Even in the dreariest of times, there was a clever twinkle in the man's pale blue eyes. His cheerful disposition and friendly nature never failed to lift William out of a cheerless mood. Ian was a good friend, one he was grateful to have in his life, though he often got the impression that Ian may have been harboring secrets of his own. For all his sunny smiles and cheerfulness, there were times when William noticed a lost and wistful look in his eyes. Ian also bore the ghosts of scars on his wrists, not terribly unlike William's, though they were far less visible. Many times he had wanted to ask Ian about them, wondering if it would help him remember how he came by his own scars, but he could not bring himself to ask.

"Look what I found in the kitchen." Ian entered the room carrying Seany, giggling and upside down over his shoulder. "The rascal was stalking your breakfast." He plopped the lad down onto the bed.

"Was he?" William gave his son a wide-eyed look of mock reproach, "I hope you saved a crumb or two for your wretched father."

"No, Papa I ate it all." Seany patted his stomach, laughing as he rolled around in the big blankets.

"He certainly did, but I've made more." Mehlyndia chuckled as she carried William's breakfast tray into the bedroom. "Ian, would you care for some breakfast? I've made enough cakes to feed the whole of Port Edin."

"That would be lovely, madam, thank you." Ian smiled then took the tray from her. "Didn't you make any for him?" He motioned with his head toward William.

"Him? Is he to eat today? I thought we fed him yesterday?" Mehlyndia teased.

William made a comical moan, "Alas, I shall starve."

Seany stopped rolling and gave his mother a disapproving scowl. "You made Papa sad, Mum."

Mehlyndia winked to her husband, "Have I?"

William reached his arms out to his son, "Oh, we're just playing, Seany, I'm not sad. See?" He grinned as wide as his face would allow. "Ian's got my breakfast." He motioned for Ian to set the tray on a little table in the far end of the room.

Seany climbed up onto William's lap, and gave him a hug. "Good. You need your breakfast. That was mean."

William held Seany tight for a moment then let him slide off to the floor. "Thank you for your concern, son," he grinned at the lad. "Go on now, get your breeches and shoes on, and go see if Elinor needs any help."

"All right, Papa." Seany smiled and ran back through the door.

"I'll bring you something in a moment, Ian." Mehlyndia said, as she followed Seany.

"He's a good lad, Will." Ian said, as he went around behind William. "I see a naturally kind heart in him. He'll make you right proud one day." He pushed William's chair to the table in front of the breakfast tray.

"Aye," William said. "He makes me proud now." He reached for the kettle on the tray, poured some of Mehlyndia's spiced cider into his cup, and took a drink. "And so shall his little brother, or sister." He smiled at the thought. "I find it so wonderful to know there is another bairn on the way, and that I'm not a completely useless man. It's overwhelming, Ian."

"I'm sure it is, Will," Ian said, quietly. "You're a lucky man." He pulled a stool up to the table and sat down, then rested his chin on his hand and looked at William closely for a moment. "So what's troubling you?"

William looked up over his cup. "Nothing, why d'ye ask?"

"You've got that look about you." Ian's face grew serious. "Dreams plaguing you again?"

"When are they not?" William made a half-hearted chuckle, "No, it's not the dreams." He pushed the cakes around on his plate idly with his fork. "I'm worried for Melly. With the little one coming, and Seany to look after, and me—" He dropped the fork and sighed. "Ian, the least I can do is to find a way to get out of bed on my own. It's not right that she should have to put herself and the child at risk just because—"

"I'm not complaining, William." Mehlyndia interrupted, bringing in a tray for Ian. "And I've told you when I can no longer lift you on my own, I shall call Elinor to help me." She placed the tray on the table in front of Ian.

William looked at her, embarrassed that she had heard him. "It's not right. A man should not burden his wife with—"

"Hush." Mehlyndia placed a hand on his lips. "You are not a burden." She leaned down and kissed him. "You're my husband. Now, eat your breakfast."

William leaned back in his chair. "Some husband," he muttered.

Mehlyndia shook her head, ignoring William's comment. "Ian, could I ask you to clear away when you've finished? I need to see to the preparations for the feast."

"My pleasure," Ian nodded.

"Thank you. I'll leave you two to talk then." Mehlyndia gave William an affectionate pat on the shoulder, smiled at him, then left the room.

"So, do you think you can help me?" William asked.

"Help you what?" Ian asked, between bites.

"Get out of bed," William answered, as he picked up his fork.

Ian froze, his fork halfway to his mouth. "You want me to come and do it, instead of your wife?"

"No, lunk," William rolled his eyes. "I want you to help me find a way to do it myself."

"Ah." Ian took another bite, and creased his brow in thought. "I see." He set the fork down and looked over toward the bed. "It shouldn't be too difficult to rig up something. I expect all you really need is something to grab on to."

"Aye, that's what I thought too." William nodded. "A handle of sorts that I can hold to pull myself up. Then Melly won't have to lift me."

Ian stroked his chin. "Let me think on it, but yes, I'm sure there's something we can do." He made a crooked grin and leaned close to William. "Perhaps we could put one in the privy as well?"

William blushed, but could not suppress a grin. "Absolutely."

By mid-day, the little cottage was teaming with activity. Elinor, ever the organizer that she was, saw to it that each of the ladies who had come to help cook, had a proper job and a proper spot to do it in. Since Mehlyndia's kitchen was quite small, most of the preparations were taking place outside on worktables, and the baking was being done in the large stone oven adjacent to the barn. Kettles of steaming vegetables and soups were bubbling away, suspended over open fire pits, and for the main course, a whole calf was roasting on a spit. Elinor mourned the huge efficient kitchen she had had in

Drumoak, with its acres of work tops and the colossal stone oven and iron cook stove — a rarity in Scotland, especially forged on Edward's order making the Drumoak kitchen the envy of the highlands. She missed her own cozy quarters and the company of the other maids as well, though she was careful never to mention it to anyone.

Prior to Port Edin, Elinor spent the majority of her fifty-four years in service to Lord Edward, the Duke of Stonehaven and Mehlyndia's father. She had enjoyed keeping the castle in proper working order, and managing the household staff, and had taken pride in knowing everything that took place within its walls. Edward often shared his thoughts with her, or sought out her advice on small matters. When his wife, Anne of Sutherland, passed away, it was Elinor that Edward had turned to for comfort. She never expected she would have ever left Drumoak, but the choice had really not been hers. Edward had implored her to stay with William as he was in sore need of her healing talents, and she would never refuse to go where she knew she was most needed. Besides, she felt responsible for William's misfortune and felt she owed it to him to stay with him. It wasn't a terrible burden for her, however, she truly loved the young couple as her own children, and now that she was accustomed to the more primitive conditions of Port Edin, she was content to manage the workings of this far smaller household.

Elinor was in her glory this day. It hadn't been since she had presided over the preparations for William and Mehlyndia's wedding five years earlier that she had a celebration to organize. Of course, the wedding banquet was far more elaborate than this peasant's feast they were planning today, but she was enjoying the task all the same.

The Blessed Mother grant this feast end on a far happier note than the wedding, she prayed silently. Grant that this celebration be the beginning of good and better times, as they've so earned it. Dragon came by and brushed against her leg, and she finished her thought aloud to the tabby, "After all, there's no reason anyone would be sending assassins to a house raising, now, is there? This day shall end peaceful and merry with a fine dinner had by all." Dragon sat and looked up to her. "They're well deserving of the peace they've come to know here, I say." She squatted to pet the cat. "It's long overdue."

"Elinor?" Mehlyndia said, entering the kitchen with her apron laden with carrots, "who are you talking to?"

Elinor blushed and chuckled to herself. "A silly habit, I suppose, but I was talking to Queen Dragon here. She's quite the listener, you know." She stroked the cat and straightened up again. "Let me help you with that, dear." She picked up a large basket.

Mehlyndia emptied her apron into the basket and sat down on the workbench with a sigh. "You're not alone in your silly habit," she laughed, "I believe William speaks to Dragon on a regular basis. No wonder the creature believes she has the run of the house." She bent and stroked the cat, then took a long breath.

"Are you feeling unwell?" Elinor set the basket on the table and sat next to Mehlyndia. "You're flushed."

"It's warm outside in the sun, I'll be fine."

"You've been on your feet all morning, you just sit here now. Let the other ladies handle the rest of the cooking. And

I'm sure Prissy won't mind keeping an eye out for Seany."

"Thank you Elinor, but I've had a hard enough time convincing these women that I'm made of no lesser stock then they." Mehlyndia sighed then wiped her face with her apron. "I grow so weary of the whispers and snickers behind my back. Is it my fault I was not raised on a farm? Josephine Ashcrofte practically fell all over herself to hurry and tell Prissy how uneven my rolls were."

Elinor watched Mehlyndia's face turn redder as she spoke. She knew it had been a difficult adjustment for her to go from being Lady Sutherland, the future Duchess of Stonehaven, to Goody Philbrick, common housewife and mother. Elinor admired Mehlyndia's determination to fit in, and felt equally irked by the snobbishness of the other wives. As pompous and self-admiring as noble women could be, at least they did not belittle each other by comparing bread rolls and whiteness of their linens.

"There now, dear, don't let them bring a pall on your day. They don't intend to be unkind." She patted Mehlyndia's hand. "After all, they've no idea where we've come from, and that you'd had no reason to learn to cook as a girl." Elinor gave her a warm smile, then glanced through the open kitchen door. "See, out there? Prissy will have none of Josephine's waspish gossip. She's giving the old biddy a bit of a tongue slapping."

Mehlyndia followed Elinor's gaze, then made a smug smile. "That's because Prissy's rolls are even more uneven than mine." She laughed out loud then caught herself. "Shh, she's coming in."

"Do you need help with the chopping?" Prissy asked,

pointing to the carrots Mehlyndia had carried in.

"No I think I can handle it, but I'd be grateful if you'd keep an eye on Seany. He's been wanting to join the men in their building all day. I've had a devil of a time keeping him out from underfoot."

"My pleasure," Prissy beamed. "I'm glad to have an excuse to get away from Josephine." She put her hand to the side of her mouth and leaned close to Elinor and Mehlyndia, "She's been into the sacramental wine again and is running at the mouth. She just called the vicar a dried up old goat!"

"Oh my!" Mehlyndia covered her mouth and giggled into her hand. "Well she is his wife, so she would know how dried up he is."

"Melly! You're wicked!" Prissy giggled.

"Aye, I've learned to adapt, havn't I." She winked at Prissy. "Thank you for minding Seany, Prissy, you're a dear."

Prissy winked back and trotted out of the kitchen.

Elinor watched her go, sighing, "That girl is such a joy. Always cheerful, that one. Simon married well."

"Aye," Mehlyndia agreed, "she's a dear. She reminds so much of..." She cast her eyes down, and picked at her apron.

Elinor nodded, and finished her thought, "Laurel?"

Mehlyndia looked up, "Aye. Laurel. Prissy's got the same streak of mischief in her." She shrugged, stood, and went to the door to look out. "I find I've been thinking about Laurel often lately. I miss her."

"It's the time of year," Elinor said, quietly, then stood and retrieved a cutting board and a large knife from a shelf. "It will be five years come the end of this month."

"Five years." Mehlyndia nodded, then wiped the

perspiration from her face and joined Elinor at the table. "At times, it seems more like fifty, and others, it feels like only five days. It's not right that she isn't here with us. She would have loved taking care of Seany." She picked up a carrot and the knife and began chopping. "I'm sure she'd be quite amused to see me chopping carrots." She raised the knife a little higher with each chop, "I'm sure she'd be pleased to see how well William is coping." She brought the knife down hard and sent the tops of the carrots sailing onto the floor. She stood frozen, then burst into tears.

Elinor put an arm around her, and coaxed her to lean on her shoulder. "Hush, now. What brings this about?"

"He spoke out in his sleep, again, Elinor. He's still trying to remember." Mehlyndia cried onto Elinor's shoulder. "He called her by name, this time."

Elinor held Mehlyndia at arm's length, looking her in the eye, "Does he remember her, at last?" she asked.

"No, only in his sleep." She took a breath and blew her nose. "Elinor, why must we keep it all from him? He loved Sean and Laurel. It seems cruel not to allow him those memories."

"I know, dear, but it's best." Elinor gave a quick glance over both shoulders, being sure there was no one to hear her. "After all, the moment he learns of Laurel, he'll remember how she died, and then why she died the way she did—"

"She saved his life," Mehlyndia argued. "Would that be so wrong for him to remember?"

"Not in itself, dear, but think." Elinor put her hands on the sides of Mehlyndia's face. "If he remembers Laurel, the memories of his trial will soon follow, and all that came before it." She fought a shudder that crept down her spin. "And what brought him to trial in the first place. Dear, we've had peace here since we've come and he's come such a long way. It's best he not remember his former talents with the herbs and...charms." She whispered the word, giving another quick glance over her shoulder.

"That is the last thing I want him to recall." Mehlyndia sighed.

"And what gain would there be in him remembering all he could do before, if he can't do it now?" Elinor said, wiping Mehlyndia's cheeks with her apron. "Would only pain him all the more."

"You mean the music, don't you?" Mehlyndia said flatly. "It was the most important thing in the world to him to be able to sit and play his lute and lose himself in the tunes. Do you think he honestly has forgotten it? I don't. Watch him when Ian plays his flute. He enjoys it well enough, but I can see it his eyes, he's missing his own music terribly." She shook her head impatiently, turned back to her carrots, and resumed her chopping.

"Aye, I've seen the look, dear, but there would be no sense telling him about his lute. He couldn't possibly play it now. Why pour salt in the wound?"

Mehlyndia looked up with a sudden, guilty blush in her cheeks. "Salt in the wound? You're probably right. Now I wish I'd waited to speak with you before I..." She shook her head, turning away.

"Melly?" Elinor asked, "before you did what, dear?"

Mehlyndia forced a smile, waving her hand as if to dismiss the thought. "Oh, 'tis nothing, Elinor. A silly notion I had last spring. Remember William's birthday last May, when Ian played that lovely tune on his flute?"

Elinor nodded.

"You see, while William was listening, he seemed quite taken with the music, and you know how he gets that far-away look when he's daydreaming."

"Oh, yes." Elinor smiled.

"Well, I happened to notice that he was keeping time with the music with his hand. It was as if he was strumming the air. I'm not even sure he was aware of it, but it made me feel sad just the same."

Elinor placed her hand on Mehlyndia's cheek, wiping away a stray tear.

Mehlyndia continued, looking to her hands as she spoke, "I mentioned it to Ian, and he said he'd noticed it too and we agreed that perhaps there was an alternative to his lute— something simple to play. So, when Father's ship arrived in June, I wrote him asking that perhaps he could send something musical back on the next ship. I thought perhaps Geoffrey, the old luthier, would have an idea of what to send. I've been looking forward to the next ship to see what comes...but now, I'm not even certain I shall be able to give it to him. Oh, Elinor, I feel just awful! You're right, it will hurt him more to remember what he's lost..." She buried her face in her hands and cried. Elinor pulled her to her shoulder in a motherly embrace.

"Oh, child, what could I possibly know? I think that was a splendid idea and I'm an old fool for my fear. We shall give him back his music, and it will be a balm for his spirit, something to chase those gloomy winter blues away from him." She rocked Mehlyndia on her shoulder for a moment, the stood back, turning the young woman's face up, persuading her to smile.

"Do you really think so?"

"Aye, I do," Elinor assured her with a kind smile, then turned to the chopping block and scooped up the carrots into a small pot. "Besides, he's remembered some things on his own all ready, eventually it may all come back in its own time. I just pray he's prepared for it when it does."

"Melly, Elinor, come on out," Prissy called, excitedly through the kitchen door. "They've raised the frame! It's time to nail the bough to the peak."

"So soon?" Mehlyndia set her knife down, and wiped her hands on her apron. "Where is Seany, is he out of harm's way?" she asked, hurrying to the door.

Seany peeked out from behind Prissy's skirt, and held a chubby hand up to his mother. "I'm here, Mum."

"Thank goodness, I was worried you were in the way," Mehlyndia sighed as she took his hand. "I wouldn't want you to get stepped on, or squashed under a log, after all."

"But Papa said I could help." He stuck out a lip, and frowned. "He said I could carry his hammer."

Elinor joined them in the doorway, and leaned down, resting her hands on her knees to speak to the boy. "I'm sure your Papa wants you to stay where it's safe while they raise the frame. That's dangerous work, and they won't be able to watch out for you, little one."

"Can I ride up with Papa then?" he asked, pointing toward the construction.

"What?" Mehlyndia gasped and followed Seany's gaze.

"Good God in Heaven! Has he lost his mind?" She ran out of the kitchen toward the men, leaving Seany with Prissy and Elinor.

"What is—?" Elinor looked to see what had sent Mehlyndia running. "Blessed Mother, some things never change," she sighed, shaking her head.

"You don't suppose he's planning to let them hoist him to the peak?" Prissy asked, wide-eyed, "It's at least twenty feet or more!"

"That's exactly what he's planning, Prissy." Elinor held Seany's hand tight then followed Mehlyndia to the construction.

William sat in the sun watching the construction of the frame that would eventually become his home. He had spent months planning the structure on paper, and having the logs hewn and notched. It would be a fine home and would be large enough, if the need arose, to serve as one of the garrison houses in the settlement. It would have two stories with a half floor for an attic. The second level of the house would protrude ten feet over the first on one side, and be fitted with removable panels in the floor to allow for quick exit, or strategic defense should they ever find themselves under attack from the native people. William thought the likelihood of an attack remote, as the natives he had come to know were quite pleasant and peaceful. He assumed the more likely function of the openings would be the disposal of wash water.

The lower level of the house would include a large kitchen he was sure Elinor would appreciate more than Mehlyndia, a sitting room, a bed chamber for Seany and one for Elinor, and the master bed chamber for he and Mehlyndia. He had made last minute changes in the design to include a small nursery off the master's chamber. The second level would have four more bedchambers, each with a proper fireplace. The rooms to the front, where the escape panels would be, would also include built-in bookcases that would conceal passages to other parts of the house. It would be a safe and warm place indeed for him to raise his family.

One of the unique features he had put in his design had been a suggestion and worked out by Ian. For all outward appearances it resembled an empty closet. But next to it, behind yet another hidden panel, would be a series of pulleys, cantilevered weights and ropes, that when pulled, would lift the entire closet to the second floor. This was how William was planning to be able to enjoy his entire home. Though he was skeptical that the contraption would actually work and that he would be far too heavy for Mehlyndia to hoist, Ian assured him that with enough pulleys and weights, that even Seany could lift a draught horse to the second level.

Though he would have rather been helping with the construction, William sat in his chariot-chair, plans in hand, amazed as he watched his design become reality. When the last of the construction beams had been notched and fitted together properly, the frames were raised, one wall at a time. Deep pits had been dug, and then half-filled with rammed earth and stone to serve as footings for the huge beams. The frames were lifted by bulls, pulling large chains that were attached to what would be the highest cross beams, while the men lifted from underneath. The bottoms of the beams would slide into the ditches and, if the planning had been right, they would stand straight. This was the most dangerous part of the job, and the one William was most worried would go wrong, but after the first, then the second wall was raised, he became more confident in his foremanship. When the last wall had been raised and the crossbeams set, William sat, marveling at the skeletal structure of his home. I'm not as dull-witted as I thought. It worked. It all actually worked!

When the frame was complete, the men let out a wild cheer, then sat in the grass to rest. William had known most of these people for only a short time. Some had only arrived to Port Edin in the past months on the latest ships that had come from France. Each family was eager to build for themselves, though most of their homes would be far smaller. Among the men were Ian, and the only other person, besides Elinor, that had come across with him from Stonehaven, Simon MacHenry.

Simon had actually gone back to Scotland after the initial crossing, and William assumed he had only come with them that first time, to see that he and Mehlyndia were safely settled. He vaguely recalled that Simon had once been a friend of his in Drumoak, and he was not sure, but it seemed that Simon might have been a soldier. William and Mehlyndia were surprised, but pleased, when Simon returned to Port Edin the following year, with his new bride, Pricilla, who preferred to be called, Prissy.

"I told you it would work." Ian clapped William's shoulder. "That was a fine bit of engineering you worked out."

"He worked it out?" Simon scoffed. "It should have fallen afoul before it started, then." He crossed his arms over his chest, grinning.

William turned the plans over in his hand and gave Simon a confounded look. "That's odd. The peaks are pointing the wrong way, look." He held the upside-down plan out to Simon.

Simon burst into laughter then shook William's hand heartily. "Congratulations, Will. 'Twill be a fine home."

"Thank you." William rolled up the plans and took another gander at his masterpiece. "I'm as surprised as you are, Simon. It's better than I expected. I'm amazed that the frame is finished so quickly."

"It isn't finished yet." Ian shook his head, looking to Simon. "Is it, Simon?"

"Why, no, Ian." Simon stroked his chin thoughtfully. "There's something missing."

William gave Ian and Simon a suspicious look. He unrolled his plans to see what could possibly be missing. "What are you two talking about?" he asked.

Ian winked at Simon with a grin. "Won't be finished without that last touch, will it?"

"Not at all," Simon answered.

"All right, what are you two up to?" William rolled his plans again.

"Why, the blessing of the bough, of course." Ian extended a hand to the peak.

"The bough?" William looked where Ian pointed. As part of the construction preparation, a large iron arm, with a pulley on the end protruded from the peak. A rope had been threaded through, and was attached to a workman's bench, meant for hoisting building materials. "What bough?"

Ian gave William a mischievous smile, then nodded a signal to Ephraim Ashcrofte, the new vicar, and Charles Blackwood, the blacksmith of the village, who were sitting on the grass nearby, both wearing the same look of smug conspiracy. They stood and went to the workman's bench and set it across two barrels. Charles held up the evergreen branch that, as part of the traditional builder's blessing, would be attached to the peak of the frame and remain there throughout the rest of the construction. Ephraim held up a hammer.

"So...who is to place the bough then?" William asked, with a slight sense of trepidation.

"The bough is always placed by the master of the house, of course." Simon said, resting a hand on William's shoulder.

"What?"

Before he could protest, Ian and Simon flanked William, and lifted him off his chair, each taking one arm and leg, and carried him to the workman's bench and sat him down.

"You're not serious..." William laughed, looking back and forth at his friends, "are you?"

"Aye." Ian and Simon spoke together, as they handed him a long length of rope.

"Strap yourself good, lad, you're going up," Ian said with a comical seriousness in his eyes.

"Absolutely!" William grinned, as he wrapped the rope back and forth around the bench and across his lap as many times as the length would allow. He looked up to Ian, then to the peak. "It is safe. Right?"

Ian leaned close to William, "Yes, but if you don't want to do it, tell me. Truly, Will, it's up to you."

William looked again at the peak, thinking it over. "How high is it?" he asked quietly.

"It's a bit more than twenty feet to the ground from up there," Ian said, still speaking quietly. "If you like, I'll go with you, if you're afraid," he offered.

William grinned, and raised a brow. "Afraid?" He took the hammer from Ephraim. "I think not. Hoist me, lads!"

The men around him cheered as Charles handed William the evergreen bough. It was no more than a yard in length and an inch in diameter. William threaded it under the rope on his lap, along with the hammer.

"Ready?" Ian asked, as he checked the safety rope.

William wrapped his left arm around one of the supporting ropes. "Ready."

Slowly, Simon pulled the rope hand over hand, lifting the bench toward the peak.

Twenty feet to the ground. Twenty feet? For a moment William had an odd feeling he'd heard someone tell him that before, then the thought passed as finally he reached the peak of the frame. He glanced down to the ground. Wrong thing to do. He closed his eyes for a moment to steady a strange trembling that began worming its way from the pit of his stomach up through his chest. Fine time to discover that I'm not fond of heights. Just hammer the bough, and be done.

"You're doing great, Will!" Simon called up from the ground.

"Just drop it in now," Ephraim added his encouragement.

William tightened his grip on the support line, then reached for the bough with his free hand and slid it out from under the rope. A U-shaped bracket had already been placed in the beam, and all he had to do was slide one end of the bough into it, then give it one or two taps with the hammer and he would be done. Easy enough. Just hold on tight and lean out a bit—

"William!" Mehlyndia cried out, "What are you doing?"

William jolted, violently, as the sound of her voice startled him, and for one, terrifying moment, he was certain he was going to fall off the bench. His brief panic was echoed by a chorus of startled gasps from below him that quickly settled. He clutched the support rope as tightly as possible, and took a long breath, then looked down, nodded to the people that all was well, then looked to where Mehlyndia's voice had come from. She was running toward the construction from the cottage. Elinor and Prissy, with Seany in tow, ran close behind. Ian ran to meet Mehlyndia half way, and stopped her from getting any closer. She argued with him for a moment, a mixture of panic and anger on her face. Oh, I'll catch it from her later, I'm sure. Elinor caught up to them and put a motherly arm on Mehlyndia's shoulder.

"Be careful!" Mehlyndia called up to William as Elinor persuaded her to sit in the shade. "That's a long drop!" She settled on a rock beneath a large oak tree and watched him through her fingers.

"I'm always careful." William answered, forcing a smile he hoped appeared more confident than he was feeling after being startled. When he turned his attention back to placing the bough, he discovered, to his dismay, he would have to lean out farther than he expected to reach the bracket. He instinctually wrapped his left wrist one more time around the support rope, which tightened, almost painfully so, as he leaned out, holding the bough with is right hand. Another strange echo flashed in his head, the drop is twenty feet to the floor. He froze, bough midway to the bracket, as the tremble in his middle made its way to his hand. Ground, not floor, there's no floor under me. It's the ground.

"Will?" Ian called up, from directly under the bench. "Is something wrong?"

William did not answer. He sat still as a stone.

"Can you answer me?" Ian called again, a concerned urgency in his voice.

William wanted to answer, but found himself unable as the strange echo in his ear came and went. Answer the question, yes or no... For the briefest instant, the recollection was clear to him, then gone again, leaving an uncomfortable tremble he did not understand. He closed his eyes for a moment. It's only the height that's shaken me. That's all. He sat, still waiting for the unpleasant sensation to pass.

"Simon, help me with the ladder."

William looked down to see every face staring silently up to him. He had not realized until then, that all the cheering and conversation had gone silent. How long have I been sitting here? He still held the bough in his outstretched right hand, and his left was becoming numb as it clung to the support rope.

"Will?" Ian spoke, calmly, as he climbed to the highest rung on the ladder, almost eye-level to William on the opposite side of the beam. "Are you all right?"

William closed his eyes for a moment and repeated the half-memory. "It's twenty feet to the floor." He opened his eyes and looked at Ian.

Ian kept his voice steady, though the concerned look in his eyes belied the calmness. "Place the bough, Will, then they'll lower you down, slowly—"

Answer the question and we'll lower you gently, all it takes is one word—yes or no. William glared at Ian, then with a sudden and inexplicable anger, he forced the bough into the bracket. He picked up the hammer and gave the bracket one furious whack, securing the bough to the beam, setting the bench to swinging, and banishing the echoes in his mind all at the same time. The people on the ground burst into cheers. William took another long heavy breath as the wave of unexplainable anger passed. "I did it."

Ian exhaled, loudly, and nodded, a slow grin spread across his face. "You certainly did." He looked down toward the ground. "Bring him down, Simon."

"Gently!" William added, feeling slightly giddy.

At sunset, Mehlyndia, as the wife of the Master of the House, rang the beckoning bell, calling her guests to the barn to enjoy the feast she and the other ladies had spent the entire day preparing. All gathered around the large table that was set in the shelter of the communal barn. The roasted calf was carved and set out on several platters surrounded by bowls of steaming squash, carrots and green beans, breads and pots of butter and cream. With Ian's help, William took his place at the head of the table with the men seated on his right, their ladies, across from them, on the left. The older children sat at a smaller table that had been set especially for them, while the toddlers and very young sat with their mothers, except for Seany. William insisted his son sit with him. When all had found their place they stood, and joined hands.

William realized he was expected to offer the Thanksgiving prayer as the 'founder of the feast' but was never comfortable in speaking prayers in public. He never recited any of the common prayers that were offered at Sunday meeting, as the chant-like, unthinking quality of them left him feeling somewhat unfulfilled. The way the prayers droned automatically, without inflection from the congregation, only heightened his resistance to speaking them. So, for his own comfort, and true to his own faith, he kept his prayers to himself, and the words were never the same, coming to him as the spirit led him.

With all his neighbors now standing around him, holding hands, waiting for him to say something, he decided on the most graceful and inconspicuous solution to his dilemma. "Please forgive me for not standing." A polite chuckle made its way around the table in answer to his jest. "Since we are honored with the presence of Reverend Ashcrofte, I believe it appropriate for him to lead us in the prayer."

"My pleasure." Ephraim nodded solemnly bowing his head. "Thank thee, Father in Heaven for the food you hath provided. Amen." He looked up. "Let's eat."

William chuckled quietly, I could have done, at least, that well.

"Ephraim, really." Josephine scowled at her husband. "The poor man suffers enough in his infirmity, the least you could offer is a proper blessing, and a word for healing—"

"Thank you, Ephraim," William interrupted her, "the blessing was perfect." He smiled, politely, at Josephine, camouflaging the irritation he felt at her well-intended, but unthinking words. "I'm not suffering more than a ravenous appetite at the moment, Goody Ashcrofte."

Josephine, pursed her lips and blushed, but said no more, much to William's relief.

"Everyone sit down, please. The work is done. It's time to enjoy ourselves."

Mehlyndia sat to William's left, Seany on his lap and Ian to his right. Next to Ian, Simon. Elinor sat to Mehlyndia's right, Prissy next to her. As far as William was concerned, these were his family, and he was well pleased to have them all close to him.

"Now, Mr. Philbrick, would you care to explain yourself?" Mehlyndia asked, stern brow raised, as she prepared a plate for Seany. "What, in the name of God, moved you to ride to the peak as you did?"

"Ian and Simon moved me," William answered with an innocent smile. "I was kidnapped."

"Us?" Simon placed his hand on his chest in mock astonishment at William's accusation. "It was your idea, Will." He looked to Ian for support. "He begged us to hoist him up, didn't he, Ian?"

"Aye!" Ian nodded comically, then looked at Mehlyndia wide-eyed, "He overtook us and forced us. He's a nasty one, your husband is."

"Nasty he is, for scaring me to death." Mehlyndia, finally, relented and laughed at Ian. "I suppose you'll next try to convince me he overtook Ephraim and Charles as well?"

"Of course I did." William said, straight-faced, "Pass the bread, please, Elinor."

"Here you are, dear." Elinor passed the breadbasket,

smiling. "It's nice you haven't lost your sense of humor. But in all seriousness," she leaned forward and wrinkled her brow to him, "what were you thinking?"

"That's the trouble, Elinor, he wasn't." Mehlyndia said, taking the bread from William. "You could've fallen you know, then where would Seany and I be?"

"I was careful—"

"And you two!" Mehlyndia shook her head toward Ian and Simon, "You should know better than to allow him to talk you into—"

"Melly," Ian held up the palm of his hand to quiet Mehlyndia. "William was right the first time. Simon and I kidnapped him." He lowered his hand, and sighed, "It was completely our plot, he had no idea what we were about. It's just, that we both knew how badly he wanted to be part of the building and we thought—"

"Ian," William tapped Ian's shoulder, "it's all right, no need to explain." He looked at his wife. "I'm sorry I scared you, Melly. But as you can see, I'm well and fine, no harm done. Please, let's just enjoy this glorious dinner you've worked so hard to organize."

Mehlyndia shook her head, and gave up the argument.

The rest of the meal was passed with polite conversation, and Ian's lighthearted quips. The ladies discussed plans for a quilt they would sew together to pass the coming winter months, and the men spoke mostly of the rest of the construction of the house.

"You'll want it all closed in before the snow flies, Will," Simon said, sitting back with a cup of after-dinner ale. "The bricking has to come next though."

"That'll go quick with enough many hands to the task," Charles said, as he pulled up a chair next to Simon. "I've done a fair bit of masonry work in my day. We'll have the hearths and chimneys up in short order. I'll be glad to oversee the job."

"Thank you Charles, I'd much appreciate it," William said, extending a hand to the man to seal the agreement.

"My pleasure." Charles smiled as he shook William's hand. "I may even find need for this lad as well." He reached out and mussed Seany's hair.

"For me?" Seany looked up wide-eyed and pleased.

"Are you stout enough to carry a bucket of water, lad?" Charles asked.

"I'm strong enough to carry two," Seany said, holding up three fingers. The men laughed heartily and Seany buried his face on his father's shoulder.

William motioned the men to quiet with a wave of his hand. "I know you're a good strong lad." He gave his son a tight squeeze. "The other children have gone to play tag in the moonlight, would you like to go?"

Seany lifted his face and nodded.

"Go on, then. Don't wander far, though."

"All right, Papa." He gave his father a quick hug, then slid off his lap and trotted out of the barn toward the other children.

William watched his son join in the children's game, merrily dancing about in the moonlight. His thoughts strayed to the new child who would arrive early in the New Year. *Perhaps I'll build a cradle then? I can do that much now.* He had not been able to build a proper cradle for Seany, and the child had been bedded in a sea trunk for his first months. But then, he had not had the opportunity to prepare at all for Seany's birth as Mehlyndia had carried him through what William had come to regard as his 'dark time'; the months of the crossing, that he had spent ill, lost in the dark of his own mind, after whatever the event had been that put him off his feet. He'd come back to the living, as Ian had put it, only a couple of months before his son's birth, and was hardly able to hold a quill, let alone build a cradle. But he'd grown steadily stronger since he woke up, and decided at that moment, that he would indeed build a proper cradle for his new little son or daughter.

Lost in his thought, working out the plan for the cradle, he hardly noticed that most of the guests had wandered away from the barn to enjoy the exceptionally warm September evening. The ladies were busily clearing away the remains of the meal on the far end of the table, when Ian interrupted his thoughts.

"I don't suppose you'd care to talk about what went on today?" Ian asked leaning his elbows on the table.

"Hmm?" William looked up to him, "what do you mean?"

Ian kept his voice low. "Something happened at that peak. That was more than a simple reaction to the height you had up there."

"Oh." William sighed and sat back in his chair. "You noticed that? I suppose everyone else did as well?"

"Well, it was fairly obvious you didn't like it up there. My guess is Ephraim and Charles attributed it to the height. You must have noticed neither of them volunteered to do any of the high work." Ian laughed lightly but his eyes grew more serious. "But they don't know you as well as I do. Something else drained the roses from your cheeks, and I wondered if you wanted to talk."

William sat silently for a moment, thinking over the sensation that had overcome him just before he placed the bough. He could not recall exactly the echoes that had come to him, only that they seemed familiar. What he did remember was the all-encompassing sense of anger that he felt. As he sat thinking, his right hand, idly, found its way to his left wrist, and he began working slow circles on his scars. He winced, surprised that it hurt him to do so at that moment. "I hadn't realized I'd done this." He held his wrist out to show Ian.

Ian examined William's wrist, "A bit of rope burn. I'm not surprised, given the way you lashed yourself to the safety line."

"Ah, that was probably it." William rubbed his wrist again, tracing the lines of the scars. "Ian?" He began then sat quietly, not quite knowing what he wanted to ask.

"Aye?" Ian raised a brow and leaned forward.

"It was almost there. But I couldn't get my fingers around it."

"The bough? It was farther to lean than we thought—"

"No." William shook his head. "Something... I'm not sure what, but something about that bench, or maybe it was the rope, I'm not sure..." He knew he wasn't making sense, but Ian had always been easy to speak to, letting him ramble if he needed. "It reminded me of something..." He looked Ian in the eye, "I almost remembered it Ian. But it was gone in an instant."

Ian drew a long breath, and rested his chin in his hand. "Your accident? Is that what you remembered."

"Accident?" William scoffed. "I stopped believing that long ago. You don't come by these sorts of marks by accident." He held his wrists out. "You should know that," he said, quietly, looking at Ian's wrists.

Ian self-consciously folded his hand on his lap, concealing the marks on his wrists. "What do you think it was, then?"

"I think," William began slowly, "I came by these marks, the same way you came by yours," he looked Ian in the eye, "and when you finally come to accept that I'm not as fragile as the robin's egg you and Mehlyndia, and everyone else believes I am, you will share with me how you came to own them."

Ian looked away. It was the first time William had known him to be speechless.

"I'm right, aren't I?"

"Will, I can't answer—"

"Seany!"

William looked up to see Mehlyndia running out of the barn door.

"Seany! What are you doing up there?" She cried frantically.

William looked through the doorway, but could not see Seany. "Ian, go see," he said, fighting a rising panic at Mehlyndia's reaction to whatever Seany was doing.

Ian jumped up and ran out of the barn. He stood in the doorway, looking to the place Mehlyndia had run. He relaxed, a wide grin on his face, he waved to William. "All's well."

"Thank God." William exhaled as the panic passed.

"What's happening?"

Ian stood in the doorway smiling, watching something. In a moment Mehlyndia appeared, a contrite Seany in tow. She led him into the barn and sat him on a bench near William.

"Your son has inherited your talent for scaring me to death!" she said, an angry scowl on her face. Seany sat pouting.

"What has he done?" William asked, not knowing if he should laugh or be angry.

"He managed to climb the scaffold nearly to the peak! Thank goodness Charles's boy, Kevin, was close by." Mehlyndia dropped herself heavily on the bench next to Seany.

"You could have fallen, little man," William said, suddenly as frightened as Mehlyndia had been. "Why did you climb up there?"

"I'm sorry Papa." Seany dropped his little chin to his chest. "I wanted to help build the house."

"You scared us to death," William said, trying not to raise his voice to his son. "Where on earth did you come by such a bold streak?"

Mehlyndia gave William an incredulous look, "You need to ask?" she said, drumming her fingers on the table. "I'd say he is, indeed, his father's son. The both of you should be sent to bed early."

William finally allowed himself to laugh. "Yes, ma'am." He held his arms out to his son, "Come over here and sit with me, Seany. We'll keep each other out of trouble."

Seany hopped off the bench, climbed up, happily, onto William's lap, and snuggled in. William smiled at the boy, and finally relaxed completely. It was then, he remembered the conversation he had been having with Ian, and that he had finally asked about the marks on his wrists. He was not surprised that Ian had chosen not to come back into the barn with Mehlyndia. Ah, well, he thought, I'll ask again some other time. It's not as important as this.

"How would you like to help me make a present for the new bairn?" he asked Seany. The child remained quiet. William looked down to find Seany had already fallen asleep in his arms. "Sleep sweet, lad."